— The God's Cycle —

Also by

S. Dorman

Gott'im's Monster

And

Fantastic Travelogue:
Mark Twain and C.S. Lewis Talk Things over in
The Hereafter

THE GOD'S CYCLE

S. Dorman

~ ~

S. Dorman
P.O. Box 172
Greenwood, ME 04255
USA

The God's Cycle
Copyright © 1994, 2014 by Susan C. Dorman.
ISBN: 978-0-578-06945-6 (Softcover edition)

Cover photographs by Ronald A. Dorman, manipulation by Nancy Jacob.

Translation of Hodr's request into the Anglo-Saxon by Marie Nelson Ph.D..

This novel contains brief quotations from the works of J.R.R. Tolkien.

Dedication

To Ron

Who makes everything possible

Return to God's House

God's Twilight/13
History in Gottheim/20
Balder's Love/41
Doing Business in the House of God/55
Family Secrets, Secret Family/68
Thinking God's Thoughts/81
God Takes Care of God's Creatures/97
The Gott'im Epistles/128
Jasper Mary/139
The Common/158

Within Without

Burning Down the House/175
Builders in Time/190
Greenhouse Gott'im/223
Leaving Gottheim/238
Bird Hunting/257
November Waters/278
Jasper Mountain Breakdown/290
Christmas in Gottheim/306

In Winter

Layer of Hidden Life/333
Daniel and Balder/346
Old Tires/354
Time on Jasper Mountain/374
God's Creatures in Winter/403
Loki/422
They Suffer in Gottheim/443
The Village in Twilight/471

Mystery Gottheim

489

Balder's Wilderness

Balder Enters the Enchanted Forest/597
He Meets His Guide/608
Balder Descending/616
Mist Limbo/629
The Count of Time/638
'Board— the Inferno!/656
His Brother Hoder/670
The Dream in the Book/677
Invitation to Ragnarök/682
Shucky/698
Balder Meets Hela/709
The Mountainside in Gott'im/724

Character Guide/728

— Return to God's House —

"One thing have I desired of the Lord, that will I seek after; that I may dwell in the house of the Lord all the days of my life, to behold the beauty of the Lord, and to inquire in his temple."

— Psalms 27:4

12

God's Twilight

Elda stepped down from the dark kitchen doorway onto the hewn granite stoop, into predawn stillness. She stood there, almost as though to lift her nose to morning's scent, so poised was she to receive the strange day. She strained for a sight of Posey through the encroaching woods, where spindly trees grew thick and tall. Twilight filled woodland and the small clearing with nebulous shadow. It made a mist of existence, as though all things were dissolving. Elda associated twilight with Norse mythology and her grandmother's tales. It was all there in the immigrant Embla's old stories from a half-century ago, the '30s. Niflheim and Ginnunga were the source of these impressions, fathomless places of creation's inception. The cold of the abyss, of vapor and darkness, merged into a mist of sea smoke that writhed about tall teeth of ice.

In the early stages of tumbledown, tangled in budding foxgrape and woodbine, Elda's house hunkered below a fir-bound ridge. It faced south, as though its long-dead builders had been concerned to catch as much light and warmth as possible in these cold Meguntic Mountains of Western Maine. They trusted a crop of rocks to sprout through the thin soil each spring, pushed up by frost. Farming won't be easy here, said these Yankees, but the land is free. Over the run of those settlers' first century, the house was cobbled together, spreading on either side of its gray granite cellar hole foundation: compounded of hewn logs, timbers and clapboard; of casements, posts, glass panes and various kinds of shingle. Asphalt roofing crumbled on the east and west ends, causing the connected barn to cant and the roof of the attached children's house to rot.

Thirty odd years ago, Everett, Elda, and their baby Balder lived in the children's house, so-called because the newlywed children of each passing generation set up housekeeping there. The extended Simon family was immense, intertwined, spread now throughout the Meguntics like the tendrils of bindweed and virgin's-bower—creepers groping along roadsides and through cutover woodlots. The rock and conifer ridge above was called Simons Ledge after the early family and its descendants of the original proprietors. The house, in its turn, had been named for the ledge. And over them all, settlers, house, and ledge, soared Jasper Mountain.

Balder was the only human left that Elda knew intimately. Everett, Balder's father, was also gone, along with Everett's father, his mother and grandmother: All once lived in this old house. But Elda's once-crowded life as young farm mother in an extended family was seldom called to mind. In some ways her life was truly crowded still because she cared constantly for what she called "the critters." So life now seemed only full and without noise in comparison to her young adult life when people were everywhere about the house and farm.

Posey must not be in those tall encroaching thickets or she would've drifted out. Elda could not now see them with definition, but she ever sensed the trees' presence. Soon the house would be engulfed in them, but Elda was pleased by the thought. She loved the tangle that most Mainers worked to keep back. Elda had once seen the word "arboloco"—a term invented for the Civilian Conservation Corps during the Great Depression to describe the depression of young plainsman who had been transported to the Ozarks for government jobs. The exaggerated academic term made her chuckle but it fit Balder's Yankee farmer ancestors perfectly and she appreciated the respect it accorded to trees. Anyone who ever got turned around in the woods would recognize the tribute.

She kept to the path on her way to the barn, fearing the interior passages that connected the house, ell, shed and barn. She did not like to meddle with all the doors. Something might fall, the barn might tumble to timbers. Balder had inspected it since snow's passing, pronouncing it "safe'n habitable fah your crittas," but she could never trust tilted appearances. Balder had the mind of an engineer. He could believe in, admire, tune, even design machinery, but his mother was hopelessly unmechanical. Metal and mechanisms were less substantial to Elda than the inner essence of a beast.

Was it brightening? She looked toward the treetops. The bristly tips would catch light soon. Then the gods' twilight would be gone till evening. Later, in sun, Elda would go abroad, seeking animals and the impending spectacle of an eclipse. Her aging eyes could deliver that much still, surely. But first there were creatures' needs to tend.

She fingered the small plastic bottle in a pocket of her worn woolen sweater, making sure of it. Her pale veined hand reached out then, pushing a bit on the heavy barn door, sliding it aside. So slight was Elda that a crack was all she needed to slip within. The dank hay- and animal-dropping smell took hold of her. A mingled scent of skunk and bear cub permeated the cavernous place. She felt for the switch that Balder had installed: A powerful 500 watt light cut a dusty swath through the gloom, reflecting from a multitude of wild eyes.

She made the rounds, working from bins in a former tack room and from the old refrigerator where she kept meat. Working around the shored interior of the old barn, Elda fed, watered, inspected, and nursed her current menagerie, everyone in some state of recovery. Here were perched birds and furry animals caged behind fencing. There was also the reptile silent in a tank beneath a heat lamp.

Rounding the corner of one tank, Elda entered a workroom. Light was beginning in wire-screened windows silhouetting a great horned owl. Perched behind chicken wire, its huge talons were locked around a T-bar. She looked a touch too alert. The woman dug in her pocket for the plastic vial containing a dark powered root. She poured the premeasured amount of valerian and worked it into a piece of raw cube steak, rolling it up along with the bony carcass of a mouse into a sticky ball. The owl was her current dangerous case, a villainess with front-facing yellow eyes, feathered tufts jutting from its fierce brows, and a wingspan reminiscent of eagles. Even though the owl was in here out of sight, its presence made the other animals uneasy. Rabbits, a woodchuck, skunk, partridge, one racoon with kits, an orphan bear cub: All were unsettled and restive.

They should worry, thought Elda....*once its wing mends*. This mighty-legged, three- and a half-pound bird had scooped up a nine pound village dog, and punctured Asa Bartlett's head with its two-inch talons. A regular dosing from Elda's herbal pharmacy kept the edge off its ferocity, giving her a chance to check the progress of its wounded wing. Even so, Elda would wear safety glasses from Balder's shed and speak softly while treating this great female. And she would hood the owl when it was ready for her to inspect the wound.

Seeing Elda, the great horn became watchful. Then it eyed the meat, complete with a dangling mouse tail. Elda donned a gauntlet for protection and opened a small feeding gate, extending the doctored meat. The owl snatched and downed the offering.

"Back soon," murmured Elda and turned away. She turned back into the barn and began cleaning out cages.

It was still early when she went outside to look again for Posey. Silent sunlight touched the naked red-tinged twigs of the treetops. The woodland bordering the weedy dooryard was still... and apparently empty of critters. When would Posey show? Elda sighed, taking the morning in on a breath.

She would look for the deer when she climbed the ridge to seek out the eclipse.

Noon was on its way as Elda climbed Simon's Ridge. May sun shed its welcome warmth on her flannel-clad back. Taking hold of budded saplings, her joints and limbs aching, she pulled herself upward. Elda's worries bunched in her mind, clustering like flowers soon to emerge on the moose maples where she climbed.

Posey had not shown at the house and, so far, was not to be seen on the mountain. Of mornings the doe would come as on tiptoe, silently stepping, a swollen shadow in the grey half light. Was she hurt somewhere—or just sore over the owl?... Even Balder had not been home. Now that was not usual!

No one was steadier than Balder. He had a regular job and also did odd mechanical and carpentry jobs; hauling in his pickup, and even snow plowing in winter. His job at the Gottheim Chair Factory, keeping outmoded machinery running, was the kind of challenge he used to keep his skills honed. Elda tried not to worry over his absence, but that was what it was these past two days—trying. Human relationships required so much of what she seemed unable to give. When he showed again, he would probably be irritated if she gave away her concern.

Another worry was the sun—friend or foe? Could she really blame her failing sight upon the sun ... and wouldn't that be pointless? So here it comes—another lonely night in a bed of tears?—oh quit, woman quit! *Quit all this worrying!*

Just keep climbing. Almost there. Life is better when there's something on the horizon. Something like an annular eclipse to watch for. Elda had been counting on this for two weeks. It was movement in heaven—even if it didn't always live up to its billing. Maybe it was the waiting and watching that mattered, anyway. Hopeful watching itself might light and animate everything. Like an eclipse, watching could show forth an inscrutable purpose ... underscored in fire and blue air. Afterward, the remains of watching would be largely unintelligible, except in that kindling still moment before God slipped away.

The pack on her back waggled as she climbed, hand over hand, taking foothold in leaf-litter among rocks and roots. From every rotten surface slick with wet, the green life of earth was starting, tender and delicate. Frost had been coaxed out of everything, rains saturating all. Elda rejoiced in seeing pale green after so many months of winter white and brown. —But would there be gaze enough for it next year?

She lay on the hard ledge above the pond valley. She looked up through a makeshift combination of sunglasses and Balder's welding mask. Eccentric, the townsfolk would think her. Laughable. Lying out here on the edge like a stranger fallen from space—blackflies lighting but not biting. She could imagine the judgment: stop work, equip yourself, climb to the ledge ... because the moon's path crosses the sun? She was already some queer by any tale, spending her meager means on feed for wild animals, putting ads in *The Village Voter* for handouts for ailing wild animals. Animals don't need help! You can't stop animals. They come like raindrops, one after the other, a flood. A strong winter could take nine tenths of a herd's casualties in fawns, but it would just come back wombs full next May. Why all the work and expense when nature supplies her own gourdful each spring?

A nearby chickadee started its patient soft calling. Now another began further along the ledge. Elda stopped her self-involved thoughts to listen. She continued peering through the doubled glass, watching for the spectacle.

Ah. The bite was on: The sky appeared to take a piece of the sun. There would be no total eclipse because the ring of light would be too wide. From reports she knew that full annularity would be a while in coming. She could sit back, eat lunch, even doze, while waiting for the moon to center itself over the sun's disc.

Digging her lunch from the pack, Elda tried to imagine other space-fallen folks watching along the shadowline: people in northeast Asia, the Arctic, Ontario, the Baja peninsula. She felt a faint kinship with them. They too, would notice a powerful withholding. Ninety percent of all that light, for a time just taken away.

She ate under pines and slept to the soft sound of the hopeful chickadee.

The raucous call of ravens startled her awake. She donned the glasses and mask, slid to the edge of smooth rock and looked up, away from the valley of the ponds. In the sky the sun's rim was just closing the bright *c*, turning it into an *o* as the invisible moon covered it.

There. Elda beheld a complete and perfect ring of burning light. And she felt it pierce her retinas with fire. With a small cry she let the rig fall, closing her eyes. Now she saw that the sunglasses had slipped out of place after donning the rig. With haste she adjusted them, feeling tears well. Why had she attempted it with the less powerful mask—when she knew that a rating of 10 was not powerful enough protection? Because Balder had no mask with the required 14. Her reckless obsessions would wreck 'em!

Elda winked the tears away and lay very still, staring up through the mended rig at the thick ring of muted light. Quiet; stillness in the sight above seeped into her. This silent coupling of these great heavenly bodies moved her with a deep impression of silence. The sight imprinted her retinas, but the quiet embodied for her mind was more eloquent than what she was seeing. It was silence soft on her spirit. As though God had come and lain down in her.

She waited. Then she removed the rig and looked around at the natural world of her own familiar neighborhood. The light revealing this world was unnaturally toned. Here, almost, was the twilight again. A brighter twilight of the gods, but still subduing everything. She felt a slight drop in temperature and the breeze was freshening. All sights were hushed in silvery non-light: the valley, where part of Hutchins Pond and the entire village lay hidden by the hill; her house standing in trees; where pines grew dark and hardwoods twiggy and the creatures slept: Every loved thing was cast in that unsettling diffusion of dark and light. Was it an almost belittling dimness? As though the scene were no longer worth the shine of its reflection after all these years. And she felt its significance dissolving.

With care she donned the glasses and mask again, intently searching the spectacle. Now it was like an eye, watching her in turn. Suddenly. Great and heavenly, staring. She was protected from its awesome power to burn and blind, yes, but it was looking at her all the same. God had gotten up and walked away, gone, leaving this Great Eye staring at her. She willed herself calm beneath the unblinking gaze ... until it looked away, becoming a small c, opening on the opposite side of the circle. And the spectacle was undone.

She removed the mask, crawled away from the edge and stood. Elda gathered the remains of lunch, her gear, and crammed them into her backpack. From there she took the deer path up to the ridgetop, intending to hike back the long way—through the brush at the top and down to a dirt road. But she was startled to find that a cut had been made by loggers, and finished off with a bulldozer. Someone had slashed a fresh road along the spring-swollen ridge. The new road was deeply rutted, spongy with runoff and melted frost.

Developers coming! The ski resort on the north side of Jasper Mountain had opened up all sorts of speculation in the town. Outloud she exclaimed, "Someone's building ovah my head. They gont look down on me from theya porches?!"

Limping, aching, arthritic, Elda came through reddening woodland on the lane toward the crumbling house. Paunchy with fawn, Posey stepped out of bordering trees. Silently she came to Elda's side and nuzzled her hand. Relief flooded the woman.

"Why Posey! Waya you been!" She knelt and stroked the little doe's long tawny neck. Posey was an undersized, whitetail doe, befriended during a day's doctoring when the herd had taken shelter in the plowed lane. The snow was deep, so deep, then. After that, they had yarded up in the garden—not uncommon at the relatively hidden *Simon's Ledge*. The finish of hunting season sometimes brought injured deer to this house of healing.

Together they walked up the long lane. As the woman made rounds in the barn, Posey followed delicately. When it came time to check on the owl, however, she backed away and wandered outside to browse on blooming tender maples twigs.

An hour later, having released a mended partridge, Elda entered the oaken and pine paneled kitchen. There dismaying shadow fell on her, darkening the peace that Posey had given her. She felt for Posey's long ears and, reassured, flicked on the light. The doe went to the sideboard and, attempting to mount, scrabbled her small split hooves on the wooden countertop.

Chuckling, Elda snatched up the canister Posey was trying to reach, pried off the lid, and held out a handful of raw peanuts. Posey pushed her moist black nose against the heel of Elda's hand, delicately picking up the nuts with her tongue. Swallowing several, she set her hooves up again and, bending her neck, reached for the salt shaker. Elda grabbed it first and shook liberally into her hand, then held it out for the doe to lick.

The woman went to the sink, washed her hands, and filled the kettle to set on the woodstove. Suddenly she was too weary to stoke the fire. She turned off the light and crept to the couch by the stove, sank gratefully back and drew on an old patchwork quilt made by Everett's mother long ago. Posey knelt and lay atop a rag rug on the pumpkin-pine floor. Peacefully she chewed her cud. May light moved across the wall and was at last cut off by an arm of the hill. Neither creature stirred.

History in Gottheim

It was still light outside when tall blond Balder came in. Posey scrambled up to meet him, sniffing then licking the small togue dangling among those in his hand. Laughing, he laid the fish on the sideboard and reached into a paper bag. Elda stirred on the couch and sat up stretching, glad of his voice.

"Better shoo the doe away, or we'll have none fah suppah," he said, giving Posey a nibble of something from the bag. "See what I brung you?" He held the something between his thumb and forefinger. The house being so dim, she could not make it out. "What is it?" she asked, rubbing her eyes.

He frowned. "It's fiddleheads is what. I could eat the bagful." He went to the wall and flicked on the light. "You gont fix'em or am I?"

"Well, I will, you spoiled kid." Never mind that Balder was approaching his mid-thirties. She stood and went to stick her hand in the bag to feel the small plump wheels of furled fern shoots. "Look at'em all! Waya did you find 'em?" She brought out a handful for the pregnant deer and led her out the door. "Boggy Place?"

Shaking his head, Balder got out the cutting board and lay the fish on it in the sink. "Hiked into Birch River afta work. Blackflies's starting."

"So don't I know it. Not biting yet, though." Elda got out a skillet, began heating oil. "Was you down by old Mason's Mills—across fum the old granite work, hidden like?" She put on a pot containing enough water to steam the coiled fiddleheads, sprinkled in some salt to remove bitterness.

"The same." He was cutting the brown and silver fish under running water. "Wasn't it you showed me it as a kid?"

"Cuss I did. Told you about the old grist mill. They had a carding and fulling mill. Prosperous, too, said Asa Bartlett."

Balder said, "Cold in heah." He went to the stove to lay kindling and blow on the embers. The door squealed as he shut it. "Kinda like the Bearces of theya day, guess."

"Yuht. Owned all that land around theya on both sides of the stream. Maybe 100, 150 years ago. Think what things was like back then."

"Blackflies like now. And no TV. Whad they do nights—visit?"

She nodded, breading pieces of fish. "Had socials, musicals and all. Dances, school plays. They read!" She grinned. Balder was back!

The fiddleheads were steaming and the fish laid sizzling in oil. She said, "What I don't know was how they stacked that monstah granite. How'd they move stuff like that then?"

"Oxen or draft hosses, with block'n tackle. Pulleys." He stood over the fiddleheads, picking through them with a fork. "Be surprised what you can do with'em. Look what you can do with a come-along—move a truck out of a mud hole with bare hands and that."

"Whad you see down theya besides fiddleheads?"

"Skunk cabbage, wild ginger, wake-robin, bellwort." He grinned.

"Good, ain't it?" She returned a grin.

Balder nodded, lounging against the sideboard his powerful shoulders at ease. His blue gaze was still upon Elda, paying attention. "Took my break when I could see that eclipse you been talkin'bout. You notice that strange silver light when it was on? That mask work OK? Know what that ring reminded me of?" He noticed her perfunctory response to all these questions and went on: Evah read *Lord of the Rings*? Story about this hobbit—theya little people. He had a powerful ring to get rid of. You might say it was a quest in reverse. A quest to get rid of power. Anaway, by the end of the fuss book, he's seeing this ring—like an eye looking at'em—every time he closes his eyes. You ought read that book, Mutha." He stared down at the skillet where she was poking at the fish. "Under certain conditions, I can see a ring in negative if I shut my eyes. That evah happen to you? Works out it's an image of my iris."

Elda was silent, turning pieces of lightly browned togue, not even looking up. His allusion to eyes and the eclipse threatened the peace his company had brought her.

She heard him go into the front parlor and snap on television. The McNeil/Lehrer News Hour on Senate legislation drifted into the kitchen. Elda turned her thought away from distress. There was something better to think of: Something was different about Balder. Gone was his more usual solemn silence. Tonight his attitude was light. Unconsciously she had seen it, but now she was aware.

Balder was tall and as good-looking as a healthy buck in velvet. He had a cap of blond, almost white hair, but when he wore his watch cap he reminded her of a Norwegian sailor, off the stormy North Sea. He could joke and wisecrack, yet for years there had been an air of grief about him.

Vietnam grief, she called it. Everyone in town had opinions on the way he had spent his time here in isolation after his tour. "In hiding," they called it. They all thought the way to deal with grief was to work like a maniac. The respectable ones said so; others thought he should drink a little harder.

But today ... today was different. Thinking about it, Elda saw that Balder was happy.

He wandered back into the kitchen, saying, "Went down to apply at the papah mill today. Ovah to G'fid."

"The papah mill." Taken by surprise, she said crossly, "Whad you do that fah!"

He frowned. "Why does anyone? Fah the money."

"God-awful place! Could get choo killed."

"Now Mutha.... " He was laughing at her!

"Theya's poison in that mill!"

Frowning, he could see that she wasn't going to lay off this saw until a tree fell somewhere. "Forget it, Mutha. Prob'ly won't get the job anaway. Getting in is like getting into Harvard. Evah man in fifty miles tries to. Didn't Fatha?" He turned, went to get the plates from the cupboard.

Elda heaped one with flaking fish and steaming fiddleheads. She forced herself quiet, said in a low voice, "What's wrong with your job at the chair factory? You make money working on cars'n pickups besides. You get odd jobs enough."

He said (mysteriously she thought), "I need more money now. Let loose of it, Mutha." Balder went back to the parlor with his plateful.

Elda followed with hers. Balder sat on a sofa, facing the TV. She sat in a woolen worn arm chair, an afghan draped across its back.

Balder said, "Fiddleheads's good."

"Not bitter at all," she agreed.

It had been years since they ate together at the table, when his father was alive, in fact. More and more, since Everett's death, the news hour has come to dominate supper. Even breakfast is now frequently eaten before the Maine morning news.

Now each sits in separate thought, eyes upon the flickering images. Balder thinks of Middle America, whose cause is before him on the screen. He has just come away from what he thinks of as a typical product of that self-involved class. The young woman is up from Massachusetts to work with her brother, an entrepreneur developing a condominium resort. Gloria thinks herself brainy and brave. They are two from a fantasy written contingent, up to tame and shape the wildlands; to make a brighter suburbia than the labyrinthine, if elegant, subdivision they vacated. He frowns. As he considers their plans for Gottheim, the frown hardens into a scowl. The plans call for the Jasper Mountain ski resort to stride practically around the base of the bald rocky giant and make a new shiny Main Street for the community.

Watching the debate on economic trickle-down, Balder grimaces and thinks of these things. Gloria Fay has a master's degree in public policy and can punch up a computer, cranking out statistically loaded reports by the bucketload—but most likely can't mop out a toilet or feed herself. Not with any consistency. He has discovered that she is an upscale restaurant dweller, as some writer-lady somewhere put it. In her mind Maine is still the District of Maine, a province of the Commonwealth of Massachusetts— as it was two hundred years before gaining statehood in 1820.

She can ski though—like she was born schussing down mountain. Must've been two weeks ago when he noticed her on Glory Trail. Jasper's trails had not been so rotten then. She was there on the lift up ahead, decked out in brightness, banishing the dreariness of mud season. When she took off down Glory, he saw her below, swift like the trail itself (and her name nearly the same, he learned later). He had to work to catch up with her, through snow the consistency of sugar up top, then through the slush below. But the next trip he was on that lift with Gloria.

Canny talker, full of fun—like sunlight glittering on the surface of the pond. A voice like honey. He was rejoicing inwardly all the way topside again. They crossed the tops of spruces, and were ready to jump the ramp together.... Just there a dreaminess entered him, coupling with a patient desire. Gloria: her smile spring-bright, and head sleek with heavy gold hair. She led them toward the near precipice that was Glory Trail. And he followed her down, this time not in curiosity but with joy.

Now, sitting in front of the television, Balder Simon considers that he needs more money. He might even go into a restaurant other than the diner—once in awhile. Love has fired a quiet form of ambition in him where nothing else could. Yet he has made up his mind not to follow in her ways. He can't. Instead, he will go after things that have always seemed good but, until now, were not greatly desired. He will buy land of his own, and a house ... or build one? Someday—daow, he's not counting on it ... though having a family is what he wants. It will depend on how wedded she is to her fantasy. Will her unconscious selfishness bruise, break his heart? It's happened before.... But, Vietnam gave him suffering in stronger form, so that Balder now knows what time is for. Time exists to squander upon the best you can find.

Lord Jesus, there it is. Happening again, after all these years.

Intent on the next News Hour segment, about possible resort development in Virginia, Elda scarcely notices the wobbling snowy reception of the TV. She's listening, staring into space, not watching. Here beneath Simons Ledge in the mid-1980s Meguntic Mountains, the only stations available are few and distorted. Thinking of the planned development on the ridge, Elda wonders. How can these people keep building these elaborate, palatial houses, such as she sees on the screen? Who has money for such places? What do they all do for a living? Not farming, not mill work or logging. Is the rest of the country so different from Maine?—she guessed. They have to come here with money earned elsewhere.

She glances at Balder who is just coming into the room with a plate of toast, cup of coffee. Work boots, jeans, flannel shirt. It's practically a uniform. She asks, "Choo see the new road up theya yet?" She gestures toward great Jasper above.

"Saw them stot logging up theya last fall. Thought they must be putting in something by the way it was cut." He remembers her after settling back on the sofa. "Waunt tea?"

She stands uncertainly, her arthritic hip giving her a jolt. "I'll get it. Maybe two dozen house sites up theya. Hope they won't be so big's those on TV."

He watches her exit: stiff tonight. A slight, kerchiefed, crooked thing.

He raises his voice. "You'll be turning middle-aged, you don't watch, Mutha."

"I am middle-age, Balda!" she calls back.

"Then what'm I coming to, deah?"

"Y'ain't middle-aged till forty!"

In the kitchen she fills her cup, dunks a bag, wanting to ask where he's been for three days. She wonders, why is it none-of-your-business if you're the one worried?

Elda comes back with her tea, eases herself into the chair. Now it feels good sitting down. She'll stay awhile, put her feet up on the straw-leaking hassock.

The last segment of the News Hour is on the annular eclipse, a public television poetic essay. There is the great eye again, looking at her, just. The eye of one of Embla's old gods. The essayist tells how a crowd of students responds almost as one, awed witnesses of the covering and rediscovering of the sun. The wholeness of the sight brings a sort of rapture to the class as they are caught up together in a joyful response.

Slowly it comes to her that she wants to tell Balder. To tell someone trusty and loved. But she knows she won't. She will only tell Posey, a whisper under her breath. Because it is Elda's way to just ... keep going. Till she can't go no more. That's what she does when things are beyond her. She will move through twilight until it's so dark she can't see. All things will dissolve in one.

In treetops, high above, late light shone on red tips and tiny blooms. Elsewhere were hints of red and green buds. In the dooryard outside Simon's old settler house, Posey stood, gulping down her fiddleheads. Came a rattle, to her pricked ears, from the duff in the woods. The little deer lifted her pointed face nervously, staring through spindly tree stems. A red squirrel leaped, scurried up the trunk. Posey relaxed a bit, drifting toward the woods. Desiring company, she began browsing her way toward higher ground. Then, climbing on quick thin legs, Posey's hooves imprinted the soft earth, still mixed with last autumn's leaves. Sometimes her split hooves gripped protruding rock, milky quartz, or glinting granite. Hearing the intermittent rush of water and wind, she followed around the shoulder of the wooded slope. There the falling sun alighted yet. Breasting a rocky crest, she found a brimming brook and smelled its clean vegetative scent. She ducked to it, taking a long cold drink. Posey jerked her head up, watching.

Now she stepped through the water and began following along the course of the brook, through emerging grasses and plants—dainty spring flowers like bluet, sessile-leaved bellwort, blue violet. The Jasper Mountain brook wound around hummocks and saplings, beneath high straight trunks of maple beech birch. The paunchy little doe found young beech with shapely limbs, alight with tightly furled buds. She stopped to tear off the tender stems and swallow before continuing on her search for companionship.

Movement off her shoulder startled her, and she looked up. There a hairy woodpecker, speckled and striped, fell fluttering from tree to tree. It inspected crevices in the bark but did not rear back to thrust for a meal. Posey went on, picking her way with nervous delicacy, lifting her pointed face to the breeze.

And still calm light lingered above as she meandered up current, but at last the shadows deepened. The brook thinned to a trickle then turned to mush with green plants sprouting. There Posey saw yet deeper shadows, standing, quiet and many-legged: three does, each filled with fawn; and one of these her mother. Touching, rubbing necks in greeting, she joined them. In dusk they stood together, chewing cud, blackflies alighting. Now the deer started back toward low ground. They sought the still waters of ponds with peepers, a mist-strewn vale, and soft bedding.

Their shelter would be darkness. Darkness had sheltered their antecedents, who settled all the mountain long long ago.

At dawn came light on the heights of Jasper Mountain. In deep shade, far beneath, six deer looked up from a sheltered cove. The bald head of the mountain was out of sight, but across the pond a fir-crowned summit floated above a wreathing mist. Distant rumbling on the highway stirred them to move. In silence the does drifted upward through hemlocks toward higher ground. The slopes of Jasper Mountain stood in ponderous mystery over the village of Gottheim.

A door opened in the ell off the kitchen of a many-angled farmhouse near the shore. Stepping out, Asa Bartlett caught sight of the many-legged shadows disappearing among dark conifers beyond the cove. His breath a vapor on the early air, Asa stepped off the doorstone and walked across the sandy weedy, but trim, yard to his freshly painted Ford pickup. He had painted it hunter green last weekend and now stood in critical appraisal of the job—as he had each morning since. The right front fender might need a touch-up. Maybe a slight but definite line with a fine brush would do it. Asa considered heading to the shed for brush and spray paint, but his stomach was growling. He wanted a cup of Decatur's coffee more than anything on earth. So he yanked the door handle, slid into the pickup.

But he stopped, cocking his head to look in the rear view at his bandaged temple. He smoothed his crewcut brick red hair, then, wincing, adjusted his horn-rimmed glasses. How can this wound be throbbing still— after two days. That owl! He ought to go into the house, get his 30-30, go up to Elda Simon's and blast its malicious head off. But, catching a glimpse of his furious face in the mirror, Asa cackled, sinking back against the seat.

Don't you just look like Buster Bearce the time we tied his pants in knots. Asa recalled the decades-old incident of the lumber baron's son who went skinny dipping by moonlight, only to emerge and find his dungarees, shirt, and socks all knotted tight and soaking wet. Asa and Wellington Bird might have run off with the clothes but that would've been theft.

Asa turned his key in the ignition, eased out onto the hot-top and headed for the diner on the highway. The camps and summer places were still vacant as he drove past. Then the road wound through the narrows among broad ponds. He thought about the folks from away who had peopled the shores for decades. Now they were being joined in the area by skiway interests. The pattern of succession, which Asa often thought about, was making new inroads of late. Mentally he ticked them off. First had lived the Indians, which he thought of as abiding here since forever—though of course he knew about the land bridge migrations. Then came proprietors, then settlers and their descendants. Next were timber speculators, then immigrants—Irish, French, Scandinavian. Now it was developers. Everybody's staking their claim in these mountains ... each new group full of dreams.

They forget, he thought grimly. We spend more time in the ground than we do walking around on top of it. "Just waya do they think they're going s'fast?" he said aloud. Maybe that was why he enjoyed tying Buster's pants in knots. Always in a hurry, those Bearces. Gobbling up the land right to left since anyone can remember. As though consolidating holdings could somehow keep them from sharing space with roots and rocks in glacial till along with everybody else.

He pulled onto the highway and drove on as the diner showed silver and maroon beneath the wooded knoll. The village of Gottheim edged a gleaming pond, sheltered beyond in shadow: the tiny houses and businesses drowsing in the dusk of Jasper's great knees. Other mountains surrounded the valley, most named for Yankee settlers who once had homesteads there. Many granite shoulders of the low ones were to this day laced with networks of moldering stone walls, covered now in standing third and fourth growth timber. Overgrown discontinued wagon roads looped through the woods. The forest floor was pocked with old cellar holes, ingrown with oak maple birch pine spruce. Moss-grown dumps of rusting tools and seamless bottles lay near more recent pits dug by prospectors—the descendants of settlers, looking for treasure: tourmaline, topaz, amethyst, beryl. There were other treasures too, buried, unseen, of which Asa knew nothing. One of these lay hidden beneath concrete in the basement of a Jasper Mountain resort condominium.

He saw Elvegy Blanchard drive out of the parking lot of the diner in her Bronco pickup, the bed loaded with manure and its powerful smell reaching out to gag anyone in sight not used to it. Asa was.

Overstreet the tower clock of the Congo Church chimed distantly, just as he entered Decatur's diner. He enjoyed the diner's smell of coffee, bubbling hot oil, and chicken soup already a'simmer. The diner's floor was uneven, covered with linoleum in dire need of fresh wax. The ceiling was peeling tin, the booths taped and tattered, but no one—even tidy Asa— seemed to notice. The regulars seemed not to see the place at all ... except in those isolated, clear moments when things were either very right or going dead wrong.

He heard the jabbering on about Elvegy as he entered the glass door just inside the glass mudroom entrance. Apparently she'd left a stench, along with that of the manure, about her brother-in-law Ithiel Whitman. Her tone was escalating of late. Fortunately for Ithiel he could brush it off with humor.

"Went too far this time," Asa heard Rensalier Simon growl. And Melvinia Sessions answer, "But Ithiel just bears it light as pie. Seems to relish it like pie, too."

Asa copied it all and greeted a few regulars and, so that he might lean back against it surveying the door, took his usual stool near the counter's elbow. He liked sipping coffee before breakfast, seeing who came in. Decatur's was the place to imbibe gossip along with breakfast. People on their way to work stopped in, retirees took up residence, and school bus drivers klatched here after dropping off the children. Recently, a resort developer had suggested that the Post Office be moved out to a proposed mini mall. God awful!—but, if so, the diner's being not that far off Front Street, on a loop to the highway, would be doubly important as communal meeting point. Asa worked second shift at the village wood-turning mill, but still he came in every morning for breakfast and a word or two before running errands or returning home to chores. The latest news was kicked around, opinions batted back and forth—from booth to booth, over the counter and back again. Every juicy subject was here. Politicians, welfare mothers, abortion, the economy, foreign affairs, plain affairs, murder.

Like what happened the year the ski resort really took off— property rates tripled as folks came from away, speculating like mad. A Connecticut landlord shot his ex and her boyfriend, then larruped round over the back roads and tried to shoot his daughter-in-law in the gut.... Over property. That was the year young people gave up thoughts of owning and just tried to adjust to increasing rents; descendants of those generations who had remained when others had fled to easier places like Ohio (Asa muses a moment upon the Ohio fever of the previous century): their ancestors still faithful on rock-bound soil. But now, on minimum wage, they are unable to afford a place. Paper corporations and other large landowners once kept everything in trees for wood products but now were beginning to sell cutover and off-aged woodlots to developers. At Decatur's diner, locals met to talk it over, complain about the machinations and perceived effrontery of flatlanders coming with threats of "a booming economy and service sector jobs." As Asa had said, "That promise of a booming economy's what scares me. Means theya's a bust some wayas down the road."

A waitress in her late fifties stood behind the counter before the order window near the coffee urn. Her gray hair fluffy and short, Melvinia Sessions' eyes glittered behind her outsized pink glasses. Her head shook with exaggerated sympathy, or perhaps suppressed laughter, so that her earings sparkled as she called out in her tinkly voice, "How's the ol'owl bite, Asa? Gut any better since yestadee? And when can we expect to see a photo in *The Voter*?"

Asa grimaced. "Daow. And it's not a bite. I ought to shoot that bud. Can you imagine Elda Simon's nursing that malevolent thing? It could come back fah the rest the town. They won't be no cats left, anahow. Someone saw it disembowel one not two weeks ago. Least they thought 'twas the same owl."

"Cuss it's the same!" returned Melvinia. "Gott'im is haunted by a demon possessed great owl. Someone ought to call Stephen King'n tell 'em about that owl."

Rensalier Simon, sitting two stools down, set his coffee mug by and, still reading the paper, said, "Things is spookier than anathin he could tell."

"What they doing now?" Asa craned his neck for a look at Rensalier's paper. "Haven't seen the town bellyache yet."

The big man drew back, glaring, tipping *The Village Voter* against his expanse of green work shirt.

Asa huffed, and turned back to Melvinia. "Your joints gummed up with molasses today? Waya's my coffee?"

Melvinia poured a steaming cup and set it before him, saying, "How many thousands of cups've I brung you over the years, Asa? Never said nothing bout how fast I got those cups poured."

"Don't you sound like someone's laundress."

"Me—married to you?—and have to wait on you at home too?" She shook her head. "When I get home I put my feet up."

"I sure was not asking, but so don't I—about the feet, I mean," said Asa (his Gottheim Academy schooling notwithstanding).

"Like any ol'Mainer, you keep working, frigging with something."

"You don't? What about those yuppie kids you was babysitting? Their parents went ovah to Farmington teaching nights?"

"In three weeks school ends'n then I'm taking hints fom TV newspersons—like they call 'emselves now. Always giving out these health tips, so I pick'n choose fom all the medical advice. Too much work makes you tense. That makes you unfit for work, they say."

"*Phew*—work less so you can work more? What's the point?"

"Whad'll you have, deah?" she said tartly, pencil poised in hand.

"Hev I become a different person since yestadee? Give me what I always have! And waya's the counter paper? Got to find out what's spooky in Gott'im." He didn't waste a sidelong glance on Rensalier Simon.

Smiling, Melvinia jotted something down and laid the slip on the wooden sill of the window between the kitchen and the counter. Decatur, the business owner and cook, was inside at the grill. Melvinia hollered, calling his attention to the order.

At the counter Rensalier grunted then folded *The Voter*, laying it by his empty plate. He got up, resettled his ballcap on his squat head, and went to the cash register at the break in the counter.

Asa snatched up the paper and spread it out before him, muttering. There, in front of his bespeckled gaze, was a story of the owl attack, illustrated by a photo of the great horned perched on a T-bar in Elda Simon's barn. Asa was grateful he'd had the presence of mind to slip out the back way at the Gottheim Health Clinic, following treatment of his wound. He'd probably be staring at his own picture now. There was enough to mortify in print without his bloody bandaged likeness staring off the front page. He by-godfreyed to himself as Melvinia, chuckling, came over to pour more coffee. "Too bad li'l Libby didn't get choo with her camera," she said. "Wouldn't that be pretty, just?"

"Yuht," said Asa absently. He had found the spookiness Rensalier referred to and was already knee deep in it. "Taking seen as only course," read the headline. Developers had petitioned the Bureau of Parks and Recreation to use the power of eminent domain to intervene and settle an impasse in negotiations for purchasing private property. Developers would then convey to the state the clutter of dilapidated camps, warehouses, and junk-filled lots on Hutchins Pond, yielding ground for a shoreline park to enhance the proposed mini mall nearby. Asa finished the article and looked up, saying, "History's making rounds again."

"It has a way of doing that," said a female voice nearby.

Asa looked over, surprised. Olive Lovejoy had slid into the seat vacated by Rensalier. "Well, ain't choo the stranger! They let you out, have they?"

Melvinia set a mug before Olive and she clasped it in her dimpled hand. She was a large, talking woman, not fat. The henna was wearing out of her hair and so was the curl. Olive's clothes were comfortable, practical, a blue blouse and skirt; her face full, only just beginning to show little lines. She seldom wore makeup, but when she had the chance she painted her nails so bright they made you wince. Her life was spent in brooding over a houseful of five or six developmentally disabled. Now her husband had a malignancy in his liver, and she was watching him waste and die. Asa couldn't bring himself to ask after Horace right off. He had to work up to it, so he said, "What's new among the retarded?"

"Well, I'm getting disgusted, that's new. Bout ready to give up."

Asa moved the paper to make room for the plate Melvinia set before him. "What's this!?" he barked. But he was relieved to be distracted from his duty of broaching the subject of Horace. He looked from the yellow mounds on his plate into the glee of Melvinia's slack-skinned face.

"That's your usual, in't it?"

"I nevah et scrambled eggs'n my life!" He pushed it away, scowling. His head throbbed.

Melvinia's grin grew. "You know y'look like a Bearce when you make that face."

"And you look like an ape!"

Olive said, "That looks good. Give it heah." She reached over with her brightly painted fingers and pulled the plate to her. With relish she began eating.

Melvinia shrank back, sorry, then went to the window and called to Decatur to fry a couple eggs with bacon and homefries.

Asa heard and was mollified. He turned to Olive. "How's Horace?"

"It's those people ovah to 'Gusty! All they want's papahs."

Asa was baffled. Then he saw that she spoke not of Horace Lovejoy—she couldn't. Olive referred to the bureaucrats in Augusta.

She was shaking her head. "All my kids waunt is someone to take a li'l time with 'em. But 'Gusty only wants papers filled out. And numbas. X many sheets, x many towels, x many times I done this, x many times that. But all the kids waunt's attention. Stopped mopping the floor yesterday to play with Tommy. Sixteen years old'n his folks has dumped'em. He was in a pink-stink—s'lonely. 'Gusty don't care. Everything's got to be on papah." She stopped talking to take another bite of toast. Asa sat in commiserative silence. After a bit she said, "Looks like I got to give up on Billy. I've had problems with him, so Horace wants me to get rid of 'em—afterwards .... "

Asa gave a slight nod, otherwise leaving the thought alone.

"Billy's still afraid of Horace, though he's so ill. Respects 'em, might say."

"That the one uses the F-word evah other word?"

She nodded. "Billy's tough, but I give 'em time-out. Ten minutes. Like with children though—he thinks it's an hour." She turned her eyes toward the paper. "What's this history repeating itself?"

"Developers caunt get their hands on property fast enough. They waunt park land by eminent domain."

"Who evah got land that way before?"

"... Well, it's not the preferred method round here."

Her eyes smiled shut. "You wouldn't be thinking—That rumor about folks being cheated out o'theya land by mill owners—that going round again?"

Asa smiled. "That's just one example. Daow, I'm talking bout history!" He smacked the countertop for emphasis. "Go back to the beginning ... what's theya?"

"Indians. That's why Jimmy Carter signed that settlement. Ah ancestors took theya land."

"Now that settlement down east was a little different. This heah was nice'n legal. They had a grant fom the General Court afta the Indians was most subdued. All this land was reward fah theya own ancestors' part in fighting the French in Canada. But something happened even after that grant."

"Tell me." She let Melvinia pour her another cup. "I don't pay's close attention. Haven't been to society meetings lately, anaway."

She referred to the monthly meetings of the Gottheim Historical Society. Asa was the chief amateur historian and knew much of what was in the books and records. He encouraged the old folks to record their recollections. He pored over town and county documents, made trips to the state archives, and generally kept the society from moldering away. Asa urged the keeping of memoirs, compilation of photos and the donation of town related antiquities, letters.

"Oh it's all theya in the records. But I should say 'the memory of records' in this instance. Doc Kimball, writing in the last century, talked about the 'convenient fire' (what gossip of that time called it), occurring afta the founders had consolidated theya holdings. Evah notice it took thirty years to incorporate this town?"

"So?" Olive's plate was now empty except for crusts, on which she was patiently spreading jam. Intent on the story of Gottheim's founding, Melvinia leaned into the counter. Just then Decatur stuck his sweaty bald head through the order window.

"Asa's eggs is ready!"

Scarcely taking her eyes off Asa's face, Melvinia reached back for the plate. She set it before him, waiting for him to go on.

Setting an egg on a slab of homemade toast, he began eating. "Somebody had to survey that land. So the proprietors sent theya sons up from Mass'chusetts to do it. By the way, that's when the fust industry was stotted here. Boiling sap. Sugaring off was the fust industry, not milling. Even the Bartletts come up and was making maple syrup 'fore a house was evah stacked together." He mopped up some yoke with a forkful of potato.

"What was my folks doing—the Gammons? They was heah, waunt they? Woodsmen, trappers, meatmen?"

"They didn't come 'til later, not in that first cultch."

Melvina drew back at the slight.

"So, they was surveying,..." prompted Olive.

"And when they gut done," continued Asa with relish, "they says to the other grantees, 'we got to assess you fah labor'n costs. That'll be forty shillings each,' which amounted to a few months' wages."

"Waunt it only fair?" asked Olive. "That's how taxes work."

Asa shook his head. "A governing body decides taxes. There was no Town, no selectmen yet. Those that balked at the after-the-fact fee had theya lots sold at auction ... in absentia. And the sons of some proprietors bought that land for nothing. Much later, when theya was talk of litigation, come the 'convenient fire.' "

"Wait a minute," said Melvinia, seeing a righteous outcome in the Gammons' late-coming. "Your ancestors was one o'those propri'tahs! You're saying your forefathers cheated folks that stayed in Mass'n couldn't get here—cheated them out o'theya land?"

"May be. No one knows for sure who surveyed, who bought at auction'n what was bought. Look up the list of grantees fom the General Court. Lots of names you never heard of! Lots you have." He swallowed some cold coffee. "But maybe sowing and reaping's took care of all that by now—evened things out. Some families hev come up'n some have gone down. Don't yours own that goodly piece north of the mountain that developers are eyeing?"

"That's Reuel Gammons. Cousins on Mutha's side twice removed." She laughed, earings swinging. "Something like that! Older I get, less I keep track. I mistrust I'm related to myself some way."

A huff of exasperation exhaled from the hot little kitchen. Decatur, at the window and irritated, said, "I note the family resemblance! You're late comin' to work, late getting this order out—just like your cousin Melviny!"

Melvinia said, "Don't know what you're so pleg'ed'bout today." But Decatur had withdrawn. Shaking her head, she picked up the order and emerged from behind the counter toward the far booth.

Glancing up at the neon clock, Olive said, "Looks like I got get back. Theya's no end o'things to do."

Asa nodded, saying, "Be by t'see Horace in a bit." She smiled. He watched her pay up and walk out, regretful that she could not stay to hear the cycle of Gottheim's history; regretful that Olive would experience her own small piece of succession—now that Horace was leaving Gott'im's cycle for good.

Asa was always ready to tell the story of Gottheim, but he had learned patience over the decades. Yes, they took his droppers, the repository of people's mental sheds filling up. With that and the archives, droppers enough, he thought, to keep the townsfolk in knowledge for three generations. But he had no children of his own to test this on. And, with a fresh reminder of Horace's passing, he realized that this generational spread might exclude a child born this week in the Guildford hospital. He would have to talk to someone at the elementary school about starting a program of some sort.

The door opens and in comes Robbie Robichaud to straddle the stool beside Asa. Robbie is a good-sized man wearing the worn working green of Asa's generation.

"That jeezly rig!" he said. "There ain't enough baling wire in the state to keep that piece o'junk together. Got to go down to G'fld and get parts for that pulp-loader. Ezzy's got the pickup today so I had to take Drusilla's TransAm. She waunt too happy. Spoiled kid." He drew close the mug set before him. "At least I ain't in the woods gettin'bit."

Robbie was another living piece from the puzzle of Gottheim's history, descended from French-Canadians who had come from rural Quebec at the turn of the century when Maine's paper mills were up and running. Robbie's father lost him his language in school when English was pressed into him. School children administered the prejudices of their Yankee elders in the hallways: "All frogs gut talk English—if they waunt get along. Hev to learn to wash'n wear shoes." The Robichauds would have retained their language in a community the size of Lewiston where the Franco-Americans were employed in textile mills, or in Guildford where they made paper; but Robbie's grandfather had come to Gottheim to work in a wood-turning mill when the paper mill stopped hiring. And his offspring went into the woods where it was quiet and free from the taunts of bigotry. Robbie never finished school. But now, besides sons who were in the woods, he had a daughter, Drusilla, who looked to be going to college in the fall. And Robbie was proud and glad that he was at last able to spoil someone. Drusilla's first choice had been the prestigious Bates College, in Lewiston, but she wasn't unhappy to settle for the University of Maine at Farmington with its excellent education program and in-state tuition.

Asa said, "Blackflies biting now, ah they? Waya you cutting these days, whose stumpage?"

Holding the ceramic mug between his big hands before drinking, Robbie drew the fragrance of coffee into his large nose. "Just cutting one li'l old subdivision in Copenhagen—on the east side of Mount Will. You know where Alcohol Rosy Road climbs into the woods'n stops?"

Asa chuckled. "Don't choo love cutting a subdivision?"

"Like I love searching for fleas." Robbie shakes his head. "The twins hate picking nits, too. They like to go in and mow 'em all down." He drank his coffee. "How'd that road get its name?"

"Whad y'think?"

"Ida know. Someone named Rosie sold sombreros during prohibition. Rosy who?—hed t'be a Roebuck."

"Deluded whiskey. Believe it or not—twas a Simon."

Robichaud burst a big laugh. "So they ain't all nice'n proper!" He looked pointedly at Asa's bandaged head. "Hear some of 'em even harbors killa owls."

"Someone ought harbor it in the bottom of the pond. Even ravens is better. At least they eat what's already dead'n keep the roads clean while theya about it."

Melvinia came and slid a plateful of eggs and hash under Robbie's nose. She went back to the cash register to wait on a customer. Robichaud reached for the salt and pepper. "Elda Simon's a strange bid herself. They say she's got bears, coy dogs, even a moose in her barn ... one time or another."

"I misdoubt the moose," said Asa, savoring the smell of hash. "But you never know. Her zoo's usually no worse'n Decatur's. Self and present company excepted."

Robbie grinned. "I run into Decatur coming out of Bearce's office on Front Street yestadee. He nearly run me down, never looked back. That in't like'im. Usually he's s'down right cuddly it's sickening."

"He was mad at Melviny earlier. Could be he's ill."

"Betta not be! He's cooking ah food!" He took another bite. "You hear what happened up't Jaspa Mountain yestadee? How the new snow-making got its style crimped—so to speak?" His grin was as bright as the fog lamps on his logging truck.

Asa chuckled. "Goldings got all bent out of shape, too, I guess."

"Well, Alvin's friend, Wilbur Hastings, was up theya when it happened—cutting for peanuts. You know how they pay people. Well, Wilbur was cutting a new trail, when he looks down through the trees'n sees this long shiny pipe, snaking down mountain. Heading straight fah the condominiums. Tons o'steel just sliding down mountain."

Asa had leaned back, elbows resting on the countertop, his coffee cup cradled on his stomach. He said, "Li'l spring rain, li'l thaw, some mud ... mountain makes pretzels out of good 16-inch pipe. They're lucky it didn't cream out a condo."

"Miracle no one was killed ... Piling up down theya, twisting itself round'n round. Took a couple dozen trees on its way down. What a mess."

The two men said all this with solemn faces, fooling no one. Melvinia had come over to top off their cups again, saying, "Think them Goldings believe in miracles?"

Robbie said, "They have to now no one got killed. Mountains don't put up with shit like that. But waya's OSHA when you need 'em? Someone ought've called'em to come look at that mess."

The two men sat talking, Asa starting on his fourth half-cup of coffee, Robbie finishing his hash and eggs.

In comes a stranger and sits at the stool one place away from the logging contractor. The stool squeaks as she turns a bit, squaring herself at the counter. Still leaning back in the elbow, Asa looks over at her, casual as real life. He takes in that she's wearing a blue bandanna and what looks like tourmaline—two studs—in her earlobes. Huh, haven't seen that before. Who wears more than one earing in each ear? Her speech is jagged giving Melvinia her order but she looks like any other working Mainer in her maybe mid-thirties. She asked for a cup of coffee and an English, grilled. Now Melvinia larrups around the corner into the kitchen. The stranger glances around and catches Asa looking at her. The stool squeaks as she turns toward him, leaning out from the counter. The words on her t-shirt read, "Naked-coed-diaper-changing."

"Well, Mr. Bartlett, if you look any harder you might just pierce another hole in my ear."

Asa feels himself change color, but he keeps on staring. Suddenly he knows. Chrischana Twitchell. Last of the Twitchells original to the area. Come back to Gottheim again. Seeing her conjures up so much historical remembering that it is moments before Asa can speak.

She is descended from Mahalalel Twitchell, the very first proprietor of Gottheim: the man who originally petitioned the Massachusetts powers-that-be for the Town, an inheritance for the heirs of colonial soldiers. Mahalalel Twitchell gave the town its first name—Farmingham Royal, after the two places occasioning the grant. In 1680 the town of Farmingham, Massachusetts mustered its own for the expedition to Port Royal, Acadia, to help roust the French out of the New World. The township in the wilds of Maine was their eventual reward for that effort. For a century after the town lots were first surveyed the name Twitchell so dominated the community that the index of Doctor Kimball's 19th century history contained more Twitchells than any other surname. Today, however, you can't find even one in the local phone book. Still, there are plenty of Twitchell place names.... Mountains, roads, ponds, streams, ledges bear the name Twitchell.

Now, here's Chrischana come back—who left town abruptly maybe fifteen years ago. Asa remembers: It was shortly before her father's death that summer. Hasn't been heard from since, not that he knew of, anyway. Bright as ever, she talks as though she saw him just yesterday. Still with that satin dark complexion and faintly exotic look from her mother's side; the Native American blood of the Abenaki Indian. She is broader though, maybe fifteen or twenty pounds heavier. Her features shockingly fuller. Looking at her, Asa feels the power of time. Maturity's more sedate gait is evident in her posture and walk. Her mysterious disappearance and sudden return, the effect is as lightning—instantaneous. Suddenly it's as though he *did* see her yesterday.

And a two-decades-old image, clear as yesterday, comes to his mind. She was fourteen or fifteen, chosen for the signature part of Jasper Mary, the proud Indian princess in buckskins and feathers, pony-mounted and dancing down Front Street as the parade wound through town. She was full of a tough, ready intelligence that could express itself in somewhat confident, not flashy, public performance. Yep, that pony gave her some trouble, Asa recalls. Back then, Chrischana was possessed of a notably sure spirit, with quiet dignity even in the midst of youthful joy. She was one to be depended upon. Many looked for her to leave town on a scholarship and make something of herself, returning now and again to encourage the youth of hardscrabble Gott'im. This plan she rejected, choosing to take nurse's training in Berlin, New Hampshire and be on hand to contribute to the life of the town. She worked weekends here in this diner and babysat evenings for a woman on the afternoon shift at the turning mill. All these hopes and works ceased the day she vanished without goodbyes to the people who loved her.

Daow. This can't be Chrischana. Not this early 1980s May day in Decatur's diner. According to his sequential perception, she should return to the stool in the same form in which she was last seen here—not in the broader body and matronly maturity of an aging townswoman. Slowly he shakes his head.

Chrischana smiles her same half-smile, and says something in the quiet voice he remembers: "Read in the bellyache that you were attacked by an owl. Do much damage?"

Flustered, again he shakes his head. "Might'o put out my eye, though."

She chuckles. "It's good to hear you say so. I mean ... in comparison with where I'm from ... the way people talk. In Phoenix they whimpah." She gave the word the soft elongated ending that she would have used fifteen years ago. Then, looking at the other man she says, "Hi, Mr. Robichaud. How's Alvin'n Ansel? They end up in the woods?"

"Cuss they did. Caunt expect them to work in a mill. Caunt breathe in theya, sawdust flying everywhere."

"And tuning skis isn't work, I s'pose?

Robbie snorts in disgust.

She says to Asa, "Good thing there was a Roebuck on hand to bring down that owl."

"You was always one t'think good of'em. People judge 'em hard but wouldn't you want one with you in a pinch?"

"More'n a Bearce," says Robichaud as a matter of fact. "Fust thing Lyman Bearce says to me after I sluiced my load coming down Kimball Mountain (on the phone later when I told 'em)—not choo all right, nothing broken?—but, 'Don't expect me to pay fah it!' "

Asa chuckled, nodding. Then, both to chide her and to satisfy his curiosity, he says to Chrischana, "You fom Arizona now?"

But, coming along with her grilled English, Melvinia crows, "Decatur's comin', Christy! Got all misty when I said you's out heah."

"Good! 'Cause I wanna ask 'em for my old job. He need any help just now?" She gives Melvinia an open hopeful look.

But, in the kitchen—sweating, flustered—Decatur hovers over the grill, finishing up some orders. Two omelets, ham, bacon, potatoes, and one drop egg. *Chrischana Twitchell's home! Home from godfrey Arizona!* What's it all mean? Bald-headed Decatur is thinking, How life carries on so plain and peaceful—year in, year out—little happening, as though it was no more than eggs on the griddle—? Is this Gott'im anamore? Not the ever Gott'im *I* ever knew.

Could he imagine not getting up at 3 a.m? …Not making soup and tuna salad and Jell-O; nor potatoes chopped and parboiled for homefries, coffee brewed by 5:30 a.m.? What's life if not that? Forty years ... with Gott'im people for my relations? ...

He shovels everything onto plates, sets two kinds of toast, muffins on the side, and all on the sill for Melvinia ... not daring to glance out to the counter where little Christy sits ... her dark skin glowing and eyes so lush, no doubt the same as on that last night when she helped him close in silence (and he knew not what was wrong). If she's back—can it be so bad?

"I see you, Decatur!" calls Chrischana Twitchell through the window in her low voice. "Can't hide forever!"

But he is coming round the corner now, worried and wary; through the door, wiping his hands and taking off his glasses (just as she remembers), rubbing them nervously with the bottom corner of his apron where it's most clean. He sets the glasses on his bland face and looks at her, bald head gleaming in fluorescent light. "Chrischana, we've been missing you," he says, chiding like, and holds out his hand.

But standing she pulls on him and, drawing his pasty face to hers, plants one on his sweaty cheek. "There," she says, a stranger in his eyes. "No need to scold. Got any fishing, hunting stories, bear stories for me to hear?"

"When'd I evah have time fah fishing?" And a stricken look comes on him.

"Well, don't take it so hard. I'm here now, to help.... That's if you can use me," she adds in haste. She stops. "I'm looking for work." This is not the response Chrischana has hoped for.

Looking at him, she is surprised by tears in Decatur's eyes. And folks in nearby booths are watching, some setting down their knives or forks, one peering over his raised coffee cup.

He says, "You know, Christy, you'd have a job if theya was one. But it looks like—if what Melviny says Asa says is true—you best go to Mass fah work." Then, stopping and starting, repeating himself in a tangled way, he continues as people gape or look a question. At last Decatur gasps in frustration, saying, "God's give Gott'im back to Mass'chusetts—if it was took fom them back then." His words deepen with the thunder of his emotion. "My lease's up next month, and Bearces give me th'news: Bearces waunt this property back. The skiers gont develop it!"

Lightning has struck the tin room, galvanizing the lot of them. Two score pair of eyes look at Decatur. No one moves.

Asa says, "Gory, it's not world's end. Theya's plenty of other locations. Open that empty place used to be Virgie's restaurant.... Won't take much getting used to."

And murmurs go around the room. Some look out through smudged windows toward the parking lot and highway. There the sun glances down the road directly from the east. Drivers leaving the valley of the ponds strike down their visors.

Robbie says, "We'll go wherever you go, Decatur. We still gut t'eat." He looks around and others, chuckling, agree.

But Decatur shakes his head, reaching for a napkin to blow his nose. "All's s'dear. Caunt afford any place else. 'N they's fixings, loans, red tape, utilities, parking.... All too much!" He reiterates it all again twice, and groans. "I'm gettin' done heah on Jasper Mary Day next month. Decatur's is finished!" And, overcome, he turns back into the kitchen.

No one follows. Offers of comfort seem vain, as stunned quiet settles down over them. For a moment Chrischana stares through the order window after the man who has turned his back to go stand again over the grill. Then she sits and leans on her elbows, staring into the murky depths of coffee in her cup. Robbie mutters something to himself about ritch bahstids, says it again bitterly to Asa, who barely answers. Robbie takes his mug and moves across to a booth where his cousin Bob Bilodeau is talking to another logger.

Asa is trying to make sense of Decatur's jumbled logic. What has Asa said that made him think jobs would go to Massachusetts? Never too good at it anyway, Decatur must be too upset to think straight. *Yuht*. There is something to this idea of land being "returned" to Massachusetts. Isn't something of the sort the subject of his ruminations lately? He looks across the diner, over the warped gritty floor, brushing the peeling tin ceiling with his gaze. *Godfrey, this place this seedy*. It offends Asa's impeccable sense of neatness. His gaze rests a moment on Melvinia standing at the dirty glass door, staring out into the littered parking lot. He sees Janie and Ethel Simons sitting in their regular booth, one idly stirring her coffee, the other looking with distaste at the old linoleum. Turning, he notices Chrischana, still staring into her coffee. She looks up at the window into the kitchen, makes a tentative move, settles back.

"Maybe he could use some help," he prompts.

She glances at Asa, coloring deeply, her Native eyes somber. "I dunno. I ran out on him years ago."

His glance slides away. Silence. And then he says, "Seen Balda Simon since y'got back? Funny thing.... He nevah married." He thought, too bad you're from away now. I could tell you a story about.... Something not quite right about that business of him staying three years in his room.

She nods in response to the pointed comment about marriage. "So I'm told." Another hasty little sentence that. "He still good with machinery.... Works in the chair factory—must be a mechanical engineer by now. "

"Daow. Just a mechanic!"

She looks away. "Good person, Balder. "

Asa nods, dying for information. His curiosity palpitating yet.

Balder's Love

Chrischana pays Melvinia for coffee and an English muffin, and lays fifty cents on the counter beside her plate. Outside she inhales the breath of spring, deeply. Leaves on beeches beside her car are beginning to unfurl. Has it been fifteen years since she last saw these green and gold buds lighting the branches like tiny flames? Gratefully she thinks of the glare of Phoenix as receding into a dream. May you shrink, evaporate, be nothing but a wash, a dry spot in the sand. Be a ghost town standing in concrete.... Bet your sky will be dirty a hundred years after.

She opens the battered door of her boat of a Bonneville, slides in behind the small wheel. Chrischana wants to get back to camp, where she left the boys, but first—got to find work. She starts the cavernous car and pulls out into the highway bypass leaving the disappointed hopes of Decatur's Diner behind. She can just see the eyes, hear the tongues marking her escape down the road. Asa Bartlett will preside over the speculations and rehashing of old rumors. Fifteen year-old gossip, freshened up again. Melvinia and everybody adding their jeezly two bits worth of recollection. Even when their facts are straight—rare enough!—they get it wrong.

Her smile is tight-lipped. Wouldn't want it any other way! It wouldn't be Gott'im without beech leaves and gossip unfolding. In two weeks I'll be sick of it.... If I could see it without the squint of self-absorption—I'd have some laughs now.

In their jeezly stories there is perception sometimes, a breadth of human experience laid bare: The stories of her people she's been missing. The diner talk reaching back, back ... into the past of what the oldest gossips can remember ... and beyond. If pieced together properly, by someone like Asa, it could tell the whole Story Twitchell. In Phoenix you couldn't be known—or miss-known!—like that. In Phoenix, who cared. Even Petey, the reason she stayed, didn't care.

Hand on the wheel and passing once familiar places, Chrischana tries to remember what she can of the story. Twitchells were the principal founders of Farmingham Royal, prosperous and prominent, before slowly descending into poverty, dispersion, eclipse. They laid out the town. But, on her mother's side—the Truemans, was Nataluk, a Native who took the local doctor to an island in Mason Pond on some pretext. What he wanted was to trade cached furs for the doctor's penknife. Dr. Lapham refused to trade, but, when Nataluk threatened to keep him on the island, the doctor disarmed him by bestowing the penknife as a gift, thereby gaining his friendship.

Chrischana could not help but remember how bears had figured in the family story: There was the teenager who was wounded and treed by one on the far side of Puzzle Mountain. The bear circled below, making sporadic attempts to retrieve him, while the boy whittled a stick then dipped it in his own blood to write "KILT BY BEAR" on his handkerchief. Such tales were why Decatur once always kidded her with bear stories.

The farm of her father, Daniel Albert Twitchell, was hillside land, neglected as was a lot of that Blackwell Mountain land. He had a potato field, small orchard, a garden, wood lot, and cut over blackberry puckerbrush. He suffered lead poisoning from pesticide applications and had to give up on the orchard. That land, she knows, is all gone now in liens and back taxes.

Father either kept his blood pressure problems secret or he knew nothing of them. The treelined streets of Gottheim blur as she remembers finding him beside the spring, and struggling to lift him into her arms. "Don't drop me, Christy," he whispered. She nagged him until he promised a trip to the doctor—and then satisfied her with an easy report of an apparently fictitious visit. Pregnant, in turmoil, forgetful of him, she ran out shortly before his death. Stopping in Elko, Nevada and thinking of him, she called Olive Lovejoy for news, and learned of his death. Traveling aboard *Trailways* through the desert, she kept hearing that whisper, "Don't drop me, Christy." Fifteen years. She's still hearing it. The words taught her to love in the midst of suffering, taught her endurance, to go on.

"I lied to Asa Bartlett!" Chrischana thumps the steering wheel emphatically: *I didn't know Balder was still single.* "Balder," she whispers. If only you knew."

They've been in the area barely twelve hours, arriving last evening as the light turned golden. They were exhausted, yet feeling the elation of a difficult journey achieved: making camp with a glad spirit, the four of them. Abenaki Notch, enclosed, protective. It was a comfort they needed. There was peace in the deep woodland beside the pool. Mountain water roared, the spring runoff, pouring greenish gold over rocks into the hole, just as she had seen it when a girl. —So cold last night, lit by great stars seen through nearly naked stems. This morning they heard songbirds, three kinds of thrush.

She left the boys fishing, something she had taught Daniel on the journey, and came into Gottheim: amazing to pass Balder's old '55 Chevy parked in the lot at Gottheim Chair. He must keep it up on blocks in winter, it looked so new. The aqua beauty Chevy, nearly chromeless compared to the '57.... It harbored their youth and shared sexuality. Daniel was conceived in the car ... right on the woods road beside the pool.

Chrischana has been circling through the village, remembering the story, wasting gas, time. The corner of Livery and Front Streets, easing the big car past the few old brick blocks, gaping at the skiers' boutiques and trendy restaurants in the old Victorian and Federalist houses. And, from back of the storefronts, gleams of Ben Hutchins Pond. The ice can't have been out too long—I guess. Rounding the corner at the common, onto School Street, past the straight white churches, and out towards the academy as the Congo Church strikes the half-hour. There is the Gottheim Academy, with its spacious central lawn encircled by well proportioned early Greek revival brick buildings. Classes will soon be over, IICE will begin summer sessions. That's Lord's Hill behind, a spur of great Jasper Mountain, and site of an old topaz mine, long defunct.

The sights and associations seep into her, a welcome distraction.... From the real problem. How can she tell him? Even how to face him? She traveled eastward from Phoenix, glibly concocting scenarios. But arriving here.... These fantasies dissolve as reality pricks at her. There is no good way to tell a man you conceived a child by him fifteen years ago and ran off in order to? ... You went to the desert, starved yourself of living green— denied him even knowledge for his rights.... For reasons—you no longer remember.

This is a bizarre plot, this tangled experience—life. He does not even know of Daniel's rich existence.... Miracles, my sons, brought out of the white hell of Phoenix.... A strange new life for her children.... Here, where they know—only one another.

She is grateful to find herself on a back street, winding her way up Crazy Knoll with its quiet old houses. Face Balder? She can't. It's as plain and smooth as one of Birch River's cobblestones. Oh, this is a devilish idea, this late coming to Gottheim!

There are other places, other woods they can camp in. Some other Maine town they can go to and live anonymously....

But Chrischana's heart is breaking. The dream of returning to her community and people is breaking apart.

In Phoenix she had taken a subscription to *The Village Voter*, under a fake name. She'd taken books out of the library by an author who encouraged her to rebuild thoughts of community. That was when Gottheim began reestablishing itself as the ideal. She sweltered in that desert city, sweating over a shirt press in the dry cleaners, and found kindly Gottheim filling her imagination. Gottheim, where people cared if you lived or died, how you lived and died. Little Gott'im, which Petey mocked and derided her sore over. Gottheim, whose people had crowned her with feathers and set her astride a pony, prancing in the midst of a parade as Jasper Mary. Gottheim made her act like a princess during those hard teenage years, when all she had to keep her in line and make her worthy was Father's pride, and that vicious pointed pitiless erring gossip. It made you want to be good—or else a stranger in some huge anonymous city. *Gott'im, I can't lose you now!*

She has reached the edge of the knoll that looks out over the railroad tracks at the end of the village. Across fields stand misty mountains. Aching within, Chrischana shuts off the engine to lean against the cool glass of the window. Above and across the street, stands the Gothic mansion of some old Gottheim family, but she takes no notice. High, inside the turret, a shadow stands still behind a window pane. But Chrischana does not look up to see. Hands now clenched in her lap, she leans over the steering well, agonizing, whispering, "Can't face him ... can't face you, can't." Filled with self-loathing, the woman whimpers.

Chrischana weeps. Long sloppy heavy weeping. Then she rests a tear streaked face against the wheel, staring out the passenger window. A wreathing mist is lifting, parting from the mountains. In the distance stands Mount Will, somewhat apart from the others. Her empty gaze rests upon its quiet summit. A collar of white mist adorns it, quietly ... and now that quiet is seeping into her. Slowly she absorbs it, like greening moss in rain or dew. It is as though the vapor is crossing invisible barriers between the known and unknown worlds ... only to impart this quiet to her.

And now, as she looks out on Mount Will, a thought occurs, a story. Sitting in that unbearable trailer in searing Phoenix, she read in *The Voter* of changes in Gottheim, along with the more familiar neighborly disputes, school questions, Water District problems; a ski resort was growing and impacting the character of the town. Resort family members trying a night landing at the unlighted Edwin Brown Field. Someone was waiting at the other end of the dark strip, headlights on to light the way. But the plane never showed, for Mount Will stood in the way. Only the young daughter, or somebody, of the resort owner survived the crash among the trees on that dark summit. Concussed and bruised, the child made her way down mountain. Somehow she made it to a little house beside a dirt road and was taken in. The man there guessed she'd been in an accident, but had no way of knowing it was in flight on the mountain above. The girl managed to call her sister, and a sisterly response loosened her recollection. She said a dark Angel had taken her from the plane and brought her down toward the light. When she looked around, the woman was gone.

Chrischana sits upright, musing, looking out on mysterious Mount Will. *A guide met her and carried her down.* The quiet continues in this resting woman. Reluctantly she turns the key, starting the big rough engine again.

The daughter of Mahalalel Twitchell, nine generations removed, sits looking up at the array of wide Bavarian gables on the Jasper Mountain Hotel. Behind the hotel and new lodges strands of lift-cables ascend, lit by the morning sun. The little rope-tow skiway, cut long ago in the dark expanse of pointed firs ... where is it now? That lone trail of her youth—gone under this pile of concrete, half-timbering, glitter and glitz. Where once was a ritualistic part of her heritage, images of fiberglass ski-toting hordes with their shiny-faced children, new cars and two homes now filled the slopes of her imagination. She remembers the yellow bonfires, the old gasoline powered rope tow, her heavy secondhand wooden skis bought with savings earned in Morrill's potato harvests. The slopes are covered in money now— No, plastic. Isn't that how people buy things like this?

Maybe skiers just needed something to keep them out of trouble. No, she wouldn't trade her rough-textured life for ten smooth ones. There's no earth in them. All I need is enough. Won't hurt myself with envy or hostility. She wanted to be alive. The boys gave her substance and purity in caring for them. Without Benaiah, Nathan, Daniel—she'd be dead inside.

Have to get the boys out of that tent before winter. She might do it in three months, in time for the start of school in August. They could enroll tomorrow until the end of this term—with only a P.O. box number. They'd have enough money for gas and food to last till week's end. They could stretch to two if the fishing was good. Hope the game warden doesn't show. No money for a license or fines.

Chrischana removed her bandanna, loosened her braid and brushed her hair smooth. Applying lipstick, she glanced at herself in the rearview. No longer having that withdrawn sightless look, her eyes had calmed since the prayer of Mount Will. ...Since leaving Petey.

She grabbed her knapsack and purse, reached in the back and took down the hanger with her good blouse and skirt. She would have to change in the women's room. *Naked-coed-diaper-changing* won't make a good impression in personnel. Chrischana glanced solemnly into the mirror. She sighed and thrust open the door.

Stepping out of the tiny condominium unit into the carpeted hallway Gloria Fay gives the Morgans a bright smile. Simply and sweetly she thanks them for letting her show them the time-share units. Walking toward the lobby together, their comments are light, appreciative. In the absence of his assistant, brother Jimmy has Gloria mopping up this morning, showing prospective buyers some of the facilities of the Jasper Mountain resort complex. She has just given the young couple—he, an investment counselor, she a junior partner in a family law firm in Massachusetts—a tour, including jacuzzi-pools-sauna-fitness center-day care-restaurant-conference rooms-ballroom *et al*. Upon reaching the commons, which overlooks the Great Room with large mineral stone fireplace, Gloria offers a business card and shiny brochure. "Please feel free to call us if you have more questions on this plan." Again the smile. "Thanks so for considering us."

The Morgans make an encouraging reply and saunter off, murmuring to one another over the brochure.

Gloria glances at her dainty wristwatch cum bracelet and makes her way into the spacious reception center just off the commons. She picks up her little purse from the desk then stops to look out the wide windows up the faintly greening flanks of Jasper Mountain. She has a lunch date down in Gottheim, but there is still plenty of time. Gloria walks over and stands looking at the still somber slopes, streaked with spotty trails—patches of snow, outcroppings and mud—a haze of delicate green now forming like a cloud to transform all.

Sometimes her feelings for Jasper Mountain approach reverence. Here upon its flanks she's too near to see the central rounded batholithic head, which gives the mountain its mighty appearance, yet she addresses it in her thought. *You are one of the old stone gods, and I am so happy to be here.* Looking fondly up these flanks, she can scarcely believe that she is actually here—at last living full-time on the mountain.

Here is where she has wanted to live since that first winter vacation as a twelve year-old tomboy. Jasper's pull on her is mystical, as though its great gravity and her small gravity tug upon one another. Jasper is the thing she has ever been faithful in feeling to, having lost interest in Christianity ages ago. Of course she loves mom and dad, her brothers and sisters, but they will always be background love that she counts on. Mom has instilled right thinking, confidence, the ability to dream, a sense of the possibilities, ambition to succeed on her own. Daddy encouraged ambition solely with funding, and this happy daughter will reap its rich harvest. Jimmy, too. This is how life is meant to proceed.

Gloria's thought scarcely touches these themes, for living in Maine is what absorbs her. The place invigorates, whereas study failed to support her in the low times. *So* glad to be finished with the rigor of academic deadlines. Staring up Jasper, she gives herself a grin. Getting through grad school is the hard part because studies are only a means to an end. Without that gold-lettered piece of paper there is no work with appeal to be had. That baccalaureate degree might as well be a high-school diploma. Like many of her friends, though weary, she went back to school once she saw the abominable rewards for kids with liberal arts degrees. The '80s are not the picnic Republicans like Jimmy, with business degrees, think it is. Kids who can't swing the money for grad school settle for the nightlife and minimum-wage jobs. And kid themselves that it's only temporary.

Jasper Mountain! Rugged face streaming with trails. Here, in the privacy of my mind, you are the mythic symbol of both intimate friendship and aloof majesty—my best friend. In my childhood winters I grew up with you, watched your industry grow. The resort thrives, but no one here sees you as I do. They can't know what you mean to me. And now I'm going to earn my own little piece of you. *Earn.* I'll never be childish, dependent, again.

Gloria smiles, her reflection faint in the glass. She turns, starts for the door, then pauses a moment looking back with a child's imagination and spirit. "And thank you for showing me Balder." Gloria will not be ungrateful.

Her small purse slung from a spaghetti strap on her shoulder, her little heels clicking over the slate floor of the lobby, Gloria is a burnished blond, tanned the year round, immaculate and classy. She pushes her way through the glass doors of the lobby just as a brown woman in bandanna and backpack, with garments slung over her arm, approaches. Gloria reads the T-shirt she's wearing, holding the door for her, laughing. "Hey! That's the way! Make those boys own up to their actions!"

The woman returns a faint smile. "Which way to the restroom?"

"Through the arch opposite the stuffed buck and turn right. Can't miss it!" Still holding the door, Gloria watches her cross the lobby. Turning toward the parking lot she finds herself thinking about the locals. A bit darker for a Yankee, that one. But the dress is all Maine. The girls are basically stylish, but the women wear practical clothes, and that's it. All on their way to becoming "old Mainers," dowdy and neat with the style all washed out of them.... But so full of character! Especially when they talk. Not possible that I should ever get acquainted with one—but then comes Balder. And he's well on his way to being an old Mainer, but he's awesome, absolute! A wedge-shaped hunk—the kind to send shivers down your legs.

She trots down the sidewalk, smiling deliciously. Gloria will not kid herself on this: She would never be attracted to just any Mainer unless he was as good-looking and witty as Balder. She admires them all in a quasi-romantic way. They're hardy, smart (but some are illiterate!), and far tougher than she will ever be. *I'm way spoiled while they have to work hard for low wages.* And she wonders if they feel exploited. They make a living—Is that enough? She should ask Balder, get an angle on attitudes to augment her study. Anecdotes will liven it.

Spying her little red Caprice against a row of dark conifer, she smiles. Gloria loves seeing her new car against a backdrop of forest green. That touch of red perks up the somber scene. Just a spot of it can give a painting that little extra appeal. Like an El Greco. A Monet. Everything has significance if you look for it. She unlocks the door and slides in, laying her purse on the passenger seat. Gloria starts the puring engine of the little sports car and pulls out into the lane.

Significance, that's it. Winding her way down toward the highway, she decides to stop at the library in search of some. The library! Way too tiny. Cramped, stacked with ancient falling apart editions. Some of those things haven't been checked out in forty years. Dark in there, too, the only light some glaring bulbs. Their hours are abysmal. She's used to strolling into a library whenever. It's frustrating to arrive at 4:00 p.m. on a Wednesday or eleven a.m. on Monday and find the door locked.

She could go down to Guildford, but she is meeting Balder for lunch and can't be late. Being a blue-collar worker, he has to punch in and out. Gottheim Chair would probably go under if he wasn't there to keep the junk machinery going.

Once in the library she rummages to find what she's after, then seats herself where light falls in at the window seat. H.A. Guerber's *Myths Of the Norseman* would have it. May light comes through the panes onto the old pages. The glass does not quite mute the singing of a dusky little bird on a budding branch outside. Gloria turns the pages, glancing curiously from title to title. "The coming of Brunhild," the "History of Frey." "Balder." Yes! She has teased him about that name almost from the beginning.

She laughed about it while picking fiddleheads yesterday. "What kind of mother names her son Balder?"

He grinned that great grin at her question. "One who caunt think about children's names. Comes up with some beauts fah animals, though. Gram give me this name. That branch of the family were Norwegians who believed in Jesus Christ but told stories of faeries and gods. Balda was pot o'Norse mythology."

"Like with the Vikings?"

"The same. "

"I hear lots of strange names here in the Meguntics. A lot of Bible names. Viking names don't seem appropriate."

But he grinned. "This is Viking soil. Nevah heard 'o Vineland, Markland? Theya south of all the other lands: Finland, Iceland, Greenland, Helluland. And, more recent, Scandinavians came here along with other immigrants." He plopped a handful of fiddleheads into the sack, and said with a touch of mockery, "Thought you knew so much about this place fom your big master's study."

His grin was provoking and she felt her face flush. "Well, I have been doing that study! Balder Simon, I know more about the statistical dynamics of this area than you do—demographics—population trends, composition of labour force, income distribution, housing costs, seasonal variations—! I know projections in manufacturing, transportation, retail, location quotients...."

He let her trail off, then said, "And it's all in your computer, waiting for you to touch a couple buttons. You wouldn't be able to think if you had no fingas!"

"I might say the same about you! What can you do without those tools of yours?"

"Got me!" Light shone through the tree stems, gleaming off of his white-blond hair as he shouted his laughter.

Gloria read on page 197. "... Balder, the beautiful, was worshiped as a pure and radiant god of innocence and light ... which gladdened the hearts of gods and men .... " The young woman sits in the mote-shot light of the window in the musty library, poring over the first part of Balder's story.

> The god of light was well versed in the science of runes,
> which were carved on his tongue; he knew the various
> virtues of simples, one of which...was called 'Balder's brow,'
> because its flower was as...pure as his forehead.

Thoughtfully she lifts her gaze, staring without seeing at the bird on the budding branch. Mmmm. It's rich. This must be the Romance my linguistic analysis professor poked fun at. I must be ignorant: I like it! She smiles a secret subversive smile.

"The only thing hidden from Balder's radiant eye was the perception of his ultimate fate."

Gloria Fay closes the book, looks about the cramped stacks behind her, and the precarious piles heaped on the floor. Someone should do something for this place. *Maybe I should.* Clasping the book, she moves lightly over the bare floor to check it out at the desk.

She flies down the highway toward what she thinks of as the grubby chair factory. A very interesting place, though. Like something out of a children's book: dark corners, wires and pipes, conveyors, strange passages, mezzanines, sloping floors, old open elevators and weird dilapidated machinery. Fresh wood shavings, old sawdust piles everywhere. What fun—talking to Balder at all hours while he worked like a fiend on some dangerous-looking contraption. (He might spend hours on one, get it running, and have to work on it all over again three nights later.) All the while he cracked jokes about the way Ms. Prescott ran the place. Gloria's impression is that the owner is eccentric. Apparently she forgoes buying decent machinery, or paying her suppliers of wood for production, in favor of spending many thousands on an elaborate generating system. "Just what we need," cracked Balder, over this system which is outsized in proportion to the company's needs: "Gott'im Chair, manufacturers of fine waste vapors."

Evidence of the jest appears as Gloria rounds Mount Morrill. The factory, spewing excess steam, comes into view. The precarious hodgepodge of disheveled buildings looks as though it will fall over. How has the weight of winter's snow spared it? Volumes of steam pile up before the dark somber face of Mount Morrill: enough steam to heat forty houses at ten below—or so Balder claims. Gloria has heard talk to support the supposition that Gottheim Chair is the derision of all the mill owners, those whose mills dot the surrounding towns in these mountains.

The little mills are scattered all over the Meguntics, providing low wages for those who can't get into the paper mill—where some can earn as much as fifteen dollars an hour. Even Balder says he will apply for work in Adirondack Paper down in Guildford. Gloria thinks it a bad idea. "Place stinks! When the wind's wrong you could smell it all the way up here. Think of its always being in your clothes."

He retorted that the wind is never wrong. "You caunt say that a weatha system spanning a quarter of the globe's a mistake."

"Why not apply as a Sno-Cat mechanic at Jasper Mountain?"

"The idea's t'earn a living."

She slows the little red car, turning off the highway onto the puddled sand and gravel lot, allowing it to roll down toward the open rear door of the mill. Gloria waves gaily as he steps out to meet her. Balder leans into the window, kissing her quick. He is as happy as a territorial loon.

Gloria's here! "Now we can swim!" he says.

She pulls back. "Like hell, fella! Snow's still on the mountain. Patches of it, anyway. This ain't no swimmin' weatha." Her blond pageboy swinging, she shakes her head.

But Balder hurries around and jumps in the car. "Turn this fuss bucket round'n head down the highway, that way. There's a turn off down theya, leads back into Abenaki Notch. Evah been t'Deep Hole?"

"Sounds cold and *is* too cold for swimming."

"Not too cold fah a ritual. Snowmelt's the thing t'get winter out'o your joints." He looks over at her striking profile, the fringed eye, the chin that juts a little too much. The chin, he decides, is the imperfection that heightens her beauty. Lord! He's lucky.

She protests. "But skiing keeps me limber, shaped up all winter long,"

"I'd say!" He grins. "But Deep Hole's fah more bracing. We need t'get the wimpiness out. If you're gont live heah now we got toughen you up."

She glances at him. "Will it make me a real Mainah?"

"Nothin'd do that." He grins. "You'll nevah be nothing but a summer complaint turned inside out. Skiers ah winter complaints—Wuss'n summer people. Least we got them trained to have a li'l humility. Only took about three-quarters of a century to whip 'em into shape."

Her eyes still on the road, she flings out an arm, belting him across the ribs. "I'll have you know that diner woman calls me *dear*. If I'm not becoming a Mainer then what's that?"

Balder can only shout. "It's no space above flatlander!" He touches her arm. "Theya's the turnoff."

Daniel Twitchell's stringer of three small brown trout is tied to a twig of the yellow birch leaning out over Bear River. The fishing pole now stands idle among the thin birch stems. Watching his little brother, he sits on a rock, blackflies clouding his solemn face. Nathan hops from rock to rock above the icy stream. Daniel is thinking for the umpteenth time that he has to make sure Nathan doesn't tumble in and get chilled. At least they are far enough away from that fall over there into what Mother calls Deep Hole.

The middle brother, Benaiah, is alternately hopping around with Nathan or wandering off down the muddy old logging road. Never spotting Mother, he always comes back after a few minutes. Daniel can sense his unhappiness. When will Mother come back? Gone looking for work in the village called Gottheim, she has left him in charge of the boys and their camp. Daniel shifts on the rock, looks around at emerging buds, into the tall thin stems of the endless thicket; up into the swollen tips, and up up to the blue northern sky. Never has he seen sky so blue. Missing the concrete of Phoenix, his glance falls back down to Nathan.

"When's Mother coming?" Nathan calls. Waving his skinny arms, the boy narrowly avoids a tumble.

"Get back here, Nathan," Daniel yells above the rush of the water. "Now!" Those rocks are way too slippery.

"Don't haf'ta!" But he hops back to Daniel, saying, "What does Dad look like again?" It has been maybe two weeks since they've seen their dad, Peter Prince. And every day Nathan asks Daniel this question. Yesterday the older boy answered, "Like a man working on his motorcycle." Now he says, "Like Benaiah with his green eyes, only bigger."

Nathan's fresh features form the word, "Oh." Then, pointing out the metamorphic swirl in a nearby rock, he asks, "How come the rocks are all curly like that? Did we have curly rocks in Phoenix?"

Daniel looks down at the stone spread by the little pool where his trout flash and float. The wet surfaces gleam with transformed mica. He says, "It's what happens when rocks sits in water too long. Like when it wrinkles the tips of your fingers after washing a big pile of dishes."

"Oh." Leaning on Daniel's knees with his thin hands, Nathan begins jigging himself up and down, up and down. Sometimes he alternates, kicking back with his feet. "When's Mother coming?"

Daniel addresses the deep fierce sky. "She'll be back when the leaves are all the way out." He drops his gaze, searching through stems for Benaiah. There he is, a gangling form in T-shirts and holey jeans, coming this way. Light shines through the woods except where dark clumps of evergreen seem to absorb it. There is a close feeling about this place. Closed in. Daniel feels the walls of the Abenaki Notch encroaching, though here they are cloaked in great thickets of endless brush. Puckerbrush she calls it.

Nathan shakes his head. "I don't think so," he says about the leaves coming out. "I'm hungry."

"So'm I," says Benaiah, approaching on the track. "Let's cook the fish. "

Unmoving, Daniel sits slumped on the rock.

"C'mon, Daniel," wheedles Benaiah. His tangled brown hair frames his wide fair face.

"You want to fillet 'em?" says Daniel at last. His own face is somewhat square and dark, a drab almost greenish color in comparison to mother's more glowing brown. His brow is wide, eyes seldom smiling. He hears an engine, quiet and too smooth to be the Bonneville's. Looking off toward a bend in the track, he tenses until bright red flashes through the stems. The game warden wouldn't have a red car. Mother was unsure if Daniel was over age for fishing without a license.

Together the three boys watch as the little car pulls up among the opening may apple near their campsite opposite. A tall man and pretty woman get out laughing, talking. She's as bright as the sun, classy, stylish. Her suit seems to shine. The man dresses like Dad, the way highway or construction workers, mechanics, dress. But he is bigger than Dad, has a quiet power. This man moves with confidence. Daniel sees these things, makes these comparisons as they come toward him.

The man smiles a little, asks, "That your camp?" seeing the fish, his smile widens. "Nice brookies you got theya. "

Daniel only nods.

"My brother caught'em," says Nathan. Reaching thin arms up to a budding branch, he begins pulling it up and down up and down, up and down.

"Don't the blackflies bother you, camping?" The woman asks this, fanning them away with her pearly manicured hand.

"Sometimes," answers Daniel, wondering what they're doing here. No fishing pole, and the woman doesn't look ready to fish—not in high heels, slinging a little purse.

"They won't bite till they're already t'lay eggs," the man says to her. He flashes a smile at Daniel and moves her off onto the soggy path through trees, toward Deep Hole. As the boys watch, she steps gingerly over some protruding roots. The murmur of their voices is soon lost to the sound of rushing water.

Nathan starts to run after them and, after hesitating, Benaiah goes too. Daniel looks away, restive but resigned. Now I'll have to go, to make sure Nathan isn't hurt. Benaiah might get into trouble too. Daniel wonders what he'd do if either one fell in. He's not much of a swimmer himself, there being no place much for them to learn in Phoenix. He wants to call his brothers away, but the strangers make him shy of it. The boys will probably just ignore him and then he'll feel like a fool. No doubt the man can swim, but what good will that do if Nathan hits his head going down? You can't tell what it's like under that water except that it's rocks rocks rocks, nothing but rocks. Why doesn't mother come back? He worries it all, taking the path.

Over rocks in the rushing water he approaches toward the fall, seeing that the man is already down to his jockey shorts, about to drop. Yelling, he's gone. Standing back, Nathan and Benaiah are at the brink, looking down from rocks into the roaring swirling waters. As Daniel nears, the roar of the river is like that of a bear roaring without surcease. He stands above with the boys now, looking down, shivering. The man's head is visible in the white water. He calls to the woman who is undoing her clothes on the bank.

Daniel motions to Benaiah and takes Nathan by the arm. Why did mother bring them here? Placing his feet just so on the rocks, he leads his brothers, keeping to the rough and avoiding the smooth and slick surfaces, watching the others as they step. At last they are on shore in the budding bushes, looking back.

The woman has stripped to her shining white slip and is stepping into the stream above the greenish narrow fall. She throws up her arms. She is gone. The boys hurry down the sloping path to see her bobbing in the shimmering pool of Deep Hole. At a little distance they see her water-dark hair molded to her head. Amid the roar and foam she is shouting for joy.

Daniel cannot be sure.... It sounds like she is crying, "I'm alive! I'm alive!"

Doing Business in the House Of God

Tidy and small, bespectacled and blond, James Fay hurried out of the men's room, nearly colliding with a woman in bandanna and T-shirt with idiotic logo. Already late for his lunch date with the boss, he brushed past, leaving her to sidestep any way she could. Mr. Fay scurried past the mounted white-tailed buck and across the lobby toward the Gemstone Restaurant. This sales dynamo was suddenly preoccupied with a new pitch: *Harry, the housekeeping staff should be wearing uniforms.*

The hostess, Karon, stood smiling a welcome by the velvet rope just inside the panelled room. She too was a member of the Jasper Mountain brat pack, people who had grown up together, winters, on the mountain. Karon was luscious in deep blue, her dark hair pinned back with matching barrettes.

Jocular, beaming, James Fay came up to her. "How'd you like to wear a uniform?"

Her smile dropped. A scowl puckered her white brow. "I'd hate it, you?"

"But you'd look good in a uniform!"

"I mean how would you like to wear one?" His smile was so maddeningly fatuous.

"Some people have no sense of humor. I am wearing a uniform. Three-piece, with a silver textured tie—for that touch of elegance." He turned smartly, still with the joke, indicating the tie with a flourish. "Don't worry, you're safe. Hostesses must look elegant too. But you know, Karon, you should have gone back to school instead of opting for ski bum." He grinned at her raised eyebrows and said, "Maybe it's not too late."

Then, craning his neck and looking past, he missed her glare. "Is Harry here yet? Never mind." He grabbed one of her menus and hurried away.

"Sure," she hissed, looking darts at his retreating backside.

—

Harry Golding, formally of a suburb outside Boston Massachusetts, is descended from Palmer Golding, one of the original proprietors of Farmingham Royal. He will take a break in a few years, his head-of-steam dissipating, loss and personal sorrow breaking in. He will settle back, feeling the emptiness of empire drying him out. In dryness he will turn his hand to less acquisitive activity, genealogy among other things, and stumble into the fact of his predecessor Palmer Golding and his initial proprietary claim in the wild district north of Boston. He will sit at his desk, looking out on a mountain far distant from Jasper, an absent smile in his gaze, remembering Gottheim as he first saw it ... a quiet New England village sheltered by a great round-headed mountain with a small neighboring skiway on its back slope.

At the moment, sitting here in the Gemstone Restaurant waiting on Fay, he is unaware of this salty fact. He came to Gottheim more than a decade ago as a young entrepreneur, buying little Jasper Mountain skiway from developers who went belly up in a bad economy. And his brother Julius later joined him. Although his touch is generally sure, Harry Golding is always amazed at the fates of finance. For instance, four years ago, when the mountain had half the trails, condominiums newly built in the area went bankrupt. "Condos of cards," went the joke around here, but the fortunes of three good people were destroyed. It happened in the wake of a real estate boom that had seen property values rise three hundred percent in a single year. There were others who lost that year. Cory, Graham.... He begins ticking off investors who lost everything during that period. They sank dollars and dreams into Gottheim area construction and properties, bought land from the old-timers—all on the basis of what he is doing here. But their timing was ever so slightly off. Interest and development in the mountain itself had not fully ripened, and in consequence everything went down under the hammer, sold for twenty cents on the dollar. Last year, even two years ago—That was the time to begin. The auctioned properties now prosper but the original dreamers are gone. He sees the timing clearly now, and is sure the losers do too.

"Did I keep you waiting, Harry?" James Fay pulls out a chair across from him.

"Not at all, Fay." He looks for Evan, the waitperson.

"Uniforms, Harry! I just bumped into one of the vulgar T-shirts—"

"Let's order, shall we?" Evan has appeared, pad in hand.

Briefly Fay scrutinizes her neat dark shirtwaist before ordering.

When she is gone Golding says preemptively, "This is your only chance to talk to me before I'm off to Quebec for a week."

Open for further confidence, Fay raises an eyebrow but knows better than to ask about Canada. He also knows he does not want to waste what time he has on uniforms. He clears his throat. "You heard me use the term 'aggregate' in connection with this idea?"

Golding nods. "I've read of the concept. A hamlet, of some sort, surrounded by no more than a score of second home single-family dwellings—the nucleus of a rural 'neighborhood.' Perhaps complemented by a working farm or other rural enterprise."

"Exactly. A more lively development concept." James Fay is beaming again, excited. "Harry, it's as though family culture is finally coming first—showing a wise, moral way to proceed in the practical business of development."

Golding smiles. A very slight smile. He picks up his martini as Fay continues.

"After decades of trial and error—From ticky-tacky crammed together over vast tracts to spacious-gracious five acre lots—we've come back, Harry, to the sense of—of what's best for people!" Fay emphasizes the words by tapping the side of his hand on the table top. "Ever since Levittown we've been trying to kiss away the very thing that's best for people. How, finally, do people want to live? They want to live in a caring community, one where they can be sure their kids will be safely nurtured." Again he taps the tabletop with the side of his hand.

Light hazel eyes gleaming, Golding aims his slight smile at Fay. With forearms propped on the table, his chin lightly resting on the laced fingers of his manicured hands, he stares at his tablemate. Harry Golding wears a brown cardigan shot with amber threads. His open shirt collar reveals a tanned throat. He has a definite and undisturbed fondness for the young man across from him, for his naivete and enthusiasm.

And tidy James Fay pitches ahead with enthusiasm. "We put at most twenty percent of the land in development—infrastructure, houses, telemark trails, even a millpond, and leave the rest markedly wild. As with condos, there'll be an owners association for maintenance—but the aggregate will have far more aesthetic appeal." (Tap tap tap tap.) "And a healthy ambience...."

Golding lets him continue until Evan returns with their salads— Golding's tabooli, Fay's crabmeat. And then, as Fay pauses to eat, Golding asks, "How much land, where?"

"Fifty plus acres. On the wild Birch River, secluded at the base of Mason Mountain. There'll be cross-country till the cows come, due to a network of logging trails on adjacent paper lands. The centerpiece will be an old mill race. Have to rebuild the dam out of the hewn granite lying around. In summer it'll be idyllic, in winter elegant, austere. Oh, and it abuts one of the unincorporated towns. Wild, Harry wild."

Losing its ironic tinge, Harry's smile slips toward admiration. "What's the problem in Copenhagen?" He asks suddenly.

James Fay stops, signals Evan for more coffee. *Why does he do this?* Lately, Golding seems to enjoy throwing him off. Just as Fay is finding his rhythm, relaxed and finely concentrated.... And, true to form, Harry hasn't even shown any immediate interest in the figures.

"Nothing to worry about, Harry. It's just that little piece on the outlet of the fifth pond along the valley. For Dad and Mom. Not enough setback from the pond due to the road. Since it's less than an acre it's undersized for regs for construction. But the board has said they will hear the appeal." He wants to say, it's personal, Harry, but that would sour the conversation ... if not the relationship. "They need a variance, that's all. "

"So, why was it splattered across *The Voter* last week?"

Fay fiddles with his napkin, taking his time. He hates being checked this way. It's demeaning, as though he were Golding's son, not his associate and the man is only thirteen years his senior. Casually he says, "Because the appeal was delayed. Look Harry, you must've read the thing. The deadline passed before they received my request."

But Golding is not in a merciful mood. "The envelope was postmarked ten days after the date of your letter inside, Jimmy. You tried to cover with an excuse about harassed assistants and constraints on your time. Don't you realize what an ass that makes you look?" His chin resting lightly upon his laced fingers, Golding closes his eyes. "I'm not sure I want you handling the village negotiations. The news of the proposed 'taking' has just hit the stands and already there's talk of circulating a petition. It's not really necessary for me to remind you that the contingency for your removal has been provided for in our agreement?"

Fay quieted, clearing his face of earnestness. He looks down, resisting the urge to scan nearby tables for eavesdroppers. This is as much as he can stand. He says quietly, "Is that what you want?"

His eyes gleaming once more, slowly Golding smiles. He withdraws his gaze, leans back, looks across the room. "What I want is for you to handle yourself better."

Fay looks quickly at him. But already the man is far away—in Quebec. Relieved, the younger man expels his breath. "I can do that, Harry. "It is a soft reply.

"Good." Golding looks at Fay, smiles.

—

The clock in the gleaming chrome desk set said 12:45. Jimmy pulled out the chair, sat down. He had not told Harry of his plan for several aggregates around the base of Mason Mountain, thinking it best to sell him on the concept first. He drummed his fingers before reaching for the phone, dialing his father at the Hancock Building in Boston.

"Dad! How's it going? How's the back?... Glad to hear it. What'd you do last weekend?... How was it out there? Your first time to the Vineyard this year wasn't it? How's Mom liking it?" James laughed. "Well she loves to give you a hard time."

He drummed his fingers on the blotter, glanced aside at the monitor. He swiveled around and leaned back, looking up at somber Jasper Mountain, saying, "It's still got that drab muddy look, but there's a haze of red higher, and green nearer the base.... OK, I guess, but she's been hanging out with a mill mechanic.... All right, but don't expect her to listen. *You* can't do anything with her, neither can I.... Yes, if it does I'll let you know. Better not say anything to Mom. Right now she's so embarrassed she doesn't even want me to meet him—won't admit it, though.... No, don't worry; the waiver should go through. Get out your plans!" Fay's voice gentled: "OK. Tell mom I love her, will you?"

Fay hung up, turned and pressed enter on the keyboard. The screen lit up, green and ready for spreadsheets. But he turned back to the mountain, absently. Smiling faintly, he ran a thoughtful finger across the faint cleft in his chin. A quiet gladness came into him. He had managed to refrain from bragging to his father about his deals. But, as quickly as it had come the peace was gone, supplanted by anticipatory glee over Mason Millrace. Or, maybe it should be Millrun. Which was the more euphonic?

The single original building of the Gottheim Chair factory was built by the Town in 1890 for ninety-five hundred dollars. Initially, Amos T. Prescott leased the property and building, formed the company and began manufacturing some of the finest chairs in the country, employing sixty townspeople. Over ensuing decades the original neat structure and property were purchased from the town and haphazardly amended on all sides, as expansion warranted. Increasingly, its outer appearance mirrored the shambling business practices of Amos Prescott's descendants.

Tidying her desk his granddaughter, Theodora Prescott, glances out the window in time to see Balder Simon get out of a little red Caprice and round the corner on his way to the rear entrance. She sighs, and gives him time to enter the maintenance shop, then steps into the hall, herself heading toward the parking lot. Exiting the building, she is careful to shake out her skirt in case of clinging sawdust. On her way to the car a shadow crosses the lot, momentarily shading it. Theodora looks up.

Oh, that awful steam! She watches as the breeze passes, leaving the cloud to shoot upward again. Such an embarrassment. She wants to hide herself in a hole whenever she sees it. That generating system is why she stopped showing herself at community functions. In the mill she won't come out of her office for fear of workers being reminded of how Jerold had used her. Once that system was installed he dropped her like a load of lumber. Theodora is weary of her continuing charade of admiration over the technological upgrading of the company. Vernon must get her a contract with the power company while the window is still open. That was Jerold's selling point. Bearces and the others have managed to get the bugs out of their systems. They've been selling to the utility for something like thirteen cents a kilowatt hour!—even though Central Maine Power is selling on the grid to Massachusetts for one cent. They are bound by law to buy from co-generators at the higher rate. She wanted to check with Vernon on his progress this morning, but he is in Lewiston on some errand for Aunt Aggie. When will he stop that infernal dubbing around on errands for her? This is a business for godsakes!

Theodora rummages in her marshmallow blue leather bag for the keys. As she opens the door of her custom painted powder blue Saab 900, Balder roars past in his '55 Chevy. Her jaw works. The mechanic is gone in a spray of gravel. *Come back!* She wants to scream. *You can't leave in the middle of the day!* Involuntarily she has raised her arm, trying to wave him back. But sudden awareness of her action embarrasses Theodora. She fumbles with the key, unlocks the door of the Saab.

Out on the highway and after some moments the woman feels calmer. The car's sleek interior soothes her. The mathematical precision of Bach's harpsichord fugues in the cassette player imparts order to her beleaguered psyche. Then, eyeing the clock, she sees need to hurry. The pre-season session is due to begin in a few minutes and reception for tardiness can be frosty. Once she was actually excluded for it. And she needs these labs! You never know what will happen: depending on the chemistry of program and people, you could be bored numb or thrilled to desperation. Sometimes you can't even remember, afterward, what exactly has taken place. It must be an effect of hypnosis. And a very relaxing one. She once joked with Brandel about getting her money back: "How do I know there even was a session?" Theodora spends thousands on IICE courses and sessions, and has donated thousands, too.

How did I survive before IICE came into my life? The dynamics of organizational development and personal growth is transforming existence for everyone. By it things are improving all over the world. Theodora herself has now an almost constant glow of anticipation about life and its possibilities—thanks to IICE. She acknowledges to herself that her affiliation with them is her prestige in this town. No one here takes her as seriously as they do. And now she is looking forward to working with Eveledore on formulating a program tailored for personnel at Gottheim Chair.

This, finally, is something she can sink her teeth into without fear of falling into an area she knows nothing about. It will redeem all her previous blunders at the chair factory. Theodora has been interested in interpersonal communication all her adult life. It gives her content, structure to her thoughts, enabling her to feel vitally connected to the world. *IICE has given me participation in the global community.* Think of it! A timid local graduate of Gottheim Academy, lacking courage even to finish a semester at Vassar—always shooting about in search of a meaningful response to life—and they were right under her nose all the time! Once boring to her, a little absurd—IICE! That oddball community that came to town every summer to study.

Theodora giggles, remembering the first time she laid eyes on Brandel. Sitting in Felicity's having coffee and conversation with Eveledore and this supposedly suave stranger, Theodora was too timid even to look him in the eye. And suddenly she was looking him in the eye! Eyes wearing shadow, liner, mascara! A face full of makeup! What a laugh she had with Eveledore over it just the other day. Eveledore.... Even her name is significant, felicitous (like the restaurant!): It is a veritable echo of Theodora. She smiles a secret smile: Of thiscourse, the other's name doesn't contain the word God like mine does. At IICE they appreciate my sensitivity to significance.

Unconsciously a frown troubles her brow. Trying to remember.... Rounding beneath the far curve of Mount Morrill she passes the state roadside park without seeing it. She sees little along the highway most days. The landscape rarely changes, a new building might pop up.... Harry Golding's resort is doing so well.... But today the burnt-out structure of that unfortunate Ithiel Whitman grabs her gaze. Passing, she looks at the charred cross-timber sticking above a blackened roof.... Like a giant crucifix. Poor man. An old classmate of hers, very popular. He has certainly endured a lot! His wife vanished, a sister-in-law that won't leave him alone....

But suddenly Theodora gives a little quiver, remembering at last. That awful rumor heard in the post office this morning! Is—can IICE really be thinking of leaving?! Upon first hearing it, laughing, she could scarcely give it credence. Her frown deepens. Can it be true? IICE actually thinking of breaking their affiliation with Gott'im?! Can't be true. *Can't.* "Let it have no real substance," she murmurs, repeating it several times.

But IICE is a far-reaching entity, she knows, and looking to reach further. Its natural they'd want affiliations in other places abroad—countries with any potential for growth in interpersonal communications. Why that's nearly the whole of the Third World! Nations on earth are in transition, and IICE is exactly the kind of organization to help them stabilize. According to Dr. Anami's lecture, every new institution would benefit from the social and psychological programs of the institute. Of course IICE must expand, but they needn't leave Gottheim to do it! Wouldn't that demean us?

Well, that can't be their intention. If they need bigger facilities, more of a world-class center.... The Golding's! That's it! The Jasper Mountain Hotel .... More seminar and conference space is planned. Oh, IICE'll see. It's just a rumor anyway. *Only a rumor*.... Theodora hurries toward Gottheim for a session at the International Institute of Coordinated Experiments.

But, later that night—Theodora might have been seen racing wildly along back roads, her headlights crossing bare branches, branches that thrash on the breeze. She would be crying, wildly weeping, tears flowing ceaselessly. Hiccups engulfing her, anguish roaring in her heart.

"*How*! *How* am I unacceptable to you?!"

Remembering the horrible session at IICE, Theodora's hands will clench and unclenched on the beveled wheel. "Why oh why don't you accept me as I am? It was you who told me initially: 'Don't be ashamed of who you are. Never be ashamed,' you said. Why? Why are you people trying to change me?"

Theodora will tremble with anguish, wail. Heave and sigh. Whimper. "Why are you trying to change my personality?..."

She will whisper it to the wind, to the grinding wheels. "Why, why, why?"

Sipping coffee from one of Decatur's mugs, grubby old Ceylon Segar sat on a squeaky swivel stool in the diner. Smelling like old tires and ripe underwear, he enjoyed twisting on the stool just a little bit, producing this squeak. Those coming in avoided the stools on either side of him. Sitting beside Ceylon Segar was no picnic. He was big in the used tire collection business. Not that he went around picking up tires.

Lyman Bearce, the lumber man, had vacated his usual stool to get away from Segar. He would not be associated with that abuser of property even by physical proximity. Besides, the smell was enough to gag a man and drive him into one of Decatur's booths. If those goddam tires of his ever caught fire they could kiss the surrounding woodland goodbye. The fire would burn down into the ground, run along the roots in the acreage roundabout and there'd be no putting it out till after the grandkids started having kids of their own. If then. It set Bearce's blood on fire to think of it.

He was a powerful, vastly bearded man who brooked nothing against his purposes. First, foremost, always he was a businessman, deliberate. Yet Lyman Bearce, with his dark hair and white beard that hid the acne scars of his youth, looked like a logger who had just come out of the woods. His forebears had been in the woods since history, setting up mills on any stream large enough to float a log. Yankee Maine had a history of illegal lumbering dating back to the King's broad arrow, a seal set on every tree deemed the King's. Houses with punkin pine floors attest to the "thievery": Uniform planks shaved to under twenty-four inches can still be found in colonial houses. That diameter was reserved for masts in His Royal Highness's Navy.

The family Bearce were relative newcomers to the Town of Gottheim, arriving only after the turn of this century. By the mid '20s they were a sprawling fixture; Beatitude Bearce, having obtained a fair parcel of forestland, was well on his way to amassing the large tracts they now owned. Lyman, one of his five sons, was a formidable and conscientious forester, promoting healthy timber through sound harvesting practices. In balancing the mills' requirements with what the woods might safely provide, his rule was, leave the best, cut the rest. His forests were almost uniformly beautiful, healthy; possessed of a quality to revive the bruised soul of almost anyone who walked them. Only once in his thirty-seven years as forester had he allowed clearcutting, preferring to achieve stands with canopies to provide support in case of high winds and storm. Erosion of his land was practically nil, the stable stands slowing runoff, reducing siltation of brooks and preventing dessication of the floor. However, last spring under pressure of the changing community, he decided to try his hand at mountain development, selling stumpage on five hundred acres to Adirondack paper for the possible subdivision of the land. Bearces could be counted on to try just about anything not unwise and not—at this date—publicly unseemly for profit.

Lyman Bearce frequented Decatur's Diner, as had Beatitude before him decades ago when it was operated by Jeffy Decatur's father. The business, that is. The site and diner itself, of course, belonged to Bearce. Sitting here in the booth by himself, Lyman thought of this. He had begun the process of exercising his option to develop this site, local icon or not.

He smoothed his great white beard with a calloused hand, one sporting his Gottheim Academy class ring. He still wore the ring after forty years. What people failed to recognize in him was his sentimentality. (He would certainly never acknowledge it himself.) If anyone had suggested this fact to Town historian Asa Bartlett he would have hooted: "That diner disposer—sentimental?" But, sipping his coffee, Bearce thought, *Not one of these people ever realized the near sacredness of this place till today.* Without betraying it by even a gleam in his eye, Lyman Bearce smiled to himself. He was glad to be the one to teach 'em! He looked around at its fixtures—the garish neon lit clock, sagging booths, chipped tabletops. He had no idea what he would do with this ugly bucket of crud. He was half-tempted to have Howe tow it into the woods someplace, just let it sit till he could think of something.

Flatfooted, Melvinia Sessions came up and nearly slammed a cheeseburger plate in front of him on the linoleum tabletop. She sent her nose toward the ceiling and sailed away.

Lyman Bearce almost smiled. He ought to demolish this place but he couldn't quite bring himself to it. Keep this thing? Lyman Bearce was good for a surprise now and then. Like four years ago when he up and ran for selectman. Folks weren't surprised that he was elected. The surprise was his candidacy. There'd never been a Bearce in Town government. Never. Bearces had always been content to influence politics through the mere expression of opinion. That was all it took.

But Asa Bartlett thought he had pieced it together, and what he came up with was Jasper Mountain. Lyman Bearce was not about to let outsiders Harry and Julius Golding walk off with policy in this town. He had to keep things favorable to his mills. He had sat back and watched the little skiway expand bit by bit and recognized that it was going to snowball into the biggest resort in Maine. The dynamics of Gottheim were bound to change and Lyman Bearce was going to be the one to affect them. Asa Bartlett was sure of it. It helped that his wife Rhetta was on the Planning Board.

A Bearce mill manager named Elmer Robbins came in, hurried past Ceylon Segar, and sat down opposite Bearce. Robbins was a generation younger than Lyman. His was a sandy complexion replete with freckles. He had reddish hair and a falsely serious mien, meant to ward off remarks and familiarities occasioned by his slight appearance. He signaled Melvinia for coffee, then began complaining about the quality of logs he had turned away that morning.

"It's a good thing Bearces made the switch," he said, referring to recent upgrading of the panels and bentwood mill. Rising world demand for hardwood sawlogs had depleted supplies to the point where quality was getting harder to come by, though the softwood mills continued to prosper thanks to Bearces' woods management and high standards. In recent years they had acquired a furniture components mill with a hunger for hardwood and the strange touch of technology. After much study, Lyman had decided upon bending the wood with the powerful tool of electricity. First developed in northern Europe, radiofrequency produced a value-added product using less wood. Robbins stirred his coffee, saying, "Now that we've got that contract with Alabama Furniture fah those bow-backs, we'll hev t'increase our suppliers."

Bearce grunted. "Already been talkin't'some. Should hev it nailed down by the fust next week." Lyman took another bite of his burger.

Melvinia set a Jell-O salad in front of Elmer Robbins. He watched her walk away, saying, "She's in a Christless pink stink. It's all over the town about this place. The old timers is boiling."

"Give 'em something t'be opinionated about, 's all. Ought keep'em happy awhile."

"Got that right," said Robbins, which phrase was habitual with him. "Heard the latest in snow-making, boss?"

"You mean freeze-dried piss?"

Robbins restrained a smile. "Only Harry Golding would brave the publicity o'that." He couldn't help grinning then, revealing a slight gap between his front teeth: "Next he'll hev 'em schussing through frozen shit. Has about the same appeal, don't it?"

But Bearce did not laugh. "It is an efficient way to dispense with two big resort problems: snow-making and sewage disposal. When snow guns spray sewage under high pressure, rapid freezing kills bacteria." He speared two fries with his fork.

Elmer was incredulous. "Theya's got to be a downside. They just haven't come across it yet."

"Phosphorus in the runoff. It'll run down'n pollute the Arossagunticook."

Elmer swallowed his coffee wrong and choked back a mouthful. Like it wasn't a dead river now.

Bearce looked disgusted and slid his plate closer to his bearded chest. To him the great river was no laughing matter. They had all grown up with the open sewer that the bountiful river had become since Andrew MacDonald built his paper mill and Magic City near the great falls. Three more paper mills were built after that, all since changing hands. They had been going at the dumping of toxic chemicals for nearly twice the span of Bearce's life. The federal Clean Water Act of the decade past had put a stop to fumes strong enough to peel paint off riverside houses, but along with many others Lyman could not get used to the off color and foam, the odor; and dioxin that made it advisable for pregnant women to eat no fish caught in its waters. Despite the Act, the river looked bad, it stank; and he could not accept that it spawned mutants and had been carelessly commandeered by corporations who ignored the rights of their neighbors. Now, in the latter half of the twentieth century, they were absentee stewards, headquartered elsewhere. No stewards at all. To Bearce the effect was that they found the river useful but hated it. But Bearce had informed his representatives in Augusta. Yes, they would spend a substantial amount of time and money wrangling over this bill. The battle would be fierce, but Bearce had thought it all through. The river should not be for the papermakers only, even if it meant joining forces with the fluff-headed environmentalists. The Arossagunticook belonged to Maine.

Yes, Lyman Bearce cared about such things, but, as everyone knew, he did not care for individuals. He cared more for Decatur's Diner, as a piece of Americana and even for its function in the community, than he would ever care for Decatur or Melvinia. He liked to see Melvinia stomp around or Decatur scratching his bald head and wondering what to do next.

Robbins was asking how the meeting went last night. "They gont avoid that eminent domain thing?"

"You read about it. We're gont request a delay on deciding that. The twerp says they look t'finish papah work on land swaps by the end of the month." (The "twerp" referred to James Fay, who was handling negotiations for resort interests.) "A selectman'll represent the Town in 'Gusty once everything's secure. But far's I can see, it's all worked out. What a haggle. Fay's crowding t'get building—like the outsider he is. A shoreline park is a good idea, though. Wouldn't want this place turning into another North Conway."

"Got that right. Had t'go theya last week. Nothing but strip malls'n outlets. Traffic wuss'n Freeport."

Bearce nodded. He doubted North Conway looked much different than the rest of America. He'd read somewhere that anyplace now looked like every place. They'd written right. It had no business happening to Gottheim.

This was the secret of Lyman Bearce and his father before him. But Beatitude never had to deal with outside forces. Not like this. The old man was retired now. Maybe he didn't know it, but he was. Forced into it by decrepitude, and his son was so much like him: Beatitude could no longer keep his dogs on the way Gottheim grew, and Lyman made sure his own orders were not superseded by the old man's.

In the time allotted him, Lyman Bearce planned to make sure it never happened to him. His influence would be sure. And Gottheim would be kept looking and feeling like Gottheim.

Asa Bartlett would've hooted, but this imperfect stewardship was but one of the secrets of Lyman Bearce.

Family Secrets, Secret Family

Catching movement off his right shoulder, Daniel looks up from the swimmers in Deep Hole to see the dull gold of the Bonneville coming through the buds above them. "She's here!" calls Benaiah, the river rushing over the falls drowning his cry. Followed by his brothers, Nathan runs up the muddy path. Mother pulls off the puddled road into their campsite well away from the Caprice and gets out wearing her good skirt and blouse. She glances at the mud spattered red car just down the track. The two youngest rush her, but Daniel trails over to the stream for his fish.

"Mother! Mother! You shoulda seen it!" Nathan tugs on her arm and she embraces him briefly. "They went o'er the falls into the hole!"

"Told you people swim here," she says. "When I was li'l older than Daniel, we cooled off here summers. There was a runoff ritual—if you were older and brave enough. I'll teach you all t'swim, come July."

She watches dark Daniel crossing the track with his stringer. "Nice catch, Daniel. Everything all right?" She looks carefully into his face. "What's wrong?"

"Aw, we're okay. The man called these brookies." He holds up the stringer. The fish are patterned and speckled, but small.

"Good eating," says Chrischana. "I'm proud of you for feeding us. We're going to need more.... I didn't get my job yet."

Daniel looks away. So hard .... Haf'ta ask her to find some other place than Deep Hole, or Nathan will drive me nuts.

"Eat now, eat!" cries Nathan, pulling on the budding twigs nearby. He lets loose a fistful, swatting Benaiah across the chest. He runs off, Benaiah after him yelling.

"Don't hurt your brother!" shouts Mother. The rushing of Bear River drowns her out.

"Can we go with you this afternoon?" asks Daniel as they near the campfire. "I can watch Nathan better in the car. The river's too dangerous,

Mother. He's gonna fall in. Or, maybe there's a park or playground somewhere?"

"He did like you said about staying off the river, didn't he?" She lays the fish on an old mossy stump beside her secondhand Coleman stove. Here are utensils for cooking, an old fry pan, fillet knife, battered dinner plates. She sets a brooky on a plate and slits it.

What do you think? "Pretty much, but he's too itchy. Doesn't really want to stay away."

Chrischana hears a murmur of voices above the water and looks up to see a man and woman coming out of the bushes toward the track. They are laughing, animated, invigorated by their plunge. Distracting her, Nathan and Benaiah zip back through camp, Nathan hollering. Each laying blame, they tear about yelling at one another. But, upon seeing the couple approach the little red car, the boys stop to stare. The young woman goes around to the driver's side, but the man stands a moment looking from the old Bonneville to the camp where the little family stands watching. Chrischana recognizes Balder. Feeling hot in the face, she turns her head away—but too late. He comes toward them. There is no evading it. He strides past the Bonneville and stands sternly regarding her.

"Chrischana Twitchell?"

"Yes, it's me, Balder. "

A frown creases his brow. "Waya'd y'go?"

"To the desert. Nevada first, then Phoenix."

They look at one another. The young woman comes up behind Balder, saying brightly to Chrischana, "You changed out of your T-shirt."

The older woman recognizes the striking girl from the Jasper Mountain hotel. Her hair is still plastered to her head, her clothing damp and disheveled.

"Had to, I was applying for work. Chrischana Twitchell." She steps forward, holding out her hand.

"Gloria Fay. Nice meet you." She shakes the proffered hand. "Balder's friend?"

Chrischana nods. "From high school. I was away." She steps back to her place beside the boys. "These are my sons." She sets a hand on each, naming them. The youngest is spinning the slit brooky around on the oily plate with his forefinger. Benaiah stands by Daniel, staring at the pair.

Taking his stern gaze off Chrischana, Balder now sets it on Daniel. He looks from Benaiah to Nathan, then back to Daniel. At last he looks again at Chrischana. And silence has taken possession of them all. His glance on her is pensive, as seeing into her. Gathering an impression of someone changed in body and soul. A person he knew once, held intimately in his thought.

Now, slowly again, he puts his gaze upon Daniel. Beside him Gloria says something, too brightly, but no one attends.

Feeling the intensity of the man's gaze, Daniel looks down. He picks up the stringer with the remaining two fish and begins removing them, gently lifting a hook from each mouth. He wishes the man would go away now, the woman.

Gloria shifts nervously, lightly brushing the tips of Balder's fingers with her own. She looks at her watch, says lightly and sweetly, "Lunch's about over. Got to get back."

"Nice meeting you," says the dark skinned woman.

Her shoes in hand, Gloria turns and walks toward the car. It is then that Chrischana notices her bare feet, the wet slip wrapped around her wrist and clutched against her palm.

Staying, Balder looks from Daniel to Chrischana once more; and, frightened now, she returns his gaze. The look she sees is very quiet in him. Dark, crestfallen. He stands a moment, looking so at her. He turns and walks away.

Several nights later, Daniel stepped from Hannah Sessions' filthy kitchen into fresh night. Stifling the urge to vomit, he'd got out of there just in time. The stench and squalor in the sagging clapboard Cape were almost unbelievable. Now, in the swatch of yellow light from its window, he checked to make sure he still had his notebook and pencil, as well as the tape recorder belonging to Mrs. Melville. He needn't have worried, for the condition of that house had precluded any idea of setting something down. He had clutched everything fiercely while inside. Did he really see Cindabilla's Uncle Ferddy slurp his spilled beer off the table scattered with chicken shit and crumbs from supper?

The stench of the pigpen in the backyard now assaulted his nostrils as he passed. He went picking his way through the littered yard, hoping his eyes would soon adjust to the dark. He found a path Cindabilla had told him of, cutting narrowly through piles of junk. Distantly, he heard spring peepers chirping. Trailing past clumps of sodden feed sacks, pieces of rusted metal, old tools and parts, a path led him by the looming hulk of an ancient pickup and on into neglected pasture at last.

Daniel was on his way to meet Cindabilla's great aunt Nellie, who lived in a camp alongside a track in the woods beyond the field. Last year's grasses were dried and stark, and shot with emerging brambles in need of spring burning to encourage fresh growth. Now he went up the pasture path toward the woods with confidence. In those woods beyond he soon saw a glow, very faint. Was it a light from Aunt Nellie's window?

Daniel looked up at stars, May stars, Mother would say—Hercules and Arcturus heading toward the zenith. Rarely, they had gone out on the desert to escape Dad, or more often gone with him, to leave the heat of Phoenix. Even with the light and pollution of the city beyond, you could see stars. Mother seemed to be learning the stars right along with them, teaching them out of an old book. Leaving the Metropolitan desert was necessary, but ....

The memory of his euphoria after she had confided the planned departure remained, but being in Maine was not what he had foreseen. It was a more impoverished, sorry experience. And tough kids at the new school hounded him almost moment by moment, sometimes punching, kicking or tripping him. He hated the bigotry of their view of his skin. The sound of their speech grated on him. In Phoenix they pronounced their r's, and the view of his skin was accepted erroneously as being Hispanic. Daniel knew he was part Native, like mother, though the fact had never excited his curiosity. But the move had to be the right thing, despite it all. Mother was doing better.

The glow in the dark woods flickered now with his movement through the trees, even as it increased. The light in there would be soft, he knew, because Aunt Nellie had no electricity in her camp. A good thing Mrs. Melville's tape recorder had batteries. Cindabilla's aunt had a wood stove for heat, kerosene for light, and a refrigerator that ran on propane. If Mother really wanted to live cheap, maybe they could rent a camp somewhere.

He was relieved that they were no longer camped at Deep Hole. Mother thought they should find a safer place, and Daniel had the idea that her joy in Abenaki Notch was gone. The cove at Twitchell Pond, where they were now, was much safer and secluded, but Mother said another move would be necessary when July brought swimmers.

Daniel was lucky to find Cindabilla a friend among his classmates, but would she go on to Hazel Newell High School next year? She knew how to read, which she said was more than a few in her family could do. " 'N they all try t'hide the fact they caunt," she had said. Cindabilla reminded him of Huckleberry Finn—wild and free. But, where Huck's Pap had been a drunk, it was Cindabilla's mother who abused drugs and alcohol. Hannah Sessions' was Cindabilla's struggling grandmother; and the old woman's daughter, Etta, was Cinda's mother. Why, Daniel wondered, do they say people abuse drugs? It always seemed to him the other way around.

Blackflies and mosquitoes were swarming him. He could feel the collar and crown of thorns the latter made feasting on him. The blackflies were biting now too, but he would not feel their bites until later when he tried to sleep.

Clutching his notebook and recorder, he hurried up to the camp and pounded on the door. "I'm here, Miz Sessions! Daniel Twitchell—for the interview."

"Just come in," came a high voice from within. He lifted the latch, pushed on the weathered door, entered and shut it quickly behind him. His back to the room, juggling his notebook and recorder, he heard her say, "Blackflies's is surely bitin', in't they?"

"Yuht." He heard himself say it the way they do in Gottheim. The pronunciations had begun slipping into his talk whether he wanted or not. Before long he'd be flattening his r's and adding extra syllables to words like "here" and "there."

Turning, he saw the frizzle-headed and bespeckled Nellie Sessions, sitting at the table. Her hands were at rest among bits of what look like rock. One of her wrists was splinted and wraped in elastic. Looking about, Daniel saw shelves with white labels, their contents in shadow.

"Sit down heah—Daniel, is it?—n' tell me the purpose of this visit.... See if I undastand Cindabilla right."

Daniel set his things on the scrubbed wooden table. He pulled out the worn ladderback chair and sat down, seeing that what he had taken for bits of rock were arrowheads—bits of quartz and flint. A magnifying glass lay among them beside her long hands, their nails clipped short and clean. Looking about, he saw that this house of Nellie Sessions was like those hands—clean and orderly and calm. What a relief to be away from the wretched house where Cindabilla grew. Why couldn't she live here with Aunt Nellie? But it was small, only a camp. There was a cot with quilt, a sideboard with pump and sink, the shelves, a refrigerator, a table and three chairs. The flame of her lamp gleamed back reflected at him from the windowpanes.

"Miz Melville, our English teacher, told us to do oral history tapes so we have something t'write about. That we learn other things besides writing that way. Cindabilla doesn't wanna do it, so she said I could have y—I mean, talk t'you about arrowheads."

"That so? 'N I say it t'th' recorder?" Nellie looked at the machine significantly. "Will I get t'read what you write?—afta?"

"Yuht ... if I get a good grade. Won't waste y'time if not." He checked the cassette to see if it was in right.

She grinned, saying it sounded fair to her. "You're a Twitchell, in't choo? Heven't had one round in a long time. Twitchells was fom the first."

Daniel wondered what she meant. Did she expect a response? "This is ready," he said. "We test it?"

"You're the boss."

"I'll play back what we said'n see if it works." He pressed stop, then rewind and play.

"Twitchells was fom the first," came her thin voice from the recorder. Across from him, she grinned.

Now He opened his notebook and said, a bit nervously, "Got questions written down."

"I'm ready." Her hair was a frazzled mixture of light and dark around her head, like a nimbus of shadow and silver in the glow of her lamp. Her glasses shone, the eyes behind a penetrating black.

He began with biographical questions, asking when and where she was born, grew up, went to school, and worked. When asked what she did on her job at the glue pin factory, she said, "I fed dowel rods to the machine. That's all. Just stand theya all day ovah that clackity-clack pin machine. It rumbles'n whirls round'n round making that sound. Evah time it goes round, it clips a course into pins, 'n they fall into a basket while the dowels get shorter'n shorter. I watch fah empty sockets'n drop in another rod. Thirty-six sockets I keep filled. Sometimes I work nights. They turn off the heat when office workers go home. Don't try that job in winter! We work in coats, mittens, hats'n stamp ah feet a lot."

Daniel said, "How'd you become interested in arrowheads?"

"These ponds round heah, and the lakes t'the west in't same as they once was. For instance, the dam by the mill down theya controls water levels. When the Indians's heah the water was a lot lower. My Daddy wanted nothing to do with the mills. So he was a caretaker."

"Caretaker?"

"Yuht. He watched ovah people's camps. He was in the woods, cutting, too. When I was li'l I go around with him, and checking on the camps. In the fall, water'd be low and I'd scout the flats fah arrowheads. That started when I was climbing round Littlehale Lake once'n saw this funny crescent shaped rock. It was about fifteen inches long, three inches wide and thick. Slightly ridged. Being just li'l, I couldn't imagine how it got that way. Lugged that thing from camp to camp with my daddy. In one camp was a botanist and he said, 'That looks like mid-archaic.' 'Mid what?' I asked. 'Archaic,' he said. 'Was likely made by an Indian three or four thousand years ago. It's an adze.' Well, my daddy got all excited bout that. Some pleased. I had my regard of him by that."

Nellie Sessions grinned, sweeping wide her arms to take the room in, with its shelves ceiling to floor. "All this, of that regard. Thanks to that botanist, scientists hev seen my collection fom early days. I've took 'em to places, showed 'em things. Theya's collections in Harvard'n other places on account of that funny old stone. Fom Paleos down to Ceramic Indians: I picked up what Mother Nature washed out fah me'n let the archaeologists do theya digging and sifting. Look't this."

She held out a five-inch piece of worked over rock, slightly raised in the middle. "That's chert formed into a clovis point. Tip's broken off. Paleo-Indians shaped 'em with a hammer stone, just hitting it from side to side—like this." She demonstrated, using a round white stone, but without actually striking.

She looked hard at him, her eyes growing sharper. "Picture this. Round bark-covered huts, or may be covered in hides. Hunks of dried fish hanging in the sun. A man in breechcloth poised to thrust a spear with clovis point into water. Dogs barking. Folks chippin' fom a log in order to hollow out a boat. Some sitting flutin' clovis points. That's how people got theya livin'. *You* could make a living like that!" She poked his dark hand where it lay by the recorder.

Daniel had been watching her, entranced. Now, startled, he stopped the machine. "Better check it," he mumbled. Fumbling, he rewound a bit, played the last words, and stopped.

"Wait a minute," she commanded, laying hold of his wrist with her uninjured hand. "You're Chrischana Twitchell's boy, ain't choo?"

Uneasy, he nodded. She was beginning to spook him. The multiple flames of wicked kerosene reflected in the divided lights of the window panes, and from her glasses, casting a spell. The blackfly bites were beginning to torment him. He wanted to rake his neck with his fingers. He wanted to speak, to hurry on with the interview—or just get out. But Daniel waited, forcing himself to stay with the assignment.

"Chrischana Twitchell's son," she said. "Theya y'go! You're pot Indian! Indians was fom the first."

Nellie curled her good hand around his wrist. "Don't push that button!" She commanded. "I'm gont tell you something, Daniel Twitchell'n I don't want it on tape!" Then she let go his wrist and sat back in her hard chair.

"Now theya is no proof o'this. If they was, I'd let the tape run. But I know for fact. Y'see, my daddy's people is millers. They all made money'n their kids is mill owners today. But my daddy had no pot of milling. We stayed poor, but did all right. Look at all this." She nodded her head, indicating the contents of her shelves.

But though agreeing somewhat, Daniel could only think how some kids in his class would say, "All what?"

"You seen these mills in these mountains, Daniel. Every year these owners meet and confirm to keep wages low, to a certain rate. They fixed it so workers who quit the mill would be blackballed—meaning not hired in another mill till six months, at least, passed. Every year, at that meeting, they agree on it. It went on five decades.... Maybe still does."

She said all this and stopped—significantly—her eyes glowing like coals, flames reflecting.

Daniel looked down. What did she want? What's this got to do with anything? He was only fourteen years old!

"All right," He heard her say. "You can go on now." She nodded toward the recorder. "When we get done taping, I'll show you my fust adze."

On his way back down the path, he looked through trees toward the distant lights of Cindabilla's farmhouse. He found himself recalling what Nellie Sessions had said about finally receiving a dime's raise last month. After twenty-five years of making glue pins, she now earned ten cents over minimum wage. He thought again how her wrist was braced against stress and pain, and wondered what it was like to stand for more than two decades in the same spot. Eight hours a day, dropping dowel rods into a pin machine. How many rods did she throw in over the years? Did she get dizzy watching them all spin around?

Sheltering from abnormal spring heat, Chrischana sits huddled against hewn granite. She is drenched in repellent, keeping blackflies at bay. The sound of Birch River, flowing through a channel between the hewn rocks behind her, sounds a note of coolness. But even the shiny leaves of beech and maple shading her give no relief from the heat. The fiddleheads left over after Balder's harvest a few weeks ago have opened into ferns at Chrischana's feet. The sound of water pouring past huge remnants of last century's industry soothes from the heat and exertion of her hike in. Chrischana's not used to walking, and her limbs are leaden, also, with defeat. Lying back, she lolls against the cool old stones of Mason's Mills. Still, she finds no thought to guide in her troubles.

And what about the problem of survival.... AFDC is promised, she has food stamps and a rent voucher. But welfare is not what Chrischana wants. Going down to Guildford, sitting in that office ... being questioned by that woman.... The awful admission of domestic degradation. The grief of it. Yet Chrischana has used nothing given her except a few food stamps.

She can accept none of this. How can she? It's the failure of everything, and, yet, even this wouldn't be so bad ... if only the ache will depart.

....She keeps seeing that light intimate touch of his new young love ... upon his hand. That intimate brushing of Balder's fingers....

How could she have allowed herself to hope? Worse, how could she have hoped ... all the way across the country ... without knowing it? Across mountains and plains, going through great Midwestern cities, on rolling farmland and into the woodland of Pennsylvania and New England.... Through all their current trials and the free familial joys of their travels. Through it she tried to keep after herself: The Balder she knew no longer lived. He had changed into a heavy, slow family man of responsibilities. His mind, like her own should be, would now be, a world away from the moony-nights-through-trees of their joint youth. At one point in her life she had forgotten him altogether—for years! In the early years of Peter's love, with childbirth and partying and the endless gabbing with other young mothers—she had been happy. It had become a fact that the Balder she knew had receded into memory, not to be known in any other way again.

....That intimate brushing of his fingers.... Chrischana feels the heat of her shame and failure rising in her, rising and recurring as it has again and again since she saw that touch.

Seeing his car at Gott'im Chair—the exact car in which Daniel was conceived!—and hearing from Asa Bartlett that he was unmarried still. These things had encouraged the false hidden hope. Seeing the intimacy of Balder and Gloria exposed it.

Oh! She is bright, that Gloria Fay.

Balder's own features have matured; his body with more muscle, heft, power. But how can it be that he seems barely aged? He is still vital, young, happy. It must be from a lack of responsibility, that true heritage of adulthood. No one can walk and laugh—as he did with Gloria, who is occupied or burdened with real life. He lives without a care!

She opens her eyes, staring up at the configuration of fresh leaves against the spaces of colorless sky.

He has a problem now.

.... That fallen look. The darkness of his expression.... With compassion, with shame, water rises in her eyes. He suspects a son. A stranger, but his living offspring. Of whom he was bereaved.

There is a path into woodland where mill foundation stones stand silent in their moldering vigil. The stones are massive, dark, split here and there by living roots; crumbling from frost and lichen, bitten by organisms too small to see. The spirit of human industry is idle here, industry once powered by water brought from above. Here boards were sawn, shingles cut; wool combed then carded, cloth dressed; and grist was ground for the ovens and stomachs of townsfolk round about. In this now secret and abandoned site, the human and material needs of the community were with constancy met. Here labor provided sustenance, fitness, aim: the feel of rough boards in hefting hands, of lanolin soft in the shorn fibers of sheep; sound—for the listening ear—of water pouring and the creaking, turning of cylinders. Here, at Mason's Mills.

All the quiet ghosts about this place are invisible, unavailable to the troubled woman who sits idle against the stone. Chrischana is here, thinking again of leaving town, finding nowhere in Gottheim, in God's House, to earn her living and that of her sons.

But now she stops her ruinous thoughts to listen. Is this someone coming down the path? Someone is singing—or chanting? She can't make out the words for the ceaseless flow of the stream. Gradually, the murmur of human speech increases, as the walker comes on:

Bear, bear keep away....

Chrischana peers through the leaves hiding her face from view. The sayer approaches, but it is moments before Chrischana understands this odd sight. Surely she knows the strangely burdened person? Yes, and another soul hardly changed in fifteen years. *Maybe a glance at her shy face will tell me of her aging ... and the stoop and stiffness of gait.*

Yes, this is the only difference in the pattern Elda Simon's ever made against stems and foliage of the woodland. She wore a red or pink bandanna, a T-shirt, and dungarees rolled up at the ankle ever since Chrischana can remember. But, what's the great thing on her arm?... a bird is it?... with a cloth over its head?

Yes. Mrs. Simon shuffles along, balancing a great living burden on her arm. It's the weirdness of the woman. Always she was weird. You could remember upon the eternal strangeness of Elda Simon like you could the gossip of Asa Bartlett. Most people in Chrischana's place, seeing this woman, would be stifling laughter. But she has always respected the older woman's ways with animals. There's something maybe spiritual in her handling and care of things found insignificant by others.

The woman stops on the path among woodland shadows, looking around. Chrischana's discomfort watching in secret grows. Yet, she does not want to startle Mrs. Simon at work. Can't tell what a wild creature might do.... She's looking for something.... A perch. She kneels at a hunk of deadfall, shifting the great bird onto it. The bird feels with its horned and feathered talons then moves off onto the branch.

Mrs. Simon sinks back on her butt, weary from her exertions; seeming to fold upon herself as though the impulse of life has evaporated. She *has* aged. Chrischana restrains a kindly urge to aid her. Better let her see the task through without distraction.

—Asa's owl is it?—stands quietly, locked to the branch. After several moments, the woman straightens up, begins loosening the bird's hood. Watching, Chrischana tenses.

A hooked beak emerges, followed by fierce frontal eyes and ear tufts. The great horned owl shakes itself off the branch, as Elda backs away. Hissing and beating, the bird tilts off. Looking fiercely back at the woman, again and again the owl moves its wings, as if mightily to fly. Failing, the bird yet manages to put several yards between itself and its benefactress.

Chrischana rises, rustling foliage as she emerges. "Mrs. Simon!"

Startled, Elda whirls. "Who's that!"

Chrischana steps out from the leaves, saying, "It's only me, Mrs. Simon. Chrischana Twitchell." Crossing through new bracken, she takes the path.

"Chrischana ... Twitchell?" But a moment passes. Chrischana wonders if she will remember—if she will even know who she is. But the other says, "Oh. The li'l Indian maid—Jasper Mary—waunt you?"

The woman must've forgotten she was once Balder's girlfriend—if she ever knew. Balder was not one to talk much about things personal. And Mrs. Simon always seemed a bit remote, ever immersed in wildlife and more absent than not when among people. Now she turns back to the bird, saying, "Caunt talk just at the moment."

Chrischana comes up behind her to watch the owl's struggle. The bird is well into the bracken and moose maple, but its thrashing has stopped. Elda says, "She's resting a bit, I s'pose.

Now, as they watch, it beats again but with more power and control. Beating, the owl flies into the branches of a middle distance maple.

Elda relaxes. "She'll be all right now." She turns toward the younger woman. "People guess I should've let the Roebuck boy finish her out of her misery, but I just caunt do that to an owl, could you?"

Chrischana couldn't help but think that anyone but Mrs. Simon would have made some statement designed to get her explaining herself in some way, maybe to talk about where she's been.

"Why not help an owl?" Christy answers, looking into her shy eyes. "Look at the good they do keeping the rodent population down." She smiles her slight smile. "Rats don't stand a chance."

Elda Simon looks away. "If I hadn't been to the grocer's that night to see it happen...." The sentence trails off.

"This is a long way from Simons Ledge," says Chrischana; flushing, aware that her internal criticism of townspeople might extend to herself.

But Elda smiles her shy smile, answering, "Had t'come a good way t'help 'em get stotted away from people. Elsewhere they might not give'em a chance."

They start down the path together, Elda with a last look over her shoulder. The owl is still resting in the maple.

Chrischana says, "There a bear around here somewhere?"

Elda nudges her. "See that track? Fresh."

Looking in the mire among sparse grass, Chrischana sees what might pass for the print of a fat barefoot child.

"Uh-oh." Startling a mother with cubs would be a project. "I always wonder what they find to eat this time of year. Flowers haven't ripened to berries yet."

"Oh, they'll eat just about anathin. Slugs ants honey rodents carrion everything. Root round like an ol'pig. They ah pigs!" She has been looking this way and that, admiring what she sees. Now she says, "Just look at all that's growing heah. Starflower, gaywings, lousewort, baneberry. Look! Jack'n-the-pulpit!" She ticks off flowers, families of flowers, as they go along; looking carefully, taking great pleasure in seeing. "But I guess you know what's good to eat and steep—being pot Indian."

But Chrischana flushes saying, "People think Natives should know that stuff, but I'm not native enough. I was raised like anyone else around here.... Like Balder was. Used to trap.... That's about it. I did some fishing, berrying of course."

Elda grimaces at mention of trapping, but she says only, "Balder knows what to eat, what not. We learned that stuff from field books, whatnot."

Chrischana feels rebuffed, whether Mrs. Simon intends it or not—which the younger woman doubts. She thinks now how far she has moved from Balder. Or, no, how little she ever really knew him. Again she sees Gloria's caressing fingers ... that gentle cutting gesture. And here is Mrs. Simon, likely unaware that Chrischana is a stranger here now. Does Mrs. Simon even know I've been away?

The older woman is saying, "Anaone can learn this stuff. A good guide would be *Grove's Basic Herbal*. All the uses ah in theya: culinary, medicinal, cosmetic. Lore's in theya too. The book's in Gott'im Library."

Not you, too.... Everybody's got something you're doing wrong. Chrischana murmurs something to signify a response. Actually, she has thought of searching out this kind of knowledge, but someday, not today.

There are decisions, and challenges enough ahead. Daniel, Nathan, Benaiah.... Her boys need a community, safe, sure. *They need a home.*

The two women walk on, more words about plants and animals spoken along the way. The trail winds back around Mason Mountain, comes to the gravel shoulder where Chrischana's faded old Bonneville is parked. She offers Mrs. Simon a ride, and, after hesitating, the woman accepts.

And last they reached the shaded lane to the old Simon house, Elda saying, "Just let me out heah. Posey might be about'n she's due to fawn. I'm afraid we might disturb her."

Chrischana watches her hobble the lane, watching this way and that. Now she seems to loosen up and walk with some grace. Just as the woman becomes lost in shadow at the far end, it strikes Chrischana. She turns her gaze away, up the gravel road toward the heat-hazed mountain.

There goes Daniel's grandmother.

Elda Simon walks past hummingbirds sipping in the honeysuckle tangled thickets about the house. At last she thinks she understands.

Her coming took away his Vietnam eyes. Her rejection brought them on again. Why did she come back—if not to be with him?

God. Worried about Balder again. He's been in his room, issuing only at night to look up something in a book. Or go look at the stars. Not this! Not when he got done with that awful war in Southeast Asia ... in his room three years. Why can't all that melancholy seclusion stay back where he left it? She sighs. Was it two weeks ago he was happy?... It's like a fall from heaven.

To her Balder Simon is a secret, hidden. She has never been able to fathom him. Yet, she, more than anyone, knows Balder. She ponders him in her heart.

Thinking God's Thoughts

By day, and outside the window, he sees green buds emerge, leaf, filing along lit branches. But at night Balder turns from surveying the jungle to see his best buddy's guts, blossoming, a curtain of blood: blood, tumult, blood, shattered bodies and friendships, blood; his mind populated with it. He might lift the sash to hear pine boughs intoning up on Simons Ledge, acknowledging the booming, hoping to displace the roar of the war, of choppers beating and B-52 bombers howling to heaven. But the wind-freshened moonlight, washing faint whiteness into the woodland, cannot take it away. If he went down to stand in the yard (and sometimes he does), and looked up to see stars in the branches, even there the war would pursue.

These thoughts the window of Balder's room reveals, as it has always revealed, since all those years ago when, as a riven veteran, he returned to Gottheim. One reprieve from the anguish of that time came during his stopover in New York. Was it Pennsylvania Station or Grand Central? There was the vision ... was it a vision?.... It was a profound sense of *Love*. God, loving the bounty of humanity Balder saw walking—like sheaves of wheat walking in God's great eye. Only travelers, commuters, panhandlers—walking, crisscrossing multitudes ... all deeply, profoundly respected and loved.

When will he be able to spit out the cud of self recrimination? If only he could forget (no not forget, but something ...) that Dana Mills is dead, that Tim has—. No. Tim Bean was a casualty of Nam as surely as if he were killed in a chopper crash on the Cambodian border or earmarked for death in Cai Lay as an enemy of the Viet Cong. Except Tim drowned off the coast of Maine while sea kayaking in a storm. Like Balder, he was never able to leave the pictures and defeats to their place in that strange, but never distant, land.

A Roccomeeco native, one of eight hundred Maine Indians to see combat, Tim Man Bean maniacally set himself on self-destruction. Not once or twice, but three times he took his tour, never fulfilled, never satisfied, ever seeking the great intensity of life. After the second tour, Balder understood that Tim's road would be both deeper in punishment and shorter in duration than his own. Tim's name will never be engraved on the Wall, being but one of that number which would double or treble the list— suicides every one. Balder looks at the stars in the dark branches, musing. If Tim had held on a bit longer.... Maybe maturity and involvement would've exorcised the torment of Tim. Eventually. Maybe. But it's too late now. Tim Bean died right before Gloria came.

Balder is one of eighteen thousand Mainers to receive the bloody baptism that crippled a generation. War. It turned the dominant preceding generation into heroes, and its offshoot into "draft evading cowards" or "emotional cripples." What's the good, the purpose, of this psychological pain? Why does he find himself in this room again—pondering pain?

Beyond his personal experience he sees the mistake of that older generation—self-deceived, impinging almost unforgivably on its children. They conceived and developed an ideal of valor based on World War II, and then, being so impressed by their mighty experience, used it ever after as a template on those to follow. That template promoted industry and profit, greasing its increase with young man in Cold War surrogate "skirmishes." What was that bumper sticker he saw yesterday? "El Salvador is Spanish for Vietnam." Each great power embroiling its young, as, today, the better-red-than-dead of the current Soviet generation is juice in a fruitless war in Afghanistan. He understands that the older generation will continue, until its passing, to exacerbate the pain, and to divide the Nam vets from the non vets with painful regret, recriminations. Balder wants none of the division. He sees his generation as a whole—wounded whole. Yeah, he has forgiven, is no longer bitter. The older generation is mistaken, that's all.

Tim has died. Balder, on the other hand, is alive. Seeing the stars. And now, even though he's back in this room, so much is mitigated. The emotion bringing him back this spring is—other. Like budding leaves on beeches maples popples, he will emerge, open and leaf in this new spring. What was cut off, taken from him in the fiery war, is not being restored to Balder (youth peace wholeness cannot come again this side of heaven, blessed be the name of God)—but something new is given. A son.

Family. People. Intimate, connected.

(One thing greatly interested him to look up: the biological pathways of conception; intricacies of how people are formed.) Sitting before a window (sending in the scent of spring), he sees these people ...like the stars up there in the dark boughs. In muscle and bone, in genetic material, they are in it together with him. He knows how Abraham felt, Abram.

That's who I was, but now Abraham. And Daniel is my Isaac. Generations could come of this. Generations—begot in a single night in my '55 Chevy.

Sitting here in the old Morris chair, looking up through the branches, he smiles.

Can I stand being told that Daniel isn't my son? My son. Seeing them there like that.... At Deep Hole! Daniel must have been conceived there. Apart from Abenaki Notch, Balder has no memory of her body (of Chrischana's high brown breasts, long dark tangle of hair hanging down). Because of her, Deep Hole is the most intimate place on earth. Isn't that the real reason for bringing Gloria there?

Gloria. Gloria Chrischana Daniel. And mother. These are the people. They are the reason Balder can live. Without them he might zigzag, flounder. Mechanical ability has given life structure, but now there are people to be responsible to. This is what the baptism in blood brought him (and almost cut him off from): the knowledge that life's meaning indwells human flesh. His brothers of the battlefield showed him this in bloody dying, some in his arms. Relatedness: deep, indelible, painful. In this becoming a father—beyond being only a son—he finds a pattern revealed: a tricornered pattern, inscribed with human faces. Father, Mother, Child.

Again comes the sight of Chrischana standing there in the budding with her three sons ... Chrischana. Older, fuller, unhappy, *mature*. She steps out of the remembered form: the tawniness; shapely, limbly, the earthy exciting smell of her. Surprising how well he remembers the quiet proud girl on a prancing pony, feathered like a bird. An icon changed. She stands now between children, fruit of her sexuality, generosity, verve.... And that look on her face.... Unhappiness yes, and something else. Fear. Somehow he frightened her, but not intentionally. He recognized his sternness toward her only afterward.

She must have been wary of seeing him ... having abandoned him abruptly fifteen years ago. Leaving without a word. Because of Daniel?

He has been in this room more than a week, an indulgence. But now his soul is steadied; it's time to leave this place. Can't leave them out there like that, homeless, camping at Abenaki Notch. It's rained twice already. Each time he fought the impulse to jump into the truck, bring them back to *Simons Ledge*. He can't just force himself on them, impose his own order on their lives.

Where's the other man, the father of the other two? For all Balder knows the man is with them now....

Gloria. Balder Simon loves Gloria and plans to divert his life into her. Into her, not into her "life-style." Their plans are so opposed it's funny. Cosmically funny. Though he is nothing but traditional—fiercely so—this match can't possibly travel a traditional road. But he will not cease to love, though Gloria will go her way—zigzagging, sure—and he will go the way he must. No matter how she tugs.

Now that Daniel has come he feels sure about building his own house. May it be like a great tree, housing many birds. Gloria and Daniel will be in the roots of its foundation. Bride and son? ...

Balder frowns, his gaze sliding down the weathered window frame. Could do with scraping and painting, inside and out. So much work this old house needs. The breeze slides under its slightly raised sash, falling cool on his lax hands. A frown deepens. He loves two women. Chrischana was the wife of his brief youth. But Gloria is his bride. When he first came into this room again, he did not know what to do with them. Still doesn't. But his feelings are sorted. He finds order in the way things have fallen: Chrischana has been faithful in raising their child. Though his being left out was wounding, he is not angry or bitter on consideration. (*What is that haunting Chrischana's eyes?*) Soon he will thank her for bearing and raising Daniel.

He shakes his head. The boy is something. Balder feels luckier than he can express. Finding Daniel is like finding gem quality beryl in the belly of a fresh-caught trout. *Don't let her tell me he's not my son.* The fervor of this hope surprises him. Sitting between the old wallpapered walls, he feels it again and again. Daniel was watching his brothers. He has a sense of responsibility. Daniel caught dinner. He understands and acts on the realities of life. Only fourteen years old, right? After it all ... how can a gift like this be delivered whole? (But he should not have subjected Daniel to such scrutiny as he did upon seeing him. The bald look will make it harder to gain his trust.)

Life! What a mystery. How can Gloria come here and fall for him, like the sun dropping into his lap? He was all set, resigned, to being only an aging mother's keeper, a tinkerer and fishing fool ... after the fires of Vietnam. It was to be a plodding existence in Gottheim. That was a month ago (and the grief of Tim's death still fresh).

Balder rubs a thoughtful thumb along the whiskers of his newly bearded jawline. The breeze brings a distant sounding of the village clock up the mountainside to him. Even after a lifetime it surprises how well the sound travels. Early morning, 3:30 a.m..

Stretching, the man stands. Time to go fishing.

—

Gloria pulls up to the sidewalk beside white washed half-barrels overflowing with flowers. She looks at her watch. Almost lunchtime. The day is breezy but beginning to heat up. *Might put the top down on my little red baby after lunch.* She picks up Guerber's *Norseman* from the seat beside her, thoughtfully fingering the old and lose binding. She opens once more to the place marked.

"*Gradually the light died out of his eyes, a careworn look came into his face, and his step grew heavy and slow.*" The words signified the god Balder's want of spirit in the wake of foreshadowing dreams. The son of Odin and Frigga, whom nothing else might conquer nor weapon destroy, would be slain by the lowly mistletoe, a parasite of the oak.

What a charming story, not at all the kind I'm used to. Brooding and romantic, sad. Before this I read only contemporary realism. Idiosyncratic and subjective, it was how she got her realism—not from actual life. But the sagas are not sentimental. She feels in them the blood and steel of thirsty swords, a dark violence of molten fires, the monstrous cold and ice of the European north.

Gloria looks up at the brick building where the Gottheim Library is housed, dim stacks visible behind the divided lights of its twin bay windows. She looks at the word Gottheim over the granite lintel of the entrance. The roots of the word must be related to words in Guerber also ending in *heim*, Teutonic or German for *home*.

She turns to another marked page. "To give light to the world ... the gods studded the heavenly vault with sparks secured from Muspells-heim, points of light which shone steadily through the gloom like brilliant stars." *Muspells-heim*, she muses. Home of fire. Nifl-heim, home of mist. She shivers with delight, smiles. Gloria is liking this mythic way of seeing things. It's like the way she feels about Jasper Mountain. Mythic imagery seems appropriate to the life she finds in Maine. Couldn't life all over the planet be expressed mythologically? Thoughts like this didn't occur to her until Guerber.

Closing the book, she opens the car door into the wind. Nearing the library door, she is disappointed to notice the sign, *closed*. Oh well, use the slot beside the door. Now she will have to come back for it instead of renewing. She drops the book and turns, staring absently off across the Common toward one of the churches.

Gloria is eager for her lunch date with Balder at the crappy diner. More than two weeks have gone by since the snowmelt ritual at Deep Hole. His long absence must have something to do with the woman they saw at Abenaki Notch. There was a quality of hardness in his continued silence in the car afterward. Gloria feels the need of reassurance. The strange separation and silence have shaken her confidence in the relationship. If not for his blunt avowal on the phone early this morning, she might believe it was over. He never spoke of love till now. It's the gift this time apart has given. But she has promised herself to be honest. I'm not capable of undying love. I know that much about myself. I know from past experience. Even so, Gloria is sure that she will go on loving Balder a very long time. Maybe she'll be loving him still at thirty, even. Five years is a practical scope for fidelity. If you can't manage it with someone like Balder ... well, there's something wrong with you! She smiles to herself on the windy sidewalk.

Gloria slides back into the sports car. On the satisfying purr of its engine, she glides round the corner and past the storefronts lining the shores of Hutchins Pond. How can Balder stand that crappy place, that greasy food! Oh well—it will be gone soon. It's in *The Village Voter*. Letters to the editor are shriveling up the page. Doesn't matter: Balder will die an old Mainer, felled by grease, not mistletoe.

Near the elbow in the counter, Balder sits at the end booth of Decatur's Diner, idly stirring his coffee. The colorful, greasy old neon clock above the order window gives him a small block of time till Gloria shows. Maybe there's time to go to the chair factory and apologize to Vernon for his unexcused unexplained absence. He owes them that. While he was out, there was only Gilbert Gage to keep things running, but he's capable. Then, after dinner here with Gloria, he'll go to the Abenaki Notch to see Chrischana. Daniel's probably in school now.

But, instead of rushing, he sips the light coffee; frowning, thinking of that walk around the mill in Guildford this morning. It took more than an hour to compass the paper maker. He had come out of the employment office and caught sight of its steam billowing on the wind. The stacks and gray monolithic structures stood just beyond the town's red-brick blocks.

The woman in the employment office was encouraged by his qualifications, saying the mill would be taking applications owing to scheduled retirements in maintenance. The state employment service was to screen all applicants. The crisp and angular woman put Balder's file in the Adirondack Paper stack. "Just between you and me," she said with a resigned air, "It's a plus that you live outside the immediate area. The company's new office of Human Resources avoids the hiring of town applicants if it can."

"Why's that?"

She hesitated. "I think the reasoning goes ... that people here think they're entitled. I'm not sure I blame them—The G'fid people, I mean. Look what we put up with. I don't need to tell you about the river. Or the smell in our buildings and houses that can never be eradicated. It accumulates, turns stale, gets staler. 'It's the smell of money,' they say. So more people ought to share in it. Look at this town. It's picturesque; views that don't include the mill are beautiful. I know—'Without the mill there'd be no town.' But they take all the sludge and spread it on woodland along the townline. No one knows what the result of that is on wildlife. Fortunately, the taxes they pay keep education on a par with that of Southern Maine. We're grateful for that. Many of us are. Schools to the east are faculty poor, technology poor, extracurricularly poor in comparison."

She stood then, looking a bit chagrined, probably for revealing so much. "We'll be in touch if you make the first cut."

It was afterward that he decided to take that walk. Balder had been coming to Guildford all his life on errands. Adirondack Paper was the single impressive fact about the would-be gracious New England town, with its spires and rooftops clustering among the foliage. Although it had changed hands twice in the last few decades, the mill was a singular legend in the county during the late 1800's. The town and mill were founded by Andrew MacDonald. Unbeknownst to Balder, he did this by quietly buying up land north of the tiny farming community of Guildford Center, and securing riverfront property around Roccomeeco Falls. A holdout against the proffered seven dollars an acre, one shrewd farmer demanded top dollar from MacDonald's agents who reported back to their boss with scorn: "Crazy fool wants fifty an acre for the rocky old headland!" MacDonald got a glint in his eye (not unlike the glint James Fay often noted in Harry Golding's eye). "Pay the crazy fool his fifty dollars for each of those rocky acres!"

For all its bold monolithic stance in the community, Balder had rarely considered the mill when he was driving around town on errands. He would have noticed only if it turned up missing. Now he thought why not take a look at the place he'd been taking for granted. If things went as he hoped, Balder would be spending his work-life to help keep the place going. So he tramped on a dirt lane beside the railroad track leading toward the company railyard.

Dust devils spun on the lane ahead of him. Enlarging as he neared, the mill spread out before him like a city; end to end in conveyors, concrete and steel. Heavy with great insulators, the girders and gridwork of substations complicated the view. Smokestacks towered, pouring forth a white mixture of smoke and steam. Electric towers strung with miles of cable and conduit were dwarfed by the monstrous buildings above. Inside, he knew, forests were debarked and chipped, wood pulp was chemically digested; as slurry it traveled a wire mesh toward dryers, presses, calendars and winders, mysteriously transformed as paper.

Now, as he walked, Balder was assaulted by a brutal, even tactile, stench—both chemical and organic. A corruption-of-vegetable stench, piercing to the back of his nares and prickling through his lower face as though he had swallowed hot mustard. Stung, he looked down into the mill yard. Rumbling clinking roaring and screeching, the yard moved with trucks, cranes, conveyors and tiny hard-hatted workers. Over all swam shadows of vapor, swift and dark upon the swarming mill yard. Walking on, he rounded a bend beside the crusted sludge-delivery building, stopping to watch dried residue of papermaking crap itself into the filthy bins. Crusty trucks were lined up to receive and cart sludge off to the edge of town.

Continuing on, Balder passed a lake of sewage, hidden behind a half-hearted screen of popples in spring leaves already flecked in dried spume. Looking at them, he recalled that when paper was first made in the Meguntic Mountains popple were considered premier papermaking trees. Today spruce was supreme and popple only filler. When they saw it quivering in the woods people said with scorn that, like weeds in a garden, it should be eradicated. Ever sensitive to the faintest breeze, the popple screening the sewage before him shivered mightily in the dry wind. At first he thought little of their dry hustling sounds. But as he peered down through the spume-coated leaves on the scummy colorless pools, the hustlings turned sorrowful and frenzied in his ears. He watched the wind whip up the filthy foam, bubbling and spitting in scuzzy glee.

Glee? He thought it then. And he thinks it now, sitting in Decatur's diner. What made him think of glee?

Later, rounding the sewage plant, he came out above the pulpwood yard where mountainous piles, from clearcuts all over the northern woodland, towered. Beyond these ranges of pulpwood, were great ridges of wood chips. He walked on, watching chips spewn out of the wood room from nozzles with necks like those of praying mantises. Truck dumps upended the beds of semis, puking out chips from distant shipping operations and wood mills; bulldozers busily worked them up into the great piles. Pulpwood had come, in one form or another, from all over Maine, Vermont, New Hampshire, even parts of Quebec. Gazing on the monstrous piles, Balder thought suddenly what a fixture it all was. Week in, week out, every week of his life, he had seen this place full of junked trees—trees cut to junks and piled to a height of seven or eight stories. He stood watching until he could absorb no more. Then he turned and walked back to his decades old Chevy.

He holds up his mug, signaling Melvinia to pour him another. In comes Huldah Littlefield with her boy, setting the toddler to stand on the booth behind Balder. He turns to look thoughtfully at little Simeon. The boy's great eyes and soft expression impress the man with innocence. Transfixed, he feels a slow smile coming.

"Hi, Balda," says Huldah. "Didn't I see y'cah in G'fid earlier?"

"Yuht. Down applying t'work in the mill. You work in theya, don't choo?"

Her fringe of hair bobs as, nodding, she settles Simeon. "Might put me on a papah machine, but fah now I'm doing custodial work. I was down't the basement last night, hosing out stock. Waste's unbelievable! Theya making way too much prep fah the storage chests t'hold."

"Whad they do then with all the extra?"

She shrugs. "Goes to the sewage plant. Turns out sludge, I s'pose."

"So they cut down trees, truck'em t'the mill, chip'em, slop'em, hose'em out, then turn it all into sludge t'spread on the woods?"

Huldah giggles. "Sometimes seems like it."

"I'd be taking the woods apart every day with a wrench'n pair of pliers. Don't it make you mad?"

"Not if I'm getting paid. Y'get use to it. You wouldn't believe the waste goes on—evah department. Wait'll you get in. If you got mad all the time, you wouldn't work theya."

She spies her sister, Polly Proctor, waving from the other end of Decatur's. Grabbing up the boy, she hurries off toward Polly. Balder watches after big-eyed Simeon as she carries him, bouncing, away.

Outside, in Decatur's parking lot, a dust cloud blew past Chrischana's Bonneville. She studied the windows of the maroon and silver diner through her pocked windshield. Balder's aqua Chevy was sandwiched between a Ford pickup and Bronco. She had not counted on this, wanting only to see Decatur and find out what his plans were when the diner got done. Chrischana's gaze stopped at the far window where Balder sat in the end booth, motioning to her. Too late to pretend she didn't see him. She felt tears coming and widened her eyes to stop them.

He was still waving her toward him as she came through the glass door of the diner. "Sit down, Chrischana?" he asked as she approached.

She sat down across from him and clasped her hands on the tabletop, pretending to study a missing chip in its linoleum covering.

This is silly, she thought, and looked up.

With surprise she saw that he needed a shave. Or, was he growing a beard? But hunting season was months away. There were plenty who got started during buck season and never bothered to shave again.

He was saying he had planned to drive out to the Notch to find her. "Sorry I waited s'long. Could we meet at *Simons Ledge* or someplace t'talk?"

Avoiding his eyes, she looked again at his darkened jawline. It was expectant, taut.   Glancing around, seeing that they were alone at this end, she said, "Well ... I can just tell you .... Yes, Daniel is your son."

She saw him swallow, relax.   She'd forgotten the way he tensed up over something important to him. And how his jaw relaxed suddenly when he was eased. She looked into his intense northern blue eyes then, not wanting to lose his gaze during this confirmation.

Balder was the one to look away now. "... Knew it!" He murmured, and turned to face her again. "I'm glad, Chrischana. Very, very glad. We made him together. "

She nodded, lightening.   Feeling a smile slowly rising in her. They looked at one another across the table, smiling. "Damn!" He smacked the old linoleum with the palm of his hand.   It stung, but he grinned.

Melvinia came over, grinning behind her outsized glasses, saying, "Don't choo two look happy's clams." She turned toward the door, tittering. "Look out! Heah comes Libby with that camera."

Little Libby Greenleaf came swinging down the aisle, clutching her camera. "Miz Sessions," she said, "How about a picture o'you and Mr. Decatur fah *The Voter*. We are doing a story on the history o'this place!" She walked back toward the order window, calling for Decatur to come out.

And so it happened that a photo would appear in next week's edition—a symmetrical grouping of Melvinia and Decatur flanking a grinning pair in an old booth in Gott'im's local diner. Chrischana would clip it out and give it to Daniel along with the strange and unsettling news that the man at Deep Hole was his father.

When Libby was gone and Decatur had retreated to his kitchen, Melvinia took their orders. Balder prevailed in buying Chrischana lunch, and now they sat back, each wondering where to go from here. At last he said, "I waunt t'help."

She looked at him with her Native eyes, slowly shaking her head. "We're a unit, the boys'n I. Together we're going t'make it."

She was letting him know that the other man was out of the picture and that she would not split up the boys. He smiled a bit, saying with regret,

"You lost the Maine way o'speaking." He was dreaming some, remembering the girl he knew.

She nodded but hurried on. "All I need's a job. Picked up a few house-keeping jobs—spot work only—last week, but we need something permanent. I was going to ask Decatur about his plans."

He grinned. "You can have my job. I in't been t'work since I saw Daniel. Chair factory must be hurting by now."

She smiled and slowed down some, taking time to remember— seeing him bent over the engine of a Chevy. "If only I paid attention when you tried to show me how engines work."

He was looking at her, taking in her blue kerchief, the long dark braid hanging down along her breast. Her black T-shirt with a winged Harley-Davidson emblem on the pocket. He looked away, out the window at the faded gold Bonneville. "That rustworks bring you all the way fom Phoenix? Must'o cost a fortune in gas."

She nodded, murmuring *a fortune,* waiting for him to continue. He ran his fingers absently over the blister scars on his arms. The sleeves of Balder's flannel shirt were rolled up. Chrischana looked carefully then at his forearms and drew back. "What's this?" And instantly she regretted the exclamation, regretted prying.

"Those are my A.O. tattoos." He rolled his sleeves down over them, saying, "From Vietnam. It was hard to avoid that stuff over theya."

"Agent Orange!? You were *in it*?!"

"Went theya afta you left. Got scared when MIT tried t'draft me. 'Twas the only way I could think of to escape."

But his humor could not bring back the ease of a moment ago. So hard to see him now, to try talking as if nothing had happened. Dimly she understood that a period of adjustment was needed, a sense of where they stood today. But it eluded her. The moon had moved off from the earth, the sun had reversed its course over the mountains. A child had been conceived, shot off toward manhood. Two hearts had been broken and horribly scarred on the mend. She felt her father in her arms, falling. She wanted to fly again, leave the ordered burger, *the world*, behind. But Balder's voice checked her.

"Look Chrischana, it was what I chose to do, fight Communism, get out of Gott'im, see the world." He wanted to take her hand, but stopped. The gentle touch might complicate the fragile new relation. "We've got Daniel. And I'm not gonna leave y'blowing in the breeze. We've both got something t'do in caring fah him. Is this right?" With relief, he saw her nod, eyes once more on the chipped linoleum. He wanted to open his wallet immediately but understood that this would only embarrass them both.

"We'll go to some court and have'em work out support payments. I'd pay t'them, they pay you, OK?"

She looked out the smudged window, bemused and sad. A little red car pulled into the parking lot. Chrischana gazed absently at it until the blond driver got out into the wind, buffeted by a dust devil. Chrischana looked toward the kitchen and saw Melvinia lifting plates from the window onto her tray.

"That'll be fine, Balder," she said, snatching a pen from his breast pocket and hastily scrawling her post office box number on a napkin. "Sorry t'rush." She pushed it toward him and stood. "And thanks for the burger. I'll eat at the counter." She walked away.

Surprised, he turned to look but saw Gloria coming up behind him. The light of her smile filled him; her great eyes, glossy swinging pageboy; her crisp classiness rejoicing him. She leaned over to kiss him, a brushing kiss, soft as the petals of a wild rose. She pulled back, startled by the scratch of his whiskers. He caught a whiff of her perfume, smooth and light, as she slid into the seat across from him.

She resolved on no mention of the one who had just vacated the booth. Nor would she be the first to bring up the separation immediately past. She would not say what she thought of the *facial hair*. "Ah." She chuckled, eyeing the food Melvinia set before him. "Having our grease in the form of the hamburger plate today!" She lifted a shapely eyebrow, smiling. "Somehow, I don't think I'll miss this place as much as you will."

"Well," he returned, "I may not have t'miss it! Nevah know what can happen. Decatur's could go down and spring up over theya." He gestured across the road with a wave of his fork. "God is spooky that way. Can't deprive a small town of its grease'n not have repercussions."

She made a wry face, said, "And who's going to see to it? The Goldings? The condominium owners on Roberts Pond? How about that new bed'n breakfast on Livery Street?"

"Maybe all! You fail to take into account the whimsey of God. Evah think theya may be some cause fah his name to be in Gott'im?"

She pounced on this. "How *did* Gott'im get its name?"

"Ask Asa Bartlett—over to the historical society. Now back to my point. Ever hear of God playing practical jokes?"

"Never." Again an arch of the eyebrow. "Why should She want to?"

"How about that time God had Noah spend a hundred years building a big boat—his neighbors jeering at 'em evah day? How about that forty day rain'n flood?"

She pulled back, indignant. "That deluge *killed* everybody. If it happened." The last was said in a mutter.

"Evahbuddy but Noah'n his family. But take now. S'pose he was t'make some small adjustment, say in the earth's rotation to wipe out the westerlies and make the prevailing winds come from the east? Evah mill owner on the west side o'town—all over the country—would have to breathe the stink o'the mills they built."

She shook her head. "They'd all just move to the east side. —No, they'd move to some place like this—and telecommute!"

"Yuht, but then property values'd plummet on the west side'n regular folks could afford t'live in the nice houses left behind. It could happen like that in Gott'im. Some minor adjustment—say in greenhouse gases raising the temperature a notch or two. *Phut!* Ol' Harry'n Julius'd have to go north fah theya snow. And Decatur'd be back in business."

Dimpling, she said, "You're desperate, y'know."

He grinned.

"Besides," she said, "Would the cause be God or man?"

"May be God'n Satan."

"What's *that* supposed to mean?"

"Didn't you say you was a college person—then think on it. Y'don't want an ignorant mechanic thinking your thoughts fah you."

Melvinia set coffee before Gloria, got out a pad to take the order. Balder looked up at Melvinia, seeing the wheels work as she wrote, knowing what the conversation would be in here after they left. Lunchtime, and the place would be full of tongues.

Melvinia paused pointedly, then picked up Chrischana's cup. She carried it to the counter and set it by her elbow. But, as Balder watched, Chrischana stood and went into the kitchen.

Gloria watched Balder. Kissing him earlier, she had seen him fold the napkin—marked in ballpoint pen—and stuff it into his pocket. Now her imagination busily occupied itself creating scenarios. She looked out the window, idly stirring her coffee, waiting for him speak. First the separation, now this. What's going on?

His voice came low. He took her fingers and began rubbing the top of her thumb gently with his own. It was an exciting, yet thoroughly tender, gesture. She turned from the window and looked in the face that was delineated in whiskers, suddenly deciding that it was sexy. The whiskers could stay, but she fervently hoped he was not growing a beard. She couldn't bear a bushy growth on that sexy face.

He said softly, "Forgive me the silence of these last days?"

She nodded, squeezing his hand.

"I got some odd news'n it unsettled me." Thoughtfully…he stopped talking, still gently stroking her thumb. The place was now filling for lunch. A noisy foursome came in to occupy the next booth. He leaned over the table, and she edged forward to meet him. Again he spoke low, thrilling her with the sweetness of this attention.

"Glory, have you ever considered kids? Having kids?"

Loosing his hand, Gloria fell back against the seat, astonished. But she recovered herself, leaned forward again and took up his hand. Gently. She smiled. It was one of his wonderful jokes. He went on seriously, intimately, his voice soft and low. "I know it's maybe kind'o odd, asking you like this ... ovah a dinah table'n all..." (here he did grin a little) ..."But it's—well, I got something on my mind." He was finished now, awaiting her response.

But she was unable to frame one. She sat there, feeling his gentle touch. Quietly, she began stroking his thumb in return. Is he wooing me? Is this what we mean by pitching woo? No one had ever bothered with anything remotely like this. Plenty of heavy breathing, groping and clutching—but never *never* anything like this. She and Balder had not yet consummated their intimacy, were still mostly sexually innocent of one another. Now, slowly, thoroughly, as his thumb wrought, he was filling her with desire. As though filling a glass with sweet wine from the bottom up. Filling her with arousal, where she sat—here! In Decatur's Diner!

His face, close to hers, was expectant. She felt his breath on her hand as he waited for her to speak. She leaned close, very close, saying, "You know I want you." Whispering, she felt meager and appealing ... the best she could be. Yet she felt it strangely small and unworthy. He had invoked deep desire, but her answering seemed uneven in comparison. Did this sort of thing take practice? She thought her sexual experience would have qualified her, but somehow, inexplicably, she was disappointed in her own response.

He said, still low, "And I want you. But do you want children?"

Puzzled, she pulled back. What is this? Is he actually asking if she wants to have children? Give birth? *Take care of kids?*

Balder was watching, gauging the emotions passing through Gloria's features, and suddenly as she looked at him it was as if she looked in a mirror ... seeing that disappointment in his face. He had seen her setback, that she was shocked: indignant and unable to cover this disenchantment.

She said it flatly, withdrawing her hand. "I'm still a child myself, Balder. The child in me needs nurturing. I need all the fulfillment that I can responsibly muster." She hurried on, her voice now a mixture of anger and pleading. "The possibilities for me are boundless, exhilarating. Do you have any idea what children would do to that? Balder," She finished raggedly, "Balder, it would not be good for them, either."

His jaw tightened. He looked away. Outside the window he saw Chrischana getting into her rusty Bonneville. He heard its deep-throated rumbling as she started it up.

God.

He turned back to Gloria, for in another moment he would've seen her drive off. He felt his breast pocket where her napkin lay.

Gloria saw this movement and looked away.

"Gloria," he said with finality. "I'm a fatha now. I found out fah sure this morning. When Chrischana left here fifteen years ago, she was pregnant with my son Daniel."

Her eyes widened. She looked out the window, seeing the dust cloud from the big car settle in its wake as it went.

Balder was saying, "I waunt t'be with you, but you got t'understand. I'm a fatha now. I want to be one. To be a fatha to Daniel ... and his brothers if they need one. Can you share me? We'll build us a big ol'house...."

But, looking at the fish sandwich Melvinia had just set in front of her, she had stopped listening.

"Heah y'go, deah!" said Melvinia.

Gloria stared at the greasy thumbprint on top of the bun, the revolting glossy tartar sauce in its little paper cup. Dully she looked around, the whole place revolting her. Clasping her purse, she stood. "I'll have to think about this," she said, eyes on the door. "Gimme time. I'll get back t'ya."

She was gone ... out to her little red car. Balder grinned unhappily up at Melvinia. "Some people in't cut out fah eating in dinahs. The food makes'em lose theya appetites."

Melvinia snorted, her dangly earrings shaking in disgust.

Gloria Fay is holed up in her bedroom, looking out at the grey flanks of Jasper, laced in green. The view here isn't like that of the reception center where she sometimes works; but no matter, for, leaning her wet face against the screen, she doesn't see it today. For the summer she is sharing her parents' townhouse condominium with her brother Jimmy. She can remember the day the resort broke ground to build these units. How she jigged up and down, excited, jabbering to her siblings, to Daddy and Mom. On a subsequent visit she ran through the white stud works, exploring the connecting units of the townhouses. She is part of this place, of Jasper

Mountain. She belongs here as much as anyone, as much as Melvinia and Decatur and Balder and that crappy diner. She'll show them. She'll convince Balder of her fidelity to it! No one is going to exclude her from this place. It is dear, dear, dear! Gloria wipes at the tears with her fingertips.

How will she show him? It takes more than selling time shares.... Or, why should she care what he thinks? Why not just let it happen? Be what you are, forthrightly ambitious and hard-working. Find what you can do to be of use in Gottheim. To Gottheim. Just hold on to the mountain, and to those dreams of owning your own place. And schuss straight to your goal, no switchbacking.

But the tears start again, her face already sticky with mascara and tears.... When there comes a soft rapping at the door.

"Open the door, Gloria. Talk to me." It is her brother, James. "Don't stay so long in there, Gloria.... Please? It's not good for you. Talk to me. Gloria? Please?"

God Takes Care of God's Creatures

In a corner of her office panelled in dark oaken squares, Theodora Prescott sat turned away from the antique rolltop desk. Behind her sat a stack of printed forms. In a posture of assumed relaxation, she tried to lounge against the desk in this tiny office from which her great-grandfather had first run the then flourishing business of the Gottheim Chair Company. Opposite sat Balder. The room was a solid piece of craftsmanship, illumined by two tall mullioned windows. It could have been a study in an elegant nineteenth century industrialist's mansion. The offices of the company were the only sound components of the now ramshackle array. The connected buildings were at odd angles, crazily leaning either toward or away from one another, variously sided in wood, asphalt, metal or block. From behind the closed oaken door came the muted racket of the furniture mill. The smell of sawdust, shavings, resin and glue penetrated here.

Theodora was just finishing up on her subject of turning the mill into a cannery. She had been reading Maine history and was intrigued by the fact that the state once had a reputation in canning. And she was uplifted in discovering that Gottheim's first industry was the processing of maple syrup. Ms. Prescott thought that Gottheim Chair could stand updating: In view of this trend, in which tourism was edging out the woodsmills as the town's leading industry, she had decided on finding an historical niche and exploiting it. Thankfully, Gottheim was practically a full-fledged four seasons area. The new mountain biking craze, foliage tours, and skiing are all here to round out the future of God's House.

"Balder," she said, wrapping up her little talk, "I'm seriously considering a merger into our historical industry, complete with old fashioned canning jars and quaint labels. It would be a sweet appropriate endeavor here under our roof, and we could have a viewers' gallery for tourists to watch the process. Now what do you think of that?" She smiled, hoping the gesture would be construed as conciliatory, though she continued to be annoyed by his recent actions ... and those whiskers.

But the smile struck Balder Simon as coy, though he credited her with genuine ignorance of this. By unspoken mutual consent they had left off the topic of his prolonged unexcused absence—for which she had attacked him and his utter lack of consideration for the business. He had apologized, offering to work the current week without pay, which she promptly noted at her desk. But the apology itself went unnoticed, a habit of hers that he recalled from childhood when they were neighbors at camp. As children they had exchanged insults across the cove of Kimball Pond, where their extended families spent part of the summer. Now that they were grown, each occupied a defining role in community life, she as a business-person philanthropist, he as irksome wisecracking mechanic. His deference today was genuine and proper, but Theodora's sometimes blind frantic personality precluded notice. It seemed a necessity for her to express the last drop of indignation over neglect. The process could be lengthy.

Now Balder thought, *The Gott'im Can Company.*

He was tempted to respond to her question about the proposed syrup cannery with a blunt agreement: We could shut down for the ten months following sugaring off. However, he did not feel like cranking up the feud again. Instead he nodded. "Will we can blueberries, apples, and other fruits in season?" He said it idly, absently. Balder was still seeing Gloria's horrified expression against the grimy backdrop of Decatur's diner.

The question checked Theodora. How could she have forgotten that huge chunk of time between sapping seasons? She felt embarrassment burning through her features and rushed to cover the error by concurring with his suggestion, then hurrying on. Her arm resting on the stack of paper on her old desk, she leaned confidentially toward him.

She was immaculately coiffed and demurely dressed in a powder blue suit, smelling of perfume. Balder restrained the urge to lean away. She had displayed coquetry before, and he found it embarrassing.

But her eyes gleamed instead with ambition. She said, "We are about to embark on something new here at Gottheim Chair, something innovative. People don't expect this sort of thing here in this industrial backwater (where Western Maine is unfortunately tangled in the shallows)."

Now she was reaching for poetry. Balder dropped his gaze. He was used to suppressing his humor around her. Sometimes he felt pity, even tenderness toward her, but her lapses into self-deceived arrogance annoyed him.

She drifted shell-pink fingertips down the stack of papers, saying, "As you know, I've become increasingly associated with the International

Institute of Coordinated Experiments." Her look was eager and bright; she used its full name to remind him of its scientific cachet. "Gottheim Chair is going to benefit from that association. I've contracted for our employees to join in testing, and seminars, specially designed to help make for a smoother running, more friendly operation here. Help will be in the form of consensus building, psychological profiles, and what I would call respect and respite sessions—where people can relax and say what's on their minds. These measures are designed to evoke a more positive attitude in the mill. Can you agree we need that here, Balder?"

As she talked, a frown gathered between his brows which she failed to notice. He hated anything like what she was proposing. Had she not displayed such bright hopefulness, he might almost have verbally savaged her on the spot. Instead, he fell back on the ploy he sometimes adopted when he felt contempt for one of her ideas. Balder leaned back and averted his eyes, frowning. "I don't know, Ms. Prescott. I'm just a mechanic heah."

Theodora sat upright, heaving her small boson, lifting her chin. He'd done it to her again; just as she was feeling at ease in the emotional reliance he must know she craved. *He was so reasonable just now over my pain and trouble during his absence.... That miserable machinery could* not *be kept in repair with only the hands of Gilbert Gage to coax it. He* knows *how much I depend on him.* Balder knew she had always loved and respected him! Together they had taken all those college preparatory classes at Gottheim Academy when it served both town kids and the preppies from away, for even though he had gone on to Vietnam—volunteered when others were burning their draft cards!—he was an intelligent man. Not like Six-pack Sam who went into the woods or turned furniture legs for a living. He had always claimed some kind of kinship to those people by his associations (and now with that awful facial hair!) but she knew he was no mere mechanic. He just used that as a copout whenever he came up against anything he thought would threaten the precious dumbness of this wretched little community!

But she had a respect for Balder bordering on fear. She couldn't bring herself to go verbal with him on this because he might shred her with his wit. She now tried to cover her initial heave of the bosom with a contrite look. And recalling his skill in ridicule, Theodora *did* feel contrition.

She sighed, venturing timidly, "Well ... I was trying to lift my employees up with this program from IICE ... but it's fine with me if you don't want to talk about it.... Incidently, Vernon thinks it's an excellent idea." She could not resist this last thrust, but she stood quickly, holding out a dainty hand.

"Thanks for coming in." At least she had learned something at IICE. You must employ courtesy and develop a habit of respect if you're to build toward compromise and consensus.

Aside from his greeting, apology, and leave taking, Balder had scarcely spoken three sentences during the interview. Going down the worn wooden stairs toward the shop, thinking of the plans for her employees, Balder Simon grimaced.

Lift those employees right up there. Up where you can hang 'em out to dry!

The long June twilight had lingered, dark was just about down. Beyond the fretful borders of the sagging Cape, Cindabilla stood near the lane awaiting Daniel. She climbed onto the great low branch of a huge maple not far from the broken gate, and looked up.

A tufted owl in the higher branches somewhere up there. Thing was on the far side, in the leaves, spitting out another mouse. Heavy old thing— swooping down on rodents all evening, killing and spitting them out; not even bothering to eat. It gave her the creeps but she was fascinated anyway. Owls don't usually do that, do they?

She had crept out her window and scurried away from the fetid and furious house. A long wait, but Daniel would be here. One thing she could count on was Daniel. Feeling the impress of jagged bark on her palms and even through her jeans, Cindabilla swung her bare feet back and forth.

A crash came from the Cape style house. She looked over her shoulder at the yellow rectangles of light that broke the dark surface of her home. Shadows crossed the blinds, and in one shadeless window she saw Uncle Ferdinand lurch out of view; heard his drunken cursing drift out. He was taking aim at his girlfriend again. Babette sometimes looked 45, but Cindabilla knew she wasn't more than 33, or 34—ancient but not that ancient. Daniel had said she went to school with his mother in the '60s.

The soft rush of quiet wings went past. The owl was at it again. "Cruel bastid," she said in her high thin voice. She looked away from the house toward the lane. Why don't Babette just leave? Why take that abuse ovah and ovah and ovah?

She leaned out, looking up the road. Is that a shadow moving toward the lane? Yep, here he comes. She slid to the ground and moved toward the lane, running like a pale stripling through the dark of grass. So cool and sweet out here tonight.

Daniel came up to her, his quiet face with its slightly Indian contours visible in the June evening. He had high cheek bones and a broad brow. She had never seen him smile.

"How's the school play t'night?" he asked.

"Cruel bastid's beating on her again—like last week. Wish she'd leave."

"Can't your grandmother do anything?" He was thinking of how there'd been no family in Phoenix for him to call on when Petey went ballistic.

"Call the cops's all. It's something t'do, but ain't much use t'Babette. She nevah presses chodges, so Gram gets discouraged." Her eyes brightened in the night. "Waunt see something?" She pulled him toward the maple.

In the shadow on the ground beneath lay an odd little mess. What's this? Then a dead mouse fell on top. Daniel started back.

Cindabilla said, "Cruel bastid's up theya."

Daniel glanced up into the foliage and saw a gleam of something. He looked on the pile at his feet, recognizing tiny bodies, legs and tails.

"Cruel, stupid horned owl," said Cindabilla. "Been heah all evening, swooping down, spitting 'em out. Someone ought shoot it!" Staring at the heap of little bodies, she said, "We ought." She looked back at Daniel.

Cindabilla's face was ghostly and there was moonlight enough to see her cloud of freckles, the pale lashes around her eyes. Her long ponytail glimmered in the night as together they moved out from under the tree. Her arms were thin and white, her chest just developing under her T-shirt. Other girls in class were stylish in comparison, wearing bras, makeup, earrings, and blouses to top their imitation designer jeans. Their shoes were petite, feminine, but Cindabilla would go barefoot as much as possible this summer. Her sneakers, bought by Gram last fall, were now smelly and shot.

Daniel's look was doubtful. "Whose gun'd we use?"

"One o'Uncle Ferddy's."

But Daniel looked off toward the woods beyond the Sessions' pasture behind the house. He fancied he could see the glow of Aunt Nellie's camp. He pictured her looking at the arrowheads through her magnifying glass. But the thought of Cindabilla's great aunt at peace was suddenly shattered by the cries of Babette Roebuck.

Daniel seethed some words between his teeth, inarticulately wondering what they could do. Should he go in there and throw himself on Ferddy—a stranger? He had thrown himself on Dad—Petey—not long ago, in Phoenix. Ferddy is bigger than Dad, but it might distract him long enough for Babette to get away.

"Let's go look in the window," said Cindabilla, turning toward the house. "If it's bad we could decoy'em. Beat on the house, break a window, something."

Through weeds and bits of trash they crept up to the weathered windowsill. The rank smell of Hannah Sessions' kitchen came out at them, along with the glare of a naked bulb above the table. There were cans and clutter, plates and pots everywhere. Chairs were askew or knocked over. A cigarette lay on the floor, burning a hole in the linoleum. A cat lapped at something under the table. Over in a corner beside the refrigerator hunkered Ferddy over Babette, yelling like a maniac. He was a demon hollering himself hoarse, right into her ear where she sat scrunched against the appliance. She didn't seem injured, but her head was down, covered with arms clasped in an attitude of protection. Hannah was nowhere to be seen.

Wide-eyed and tense, the children watched as long as they could, but Cindabilla soon pulled Daniel back. "She's all right. Let's go get the owl. We'll climb in Uncle Ferddy's window'n get one o'his guns. One of 'em's bound to be loaded. He's like that. Surprised he never threatened Babs with one." She shivered, thinking of an ever present dread. Maybe she'd come home some night to a scene of blood.

Threading through junk, weeds, and swatches of streaming light, they moved toward the dark end of the high-gabled cape. Cindabilla clambered over the sill and in through a tear in the screen. She landed on a pile of dirty clothes, popping up to whisper, "Wait heah. I'll hand out the gun."

Daniel stood peering in as she moved around. Light from the kitchen at the far end of the house slashed into the open doorway. He saw the shade of Cindabilla crossing and recrossing the bright line made by the open door. At last she handed out the gun and climbed after.

"Just what we want," she hissed. "His bid gun—loaded'n ready t'shoot."

Going down the lane, she asked, "Your aim ana good? We'll shoot that owl, run back'n dump the gun on the clothes pile. Tomorrow he'll probably know 'twas me done it—if he even 'membas it then."

"I never shot a gun," said Daniel, a bit breathless. "In Phoenix only gangstas had guns."

"When we get done, hightail it t'the woods'n you can tell me bout Phoenix more." She nudged him. "There 'tis, on the other side in the branches," she whispered. "Gimme."

She crept beneath the overshadowing boughs with the bird gun, lifted it to her shoulder, took careful aim, and squeezed off a shot. The explosion tossed her back, a light thing. The owl dropped with a thud onto its pile of prey, bouncing a bit. The children ran back across the weedy yard and rounded the corner of the house, breathless. Cindabilla threw the gun into the room. She heard it miss the clothes pile and bark on the floor. There was another explosion.

"Shit!" she squeaked, and ran away around the corner at the back of the house. There was a pigpen and, beyond, the trash-filled yard with the old pickup. She panted and squeaked with excitement, looking back to see if Daniel followed. He knocked into Cindabilla and they tumbled into muck that Hannah Sessions had raked out of the pigpen that afternoon. Rising, stumbling toward the pasture, Daniel puked. But Cindabilla was laughing, freely cursing as she followed, bumping him. "Fuckin' pig shit!" she squeaked at the end of her cursing.

Over and over she said it, as they ran down past the abandoned '40's pickup, tripping over junk. "Fuckin' pig shit!..." They made it to the pasture and went on towards the woods. Daniel looked back toward the hulking tumble-down barn and sway-backed Cape, thinking he heard something— screaming? But he kept on, Cindabilla's laughter and his own ragged retching diverting him.

On and on they ran until at last the great arms of the woods received them. Daniel knew where he was heading, whether Cindabilla followed or not. He was far ahead of her now, on his way to the stream. All he wanted was to drench himself in the rocky waters. He rolled under the current, careful to avoid the rocks cropped out here and there. He clawed at himself, futilely scraping at the muck on his clothes. He wriggled out of them, flopped over suddenly, looking for Cindabilla.

She stood a little apart, already down to her underpants, dunking her T-shirt up and down in the stream. He saw her thin body, faintly agleam, her breasts like buds. She was giggling, cussing a stream of filthy words, and looking over at him with what seemed a face of pure wicked glee. It wasn't quite light enough in the woods for him to see it clearly. "But we got that owl," she said, breathless, repeating it over and over. "We got that stupid bastid fuckin' cruel owl!"

At sight of her Daniel felt an erection coming on, even here in the cold water. He struggled up, lugging wet clothes under a nearby arched snowmachine bridge. He went further upstream and began again, furiously dunking his clothes.

He heard her call out, "Daniel! What choo doing over theya?!"

"Here's where you ain't. We're not doing anything, Cindabilla!" His voice was cracking and shrill.

"Who said anathin bout doing anathin?" Her voice echoed toward him under the bridge. She was wading after him, her teeth beginning to chatter.

But Daniel did not look toward her. "Stay over there till we get dressed." His voice trembled, the words stuttering out. "W-we're t-too-young t'do anathin'!" He was shivering, his sexual urgency now abating.

Cindabilla giggled, but turned away. She climbed up over the rocks onto the bank. "Good thing water's high this time o'year," she called, wringing out her T-shirt. "We'd nevah get fuckin' pig shit off us." She was squeaky with laughter and kept hearing that explosion inside Ferddy's bedroom, the one he shared with Babette.

Her thin arms and hands worked over the jeans, twisting. Never get the water run out of 'em! "Daniel, I caunt get the water out o'my jeans'n I in't wearing 'em wet. Way too cold!"

After a moment she heard him yell, "Well, put your T-shirt on then." She felt energized, exhilarated. No one ever wanted to do anything with her before. Daniel was surely just about saying he wanted to do something! Glorying, she felt luckier than anything; and glad, too, that nothing was going to happen. It meant that Daniel was to be trusted more than anyone. More, even then Gram or Aunt Nellie. —Neither one knew what to do with her anymore: Cindabilla was too far out of hand. She pulled on her T-shirt and called for him to come over now.

When he came up out of the water and saw her in shirt and underpants, he wanted to protest, but decided not to be bothersome. It would be all right as long as he didn't look at her. He started up the path a little ahead of her in cold clinging jeans. Water trickled down inside and the cuffs dragged in the dirt. "C'mon," he said, trying to jam his hands into the pockets. No good. His teeth chattered fiercely, and he flapped his arms. "N-now what'll we do?"

"You're gont tell me bout Phoenix," she said, a little behind him.

She's so tough, he thought, makes me feel wimpy in comparison. "No," he said. "We got t'get warm! Let's go to Aunt Nellie's. "

"Daow," she said, sounding like Hannah Sessions. "We'll just jump up'n'down and beat the trees with sticks. That'll keep us warm."

He jogged along the path, swinging his arms. All he wanted was warmth, but he said, "Whad y'think happened when the gun went off? Thought I heard someone screaming."

"Let's go back 'n' look in the window."

Jogging through the dark, careful of roots and rocks, they speculated on the uproar that must have been caused by the discharging bird gun. Laughing, Cindabilla spun ideas for escaping retribution. She did not really care. Gram didn't know what to do with her and that meant liberty.

When they reached woods' edge, Daniel grabbed her jeans and wrung them out. "Put 'em on. You won't believe the trouble we'd get in if anyone saw us like this."

So, hopping on one foot then the other, Cindabilla got into her jeans. Coming down through the pasture, they noticed a flashing glow coming from beyond the house. And there was another flashing, blue, coming down the road.

"Police," said Daniel. "We're in trouble now."

She grabbed his arm, pulling him toward the corner when they reached the yard. "Theya won't be trouble fah us if I get in bed 'fore they get here."

She pulled herself over the sill and into her dark room—the room beside Ferddy's. Her pale face glimmering in the opening, she said, "Go back t'Twitchell Cove'n I'll be down tomorrow. Let you know what happened then."

He heard her moving around, probably taking off the wet jeans. Then he watched as she opened the bedroom door, letting light stream in. He heard voices of the police come in with the light, questioning. Cindabilla rubbed her eyes against the brightness, yawning and stretching as she headed toward the kitchen.

Daniel crept away as quickly as the strewn yard would allow. The police might check the area, so he had to get out of sight. He went down past the old barn that loomed like a small mountain over the farmyard, then took its lane to the road. Glancing back, he saw the ambulance, its red lights still flashing, mingling with the blue of the cruiser. He watched as the paramedics loaded an occupied stretcher. Then, in a spray of gravel, it leapt away, took the road and flew down toward the highway. Daniel saw the lights vanish below hill-crest.

Feeling a pang of dread, he stepped into the road. Who was on their way to the hospital? *Don't let it be Gram.* Cinda might as well not have a mother, so little use was she to her daughter. Walking on toward the crest of the hill in the light of the stars, his breathing slowed. He grew thoughtful and calm. What will the cops make of her wet T-shirt? No, better not think about it. Not if you can help it.

But he felt a strange exuberance. Daniel wasn't sure he could help thinking of Cinda and her budding T-shirt.

Gottheim's police officers stood in Sessions' yard, looking at the stiff, staring owl. It seemed to be in shock. Scattered in the bird's agony, the prey pile was strewn at the base of the rugged old maple. But the owl had worked its way out of the shadows, its tufted face and great gleaming eyes staring up at the officers in the light of the stars.

"Those eyes!" The woman said.

"Gawd! In't that th'owl's been terrorizing Gott'im?" said the man.

"I guess. They say it's right out o'Stephen King."

Lifting the flap on his holster, the man said, "Ought put it out of its misery."

"Wait," said the other officer. "What about taking it back t'Mrs. Simon. She's got a permit fah this kind o' thing. Fixed it up before."

"How'd we do that? Look at those talons."

Doubtful, the woman looked around. "D'know. I'd go ask Miz Sessions fah one o'her feed sacks. Stuff it in that with a broom or something. It caunt have no fight left now. I'd say it's half dead anaway." She strode off toward the house.

The other stood staring back at the great malevolent face of the horned owl. Never know what a night might bring, he thought. Guess Babette can relax for a while anyway. He smiled, wondering how it would read in *The Voter*.

Out on the highway Daniel averts his face from oncoming headlights, yet he is vigilant on this stretch, moving off the shoulder when it seems wise. Traffic can be either heavy or sparse this time of night, and the highway is two lanes, dark. But it is wide and smooth with fresh asphalt. Jasper Mountain has seen to it, the owners having friends in the capitol and Blaine House.

Daniel skips over some hunks of stuff gleaming whitely in the black road. What is this stuff? He bends for a piece, examines it. Drywall, coated in plaster. You never know what will let loose on the highway. He walks on a few hundred feet, coming to a couple chunks of wood, some scattered strips of bark. Glad I wasn't here when these things fell. Once, just about here on the approach to the Twitchell Pond turnoff, he stepped on broken bits of concrete, and two blocks of it lay just off the shoulder. That night, recalling Mrs. Thurston's hints, he did not tell Mother about the debris. Because he wanted to justify Mother's faith.

Mrs. Thurston was a sturdy group leader at the middle school, and a good assertive woman, mother had said after the woman's implied censure. She kept silent that night when Mrs. Thurston dropped him off at the campsite after learning he had no ride. Later Mother told him of her faith. She would not check his freedom to walk where he desired, in part because she would not be able to drive him around, as could other mothers with reliable cars.

Daniel is glad of his freedom, enjoying this feel of the rural night about him as he walks along in silence. There are no gang bangers to trouble him in Gott'im. He likes the freedom of his feet, now that they are out of the city. They can bring him anywhere, out of anything, if he is patient.

He comes down into the open beside the pond, looking across starlit waters. The black contour of the surrounding hills, edging the still sky, soothes him. Thanks to his exertion, the wet clothes no longer chill him. His thoughts rise. He is going to tell Mother about Babette. At last he might even broach the subject of battered women. Why did she take it so long from Dad—Petey?

Walking at night is good for thinking. On this road beside the pond the strange new idea surfaces again, as it does whenever he is alone. He has told no one, not even Cindabilla. A new father.

Mother said he has to meet Balder. It's bad enough just knowing the fact. It makes him hoppy as a jumping bean. A new father. The idea jumps around inside ... where everything goes on. The trick is to keep it all in there. It can't show on your face. How can that man at Deep Hole be his father! What he remembers is that creepy look in his eye. Hugely, the world goes on around you ... but inside is where it makes itself known.

He remembers the letter Mother got today. The way she stared at it, held it so long in her hands. How still she went, but how far away. Then suddenly she looked to see if he was watching, and crammed the papers into the envelope again, stood and went into the tent.

Daniel couldn't help but wonder. Does it have something more to do with him? But maybe not. Things are always happening to adults and being hidden from kids. They don't know, but kids can worry more about parents than the reverse. He has always worried about mother.

But things are better for her in Maine.

If he can just get used to it himself.

Dear Chrischana [fifth draft of a letter],

You know me well enough to understand that I would've been right there with you, loving you, caring for our child, all those years ago. Maybe you didn't want to burden me. Maybe you didn't want to subject Daniel to the stigma of Gottheim since it was different here in the '60s. Maybe you didn't want your father hurt by it all. Maybe it was all this. However good these motives, pride was in it somewhere: the belief that it was all on your shoulders and no one else had any help, any say. You acted like, since you were the one pregnant, no one else had a part to play, no one should be permitted to bear the burden with you—not me, not your father, not God whose power ignites life.

Can you, acting alone, conceive, spin out the vast array of chromosomes, the genosphere that lives in the continually dividing cells which form a human being? Was it your plan to sit and knit, to fashion together the intricate eyes and world of sound, the knees that crawl, the tiny hands and innards, the living quivering heart of a human? Did you take any thought about how to construct one? Did you design the interconnected, resilient and generous realm required for its support? If the answer is no, please have the humility to share the upbringing of our child with me.

Please don't think that God is not with you, that God cut you adrift because of our backseat Chevy joy, our mysterious fumbling that led directly to Daniel. Is it anything but our selfishness that makes us separate warmed skin ecstatic sex from the act of conception? The only shameful thing is the way we denigrate it, slight, rob its meaning of importance, say that our sexual union "accidently" created life. In a moment when our desire reached its climax, God was there. The shame is in denying that our sexual expression is an intimate collaboration with God. It's the only way that any of us can come here and together share the realm of life.

For Christ's sake, Chrischana, let me share in Daniel's *past* upbringing. Let me provide some of that support now. I arranged for you to receive child support payments, but there's more I want to do. The man you were married to (or live with?) maybe helped to raise Daniel, so I'd like to return the favor by helping with the other boys, Nathan and Ben (that name right?).

Be reassured. I know from battlefield experience and its aftermath that there's such a thing as retroactive prayer. Prayerful regrets can mitigate the sorrows of the past. Please, please accept the enclosed check for back support. They are expecting you at the courthouse and the bank. I would be proud if you walked into Gottheim Savings and presented the check to start an account for yourself and family. It's a part of my savings, but still not as much as I'd like to give. The rest is needed to help me start building a house, or maybe restore *Simons Ledge*.

I haven't talked to Mother yet, but I will. Then I want Daniel to come here and meet her, spend a little time with us and, if she's OK with it, have Nathan and Ben (?) come sometimes too. I want to be a friend to them, and to you all. Please don't deny me a part. Write back and say I can. Or come visit.

It's true I have a woman friend now, at least I hope so. But you aren't alone. I will always love you, Chrischana,

Balder

At IICE they had shown Theodora her problem: She has always believed there is no help for her in the world. "This seems to be the defining myth of your identity. It can be traced back to that first incident and pattern of your mother's inability to console you." Oh, the clarity of this revelation. After the initial trouble to her soul (some of the simply awful stuff IICE revealed!) ... well! There *is* help for her in the world! Everyone else finds help, and now that she knows what her problem is, she will find it too! I will change my myth, that's all. The world is my store—I *can* take what I need.

Then why is she paralyzed with fright in the gleaming kitchen of her spacious townhouse condominium? Just the sound of that awful chipmunk thrashing around in the cupboard under the sink, angrily chattering—oh God! What can I do?

All the Hepplewhite chairs from the dining room were piled against the cupboard doors, ensuring that there could be no escape into her seasonal home. Why doesn't the thing simply vanish, slipping out the way it had come—on the water pipe...it must've been the water pipe. Why doesn't it just scrape the mousetrap off itself? Is it injured, in shock, unable to think?!

"Why are *you* chattering at *me*?!" screeched Theodora. She kicked the side of the cupboard. "*I'm* the injured party here. You are the stupid animal-witted intruder! Why did you come here in the first place?!" she shuddered. "Ohhhhh! those stupid contractors and their dim-witted carpenters!"

It was a helpless mutter under the breath. Why are *men* put in charge of building houses, anyway? They have no concept of thoughtful design construction. A woman would've known that holes around pipes should be perfectly snug, that foundations should be thoroughly inspected.

She was near tears. Who could she get to come take this thing away? There is no concierge, the groundskeeper was gone, so was housekeeping. Maybe some other Jasper Mountain employee? But it was after hours in the off-season; staff were limited. Besides, she felt embarrassed calling about a chipmunk. She was too harassed to assume a proper demeanor over it.

Hands on hips, she kicked the cupboard again, just to see if the creature was still there. She heard it clinking among the things under the sink. "You awful little beast! Why don't you just die! I would at least be able to carry your little carcass out in the dustpan."

Theodora walked into the living room among the elegant Thomas Moser furnishings, wringing her hands. "I shouldn't talk that way," she whimpered, beginning to cry. "It's one of nature's dim children. I can't just wish it dead." *Think how scared it must be.*

But the animal was chattering again.

The doorbell rang. Theodora froze. Her glance slid to the gilt framed mirror in the entranceway. She was a mess, her auburn hair falling out of its red ribbon, her mascara smudged. Whoever it was would know she was in here.

"It's your neighbor next door, James Fay," came a voice through the door.

With another glance at the mirror she went and peered through the peephole, scrutinizing him as he stepped back to give her a view. Of course she knew of the bespeckled Mr. Fay by reputation.

"Is there something I can do for you? I ... couldn't help but hear. You are in some distress, Ms. Prescott.... Isn't that what neighbors are for?" She wiped hastily at the mascara under her eyes and set her white hand on the deadbolt. In the village she never used the deadbolt, but Theodora did not feel quite safe on the mountain. Too many strangers. Slowly she turned it and slid back the chain. Opening the door she said, "Please come in, Mr. Fay," and turned toward the kitchen area, unable to look him in the eye.

"There appears to be a chipmunk or something in my cupboard. It must've come up the pipes...." Leading him to the sink she saw the ridiculous stack of chairs piled against the cupboard doors—as though seeing it for the first time. Theodora gave an embarrassed little laugh, saying, "I don't think he's escaped, do you?" She looked at him then, flushing deeply. And her fingers flew nervously over her hair, pulling out the loose ribbon.

His smile was brief. "I guess we all have our ways of dealing with crisis." James Fay turned and began removing the chairs one by one.

His tone was brisk, impersonal, encouraging. Theo stood back, somewhat eased of her embarrassment, but still apprehensive over the rodent in the cupboard. She edged against the back door, fearful that the animal would leap out and scurry about the floor. She shivered, picturing a hairy thing rushing among the chair legs. As quietly as possible, she turned the deadbolt on the back door, slid back the chain and set her hand on the doorknob, ready to flee.

James Fay was squatting before the open cupboard, and it was then that she noted his manner of dress. He wore a perfectly pressed three piece suit, and seemed as fresh as though he were starting the day. His dark blond hair was crisply cut, his neck tanned as though he spent all day biking over the slopes of Jasper Mountain instead of wheeling and dealing for Harry and

Julius Golding. James Fay was a compact young man on his way. Now he was in her kitchen, answering her distress.

He's a strong person, sure and secure. But I'm humiliated, an imbecilic hand-wringer, scared of a chipmunk. Why can't I be tough and competent like the feminists? I *am* a feminist, she reminded herself. We're not all made of Kevlar. Was he six, five years her junior?

"He's crouched in there by the hot water heater," said Fay, looking up. "It's a squirrel, red squirrel I think you call it."

"You mustn't take it up in your bare hands." Her voice was squeaky and shrill.

He smiled up at her. What a little spook. She's as fragile as a squirrel monkey ... with those smudged eyes. All she needs is a tail. She'd probably run away if I approached her on the street.

"I should've brought leather gloves," he said, still smiling. "Have you got a pair of tongs?"

"Tongs?"

"Kitchen tongs. Like for picking an egg out of boiling water."

Trying to think, she made a move as though to approach a drawer. "Will it?..." But she went bravely ahead, pushing back a chair and beginning to rummage in the drawer.

"Here," She said at last, handing him the tongs. She tried not to look in the cupboard. A sight of the squirrel hunched in there might be too much for her. She had a thousand reasons to protest this method of handling a squirrel, but no words would come. Just let him handle it. He's willing, has the nerve. She took her place by the door.

He approved her stance, saying, "Hold the door open while I bring him out. Then go down to the back door. I'll take him down that way."

Theo's mind was a jumble of objections. Would he take it by the tail? Could it swing up and bite him? What if it wiggled lose, jumping at her throat on the way down? —Another neighbor might come up the walk as they were coming out and disturb the whole process.

Fay reached inside the cupboard and there was nothing for her to do but open the door and go downstairs. At least if it got loose, she would be out of the way. At the bottom of the step she opened the door and peered out. The air had cooled and Jasper was beginning to cast its great shade across the valley. The parking lot was half in shadow. She heard James Fay on the stair and opened the door wide, hardly daring to look over her shoulder. Stepping off the path onto the bordering mulch, she watched him come out. The red squirrel looked plump, larger than she had expected, between the tongs. Its round dark eye was circled with a cream colored eyelet. How still it looked, funny and fat. The little thing must be terrified but at least it was free of the trap.

He set it down in the mulch and stepped back. Looking for it to hurry away, they both backed to the doorway but the squirrel just stood there, at first looking about and considerably slowed from a normal squirrelly pace. Tentatively, it looked this way and that. The man stepped out and nudged it with his foot. It hopped a bit, jerking, but looking up at James Fay.

"Go on," he said to it. "Go do whatever it is squirrels do in the evening."

But the rodent continued gazing up to him.

"Maybe it'll leave if we go inside," suggested Theo.

They stepped back, peering through the screen. The squirrel continued looking at him with what seemed a faint appeal. At last the tiny creature turned and, with a few jerks, started into the shrubbery along the wall.

Oh dear, thought Theodora. What if he comes back?

"I don't think he'll be back for more of that treatment," said Fay as though he had anticipated her.

"Maybe not," She said doubtfully. "But now he thinks you're God and will come back, trying to see you again. Did you see the way he looked at you? And he was so quiet in your hands—tongs!"

James Fay was tickled with her talk. "I don't think so," He laughed, "But you might want to get those holes plugged anyway."

"No, really! He thinks your God!" Now that the ordeal was over, she felt featherlight and a bit reckless. "He'll be like Marco Polo—telling all the other squirrels about this strange dangerous land and its God. These condos'll be crawling in squirrels."

Fay grinned, taking her elbow as she went a little ahead of him up the stairs. At the landing outside her kitchen door they stood lightly talking. She was grateful and he was enjoying her company. "I tell you what," he said, looking at his watch. "Why don't we go get something to eat?"

"Marvelous idea! My treat! You were so helpful, and I owe you *some*thing. Just let me go freshen up and we can walk over to the Gemstone."

"I can't let you do that," he said, embarrassed. "And I thought maybe we could go into town and try that wonderful little Below Street Bistro. I think they're falling on hard times since the end of the season."

She supposed that the cause of this embarrassment was a quaint residual pause at letting the woman pay. But Fay was smarting under the recollection of his treatment by the hostess whenever he took a date to the

Gemstone. For some reason Karon kept seating him off by the kitchen when he came in without Harry or Julius. When he was on his own he ignored her choice of seating, but you couldn't very well do that with a date by your side. Could she be jealous of his dating? But she had never seemed to care for him that way before ....

Theodora smiled brightly, adding light to her pale complexion. "Below Street is lovely. I'm sure we can work something out on the question of whose treat. I won't be five minutes. Would you care to come in and wait?"

"Thanks, no. I've got to go next door and let my sister know."

"Oh. " She remembered his sister now: Gloria Fay, the bright young woman who spoke at the meeting to keep IICE from leaving town. Trying to hide her disappointment over the possibility, she yet offered: "Would your sister care to join us?"

"I doubt it. She's been depressed lately. Hides out in her room when she's not working. Probably be glad to have the place to herself tonight." He said this dismissively, but was unable to rid himself of a suggestion of woe. He would be glad to get away from her morbid brooding behind that door. He wished she'd give it up. Was it something to do with that mechanic? He wondered—for the nth time.

"So sorry," said Theo, displaying a long face. Then, hurrying on in her scattershot way: "Maybe she'll snap out of it soon. It happens to me all the time, and then, next thing you know, I'm snapped." Inwardly cringing, she smiled as though it had not been awkwardly put. But the lightness she felt over the squirrel was leaving her. *No doubt I'll make a fool of myself and lose his attentiveness well before the evening is gone. Worse, earn his secret ridicule.*

With a wave she hurried in, shut the door.

What a noodlehead, thought James Fay on his way to the townhouse next door. He had already placed her as the owner—one of the owners?—of Gottheim Chair. The pathetic furniture factory was falling apart at the seams, but it wasn't a bad piece of land there along the highway ... picturesquely situated under Morrill Mountain. He checked himself. Was he doing it again—thinking of people in terms of their property? But you couldn't very well separate people from what they owned before you got to know them. He grimaced, recognizing the pun.

"Gloria!" He went through the dining area. "Gloria, I'm going out!"

He orders the certified Black Angus steak, and she the plank roasted salmon. Together they contemplate a daintily loaded pastry cart nearby, anticipating desert as they await salad. Will it be bittersweet chocolate cheesecake, the peach tart, lemon cherry torte?...

"Gregory works like a demon on these desserts," says James Fay, as the salads arrive.

He set his coffee down to spear a spinach leaf glistening with olive oil. "Because they pay their help one-third more than any restaurant in the area, staff is loyal. Since Christmas Day opening they've had zero turnover. But the business is so seasonal...." His look is dubious. "I don't think they're—and she was an investment counselor who should've known better; runs the financial end, y'know. They've turned this ugly old basement into a cozy atmospheric place. Look at that brick, the polished brass pipes." He shakes his head. "They should have waited a year, maybe two." Listing their difficulties one by one, he emphasizes each with the side of his palm on the gleaming granite tabletop. "They do have their niche, however. The place has virtually absconded with their lives, so they make it by dint of perseverance. IICE will be throwing business their way this summer, of course. Who knows? They may get by. Obviously they love it. They're in their mid thirties but have given up thoughts of a family until this thing flies.... About your age, I'd say." It was an obviously leading statement.

As he looks at her through the glow from hand-dipped candles, Theo thinks, It's the first personal reference he's made. His talk has been of business, at first the Golding's shoreline park and its opponents; then of the recent victory in securing the compromise without eminent domain proceedings on parcels involved. She smiles, not at all unhappy that the conversation has been only his. "That's about right, James." She does not reveal her exact age.

James Fay repays the smile with a grin. The monkey eyes are gone. Theo has changed into something blue, possibly her best color, and tied her auburn hair back in a blue ribbon. The woman is like a bouquet of tiny flowers. Her nose is a tad long and her chin too recessed, but she is elegant ... if aging. Even so, he is having a hard time thinking of her as anything but young. She'll be helpless and young the rest of her life, as trapped in her own nature as an injured squirrel in a cupboard. It's not fashionable anymore for women to be helpless, but if it were, Theodora Prescott would never have to fake it. She will need help as long as she lives.

So will that business of hers. He reminds himself that this is only an observation. So far he has managed to refrain from broaching the subject of Gottheim Chair. How long he can refrain—Well, lately he's not so confident. Just when he begins to congratulate himself on a personal victory, the good air of the accomplishment actually seems to precipitate a fall. And there he is—finding himself hitting moguls on the fragile snow of a new friendship. *Afterward I recognize it*. Karon is puzzling. She's got no business interests, so how did I earn her ire? We've joked since childhood, now suddenly she turns evil. But Theodora is a good girl. Going to like being her neighbor.

The salmon and steak have arrived, odors of the charred and roasted mingling pleasantly. They murmur appreciatively over the dishes.

After a bite, he says, "Funny. I don't remember seeing you all winter—Or ever—at Spruce Grove. Of course we've always rented it out, summers. You didn't just move into that townhouse?"

"On no. I've lived there almost every summer, sometimes only part of a summer. Most people in Gott'im own as an investment, and to have a place to entertain visitors. But you must know. Your folks have had the place practically forever, haven't they? In the winter I rent to skiers, but I like getting away from the village in summer. It can be so peaceful on the mountain." Sheepishly she adds, "I'm not much of a skier, anyway."

Oh, why am I always so apologetic and inferior about the way I live? Or else I'm constantly trying to put a normal face on it. Isn't it perfectly reasonable—normal even—for a person to get out of gossipy insular Gottheim in warm weather?... It *is* only to the other side of the mountain ....

But Fay is saying, "Now that I work with Harry on the project, I want to build my own place. I'm head over heels about the area. So's my sister. Always have been. I think Gloria's a bit wacky over the mountain. Like it has a personality or something. Anthropomorphizes it something awful. Skiing is the thing, though. Actually, business is what really gets me schussing." He takes a turn at feeling sheepish: "Guess you can tell by the way I talk—"

"Or from the pages of *The Voter*." She smiles provocatively. "It's always James Fay this, and James Fay that."

"Yes, well. There's that...." He does not like what he reads in *The Village Voter*. Except for the parts that provoke or advertise, the little rag bores him numb. He has stopped reading it. There are always others around to crow over its latest spin. Harry enjoys it, of course. If this project were going on in Boston, it wouldn't even make it into print. Small town spite's all it is! In fact, if James Nutting doesn't ease up—once this venture is through ... maybe I'll just get out. That sourball crank editor is nothing but a knee-jerk hypocrite. Like Nutting has no knowledge of the constraints of business success! Even his silly self-important weekly makes its concessions. Has to! —But ... it's nothing to do with little Theo.... He smiles at her.

"Are you teasing me already, Theodora?"

"Oh no!!" She is wide-eyed. "I think it's wonderful!" She ducked her brow, saying, "I'm only glad it's not me! I couldn't *stand* being in the paper all the time."

"Well, now that IICE has made its plans public, maybe the heat will be off me for a while. Give Nutting something else to focus on. He—he's not related to you or anything? I hear that paper has been in his family since the dinosaurs."

"Oh yes, and you can't get him to part with that horrible old machinery. Can you imagine—in this age of electronic production values? He should turn that place into a living museum. Really. If it weren't for its thunder—and the way the whole block shakes when that old press starts up!—people would stand in line to get a look at his shop. I'm surprised he gets anyone to work for him." Drained from the eagerness of her initial response, she sits back. "But people here will do anything, jobs being what they are. Now what was your question?—oh yes. We're not related that I know of."

James Fay is amused. From what he's heard, she might have said the same about herself and decrepit Gottheim Chair. But, likely, Nutting relishes his job as much as he does his attacks: with fierce obsessiveness.

"But, you know," she continues, sitting forward again, "About IICE—I am personally concerned." She sets her napkin delicately aside to pick up her dessert fork as the dish is set down. "We've *got* to do *something* to keep them from leaving! This town *needs* them. You have no idea. IICE gives us our intellectual stature. It's just a *boon* that they've done the courageous thing in announcing their intentions at the beginning instead of the end of the season. They could've waited till then and skipped out of town, gone forever, and free of the heat and tumult that has now assailed them from all corners. Maybe Gloria told you: Our Committee for Community Alternatives to IICE is hard at work composing a response, and, incidentally, is developing an aggressive program of alternatives in case we fail in persuading them to stay. Confidentially, now that you people are increasing facilities at the mountain, and with the proposed upgrading of Gottheim itself, I think their talk about inadequate conference space—Well, it strikes a false note. But it has had its benefits. We've been jolted out of our small town complacency ... into taking a really hard look at ourselves."

Fay is beginning to tire of this talk. His fork slices through layers of clotted cream, currants and chopped pecans. He regretted her indulgence of three cups of cappuccino. The caffeine is not going to let the woman slow down. Secretly, he laughs at the IICE upheaval—while remaining outwardly commiserative with the village. Their desperation is comical. That early warning tactic of the institute's was brilliant. All the commercial interests in town are buzzing like a hive of Africanized bees, galvanized to appease this inclusive bunch of academic witch doctors.

If she could just slow down. There is something he wants to grill her about. "Care to take a little drive in the twilight before heading back, Theodora? Maybe take that high stretch along Uncle Righteous Ridge?"

James Fay's BMW creeps along the backbone of the ridge named for an old settler who had stamina enough to set his farmstead up where frost was not apt to settle. He did not choose it for the views, but Righteous Ridge has romantic views on either side, the best of Gottheim in the area. Spangled in old neglected apple trees, it now bears the scars of burgeoning upper middle-class development. Below, lights of the village prick through the still deep shadows of the June evening. All along the surrounding summits they see the afterglow of sun's departure setting faint rose edging upon the deep blue contours. Looking out, Theo sighs. Here is benediction of day's end upon Gottheim.

Fay does not want to do anything so obvious and loaded as parking along here. He satisfies himself by creeping back and forth along the ridge road. Together they are silent, absorbing and being absolved in the tranquillity of the summer eve's transition from light to dark. They are attentive to the view's call upon the spirit. The flow of caffeine and conversation has ebbed. Earth's radiation into space above has taken off their cares, dissipating them upward, toward that realm without end.

"Nice," is all he can say, quietly. Then, "Nice how when day closes we can look up and see it all open before us. Look at the stars just beginning."

She agrees, dreamily. It is tempting to relax a bit now. Even here in this car, on this ridge, with someone new. Someone Theo wishes she could impress but knows from past experience that it is hopeless. He's so young important intelligent charming. She remembers seeing him here and there with various dates. All young vivacious self-possessed and ski slope rugged. Her dithering temperament cannot possibly interest him beyond this bright moment. Theo is conscious of his arm beside her, the beringed hand resting lightly upon the gear lever. James's masculinity is compact, well knit, and she feels now an acute and pathetic sensitivity to his sexual presence. She sighs. Maybe the squirrel will come back.

Yet James Fay is thinking how lucky he is to be sitting next to someone who doesn't find him overbearing and a bore. In clearer moments, he sees the effect that his overly buoyant self-centered conversation has upon his dates. In the past ten years he has been attracted to the rich skis types, but rarely it goes beyond the first date. He sometimes suspects himself the butt of jealous jokes and, at times, has to credit it to his own pomposity. But attempts at training himself away from it only end up amounting to hiding it. He isn't very good at it, either. Theo *is* quite—a bit ridiculous ... But if anyone can understand that he can.

Back there, in the restaurant, he planned to ask her about that millwright, Simon; the one Gloria.... He works for Gottheim Chair. But now, with evening stealing through the window.... Cannot bring himself to break the peaceful mood. Inject that note of self-interest.

This benediction.... It's not something he experiences often. James Fay smiles, remotely. Neither does he rescue squirrels from a cupboard every day.

Are there darker stretches of highway than those in rural Maine? No streetlamp mitigates the glare of oncoming headlights. With brights on, one drives through a tunnel of trees, attending to road signs with silhouettes of farm machinery or leaping bucks. So dark, the two-lane highways at fifty-five miles per hour are not what James Fay would call safe.

And tonight his vigilance is no different, yet, suddenly charges a hefty horse—! God-a-moose! A young moose, rackless, with monstrous legs just crossing haplessly into his highbeams. Fay's foot jumps to the brake. In his ear comes screaming. Relentless. *Screaming screaming screaming*. Swerving, the animal turns to outrun them, headlong. And Fay's foot is mashing the brake, mashing, mashing. The tires burn pavement, trebling the relentless screaming. Every moose collision story ever heard comes into his mind, boding fatality. Visions of great hooves breaking through the windshield, a massive back—flashing on him, even as he mashes with all his might. The headlamps brighten the gaskins, fetlocks, and straining thews of the animal's rear, approaching even as it runs.

Bumping and thudding, and that screaming as the bumper hits those thick legs. Then, in a lit spray of piss, the moose is gone, flying off the passenger side where Theo is clutching the dash. The scream is clipped off in a relieved whimper. And, accelerating once more, he looks to see her head turned, tracking the sorry beast still yellow in the beams, racing now alongside them off the shoulder.

Anguished, she sees the creature clipping through the thickets. *Baby, helpless child.* Theo feels its desperation, its throttling terror. Innocent discomfited spirit reaches out from it, brushing her own.

She hears the quiet voice of James Fay. "It's all right, Theo ... alright ... it's okay now...." Over and over he says it, gently assuring her.

We made it. The creature is okay. The moose ... us, Theo.... We're going to be all right.

Watching through trunks that crowd the downslope, Elda Simon creeps down along the moldering stone wall. In light shooting through, things are plain enough. In shadow the problems lie. Still, she guesses there won't be any trouble spotting Posey's fawn. Why did Sugarloaf have to be born albino? He'll be a doomed deer. Imagine a white buck—or even a fawn—making it through a single season.

Here's a new section of blowdown, a field of light, and she sees that the trail is obliterated. No, not blown down ... the damage is too extensive. These are leavings from logging. National Paper's been through since her visit to this part of the mountain last summer.

Posey, Posey. She wills the deer to appear. The does are off alone somewhere, in seclusion. Each with a new fawn, they will enjoy a quiet isolation. But she can't seem to end her urge to check on them. That white fawn is so dainty and tender. The innocent light of it tugs at her. Every time she catches a shy glimpse of Sugarloaf…it feels like entering fairyland. Posey, Posey, why have you given birth to a storybook creature? When the bearded boys get wind of him, his life goes. Why-oh-why do they want a dead trophy instead of a living glowing animal free to wander the hills?

She tires, having searched all morning over these old hillocks; climbing painfully now over the bleaching bones of hardwoods and the burned brown sprucetops, broken fragments of human industry.

The boys'll be coming soon, a new worry. Entirely different. She has to get down from here to see Daniel. Kinship bewilders Elda. She can scarcely believe she is a grandmother, did not even dimly foresee it.

Almost she could wish to be like Balder's grandmother. Priscilla had a lap wide enough for three children to climb into, a neck strong for them to latch onto. The old woman, her flesh plump and jiggly, was always in smiles. Did an awful lot of baking, or else sat rocking with grandchildren lolling all over her, storybook in hand. Flour was everywhere in her house, children dusted in it, flour sifted onto tables, chairs, the scrubbed wooden floor. Priscilla set them each up with a ball of dough, tiny rolling pins, cookie cutters. While Elda—who lived in the house with one of their sons, Everett, and grandson Balder—was always out with the farm animals: Blue Boy, she recalls especially. There were sheep, pigs, chickens, and geese ... what else?

She dreads this meeting, this collision with a new grandson. What does she know about fourteen-year-olds anymore? You can't play with them, she remembers that much.

Clamoring through the leavings, she has lost the old stone wall, a sure guide in her descent toward *Simons Ledge*. He is from Arizona, think of it! Doesn't know about things like settlers' stone walls. He can't know they hold the earth of Gottheim together. That without them people would forget the salvation of rocks, the old ways. Daow. Can't understand why they aren't marrying, now that he's found her again. Balder always did things his own peculiar way. (Guess I know where he gets it.) Still, she thinks that is no way to handle it, but it's no business of hers. She has her own worries. Going blind is no easy task.

What can she say to a fourteen-year-old boy? You want to bake cookies? Elda doesn't think so. —What really troubles her is his plan to "restore" *Simons Ledge*. So nicely settled now, after all the upheaval of living there with the Simons, of being a virtual stranger, awkward in her task of mothering, having to act like living together was normal. Extended family was all she knew—from childhood!—yet she never got used to it. What a relief, after the grief of dark river partings, to sink crab like into her hole in *Simons Ledge*, free at last to be true to her own nature. Will he really disturb all the foliage-spangled habitat, cut it back, make the yard again, rehabilitate and extend the old garden? And drive all the animals away with those kids!

Three boys coming for visits—if she and Daniel work out. Did he really expect her to said, No, Balder, this won't work after all? That's not how she does things. She does things by just getting along. You don't say, no, I don't want to. When was she ever able to do that? After all these years, she wouldn't want to be that kind of person if she could.

Now, leaving the light of the clearcut, Elda is back in the shadowy woods. Here's the discontinued settlers road, now only a path, to guide her. Soon an overgrown cellar hole will be on the right, an old granite-lined depression bristling with trees, some trees with two-foot diameters. The old Leroy Trowbridge place. People there lived like all those folks whose children now populate Gottheim, working in the woods, keeping the mills running; build the condominiums, operate heavy machinery, clean house, wait on customers. Back then—and not that long ago either—the Tituses cut two hundred cakes of ice down on the pond, kept milking cans on ice covered with sawdust in the ice house, sold cream, fed skim milk to young farm animals, especially pigs. Hogs were raised, dressed, butchered. Salt pork was kept in that cellar, hogshead cheese, smoked hams, pickled bacon, lard that made the lightest crusts and oatcakes. Kept them in good food all winter. Long winter. Lord, she remembers helping in all such preparations. Bringing in the wood! People keep hogs today, too, though. Elda couldn't abide the killing, watching her animals frantic, helpless, aware.

How did Daniel grow up? She doubts his mother kept pigs in Phoenix. The idea tickles her: hogs penned in the desert, next to bright concrete, squat between stuccoed strip malls. Let people remember what food looks like when it walks around: plank-skinned bristly, with glistening snouts. Hoofed, buttocked, curly tailed. Did he see nothing but buildings all day? Find shade beneath cactus?

What will Balder do?—a father! He'll take Daniel fishing, show him a wood mill, and the workings of pickups, how the press operates down't *The Voter*. You don't have to think of what to talk about when you do stuff like that.

The old road merges with the sand and gravel of Fox Hill Road. She calls off her search for Posey and Sugarloaf. Elda passes roadside virgin's-bower. From the corner of her eye, she notes daisy fleabane, hedge mustard and corn speedwell under the eaves of trees and among the rocks. The warmth of late June encourages her. July is on its way. Chrischana will leave her camping place down at the cove. Elda worries about her. Where will they live now? Her and the three kids and no roof. Balder said he took care of it, but how? He never tells her things. It's none of her business. And what meddlesome thing would she do about it anyway?

What a way the world has! A month ago she was middle-aged, now she someone's grammie! Life is crowding up again, has turned itself on its ear, presenting complete strangers in the guise of one's flesh, two generations removed. She's got genes in common with someone named Daniel Twitchell!

The road winds down, down. For a few paces, the ponds open before her, the blue and brown edged in green; limpid waters like a fringed plate. Maybe Daniel will be interested in the great horned owl. Or will he just think her an odd old lady? Will he find it neat to feed an owl? Can he do it without getting hurt? An injured owl. That's some conversation piece!

Daniel Twitchell. A Twitchell, in Gottheim again. What would Asa Bartlett make of it?

"Your mother might've told you: Talking don't spook'em, but noise against the boat'll alert 'em. Knocking oars, dropping things. Gut be careful with the tackle box, the well lid...." Balder and Daniel are sitting among the gray stumps and rocks near the weedy shallows, floating in the green and white wooden boat.

They puttered over the pewter platter of Loon Lake at first light to fish for bass. "A sport'll set out five, six different rods with as many lures, tryin't get bass.... Turn the boat into a reg'la supermarket." He grinned. "...Well, I might change bait, switch buzz bait fah jigs, go to a spinna, try grubs. Depends. You might try practicing with one kind to start, then move t'nother."

Daniel sits in the boat, facing his father over the shiny clutter of an open tackle box, with a beat-up ice chest acting as a live well. They have thermoses and a lunch box with sandwiches, chips, fruit. Orange life preservers are within reach. Daniel is in a T-shirt, having taken off the sweatshirt he had on against the early morning chill. The last of the mist has vanished and sun falls now on his sallow arms. By the time July arrives, his coloring will turn golden brown ... now that he is getting more sun than he has since leaving Arizona. In response to the stream of talk Balder pours on him, he says nothing. Talk about bass fishing: largemouth, smallmouth, tournaments, spawning season, range. He doesn't know what to say, so he sits slumped, just listening, or casting his line. Sometimes it snags, and he rips it back, snarling the line.

"That's all right," Balder says when it happens. "Got expect snags'n a place like this." But he is beginning to run out of talk. Being a father isn't as easy as he imagined. Just three hours into it and already he feels the weight, the perplexity. Actually, he felt it two and a half hours ago. Chrischana warned him to take it easy, not expect anything at first. "He's a quiet kid at home, more so with strangers. You take an engine apart a piece at a time and put it back together the same way, right?" Patience, he thinks. And Balder's native New England reserve with strangers should aid in this spot, but his excitement has crowded his common sense. Maybe this natural running out of steam will help...?

As the darkly bearded man's talk slows, Daniel looks away. He feels sorry for him, but can think of nothing to say. Nothing that won't sound awkward or forced. Even so, except for this strange man sitting opposite, trying too hard to be something to him, Daniel is having a pretty good time ... just sitting in a boat in a lake full of shining water, stubby with stumps in the shallows. He likes casting his line, searching for the feel of it, seeking a strike. But the strangeness of the man's role, the weirdness of being alone with him.... Daniel might have been relaxed and excited in the venture if the man were, say, a church youth leader or scoutmaster. Anything but a new father.

Dad—Petey—was good at this sort of thing; like taking him on his hog into the desert. Once or twice, maybe, he suspected that Petey wasn't his real dad. But it had been impossible to broach the subject with Mother. The fact that he looked like Mother and nothing like Petey, where Benaiah and Nathan looked a lot like Petey, couldn't be relied upon. Lots of families were like that. And Petey never showed a preference, so this allayed his suspicions. It is a relief to know that Petey isn't his father. Maybe it means he won't become like him, and drink and turn mean like him. More and more, now, since Mother told him the news, he thinks of Petey as ... not

Dad. It makes him feel strange every time he looks at Benaiah or Nathan.
Especially Benaiah. There has always been a ... slight—a distance between
them, as if they weren't quite related. Now he knows why. But Nathan is
different. He's a little kid and needs someone to keep an eye on him.

They are silent in the water among the stumps. Balder says nothing
for several minutes. They sit in the boat, one at each end, casting plastic
worms on the surface. They get nothing, and for a moment, each sees the
humor in those plastic worms. In silence. After a bit Balder looks at him,
saying, "Y's'pose this is what they mean when they say 'dead in the watah'?"

Daniel would shrug, but then he thinks of something, and says, "I
always picture coffins bobbing around when someone says that."

Balder grins. "Thought I was the only one with that mental image."
He feels his jaw relax, his next cast is leisurely and deft. And here it is—
running off with his line. Daniel watches him play it, leaning toward the
action. The line closes toward the boat as the flashing of the bass nears.
Daniel grabs the net and leans out toward the finny creature. At last a heavy
largemouth gasps in his net.

Later, they sit eating baloney sandwiches prepared by Balder before
dawn. Munching away, he says, "In Gott'im, people like getting out after
working all day'n fish fah togue'n squaretails. You see'em standing
alongshore, casting away. You don't get big bass like y'do togue. Winter's
too cold. They say it takes bass 20, 25 years t'get near five pounds. That
largemouth in the well theya's prob'ly old's you."

"People throw those things back?"

"When they ain't eating 'em." He grins. "Sports y'see on TV are
reg'la fanatics about bass, wanting to give 'em a chance. But I like t'bring
supper home. It's rare I catch more'n I eat, freeze, or give away."

Daniel looks off toward the low summit of Loon Mountain, its
contour jagged with conifers, its sides soft in foliage. Above, clouds have
drifted across, white and few. The air, while warm, is mild compared to the
glare of Phoenix. By this time it could be 110 degrees, breathless and hot
enough to fry your brain if you stayed out in it. He'd be inside reading,
watching his brothers and breaking up their fights to the hum of the air
conditioner. Maine seems like a painting or photograph to him, one he can
live in.

With the corner of his eye he catches movement, across the bright
water. There. A long homely face, dark and crowned—an unwieldy
crown—emerging from water among weeds. His first moose.

He says so, without moving.

Balder looks toward the shore beneath Loon Mountain. The moose mounts a bit, emerging more, its dark rack festooned in green weeds. Balder glances at Daniel, who can't seem to take his eyes off it.

The boy thinks it's like something from books, fantastic.

His father says, "Have t'see one up close some time. Look into its eyes. Pure dumbness. You'd nevah call a human being stupid again. Creature's eight, nine foot tall. If one's evah close enough'n irritated enough, it just might stomp you t'death."

Daniel looks doubtful. The Moose seems pretty placid to him. After a bit it clambers out of the water to wander along shore. Soon it steps long-legged into the shadows beneath the mountain. "Are there bears around much?" He asks, still trying to catch a glimpse of the moose through the trees.

Balder nods. "What choo waunt is don't surprise 'em. Let them know you're in the woods. Hearing noise, they take off. Bear's faces almost all nose. They smell ya if the wind's right. If you come across one, stay calm, don't run. They bluff pretty hod, though. Scare the crap right out o'ya t'see one charge. Nevah had it happen t'me. Last figure I read was something like twenty thousand bears in Maine, so you're bound t'see one some day."

The calling of a loon comes across the lake. A two-noted call, at once lonesome and solacing. From some distance down the lake comes an answering. Daniel says, "I hear loons on Twitchell Pond. Sometimes at night they sound pretty wild."

"It's defensive. Alerts other loons to theya territory. They go all out t'protect eggs, chicks. They'll dance themselves to pieces, trying to get boats to back off. On predators it works pretty good, but it only encourages humans. The more they dance, the more people move in. A loon goes nuts, running atop the water, wings flapping. Its cries sound like laughter t'people, but it's really disturbed. Summer folks love'em. Once a woman fom away, staying too long like a loon itself sometimes will, about died trying t'get one loose from the ice. She had an ax in her canoe'n was chopping away at that ice—to give it some straightaway—and fell in herself. She had tried to walk on ice an inch thick." He grins. "And they say the bird's loony."

"In the desert I saw snakes," says Daniel. "Sidewinders are spooky, moving across the rocks'n sand." He demonstrates the snake's movement with his arm, a swift, lateral looping motion.

"Go out to the desert much?" He takes a swallow from the thermos and blots his mustache with the sleeve of his T-shirt.

Lacking expression, Daniel's dark eyes are like charcoals. He shakes his head. "Once in awhile we rode out. Mother'n Dad both have hogs."

"Harley-Davidson?"

He nods. "She had t'leave hers."

Balder's gaze is solemn in return. His sense is that Daniel is telling him she misses the motorcycle. If so, it's the first personal reference he's made. Balder wants to know more, of course. He wants to know why Chrischana came back. She must not have been married to that other man: All the boys' names are Twitchell.

But he pauses, saying nothing. Then he asks, "Your brothers fish too?"

Daniel hesitates. At last he says, "They try."

Balder grins. "That bad?"

You grin a lot, thinks Daniel. The man is like a monkey.... But he's okay. —*God, this is totally weird.*

It would be a surprise to Daniel to learn that Balder's grin frequently covers a mass of calcified agony. And Balder is thinking, Can't get him to smile. He's not the kind. This kid has been through a war. He seen casualties. He is one.

He looks at his wristwatch, puts a cover on the thermos and starts packing things up. He stops a moment to study Daniel who is crumpling a wax paper bag. "You still okay bout coming to *Simon's Ledge*?"

The boy nods. A new grandmother, too. Will she grin a lot? Will she try to hug me? He looks off toward the trees, tree shadows, wishing the moose would reappear. There are worse things than being hugged. He thinks of Petey on a rampage.

Balder turns away, chokes the engine, and is about to pull the rip cord when he turns back. "You were kind of surprised by my new beard this morning.... I'd like you t'know why I grew it." He pauses, making sure of Daniel's attention. "Theya had t'be a great change ... cause I got a son now."

He uses that word "great" on purpose. He would like to communicate to Daniel how the heavens have changed. That the solar system has rounded a curve, and his view of the universe is new.

But Daniel is thinking, Great, *weird*, change. *Totally weird.*

He had been warned about his new grammie's head gear. Yet, upon his entrance into the gloomy front room, he was taken aback. Elda Simon came out of the kitchen with young birds in her softly spun sandy gray hair. They were four baby birds, and their tiny sharp beaks and round eyes pointed toward the ceiling; giving his grandmother a crowned, jeweled appearance.

Her face was flushed, sagging and thin, hollow cheeked. Her dim eyes were the shiest he had ever seen. Creaturely shy, and peering. Somewhat wild, he thought.

"Hello, Daniel," she said, holding out her thin hand. "I'm pleased t'meet choo." The hand in his felt like a thing of bones, fragile and long.

"Did you get choo some bass this morning?"

"No," he said. "Grandmother. Balder caught one, though."

The man went into the kitchen, his gaping fish adangle.

Daniel looked about the room, taking in bookcases under dim windows crowded with dark lilac leaves. He had seen their dried blooms outside. There was an old console television, ratty looking furniture draped in old afghans and quilts. A tuft of dingy stuffing stuck out from the arm of one chair. Even so, the room was neat and clean, everything in place. The worn wood floor was scattered with rugs, once colorful. For all the room's apparent cleanliness, there was a faint animal odor.

"Dahsn't mind my looks just now," Mrs. Simon was saying as she followed Balder into the kitchen. She seemed ill at ease in her own living room. He could tell she wanted to move about, do anything but stand there talking to him. Her voice trailed back, and he moved to follow. "These babies was abandoned—afta theya nest blew down in that storm two days back. I been feeding them. Theya s'weak I had t'pry theya li'l beaks apart."

Daniel entered the kitchen, remembering the night they spent in the Bonneville, thinking of that storm. "Whad you feed 'em?" he asked.

"Milk soaked crumbs. Gaunt graduate 'em to cat food mixed with mashed worms."

The kitchen, like the front room, spanned the house. More light came through its windows, a filtered green light, where vines glimmered at the glass. The counter, or sideboard as Cindabilla would've called it, was gleaming wood. Tins, brassy and colored, lined it along the back. Balder stood at the sink, water running. He was filleting fish, attentive, but saying nothing.

Mrs. Simon walked over to him and peered at the fish. "That's a good bass, Balda," she said.

He grunted, looking over his shoulder at Daniel. "You can sit at the table, if y'waunt."

"That's okay. I sat all morning."

"Yuht," said Balder, grinning, thinking maybe he should bring up the moose sighting again.

But Daniel is startled suddenly by scrabbling across the floor. Two chipmunks, tails straight up in the air, come out of nowhere. They are on the gleaming countertop. One has pried open a tin. Now, their bushy backs bent, their hind quarters twitching, they grab for tidbits. Peanuts, he sees. Turning them rapidly in their tiny paws, they send specks flying.

Balder grins at the look of astonishment on Daniel's face. "That's Dip'n Chale. Forgot to tell you about them. They come in through holes in the stone foundation. Holes behind cupboards, too."

The scampering sent the birds from grandmother's head flittering about the room. Daniel's eyes widen, watching them flurry in circles, crisscrossing below the ceiling. Slowly, he shakes his head. Nathan and Benaiah are not going to believe this.

Balder is grinning again. "More's in the barn. What choo got out theya now, Mother?"

"Not much just now. A rabbit, couple rabbits. Fox from an illegal trap. Birds. Young moose with damaged tendons in his hind leg. He'll be all right; just keeping'em quiet so he don't go lame. Oh—an owl. Quite a story, that owl. Keeps getting shot."

The owl! thinks Daniel. Got to see that owl. The one that sent Uncle Ferddy to the hospital ... and stopped him beating on Babette! This place is better than a—a book! It's *being* in a book. He's beginning to wonder if it's worth all the weirdness, the babysitting and comfortless camping with little brothers and hordes of biting insects. It's almost worth the hazing he got in middle school (not quite).

"C'mon," grandmother is saying as she crosses toward the back door. "I'll show you."

Daniel follows, looking back once at Balder. The older Mainer grins, his teeth flashing in the dark foliage of his face. His cap of hair gleams whitely, vivid in contrast. Daniel smiles back. He turns and steps out onto the granite stoop.

He's on the path among the green overgrowth, smiling all the way to the barn.

The Gott'im Epistles

Dear Miguel [fragment of a letter from a resident of
Quaker Plantation],
Howz it do? Thanks for your last.
[...]You remember my blather that most of my
ancestors were Welsh coal miners, but probably don't
know how it was for them. As children they carried 50,
60 pounds three hundred feet to the surface, in order
(ultimately) to make profit for wealthy mine owners.
Virtual slaves, denied education, forced to pay a
perpetual bill to the mine owners for bare necessities.
With their breaking bodies they brought up the fuel that
warmed all England and blackened the skies of London.
I haven't forgotten this, so I'm on your side. I admire
your forthrightness, and your feelings, and especially
your paintings of people in their place. But here's where
I differ. You wrote, "They don't love art," of MFA
students who failed to repress visceral reactions to your
paintings. You even suspected them of racism for this
reason.
Sweetie, you know what a reverse snob is.
What's a reverse reactionary?
You write me that "People want nice, sensical
romantic images instead of the tortured realism of these
fragmented souls." Yes, many do. But does your love of
art condemn those with an affinity for whole images?
Should the classical or romantically inclined be pushed
out of the gallery because your full-hearted gritty realism

doesn't nourish them? Can everyone enjoy the same dish? Should people who can't eat broccoli quiche starve? How can people sit at the table when their food is taken away by peer pressure? Or by the authority of teachers like yourself?

You said something good about the arrogance of painters whose sole object is themselves, as opposed to the breadth and interconnection found in community: "Finally it's the cause and the impact of work that counts, not the painter." Wow!! Maybe you'll consider reading one of the portrayers of rural Maine. Carolyn Chute has just caused a ruckus here with the *Beans of Egypt Maine*. These earthy writings tell some of the stories of this place. It might work toward establishing a rapport between wasp and chicano. The coldness and ego of Mainers in a certain socio-economic slot might have more in common with your arid village counterparts than do those middle-class mindset suburbanite Latinos you tangled with.

(oops—my reaction is showing.)
Later, El

Dear Editor,

Now that snow cover no longer hides the mess, I'm writing to express our indignation over the unsightly places one finds in Gottheim's lovely countryside. We're skiers who've moved up here weekends in order to enjoy the beauty of these mountains. Some of our neighbors in this rural neighborhood don't seem to care *what* the place looks like. Junk vehicles, parts, assortments of trash, rags tied on trees as *decorations*!, refrigerators, bedsteads—an old dental chair set out for passersby to admire?! I'm tempted to call some authority to make abutters clean up. But we want to give neighbors a chance to do right on their own. Have mercy on your neighbors who have put a lot into their homes and lawns, and appreciate the overall aesthetic framework.

Joe and Mrs. Sixpack, you know who you are. Please get to work on this right away.
Jamie and Frederick Sludlinger,
Quaker Plantation

Dear Chrischana,

I figured Gottheim was small enough, if I sent this letter to the post office you'd get it somehow. I was surprised as hell to find you and the boys gone, but on second thoughts wasn't. Can't really blame you. Last night I dreamed a gorilla was beating the shit out of me. Drinking did it, like it did to you. You had a hard time.

You know it's not easy for me to write this, but I miss you so damn much. I love you dammit Christy. Never realized how much till I came home from school and found you gone. Before I always promised to mend my ways, and you always gave me a chance. Guess I ran out of chances after that last binge.

No more binges, period. I need you so much, Christy. I recall every inch of your body. All your loving ways, how you put up with so much, so long. Remember the Sunday mornings in bed? Remember the funny papers on the floor with the little guys, or that last long desert ride? I miss the little bikers so much.

Christy, I'm human, flawed. I know it. Have mercy. God, if you could just exercise that famous sweet mercy one last time. This time I'd get counseling—like you always said. I'm ready for it now. Just write and say you're coming. I'll go into counseling the day I get your letter, even join AA. You know how good I can be when the devil's not around. Together we'll keep him away for good.

Think of the boys. They can't be doing well. You've got no money, family (I remember that much). Please take my week's pay, here in the envelope, and get what you need. Write and I'll send more, the expenses to return you all, if it means having to drop out of MMI. Hell, I'd hock my tools to get you back. My life back. Please bring back my life, Christy.

Peter

Dear Editor [three drafts],

Some of you may have heard of the grants from the Maine Humanities Council, being offered for the purpose of studying and making known town history.

This could include studies on the following: genealogy, antiques, back issues of *The Voter*, letters and records of every description, oral history, architecture, songs, poems, literature, and just about anything else you'd care to name.

Some of you in the primary grades, middle and high school, churches, adult education, fraternal orders, the Grange and what have you, might be interested in applying. What are your separate histories? For our part, we here in the Gottheim Historical Society are hoping to present a series of discussions on these topics and more. We're interested in questions such as, what has small-town life contributed to the formation of American culture, what do we contribute now, and is there a future contribution to be made?

We're also interested in how great Aunt Fanny braided rugs and did she use peppers when canning corn? And what date, precisely, did the peavey make an appearance in the woods around Gottheim, supplanting the cant hook? Can anyone shed more light on our clock's origination? With the post office commenced on a search for new quarters, might now be a good time to search out the history of the mail service in town?

Methods of dissemination might include plays, short stories and songs, a theme parade, art projects and puppet shows, or displays: botanical, artifacts, and old-time craft.

Some of you understand how interesting and absorbing this all can be, and how it to might elevate the children hereabouts beyond a mass culture purveyed through your televisions each night.

Don't forget your local stories of the supernatural. We got tales of hauntings in Gottheim and towns roundabout to yield a small body of folklore. How about forming story groups designed to scare history into the ignorant?

Asa Bartlett

Dear Editor,

We the undersigned are looking for a new meeting place for early morning coffee. This is the unofficial Gottheim selectmen's critics and old gossips' coffee club, meeting in Decatur's every morning. We'll be needing a dite o'donuts, bacon and eggs, flapjacks, coffee, what have you. To begin after Jasper Mary Day. We have a little more to do than a man on the town, but not so much as to prevent unofficial meetings absolutely essential to maintaining town business. Send suggestions to *Entrepreneur de bois*, P.O. Box 47.

On behalf of Decatur, we are some exercised but, owing to financial consideration, won't mention at who.

Etc.

Dear Editor,

The Committee of Community Alternatives has assigned me to oversee the compilation of studies designed to find direction for Gottheim's future cultural and economic stabilization in the wake of IICE's previously announced departure. Negotiations are, of course, ongoing, and, after our hard work, there is no reason to hope that the Institute may continue to return each summer. My first step is to initiate study circles designed to bring the diverse minds of the community together for discussion. Area businesses, art, theater, and church groups, and school organizations will want to choose representatives to attend these directional sessions. The initial meeting, to be held in the multipurpose room of Hazel Newell High-School, will be announced when all parties have chosen their representatives. Write to the committee care of me at P.O. Box 1070, Gottheim.

We on the committee have high hopes of a bright future for our town, and are looking forward to your input before the end of the month, if not sooner. Remember, this is *your* community. *Your* commitment is vital to our effort. There are exciting times ahead in Gottheim.

Gloria Fay

Balder,

I'm sorry to take so long getting back to you on your "proposal," so convincingly (and charmingly) put in Decatur's Diner a few weeks ago. You really threw me. I'm sure you know this.

I want to be thoughtful and complete in my answer. In fact, a *lot* of thought goes into it. Your ideas have forced me to focus on the big picture, to quit drifting along in my childish joy at just being in Gottheim at last. I'm astonished over your being a father. But it's helped me focus, as I'm sure it has you. You are on a new path, one (I see now) you hoped for all along. We are very different people in our pursuits. No matter the psychic and physical attraction between us, the determining factor must be the direction of our individual hopes and dreams. They clash. Hopelessly.

For instance, I strongly believe that the ideal size for a family in our present era is two, a family of spouses. Humans must consider the strain upon our planet's resources, and act accordingly. Naturally, I'm realistic enough to see that others aren't going to fall in line with this. I have no fear that we as a species will die out through lack of breeding! But there are just too many people in the world today, and I've got to do what little I can to keep competition for resources down. And a responsible thing to do in the face of *Malthus's Dismal Theorem* is refrain from bringing more people into the world. In the case of your son, of course, it's too late. (Yes, I see the irony: In the case of my own presence, it's too late as well.)

And I am honest enough to admit that the argument of competition for resources has a personal taint. My own life would be drained by a family of children. Even one child requires an enormous amount of energy and expense. One sees women shriveled up by the demands of family. Worn out, yet unfulfilled. I wouldn't have a child and then deprive it of the things it wants. Take sneakers. Currently one spends as much as sixty dollars for a decent pair. Multiply this by all the child's other desires and expectations. In another age, an agrarian age, children were an asset. They worked to keep the family going. But today, in our consumer oriented society, they're a liability, a drain on family resources. Also, the real work of being there for all the details, the logistics of family life, falls to the woman. Currently men require prodding to fulfil their obligations in regard to sensitive caring, or plain household chores. Such prodding, such work is never-ending and there's no vacation from it.

You speak of building a house. I can visualize the kind of house you want. One full of kids—kids hanging out windows, and giggling under the covers, whooping out of control. A place where they can safely get into trouble, and grumble while being made to do chores. You don't want a house with TVs, computers, VCRs, white drapery, a dishwasher. But the kids themselves would not want to be without these things. You want a house that can stand up to dogs, cats, flying parakeets, or goldfish wriggling on the floor in a puddle, a house with gooey fingerprints on the furniture. I can tell you, Balder, that is not what I want. Perhaps one day I will indulge in such a daydream. I can't rule out the possibility, or the urge to romanticize over it. But I hope to God that's all I allow myself. Life is so much more than this squalor would permit.

Looking back over the course of our relationship, I now see hints as to the kind of man you are in regard to lovemaking as well as housekeeping. We differ here as well. At first it perplexed me that we never made love. Now in light of your fatherhood I'm more perplexed. All I can think is that you've changed since Chrischana's child was conceived. Coupled with our abstinence, little things you said lead me to think you now believe dating should be an activity for selecting a mate. In other words, sex is to be a serious matter, robbed of its spontaneity. And no longer a playful encounter. I remember your crack about people seeing it on the level of skateboarding. You disparaged it as a diversion like table tennis. These remarks may be a cover for phobia. By confining sexuality to marriage and procreation, you stunt it, closing off the great field of freedom it deserves. You've managed to turn the joy of human sexuality into a form of drudgery. This is repressive and a bit sick.

Making an effort at honesty, I'll admit to an occasional emptiness in my pursuit, but remain convinced that this has more to do with an inappropriate choice of partner than to the lack of marital union. But Balder, I had to overcome quite a bit to achieve my liberation (I was raised Baptist), so I'm not about to revert to traditional morality.

Please don't be offended. I'm trying to be as honest as possible. I wouldn't want to be false either to you or myself. I avoid self deception. Isn't it only right?

Finally, we come to the most profound part. Love. Our love must not be lost in all this, but it's what I fear most. Looking back over this letter, I see I'm no closer to solving the dilemma love poses. We love each other. But for how long? And under what stresses will our love fail? Will the present conflict signal the beginning of love's failure? I don't know. And I don't know where we go from here.

I do love you.

Gloria

Dear Olive,

Please accept my condolences on the death of Horace. I won't trouble you trying to express sympathy. Please, if there's anything I can do? Maybe we could go fishing as we did in the old days when it was you and Horace, and Griselda and me. You just got to get some rest. I keep thinking of the strain you been under, straightout. Couldn't we just do something to remember him by? Talk of the good times, or something, as a memorial to him? Oh Lord, when it all ends, Olive. I still miss her.

I'll be by, of course. And see you at the wake.

Asa

Dear Editor,

Many people know that Horace passed away last week, and have sent their condolences. Such an outpouring of food and help at home, and, well, just plain—their presence, you know. I appreciate it ever so much. As one put it, it's hard when it all ends. But you folks, you folks have made it so much more bearable.

I won't be doing my news for a while. Please send your neighborhood items to Greta Blake. She'll see they get put in the paper.

Olive Lovejoy

Dear Editor,

Won't someone explain to us at Hazel Newell why German has been cut? Don't people realize the place language has in our college prep? This doesn't even mention the other cuts made. Don't people in this place care whether kids here get a decent education? Recently you eliminated half a million dollars from our budget because of higher property values. Why? If, as everyone says, property values have tripled in one year, why are taxes being cut? Shouldn't it be the other way around, taxes raised?

Gottheim Academy recently received a donation from an alumnus for five million dollars. This person graduated from there at a time when town kids, not just preppies, were also educated there, tuition free. If Hazel Newell had been built then, wouldn't that alumnus have attended and left us the money instead?

I heard one of our neighbors say that we ("kids today") need to learn to do without. The same neighbors just bought an eighteen thousand dollar car. Is this how you do without in the 1980's?

Jenn Trowbridge

Dear Editor,

The little girl who wrote last week about Spanish or German being cut just doesn't understand the burden these taxes put on folks. *Wages* haven't gone up to cover taxes. *That's* what we pay them with. We got to get some relief or people will start losing their property. What are they teaching in school, anyway?

And what good does a college education do around here? You have to leave to use it.
> Minnie Virgin

Chrischana,

    I guess you know what would be happening to you if I had you here right now. Seeing my check returned without cashing—no explanation, no nothing, not even asking how I am—made me mad enough to choke you skinny. Good thing your in Goddam. I felt like killing you. I don't care if they lock me up till I stink.

    In fact, I'm coming to get you. This note, I just decided, is a little something to get you thinking. Don't go believing I'll change my mind when this binge goes. I'm for the mailbox now.
> Petey

    P.S. Thanks for returning the check. Now I know for sure you're in Godham.

Dear Editor,

    Just a reminder about the upcoming Jasper Mary Day. We need more, albeit last minute, entrants for the parade. Kids in costume, animals, theme floats, baton twirlers, anything. We have enough veterans on motor scooters, but if that's all you have, you're welcome.

    There will be booths on the common, the Franco Fiddlers, used books for sale on the sidewalk in front of the library, the quilt drawing, art displays, refreshments and the ever popular logging competition. Can Alvin Robichaud hang on to the golden axe one more year? Don't forget the dueling guitars and the pie contest. Cast your vote for this year's Jasper Mary at Pardner's drug, the Foodliner, or Cross's Hardware. There will be fireworks as usual on the Academy lawn at 10:00 p.m.
> The Jasper Mary Day Committee

Dear Chrischana,

    Please forgive and ignore if you can the last letter I might have sent you. I think I wrote you when I was drunk and am sorry if I did. I would never harm you if I could help it. I want only to love and treat you with the respect you deserve. You put up with a lot because of me. But I love you and the boys.

Please, can't we talk? I really want to come there and see you all again. With counseling we can work it out. We've got to. I just can't give myself up for lost. Or us either.

I'd ask you to call me, but can't blame you if you don't. I'll pack up everything—my tools—as soon as this season at MMI ends, and drive to Gotheim. I don't expect to stay with you, but just want to be close, know you and Ben, Daniel and Nathan are near.

Love, Peter

Dear Dad, how are you? I am fine. Here is my pitcher from last year in case you lost yours. Don't forgit what I look like OK? Send me your's. Bald door is nice. I love you.

Nathan [letter was not sent.]

Jasper Mary

Back...back... remote in fleeting mists about the Meguntic Mountains....
Long ago there nestled a scattering of cabins high above the foggy ponds of
a wooded vale. The people there were hardy, early astir, lighting fires and
milking the family cow. They looked out from hardly won dooryards upon
a world misted over, the smoke of their stone chimneys sinking to mingle
with the clouds of the New England pond valley. Below, in those vapors in
summer, lived remnants of the Arossagunticook Natives who then populated
mountains along the river of the same name. The hardy pioneers of
Farmingham Royal, as they first named the town, looked down upon the
natives both literally and figuratively—deeming them shiftless, childlike and
slothful in comparison to their own rigorous, high-minded and provident
Yankee and Puritan descent.

Away through Mountains wound the Arossagunticook River,
toward the distant sea. The river was checked and channeled by the dark
bulks, which had once been sharp and high but were now ground down and
low, rounded by monstrous implacable ice that hunkered mile-high over this
part of the continent. An age had passed. Debris-laden tongues of ice had
melted out of the valleys, leaving the Arossagunticook and its tributaries
flowing seaward; some of them scattered with specks of gold, all of them
paved in part with smooth cobble, a legacy of glacier's patient exercise upon
the sharp heights.

Downstream from the pioneer community of Farmingham Royal the
river fell, great and creamy, over rocks where salmon leaped in season,
ardently searching for the exact streambed where they were spawned two or
three years before; before the epic journey of life that brought them full-
circle to the pure and home-scented place where they began.

Here, above these falls the Natives called *Roccomeeco*, a woman
was born to be great among her people by being the servant of all. Jasper

Mary. She was a full-blooded Roccomeeco Native, satin-skinned, dark eyed and solemn-seeming, yet full of the lore of her people; able to convey, with a deft story or incident, a world of truth to her hearers. Along with her knowledge of herbs, root, and flower, and a detailed understanding of skies, Jasper Mary kept the lore of her adopted faith, the Catholicism so dreaded and feared by early Puritans, and belittled by their settler descent. The natives had been taught by voyaging Jesuits, their Catholicism assimilated and flourishing transmuted among the natives of the Meguntic Mountains.

Jasper Mary grew to be an itinerant herbal healer, traveling the river's valley from its obscure sources in the northern mountains to its mighty meeting with other such rivers in a bay near the sea. Jasper Mary learned the river's creatures and their ways, its shoreline features and flora, its legends and histories and hauntings. I knew where the white heron nested, where leaves were good for fever, how to glean from carrion the stuff to make boxes and pouches and poultices. My quill boxes and purses were sought after, the pioneers bartering for things from their store. And Jasper Mary knew each settler along the great tortuous length of her river, watching of their comings and goings, their uprisings and downfallings. In telling herself their stories, Jasper Mary came to understand their strange ways.

All the world of the Arossagunticook was hers to observe, hers to catalogue, hers to watch over in prayer. The settlers' knew this. Yet, by those of Farmingham Royal and other settlements roundabout, Jasper Mary was most known for her treasure. For, although every household had been touched in some way by her medicine, and though many heard her familiar throaty voice weaving stories, or chanting to the Virgin and her holy Son as she paddled down river, the thing most spoken of in every home was Jasper Mary's treasure. It was thought that Jasper Mary knew where tourmaline was hidden. She knew how to find beryl, jasper and gold. She knew where crystals grew in white clay, "as though raisins for the plucking from plum pudding."

The stories she told were those of her travels along the river, of her adventures among the wildlife, of odd backwoods characters from her forays into deep wilderness. She liked also to tell the tales of her hero Culuscap, a mythic Dawnlander who had some characteristics in common with her Lord. The English and their Yankee descendants said that Culuscap was just another Indian and that he possessed no greater qualities than those found in any Indian chanced upon along the river. But, to the Abenaki, Penobscot, or Passamaquoddy, Culuscap was the human embodiment of heaven and earth. He was, if not actually born of his grandmother, then raised by her. He had a mischievous or evil brother, was always ready to accept and meet challenges, responsible for creatures, and helpful in forming the surface of the earth. The mythic Dawnlander, while full of a sinewy temperament, was also capable of being temporarily deceived.

The end of Culuscap, as Jasper Mary told, was death at the hands of his brother. Yet there was a persistent, lingering belief among the Natives that Culuscap would return once more to help restore all things. The English scoffed at this, saying Culuscap was just another dead Indian, and asking when his dust would rebuild itself into skin and muscle and bone; when would it grow eyes and see again?

Many of the Indians stopped telling the stories of Culuscap. They told stories of a hapless character named Jack, instead. The many asinine adventures of Jack—a derivative of the English Jack-and-the-beanstalk— kept them entertained. This Jack was also a Native, not very bright, but who nonetheless managed to scrape by with the help of kindly fortune. Jasper Mary still told the Culuscap stories to Natives, and also to the children of settlers. Oddly, once grown, the children forgot the stories, although some would listen raptly if one of their little ones chanced to repeat what was heard of him from the healer. Others would simply shake their heads and laugh.

She was buried near a tributary where gold was known to wash down out of the north. Today, nearly two hundred years after the mists closed over her grave, Jasper Mary is most remembered for her famous curse. She is less remembered for her murder by thieves bent on unearthing her treasure.

As the tale goes, one of them later bragged about the deed while on a binge. But the other kept to himself afterward, relating the story only once, to his sister when he was ill. He told of Jasper Mary's calm facing of death; how she had said she was old and, like the salmon, ready to return to her source-stream. And that she had always wondered what the face of Culuscap looked like; that she believed it was as the sun burning mist off a pond, reflecting out of the water in morning. The hard thief did not believe her, suspecting a bluff to disarm them. He ended as a hermit in the woods. Or maybe he hanged himself. A corpse of nibbled bones was found scattered beneath a weathered noose not far from Jasper Mary's grave. But the other thief knew that her treasure lay elsewhere.

Though her death was written in local history, it is the curse of Jasper Mary that lives on in the collective mind of Gottheim today. Two towns to the east, on a tributary called Sabbath, the healer was once turned away in a snowstorm by folk unfamiliar with her.

They had come up from Massachusetts intent on settling a goodly piece of land in the District of Maine. One raging night, they were startled to see a strange Indian calling at their isolated cabin.

"Shelter me!" I, Jasper Mary, cried as the wind tore.

"Nay, but we know you not!" hollered the householder through a crack in the latched door.

"All you know is I perish!"

Yet they would not be entreated. Thus, Jasper Mary uttered her curse, and went away through obscuring snow. Her voice fell, half absorbed by the snow, saying, "Curséd the earth of this place. Endeavors not prosper here!"

Two hundred years after, the people of Gottheim and Quaker and Copenhagen remember the curse. Today's descendants of the old settlers still watch along the rapids of Sabbath River to see what prospers. They notice the thick beds of poison ivy growing rank and dark and laden with noxious white berries. They see that the streambed holds no fish, having absorbed toxic tailings from a hundred years' old abandoned mine upstream. They point it out when a business fails on the ground of my curse.

They shake their heads ominously. But they do not laugh.

It was the cool of morning when Chrischana climbed through the ravine between old hills to reach an overgrown lane leading to Twitchell Farm. The old place is high on a knob of Blackwell Mountain called Buck Hill, so far from the highway that traffic is scarcely heard. Both the knob and rounded off double summit of the mountain are clearly visible from sections of two roads that also parallel the curving river. The mountain is of the same batholith but much lower than nearby Jasper Mountain.

Morning's early coolness has now withered away, and the exertions of her climb dampen Chrischana. She takes a few swallows of water, caps her recycled juice bottle and rounds the last leafy bend. The house is still lost in the leaves, and she approaches slowly, partly for the tender associations, partly in sorrow for the house's neglect. Olive Lovejoy has warned that during the years of Chrischana's absence Twitchell Farm was continually vandalized.

As a girl her feelings were ambivalent, sometimes appreciative, sometimes irritated over its isolation. But more often she was glad she had to look far to see another dwelling, though her girlfriends sometimes wondered over this. "Don't choo get lonely up theya y'self?" Babette Roebuck would ask her again and again. The hill had been named for one Philo Buck, who went mad because water could be hard to come by during the dry season. In those years he lost a crop seemed nearly every August.

But on this side of the hill water from springs could be found. Sometimes the hill would almost burst with water.

She comes to a rusted gate, locked shut by Enan Pale who bought the old place at tax auction during her absence. She is on top of the hill, the mountain slope above her now visible, and clearcut across its flanks. Maybe 550 acres in soft green. Had she seen the cut last year, she would've been saddened by the ugly brown wounds slashed across the slopes. Daniel Albert Twitchell supplemented his income setting traps there, and his daughter learned from him. She knew how to skin the animal, scrape, stretch and cure pelts; check traps early and late to avoid unnecessary suffering. She justified her trapping as a way to keep disease down in fur-bearing populations. Back then. Not now. Now she feels the helplessness and fear of the trapped.

She slides under the gate. The thickets thin, and Chrischana sees the house, darkened by the beloved crowd of old maples in the dooryard. The roof of its porch is fallen at one end, the floor rotten, a pillar askew. Debris spills out one window, littering the porch: shattered glass, tattered curtains, stuffing filthy with mildew. Coming around the side of the house she walks on pieces of asphalt shingle, splintered wood, the foxed backs of old and familiar books. She looks to see that the inset structure of the early Greek revival doorway is still intact, but the door itself is gone; the walls on either side agape. As she peers in, the smell of must and decay assaults her. Chrischana recognizes the old bedsprings tossed willy-nilly, the upended bookcase, the slashed-to-ribbons couch where her father sometimes snoozed. Just beyond the door frame, the tiny crooked stair winds toward the second floor, its treads showing worn where once she carefully placed her young feet, dreaming of previous inhabitants of the Twitchell line. Someone must have worked hard, getting that bedsprings around the stairwell's corner. She steps back. Belowstairs, and under the gaping separation of floor and foundation, a black cellar hole lurks. The massive slab granite foundation stones have been jerked from their moorings. In disbelief she stares at them, puzzling. How could such heavy big things be moved? Was it but frost causing them to fall inward?

Still wondering and staring into the bleak dark below, Chrischana is aware of salt taste in the corners of her mouth. She licks her lips, the salt blending with saliva. Till now she had been unaware.... Chrischana has been silently weeping.

Chrischana takes the old settler's road, the twitch trail down toward the Lower Intervale Road which travels alongside the Arossagunticook River. The intervale is good bottom farmland, hidden in spots from either the river or the highway. She is hiking to Gottheim, on her way to celebrate her first Jasper Mary Day since her return to this place from which she sprang. In the village she will meet her children and Balder, and together they plan to watch the parade.

It's still a long walk, on top of the early morning's climb, but it will give her time for reflection. They can't take this camping much longer, Daniel especially so. So much falls on him. She now knows what she will do with the money Balder has given her. A down payment is all it will take to secure part of the old property. She has heard that Enan Pale is thinking of putting it on the market. An article in *The Voter* tells of funds available through Maine State Housing Authority, loans for first-time low-income buyers. Balder's money—Daniel's money really—is enough to secure one of those loans. But sadly, the old house is beyond repair. Will that nix the loan? *Look into it, that's all. Just have to check.*

A view across the river opens out as Chrischana walks along. Tiny in the distance she sees that burned-out building on the highway beneath Morrill Mountain. Odd—this view of a blackened cross-timber jutting above the fallen roof. Ithiel Whitman's building, isn't it? From here that cross-timber looks like a crucifix.

She passes the Franklin P. Mills farm, a connected dwelling with smaller attached house, stout ell, and unpainted patinaed barn; the main house with those austere Federalist lines. Already the yard is choked with bales in wagons, spilling over, ready for the conveyor to the open loft. No one in sight to load it with the hay. As she passes, its green fragrance fills her nostrils. The family may be in the village, joining the gathering townsfolk for the parade.

Sweating, breathing hard, she picks up her pace. Lonely this last piece of the walk. For a moment she almost wishes Peter was here, walking alongside. There had been good times, too; and companionship. Peter could be entertaining, funny, loving even ....

Chrischana can't wait to meet the others outside the Bond Block. Should she really try to get something going up on Buck's Hill? Oh for a house to hold, shelter, comfort them. A safe place. She must, they all must live in the Town of Gottheim with her people. No harm will come to them here. *Forget about Petey. Don't think of him again.*

Tucked into foliage pricked by white steeples, the village of Gottheim lay in a gleaming valley of waters. From a distance it was a dream of New England, settled by descendants of East Anglians, steeped in peace. Looking down from above, was there anything of evil to be seen? Could the high view show nothing sordid or cynical to recommend it to contemporary literary interest? Maybe the stream of soot that occasionally shot skyward from a village mill currently working the bugs out of its new generating system? Even this process was performed according to strict federal regulations, so that, if the smoke was dense and particle-filled it was intermittent. And didn't it lend a kind of pungency to the scene? That little touch of dark and soot which kept it from becoming unreal?

Watching from above, the dark Angel descended down past the summit of Jasper Mountain each year to watch Gottheim's annual parade in her honor. For many years, in the early decades perhaps, she likely found clean mountain air. This year she traversed low level ozone, sent northward from the vehicle-infested eastern corridor. Now the Angel crossed over the opaque, smelly Arossagunticook, silent witness to the river's corruption by a paper mill farther upstream. Even so, the scene below the spirit was, on the whole, fair; like a garden dotted with white, and wild with rugged plutonic beauty. Even the tiny charred cross-timber, cocked at an angle, jutting above Ithiel Whitman's small white burned-out building by the river, did not mar the garden's beauty when seen from above. Did the people of Gottheim deserve the beauty because they were scattered and few? Did they deserve because of their ancestors' struggle to make and keep the Town habitable? Or did they deserve this beauty?

The dark Angel—austere, agéd, composed—drifted down each year to the far end of the village above the Greek revival rooftops of brick-built Gottheim Academy. She peered down through green leaves at the colorful assemblage of parade participants on the wide central lawn below. Already the band music was lifting, its drums beginning. Small children picked up their tiny streamered bicycles. Floats lurched into place behind tractors, four-wheelers, or on the decked beds of pickups; each with its theme of historic, recreational or occupational significance—anything to show the value of life as it was lived and felt in the community: logging, farming, and teaching. There were tableaux of sport fishermen, of wildlife, homecraft and quilting; of hunting, dogsledders, of skiers crouching and descending a hill of painted wood and cotton batting.

Slowly, the high school band leading, this living line made its way off the wide sloping lawn, filing down School Street. Approaching toward Front Street and the Common, it passed the vanguard of sidewalk watchers. Along one side of the common stood the churches. Below their large, four-square steepled whiteness, stood happy white people of every age and description ... with, in these mid-1980s, a very few alien dark faces from India, Asia, Africa, or the Middle East: These offshore representatives of the International Institute for Coordinated Experiments, dotted the white crowd assembled beneath the dark Angel's gaze. Without their lush complexions, flashing smiles and vivid eyes, the crowd would be hopelessly pasty and bland. The Angel understood: For these people of color, such whiteness in the town's streets was like a wall, an impasse, never to be penetrated by intimacy in their brief sojourn in New England Gottheim.

Under the Angel, and merging with Front Street, snaked the line of music makers, marchers, horse-mounted participants. Floats and vets on motor scooters, the gleaming humpbacks of old model cars, all followed by silent red or yellow fire engines from every community roundabout Gottheim. The Angel drifted, searching the crowd with her quiet American Indian eyes. Her solemn gaze intent, penetrated every joyful heart or sorry hidden thought of each one below her gaze. She was also deeply aware of the collective spirit expressed. And, invisible to the people, imps—naked and ridiculous—scurried among them, cavorting before her eyes. These raced from one cluster to another, mocking and grinning, laughing, winking, playing pranks.

Through chinks between storefronts came the gleam of Hutchins Pond, reflecting sunlight among the marchers and watchers who were otherwise shaded here and there by large old trees, standing at intervals along the main street of Gottheim.

Moving majestically above the parade, the dark Angel matched her pace with that of this year's Jasper Mary, the Angel's namesake riding below. The girl sat restive, astride a dancing brown pony, its halter trimmed in the dark feathers of ravens. Like some of her predecessors, she was part Indian, a fourteen-year-old whose great great great great great grandfather had once posted tokens at portages between lakes to the north. But this knowledge was now lost to the girl who rode tensely, trying to keep her ahistorical mount without a loss of dignity; but finally slithering in agitation to the pavement before Cross's Hardware. She loosed the reins, determined now to walk flat-footed to parade's end in her moccasins.

Now the dark Angel above felt an added weight of glory descending behind. She glanced quietly back at lucent clouds approaching, a great multitude of witnesses descending toward the crowd. This vast throng, full of faces, pressed above her, watching with the same austere attentiveness of Jasper Mary herself. Pressing gently upon the hometown scene, the great cloud of watchers shed a quality of fullness upon its descendants below.

The true Jasper Mary, who descends from Jasper Mountain each year to see her parade, now lowered toward the dismounted girl, speaking some quiet words in an Algonquin tongue. Immediately the girl reached out and took the pony's reins again, throwing herself upon its back. She sat straight, tangling her fingers in the pony's black mane. The aura of the crowd on either side swelled with applause and whistles. The little pony and its rider went dancing along Front Street, the ancestors of all looking on from above.

Daniel, Balder, Nathan, Benaiah, and Chrischana stood together outside the brick block where *The Voter* was weekly published, watching the parade pass along Front Street. In Balder's hands was a grease-spotted bagful of chocolate chip cookies, and, as fast as the boys could dig for one, they dipped chocolatey hands for another. Chrischana had arrived at last, just in time to see this year's Jasper Mary slither to the pavement. The woman watched the girl continue several paces, her hand still futilely grasping after the pony's halter. Chrischana smiled. "Same thing pretty much happened to me the year I was Jasper Mary." Bending to Nathan and Benaiah, she said, "Watch'n see if she climbs up again."

Nathan, all hyper movement with skinny limbs, leaning out into the street, watched the Indian girl in buckskin and fringes lunge for the pony and take to it again. He shouted with the crowd, tugging on his mother's wrist and gesturing. "Did you get back up on the pony, too?"

"Yes'n it wasn't easy. I was deeply embarrassed."

"Deeply, Mother?" said Benaiah, mocking. The sun had brought out his brown freckles, leaving the rest of his skin as fair as ever. "You'n Daniel always put things so funny. Why don't cha say 'really', like everybody else?"

Balder said, "If I know your mother, Ben, I'd say she's not like evah body else." Then he grinned at her. "Good thing!"

Chrischana smiled, her white teeth crisp in her glowing native features. She looked over at Daniel, who returned her smile. His own sallow skin had taken on its accustomed summer glow. She was glad of that smile. Daniel was a happier boy than he had been. They had all benefited from Balder's influence.

"So, did everybody vote for you to be Jasper Mary?" asked Nathan. He moved constantly, alternately hanging on her or pulling away and waving his arms at nothing in particular.

"Not everybody. Of course not. But enough to get me on the pony. Once you're up there y'wonder why y'wanted it s'bad. Everyone gaping at you, watchin' if you'll flub up. I'd never want t'be Jasper Mary again."

"You were one of the best damned Jasper Marys this town ever had," said a quiet voice behind her. "I remember that from my summer trips home."

She turned to find the keen stern green-visored face of James Nutting gazing at her. The editor had come out of the newspaper office to watch the parade. He had been standing behind them, quietly, ever since Chrischana made her way through the crowd. Nutting had what, to some, was the disconcerting custom of quiet. He could be a surprisingly invisible observer. Some called it the ability to eavesdrop undetected.

Chrischana chuckled. "Like being unable to ride a pony is an asset."

"Most of 'em can't ride," he said dryly.

Now, from the end of the parade came the whooping of fire engines. James Nutting said, "This is where I get out." Then, looking at Balder, but taking in the rest of them with a gesture, he said, "Come see me after the parade. I might have a job for someone." Then he was gone, threading his way back to the wood and plateglass office door.

"Wow!" said Nathan, pretending to kickbox Benaiah. "Did y'see his hands? They were purple!"

"I'm gonna make you purple," said Benaiah, fiercely yanking his brother's upraised leg. Nathan lost his balance, tumbling into Daniel. Chrischana put her hand on the middle brother's arm. He jerked away. "He's always provokin' me. I don't haf'ta put up with it!"

"You hev t'learn self control like th'rest o'us. You too!" She said sharply, wheeling on Nathan who was sending faces. "You both—of all people—know how important that is."

The gaze of Balder was upon them, watching this family episode unfold. Huffy, Benaiah turned away. Nathan was sober for a moment or two. Then, blaring, the gleam of firetrucks approached, drowning every other sound.

Where Front Street turned back toward the highway, the parade was disbanding in Decatur's parking lot. Above them, the Angel Jasper Mary began ascending toward the mountain. Likewise, the forebears of townspeople, both Yankee and Native, ascended too. Like so many cottony seeds on the winddrift, they dispersed, drifting toward the four directions. Into the blue they went, and beyond, toward black reaches where starlight struck through thinning atmosphere.

But one seed, one ancestor, stayed behind. Ruddy and robust, this ancestor descended, going down through the roof of the diner. He stopped by the grill at Decatur's elbow. The bald bespeckled man, aproned, sweating, stood frying burgers in anticipation of lunch. Already, participants of Jasper Mary's parade were pouring in for—as they supposed —the last lunch ever in the decrepit diner. The ghost of Dewey Decatur could remember the day this diner was lifted from the old Atlantic and St. Lawrence Railroad to this spot near the loop to the highway. Earlier, in the middle of the last century, the railroad had elevated Gottheim beyond its prospects just when the village was looking as though it might fade. Neighboring Copenhagen, for a while more prosperous, was bypassed and sent into decline instead. Dewey, the ghostly former proprietor, watched his son work the grill.

True to its habit in trouble, Jeffy Decatur's mind was working over this, that, and the other thing. He wondered if he had strength to stay on his feet, worried that the pie and Jell-O salad were enough. Would Melvinia, Linda, and Annie get the orders out on time? Already these were overflowing at the window. An ungodly amount of burgers and bacon and steak were growing beneath an exhaust fan seemingly unable to budge the breathless heat in the kitchen. But the roar out front covered his burbling agitation. Whimpering, he muttered about it all. Decatur wrestled with his great grief at having to end it all today. Today! The day his life took one final nasty turn.

"I'm glad you're not heah t'see it, Fatha," He said. "What would you do t'see Decatur's Dinah coming to the end this way?"

Putting his ghostly arm about Decatur's round sweaty shoulders, the ruddy angel smiled. "Don't matta a jot, Jeffy," he said. "They's lots to do in life. No end of things to do, now, and afta."

Jeffy said, "It's all I'm useda, this dinah. All I evah wanted to do. All I evah did."

"Daow," said the angel. "You forget the potridge huntin' we done in season. 'Memba all them bids we got those Wednesdays? Taken Wednesdays off to go get some woodcock?"

But Decatur muttered, "You was always heah, standing on this spot, grillin' 'way...."

"Nope. I'd take Wednesdays off. 'Memba them stupid spruce grouse? Dumbest bids y'evah did see. Won't beat way proper—like potridge. Just stand theya so's to get its fool head blowed off. Why, I never let you shoot 'em, 'twas so unsportin'."

"Waunt the air s'good in season?" reminisced Jeffy with a murmur. "The way the sun looked, turning the woods gold in evening, goin'home? Then it'd sink behind the mountain'n all'd be back in shadow, like when y'stotted."

"Yuht, Jeffy boy. Just like that, all sunk t'shadows. Life was like that in Gott'im. Course, it always bust up again, mornin', but we f'get that— feelin' low, like. Just wait, Jeffy. It always comes back gold again."

His son said, "I could retire, s'pose. I can still walk'n get around good's evah. A bit slow, with these pains'n all."

" 'N you got friends, all retired, in't they—'bout? Always hangin'round heah. Can spend moah time with them.   Let someone else stot coffee, mornings, somewayas other. You just set theya drinkin'it!"

Decatur slapped cheese on four burgers, reached over to lift a basket of fries from hot oil, give it a knock.

Dewey Decatur continued comforting his son. "It's not s'hod— dyin'. Now now don't go getting all worried again! I know it looked bad ... way I went, cancer'n all. But then I saw 'twaunt nothin'. Only seemed bad at th'time. But, I tell the truth, Jeffy. It's nothing compared t'afta. You believe me, now."

Decatur was agitated again, appearing not to notice, shovelling burgers, dumping fries.

His father chuckled. "Y'know, them spruce grouse in't s'dumb. It all tuns into somethin' else. 'Memba how that potridge tasted? Just lightly grilled, a li'l onion, diced bell pepper ... keep's a body in repair." The ghostly arm continued around Jeffy's shoulders. "It's like that with us. We all go fah somethin'. Got to nourish the ground, put somethin'back we been takin'way. We all get our turn. It goes down, comes back up again'n we feed young'uns, comin'up behind. Dyin's deep, no doubt! Deep to see what happens. All s'many stories fah God to fill his book with. Retire. Set'n watch stories unfold in th'town. You got your story, I got mine, Melviny's got hers'n they all come together like Sad'y night suppah, all dished out. God eats theya too. He's got a kind'o fondness fah this diner, y'know. "

Decatur smiled, wiping his sweat prickly cheek and forehead on his soiled and salty shoulder. "I can do it," he muttered. "I can do it."

"Knew you could," said the ghost. He turned away, going into the wall. He walked through Melvinia just as she grabbed a pot of coffee to service the counter—where plates and elbows crowded, punctuated with greasy salt and pepper shakers, napkins, and sugar in tall glass dispensers. He sat above the countertop floating next to Asa Bartlett's head, his leg crossed over his knee. Asa was leaning back against the counter as usual, propped on his elbows, surveying the crowd. The ruddy angel said to him, "Glad you could make it t'the closin', Asa. 'Memba times when your fatha brung you in fah doughnuts'n milk, mornings? Steam'd be on the windows, it still cold'n dock outside?"

Asa Bartlett lifted his glass, cooling his forehead with it. He smoothed his brick red hair down. Came a smile on his face with a far off look. Those crispy fried doughnuts ... not like them delivered in the truck, mornings now. Crispy, yet soft ... fresh, hot ....

—

The office of *The Village Voter*, which they now entered, occupied the ground floor of the Bond Block. Daniel took immediate note of its large press, a small job press, proof stone, and tall glass type cases: all filling the room to the back of the building, where the door opened on a closet-sized office.

In front stood the counter where advertisers, town officials and the various Town correspondents conducted business with the editor, whose cluttered desk sat behind. The counter faced large, gold-lettered plate glass windows looking onto Front Street.

Approaching with his family, toward the counter where Mr. Nutting stood, Daniel saw that the interior was far from clean. It smelled of gasoline, grease, dust and printer's ink. The nutbrown floor needed sweeping. Loosely knit dust balls had collected in grimy corners. Beyond the counter Daniel noticed a heap of slashed paper beneath a giant cutter. On the ink-stained floor around the Miehle press were scattered bits of broken metal. Now the great press itself filled his gaze. Around him, Balder and Mother talked with Mr. Nutting, while, chirping over everything he saw, Nathan hopped about like a cricket. But Benaiah, too, stood fascinated by the silent behemoth standing like a presence, filling the room. It must have weighed several tons, and appeared to be powered by a gasoline engine—if it could in fact be animated.

"How's the ol'blue babe behaving, Jim?" Balder was asking. "In't been that long since we commiserated over the ol'thing has it?"

"That's what I want to talk to you about, Simon." Nutting's long leathery face beneath the visor had a greenish tinge. His brown eyes were intent but opaque as a couple of pebbles. "It's about time for that overhaul we talked about. How soon can you do it?"

Balder ran a hand down the back of his head, considering. "D'know. Might stot Monday night, s'pose. If it takes a while, go nights during the week and hope I don't get stuck at the mill."

"Well, don't worry if you get hung up. We're all set t'go down at Farmington Press till the job's done." Nutting looked at Chrischana across the counter then. "This place is filthy," He said.

She smiled. Nathan, standing behind her and smoothing her long brown braid with his fingers, said, "We haven't seen anything like it since the dry cleaners in Phoenix!"

"Nathan!" exclaimed Chrischana. She looked at the editor, flushing. "Are you offering me a job?" She could not keep the hopefulness out of her voice.

But the editor said, "I'm offering one to Daniel."

Daniel glanced at Mr. Nutting and saw that he was looking intently back. "Young man, I need someone to clean up around here, run errands. Maybe even learn to set type. Would you be interested?"

"Sure," he said. It was something he did not need to consider. He wanted the job. But —me? he wondered. They had not met till now.

The editor must have noted that something quizzical in his eyes, for he said, "There something you want to ask me?"

Daniel nodded, returning the brown gaze with one of his own. "Why me?"

A slow smile worked its way through Nutting's gaunt green features. Then it was gone. "The English teacher, Mrs. Melville, recommended you." He might have added some of her praise, but James Nutting didn't believe in such attempts to instill self-esteem. He thought self-esteem came subtly, slowly, through working well. Curmudgeonly Nutting refused to pat young people on the head.

Wonderful, thought Chrischana. Quietly glowing, she turned to Daniel.

Benaiah wriggled his way between Mother and the counter. "I want to sweep, too," he said.

"I only need one."

The boy pulled away and went to the door to stare out.

"I need you Mondays, half a day, and Wednesdays. It might work into more. Have any trouble getting to work?" Daniel looked to Chrischana.

She said, "I think we can work it out."

"His day to take it easy in the office," said Balder when they were out on the sidewalk again. "He does births'n obituaries on Sad'days."

"O-*what*-you-airys?" asked Nathan.

The parade watchers had disappeared, leaving Front Street to those on errands. Most people had drifted over to the common for more festivities and concessions. Balder looked down at Nathan. "Obituaries. They go in the paper, saying who died. Births'n obituaries tell who's gettin' started and who's gettin' done."

"Anybody we know?"

"Not so far's I know." He grinned, stepping back as a woman in jeans came brushing past to get into Nutting's office. "What's a rush, Elvegy? Big sale at th'greenhouse next week?"

"Oh, Balder." She recognizes him, gasping, clearly distracted. "Didn't see you with that beard."

"You'd be s'prised the numba people saying that lately." He looks strong in her face, seeing that she is too upset to notice her old classmate, even now failing to acknowledge Chrischana after an absence of fifteen years. But Chrischana recognizes Elvegy Bisbee, a former high school field hockey star. Her twin, Albinia, was once Chrischana's rival for certain boys.

Her hand on the doorknob, Elvegy stays. "I couldn't take it anamore, Balda! I finally got the court'n state police to find Albinia. My twin's murderer is being exposed!"

His mind suddenly putting it all together, he stares at her. They all stare, transfixed. The woman is electric with purpose, and looking ravaged by exhaustion or grief. No one seeing her now would be able to say how she looks ordinarily when composed and working in her garden, or tending plants with subdued concentration in the greenhouse at Blanchard's Fields. Elvegy Bisbee Blanchard is bent out of her customary calm, has largely been so since the disappearance of Albinia. Frantic, scarcely glancing at them, she says, "C'mon. Come with me into th'Vota'n you can heah all'bout it. Ithiel's gont'pay!"

Held by intrigue, they follow, Chrischana wondering vaguely if she shouldn't be taking the children away.

Beyond the point of mere curiosity, Ben and Nathan's small faces are blanched, gripped. Even Daniel is rapt over this revelation. It is as though Elvegy's devastating story, told there among the fibers, muscles, nerve cells of her being, has gone into their deeply impressionable souls.

Chrischana glances quickly at Benaiah, his pique over rejection gone, a thrall to this fierce unfolding. What has happened to Albinia Bisbee? Is it Ithiel Whitman, the class personality? How can it be? It must be someone from away. People I know aren't murderers, least of all Ithiel. I dated him before Balder. Chrischana is sucked headlong into the mystery, into the storm of Elvegy's spirit, helpless to heed the hesitation she feels for the children.

But Balder Simon is more familiar with the story of Ithiel and the twins. And, hearing Elvegy, he recalls that look of fear on Chrischana's face which he saw at Deep Hole. And he glimpsed the significance of her return to Gott'im. So now, ushering them all into the office, he gives her a keen look, saying nothing in response to her torn unspokenness. The consternation in her grave Indian features ....Jee-zuz, he says to himself. Do you know what you're doing, Balda boy?

Kinetic Elvegy is calling the editor away from his typing. "Mr. Nutting! The day I told you'bout is heah! They'll have to try Ithiel fah murder now! I come t'give you my quote. Put it in your next edition!"

He rolls back his squawking desk chair and grabs his note pad, comes to the counter. Chrischana, Balder and the boys hang back, but Elvegy waves them close, saying, "These good people—Godfrey! it's Chrischana Twitchell! You're just in time t'see what an evil maniac our class voted Mr. Congeniality. Ithiel Whitman is—" her eyes grow large and shiny. She gestures toward the window. "She's being—" An agonized groan tears up from within. Helpless, she bends to the countertop worn smooth by the elbows of Gottheim's generations: weeping with violence, the whole of her psyche pouring forth.

Gaping but mute the witnesses look on.

From somewhere James Nutting produces an old box of Kleenex, and, discarding the first two as dusty, he begins feeding her clean tissues, one by one. The crumpled human takes them in on curled fingers, crushing them against her weeping eyes and wet nose. For long moments she gulps and hiccups. Then, subsiding, still clinging to the countertop, she gulps back her grief. She quiets.

Out of profound silence, Elvegy stands upright, again gesturing toward the window. In a low voice she mutters, "They ah breaking up the concrete he poured over her four years ago."

So it happens that the monumental treasure of Albinia Bisbee Whitman's body is extracted from the basement floor of the Pine Hill condominium. Right where Elvegy Bisbee Blanchard said it would be.

It was no small feat of studied deduction which led her, after many months of turmoil, to pinpoint its resting place. But to convince the authorities—years. Years: There lay the crushed remains, the wretched human leavings; while those in charge dreaded the sight of Elvegy Blanchard coming. For years Ithiel made people laugh, played with their sympathies, put up a brave front. Ebullient, likable, embraced by the community, but so arrogant and deceitful that he boasted to himself that his savagery and irreverence would never be exposed. Who could believe that warm jovial Ithiel Whitman would harm anyone, let alone his wife, whose disappearance and apparent desertion he mourned?

Oh, it was all right, he told himself: She had it coming. She always had it coming. And finally it came to her. But it wasn't going to ruin his life—a pile of skin and bones and hair. Put on this earth to provoke him, he guessed. God, how he hated to see her twin coming—so like her. Having to smile at Elvegy, try to soothe, reassure. Having to watch her run around with that pieced-out plaguéd story of murder. Why didn't that goddamn Blanchard do something about her?

—

James Nutting steps to the gate in the counter separating the pressroom from customer service. He walks to the door, holding it open for Balder and company. "I know you folks will want to get over to the common or something," he says, leaving them no choice but to be on their way. And, spent now, staring at the floor, Elvegy makes no further claim on their attention nor any attempt to say goodbye. As they exit, Nutting gives Balder a dry look, thinking, *You've got a lot to learn about fatherhood. You don't subject children to this.*

James Nutting was once the father of children. The husband of an academic, too. Once upon a time, and in Toronto. Children suffer the most in divorce. Some things are too intense for children to endure. The revelation of murder, for one.

He was a newspaperman in that city. Any city would do for a dream nurtured since childhood, in this very office; his father's office and his grandfather's before. A hope nurtured right here at the proof stone on the other side of the counter. He had to get out of this stifling village. So he left the proof stone and Gottheim Academy in the early '50s, stretching to the task of establishing a reputation in journalism. Thoughts of a career at *The Village Voter* numbed him. He was fearful of Sinclair Lewis's "village virus." The idea off settling into the complacent, self-satisfied status quo— the Town columns concerned with who ate where last week, headlines bleak with purchased property or the petty minutia of selectman's meetings, school board wrangles, continual tension over property taxes, endless rounds of school sports coverage—it was more than he could tolerate. That was before Boston College, before his stints at Midwestern newspapers and the big break in Toronto in the '60s and early '70s, where he was, at first, exhilarated but ultimately enervated by reportage on university demonstrations, sit-ins, riots, bomb threats, arrests. Toward the end, he could not shake the creeping conviction that he was merely pandering. His thoughts began returning to Gottheim, to his father's concentrated face beneath the ancient visor he himself now wore. And, to his bemusement, he began to yearn for the village and the din of the old flatbed cylinder press.

For a while he fought it, like an immune system recognizing invading antigens. But, in his reading, he came across Ruth Moore's *The Walk Down Main Street*, reminding him of the rich interplay between townspeople in small town Maine. Gladys' Hasty Carroll's *As the Earth Turns* surprised him with its sure language, calm spirit and lament over the decline of small family farms. These and other Maine authors had the good sense to portray with fidelity an idea with growing appeal to him: Small-town mores, so often transmitted with pettiness, could actively work to preserve cultural identity. He had to smile, finding that this was no longer a negative virtue to him. He was freed in believing that this ancient mechanism for keeping people from doing damage to themselves and others need not always be viewed with a cynical eye. Gossip and censure could be tolerated with humor when the offshoot was a positive model. Living and working to preserve a good name was not, in itself, an evil preoccupation, as once he supposed. It might save an individual, a family, an institution much needless pain.

He's been here ever since, preserving even the old press ways against the pressures of progress. And sometimes he smiles inwardly at the realization that he is now the troglodyte he once abhorred. Even so, the nature of James Nutting is essentially unchanged: He was always a rebel.

Closing the old wood and glass door behind Simon and the Twitchells, he turns back toward the sagging Elvegy. "Will you have some tea while we talk, Ms. Blanchard? It won't take long to heat the kettle."

Out on the sweltering street, the five walk slowly toward the Common, blinking in the light of day, trying to process this charged encounter.

Passing beneath the shade of an old maple, Benaiah breathes, "Someone got murdered—and buried in cement ...." His arms and freckled features begin loosening. His face takes on a look of awe. But Nathan's pinched little face looks up at his Mother. He is silent, blanched. I'm scared, his large eyes seem to say to her. She draws him near. Clinging together, as one, they walk on. Benaiah catches her arm, she lets him hold her hand. Walking slowly behind, Balder and Daniel look on, matching their pace to that of the trio ahead.

No one says anything. Each mind is busy with its own thought, the children especially haunted by pictures. A cement truck backs up to a prone body. Dead, or alive? Wet heavy stuff flows out, battering, crushing a human face, a human body, a woman. Bony contours harden in concrete. The face in the truck cab is savagely grinning. The drunken face of Dad.

Quietly, Nathan begins crying, wiping at his tears with hands filthy from chocolate and the dust of the window ledge at *The Voter*. Chrischana holds him harder. Her grip on Benaiah's fingers is so painful that he prys at it with his thumb.

Maybe Daniel'd kick me in the butt, Balder is thinking, *do me a favor.* The look he recollects from Nutting could not have been more dead on. But even now, some small corner of his mind holds to the thought that what he has done in exposing them to Elvegy's agony is not misplaced. But the cost is high. These kids will probably not be able to sleep for nights to come. But maybe they are clear now of whatever danger there was in Phoenix ....

Chrischana's thoughts are increasingly more disturbed. Withdrawing into herself as she walks, attention to the pain of her children fades. Whelming memories, evil memories, wrap her in a blistering haze. She thinks of Petey's notes and grows dry. The heat of Phoenix has come back on her, searing. Sealing her in slow paralysis. From somewhere outside this burning, she recollects her mind upon arriving in Gottheim, how it sustained her over the months, and even after Petey's disturbing note: the people of Gottheim, her people, would not tolerate spousal abuse in their midst.... She had forgotten much about life here, especially that of families other than her own. But now this about Albinia and Ithiel, about Elvegy's grueling quest, and the helplessness of Babette Roebuck under Ferddy Sessions. It would take more than being voted Jasper Mary, more than a parade or being elected to wear buckskin, fringes and feathers.

There comes an unconscious check in her dazed gait, slowing the entire group. It's as a revelation, coming to her: *Jasper Mary was murdered for her treasure.* Petey will surely come here and try to take the treasure of Gott'im away.

Behind her, Daniel was also thinking of Petey ... and Petey's face hovering over wet concrete. The man will be coming after her, he is sure. He saw the postmarks on a couple of letters. Now he imagines Petey coming out of the Post Office. Petey, walking along Front Street ....

Daniel jerks his head up suddenly, looking at Balder. Balder is drawn from his own thought, finding the gaze of his son. Terror is flashing out of those eyes.

No, Daniel! It won't happen. *We won't let it happen to Mother.*

If only there were some way to assure him of this.

But, at last, Balder is certain. Chrischana has come back to Gottheim for the saving of her life.

The Common

News of doings at the Pine Hill condominiums went through Decatur's Diner when Gilbert Tuttle drove down from Jasper Mountain, purportedly for lunch. Pudgy, with a slight waddle and fluffy hair sticking out from his ball cap, Gilbert had been mowing grass outside Pine Hill when State Police arrived with the warrant, Elvegy's lawyer, and a jackhammer operator in tow. The site was cordoned off at the door but, out back, Gilbert lay between clumps of arborvitae, peering into a basement window. He saw a woman and two kids routed from the morning's laundry, and in no time the place was full of officers and others, working to unearth the remains of Elvegy Blanchard's twin sister. When the place filled with cement dust and noise, an officer opened the window, ending Gilbert Tuttle's career as outside witness to the proceedings. His new role, of tattler, commenced. He made it safely down mountain, streaked over the highway toward the last good lunch in Gottheim, burst into Decatur's, red-faced and important, to spread the news about the body breakout.

Huffing, he finished, "Elvegy Blanchard finally gut someone t'listen to hah," and plunked down next to Asa Bartlett, trying to appear nonchalant. But the big news had agitated him out of any dry demeanor he now tried to achieve. Next moment, breaking through the resultant roar of conversation, Tuttle stood, loudly proclaiming, "Guess I'd betta head ovah t'*The Votah*'n and tell old Nutting. He'll be wanting a quote fom an eyewitness."

Bespeckled Asa said, "Can't imagine what Albiny'd look like after all this time under concrete. But choo know, people won't believe he done it even if her poor bones prove it. Ithiel Whitman's too popular fah folks to stand any monkeying if Elvegy is wrong. Shouldn't you have waited before coming down here to spill the beans? S'pose it in't true? S'pose nothing's there?"

Flushing, Gilbert Tuttle saw the flaw in his dance as town informant. He huffed back to his pickup and pulled out, narrowly missed by an eighteen-wheeler rounding the curve and over the limit. He was in a rush to get back to the ski resort, but he needn't have bothered. Even as the event unfolded, a multitude of scanners were tuned to it. News of the investigation buzzed through the festive community and onto the Common, spilling over to stir the little crowd around the secondhand book table outside the library. Patrons at art displays, concessions and craft booths were set humming. Participants of the ax and chainsaw competitions were thrust from the limelight, then distracted, by the news. A few of the town's teens swarmed to vehicles to go up and test the gruesome rumor for themselves. A carnival caravan of rust buckets and pickups rattled and roared out to the highway, heading for the mountain.

Subdued and expressionless, Daniel Twitchell was wandering the Common with his friend Cindabilla when her cousin Albertine rushed over to offer them a ride. She gave him a dirty look and he turned back toward the street. Cindabilla, in overalls and a T-shirt with her toenails painted a rich purple, chewed on the ends of her long honey-red ponytail, a habit of hers in nerve wracking situations. "Assholes!" she exclaimed, her light eyes narrowing. "Why'd they waunt go look at Albiny?! It's like a big party t'them!"

Daniel shook his head slowly. He kept walking, his hands jammed into his pockets, gaze on the dried beaten grass of the Common. He was unaware that this bit of land had been deeded to the Town by its founding father, his ancestor Mahalalel Twitchell, to be used as its green for all time. Daniel scarcely noticed the empty cotton candy cones, hot dog wrappers, styrofoam cups and shiny gum wrappers scattered against the stalls. He had been looking forward to this day, to his first Jasper Mary parade, now that he and his mother and brothers were in Gottheim.... But the whole thing had soured.... Frowning, he glanced into the white sky, wondering why the sun yet shined.

Babette Roebuck and Chrischana Twitchell stood before an exhibit of woodland watercolors, quietly talking about the discovery of Albinia's body. Like last time, when Babette carefully avoided mention of her own brutal boyfriend, Ferdinand Sessions, they spoke once again about spousal abuse. Ferddy was still laid up from when Cindabilla filled his buttocks with buckshot. Of course, Cindabilla had steadfastly denied all accusations. He was healing some, and Babette had not been attacked since. But the owl was a lot on her boyfriend's mind.

"Heah's the card of that place I was telling you bout, Babette," said Chrischana. She held out a purple business card. "Remember, we got a place to go f'help in time of need."

Babette hesitated, then reached for the card. She was a thin woman with bottle black hair, partial to wearing pastel halter tops with jeans and gold braided sandals. She loved the sleek new Mustang she drove everywhere, bought with her dowel mill wages. Babette had lost a child in the womb because of one of Ferddy's drunken blows. Now it looked like she would never be able to conceive again. Her once smooth skin and blue eyes had made a baby-doll face irresistible, but now, at thirty-four, confidence was gone, her good looks seamed and scarred. She read Chrischana's card. *Abused woman's advocacy project.* The words shamed her, but she thanked Christy in a low voice, adding, "And thanks fah telling me bout what happened in Phoenix."

Briefly touching the other's shoulder, Chrischana nodded. Admitting her suffering and humiliation at the hands of Petey Prince had been difficult, but there had been a small gift of relief in that telling, even in the sharing out loud of that grief.

There was nothing more to say. The two women turned away, ostensibly studying the exhibit before them.

Seeing them there, a tall ungraceful woman threaded through the crowd toward them. She wore outsized glasses and a blond ponytail, and the members of her body moved as though imperfectly acquainted with one another. Hers was the red secondhand Subaru with hand-painted bumper stickers, one of which read, *If you object to logging, wash your butt instead of buying toilet paper.* Wearing paint speckled corduroy overalls and T-shirt, the self-styled sometime neopagan came up to them, grinning. "Babette! You're interested in one of my paintings!" She laughed like a horse from a face that might've belonged to one.

"Uhm ..." stuttered Babette, smiling, looking away.

"Just admiring the lady slippers," interposed Chrischana. "You can really sense theya delicacy in the paintings." The other was still shyly silent, so Chrischana introduced herself as an old friend of Babette.

"Eloise Patadoe," said the other. "(Now you know, Babs, I have to kid.) No really," she whinnied. "It's my name! Tell her, Babs. We used to work side-by-side, planing dowel rods at Blodgett's. Thanks for the compliment," she said to Chrischana. Indicating her portraits of the wild woodland orchids, she said, "These things are icons. The academics and humanists broke all the Christian icons but then discovered they still needed icons. 'We need icons,' they said, and that made it okay again."

Chrischana smiled. Babette looked bewildered. There being no other reaction, Eloise said, "So, you were born in Maine?"

Chrischana nodded. "Grew up heah."

"In the village?"

"Up on Blackwell Mountain. The old Twitchell farm."

Smiling toothily, Eloise said, "I've been in that beautiful old wreck, painting its angles. Teen-agers go up there, have a high old time—both senses of the word! How much longer you think it'll stand?"

"D'know. Was up theya speculating early today. I'd like t'see that painting sometime—not in the market now, just." She added hastily.

"Come out to the studio in Quaker town. Watch those rocks on the Quarry Dog Road, though. You might bottom out. Can't miss my goat yard. Mine is the only other place without a dental chair in the dooryard. Ya see that awful letter in *The Voter* a couple weeks ago? Woman wants to turn the mountains into suburbia. She must think property values are the sun. Hasn't got a clue what it takes to—where else can you store things when the shed overflows? Someone should tell her—maybe I will!—that the place she complained about is owned by descendants of the very first settlers in Quaker town. Besides, the chair looks dandy!"

Babette was looking again at the advocacy card. Chrischana smiled seeing her slip it into the pocket of her jeans. Eloise paused, and Chrischana asked how long she had been in the area, painting and, "raising goats, is it?"

"Oh, I washed up in Quaker on the back-to-the-land movement spawned here in Maine by the Nearings, maybe a decade or more ago. "I've got the goats, a garden, and painting (can't make money on that!)."

"She can too, Christy," said Babette. "I saw an exhibit of hers down't Naples. Wouldn't believe the people buying 'em theya."

"They don't buy 'em here," Eloise whinnied. She gestured to show how people stayed away. "They can't stand my personality, my clothes, the smell of goat, my uppitiness, or whatever. They cast their eyes up or down or sideways when they see me coming. Wear this pointed little glare or frown. Anything to avoid acknowledging my existence. –Or they'll just stare at you daring you to speak. I display the watercolors here to remind them that *I* at least acknowledge my existence." She said the last with a shout directed at the Common in general.

Chrischana laughed her throaty laugh.

Encouraged, Eloise continued. "It's the famed New England reserve, taciturnity, whatever, which is really just a throwback to English snootiness. Cold, very cold. (present company excepted, no offense meant, girls.) Maybe they can't stand me because my descent is verbose Catholic Celtic, and darned if those Angles don't just hate us for it, if they did invade the place we had first, namely the British Isles. People think the British part is the snooty part, but it's the other way around. Practically the only thing to crack that reserve is a stint away—among strangers. Because then they know what it is to be a stranger in a strange land. The friendly ones are those who went in the service or college someplace. They come back here either chastened or broadened by a taste of life with people they aren't related to."

Ponytail swinging, Patadoe shook her head. "One thing you didn't want to do on moving here is offer suggestions. Big mistake. Nothing so uppity as someone from away with an idea of how to do—anything! People've been run out of here for that! They couldn't take it anymore— having a brain and not being allowed to use it. But things are changing. Folks from away, office people, begin outnumbering locals. The fact that Goldings and their skiers have money makes a big difference. You can't win a peeing contest with someone who has forty million bucks!"

Babette and Chrischana looked at each other, smiling, embarrassed, shaking their heads. The trampled space around the art exhibit got wider and wider, emptying as people veered past the foghorn of Eloise Patadoe's voice. Trying to cut through the mist of indignation surrounding her, she continued. "And gossip! The men are the worst! The sweetest people— nice li'l old ladies or teenage boys'll shred you like a pack of mangy coyotes. Can't wait to see some of 'em hung out to dry on that judgment day of their ancestors. They think they're good because they don't smoke, drink, cheat or say fuck."

As, lips flapping, Eloise blared on about the evils of Gottheim's gossip, Chrischana looked out over the old Common, stretching away in movement and color beneath scattered shade trees. The bawling of chainsaws came to her ears from a knot of people near one end of the green. Amid the buzz of static and screeching feedback, the Franco Fiddlers ended a set at the other end of the Common, up on the old gazebo. Her gaze wandered toward the fire station across the street. The engines had returned to their bays since the parade. She glanced back at Eloise.

"My problem is in being bereft of the 'propa humil'ty.' D'you know they wouldn't even tell me about town meeting?—what it was about, where it was held, *when*? I'd ask about it and get this evasion. If it weren't for *The Village Voter*, new people wouldn't know *what* was going on. Not that I appreciated the village rag back then. Bored me cross-eyed. Those town columns! I mean, can you really care that the Goosepimples came up from Lewiston to dine at the Frecklefaces on Sunday? That Bert and Gertie

Petunia went shopping in Waterville and came home with two hamsters, one black and one brown? Or how about those help-wanted ads? 'Models for TV and national magazines, no experience necessary, for details call this toll number.' The community bulletin board's handy, though. And Nutting, the editor, isn't bad, either. He can really think when there's something to think about besides sign ordinances. Maybe it was even his editorials that gradually drew me in, or the letters to the editor. Anyway, now I can't wait to read his ol'bellyache each week. It's like following the endless story of Gott'im."

Suddenly, cutting through the cacophony of the Common, the deep-throated town siren blew. From all over the green, men came running toward their vehicles. Many ran to the fire station to hop aboard the gleaming machines and rumble way. Even as the trio watched, the bright engines flashed and screamed out of sight around the corner onto Front Street. An old car approached along the street near the exhibit, slowing to where Chrischana, Babette and Eloise stood. Daniel leaned out the window of the crowded backseat, where Cindabilla was also visible, calling to his mother. "We're going up Blackwell Mountain! Someone said the Twitchell Fahm's on fire! Meetcha back at camp latah, okay?"

But Chrischana stood abashed and unresponding. Before she could gather herself to answer, the car listed away. The Twitchell Farm! The farmhouse had stood there only this morning, lonesome and memory-haunted. Can it really be burning?

She heard Eloise mourning, "There goes poetry!"

And Babette had taken hold of her arm, murmuring. "Ah you all right, Christy?"

No, she thought, and felt a prickling sensation starting behind her eyes. As a force of emotion welling, the morning's tide of grief surged again. It heaved up fully loaded with sadness and anguish and fear. Chrischana fled.

She had to get some place and hide. Flooded, her gaze sought the row of buildings beyond the Common's crowded edge. There was the open doorway of the library, gaping and dark within. Swiftly she made for it, weaving through the throng. Snatches of conversation, about concrete and a body and fire, pelted her as she went. She swerved past piles of picked over books and hurried up the granite steps. Momently, the library's darkness cooled her, and the privacy of the cramped stacks beckoned. Tucking herself away behind the dim loaded shelves, she sank gratefully to the wood floor. But the tears did not flow, nor the sobs she thought she had desired.

She sat back, lolling idly against an old shelf of biography. She let her face lean on the bindings that held printed pages of people's lives. Lives that were worn out, sorrowful, depleted ... like her own. She sighed, thinking of them. Lives lived out, done. Dedicated, challenged, achieving. Withered or splintered; depressed or uplifted by temperament and circumstance. Again she sighed. What is this strange experience we hold in common? So commonly we go on, day by day, task by task. What keeps it all together, fitted out with atoms, molecules and cells ... charged with the current of life? Does it go anywhere, mean anything, like I was taught? But others had also taught that we are just mishmash, happening together during an aberrant break in the chaos.

Another sigh. She turned on her hip, ran a fingernail idly down the spine of a volume, wondering about the life within: did C.S. Lewis know, the author of the Chronicles of Narnia? She had read them to her children. He understood life, didn't he? An Oxford don, rational; yet with a blazing imaginative streak sure to have originated in another world.... And now returned again back to it, whole?

She thought of Daniel as a mewing babe, emerging out of bloody earth, smeared life with an innocent gaze. Her first. His life, like in these books, concretely freighted with the elements of a story. That's the way Daniel would think of it. He told her not long ago that life was a ... a story in a body. Is that it? Is God merely after a good story? Does he only require interesting reading?

The tears of this morning, moments spent walking on fragments of her life, the lives of mother and father, and father's mother and father: The people were story and life. They held her in their blood, every one of them. She had learned this in her reading, that she was carried in their DNA, down through generations, as surely as if they'd passed her in a handbasket. A vast intelligence inhabited the replication of her genes, precise in its myriad chromosomal thoughtfulness.

Maybe I haven't studied biology for nothing after all ... still time for that nursing career, right? She lay limply, smiling, grateful to forget fear, wishing she could sit here quietly musing forever.

But the hardness of the floor stirred her to movement, and she decided that the comfort of this place was strictly spiritual. Better go look for Balder and the kids, scare up some lunch. She rose wearily, shaking with hunger from the morning's hike. She bent to brush the dust from her knees.

Did Daniel sound like a Mainer just now?

What mockery would Petey make of that? No. Don't think about it.

—

Afternoon on the Common, thought Gloria. My First Jasper Mary Day. She enjoyed the culture of New England Gottheim. The place has artists, a theater group, an academy, IICE—skiing! It's a cultured resort community coupled with the more rowdy blue-collar element. She rejoiced in its being much more than the constricted little hamlet of cliched small-town America. You could breathe here, influence things, give of your training, your talent and imagination. And you can *see* the results of your efforts in this place. Here you can experience significance.

She was out of the condo, out of her room for good. Ready, eager even, to see Balder. She had hoped to see him here, planned to just bump into him. But she had said it all in the letter, given him something to think about. She had nothing more to say, but there was a bit of worry ... that he had not responded yet. She had been liberatingly honest ... and now it was just the waiting—to see what came of it.... *Do you know how often I think of you, your humor, that grin?* Miss you, even those whiskers and that awful scarring on your arms. She stood in the shadow of the gazebo, scanning the crowd.

But people kept stopping to talk. She must've seen every committee member, Chamber of Commerce associate, or IICE delegate she knew. Where is that old New England reserve when you need it? —Well!— Many of these people aren't Mainers, but visitors or transplants like me. No wonder there is kinship, warmth in them.

Since that day of disillusion in Decatur's Diner she found more comfort in the newcomers. But it was not what she had expected, hoped for. The dour old Mainers would never let her forget that she wasn't one of them. Do they practice that stone face in the mirror each morning? There are a few, certainly, who aren't suited to it. They really work at stemming expression. In Boston we gave it up before I was born.... Conversely, does Balder have work allowing himself the luxury of that grin?

Would it kill them to yield up a smile now and then? Wait—there's a blond head at the hotdog stand. A frown puckered. *No,* she thought, *not broad enough in the shoulders.* Behind her the Franco Fiddlers trooped onto the bandstand, began opening instrument cases, fussing with amplifiers, joking. She smiled as one cracked a dumb-Yankee joke. Well, turnabout's fair play! A frontal on all the Frenchman jokes endured over the generations. Some were now even opting for reverse assimilation, rejecting what their parents had strained for. Here's insight, she thought: This is where the more voluble expression in locals will come from. That warm French temperament can come out of hiding now.

Is that him in that group way down by the logging competition? A white-blond head and tall athletic frame. Gloria began moving that way, checked twice by friendly acquaintances. She moved on, smiley polite, but firm. Oh no—he had Chrischana's boys with him, two of them it looked like. At least the woman herself isn't with them. Her worst worry had been that they'd come to Jasper Mary Day as a unit. (Don't even think the word family.) *Relax. Balder, you will not get to me.* I am what I am. I will not change for you. I must not be dishonest. Cannot pretend to be thrilled with your ideals.

The chainsaws—two of them in a heat to sever logs—were deafening as she approached, lightly set her hand on his shoulder. He turned. *Oh those ice-blue eyes.*

"Glory be t'Gloria!" He ducked to say it low, into her ear. "Can we talk sometime?"

She smiled. His ear was still bent to her and, low, she pleaded into it. "Now?"

He straightened to grin down on her, and she noticed how thick and dark his beard had grown. He shook his head, raising his voice. "Caunt! Bonding!" He stood back a bit, with the boys.

Brightly she hid her letdown, irritation. "Of course! Bonding!"

"How about tonight? Honest-t'-God date! The movies in Farmington, Fiddlehead Restaurant—The works!"

"Ooo, that's it!... The '55 Chevy or the Caprice?"

"I can afford t'be wishy-washy on this!" The saws stopped suddenly and he grinned over his loud pronouncement.

She sparkled with laughter. "Well ... okay, I'll drive then! Can't give up an ounce of control, can I? *Simons Ledge* is up that road above the second pond?"

"Yuht. Betta make it 5, 5:30—theya's the drive down."

"Of course." Suddenly self-conscious, she looked at the boys. The younger looked like he could do with a wash. The other was tousled and taller. "Are you enjoying the competition?" she asked them. No response. Gaily, "Have you ever seen competing chainsaws before?"

After the perverse manner of children, Nathan had suddenly reverted to a strange-adult-abashed silence. Ordinarily, she supposed, Benaiah probably wouldn't have responded anyway. The two simply stood there, staring at her. And Balder made no attempt to intercede. In the past he had been so sweet at soothing the little rudenesses and rejection of Mainers. But—these aren't little Mainers ... are they? Suddenly she was abashed.

Now (desperately bright), "I always worry: The saw'll kick back, a log will rebound, something.... A sliced chest wouldn't go over very good...." Words were failing her.

She raised her hand abruptly, grinning the glistening middle-class grin that meant nothing. "See ya!"

Gloria turned and fled.

"Something tells me weah too late," said Balder, driving, his hands on the wheel, one elbow at rest outside the Chevy window. Already, down the highway, they saw the diner's parking lot emptied out, one straggler pulling away. Looking on from the passenger seat, Chrischana murmured agreement. Slowing, Balder downshifted.

"I'm hungry!" wailed Nathan from the back seat where he was tussling with Benaiah. The younger had started it with a few injudicious pokes, and his brother escalated with jabs and punches. Grunts and thumps issued out of the back seat.

Chrischana turned, hissing. "If you don't stop, I'll make you get out'n walk! Balder, pull ovah, now!" Gravel growling under the tires, the car scraped onto the shoulder. The woman glared at the thunder-faces looking up at her. The boys lay tangled together, locked in arrested battle. She swatted at him, saying, "Nathan, get on the other side of the car!" With one final pinch of his brother's arm, Nathan rolled to the far end of the seat. Ben gave a quick slap in return.

"Is it necessary to embarrass yourselves'n me in front of Balder?!" (Pause.) "Well is it?! Answer me!"

Nathan's lip quivered. Ben looked sullen. Chrischana's gaze grew sharper.

"He started it!" (In unison.)

"Answer!!"

Benaiah shifted his look past Balder's blond head, which had not turned to look at them. "I'm sorry," he grumbled.

"Me, too." Nathan's voice was more positive, but thin and subdued.

"S'right," answered the man. He pulled back onto the road and coasted down toward Decatur's. Chrischana continued glaring at the boys. "Don't cross ovah the drive-train," she warned Nathan.

"Is that what that big bump is called?" he wondered aloud.

"The same," answered Balder. "Sometime I'll show y'how one works."

"Great!" said the boy, fully revived.

"You too, Ben."

No answer. Then, "Okay. " (Still cloudy and low.)

They pulled up to the glass door, where a sign shouted, *CLOSED*, in big red letters.

"That's the end o'that!" said Balder. But he did not pull away.
They sat there, the aqua decades-old Chevy idling before the dining car from
the old *Atlantic and St. Lawrence Railroad.*

People around here, even sometimes people from away, knew this
history. The minor iron god, the railroad, was once worshipped here, along
with the other gods of progress and profit. Yes, even by the thrifty people of
Western Maine. Beginning in the nineteenth century, when the steam
whistle and steely rumble were first heard in these old hills, pious
parishioners would sit in Gottheim's pews, listening for the whistle, while
droning hymns but thinking hard about some future destination, whether
near or far.

... This is all as Eloise Patadoe would have it: Droning, they sat
and thought how many board feet, or how many bushels of potatoes or
apples they'd get to the markets in Portland, Boston—heck, Brazil! They
heard the morning's text, thinking of bonnets, newfangled sewing machines,
books, periodicals, gadgets for peeling apples (just stick one on the prongs
and turn the handle!); stuff chugging its way to them in the mountains. The
Meguntics, which their ancestors brought them to, wouldn't be so isolated
any more—*Hallelujah!* A second sacred hymn, and the droning acquired
some vigor and a lilt. They were singing for real now, ready to hear a
sermon about loving one's neighbors and welcoming a stranger. It will be a
lot easier with that new piano for the parlor is on its way.

But this is all cynicism, sour grapes. A failure to show the proper
humility before the great gods of science industry progress. "Genius" and
"perspiration" changed our common culture: the way we want to spend our
days, or cultivate our nights. To suggest a better use of genius would be
uppity. There's no matching the way we get things done now, save lives,
transport lives, counsel lives. Heck, we're on the verge of creating life!

These are the things Eloise Patadoe says when she can get anyone
to listen. But they don't. She's too mouthy, too awkward, a slob. Avert
your eyes! Give that woman a wide berth!

"Now whad we do?!" Nathan popped up from the back seat, stood
on the drive-train, his gaze on Balder's in the rearview.

Balder gave the sign a last look, peering past Chrischana at the
streaked windows, the dull metal and maroon of the diner's exterior. Place
is older than I am, he thought. *Everything passes, just so.*

"Well," he looked into the rearview again. "What say we go up
t'the house fah taco salad, something."

"Yeah!" yelled Nathan.

Balder pulled the Chevy slowly along, grinning at Chrischana. She
had turned in her seat and was looking back at him, leaning against the door.

He thought about the day she had, its many losses. The T-shirt she wore was lettered, dark green with a line drawing of a raised fist clenching a set of pliers. *Defend God's Wilderness.*

Balder looked away. He shone his self-mocking grin out the windshield, easing the Chevy past the classic, but now abandoned, piece of Americana.

He said, "We'll just go up ovah home."

— Within Without —

What life it is, and how that all these lives do gather—
With outward maker's force, or like an inward father.

—from *Within and Without*
George MacDonald, 1855

174

Burning Down the House

The pond on her right yet reflects sunlight as Gloria signals a turn to point her Caprice up the mountain road. The radio beats out frenetic heavy metal but, gripping the wheel, she scarcely hears its screaming. This music enflames her subconscious, tightening muscles along her neck and back. Gloria Fay's brother James would be happy to say it's music to set fires by— if you are interested in burning down your own house.

The hill road leading to *Simons Ledge* is steep. Her tires spitting gravel, Gloria presses the pedal to the floor. I hope Balder is done bonding with Chrischana's boys. *Don't really want to run into them again just now.*

Wonder what he'll be wearing?—not the flannel and jeans. She tugs on the rearview, glances into it, scrutinizing her eye shadow. Is it the best shade for a summer evening, casual?—or too dark?

Eveledore lent her the makeup late this afternoon as they sat in the other's condo, sipping Diet Sprite, laughing and plotting strategy for the campaign to energize Gottheim.

If only Balder would show some interest in the focus groups. Surely he's read about her activities in *The Village Voter*. He might even collaborate with Theodora Prescott at the Gottheim Chair Factory by encouraging production and maintenance people to take part. This has been Gloria Fay's advice to mill owners and business people.

"Reach down and tap into the vast potential of your associates," is how she put it. Some were enthusiastic, but others seemed uncomfortable at the suggestion. One looked very dubious, and another actually smirked. That staring, standoffish Lyman Bearce never even bothers with the sessions. The second most powerful man in town, if you count ski magnates Harry and Julius Golding as one. And you can't expect them to come. At least Mrs. Bearce was there, a sensible, articulate woman, older.

The brainstorming session at Eveledore's turned into a giggle fest with Gloria's comic description of their faces. What! —involve the employees?!

Sometimes Gloria feels like knocking their cold or grinning muttonheads together. They just can't stand to democratize the process. Probably think it would be like inviting shop class to a meeting of the honor society—but it's absurd to compare the business community's sheep-headed mediocrity with aspiring intelligence.

Evela said this reaction was typical. She's been facilitating IICE seminars in Gottheim for three years and is familiar with all the lumps, people smugly satisfied with the town as is.

"But these are the 80's! Things are changing, they have to! The sod's been cracked, Gloria. We've broken them in for you. It's so much better than it used to be. When I first came, people here were a bit less inclined to involve themselves in things we proposed. And I've heard horror stories from the mature members of hostile resistance. So maybe your seeds will slip right into the broken soil and germinate. You know that they really do take to you. They are impressed by your graduate study, flattered by the attention of your happy personality. The town's come a long way, but I think you could be instrumental in helping it go further."

The kind words were balm after the childish snub of Chrischana's kids.... And Balder's hurtful failure to smooth things over when it happened early this afternoon. If he will just give a little nod over her committee work. Nothing big—just a sign that he is even aware of it.

Of course, I haven't tried to get in touch since the letter I sent him... hoping he would make the first move.—But it works both ways! If only that missile from Phoenix had never penetrated the woods of Gottheim!

The curve in the steep road distracts her. She has come up this way before—once—just idly and apprehensively trying to spot out the place where he lives. But the house was not visible from the road. That day she went past his lane, way up the hill, past a few more lanes, all the way to the mysterious dead-end at a logging track. The woody hills below great Jasper Mountain are woven with them... intriguing places... With a start she realizes that *this* is Jasper Mountain. The very backside of her deity! Balder lives on Jasper Mountain, too! He always has.

She may now engage herself at night thinking of his being just over the mountain from her. Just over this great monolith. Asleep and tenderly godlike, just beyond her great God, Jasper Mountain.

Switching off the commercial break and the rude rock-and-roll, Gloria smiles. Great to believe in what I love! And not be a Baptist anymore, have to sit in church and be oppressed by its mores, its superior insularity.

There's his lane. Secret, tangled, beckoning. Oh, please let the Twitchell kids be gone. Please let it be enough for today. (Where's

Chrischana's man, the father of the other two?)

Having released the Caprice from the madness of music and pressure on the gas, she wants to calm down now. Be leisurely on this green lane... Tree bordered and dusky, with gleams of light pouring through... The lane is glorified with amber and emerald green. Silent, she rides slowly, the car gently dipping in and out of ruts, deep in the sensation of trolling through gemlight. The woodlight is mysterious with penetrating shafts. It could be a haven for fairies. Something out of Tolkien. Still slowly driving, she turns her head more toward the source of golden light.

Then, on a sharp intake she holds her breath, slows, stops the Caprice. Among the shaftlight stands strange beauty. Delicate beauty, small. A... china white fawn, gleaming like some fragile being from another world. Is it real? Should she blink just to prove it imaginary? But she can't. Gloria cannot look away from the quiet gentle sight. It will never come again. She must imprint the image, fix the fawn in her feeble mind. For all is fragile, feeble. She sees it now. Everyone, everything... tender and bruiseable as this deer.

A white etching in hazy green, the fawn is backlit with hushed light. It stands as though hallowed, transfixed.

Now Gloria understands that her presence, watching from the car, has entranced it. As though its miniature beauty is poised for her sake... Its helpless innocence transforming her. She will never be careless with anyone again, never give harm. She will not vaunt herself, scheme or grasp. Oh, that this moment might last forever.

Suddenly comes a blast, echoing. Gloria drops out of her dream, awakening to see the fawn flinch. It pivots, springing away into the dusty shafts of light. And a reddish deer leaps up out of nowhere, herding after it. Stunned Gloria sees the tawny rump vanish among the trees, its white tail flying.

Peripheral movement takes her gaze to the head of the lane. On the foliaged corner of the dingy house stands a small figure in T-shirt and jeans, wearing a red bandanna. Cradling a gun. Outraged, Gloria presses the accelerator, speeds thumping toward the figure.

Elda Simon has long since changed her tactics. She will cease desiring to see Sugarloaf: She must prevent Posey bringing her white fawn to the house. And Posey herself must not come. To do so would only encourage the fawn's presence. So Elda Simon lives in a dither, waiting, watching lest they come in her absence. She stays home and does not make rounds in search of ill or wounded wild animals. Instead she tends those she has, cleans out the barn, shyly speaks to Chrischana's children when they visit.

And she tries to prepare for Balder to do his worst to the house.

She continues to be baffled at Chrischana's status here in Gottheim. Apparently the young woman has returned to town only as Balder's friend. And Elda fears that, except for his attention to the children, he is going against the best in all: his application was accepted at Adirondack Paper; he has plans to refurbish *Simons Ledge*, and he rejects the mother of his only child at a time when she needs his help.

None of this is right. And the last is not like him at all. But it is Elda's way rudely to shove off these concerns as often as they show their faces. It is none of her business to speak of these things, only—apparently—to obsess over them in her mind.

But she does feel safe in understanding that no one knows Balder as well as she does. Even so, she scarcely knows him at all, she guesses. Don't I know his heart anymore? Well, she knows the contours of his serious face, and how it puts on a grin in the presence of others. She knows his inner gentleness, his outward mocking grimness born mostly of Vietnam.

She knew him from a babe on the breast... but he knew her from the womb. Embla had cleaned off the blood and placed him on her chest, and when Elda said thank you, he arched his live back and looked into her eyes. The eyes of newborns, she knew, were not fully focused, but he looked right into her eyes. She pondered every so often over this scrutiny of the newborn. What did it mean? She could not pass it off as signifying nothing. He *did* attend, evidence of a pre-birth bond. And puzzling it out she came to understand that it was her *voice* Balder recognized. He knew the voices he heard in the womb from the moment his cochlea were fully formed. Probably the aural sense provided his only stimulus from outside the womb. And donning human experience, he hadn't much else to work with.

Stopping at home, resting, he speaks little. Sometimes she thinks she resents this, but mostly only that she *should*. She's never been much of a talker herself. Someday she will finally grasp that it is nature to her to receive almost nothing from him. All she really needs is to see him at peace, even happy. (Hopefully, in a house of his own somewhere, now that all this is happening.) Will he be at peace now...with Daniel?—After the terrible fires of Vietnam? His life must be whole—occupied, at least. *I'll be at peace when he doesn't need me.*

In her heart, Elda would be needed by no one. That way she can give herself wholly to animals. (... While diminishing sight allows, this twilight that seems to be coming to her.) The littleness of creatures, their cunning simplicity flightiness agility grace, their unconscious verve. The squatting toad, self-assured fox, sleeping dove. Only this. Everything else will take care of itself.—Even blindness? How then will she experience...?

Stop.

Now she stands at the corner of the overgrown house, gaping as a red convertible halts in the boiling gravel, a young person flying from its door. Elda steps back in consternation. She turns, hops stiffly toward the back door, still lugging that heavy gun.

But Gloria is too fast for her. Flying after, she grabs the older woman's bony shoulder, steps angrily into her path. "What's the idea— shooting at that helpless fawn?!"

Each is furiously breathing, their overwrought features inches apart. Elda sputters but brings up no answer. Trying to wrench free, she turns her bemused face away.

Then, beyond Elda's head Gloria sees Balder pop from his '55 Chevy, as out of nowhere, hollering. "It's only Mutha, Gloria! Wait a bit!"

She is distracted enough to note that he wears jeans and a corduroy jacket, a striped tie against the dark shirt. He lays a hand on them, saying, "L'me explain y'each to the other. Mutha, this is Gloria Fay. We been dating since spring. Gloria, this is Mutha. She's not the dangerous hand she looks. She was only scaring off Sugarloaf. Hunters likely'd kill him, if she didn't. He durst not be used to people."

At this Gloria sags, her face crumpled in sympathy. "Oh, Mrs. Simon, I am *so sorry*! Please, I completely misunderstood! I should have known—Balder's told me of your interest in wild animals. I should've known. I should've!" She pants and ceases, her features still absurdly contorted.

"S'all right, deah," says Elda. "Cuss you'd think I was harming him; cuss you would. S'all right." Looking shyly at Balder, she starts toward the house, saying, "Well, I expect you waunt get away now. Nice t'meet you, deah."

Chuckling, Balder stops her. "Hold on, Mutha. Caunt brush us off that easy. We all got get acquainted!" He grins at Gloria. "Got time fah tea, ain't we?"

"Yes! Sure! Tea's great!" Gloria smiles on the fallen old face. "We've hardly spoken. I can't let my rude treatment be all you know of me." She gives Elda an imploring look.

"But—house's a mess... kids'n all, whatnot—theya gone now," she hastens to add.

"Be easy, Mutha. Got to meet folks proper like'n all." He gives her a grin.

Unaccustomed as she is to its warmth, Elda loosens a bit. Still, her look is dubious. His grin grows.

"Well... I guess I can stand the mess if you can."

—

"She really is sweet," said Gloria, as they coasted out the lane toward the roadway in her little Caprice. "Terribly shy.... There is *no* mess in that house!"

Preoccupied, Balder grunted his agreement. He was off the subject of mother. His darkly bearded face, beneath a blond head with sugar bowl haircut, was turned toward her. She felt his gaze taken with her and, when the road permitted, sneaked a peek. He grinned.

Out on the highway, lightly she said, "How was the bonding today?"

For a moment he said nothing. Then, "Glad you asked, Glory. I can warm to that subject. Have any idea how *real* kids ah? Theya's no telling how they'll be. Chain reaction from the moment they explode out of bed. Doaw, take that back: Nathan explodes out, Benaiah slouches. Daniel comes yawning'n scratching his head. But when they rev up, it's something to behold."

"Oh kids are real, all right. Have you had to clean up after them yet?" She couldn't resist a little innocent needling.

"Well, you saw the house. Didn't looks'bad, did it? We got caught up before driving'em home." The grin again: "Have to admit—Chrischana whipped 'em into action some."

"Uh haw," came the knowing response. She smiled, but there was an inward sting. Chrischana had been there.

He said stoutly, "Don't really believe I couldn't'o got them to do it myself. Couldn't very well shut her up, could I? We worked on it together." He was irritated to find himself explaining so much. "What's the big deal? If I have to clean up after 'em, I will. Mutha taught me." At another twitch of her mouth, he said, "All right, so she made me. Been wiping my bottom since before I was a toddler!"

"Well, good for her!"

Softly, he replied, "S'pose I get no credit—won't pin no rose on me?" He reached out to smooth a stray strand of her sleek pageboy. Gently he curved the strands around her ear, letting his finger linger. "I could kiss that sweet ear, I could, Glory." His voice was soft and low.

"Please. Do."

He leaned close, softly wetly tickling her ear with the tip of his tongue. A faint acrid taste made him withdraw a bit. "Sweet," he murmured, now moving still nearer.

They were on the highway, wind-buffeted and zooming down country toward Farmington. "Why won't you love me, Glory?"

"But I do. You know it."

"Do I?"

"Balder Simon, I *said* I did!"

"Uh huh."

"Balder, you're making me mad."

"Guess so."

(Pleading) "Why can't you be nice?" Her eyes in the rearview gleamed irritation at him. "I'll wreck!"

"Guess y'betta pull over. Up theya's the roadside park."

Evening shadow was beginning to settle over the Meguntics, the sky still light with summer dusk. She parked a bit above a small group of willows rustling gently down by the river. Balder said, "I waunt your love, Gloria."

"Balder, I *do* love you. *You* are the one who will not make love." She turned and put her arm on his corduroy shoulder. Gently she rubbed his bearded cheek with the back of her thumb. He said nothing, made no move, and hardening up, she pulled back. "What is this, a new twist on the old argument?—If you love me you'd have my child?"

He looked at her now, her face knotted and stricken. He grinned that maddening grin. "Maybe."

She sat back, staring out the windshield. The breeze reached them, the leaves of the willows, gently lifting, falling. Bitterly she said, "I suppose you'd like to pull down under those willows and get all cozy in the shadows. You know I'm for the lovemaking. You've always known this. But— instead—it's, I take down my panties, you'd unzip and we get right to making babies."

But, seriously, low he said, "We could be married down in those willows." His finger moved gently down her arm. A soft slow movement, barely touching. He had time, eternity, to treat her so. She felt herself pooling beneath his touch. "We can be married in church first," he finished.

She wanted to stiffen, but she heard herself saying, a syllable at a time as though mesmerized, "well... you... can... for... get... it." She was clear, but not loud for she did not want him to stop. And, slowly and low, word by word: "Balder, where is your love for me?" (*Aren't my dreams and goals anything to you? I showed interest in your newly found fathering. Can't you encourage me in my Gottheim work?*)

But his voice was beside her, intent in her ear. "My love for you's in my dive into home life. Get married, and we'll plunge in theya together. Do all the dirty work of raising kids together. Just pour ourselves into it. Glory 'n Balda. Do it together."

Her voice, still mesmerized by his touch, answered soft and low. "... Not possible...."

Very gently he withdrew. "Maybe y'betta start the car."

—

In her bed during the small dark starry hours, she thought about it. The movie, the conversation, the meal. Outside the window loomed Jasper Mountain, blotting out a large part of heaven. If she were back in her women's studies class, she would have mentors, peers, to hash this over with. She should get together with Eveledore tomorrow. But then again... maybe not. Gloria thought of the seething women, angry, railing against millenniums of oppression, abuse. She remembered another course: Dr. Velma Arlington's harsh manner toward the young males in class—small town boys who didn't have a clue. If they'd known what their course in Communications was going to be like....—But the professor's style was _meant_ to be confrontational, challenging, and taken impersonally... Yet Gloria was sure they felt personal rancor. But the girls in Dr. Arlington's class were inflamed by her vision. Gloria felt its fire even now and, under that influence, how could you help but see the white house of male domination burning? Sometimes I long to see it burn. (What is this Balder's pulling? It fits—and doesn't fit—the pattern. Be careful. Paternalism can be very slippery.) Grimacing, she remembered Ithiel Whitman's wife found only this morning—buried in concrete, the victim of murder, abuse. It's not just rhetoric. Men _are_ out to get you!

Get a grip! Balder? It's nothing to do with him. Get a grip! She punched up her pillow. If she could not find the word she nonetheless recognized that it was his spirit that was different.

She glanced up at the mountain, good Jasper, and grew quieter, calmer. His grandmother did right, naming Balder after some old god. With that old beard he looks like one. How can his beard grow in black with his hair so white blonde? What a contrast. She grinned: facial hair, professionals call it—on purpose to denigrate beards. Balder would probably grow one for that reason alone, then make some crack about Egyptians shaving their slaves.

She had dropped him off at the end of the lane near the tree-tangled house... strange house. The kitchen in back beneath the ledge, Simons Ledge. A house drowning in trees. Front room and kitchen back-to-back, sharing a wall and the chimney. And the whole of it swimming in the overgrowth of green light. But she had not been comfortable there. The house was decaying, its furnishings dilapidated, the atmosphere musty and dim. Alien to me. I need a fresh, bright, shiny habitation, full of new, bright things.... It has a deep history, _Simons Ledge_, but that's _all_ it has.

Her reverence was dutiful, certainly, but no matter how she...—that house was better burned! Respectfully, ceremoniously _burned_. Build a new one. An exact replica if you must. But _please_—purify the ground of that rotten old structure.

She rolled over, entangling herself in the bedsheets still fresh smelling from tumbling in the dryer. He had told her about starting at Adirondack Paper, lampooning the orientation sessions of Human Resources. The marshmallow toss, balloon blowing, role-playing, etc.... She had had to laugh, his take was so on the mark. But Gloria understood the importance of such testing, such play. It was crucial to get a handle on the employees in order to develop a harmonious atmosphere on the job. He should take it in token of the corporation's wanting to get it right. It took the 1980s to really evolve the world of work toward a more compassionate sense of community. A corporation is really a community of people. If the place stank and had an abominable exterior, at least Adirondack had a decent managerial *soul*.

That stench!! Balder will have to shower till he's blue. But his clothes will be clean when we meet. He'll probably have two sets of clothes—*never* get the smell out completely.

When we next meet.... She paused. Or?... will we ever? Where does this doubt come from?

He had stood outside the car, looking down on her... the soft sighs of night about them in the dark. What was it he had said? Goodnight... you know where to find me... Simons Ledge... What was he saying there?

That she had to call him?

(Or, is this hyper-imagining?)

Then she had turned the car around, nosing slowly back on the lane toward the road where stars awaited, not thinking of what he had or had not said, but of the white fawn. In fact, she had stopped to look for it in the dark. Would it gleam out, a living delicate icon? Staring through the darkness, such darkness all about the tree-tunnel... with that faint starlit gleam at its end. Except for that it was an empty dark; silent, the fawn long gone.

Gloria lay in bed, unseeing, thinking about the little deer. Is it true? All those things revealed upon seeing Sugarloaf? Could I really become like the fawn? She sighed, turned this way and that. Now on her back again, staring out at Jasper.

No. She would never be like the fawn. She had only seen him. Seeing doesn't translate into being. It can only set up a longing inside. Probably I will forget. Forget all the virtue seen in its little bit of being.

Fair weather this morning in the Meguntics. Descending from Gottheim into Guildford, Balder looks toward the vast cauldron in the river valley where Adirondack Paper sends up smoke and steam. Vapor, pouring densely off the paper dryers within, piles up over the valley, drizzling. Looks like Guildford has its own weather breeder, hunkering like a hurricane at sea, circling; gaining moisture, momentum, force. Maybe one hundred years it sat there, swirling out its own smell and weather.

Get used to it, Balda boy. Your hands and tools are used to help keep the place running. Go down into the maw and do what they tell you. Help cook those forests, keep madly spinning out the paper. Take your part in turning spruce and birch woods into envelopes and office paper so folks down in Washington and Harvard can make work grinding out studies. You've been looking all your life for a way to help 'em keep occupied, out of trouble. Go down Balda. Go down into Egypt and lend those poor boys and girls a hand. How many bricks can you help make today for old Pharaoh's monument? He'll be sure to stop by, when you're up in the chip loft or down in the digester basement, and give you his personal thanks.

He was down in the basement, sweating it out under a five-story pulp digester. He had thought it impossible to sweat more than he did in the Kraft mill, where it often reached 120°. Wrong. Nineteen tons of woodpulp, liquor and steam were cooking above him. It would be his job to change a blow valve. As the digester heats, the blow valve releases pressure from the load. Reaching maximum pressure, the great digester begins quaking. The first time he felt this he was just entering the area under the pink glare of the sodium vapor lamps, the sharp caustic smell of white liquor in his nostrils already quickening his senses. When the quaking started he thought the monster was getting ready to blast off. It's not war exactly—but you return there.

He had read of that happening once, somewhere in a community down South: a digester ejected onto a block of stores during business hours. Balder backed up, ready to flee, until he noticed his mate continuing onto the platform as though this quaking happened every two hours. During what should have been a normal blow, its seals giving way, the valve had come apart choking on an errant eight-inch rock from the wood yard. Digested pulp stock 180°F flooded out. That was the day of his on-the-job baptism into the life of Adirondack Paper.

Working, beginning to feel the telltale slippery film of white liquor sticking to your skin, comes a point when you begin to wonder whether humor has enough thrust to carry you through these conditions. You begin to notice if OSHA's safety requirements are being enforced. Are there eyewash stations near your next job? Can you get a shower before white liquor starts breaking down your skin cells the way it takes apart the lignin of cellulose? Digesters, lines and valves, wood and skin cells can only stand so much heat, pressure, chemical burning. The nerve endings of the millwrights' skin (sooner or later) will tell: you've been burned by white liquor.

Even so, driving down into Guildford, Balder is sorry to understand that probably you *can* get used to working in a paper mill; that exposure and familiarity can inure you to just about anything. Even a place that is an exact spiritual replica of hell. Paper is made in hell.

Chrischana and her son, Benaiah, were hiking up through tired greenness, greenness spotted here and there with the light of late summer. Goldenrod and asters were already showing in the warmth of the July day. In absolute stillness, they rounded a thicket of beech and yellow birch. No movement of creatures, whether raven or squirrel, broke the heavy hush about them.

Benaiah, older son of Peter Prince, was quiet, tired, but just now uncomplaining over the steep ascent of Buck Hill, a spur of Blackwell Mountain. Perking up, he spied something of interest and hurried along the track ahead of his mother. Chrischana approached the scorched thickets, their leaves curled and brown. Silent, hushed, she saw first the pile of corrugated iron, twisted sheets of roofing washed in rust. Once the crown and protection of the house where she was raised, the roofing had been heaped up in ruins by the hands of firemen in the wake of what vandals had done. She came closer, stepping gingerly, peering into the pit of the great cellar where blackened timbers had fallen every which way. The beams glistened with hardened black bubbles, as though having effervesced out of a charred interior. If sawn through, would a cross-section of white be revealed? Idly she wondered it.

She was weary from her climb but did not think of resting. Chrischana was hungry to look over the fire cleansed remnants of a former existence. One that had been very dear to her. More dear in memory than in actual experience? She would have to muse over that. Memory was so often accused of romanticism. But Chrischana, part Native American, part Yankee descent, wasn't so sure. Doesn't the sap pressure of youth prevent full consideration? Maturing, we bring a more complex, complete understanding, memory enriched by experience. She had read somewhere that the first forty years of life were original text, the last forty its commentary.

Fire cleansed, she thought again, looking at the debris. Everywhere here is starkly brutally clean. Her gaze read the now open walls of the farmhouse cellar. What had once been the dark mystery of the cellar hole, hidden by the house overhead and the skewed foundation—now open to heaven. Master builders had placed this stonework, precisely, in a bygone era. Once granite, its color now was red. Except for this fire bought ruddiness, the stones might be taken for quarry-fresh; and placed with exactness, as once stones were so placed, each fitted to the shape of its neighbors. No mortar had been used.

She did not want to disturb the silence of her meditation, but she must be attentive to Benaiah. There he was, limby and balancing along a plate atop exposed cellar wall. "Be careful!" She called, "The stones on theya might not be stable."

It had been her plan to come alone, but Balder's son Daniel, her oldest, needed a break from watching Benaiah and Nathan. He had enough watching Nathan, the youngest, and Ben's presence was always a temptation for Nathan who relished provoking the middle boy. Also, she wanted Ben to see the hillside and remains of the place she once knew. Now the boy said nothing in response to her call. Provokingly, he kept right on, placing one foot exactly in front of the other. From Nathan she would have expected flightiness but surer obedience. Now she must contend with Ben's obstinacy.

"Did you hear me?" She called. "Remember what we talked about... You could come only if you were obedient."

Over his shoulder he said, "I *am* being careful. Can't you see? My arms are out.... I'm balancing." But his tone said, *You imbecile.*

Chrischana stamped her foot. "Get over here!"

"Awww..."

"Right now!"

Benaiah flounced down off the plate onto the bed of ash where the ell once stood. He stomped toward her around and over charred timbers, kicking them as he came.

"Listen," she said, taking hold of his shoulder. "I trust your agility (probably betta'n mine). But I don't trust your judgment. Will you walk where I say... or do I make you sit over there on that stub?" She pointed out a fresh stump where the firemen had sundered a maple.

(Stalling) "What's agility?"

"Your powers of balance and coordination. *Well, will you?*"

"I have powers?" His freckled false face brightened.

"You have powers of obedience. We talked about this before. Obey me."

"Whad you say to do again?"

"Go sit on the stump!"

"No you said if I did it your way I didn't have t'sit on the stump."

"That was before y'give me a hard time." She turned and marched him to the stump. "Now just sit theya!"

Sulking, he sat down heavily. A scowl settled, hardening. He watched her step away, heard the crunch of shattered glass and ash beneath her worn boots. In T-shirt, cutoffs and bandanna, her figure receded as she went back to the cellar hole. Ben screamed, "Someday I'll be grown'n you won't be able t'do this to me!"

Dryly the word drifted back to him, "Hallelujah."

She stood on the brink, the massive hearth, beehive oven, and broken chimney with foundation now had her attention. Its bricks, scattered or heaped among the cellar full of haphazard charred timbers, were the off-pouring of an immense chimney that once towered above. A few bricks lay on the ground at her feet. She stooped to pick one up, examining its cleanliness and heft. Could they be reused, she wondered, tossing it down onto a piece of granite. But the brick fell apart like a chunk of dense cornbread. Then, striking the granite with her foot, she found that this foundation stone also broke, if not so readily as the brick. She had yearned to salvage these materials but was now bereft of this hope.

Hush returned to the ruined site in hope's vacuum. She looked back again at the monumental center of the ruined house: hearth foundation, fireplaces and beehive oven. This great brick-and-stone heart/core once provided warmth, cheer, and the preparation of nourishment. Dimly she saw her ancestors maneuvering the great stones into place with the aid of oxen or draft horses. Intently they worked, placing the great stones with skill, laying with unconscious knowledge the individual components of her care. She could not—she *must not* let it all go for nothing. She looked earnestly about her. This place, even scorched and cleared into piles as it was—must not go into other, less caring, hands. She thought of Balder's support check, the lump sum he sent her after learning the truth about Daniel's conception. The money was now in an account of her own... for the heritage of her children. And their children. We hold nothing for long, she thought. It's the passing of the genetic handbasket that matters. What better legacy than a piece of ancestral property? Buy this land, if I can... It will mean a hasty shelter of some kind... But can I buy some of this piece, having no credit, no permanent job?

She shook her head. This burned-to-ashes relic. No—just a hole in the ground. Chrischana smiled halfway. My ancestral relic is a hole in the ground... lined with clean ruined stone. A hole filled with burnt timber and brick good for nothing but powder. And yet—she was suddenly light and lively with this thought. We will have something at last.

If Enan Pale will sell... at terms I can handle.

As she walked around, half-smiling, musing, her middle son sat by the scorched and sundered maples, scowling. If he had been Nathan, he would have peppered her with questions, observations, cheery little subtle attacks on her strictures. But Benaiah's temperament was quieter and he was older, more grudging, and beginning to internalize his rebellion. More like his father Petey, he sat solemnly chewing the cud of retaliation.

Suddenly he pictured himself grown-up and smacking her. If she provoked Dad when he was drunk he would smack her.

But, at once, a frightening feeling came over him. His eyes watered and he scrunched them up, remembering—seeing—how mother had crept into the boys room, locking the door behind her. He could hear the faint click in his head, still. Lamplight had sheeted into the trailer window, silhouetting her; a trembling shadow, softly rapidly breathing. He had whispered, "C'mere, mother." Either it was very late or very early. The drunken cursing at the other end of the trailer had finally ceased, without disturbing his brothers. That night only Benaiah had been awake to throw open his bunk to her. And she had climbed in. He sat now on the stump, remembering her wet face next to his. And his thumb, wiping the tears away.

Ben turned away, hunching his shoulders, trying to withdraw into some sort of hiding. He was frightened of the vengeful thoughts that sometimes sought residence in his mind. *Mother, mother...I won't hurt you. Help me. Please get these thoughts from my mind.*

"You have powers of obedience, Benaiah." She had said things almost like this before. He had powers of obedience, of balance, and coordination. Usually he did not care about such things she spoke of; self-control, goodness, sharing. He could say them by rote, as though repeating lessons for geography. There were mountains, forests, plains, shorelines... all kinds of boring land. There was generosity, and kindness, courtesy, and goodness—things, she had said, of the spirit. "You can obey, Benaiah."

Rap. Rap rap rap. Benaiah heard it from somewhere, knocking. He looked toward the lane which had been so still. What was that? It came again. *There are no doors in the woods, but someone is knocking.*

From across the gulf of the ruined cellar, came Chrischana's tiny voice, drifting toward him. "Hear that woodpecker?"

"Sounds like he's knocking on a door," Ben called back.

"Don't it?"

"Think I'll go see if I can let'em in. Can I get off the stump now, mother? I'll only walk where you tell me."

"OK. Go look at'em, but don't get past the sound'o my voice."

He slid off and, listening, quietly moved toward the trees. The knocking came again and, looking up, Benaiah saw a huge red-crowned woodpecker clinging to a bald patch on a hemlock tree. Rearing back, its pointed bill fell with tremendous force, powerfully thrusting, excavating toward the tree's core. And Ben marveled that a bird, usually such fluttery flighty things, could be so big, strong, and sure.

Later, speaking together of Jasper Mary and her stories, they went up mountain toward blueberry patches scattered plentifully over the rocks. The mighty Abenaki healer had once roamed these hills, eating the earlier generations of this fruit. One of the stories she told the native and settler children was of the mythic hero Culuscap's gift of fire and its many uses for his people. Was it not Culuscap, asked Jasper Mary, who showed us the cultivation by fire of blueberries? Just so the healer passed on the ancient wisdom of her people and of God.

She taught so because each generation wrestles with the same obstacles and difficulties of spirit. The way up and down the mountain is narrow and tufted with puckerbrush. You cannot escape good-and-evil's struggle that you are born into. Even so, between birth and death, there is one thing common to life: the fact of Culuscap's comfort and Culuscap's return. With the Virgin Mary's son, Jesus, you can face anything. This is how I, Jasper Mary, tell it... if you will hear me speak. If you will listen to my stories. Sit upon the scorched stump outside your ruined house, listening to the voice of your ancestors. Do you hear my voice?

Builders in Time

The youthful Balder attained his full stature with marvelous rapidity, and was early admitted to the council of the gods. He took up his abode in the palace of Breidablik, whose silver roof rested upon golden pillars, and whose purity was such that nothing common or unclean was ever allowed within its precincts, and here he lived in perfect unity with his young wife Nanna (Blossom), the daughter of Nip (Bud), a beautiful and charming goddess. [Guerber, H.A., *Myths of Norsemen*]

Balder and Daniel were up on the roof of the children's house, part of the old extended farmhouse; shoveling off what remained of ruined asphalt, prying up rotten boards, and throwing it all into a heap on the ground below.

"Watch how y'walk theya," cautioned Balder to his newly found son, Daniel. "Expect t'find more rot under that patch. Don't want Chrischana suing me f 'negligence if you break y'leg.

His arms full of shingle, Daniel nodded. Sidestepping the patch, he descended to the eaves and tossed his armful out onto the pile with a crash.

It was hot, hot even for August. The leaves over their heads and on into the nearby woods were tattered and dark. The springs of earth were receding under the rainless skies. A torpid quiet sat upon Gottheim. Fire watch, fire flights, the ban on burning, all enacted. Area wells were drying out. Yet, *Simons Ledge* had plenty of water; whether because of the ledge above or the gravel beneath, the plot had an excellent aquifer. Maybe the well had gone dry once since Elda's marriage to Everett nearly forty years ago. Wells went dry in this kind of weather, but that of the old settlers' house beneath the mass of towering rock was not one of them.

While they worked, Balder asked Daniel about his job down at the newspaper. Was the boy privy to secrets too damaging or explosive for print? Was *The Village Voter* in line to be snapped up by some big-city consortium? Did he have a chance to proof copy for what the Ezra Simons had seen on their vacation to (*gasp*) New York City?

Daniel had smiled but slightly over these questions, answering a taciturn no to each. Yes, he had been sweeping, running errands and, lately, doing a little proofreading. He didn't say so, but he thought maybe Mr. Nutting might use him more in this capacity.

Kneeling, Balder pulled up shingles. He was late beginning the renovation. There had been no money to start. He had told Chrischana that the money he had given her was only part of his savings, but it was everything he had saved while working at Gottheim Chair these ten years, at least, after Vietnam. Now every day he was grateful that the money had been just sitting there accumulating, waiting for the son who, without his knowledge, was progressing through elementary school in a desert western city far away. Ambition had been a way of grasping exhilarated at life, but following Vietnam's fires, ambition could never again spur him to life. Only the presence of people to whom he must commit all.... Rebuilding this house had not occurred to him before. Now it was just something to do for the universe, for Daniel, and the others. For Gloria. Using the faculties in a focused, constructive, disinterested way was what life demanded. And human expression of matter could be busy indefinitely in quest of... well, it wasn't the accumulation of debris, or futile grasping after dominance.

He wiped the sweat from his forehead on the grimy shoulder of his T-shirt. Balder picked up the prybar, began breaking up rot in the roof. What a relief. People can beget more people. Once the bank account had seemed almost a mocker—at the very best a cushion for mother's old age, and he would have given it all with relief. But how much better children! People, beginning again and again. You can deny love, discourage, resist, trash it even. But nothing can change its nature. Nothing can alter the pressure of love.

Its channels can change, its water courses. Working on the hot roof, he could see it in a figure flowing out from under the ledge above the house. It coursed under the dry ground, beneath and through the roots, heading for this house. He looked over the roof ridge past the settler's house and imagined its leading-edge, foaming through the trunks, glinting among the stems. After Vietnam, he had hidden himself in the crevice of this tree-gripped rock, and many years later the water came down and out to him of its own accord. Love had been coming. Here, of all places. It was taking up residence in this house. But with Gloria, too? Maybe. He had done what he could to convince her. But finally it was up to her.

Daniel edged down with another shovelful and watched it drop with a clatter. What a relief to see the pile building below. This roof ripping was tedious. Why couldn't he use his Saturday for something besides "wuk." A swim at the Cove with Cindabilla was wanting. Sweat was dribbling around his eyes, down his cheeks. He flung it from his hair with a shake of his head. Daniel trudged back to the corner where roofs abutted.

Balder was already raking together another shovelful. When will this end? When will the man say, "Let's eat," or "Go get a drink"? Why is there so much having to *force* yourself to do things in life? Why can't life just consist of doing nothing? God is great, he knew. Why doesn't God just say, "Do whatever you like; here's food, clothes, house, transportation, live off my bounty—oh, and no more sickness, pain, starvation"? Does God think we can't handle it, or what? We sure have to handle all the other stuff.

He thought about Nellie Sessions. And what she had said about the owners setting wages in all the mills about Gottheim. Balder's comic question about damaging secrets recalled her story again to his mind. All she has in life are those broken arrowheads, bits of rock shaped by hands that are now nothing but soil. Her wrists pain her, all day she feeds glue pin machines for ten cents over minimum wage, and no health insurance, no retirement, no respect. The people around here all work like that, in mills; or cleaning up after tourists. Even mother aches for a steady job cleaning up after them. Place is saturated in alcohol, too. Seems Nellie and Cindabilla's grandmother are the only ones of that large family who don't drown themselves in Budweiser or those toxic sombreros they drink. He knew they were toxic because he made the mistake of sampling one of those coffee brandies one night. When the spinning stopped, he dreamed he was slapping the crap out of Nathan. Those bleary slack faces of her alcoholic uncles and aunts. No wonder Cindabilla talks of getting out of Gottheim before the sickness gets hold of her too.

I'm definitely going to college. He had learned enough in school about self-esteem... and put that together with what he had been hearing and seeing around here. If your boss respects you and your work, it shows in pay and benefits. If your boss thinks you're not worth it, you console yourself into a stupor.

Daniel dropped another load of shingle and splintered wood onto the heap below. It rebounded, and he sneezed as dry rot got into his nostrils. He turned and saw that Balder was having to dig hard, getting the rot out of that corner up there. He was on his knees with the prybar, digging. The boy looked back over his shoulder down at white plywood stacked in the dooryard. They would be sheathing with that. "Except fah the foundation, roof's most important pot of a house," Balder had said. "Roof's no good, rest will rot away, too."

But Daniel could not help wondering why the man bothered with this. Why not just tear it down and start over? What does he need a big house for anyway? That solid part of it—the oldest house—was big enough. He and his brothers had stayed nights just fine in those extra rooms upstairs. The wallpaper is yellow and old, gloom saturates the place evenings.... But Nathan makes so much noise it doesn't matter. Gloom can't survive in a house with him.

Maybe he should broach the subject of area wages with Mr. Nutting. Maybe not. Man's as tough as an old butternut husk, hardly ever speaks. Don't think the editor is one of them... but what if he is? And what if Nellie Sessions is plain wrong?

Balder leaned on his rake, regarding his son. He saw the knot in Daniel's brow, the concentration in his eyes. Boy's sending up smoke signals. Can almost see that smoke shooting to heaven.

Daniel glanced at him, catching Balder's regard. The man said, "You'll be sliding off the roof on that sweat in a bit." The Father grinned at his son.

"Get enough of it, maybe I'll swim."

Balder grinned bigger. Daniel could make him glad responding well to something. "Swimming, huh. Maybe you betta eat first. Let's call it quits fah t'day."

He caught Daniel's half-smile and thought it was almost worth being deprived of his company for the afternoon's work. No way he could stop now, not if he wanted to get this roof on before the fall rains. He was still trying to get the hang of this father-son thing. He liked the quiet companionship of his son, but saw it costing Daniel. *A father's influence could be important, but shouldn't be heavy-handed.* Can't make the mistake of just pouring out all my thoughts and personality on him. Drop a hat and I'd share all my experiences, understanding....

Balder was learning, but he groaned inwardly. Four short years and Daniel'll be gone... Maybe to college, a trade school, whatever he wants. Boy can't see how short time is: Looking, he sees it endless... Maybe so. Balder thought of Vietnam and its aftermath. Yes, time is short. And it is long.

"And her with *four* kids!" said Melvinia, gurgling with suppressed glee. "Should be ashamed of hah self! But nobody feels shame n'more." Her sagging features turned aside in a knowing look.

" 'S truth!" exclaimed Asa Bartlett. They stood together inside the old high-ceiling post office. Asa's hands were full—with his lunch, a flier from the grocery, a packet from the insurance company on his medical plan, some bills, and a *National Geographic*. They were both gossiping away like it was excess gravy scooped up with a thick junk of homemade bread. You could almost see them smacking their lips.

On the way to his box, Learned Gammons poked a narrow face in, saying, "S'what happens when they stot getting ambition. If she just stayed a waitress—good enough f'anybody, good enough f'you, Melviny—none o'that'd've happened. The minute a woman goes out o'town, steps up to being a bank teller and gets throwed in close with a handsome face... Whad you expect?—shake hands'n how'd you do?"

"Lack o'shame," said Asa, his horned rim glasses sliding down his sweaty nose. He shoved them back into place with an immaculate forefinger. His nails were clipped and clean, as though bleached, his crewcut sharp as a razor "This TV culture's gont harm all the little ones. None' o'this went on thirty years ago in the '50's—not like now. Too much shame back then fah that. If we could just bring back shame." Gottheim's amateur historian shook his head, as though mourning over a piece of broken delftware.

The three wise people stood there shaking their graying heads, the prune-like creases of their faces flapping. They knew best. Anybody with sense could see it. If only young folks'd'listen to them. If only the young could see how much betta it was to be all wore down than excited about what they called life's possibilities. If only 35, 40-year-olds'd give up theya notions of fulfillment. Just take to duty and let fulfillment find *them*. Kids'd fare betta. We all gont be dead in a few years anaway. Might's well do the right thing while you have the chance. (Flap flap flap.)

Melvinia had flipped through her mail and stepped out into the glare of Front Street, Asa following. They stood gossiping five minutes more, mail in hand, then went their separate ways: Melvinia to her babysitting, Asa striking out toward School Street. He would go wind the tower clock in the Congregational Church before beginning the afternoon shift at the wood mill.

The Church was one of three, tall and white, all anchoring one end of School Street at shady intervals. They gave an imposing solidity and sureness, a sanctity and peace to this stretch of Gottheim's thoroughfares. Asa approached one of the two—Congo and Baptist, crisp structures painted in 15 and 12 coats respectively, one for each decade since their building. Two other churches in town, an Episcopalian and Universalist, were a trifle peeling and dingy, their congregations thinner and maybe a bit worn at the heels. Only one Church in town had the tower clock, but all pointed their white steeples skyward, pricking Gottheim's greenness, visible from lanes in the Village, and from some distance on the highway.

Asa enters the side door of the Congo Church standing at the head of Front Street looking down its length toward a facing monument at the far end. The Revolutionary War Minuteman stands erect near that point where Front Street veers out toward the highway. The granite statue was placed there at about the time the Episcopalian Church was being mooted by an earnest little congregation that met in a house at the edge of town in the 1870s. It was 10 years after the Baptists succeeded in shouldering their way up with the Congregationalists in a steepled structure of their own.

Asa opens the door to the tower where a narrow ladder staggers up through gloom. He sets his mail on the wall brace nearby, grips his brown bag lunch with his teeth, and begins climbing hand-over-hand into the tower above. He passes the hanging length of pulley chain, next the ladder, weighted with a boxful of gravel. Over a span of the past half week, by degrees, the box had fallen twenty-five feet toward the floor below. As he climbs, the clock overhead begins striking the noon hour. One... two... three.... Asa waits, bracing himself between the dark wooden wall and the ladder, as the deep tones boom out. In the Village below some might glance up toward the gonging. Others will scarcely notice the mellow strokes, and a few will not hear at all. Asa thinks of this, having been in all these attitudes himself. He unwraps his pastrami sandwich and takes a bite, as the hour falls.

Again he begins his ascent, the tower's must deepening in his nostrils. The rhythmic ticking of the clock increases as he climbs. Asa thinks of its sureness as one of his benefits, and comforting. He is paid only $300 per annum to wind the clock biweekly, and has climbed the ladder 3120 times over the years. One time he took the trouble to multiply it out, but that was 20 years ago, when it was one third that number. He has never taken a break from the clock, winding it twice a week in sickness and health. He even wound it during his honeymoon and the week in which Griselda died. Asa is wedded to this work. His wage has not varied in thirty years.

Aside from these comforts of the ticking and the routine, winding the clock yields the benefit of insight. Climbing in the ticking stillness, Asa has time to think. Standing at the top of the tower admiring its gleaming brass works, turning the crank to reposition its weight, Asa can focus on time. He thinks of Time's oddity and riddle, of its strange elusive characteristics. Yet sometimes he forgets about time as he climbs. Sometimes Asa thinks of other things.

Winding the old wooden handle today, he thinks of Olive. Asa is loving Olive Lovejoy.... He guessed that's what it was. Now that Horace has died. He never thought much about Olive before. He had recognized that she was a good companion for Horace, being a firm and definite soul. Her spirit is more solid than human flesh. So many are ill-defined, unstable and unsure. They are as changeable as the color of Hutchins Pond when the varying sky moves over its waters. He has seen the pond in every color, from the deepest heartbreaking blue, to live green, golden, silver, pewter and black. There are even times when it's colorless. The varying wind gives textures too numerous to mention. Griselda was like that. Olive is not so entertaining but, now that he is nearing 60, Asa is content with that.

Being married to Griz—*I had enough entertainment to last two lifetimes*. Olive probably felt the same about Horace before he settled down and got on with the business of loving her. Asa chuckles in spite of himself. It took heart disease and cancer to settle the boy down. The way he wanted to use his time at the moment—that was how Horace used it. A very entertaining guy.

But Asa wants only so much entertainment. He wants to work, to read, go for hikes, berrying. He particularly likes a focused rummage through documents. All a bore to Griselda. Distraction was how she filled her time out of work, even once or twice distraction with Horace. Sick with anger and sorrow it made Asa. Sick in his level fastidious heart. The messiness of her life was a terrible weight on his orderly soul. He tried to speak of this with her, but she thought him merely self-righteous, blaming Asa for trying to constrain her blithe spirit. Said it was his duty to loosen up. "Quit making me the bad guy, Asa. You'n this town. You're so good'n pure. Don't you realize how that makes it on others?" Every time she said these things it set him on edge. He was 20 years understanding her attitude: the blithe spirit in her was one of self-righteousness.

Oh, but they had some good times together. Asa loved her better than anything, even history. He loved her like she should have been loved: with all his goods and patience. And it was sure to take little of the latter, but he was ready to love Olive that way. In youth he overlooked Olive, craving Griselda's spontaneity and fun. Now he wants the definitiveness of Olive. That and her brightly painted fingernails.

With a groan, Asa unbends from the task of winding the clock. He has winched up the gravel-filled box for the next half week. His aged muscles have taken their painful shot of lactic acid, and he is fit for another three-and-a-half days. The idea of this job for a pittance was Asa's. When it fell vacant thirty years ago, the church wanted to electrify the clock. Now, Asa pops his brick-red head out the little window next the Roman numeral XI in the east-facing clock. He remembers wanting to save the rituals and romance of the great timepiece. Back then, he had a telling premonition about that proposed move to modernization.

The four clockfaces' windows let in the dusty light but he opens them to let in air. If need be, you can set the great pointing hands of time from here. Anyone chancing to glance up from below will see the tiny disembodied head of the historian, peering like an imp face from the great white dial that is set roundabout with black Roman numerals. "How fitting," remarked Eloise Patadoe once, upon seeing this. "The historian as imp, watching from his tower clock while tiny mortals walk to and fro, forgetting." Asa, if he had heard, would have retorted that it was not enough to scare history into the ignorant. Only by becoming history do you learn from it.

Asa Bartlett saved the Congregational Church Tower by means of his twice-weekly hand labor. His faithfulness keeps it from the ravages of automation. In the 1950s and 60s, when convenience became the overwhelming standard, its peril to antiquarian timepieces was little understood. Friction, resulting from the attachment of the motorized chain to Gottheim's clock, would have ground its precision gears away. By spending a little time here each week, Asa preserves the works that may continue to animate the town's timepiece for centuries. Since that ignorant era of the mid-20th-century, the brass works of clocks all over New England, the Midwest, the South, and in California, have been destroyed by electrification.

Sitting in his gleaming mountainside office looking out on the green slopes, Julius Golding appreciates Gottheim's village clock. The ski magnate is a cultured man, aware of the venerable history of tower clocks. He likes thinking of antiquarian clocks ticking away over the small-town face of the nation, gifts from the old heroes of materialism. From the start of the Industrial Revolution in England, until after the turn of the 20th century, the heroes donated tower clocks to ensure promptness in their employees. With a faint gleam in his eye, Julius reminds himself that eventually materialism destroyed the necessity by providing cheap ubiquitous wristwatches... which, in turn, he supposed, elevated the town clock to its current status of icon, an austere reminder of earlier ways and more picturesque bucolic times. For Julius they epitomize the calm solemn beauty of the traditional New England village.

Cities, towns, villages, and colleges have their prosperous patron saints of heroic materialism, someone in the Andrew Carnegie template: one who employed largely, cheaply, and in unsafe conditions; but then disseminating altruistic culture throughout the community. Mitigated hypocrisy, he supposes. Culture abounded from the coupling of capital and labor, in the form of libraries, museums, in donations to civic organizations. Yes, Golding credits labor, but his firm belief is in capital as the primary force behind any endeavor. He ticks off the names, all timber and mill families, who, for more than a hundred years held preeminent positions in Gottheim. The tower clock—with its chiming of the hours, the quarters and halves—reminded everyone, subliminally at least, that these people had the real sway in town. Townsfolk at the turn-of-the-century were also reminded by a glimpse of the mill owner in somber three-piece suit, watch fob glimmering across his expanse, further evidence of his keeping the hours of the community. Julius looks out on green mountains, thinking: Not the sun, but the man with the money determines when work will begin.

Times have changed, he knows. Gottheim's mill owners have steep competition for that preeminence now... in the persons of himself and his brother Harry.

Each winter he looks out through falling snow in these mountains, out from this perch on the rim of Western Maine. He sees necklaces of iron and steel, of concrete, brick and glass, adorning some of the monolithic bosoms of the Meguntics with new chairlifts and snowmaking lines. Necklaces set with the gemstones of trail groomers, hotels restaurants shops condominiums. He reminds himself that it's all capital-intensive, everything in continual need of refurbishing or replacement or addition... And he wants to add mountains to the collection.

Golding is fit and tan from outdoor activity crammed into his full schedule of flying and franchising. He looks out past the green slopes into the more distant north where lies the great lumpy blue counterpane of the Meguntics: but just now he thinks of what is going on in the south behind Jasper Mountain, down in the Village of Gottheim. Clouds of dust are rising, jackhammers pounding away; there's blasting and the endless rumble of dump trucks loaded with fill. More trucks will come, heavy with concrete and steel; stucco, lumber and glass. Already there are hardhats working in steel-toed boots, two-way radios in their hands. If all goes well, builders will be busy in Gottheim. After stalling for a haggle over politics and property, townsfolk will permit a business boom at last. Julius allows himself the luxury of a gleaming eye once more. Here's the trickle-down some have been dreaming of.

The knock at his door is so tiny, timid; so slight that at first it does not register. When it comes again, he turns from the view back to his polished kidney-shaped desk. "Come in, Amanda," he says. "You don't need to knock—ever."

His niece opens the door softly, softly enters, quietly closes it behind. "Hello, Uncle Julie." But her small white face speaks to him more eloquently than the words. It reveals that she is quietly glad to see him. He has nieces and nephews, children of his own, who speak familial greetings—but not as Amanda speaks them.

Amanda is the small living daughter of the Goldings' dead sister, Frances. Frances died last summer in attempting to locate the unlit runway of the Gottheim Airport, shortly after dark. His headlights on at the end of the runway, Julius was waiting below. Waiting to guide them in. In the east stood Mount Will. Looking off toward the lights of the village, he never even glanced at the dark bulk in the dim overcast. His thoughts were on the resort sponsored concert of Celtic music that they would all be enjoying later. All the Goldings would be there with interested townsfolk. He waited that night, past concert time, in mounting uneasiness. Uneasiness turned to dismay, and terror as he realized Frances was not coming. They had talked on the phone just before takeoff from the airport in Beverly. Nevertheless, he then hurried into the village to call, in case she had turned back after takeoff: calling only to discover from her oldest son that she had indeed departed in the long-overdue Cherokee 180.

Only Amanda, an eight-year-old at the time, made it down in the drizzle. There was a story in town that a dark angel led her downslope through the trees, over rocks and streams. Her sister told a reporter from *The Village Voter* of Amanda's initial account, which Amanda herself no longer remembers. She's back from the experience now, a surer quieter child. But she was always the quiet Golding, and Julius no longer feels apprehensive for her. He has come to feel more apprehension for himself.

The necklaces on the side of this mountain still matter as much as before. In fact they matter too much he is sure. Collecting them has become an obsession, a narcotic, occupying his psyche and senses with their oversight and increase. There is nothing... what *is* there to be desired?— truly desired?

Sometimes Julius thinks of Edwin Arlington Robinson's poem about Richard Corey, the wealthy and influential townsman. Yes, Golding cares for his family; more than ever, in part because of Frances' dying, in part because true desire has so ebbed. Why is it that even family can do nothing to banish this rasping emptiness, this obsession with trying to fill...? That fictive Maine townsman, Richard Corey... who glittered as he walked and all the townsfolk looked at him... But it couldn't stop the fatal placement of that bullet.

Looking down at Amanda's wistfully smiling small features, he feels a faint tenderness welling. But it subsides on his recognition of it... Yet he will not let its fleeting dissuade him of its reality. Amanda will have his unalterable affection, if he fails to feel it much himself. Feeling is not everything. There are other truths one can be faithful to... somewhere.

"What can I do for you, baby?" he asks the girl standing before him. She is dressed to go swimming. A pale shift with leaf pattern covers her swimsuit. Stray wisps of hair escape her ponytail.

"Will you take me swimming? I want to go to the town beach, on the pond."

"Poor girl. Am I all you can scrape up for company?" There is much to do this afternoon. He glances at the rolls of architectural prints stacked on his desk.

"But you're the one I want, Uncle Julie. Please?"

Deeply reluctant he hesitates, then says, "All right. We'll go down to the pool."

"But I want to go to Hutchins Pond and see the kids from my class."

Turning away toward the blue view, Julius hardens, but not visibly. He does not like to see the grubby locals swimming at the town beach. He does not like to be looked at.

"All right." He speaks slowly, turning back at last. He'll wear dark glasses, take a book. "The pond, then. We can pick up sandwiches on the way."

Amanda smiles a soft confident half smile.

The man walks away from the stack of lavender rolls piled on his desk. Julius Golding climbs Mount Will every day. But the only angel he ever sees there is Amanda.

Rhetta Bearce looked out her kitchen window. There sat Decatur's Diner—vacant abandoned decrepit—just beyond her otherwise elegant gardens. She looked with distaste at the dim hole that led to the dining area, at the brown outline where kitchen walls once abutted the exterior of the faintly rusting maroon and silver dining car. Through the hole she could make out a contour of an old booth, faintly backlit by a grimy window. Had it not been for her irritation and disgust she might have lingered gleefully over the pathetic impression of the diner's dereliction. But just now she was furious over its mere presence.

Lyman Bearce, her old sawhead of a husband, had the thing set there solely to vex her, to put her precisely into this state that she now enjoyed (as he would have put it). That was the south side. Did he expect the garden to get up and go elsewhere for light? No. He relished her vexation so much that he was willing to blight the prospect of the beautiful house and its surrounding gardens and grounds.

Those sweet neat rows, clod-lined and floral bordered, just coming into longed for fullness; chockablock with leaves and heads that Rhetta had planned for and designed on paper; each year changing the pattern and elaborating this form or that. What she most enjoyed was to adapt one of mother's old quilt patterns, whether snowflake, thistle and shamrock, hens and chickens, anything lovely. Winter she stood at the bedroom window, gazing down on snow and visualizing vegetables, showy flowers; remembering and projecting summer sights from the high perspective.

Now, in the heat of August this greasy monstrosity, this old *train wreck*, was shadowing the color and beauty of Rhetta Bearce's lacework. Oh *how*! Just show me how to get back at Bearce and rid my plot of this ugly—competitor. There, the word was out. Once she thought of Decatur's Diner as ancient hussy and rival for his affections. But no more. Rhetta rejoiced over its closing as no one else in town, not because of the old rivalry but because its passing would ultimately sadden Bearce. *And he did it to himself*! She felt the twitch of a wicked smile play at her lips.

Years, maybe decades, had passed since she had mourned time he spent there conducting his business. His brothers both enjoyed the Victorian offices on Front Street, but, before this boom, Lyman had always preferred the diner's counter. Yet now that the space was wanted for some silly new boutique or other, the endless cups of coffee and powdered donuts, cigarette smoke and grease were out. It would be a sacrifice, she knew. He liked the smell of the place almost as much as that of ripped pine.

She turned her eyes from the sight of the old diner, drifted through the eclectically furnished rooms, and out onto the piazza (as it was called in the old days) to tidy her floral rattan wing chair and matching ottoman. Here she had her cozy cool summer corner set up as she liked, screened in with the storm windows put away. Once the kids were gone, Rhetta discovered that she had been building a nest here over the years. Now it was as comfortable and nurturing as she could have liked had she given thought to such things in her active youth. This was her place inviolate. The rest of the house was more or less a museum, a three-story mansion with mansard roof, complete with cupola and gilded weather vane; painted paneling, columns, piazzas with balustrades, even porte-cochère entrance. It would have to be decorated entirely for the period then, of course, but this place was bound for the National Trust when they were gone. She smoothed the old antique quilt upon the back of her chair, straightened the stacks of *American Heritage* and horticultural magazines beneath the waxed tabletops on either side of the chair. She stood with an ache, slowly, and walked her perfect posture back through the perfect rooms into the kitchen. Hildy had cleaned the place to a T. But, failing to notice, Rhetta stood once more over the sparkling sink, looking out the window.

Ugh. Maybe I can get Hezzy Kimball, or maybe Kenny Carter, to move that thing... Both strong men, able to stand up to Bearce's ire. She sighed. Lyman would just order it right back. And she would have it moved... again.... What good gossip! Turning ever more eccentric and quarrelsome, the Bearces are at it again. Do I really want that?

No, and yet... The dignified Rhetta Bearce giggled. But it came out as a cackle, alarming her with its untoward echo in the room.

Cackling?

A shadow fell swiftly down across the window, and she gave a small involuntary gasp. There it is again. That old owl. Horrible scruffy alien thing! She had not seen anything like it for hunting—in daylight! Rhetta glanced at the Black Forest cuckoo clock against the green tiles above the stainless steel refrigerator. Two o'clock.

She went to the closet in the pantry, got a broom then went out into the heat of the garden. The woman looked over her neat rows, intersecting lines of carrots and beets, broccoli and cauliflower, four colorful strains of cabbage, six kinds of lettuce and much more. But the owl had disappeared. Rooting around where she couldn't see? Great for keeping rodents down, good for keeping out jays and crows. But this aberrant owl tears out the plants themselves.

Mrs. Bearce walked among her vegetable designs, looking for the great horned owl and signs of damage. Why has Elda Simon persisted in repairing this bird's fortunes? The menace has been shot twice by various village people but the girl mends its wings each time. What is the matter with someone who can't recognize a favor of fate when it visits? God knows we need such favors around here—the way Gottheim's been going. All that entrepreneurial elation, with its noise, dust and ugly new superstructures. And, yes, she admitted to herself, a loss of prestige for Bearces. She did not like this new acquaintance with eroding significance, now that ski people were in the ascendancy in Gottheim.

She had come down through the garden toward the diner, but now she stepped from its shadow toward the marigold border, looking off down past the house. There was the gleam of Hutchins Pond, and toy village rooftops and steeples amid the comforting foliage. But there dust was rising, and a distant rumble. Unpalatable food for her affronted senses! An eerie *vaBOOM!* threw sudden echoes across the valley and up the hillside at Rhetta. Blasting!! Trying to place the foundation for one of their hideous simulated Gothic structures, no doubt. Or was it to be stylized Italianate or Greek Revival? They change the design as often as she picked up a week's edition of *The Village Voter*.

She whirled. Where is that owl? She went back through the intricate rows, stepping gingerly, hoping not to startle it up. The old thing might attack her as it had Asa Bartlett. But Mrs. Bearce wasn't afraid. Suddenly she stood at the gaping doorway of Decatur's Diner. Might as well have a look. She set the broom handle against the metal skin of the diner. Years had passed since she had been inside. Rhetta set her hand on the sticky door frame and jerked it back, glancing quickly at the grime coating the frame. On hands and knees she climbed past the iron wheels sunk in the dry August field. The sun, shedding itself savagely on the metal exterior, had turned the diner into an oven. She pulled herself up awkwardly and looked around at the dingy linoleum-covered tables, the worn counter and plastic covered metal stools.

There's where Asa Bartlett used to sit with his father in the old days. Later, he came alone, mornings, after Griselda went to work. There was a selfish one! *that* girl. Griselda Gammon Bartlett. The gay girl grew ever more selfish as the years wore. What is it about selfishness... always popping up just when you think you've got it licked? Rhetta had found it a negative strength of her own psyche in this endless moiling over Bearce's Bearcisms. The man was as obstinate as—as herself. She coped with the challenge through escalation. Sometimes she actually believed she could top him. But, in moments like this, thinking of Griselda—she saw herself (the cackling still ringing in her ears).

She had become a boxy-shaped older woman with wavy short hair, perfectly coiffed; her body in that state of ineluctable deterioration—headed for the bone bin, no detours for historic preservation. No keeping it lively, fit and glamorous, as she had managed with the house. Yet, for all this disintegration, the spirit within (its negative aspects, that is), seemed ever more powerful. Wasn't selfishness once only a tiny nuisance motive, barely on the periphery of consciousness and easily quashed? It was fast becoming an invigorating reason for being. How much of my relationship with Bearce is this continual one-upmanship? Is there anything else to this union? Are we simply united in our mutual monolithic selfishness? Maybe I can escape this almost continual self encounter if I no longer have him to war with.

If she were severed from him it might render her harmless. Stop the cackling, at least. Standing here, sweltering in Decatur's Diner, she tried once again (as so often before) to visualize divorce. But, again, it was plain as the white August day. Financial settlement, its aftermath and enforcement would only intensify the struggle. God! She would never be a harmless little old lady! She would endure this mounting malignancy forever. Till death do us part. There's a settlement impossible to argue over!

Bearce, Bearce. How did it come to this? We loved one another! We thought we did. Doesn't it amount to the same thing?

Turning to leave the diner, Rhetta started back suddenly. Confronting her were the great yellow eyes of the horned owl. She gasped as the big female blinked once and coughed up a dark viscous ball.

Glancing down she saw a tiny dried heap of them littering the floor, furry undigested discard of the owl's insatiable appetite. She looked from this refuse to the owl's enormous sharp talons—clutching the edge of the diner's order window.

Mrs. Bearce shuddered inwardly. The owl had nearly blinded Asa last spring. But Rhetta Bearce refused to show fear. Staring straight into its flat symmetrical face, she said, "Why don't choo go back to the night, waya you belong?" It was her low voice saying this, and she decided to agree with it. "Yes. Go back where you belong."

Its face a frost of feathers, the great horned owl stared back at her. Then, to her deep amazed relief, the owl turned its head and lifted away. With a beat of its great wings and slow winking of its great owl eyes, the raptor swept past. Out through the door of the diner it lurched, sweeping heavily over Rhetta's garden. It lifted up past the dormers and mansard roof, coming to light on the gilded device above the cupola. The weathervane was a replica of a fallen white pine. It had been her first anniversary gift to Lyman.

He loves his white pine, she thought ruefully. His money trees. No, she corrected herself. Not just for the money. Lyman loves white pine. He takes care of them, always loved their long-armed beauty, the way the strong boughs hold themselves ready to heaven. He loves them in every stage of growth, from a wispy seedling.... Her eyes swept the place. And he loves this wretched old diner. Not because I hate it, but because he loves it.

"Go on!" She called to the owl from the doorway. "Go!!"

She watched from a distance as it fell sweeping down. The owl flew off into the great dark pine woods bordering the north side. In the vacuum left by her cathartic cry, Rhetta Bearce sat down on the gritty floor of the doorway, peaceful. For a moment she surveyed the garden. The shadow of the diner was shifting.

About to slip down into the dry grass, she noticed the cough balls lying near and picked up two. They were soft and dried, and, after a brief examination, she slid them into the pocket of her smock. Mrs. Bearce had an old birch burl bowl that she kept for such natural curios. Periodically she changed its contents, adding new things. These would make a nice addition to the tiny bird's nest, galls and colorful fungus she now kept in the bowl. From time to time she would feel the softness of the cough balls, remembering the owl's great horned face so near.

Beneath Mason Mountain, a tent sagged among the tangle of bug-eaten green. The Twitchell camp sat beside the stream where thriving mills once stood. Dark and weathered ostrich ferns, growing next to the pooled and sluggish stream, indicated where fiddleheads emerged in the spring. In the shade-dappled woods one could see the water level fallen owing to August drought. An extended spell of waterless weather showed in the dark and droopy green, and low water.

Here Chrischana's children bathed and washed out their under things, their jeans and socks. Wilting before the fire, the little family cooked their meals. But now a ban against burning was on, so they ate peanut butter and fruit from the Front Street Foodliner. Submerging milk in one of the stream's pools, they scarcely kept it cool. Chrischana had jobs babysitting and cleaning for rusticators. The money Balder had given her for the boys' support was still sitting in the bank, waiting upon her hope of Enan Pale selling at least part of the burned-out Twitchell Farm.

The old house was no more, and the land little more than stone. But there were still some large maples in the old dooryard, and the tall sugar maples, bristling downslope below the lost structure, held promise. Maple syrup could sell almost like liquid gold. She hoped to buy tubing, buckets, and an outdoor evaporator in order to process the sap next spring. Twitchell Farm Maple Syrup. It had a quiet sound, for a modest business. The sun will coax hidden life from underground roots by day, nighttime cold staying the flow until next day when it will rise again. The boys can tend the process too, boil the sap, watch it thicken. If they'll lift their feet, they'll earn—and learn—a lot from this. Chrischana almost grinned a secret sweaty grin.

All the dishes were in the stream on a sandbar before her. She scoured them with sand washed down from Mason's rocky sides in spring. Good cleaning agent, sand. The boys wash their jeans in it too. No pollution, no phosphates when there's lots of sand.

A distant sound... of engines... approaching through the woods.... In cutoffs and T-shirt, her brown braid lying along her breast, Chrischana stood looking over her shoulder toward the sound. Downstream and opposite, Nathan looked up from the pool where he sat submerged to his armpits. He had heard the engine before Mother, but was busy digging for artifacts, his fingers burrowed in the muck. Among his finds since moving to Mason's Mills were sand-smoothed bits of colored glass, bits of chipped stone that he thought were arrowheads, and some flakes of clear mica. Now, when he saw the dark gleams of the square vehicle jouncing through foliage, Nathan clambered quickly from the pool and splashed over to stand by Mother.

The shining Land Rover pulled to a stop at a discreet distance from the domestic scene, and two men, casually dressed, got out. At first neither were familiar to Chrischana. It was time now to face the fact of her trespass. But she was reluctant to leave this place. They were happy here and tired of moving, setting up camp anew each time. This place was to have been the last stop before home…. Is there a home?

The short, bespectacled blond man came straight to her, full of energy and zip. Something familiar about him, after all. He would suggest in a friendly way that there would be no need to call the authorities, provided…. The other man was tanned, darker, aloof; his face aquiline in profile, obscured in sunglasses. Avoiding glancing her way, he looked over the monstrous hewn foundation stones of the old mill and dam. He surveyed the surrounding terrain, the lay of the stream among rocky shoulders. The zippy younger man surprised her by extending his hand. He actually reached for hers before she could think to offer it. His grip was firm if brief.

"James Fay. Beautiful stream, Ms...."

The brother of Gloria, Balder's girlfriend…. She found her voice. "Twitchell, Chrischana Twitchell." Levelly she met his gaze, which glanced past her at once. She recognized him as the man who was always finding his way, unpleasantly, into the pages of *The Village Voter*. She felt Nathan nuzzling at her side, but she was not about to introduce him. James Fay was in a hurry. The other man was keeping his elegant distance.

Nuisance time, James Fay was thinking. A squatter. Just what we need to hold up the project. He had summed her up at once, noting the slogan on her T-shirt. *Imagine water*. Imagine no squalid squatters, he thought, saying again, "A beautiful setting, this stream. An old mill site, I understand."

Waiting, Chrischana said, "Yes."

"We're going to buy it," said Fay, not bothering to elaborate or soften.

"That so? Who owns it now I wondah?" She was inquiring politely, to pass the time. Mr. From Away caunt hurry me out of my dignity. Be interesting to see how busy-little-man puts it to me.

He thought better of his lack of elaboration, which might be useful in nudging this woman into place. Some other place. "You know Enan Pale. He owns a lot of these old places, sells stumpage off them."

"Hey!" exclaimed Nathan. "That's the man we want to buy Twitchell Farm from, Mother!" Nathan did not take his eyes off this sleek stranger. Fay was immaculate in chinos and open throat shirt. Nathan was fascinated by the thin gold chain around his neck, and the heavy gold ID bracelet on his wrist.

Chrischana smiled at Fay, rocking Nathan a little where she stood.

"Place on Blackwell Mountain that burned?" Fay was surprised, doubting they could afford anything…. But you never knew. Perhaps this is a happy coincidence. Taking them at their word instead of their looks is one way to deal with the situation.

"Thing is," reflected Chrischana, "He don't seem t'be interested in selling. Won't even see me. Probably thinks I don't have money—but I do." She smiled her half-smile.

Fishing in his breast pocket, James Fay came out with a card. "Take this to his office and say I sent you. Mr. Pale will see you."

She leveled her gaze at him again. "I'll do that, Mr. Fay. In fact, we'll go now." And she thought, I'm sure Mr. Golding will appreciate the privacy. She wasn't sure which Golding, but it certainly was a Golding.

"You do that!" James Faye looked with distaste at the dishes lying in the amber water on the sandbar.

Theodora raised eager unseeing eyes and set the receiver back in its cradle. She began pacing among the Thomas Mosher pieces in the open room, lacing and unlacing her slender fingers, fiddling with a loose strand of hair. Theo went into the dining area and ran a thoughtful hand along the perfect curve of an isolated Windsor chair. Gloria Fay was coming to dine, luncheon, next Thursday. Now there was planning to do, and it must be a memorable meal, absolutely gracious. She must make friends at last with James's sister.

Let me see.... Asparagus and potato soup? Not for a hot day. Something shrimpy, green and cool? A salad, iced tea? Simply fresh fruit for dessert: pineapple, strawberries, apricot, a hint of ginger.

Standing by the buffet she fidgeted, opened the drawer, pulled out two cookbooks. Will we be friends? We *will* be friends. Be positive.... So much in common. The International Institute for Coordinated Experiments. And James. What else? Gottheim. We both care for this humble old place.... We're going to make Gott'im shine. Some of the old fogeys are against it... but once the noise and rumbles subside—there'll be a cinema, more shops, a Bohemian coffee house. But it's more, a new spirit, an up-and-coming attitude! And everyone involved! That's what it's all about.

And love. She had glanced into the mirror over the buffet, saw her eyes shining. James Fay. We are so good together. Kind man, not like the ones who.... A Baptist! Of all things. Who would have thought I would ever consider being submerged in a tub—in front of a church full of people! Weren't Baptists rednecks down South? But there are classy black Baptist congregations—people with real intellect, leaders in the country. Weren't their churches instrumental in fomenting Civil Liberties?

Of course it's bigger than a tub. The Reverend, or whatever they call their ministers, will be there in the water with me. And others will be baptized and we'll all be robed....

Will we be engaged? The baptism will signify something... beyond dating. We're definitely dating. Surely Gloria will acknowledge that! She must acknowledge it merely by excepting my invitation.... I'll be baptized for God's sake!

This is all the stability Theodora Prescott has ever searched for. Being married, finding God in this way, will do it. No more looking here and there, high and low, like in the minister's sermon. Throw out a shelf full of New Age books, Eastern thought, fad psychology.... maybe even IICE. (James hates IICE.) Remember that brush with Catholicism? But this is it!

...What are doubts...? She wandered into the kitchen. Just think of James and a future with him. It settles you. Engaged, married. Yes. Or— no? Goose. Just wait. It will all appear at some point.... Come together. And this lunch—it will bring friendship, a type of intimacy with James's sister.

She noticed the kitchen, how it gleamed after Melvinia's cleaning. Theo knew she was lucky to get her after the diner closed. Melvinia Sessions does not mess around. She got the job done—if she did keep Theo in her place. Melvinia hated uppitiness in anyone. She makes cracks about people from away, mocking them behind their backs, commenting dryly to their faces. They must guess she doesn't think much of them. Well, she values practicality over—learnedness. Theo made a point to be respectful of Melvinia, dreading to think what she made of her. She didn't dare mention rebuilding Gottheim to her. Melvinia roared at such ambitions. "Reg'la Disneyland, this new Gott'im! When's Goofy coming? Donald Duck gont live he-ah too? They ski?" She started ticking them off on her fingers: "We got nevah-nevahland, Frontierland, Tomorrowland, New England. Meguntics had nothing until IICE took up with Goldings. Whoopee! Gont have a good time at last!"

Theo had laughed in spite of herself. She always did. Whenever the older woman got going, she saw her point as plain as pie. That's me, she thought.

Uniform in her flagrant inconsistencies, Theo. Whomever she was dealing with in this moment, that's where she found her identity, her definition. She was convinced of anything you put to her—as long as you stayed in the room. As long as her nose was still in your book, your editorial. When Balder rebuffed her efforts to bring psychological evaluation to Gottheim Chair, she had had to return to IICE for further encouragement in implementing them. Balder never did fill his out, and then he left to work in the paper mill. Only be convinced yourself, and you had her heart entire. Spend the afternoon and you could build your palace in her. In the evening someone else would have the throne.

James Fay saw much of this. She was his, he did not doubt. But what a watch she'd need. It would frustrate him, he knew. So he deliberated. There was time.

"You got that right," said gap-toothed Elmer Robbins to the older Lyman Bearce. Cup in hand, tugging on his ball cap, he moved away from the coffee machine to let large Robbie Robichaud have a turn. You-got-that-right-Robbins, Elmer was sometimes called.

People were coming and going in the early morning around the coffee pot in one of Buster Bearce's oil, gas, and convenience which were sprinkled throughout the county. It was just down the highway from where Decatur's Diner stood until recently. The store was cramped and dim and crammed with little convenient items.

"We don't get that rain," said Elmer, "fires gont get out of hand fast."

"Gusty's got get those permits tightened down," returned his boss Lyman Bearce, referring to the state capital, Augusta. He took a gulp of coffee and smoothed his great white beard. "No more permits till rain comes."

Robbie, the logging contractor and pulp truck operator, interjected. "Those trains is what's setting things to blazes—lighting that brush along the tracks."

The men around the coffee machine agreed. There was a letup in the heat today, but rain was still badly needed. All was tinder dry, the ground either like concrete or dust flying away. But fires showed, and volunteers were constantly on alert.

"Been in the woods lately?" Robbie continued. He was a big man, in his late fifties and dressed in soft green work clothes. "You can feel the static in the pine needles when y'walk."

"Evahbody wants t'know when the dust gont settle," said Elmer, referring to construction in the village. "I tell 'em when snow flies."

" 'S'about the size of it," returned Bearce. "Nothing'll stop the developers but a glacier. Tearing down's going on till you don't know the place."

"Least we got a cap on strip development, with that agreement the town got from them," said the contractor.

"Don't bet on it," returned the lumberman. "We put a check on Jaspa Mountain, but theya's plenty others coming. If you think folks won't sell along the highway, you're full o'shit. Money's too big."

You should say it, thought Robbie. He implied his thought by saying, "What's going in waya Decatur's was? Thought that'd be up and selling something by now."

Bearce actually smiled. "Just have t'wait'n see."

Robichaud drew back, faintly affronted, staring at the lumberman. "No secrets in this town. All comes out in town records, finds its way into *The Voter*. Nothing slips past."

"But you ain't heard nothing yet." Freckled Elmer smiled, feigning knowledge he didn't have.

Robbie thought he recognized that smile, and began to think Bearce had no buyer yet. Old bastid probably wants too much for it. He swallowed some coffee and changed conversational course. "That group of IICE's— what's it called—with all the meetings? Gut big changes in mind for the town."

Lyman Bearce almost chuckled. "You'n your rig got nothing to fear. Like to see 'em change the way you haul logs. Little girl, in heah come telling us—been heah generations—how to *fix* Gott'im!" He did not refer to Gloria Fay by name, and he had nothing to say about IICE and its community alliances and committees. "Gott'im needs fixing! Hell, she's cute, her'n those frigging little studies. Next thing she'll be telling us how to run sawmills. Maybe she's another Theodora Prescott."

The listeners around the machine guffawed but Lyman Bearce drank his coffee and looked disgusted. Theodora Prescott's furniture mill was a disgrace to all the mills around Gottheim.

"Like to invite Miss Fay to the veneer components mill'n show her how we bend wood." Elmer suggested this with a sly grin. "Wondah how she'd do under a jolt o'that juice?" He referred to the new technology for bending hardwood.

"You been hanging out with the boys fom the paper mill," said Robichaud, thinking protectively of his daughter Drusilla. *Either that or it's your fathers in you.* He recalled the story of a Robbins who stole settlers' children and sold them to Indians for spite. "Maybe you talk like that because you're afraid someone will call you good."

Elmer chastened his sneer into a grin. "Good's one thing I caunt be accused of!"

"Got that right!" someone mocked. The men around the coffee machine laughed.

Robbie Robichaud walked away. Lyman Bearce turned to watch him go out into the sun.

The two young women sat on the deck of Theodora's condo, looking out over the Meguntics through sparse leaves. The view of mountains was framed by tall gray birches and quaking aspen. Beyond the fluttering leaves, mottled mountains stretched beneath speckling clouds toward the mysterious heart of the state. The air about them was sweetly warm and dry. They had just finished the light lunch and were sipping iced coffee and cream.

Gloria sighed. "Just look at it. This is why I love it here." Her gesture took in the heavenly scene.

"And to think I've lived here all my life," enthused Theo. She so wanted the other to see her absolute fidelity to this place. (...In all but that abortive half term at Vassar.)

"Yes," said Gloria, dismissively. "But you know what I've noticed about people who have never lived anywhere else? They seem practically immune to this beauty. It's like they don't see it.... not Balder, though," she added.

Oh, there was a topic with which her hostess could impress Gloria. Theodora knew as much about the mechanic as anyone. After all, he had been in her employ for several years—until he went off to that awful paper mill; and they had practically been childhood chums... sort of. Gloria was attracted to Balder, had dated him earlier in the summer. But who wasn't attracted to Balder? Something had gone out of Gottheim Chair since his departure. The whole place seemed less substantial now, more rickety. Endangered. As though his absence revealed the company's decline.—Or actually precipitated it? Revealed it, caused it?—*Oh, I don't know.*

What she was certain of was her mounting unease, increasing sense that the place was a figment, doomed to ultimate—imminent?—collapse. Great-grandfather's once nationally prestigious manufactory! Gottheim Chair had always been there, the bulwark of her life, as fundamental as the woods or mountains. As a child she knew its magic, wandering its labyrinth of passages, compartments, strange great halls of machinery; discovering its hiding places. But, as an adult, she took it all for granted. Now she had offers, people wanting to buy—for its location. *To demolish it*! And, cringing every time she considered it, she was tempted.... But, if she allowed someone to obliterate the mill, dissolve its workforce, put up a ski shop or condominium... it would empty her life... point to the awful vacuity of her existence. What would she *do* without Gottheim Chair? What would she *be*? (—Maybe James's bride? If only—)

Yes, often she gave the mill only minimal attention.... Then again sometime she gave it *too* much, obsessively planning changes that weren't apt, without really understanding—anything to be involved in her ancestral concern. It wasn't until the void of Balder's absence that she realized how much the mill was part of her identity. My *raison d'être*! All coming to an end? Oh Balder, can't you see—they want to tear it down!

It had all been moiling around in her mind for weeks. The new relationship with James was comforting, hopeful, and Gloria was here at last... but these things would surface unexpectedly. Naturally, like organic scum on a stream or in a well. Now, slowly, she responded to Gloria's statement about Balder. Her tone was careful, measured and out of character. "Yes, Balder sees things... to some extent. The beauty he sees. But some things he misses entirely. And other people—well...." Thinking of the jobs that would be lost if the mill went, she added, "People here work so hard. Actual workaholics. So they can't always notice the beauty."

"Alcoholic, too—they aren't making enough money here, you know." This response from Gloria was a trifle pointed. She stopped, then went on. "But Balder?—miss something about the mountains?" It was both leading and impatient. Theodora's feeble grasping after insight did not interest her, not when the woman paid her employees so little. *She practically pulled up to the door and <u>drove</u> Balder to the paper mill.* Gloria could be fastidious in her low-key display of respect for Theodora. She would not crush the woman's self-esteem (what there is of it) with a reckless demeaning of her. I can't abide that. I will be bored donkey's days if it will spare someone so fragile a little humiliation. People accused you of patronizing, but how else can you be kind?

She said, "But you are right that he can miss—well, like when it comes to the interests and needs of women in the 80's. Let's face it, he's a Neanderthal at his dressiest."

Theo could not bring herself to fine-tune what she was getting at. To do so would reveal her insecurities. She couldn't do that until she felt... until she discovered just how acceptable she was to James's sister. The cozy feeling she had hoped for was eluding her.

She swished the ice cubes around in her glass, thoughtfully. Suddenly she burst, "What can you make of his going to work in that place? He never cared so much for money before, and that's the only reason they work there. He might find mechanical work engaging, but that's not it. Not in that place." She reached for the pitcher and began pouring more iced coffee.

Gloria said, "He wants to renovate that old house of his, and wood mill wages are notoriously low—at least they would be notorious where I come from. Isn't that why they're workaholics—so they can survive?"

The implication was rude... but perhaps unintentional... yet Theo took it in her usual way; as though it was not meant for her. In company she'd gloss over a slight... only to feel its force later when alone. Then it would undo her. But now she agreed casually, and picked up the topic.

"Renovate *Simons Ledge*!? The whole thing? He'd be better off tearing down all but the central house. He should take off all that clapboard. I think that's an original log house under there. It could be a real piece of rustic Americana."

"He does intend something like for that part he calls the settlers house. But he's also got these ideas for the rest of it... a real familial setup that makes my head spin thinking of it." She stopped.

"Really?" Theodora held still, expectantly.

But Gloria would not be prodded. She could not bring herself to share a confidence with a woman whose mind was like a restaurant table after a party of eight. Whatever her relationship with Jimmy! No intention of involving myself in *that*.

The pause embarrassed Theo. Rushing to fill the silence she said, "Balder has a son now, I guess, and he's all worked up over parenting... like a kid in a candy factory. Who wouldn't want to be loved like that after being alone so long? We all knew there was something to the Chrischana-Balder thing, but thought it would progress to marriage.... as things did in Gott'im back then. People didn't get pregnant or if they did and didn't marry, the girl had to leave in disgrace. If he had known, he would have married her. It wouldn't have occurred to anyone that she wouldn't want to! But, not knowing why she left.... well, he never made it to college like he planned. Can you imagine someone with a broken heart taking refuge in Vietnam! He could have been designing state-of-the-art furniture mills, walking around in a suit with a roll of blueprints under his arm. Can you picture it?"

Gloria grinned over the conjured image, but a private look passed into her gaze and she turned from Theo's eager face toward the shadow-dappled array of mountains.

Theo turned away too, disappointed over the other's aloofness. *We will never be sisterly. Never.*

Evening. Theodora is on the deck again, standing at the rail, a glass of white zinfandel beside her elbow. She must have her wine now for James will be here soon. He is a faithful abstaining Baptist. She looks out toward the hushed contours of evening's rest. But, like the trembling leaves of quaking aspen beyond the rail, Theo is restive, her thoughts a turmoil of old faces.

The faces of her father and his cronies, the mill owners of yesterday. They mingle with contemporary faces, older now, the ones owning the mills today. When she was a little girl, they came to the house in Gottheim—the old faces—to play cards, smoke cigarettes or cigars, schmooze. Only they didn't call it that then. It was simply the old-boy jokes they shared between them, grinning. I bet they are at it still. Only they never dare include me. How could they? Theodora Prescott, mill owner. It's a silly oxymoron.

She swallows the wine. *But it is true... what I heard as a child, playing beneath the card tables....*

Apparently her memory had submerged it... until Gloria's remark of this afternoon... coming back to her now, its pointedness growing until it pierces. They don't need to include me. I'm included *en famille*. It was all fixed decades ago. Like the wages of the workers. No one would make more than what the mill owners, together, decided. The stewards of the community....

Leaning over the rail, anguish in her thin gut, Theodora trembles. She jerks herself up, knocking the long-stem glass with its contents down into the junipers below. It's no different from the publicized squeeze put on pulp truck operators by the paper mill. No—it's worse than that. That was done by strangers, absentee owners. These employers are related to the community—my relatives, some of them, for godsake!

My relatives, me. Demeaning the labor of people.... –There's practically no one here not related. Among generations of locals, if not by blood, then by marriage. Why do we keep doing it to ourselves!?... Can I look them in the eye... Lyman Bearce, Enan Pale, the others—and say it?

Theo feels her face twisting, bleared with tears. All my little plans for improving Gottheim Chair. For lifting the employees up on some fantastic cloud. She can hear Melvinia's happy mockery: "When's Goofy coming, Donald Duck?" The shame of it piercing through her thoughts, making a shambles of Theodora's mind. Balder's scorn of her silly plans—sticking to her like burdock and nettles.

Teary-eyed, she looks up at the rustling popples. Unceasingly rustling. She turns, withdraws into the townhouse, closing the French doors with a click. Anyone looking up was bound to see her there, toiling in tears... someone bound to hear her crying. If only I could flee, anonymous.

Can Gloria have known?

She stumbles through the living room, wiping tears. Did she find out somehow?... Someone telling her? Unthinkable... even with all our studies. No one would tell. Who knew to tell besides the conspirators?

What if... oh God, I cannot confront Lyman Bearce. Someone powerful like that? What would he do if I did?

Throw me in the booby hatch, that's what! And they would all back him! They'd get into the files at IICE, or ferret it all out somehow, and *throw* me to the loonies!

"Woman's finally gone off her rocker. We always knew. Caunt count on a thing she says. What's needed is pity: Theodora Prescott—

madwoman!"

In woods beneath a shelf of Jasper Mountain towering above the Simon house, Benaiah Twitchell discovered a monolith: horizontal, long, and maybe seventy feet high, merging with the steeply wooded slope behind. It was possible, the old settlers knew, by circuitous route to bypass the ledge above and come down from remoter reaches, to walk the great rock and gently descend to the forest floor above the house. Surveying it, Benaiah did not discern the monolith's vast and mysterious connections with the giant soaring distant and far: far beyond the house, the rock, and his own young thought. He saw only the great face of this rock, split here and there with slender trees, and topped with more bristling forest. In places it trickled water from some secret source. To him the great rock was of storybook proportions, the grandfather of all stones. In moister days a stream ran under it, cooling and full, falling down toward the pond well below. Even today, in the midst of the driest season Gottheim had seen in three decades, there were pools, soft dark earth and green things growing; because of those trickles from the rock. He looked in the damp spots and saw the split imprints made by the dainty feet of deer. He also saw their round droppings in the streambed between its rooty banks.

To Benaiah, reader that he was—and Daniel read to them, the great rock was like something out of *The Hobbit*. He thought of the road to Rivendell and of Mirkwood. Trolls might have been formed out of rocks like this one. Following between the streambed and the giant rock, he saw the rock sloping down toward him, and discovered that he could easily climb the slope to come out atop it. From there he looked out in the direction of the house hiding among the trees, toward the pond and village, yet he saw only trees. He turned away and wandered over the surface among the popples, maples, beeches, birches, until he came to a tight group of three trees. He walked around them, speculatively, thinking he might build himself a deer stand.

Benaiah shimmied up one stem, grabbing a branch, hooking it with his arm and then a leg. He hoisted himself into the tree. Now he climbed higher and looked out. There was a corner of the pond and roof of a mill. Distantly, he thought he heard the drone of its separator. And dust was stirring here and there. Remotely, the clock in the tower above the Congregational Church struck the half-hour.

Working on the project over the afternoon and next morning, Ben made progress. He dragged bits of two-by-four, scraps of plywood; carried hammer and nails—all from Balder's rebuilding project. He had rope to help him climb, and haul up the scraps and tools. For hours he worked, hoisting and hammering. Sometimes he stopped and looked out into the trees or down to the rocky leafy mossy mushroomy floor. Excited, he thought of deer bear coy-dogs raccoon bobcat fox, all coming into range. You could really do something here, in these woods.

Little by little he had got used to Gottheim, and to the woodland that once terrorized him. He remembered the way he had paced the woodland track, hoping for Mother's return—when they first came to Maine and had to camp in Abenaki Notch. Trees trees trees, nothing but trees. No telling how long you could stay lost in them... endless maze, every turning like the last. There was no way to tell here from there. Hardly any houses to be seen— when any house was safety, security. From the window of the Bonneville he looked for houses, seeing miles between each one. A long road from Phoenix had sharpened the little Twitchell family's longing for home, for Mother's grateful Gott'im, as she called it. But, when they found it, to Ben it was no place at all. Trees. Only trees... and rocks, and the fear of being lost.

But now Benaiah saw houses everywhere. They lined the road, packed and populated the rural world he was coming to know. And the country was becoming a city to him, filled with what he wanted, things to do. The woods held out the promise of exciting encounters.... Especially if Balder would let him use his hunting rifle this fall. It was a beautiful nut-brown 30-30, and Benaiah was aching to try it. Maybe, if Balder saw how hard he worked on this deer stand.... well, the man was sure to let him use a gun.

Balder likes to see people doing things for themselves. Don't like to see'em lying like lumps in front of TV. Summer reruns of The Ninja and Knight Rider aren't awesome to him. Mrs. Simon took care of wild animals, but Ben knew for fact that there was deer meat in the freezer. Balder got his buck last year. Even Mother got deer when she was young.

Having just sweated it into place, he stretched out on the small scrap of plywood but found it far from level. Phooey! But—good enough. He peered over the edge. Two scraps to hoist up, then back for more to make the railing, a place to rest a gun barrel.

He sat up, leaning against the trunk. Ah. My first little house. I can bring my blankets up here, make money raking leaves this fall then buy a Coleman stove. Cook breakfast right up here!

Benaiah squinted out the sights of an imaginary rifle. He began sighting along the forest floor, carefully aiming.... He touched the trigger.... What's that in the leaves? He held his breath. It was a deer. No, two deer! A red one, and a white.

Posey and Sugarloaf!

Always he had hoped to see them. Softly they approached, browsing on the leaves. And he looked on. He watched for several minutes, until they knelt among a clump of seedling fir. Resting, they lay, chewing chewing chewing.

What would they do if they saw me? he wondered. Bet they'd let me near.... Posey and Sugarloaf.

He leaned out a bit from the platform, calling softly. Posey looked up, watching momently. She kept chewing, turned away. Sugarloaf looked, too. But the fawn turned to white china, staring as though a statue, with eyes like pink glass.

Every time he went into the woods below Simons Ledge he brought something from one of Elda's tins. But he had never seen a deer nor had a chance to offer anything. Now he felt in his pockets for peanuts. He had filberts, too. So, still looking down on them, he held out a peanut, saying softly,... "Peanut Posey, peanut." And she pointed her face up at him. He saw the delicate fluttering of her black nostrils, the mild white rings around her eyes. She was nervous, but, if he was careful....

He turned and began feeling his way down, sneakers pressed against the trunk, the rope cutting into his palms. All the while he spoke softly of the peanut. Maybe Posey will even smell Mrs. Simon on the peanut. Didn't she say molecules of things and people stick to other things? And that's how animals pick up scents. Makes sense. (He smiled over the homophone. Daniel would.) "Peanut Posey, peanut."

His patience paid. Standing now, the deer briefly stayed as he let loose the rope. Softly he approached, holding out the treat.

Gently, Posey picked the peanut from his fingers. He held out another for her fawn. The small white deer stretched for it, and Ben looked down on him, studying his form. The great pink eyes, pink insides of its ears, white bristles softly trimming the delicate features. How thin and strange its limbs, like dainty sticks. The nervous innocence of its spirit appealed unconsciously to Ben. His eagerness abated.

He emptied his pockets to the deer and brushed their coats with his palms. Sugarloaf seemed attentive to his mother, as though connected by invisible threads. Taking cues from her, it was as if the fawn had no thought but Posey's thought.

All of Benaiah's own thought was set on them. In feeling their noses with his palm as they picked up each nut, touching the hairs of their hides, he thought of their molecules mingling with those of his hand. Seeing them with attentive eyes, the image of deer imprinted him with their truth. He might have gone into the forest with them, a deer inhabiting Benaiah's body.

Why would anyone want to shoot a deer? No one could pull a trigger on Sugarloaf.... would they?

But he had eaten meat from Balder's deer. Even Balder had pulled the trigger on an eight point buck last year.... *I was building—I was going to shoot one.* It's true what Mrs. Simon said. Posey would wind up on the dinner table.... Sugarloaf end up a statue—stuffed. All because he was white as a sugar cube and a good target.

Still rubbing their sides, Ben thought very carefully. *What if Sugarloaf wasn't white?* Couldn't his coat be dyed? Maybe made two-tone, like camouflage to hide his hide. He smiled over the double meaning. It was something Daniel would think of, and Ben did because of his brother's influence. "Hide your hide, Sugarloaf," he whispered, rubbing him.

The boy looked through the stems and understory of young hardwoods and firs. He listened to make sure no one was around. He looked back down at Sugarloaf, struck by the contrast he made with the greenery. If he could carry the fawn away from this interwoven greenness, off this great rock (even if it was buried in woodland far from the road).... Benaiah wanted to bring Sugarloaf down to their bedroom at *Simons Ledge*.

Now, seeing that the nuts were no longer forthcoming, the deer knelt down again among the seedling fir. Ben saw that they wanted to rest. Softly he stole from them and headed for the sloping end of the big rock. When he was down by the streambed he quickened his pace and made straight for the Simon house.

What would she have that I could use to color his hide? He had to hurry, do the job today before they disappeared somewhere up on the mountainside. Think dummy, think. Maybe food coloring in the kitchen cupboard? Mix them together and make a muddy mess? He had experimented making frosting once back in Phoenix. For sugar cookies. And Daniel had laughed at them and asked if he had used Ritz dye. Sugarloaf will be so ugly that no one will want him even if they could see to shoot him. But how do you apply it?

His mind busy with possibility, Ben came down toward the house. You could see it better now that Balder had hacked away some of the old lilacs and vines. From the roof of the children's house came the sound of hammering. As he approached, Ben could hear Nathan's incessant nattering, as Dad would have called it, but muffled and indistinct. Brat was probably upstairs driving Balder up a wall.

Once inside, he made a quick pit stop, then crossed to the knotty pine cupboards. He pulled himself up on the sideboard and opened the cupboard door. He peered inside and began rummaging among small containers of sweet basil, dill, oregano and chili powder. Where were some things of food coloring? Doesn't she ever bake cookies? He hardly heard the approach of the others, though Nathan was squeaking away about dorky Cabbage Patch Kids.

"Need help?" asked the man, seeing Ben settle back in disgust on the countertop. What choo afta?"

"Food coloring," was the terse reply.

"Caunt 'memba last time I saw food coloring. Might be some up top, though." He reached up into the highest shelf, behind the dusty jars full of macaroni and dried elderberries. "Food coloring!" He handed down a small box containing colored vials.

"What's *that* for?" asked Nathan.

"I was curious about that, too, but didn't think it polite to ask."

"Nathan knows nothing about that!" growled Ben. "I'd tell you but *he'd* mess up my plans."

"Caunt have that!" said Balder cheerfully, grinning at Nathan. "You ain't been to the barn t'see what mother's got out theya today. Ain't had a chance, we been talking all morning." He raised his voice as Nathan headed for the door. "Don't go touching those raccoon kits. They look cuddly enough, but you dassn't."

"OK," said Nathan, slamming the screen door as he went.

Ben slipped down from the countertop. "I was building a deerstand up there'n I saw Posey'n Sugarloaf'n had this idea to help'em." He stopped to see how Balder was receiving it.

Arms crossed, the man leaned against the sideboard, his thoughtful gaze on Benaiah's freckled face and green eyes. Stroking his dark beard, he said, "Yuht.... Go on."

"Well... they're up there in the trees, resting on that giant rock—the one with trees on top and a brook under it?"

"Great rock."

"I could dye Sugarloaf so hunters don't shoot him this fall. If I mix these colors, they turn brown." He shook the coloring box.

"Well... lots oh' things come to mind about this plan and I can see you're in a hurry t'get back up theya—but I got my doubts about the permanence'o this dye. First rain come along might wash it off. Clothes dye'd be betta, but we have to buy some. Time we got back they'd be gone."

Ben's face fell as Balder continued. "That don't mean you caunt have it on hand, case they show again sometime.... But consider this."

The blond darkly bearded man moved away from the sideboard and began to wander about the kitchen, occasionally stroking his beard or talking with his hands. "Seems like you seen something special about

Sugarloaf. ... But you was up theya building a deerstand, getting all set to get your first buck."

"You got one last year," said Ben, watching him.

Balder grinned. "Deer's here partly coz other critters got eat. Eating out of the woods means seeing your food before its dead'n watching its death throes.... Instead of picking up a package of meat at the market."

"But he's special, like you said. So is Posey." He turned and began taking lids off the tins on the sideboard, filling his pockets with nuts.

"Yuht. We know em'n that makes'em special."

"They act... so... gentle...." He wanted to say more but didn't know how.

"Trusting, too. They can tell how we feel about 'em."

"Yeah," said Ben, awe lighting his face.

"So naturally we want save'em. Don't want no black barrel aiming down on them." Still talking, he went to the refrigerator, rummaging for sandwich fixings to put on the sideboard. He got bread from the bread box and began making sandwiches. It was as though he were thinking aloud as he went on addressing all to Benaiah.

"Maybe everything's got its destiny. Not that every step's cut in concrete on into the distance. Theya's what you might call leeway—f'what you will. Take Sugarloaf. All white. It happened, so we got take it into account. But he's not just some albino fluke o'nature *the end*. He's an albino buck born to Posey on Jaspa Mountain in Gott'im Maine with friends by the name of Benaiah, Balda, grandmother, etc..... take into account that he's born in a world that wants to fix him in Time by claiming a li'l of his glory, to show it off a bit. ...Stuff and mount him to make their own li'l lives seem more colorful. But there's us, the others that want to see him run free—in beauty. Maybe t'nevah get a glimpse of him again. ...Or, maybe see him once in a while high on a ridge, pure white and crowned with a mighty rack. It's all this he was born into."

Ben was listening hard, snared in the complexity of Sugarloaf's life.

Balder continued. "We're scared to have Sugarloaf end up dead, stuffed, others gawking at'em, shaming his glory, stealing his life. Because we love him."

His gaze upon Balder, Ben nodded.

"His maker might've felt the same when making Sugarloaf. Maybe feels like that about everything made and while planning what to make.

"Maybe They was sitting at the kitchen table talking, the Maker and His Friend. All manner of creation flows off them during the conversation: spiders, worms, lilies, clouds, peas, nuthatches, chickadees, bumblebees, red foxes, ravens, voles, asteroids, planets, suns and some of that gaudy stuff like palm trees, frangipani, scarlet macaws'n crocodiles.

"He's saying, We'll give the people free will so they can decide what they'll do. We don't want to make puppets, do we?

"She says, but if we give'em free will, it means letting them do what they want in creation in accordance with its laws. And we could give them Time to be builders on it with us.

"He's glad She says this. So He says, They can learn about us that way.... Things like what kind of spirit to have when they go get their food.

"But then one of'em says, That means designing, creating it in beauty and just handing it over. What if they in't trustworthy? Should we just give'em a white deer'n let them shoot it, stuff it'n stare at it? Let that neat deer get all moth-eaten and dusty?

" 'N the other one comes back with something and they go on like this, back-and-fourth polite like, f'the equivalent of one trillion years or so. At some point during the conversation, the Maker has a … a small… — takes from his pocket a hard something in His hand. May be like a marble. Sometimes he rubs it gently with two thumbs, thinking strong and tender thoughts about the coming creation. Then it grows a bit."

Balder looks over at Benaiah to see if he's still with him.

"One day His son coming, stops by and says, Ma'am, Sir, you still talking about that?

"Whole lot'o nodding, What do *you* think?

"Considering, There's *something*... but let me think it ovah a while, and the son goes his way to a favorite thinking place, some rock overlooking the water somewhere, or a big rock in the woods, comes back a few thousands years later, saying, What you need's someone go down theya and mumble around with 'em, show'em we're heah. Y'caunt just get a guitar'n start with a cool riff unless someone shows you how and where to put your fingers. Waya's the inspiration? You show me how to respect creation'n I'll go down with'em.

"So they all agree'n off he goes, comes down—out Mary's womb in Bethlehem.... Kinda like Sugarloaf come out of Posey on Jaspa Mountain."

Balder scraped excess mustard from the knife back into the jar. He looked over at Ben, having stopped and started on the sandwiches several times. "You knew they mounted Him on the cross—? Good Friday, Easter and all. But that's waya the destiny comes in. Where Sugarloaf's and all our destinies come in. Ben, someday I might walk into the lobby at Jaspa Mountain Lodge'n see our white deer mounted theya. But. He'll be gone. And I'll just be looking at his fine clothes."

Shaking his head, Balder stacked the sandwiches on the plate. "That don't mean I won't be sad. I'd be awful sad to see him standin' theya.

Maybe that's his Maker, showing us how it feels."

Balder looked at the boy. "You believe that story, Ben?"

Slowly Benaiah nodded. His eyes had been looking far away, but now they looked up at Balder. The boy nodded again, saying softly, "I do."

Balder grinned. "I was hoping."

He pushed the sandwiches toward Benaiah and went to the door, saying, "Gut to get your brother." His hand on the screen door, he turned. "By the way, Mutha might just have something to say about that deer stand of yours being on this side of the mountain." He thought a moment. "She's probably too shy to say it, though. I hunt in townships north of here. You can come with me this year—if you want."

He pushed through the screen door, letting it slam behind. Ben saw him disappear into the glare.

Greenhouse Gott'im

Dear Editor,

Following our joyous encounter with Gottheim's Jasper Mary Day, we decided to search out the sights of her life for ourselves. Imagine our horror upon discovering that awful tire dump at the site where her treasure is supposed to be hidden. This immense and hideous hoard is kept behind a wide strip of trees, but does that matter when millions of dangerous old tires are piled up behind it in monstrous black mountains? How this has been allowed in our beautiful little Township of Quaker, and sanctioned by the DEP, is beyond me. You've written about greenhouse gas in your editorials, well, what do they suppose will happen to the air if those piles catch fire? Also, imagine the groundwater, our precious well water, being contaminated with oil from a meltdown there.

Why, may I ask, is Ceylon Segar permitted—nay, *encouraged*—in this outrageous misuse of the property by the very department supposed to be protecting the environment? We appeal to the authorities (both publicly in this letter and in a copy to their offices) *to think*! This part of the state is less and less the paradise we supposed on moving here. It's enough to turn us into rabid environmentalists! Make no mistake, Mr. and Ms. Legislator. We shall sue if anything happens to those tires!

Jamie and Frederick Sludlinger
Quaker Plantation

Dear Editor,

People in Gottheim have known me all my life—my relatives, neighbors and friends. They know the kind of man I am, really. A man who helped raise money for the Knights of Christos Christmas fund. I donated labor and materials to help rebuild the burned-out places of my fellow townsmen when their own houses caught fire. I served on your boards and committees, volunteering many hours to help keep our town viable. Working together in these various organizations and activities, we joked and laughed, told stories of town life, and just plain knew each other as you can't help doing in a place like Gottheim.

It was a terrible verdict, taking away my name and freedom over something I am innocent of. It was not premeditated murder that put my wife Albinia under concrete in the Pine Hill condominiums. Everyone knows that Albinia and I had a good enough relationship. We did have a passionate relationship, but she would not want to see me sitting here in Thomaston for what happened between us that awful night. I know this beyond doubt, and am asking you to consider the situation in its proper perspective. You know there's no real murder in my heart, just as Albinia knows it there where she is in heaven. I am certain she has forgiven me, just as she always did.

Yes, her death was terrible, but understand. Domestic violence is not the same as violence between strangers. We are, were, flesh and blood people no different than any couple. No different than any of you. And with strong personalities such as ours, there's bound to be passion enter into what would have been regular arguments and disagreements. But you can't make that the same as violence between people who don't know each other, aren't married and so forth. You all know I loved Albinia and would take back what happened, if I only could. It was an accident. I was scared and so did what I shouldn't, namely the concrete. A mistake and I'm sorry. I should have called the police immediately.

God knows my heart and that I am now a born-again Christian, forgiven by God but in need of forgiveness by my neighbors. Please folks. You know me. Have worked with me, eaten with me, had good times together. Let me hear from you in my hour of need. Look into your own hearts and see if you can recognize me and Albinia there in your own relationships. She wouldn't want you to turn your backs on me.

Ithiel Whitman
[State Prison]

Dear Editor,
This is just to thank the people of Gottheim for the neighborly assistance in the crisis we have with Uncle Cyrus Brook in Jericho this summer. We're grateful for the gift of water from Hutchins Pond since the brook all but dried up this month. Seeing

the water truck pull up at the town office loaded with your good clean water (which we can't get even though we're on the Arossagunticook River) really lifted our spirits here. The folks outside Jericho Village proper were all set—that is, the ones whose wells didn't dry up. The rest of us are glad to see water again.

We might even have to postpone the opening of school because we can't support the needs of the building till we get water again. The hydrologist from the US Geological Survey has blamed the water failure on last winter and spring when we didn't get the necessary rain and snow amounts to keep aquifers up where they need to be this time of year. The unusually dry weather has near dried up Uncle Cyrus at its sources, at least till we get good rain. Since the middle of July we've had only 0.15 in. when normal for the same period would be 0.60. But it's been a year or two since anything was normal, and we're hurting now.

We've never seen it this low. Just hope and pray the good Lord knows what this is all about and see we get our rain this fall, if not sooner. And the people all said amen.

Alfred Tuttle, selectman
Town of Jericho

"Trout's hurting," said Hannibal Poulin to Pete Prince and Balder Simon at lunch. "Layin'low in pools where they ah easy pickings fah raccoon, mink, crittas like that.... In't enough water to float a frog, some places."

They were up on deck outside the new co-generating conveyor building, above Arossagunticook River, overlooking on either side the twin towns of Guildford and Spain. Their hardhats were off and the stinky breeze blew on them, carrying off sweat from their paper mill labor. The steam of papermaking poured off, blowing down valley between the two towns. High overhead thin smoke, from a combination of bark and chipped tires, burned off into the atmosphere high above the houses and businesses. The scrubbers would have eliminated the smoke entirely, but there were bugs in the system just now.

"In't but half of it though?" agreed Simon. "What's spawning gont be like come fall? Fishing'll be down two years. Look't that water down theya. Evah seen it s'low?"

Looking down from five stories where they could see lavender brown shallows beneath the scuzzy surface, Hannibal Poulin shook his dark head. He had a beard and it waggled as he talked. "Nevah. They said this watershed's worst hit in the state."

"We usually get less rain in the mountains, but you'd think snow melt'd make up for it." Simon said this and took a bite of his liverwurst sandwich. "Not this year."

"The mill keeps it low on purpose, does it?" asked Pete Prince. An apprentice millwright to papermaking, he was new in the state as well.

Poulin answered, "They prac'ly own the water. Got to balance the amount available with what's needed for waste treatment'n storage. They like to have four months worth stored to get through wintah."

Prince took a swallow of Coke and wondered aloud about the number of squirrels on the road. "Keep hitting those things. Drive along the highway and suddenly, *thunk crunch*, there's another dead one in the rearview mirror." His face was ravaged, but there was humor in it and widely spaced light eyes, greenish. He was a likable guy with a Midwestern accent. Something familiar about him Balder thought, as the man continued. "You're driving, see one coming, try to brake, but the damn thing can't make up its li'l pea-sized mind whether it's coming or going, crossing or not crossing. But you're doing 55 with one of those honking huge logging trucks on your bumper. *Thunk crunch*, another smashed squirrel. They go like that all year?"

Simon grinned. "Usually see a lot o'that in the spring, early summer. Theya young squirrels—don't know no better. Theya was a bumper crop'o acorns'n beech nuts built up the population last year. Now, with the drought there's not much fah them to feed on. Last spring theya was a record litter count. Guess they feasted'emselves to the brink of famine." He grinned again.

"Fire danger's worst thing," said Poulin. He had opened a carton of milk and, after a swallow, blotted his mustache on his grimy shoulder. "Color's gont be off this year. Maybe it'll keep the leaf peepers off the road though. Those buses is worse'n pulp trucks any day. Tour bus drivers just don't know how t'drive two lane mountain roads. Saw one almost run off the highway last year when he wasn't expecting that passing lane to end."

Prince raised a skeptical eyebrow. "I dunno. Those trucks look like they carry a whole damn forest full of tree trunks. They call 'em pulp trucks: you get a load dropped on you in one of those curves—you're mashed to pulp. *Thunk crunch*."

Simon grinned. "Where you from? The desert? Cleveland?"

"In fact," he answered, smiling, "I lived both places, one time or another."

"My wife's name is Twitchell. Our kids are under her name 'cause it's a common-law marriage."

Peter Prince was sitting across from an alcohol abuse counselor in the large grubby room of a house-shop on Main Street in Jericho. He had been in the mountains only a short time, and this was his first real friendship. He had met Hermann Gottesman at an AA meeting two weeks ago. Hermann was a vast, powerfully built fat man, balding, with a ponytail and a surprisingly tiny voice. In aiding his fellow alcoholics Gottesman found a meaningful outlet for his somewhat desperate passion.

He ran a cafe in Jericho, downriver from Spain, an oddity attracting disaffected high school students, kids seemingly uninterested in cars, sports, dates and clothes, with a bent toward self-expression philosophy books art or other weirdness. Gottesman was adamant about keeping out the drugs, even cigarettes for the underage, but he provided an otherwise free atmosphere where kids could talk and drink sodas or coffee and play games like chess and Scrabble, but also pool and ping-pong. Over in the corner were Pacman and Atari for the electronically inclined.

It was 10 a.m. and the two men sat across from one another on dilapidated couches in the midnight blue *Kids Cafe*. The door was open and a beam of sunlight fell into the dark interior, full of dust motes and smoke. There was also dingy light from the front and side windows. Peter Prince was referring to the vast void left in Chrischana's wake when she ran from Phoenix with the boys; leaving him alone with the strange idea that she no longer believed him sincere in his repentances: "Sometimes I can't blame her, and sometimes I hate her for leaving." He exhaled, staring up at a smoke ring slowly rising to disband. He took another drag on his cigarette, saying, "After she left I'd binge, and hate her. Before she left, I'd binge... and then hurt her. Hell, Hermann, why do I have to say these things? All this goddamn honesty stuff.... Yeah, I figured I could handle it and my hurtin'her days were over.... but then I think, Wait, I said all this before, felt all this before... and it always came back again. The uncontrollable rage. So, I admit it to myself. Shouldn't that be enough to make it go away?— confess your sins and all that?"

"Should it?" prompted Gottesman, solemn-eyed and bespeckled. He had a degree in psychology and another in philosophy from an early stage of his career to the bottom and back again. Since then there'd been training in substance abuse counseling. Now he was a committed 12-stepper who had salvaged existence with the aid of Higher Power. After his last detox seven years ago, in New Hampshire, he had come to Jericho following a detour home to New York, found this boarded-up derelict storefront, rented and equipped it with used appliances and furniture, put in a bed for himself in a back room. On top of one of the many bookcases lining his wall sat a large piece of pegmatite, stone blocky with huge grains of mica, feldspar and quartz. He called it his Higher Power, not out of superstition, but as a symbol of what was above him that he could not see. Desolation in his formative years had blocked such beliefs from him. Hermann Gottesman was immensely strong. It had taken a long acquaintance with alcohol to convince him of something stronger. His habit was stronger than himself, taking everything from him. Now, every day, he had to rediscover that there was Something stronger than either of them.

Peter opened a fresh pack of Viceroys and lit one. He exhaled and said, "Before I found out... while I was finding out that college wasn't for me, I was assigned a short story I couldn't get out of my head. Can't remember the author but the title sticks t'you like a burr. 'A Good Man Is Hard to Find.' Story about this 'good Christian woman' who called strangers 'good men'—even one who was about to kill her. Her own son she condemned to death without a thought. That's me, that's my mother." He said it with bitterness.

Hermann nodded. "Flannery O'Connor's story. Acclaimed, but has its flaws. Parts of it are unconvincing. Other parts are quite chilling." He took a swallow from the liter bottle of Coke that he kept by his side. Now, looking at the haggard but handsome face of Peter Prince, he understood that the green-eyed man was in line for destruction... if he left the course he had set in stopping at Alcoholics Anonymous. If he turned around in the middle of this road, he would be destroyed.

"Hermann. I have an awful twisted—twisted feeling sometimes. Like I feel myself slipping... mentally. A godawful rage. I think something evil is just around the corner, waitin' to nab me—sometime. Other times—it completely slips my mind. Then I think, That evil guy's not me. He's gone forever.... And I feel like, Hell, I'm here in Maine—I'll just drive over to Gott'im and drop in on Chrischana'n the boys. Just for a visit." His gaze had been drifting around the room, slipping now from Hermann's almost tonsured-looking balding head into his eyes. "What do you think about that, Hermann?"

Hermann's answer was prompt. "I think it's a very good sign that you're willing to ask someone else what they think. You're beginning to get that you don't know everything about this disease. That maybe you do need counseling." And he thought, without saying, You're still flip-flopping back and forth between remembering and forgetting this fact. He had seen Peter Prince's bull-necked bravado more than once. The nature of self is glib, making self-understanding a very slippery business. You wanted to lecture, tell clients what's what, but it wouldn't communicate.

Prince ran his restive fingers over the frayed arm of the couch. Humbly he said, "And your counsel would be?..."

"To wait. Wouldn't you expect a great deal of emotion being mixed into a meeting like that? That it wouldn't really be just a casual undertaking?"

"Nothing casual about it," he admitted. "It'd be a big thing for all of us. Like going through the de-barker over at the mill." He formed an o with his lips, breathing out another smoke ring. It rose, wafting toward the light of the open door.

(Editorial): We don't usually comment on the national, international, or planetary in this space. We try to stick to the hometown issues, keep things simple. What kind of place is Gottheim? How can we help make it better? Should we keep Front Street as our Main Street in Gottheim, or should we allow a mini mall on the highway, complete with post office, to replace it? Do we want directional signs uniform and small, clustered, or strung out along the highway. Do we mount a campaign to keep chain stores out, or should we encourage their presence to provide the nearby, lower-priced alternative? Are we maintaining perspective and balance on the local environmental and economic fronts? These and other subjects most often occupy this space. This town and its neighbors are properly our sphere of concern, and we look to our community if we are to be happy and well, raise our children safely.

Yet today we want to shift the focus outward, wider; perhaps look down upon little Gottheim from a distance, and then look out around us to the atmosphere surrounding our tiny community. We may have to blink back tears caused by the smoke of spot fires. Up here we can plainly see that Gottheim is tied to every place else by what is normally invisible, namely the atmosphere; or in other terms the climate, which in times past was beyond our human intervention. Mark Twain's famous quote notwithstanding, it is time we started doing something about the weather.

Us, do something about the weather? What can we do about the weather? Maybe you're wondering, even saying aloud, the crazy editor wants us to do something about the weather. Is it bad enough that wells are dry and fires burn and crops wither before reaching fruition? We can do nothing about these things, yet the editor of *The Village Voter* wants us to.

But the editor is not crazy enough. Considering the equally ruinous deluge of two years ago, we must get a lot crazier and suggest that this wildly inconsistent weather is the result of the greenhouse effect. El Niño and the North Atlantic oscillation are held to cause the fluctuations, and studies are of course ongoing. But there is evidence showing that these have been dramatically influenced by global warming. The Legislature as a whole is unwilling to mandate the curtailment of emissions until findings are definitive.

In this space, we put it to you that crazy is our current course of doing nothing "until findings are definitive." There will be no definitive findings until global warming effectively strangles our planet. The president and legislators do little, under pressure of industry lobbyists who obfuscate the issue with talk of definitive findings.

Gottheimites, there _is_ something you can do about the weather. You can write your congressional representatives. You can trouble the sleep of senators Cohen and Mitchell, of representatives McKernan and Snowe. Send them scrapings from the bottom of your wells, ash from the burnt-over sides of Twitchell Mountain. You can ask them to represent Gottheim and the State of Maine instead of the suits walking the corridors of our national capitol. Let the gentle persons from Maine understand that we here in Gottheim want water. We want rain. And we expect them to do something about it. J.W.N.

Dear Editor,

I won't ask why you printed that letter from Ithiel Whitman, proclaiming his innocence of murder by strangulation of my twin. You would only answer that the First Amendment guarantees every view an expression, that as editor you have an obligation to present them, no matter how reprehensible, so people can make up their own minds. That's why I fully expect my page space after Ithiel Whitman's sickening self-pitying plea.

Your editor's note at the end of these letters states that you have the right to refrain printing any letter. In other words, you personally _chose_ to display his fabrication, that slandering use of Albinia Bisbee's name—someone who couldn't come up from the grave or down from the skies to protest these lies.

He justified battering because the evil in him makes him think everyone is alike. My sister was a good person, but the evil in Ithiel always accused _her_ and provided an excuse for the beatings.

So, Ithiel, you say we are all exactly alike. We all work raising funds for worthy causes, we all help put on Jasper Mary Day each year. All the people in Gottheim meet, eat, and have fun together. And we all quarrel with our spouses and lose our tempers. We all abuse each other, strangle each other, and entomb one another in concrete.

If it says so in <u>The Voter</u> it must be true. Isn't that so, Mr. Editor?

Elvegy Bisbee Blanchard

"Look at these thins."

Cindabilla is provoked. She is walking with Daniel through her withering pumpkin patch, kicking at the puny specimens with the ball of her bare foot. One of the little things bounces on the concrete-like earth, its withered stem and dry leaves rattling.

"Clouds is comin'but d'you think it'd rain?—maybe that light stuff fell yestadee, pretend rain. Enough to make you mad's all. Theya irrigating like mad round heah, trying to keep evah thing fom drying on the stalk. But if your brook's dried out like that one back of the farm—kiss it g'bye!" She gestures beyond the corner of the barn where her pumpkins lie ruined. "Look at those leaves out theya. Evah seen leaves go fom green t'brown before the end of August?"

Daniel says little, walking beside her. Tomorrow's return to school occupies his thoughts. He is ready for it, even eager to walk the concrete floor hard beneath its waxed linoleum; glad of the straight ranks of metal lockers, all identical, uniform. The heat and laxity of summer, along with its contrasting discipline of work, part-time work at *The Voter* and labor on the Simon house, bores him. He is hungry for assignments and the challenges of the classroom, the glittering eye of a Mrs. Medford and the dry stare of a Mr. Clough. This year he is going to work for them; this year go straight ahead without looking aside at his classmates' dubbing around. That's what they call it. He calls it goofing off. Last spring they tormented him. But hazing's over now. He has earned enough respect to get by. He will be expected to goof off with them, make a game. No being goody-goody, no actual studying, no being nice to teachers. Well surprise, you guys: goody-goody is caving to your pressure: Be good by being bad.

He could spare himself the trouble by hanging with the honor society types, the kids who know they're college-bound. But their's isn't the company he enjoys. It's like they've been dunked in bleach, squeaky clean. Give me the real kids, Cindabilla.

You can study—invisibly. He did in Phoenix and had friends. Hit the books and mind your own business; have fun at lunch, after class, but quietly learn. I can do it here. Don't volunteer anything. Won't raise my hand in class, ever. His dialogue with teachers will be in the essays, reports. They won't get him to speak in class and he'll see the disappointment on their faces, but they'll get used to it. Daniel Twitchell goes quietly about what he wants, balancing the forces in his life.

Life outside learning is not so simple; not at home with mother and his brothers, especially when Petey was there. It's not simple with Cindabilla anymore, either. He has been trying to get her to go back to school with him. She wants nothing to do with Hazel Newell High. She's got to see that the only way out of her life is education. He tries hard, but can't seem to put it convincingly. To Cindabilla, high school in Gottheim, Maine is a dead end.

Plaintively, still kicking pumpkins, she says, "Daniel, sellin'these thins was gont pay f'my education! Now I got no money t'get out of Gott'im."

He says nothing at first. Daniel is relieved that the pumpkins aren't working out. He has seen enough of urban life and is aware of its dangers. But maybe lack of money won't stop her. Cindabilla is determined to leave.

He watches her fidget, pick at the vines with her toes.

"Can we go down by the road? I'm supposed t'meet Mother...."

Together they approach the overhanging branches of the big maple where, a couple months ago, a great horned owl fell out of the branches, agonizing. Thinking of this, he says, " If you leave, what's it gont be like fah Babette 'n Gram? Uncle Ferddy might stot giving them a hard time again." It is the only argument he can think of at the moment.

Cindabilla shakes her emphatic head, her ginger ponytail waggling. "Daniel, I'm not about to cut my education in order to babysit grown-ups. Why don't Babs get wise? I told hah, when I'm gone, Ferddy'll stot up again. Caunt prove I shot 'em, but he knows. He won't hurt Gram. Babette's only one he'll hurt—unless he kills her'n gets someone afta." She thought a moment. "He might hurt his kids if he had any. Fucking bully. Shit f'brains. Thinks he *owns* Babs, like she's his truck, o'one of his guns. Like suddenly, coz she's close, a woman caunt be her own, control her own looks, thoughts, anathin. Like, if she does, it takes something away from him. She's got do evah thing his way or she's a traitor. I tell hah get out of Gott'im before he kills you. She shakes her head, says I don't know Ferddy, that he'd track her down. I said Ferddy don't know nothing but Gott'im and he's scared to go look for hah. But she looks away, says she's scared, too. I'm telling you, Daniel, I gut get out of here fah I get like that!"

They are out on the road where the rounded old heads of mountains are shouldering, protectively. Daniel looks toward their darkly crowned summits. The sky here is smaller than it was out around Phoenix where the mountains stood distantly. Weeks have passed since he seriously thought of Petey intruding here. Most times he thinks that in Gottheim the Twitchell family is hidden, secure. That the world lies out that way, far beyond the river-split hills. That Petey would never come to such a remote place. But Daniel recognizes Cinda's description of Ferddy in Petey Prince and wonders, Is there a difference between them?

Ferddy seems permanently lost in the bottle, submerged. Dad has some goodness about him.... But it seems like he's going to stay out of the bottle, then sooner or later falls back in.... Ferddy has Gottheim to anchor him, tie him to his true identity. Without Gottheim, he'd lose what definition he has.... Petey can go anywhere because he has no place to be out of, no place he cares about. There's no Gottheim for him, like Mother has. Now, Cindabilla has brought it all back, how Pete mocked Mother's memories of Gottheim.... He looks over at the girl.

Under this scrutiny she turns to face him, exclaiming, "*What*?!"

"... Nothing...." Struggling inwardly and unable to confess, he shrugs. *I don't want you to go.* Maybe I should say it.... But she already knows.... Made enough arguments, objections. She knows I don't want her to leave Gottheim.

Dear Mr. Fay,

You raised enough dust into the atmosphere, into our homes, nevertheless, we wish to extend congratulations upon the Jasper Mountain Resort Association's recent construction project. We regret, of course, that the design of the building is stylized, but at least the materials appear somewhat authentic.

As you know, most of us on the Planning Board are members of the Architectural Heritage Foundation, so it is natural that we object to aspects of your latest proposal for the so-called Gottheim Inn. The design is out of proportion and construction materials don't meet the standards we agreed upon. Stucco? Think, Mr. Fay, think! This is a New England village, not a Floridian mall. You say you have spent a lot of money to design authentic structures? Well, you're going to have to spend more—to make them clapboard or *brick*. We've yet to discover an original Yankee village containing so much as a smokehouse made of stucco.

Why is there so much difficulty executing your promises? Count your skier visits, sir, and see if you can't translate them into the brick you spoke of.

Sincerely yours,
Rhetta Marie Bearce

Blindness takes time. It's what Elda surmises while hiking around the crest of Mason Mountain on a September afternoon. She is trying to follow a deer trail. The dark boughs of hemlock brush her thin shoulders, arms and hips, as she passes. It is the soft caress of woodland upon one of its caretakers. Her backpack empty except for the litter of lunch, Elda is on one of her rambles, having no other purpose in mind for this drab Sunday afternoon. Her old hands are stained purple with late blackberries. Whatever she finds unlooked for on her way is welcome, especially as a distraction to thought. She has been tracking changes in her vision. Such as a difficulty in reading signs and seeing detail. There are spots everywhere— exactly where she wants most to see. Yet the great leap into darkness is.... It doesn't happen.

Once blindness started happening she gathered courage and read about its various forms—an emotionally difficult task in itself.... Maybe if she got a much stronger pair of reading glasses from Brown's Variety? Biting her lip and frowning she considers that the optometrist in Guildford might be able to help her... if she could stand to sit in some chair in a darkened room and be pronounced upon.

It must be macular degeneration and not cataracts. That would fit.... There are two kinds, one especially terrifying, escalating to complete blindness.

... There would be no cure, for either form.... the thought of cold instruments acting upon the delicate mechanisms of sight was impossible to contemplate anyway. She would prefer prayer to such professionalism. A woman like Elda Simon might have to be led out blind, leaning on a stick.

Downslope a woodpecker hammers in treetops. Earnestly she searches for it down through the trees.... Something's different. Something's changed since I came here with the owl in spring.

A raucous cry overhead takes her attention. Wings spread, dark pinions flaring, a raven swooped toward the woodpecker, driving it away through treetops. Through tiny new clearings she sees it come and go.

That's it. Loggers have been here since the Twitchells vacated.... but not with wholesale cutting. As she comes down, she sees two neat plots, widely spaced with lanes leading away. More?... A network signifying development.

Taking one of the lanes and coming to a yet wider lane, Elda follows through trees, gloom upon her. Here! In the heart of history! The old mill and abandoned settlement of the century past, disturbed in its profound rest. Some would be glad to see it happen, a new kind of life—not Elda. She mourns.... All gone in a blind evanescence of *dollars*! Mason's Mills, gone from Gottheim—never to be heard from again! She is shaking. Oh, what is happening to me? Never let these things bother me. Not like this.

A gleam through trees? She turns slightly, trying to see with a still unpracticed peripheral vision. A car, parked... people!...

Too late for Elda to make a retreat, the young couple approaches, one waving. Too late to slip back into the trees, be the furtive creature she is at heart. Oh, for the puckerbrush now.

"Mrs. Simon, Mrs. Simon!" A woman's voice calls, glad and light. They come near, and she sees their blond heads. A man and woman in their Sunday best. It dawns on Elda that this is Gloria Fay, the young woman Balder was seeing—was it a month ago, two? Who's the young man—her new boyfriend?

"Hello, deah," says Elda. "Good day fah walkin'."

She bucks herself up for the encounter. She can act as normal as anyone.... If you just keep it up for a minute or two, you can escape without much awkwardness. Then you get the peace of your own thoughts again... no matter the quality of those thoughts. They are preferable to small talk with strangers. She sends out her shy smile.

Gloria had seen the figure with its bandanna, recognizing the mother of Balder. So much time had passed since that evening when she saw the white deer, and Mrs. Simon with the gun. Too much time... since she had seen Balder. *Balder, oh Balder.*

Gloria hurried toward her, leaving James Fay to catch up at his own pace. But not before urging him in an undertone to be friendly.

"Of course," he had returned, but in an afterthought adding (jocularly), " Sis, I need a bit of befriending myself—for Theodora, you know. You can warm up a little. She's been upset lately, nervous. I don't know why"

"Well okay, since you're so sure about her."

Gloria introduced them and the three spoke of the weather, quickly exhausting the subject. With her usual excuse about the animals' feeding time, the older woman began to move on.

Gloria blurted, "How's Balder, Mrs. Simon? We've both been so busy—haven't talked much lately. I heard he was working on the house?..." Clutching her purse in one hand, she ran two fingers beneath strands of hair blowing across her eyes in the slight dry breeze.

" 'Bout got the new roofs on the old parts, I guess. Finishing up shingling now. Get it good'n snug fah wintah."

"Yes!" said James Fay. "Roof on by winter. I'd like to get our roof on myself. Right here, in fact. Mason's Mills is going to be a unique subdivision. One with a friendliness families rarely find today." He spoke quietly, with a childlike enthusiasm. "We're going to maintain the integrity of history here. Might even dam the stream again, re-create the old mill pond. The children can skate on it in winter. Sis and I are each going to build here, as well." He smiled at Gloria. "That is, if I can talk her into it."

His words warmed, and he began speaking of his philosophy of development. "It's the ideal that we've always known—as New Englanders. (We're from Boston, you know.)"

He gestured. "We plan a small common here, as in a village. Everyone will own a small lot and hold adjoining lands in common. It will be private yet maintain the sense of community so essential to families. Hiking, skiing, skating, horseback riding, they'll have it all...."

Mrs. Simon's gaze had already glanced away. Still smiling politely, she started edging past.

Embarrassed, Gloria interjected with a question about the Simon house.

"I'spect you just betta come see fah y'self, deah. He'd be glad t'see you coming, mentions you fom time t'time." There, thought Elda. Must be what's on that girl's mind. I can go now.

She smiled, slipping away, leaving brother and sister to their new plots. Elda felt sure she would not enjoy the ground around one of her favorite haunts again. Maybe... maybe the young man's plans weren't really—how could she judge it outside her lights? But where was the historical integrity she longed for? Was there benefit where benefit should be? Who were these families going to live here, not a Mason, that's sure. Though their ancestors once built the mill, they could no longer afford to live in such new places. But there. Life had to continue. Young families, whoever they were, had to live someplace. And Gottheim was a very good place to live.

But Elda's thoughts on the subject were nebulous and unsure if deeply unconsciously felt. No bitter thought long inhabited or motivated her. Simply, Elda Simon would be gone from Mason's Mills. No one would know of this natural withdrawing, this leaving to others what their from-away dollars had, in legal tender, purchased.

Not all Gottheim's citizens will look at it this way. Everyone has a point of view. When Eloise Patadoe, artist and homesteader, reads about the new Mason's Mills in *The Voter*, she will fume, maybe even plot with innocent good humor. She'll comment that James Fay will put a bronze plaque there, fixed to the old granite, commemorating the old way of life, nostalgic. Children will climb on the monument, pretending to be Indians and pioneers—no. More probably earthlings and aliens. Whatever it is kids will be playing in the late '80s and '90s. In the year 2001.

Leaving Gottheim

Sunlight kindled in the mountains as two teenagers crept along the train's length. There were cars loaded with logs, with finished lumber or with wood products—all bound for away. There were tankers and trailer-loaded cars, and empty freight cars, from points north. Early on a school day, and no one else around, a boy's voice went on earnestly, hurried and hushed, pleading with the girl to change her mind. Asking her to remain in Gottheim.

Dressed in denim from head to foot—blue denim, jacket and jeans, black canvas sneakers—all brand new, Cindabilla Sessions crept along the siding, Daniel tagging after. She slipped down off the gravel into the wildflowers and weeds to wait. On her back was a new nylon book bag, also bought new for school by her grandmother. But the pack contained a change of clothes, toiletries, sandwiches, and a small piece of feldspar, studded with dark garnets—a memento from the old quarry on Uncle Tom's Mountain.

Daniel Twitchell wore blue jeans and the leather jacket Peter Prince had given him last Christmas. His ball cap shadowed his Native American gaze. He plopped down beside the girl, one hand gesticulating while the other held biology and geography texts to the his chest. Gone is the habitual guarded or solemn look of him, replaced by a face puckered with concern. And still his quiet voice pleaded.

Now she was counting out the contents of her pockets, and he began emptying his own, still protesting. He blamed himself for not bringing some savings to bequeath her. If she went through with this scary plan to arrive cost-free in Boston, she would be needing every cent. But Daniel had not been thinking of anything remotely like this when he climbed out of bed earlier. He should have known something was up when she arrived happily and unexpectedly beneath his window at Simons's Ledge. It was well before the school bus was due to lumber up the hill. If only he had not allowed himself to be hurried away from the house. He might have brought food *and* money.

"It's betta this way, Daniel," she was saying. Goldenrod dust got into her nostrils and she sneezed. "I'm not stayin'heah, and theya's no way to Boston without that punkin money."

His brown eyebrows shot up. "I'll *give* you the money to take the bus to Boston. We... we could get Eli Simms to take you to the station in Portland—or Berlin. Simple'n safe!"

"Daow! I'm going this way, Daniel. Now shut fuckin'*up*!"

Daniel sank back, silent and disturbed among the asters and goldenrod and pearly everlastings.

But Cindabilla was on her knees, nervy and alert for the movement of the great empty boxcar above them. The train must be moving in order to preclude some official's keeping it back—should she be discovered climbing aboard. She had studied these movements over the past weeks, aware that the engine ahead was set to pull the train off the siding for the haul down to the eastern seaboard.

Now, with a piercing screech and jerk forward, a clanking and rumbling passing from one car to the next, the train above began to move. Heart thumping, Cindabilla leapt up. Her backpack bouncing, she scrambled onto the rail bed and began running alongside the cavernous boxcar, trying not to trip on the ties. Grasping the track of the car's great sliding door, she hauled ass, flinging herself up onto the gritty floor. Clambering to her feet she turned to wave but saw Daniel running below. His eyes were wide and glistening as he grabbed hold. Hauling with his free arm and clutching with a leg, he gained a hold. Cinda pulled on his belt loop and Daniel rolled across the filthy indented floor, still clutching his school books in his arm. He lay there panting, spread-eagle and groaning, feeling the jerk and roll of the train. He turned his head and saw the distant backs of houses sliding past.

She stood over him now and he rolled back his eyes, looking up into Cindabilla's gaze. She did a bit of footwork to keep her balance, grinning down on him in wicked glee. "Going t'Boston, Daniel," she said. "Fuckin'goin't'Boston with me."

In the Simon house they moved about like ghosts, quiet, yawning. In the bathroom upstairs, two boys leaned over the sink, brushing their teeth. Balder padded around downstairs, tucking in his flannel shirt, looking for his work boots, yawning and stretching one last time. He found the boots by the couch and sat down to put them on. Out the front windows he saw the colors of the sun still stoking in the east and trimming high leaves with new light. He went into the kitchen where Elda was heating oil in the iron skillet. It was their week to have the boys, get them up, fed, ready for school. They had to be down at the end of the lane before the school bus, alive with kids, lurched to a stop.

Balder opened the bread bin and took out a half loaf of wheat bread, went to the toaster on the sideboard and tossed in a couple slices. Mrs. Simon began cracking eggs into the crackling hot skillet. Her mind was on the wood mouse in a nest just under the sideboard cupboard. The tiny orphan might fit comfortably in a thimble, so small was the creature. Elda was in the midst of nursing it, and would rather be over there crooning it a tune... but first these had to be fed. Soon they would be out of here.

Balder took the steaming kettle off the back of the gas stove. Maxwell House instant was already in the bottom of his cup. He poured boiling water over it and the fresh coffee smell roused him. "Want some?"

"Got mine," she muttered, grabbing her cup from the back of the sideboard. "How's toast comin'?"

"Two more slices'll have it." He popped them in and went to call the boys. Nathan and Benaiah were already downstairs, but still sleepy and subdued. Nathan, Balder knew, would soon be bouncing around. He watched their bent backs where they rooted under the couch for sneakers.

Nathan was saying, "What's Dad look like, Ben'ah?"

"Stop asking me that, geek."

Balder tucked away the scrap of conversation for future consideration. "Waya's Daniel? Your brother's usually down first, now school's on."

"Still sleeping!" sang Nathan.

"Well go wake'em!" returned Balder, grinning. Nothing like a Nathan to get you moving in the morning.

"Yes Sir!" yelled Nathan, saluting. Like a deer up a slope, he took the stairs. Balder heard the boy issuing mock orders in a high-pitched voice, the sound of Daniel's door banging open. His grin widened. This family organism! It had almost as much movement as an active battlefield, and a lot less tension and grief. Place could use a few more critters, he thought. His mind went to Gloria. She had called him. At last.

He heard Nathan slamming around upstairs, but missed Daniel's answering comments. Nathan's squeaking accelerated, more doors banged. Then, suddenly, silence. Balder stood at the foot of the stairs. Nathan appeared at the top, his hair still tangled from sleep, bare toes curled around the lip of the top stair, socks dangling limply in either hand.

"Can't find'em," he said. "I looked in all the closets. Maybe he's hiding in that other part?" He gestured in the direction of the attached children's house.

"We called downt'Sessions. Cindabilla's gone, too. They'll probably turn up at school, but choo might want call theya later—find out f'sure."

Balder stood by the drainer of the dishwasher in the Farmingham Royal Tavern and Inn, talking to Chrischana. On seeing him come through the screen door, she had stopped work. Steam rose from the stainless steel washer as she stood drying her hands on a towel. Stepping back to glance at the ticking grandfather clock through the kitchen door, she said, "I'll call ovah theya in about 20 minutes. That should give 'em time t'get to homeroom." She mopped at her forehead with the dish towel. "Sorry you had t'come down heah for that, Balda. Late fah work in't choo?"

Balder grinned. "Got your Maine way o'speaking back, complete. Know that?"

She nodded. "Sometimes I lapse though."

"Well, look," he said. "I ought be apologizing to you. I was scared whole way down heah you'd want yank'em back from me. Guess you can't just tie kids up, chain them to the bedpost, huh? They got legs and can get away from you." Again he grinned.

She smiled a half smile. "I feel sorry fah you. You're just getting started. Can't see all that can go wrong yet." She grew grave and said thoughtfully, "The beard's getting longer. How long you gont let it grow? Till you get the hang of this father thing?—but you are doing a good job, Balder. Really." She could have reached out to touch that beard.

Unsettled, Balder sensed it. She understood about the beard without being told. Or, maybe Daniel did tell her, though he couldn't picture the boy saying so. How tempted he would have been by that touching gesture, even yesterday. But two things had happened to make him... set a distance between them. He damped down the grin and thanked her. Then he said, "Your names are all Twitchell.... was that always the case? Guess I nevah felt right asking Daniel this...."

She looked away. "Well Balder—his name was—is Prince." She looked back at him. *Be honest, not ashamed.* We... had that commitment but, no, we never did marry—legally. On the other hand, the law did consider us common-law married I guess."

"Uh huh. Well, like I said. I wondered."

He excused himself on account of work, said goodbye, stepped out the door and down the steps to his pickup. After getting a jumpstart off the Chevy before coming down here, he had left it outside idling because the battery was low. There were jumper cables under the seat for after work.

Someone in the parking lot at the mill would give him a jumpstart. Maybe Peter Prince.

It was something to think about on the way to work, anyway. That, and the fact that Chrischana would have to be told. Balder didn't think she knew yet. The man. The one who must have been cruel to her... causing her to flee back home. Here. If not in Gottheim then somewhere nearby.

Driving through the village he thought about the other thing. Gloria had called last night, inviting him to dinner... which he declined.... then turned around and invited her to supper. Supper at *Simons Ledge*, this week, his week with the boys. The silence at the other end of the line had been long and intense. That silence had troubled, refreshed, and intrigued him— in that order. Then she said yes. Glory was coming.

Out on the highway, Balder opened it up. Ahead, some tour buses trailed one another into a curve. One, two, three of them. Leaf peepers. And the foliage doesn't look that good, either. Lots of leaves—here and there—already gone. A pretty spotty picture for them. But the tours come anyway. Once they get those things booked in advance.... Jeepers creepers peepers! Glory's coming!

Cindabilla slides the lock shut with a click. She closes the commode inside the tiny compartment and sits down, her heart pattering. Now she gets to her knees on the toilet lid to look at herself cross-eyed in the mirror above the little stainless steel sink. Ballooning her smudged cheeks, she blows out a long breath. Cinda gives two squeaks and sinks down, sighing. But she stands again, turns on the tap and bends to drink thirstily. The train lurches, and she sits back, relieved.

Daniel should be holed up in the lavatory in the next car. He *had* to make it past the conductor. She smiles at the thought of serious Daniel hunched up on the flush. He's got enough time to think about it now. Probably kicking himself, smacking his forehead. Wondering why the fuck he hopped a freight with Cindabilla Sessions, bad girl from Gott'im. So exciting! She begins humming John Cougar's *Jack and Diane*, more excited than she has ever been. It's only beginning: *I'm going to New York City!*

Pulling away from the station, the train builds slowly toward the rhythm she has become accustomed to. It's smoother than the freight, much smoother. The hours they spent on that rattling old clunker. Seems like days. But we bypassed Boston, never stopped! New Haven, that was the surprise.

They had peered from the doors of the rusty old freight car out on the crumbling old cities and suburbs moving past. She was amazed by the vast clutter of buildings, highways, streets, rail lines, masses of slow or stopped cars; the unbelievable glut of wooden houses concrete steel brick glass. Houses jammed together, mile upon mile, hundreds of thousands of houses, millions? Where's earth? It's disappeared. How did these masses of tiny people come to live like this? No way you could give'em all a reverse nod. No way whatsoevah.

... But, there would be no need to say hi to everyone here like you did in Gottheim. No way they'd know who you were to get mad and say "stuck up." Maybe that's why people can rob murder strangers, just jump out of the crowd and... so easy. All faceless. Heard that word faceless, now I know what it means. All those people and all those houses and all those cities everywhere. At home people don't kill strangers, only people we know. See Daniel, she'll say, already my education's on.

She dusts the rust off her denims, dusts off her arms, shoulders, legs. Cindabilla takes off the jacket Gram bought for her, inspects, brushes off its back. This new outfit. I'm *dressed* for New York City. Dreamed of that place ever since Aunt Sally came back from West Germany and told of Greenwich Village, the lights of Times Square, Statue of Liberty, Empire State Building, World Trade Center, Grand Central Station....

She stands to wash the rust off her face and hands. It must be a gift that that dirty old freight car wasn't going to Boston after all. When it stopped, they climbed down, crossed double rows of tracks, came to an Amtrak station, climbed on this train for New York. The lavatory was her idea. "It's all worked out fah us, Daniel. All we got do is stay locked in till they call Penn Station or Grand Central, whichever comes first. Then we get off, no ticket necessary."

After the fruitless call to Hazel Newell High, Chrischana left the clean stacked dishes of Farmingham Royal Tavern and got into her old Bonneville 500. She fired it up and pulled out around parked tour buses to start looking for Daniel. First she drove out to Sessions to talk with Hannah, Cindabilla's grandmother. Babs and Ferddy were at work, one to the spool mill, the other to the town garage, but Hannah would be her best informant anyway.

"No, no, they in't heah," said the old woman, peering at Chrischana from behind a few greasy strays of gray hair. "Cindabilla was up fah light, though. Heard hah root round in the kitchen. Left awful early. Say they in't been t'class this morning? Well, I'll just saddle Jimmy'n rattle around the puckabrush, see what I find."

Chrischana drove back to the village, poked about the streets and lanes, parking lots. It looked like these two were up to something, darned if she knew what. It wasn't like Daniel to skip school, but he was close to Cindabilla whose name was synonymous with truant.

She drove out to Bearce's lightless convenience store. Young Wilbur Twombly was at the cash register, no one else around. "Seen Daniel Twitchell or Cindabilla Sessions in heah? The boy kinda dark, she's got a light ponytail?"

"Two kids missing fom the high school?" Wilbur, hardly more than a graduate himself, had almost dropped out once: He could read already and had planned on becoming a rock star. Yet he had persevered, randomly, and ended up with a summer school diploma, just a step or two behind his class. Today he was on at the store. Nights were gigs in the area.

Chrischana stared at his long acne-pocked face. "You heard this already?" She glanced up at the lit face of the clock above the counter. Almost ten.

He shrugged. "It's Gott'im, in't it? Haven't seen 'em. But if I do?—send 'em back to Hazel Newell good'n propah."

Robbie Robichaud stepped in, large and in workman green, ready for coffee in the cramped little store.

"Hi, Mr. Robichaud. You seen my Daniel'n Cindabilla Sessions, Hannah's granddaughter?"

"Whad they look like?" He grinned. "No, ain't seen 'em. Why—they skipping school?"

"At least," she said, trying not to let worry into it.

"Oh, they prob'ly went to work in the woods!" He grinned more and Chrischana smiled.

"Well, give Elda Simon a call if you heah anathin." She stepped out the door.

The tower clock was striking ten as she drove along Front Street again. Could be they're hiding out at the Cove—smoking cigarettes and dreaming big on something together. She started to turn the Bonneville around in the Foodliner parking lot. Asa Bartlett, the clockwinder, was coming out, one arm wrapped around a bag full of groceries. She leaned over, rolled down the passenger window and called out, "Seen my Daniel?"

He walked over and leaned in his dark red bespeckled head, the bag crackling against his sweater. "I heard they was missin'," he said, shaking his head. "Prob'ly playing hooky, s'all. *You* nevah skipped school, I spect. That Sessions girl—no wondah. You know her mother was high on drugs night she give birth t'Cindabilla. And they say that Etta's father himself was drunker'n a stone night *she* was born. Runs in the family!"

"Gut go now," snapped Chrischana turning her face away. She frowned out the windshield and Asa stood away. The woman drove off, muttering.

The big Bonneville 500 bumped along the dippy lane that led

toward the Cove. She rounded the curve of an elder thicket and a brown half moon shoreline came into view. There lay the sheen of Twitchell Pond. They had camped here early in the summer, when the water was still too cold for swimming. There was the tree, a great knobby white birch, ancient, massive and full. The spreading branches upheld its great dark green crown. Mostly, birches in the area were tall spindly things. But this one, with its many spreading limbs, had always reminded her of a tree goddess, one of those dryads or nymphs or whatever they were. Like a great she-being about to step away and wander waist deep into the water. Sleeping beneath her branches, they had heard rustling leaves, lapping water. They sheltered here after disaster at Deep Hole, when the walls of Abenaki Notch closed in on her.

The pilgrim Chrischana got out of the car and sat on a hewn log. It was a bench in cross-section, flat on top, and curved like the shoreline. An ancient seat for the rituals of generations of young Gottheimites, carved with the many initials of teenagers now grown up. And teenagers gone, too. Idly she wondered about them, tracing the old engravings with her finger. K.C., romantically tied to W.B. Did they grow old together, wither, lie in the same grave? Maybe the soil they became together was now part of that graveyard across the pond, Twitchell Cemetery. She looked across the glimmering expanse toward the opening in trees, where the brown lawn sloped to the shore. Have to grow old first, Daniel!

She shook her head. Skipping school. Daniel and Cindabilla were far from dead, but Chrischana herself was quietly inching up on it. She shook her head again. Dead already? It's only skipping school. Small's my power over my own mind. Daniel is holed up somewhere, safe, but this mind rattles off on extremes.

Where in the name of God *are you*? *Where*?! She crossed her arms, wearily bowed her head. Resting, sighing deeply, her brown braid hanging down, she closed her eyes and asked for something with words.

On the highway into Gottheim she saw Abner Chapman. He was walking the shoulder, his sun darkened face a pucker of grim concentration. She pulled over, got out, approached the man in his now faded fatigues. She doubted whether he had been to the Army-Navy store since his tour in Vietnam. Coming up behind him, she coughed while still several yards back in case he was unaware of her presence. "Morning, Abner. Got a minute?"

Startled and wild-eyed, Abner turned. But he saw it was Chrischana, an old classmate and friend. She had stopped to speak to him a few times since her return, once buying him a cup of coffee. He knew she had children. Now she began telling him about Daniel. He may have seen them because he was about on the roads, early and late. Habitually Abner walked the highway, the streets, sometimes in anguished concentration, sometimes alive to the doings about him and ready for conversation. At those times his eyes would relax. Or, he might be like a ghost on his feet. Maybe he had seen something though—sometime?

In the doorway of Buster Bearce's convenience store across the highway from them stood Robbie Robichaud's twin sons, Alvin and Ansell, watching. They had come into Gottheim to Kimball Supply for bar and chain oil, a new set of files, and were now on their way back to the woods, coffees in hand. "Theya she is," said square-faced Ansell to his identical twin.

"Might we could beat the bushes when we go back fah'em" answered Alvin.

"Might," Ansell agreed.

By the time they got into Alvin's pickup and pulled out toward Copenhagen, Chrischana, disappointed that Abner knew nothing about the missing kids, was on her way back up to Elda Simon's.

The older woman had just come in for a cup of tea, looking to revive herself from morning chores and a brisk ramble in search of wildlife in need of her ministrations. She had also kept an eye out for Daniel, returning distracted by the sight of a deerstand—half built—up on the rock above the house. Water boiled out over the bag as she tipped the kettle, releasing the strong scent of orange pekoe and other black teas. Was that Chrischana's kerchief passing the window?

She went to let the younger woman in. "Find 'em yet?" She had missed seeing the furrow in Chrischana's brow.

"No, but it's not certain theya together. No one in town's seen 'em. Was hoping they'd come back heah... somehow."

Elda shook her head, saying comfortingly, "Have a cup o'tea with me, deah. Maybe we betta call Balda?" She went to the canister on the sideboard for another tea bag, feeling guilty for dwelling on that deerstand. Here was Daniel, missing, and all she could think of was that stand. Who could have put it theya, half-done? Seems twas one of the boys. That job of hammering showed the hand of a child.

Chrischana stood by the gleaming wooden sideboard, absently watching the little woman pour her a steaming cup. She took it, saying, "Let's not call'em just yet. Still early. I don't believe harm's come to'em."

Elda nodded, sipping the hot tea. "He'll probably call on break, anaway."

—

Asa Bartlett sat in Olive Lovejoy's kitchen, eating an egg salad sandwich. She sat across from him, large, solid, talking. Her red fingertips fluted the air from time to time, speaking along with her words. Light fell through the double windows above the sink, aglow with dust motes. The flecked Formica table top was set for two, trimmed with Jell-O salad, thick slices of tomato, a wedge of head lettuce and a pot of tea. Now that Asa wanted to marry her, Olive had given over her care of the developmentally disabled. He didn't think he'd be able to live in a house full of disabled people—or any other kind of people. All he wanted was Olive. Their plans were up in the air like the dust motes and Olive's red tipped fingers, but she spoke of going up on the mountain to do domestic work once the season got underway.

The disposal of dwellings had not yet been settled, there being two houses between them. This house of Olive's was a three-story turn-of-the-century Sears catalog house. It had polished hardwood floors and rag rugs, and leaded glass bookcases flanking a stone fireplace overlaid with oak mantelpiece. The matching oak floor molding was eight inches wide, three inches around the door frames. A solid oak banister ran from the ground floor to the landing. In the kitchen, where they sat talking, linoleum with hand cut insets gleamed across the floor at their feet. Built among traditional New England houses, its wavy concrete block exterior was once an affront to the classic or gingerbread aesthetic of the purest. But some of these traditional houses had themselves been converted into bed-and-breakfast establishments and set to work. The function afforded their owners to keep up the appearance of prosperous ease. But many were new owners from elsewhere, aware of both the commercial and historical value of these structures, and pleased to cater to the tourist and seasonal trade; join the class of small-business persons who could, with a bit of capital, earn a living in Gottheim.

In the country setting, white and tiny in the distance beneath a low mountain ridge of Jasper Mountain, Asa's extended farmhouse overlooked the pond. The farmstead, comprised of the big house and bits and sections of other houses from a bygone time, had been in Asa's family for generations; the not so gentle hardly fertile slopes steadily farmed since that first clearing soon after the incorporation of Gottheim. Asa was the one to give over farming full time, after the passing of his father in the 60s. He kept it in hay but the livestock were mostly gone and there was a healthy assortment of cats to keep the place clear of rodents. This mill worker's careful craftsmanship, and attention to historic authenticity, combined to keep the house as neat and austere as any 1800s connected dwelling could be. In spring nine huge maples yielded numerous quart jars of syrup. When hung with spanking-clean galvanized covered buckets and seen from afar they resembled jeweled giantesses in the sun.

Asa and Olive were inching up on retirement age. Now they wondered aloud if such a condition really existed—retirement. However much they talked of it, the question always came back: "What'll we do then?"

Olive's earnings had gone in Horace's illness, but Asa had carefully and scrupulously set something by for the event, yet neither could imagine not working. What would give the day its shape and supporting activity? Asa had suffered bouts of depression, over the course of his fruity life, and understood that work kept thoughts occupied, holding the undesirable ones at bay. Whatever the pace, trotting or plodding, his plan had always been to die in harness. Now, to the clinking of flatware, cups and plates, the loving couple talked of these things. Slowly a plan emerged.

Either of these two houses could make an ideal bed and breakfast. Both would. "I could do all the handiwork, keep'em repaired inside and out. Yardwork, neat and trim out front," he volunteered. "We could have our own private areas, keep us separate from the guests'.... Think of a house providing a living, making money!" He pulled his apple crisp toward him, sliced into it with his fork.

"Well, it's the local economy now, Asa," Olive said, then took a sip of tea. "You couldn't imagine selling mulch hay—whole crop—even five, six years ago. Now developas all want it fah landscaping. The power company, wanting so much fah that new right-of-way."

"But think of us employin' people! Imagine givin' orders to people round heah? I dunno."

"You'd hire a contractor, wouldn't choo? Do it that way. People want work. Melviny'd love working with folks she knew, stead of strangers. Could maybe persuade Decatah t'do breakfast, one place. I caunt do both, you know. He'd have to sharpen up a bit, though. Learn a little fancier way o'cooking. Maybe Chrischana'd work fah us."

"You heard about her boy? Him'n Cindabilla missing? Wondah if they found them yet."

She nodded. "I betta get back on the phone, find out. I been callin' all morning trying to find out if anybody seen anathin'."

"Yuht, betta." He stood to kiss her. "I gut wind the clock before my shift!"

It was a long day. Although Chrischana had not yet reported Daniel missing, the Gottheim police were already keeping an eye out for the boy and Cindabilla. One of the officers thought there was cause for concern:

Late last spring there had been two attempted stranger-abductions in the town of Percy. Someone in a new Bronco had tried to entice adolescents into going for a ride. Teenagers were a fixture, walking the shoulders of highways and back roads. How else could they get around? If you've got no car and want to see your friends outside of school, you have to walk. Few parents have time to drive here and there, ferrying kids back and forth. That's why late bus has always been provided for in the school budget. Afterschool activities would be impossible without it. Though things have been quiet since the too unsolved incidents, the culprit must still be at-large somewhere. The Bronco's license, known only by color—black numerals on white—was in-state.

At noon Chrischana talked to Balder but encouraged him to stay at work. It was still too early to suppose this was anything but truancy. She was determined not to be alarmed. But Balder, unaccustomed as he was to child-rearing, was worried. Woods around Gottheim were as large as the states of Rhode Island, Connecticut.

"No need to worry," returned Chrischana. "Cindabilla is some woods wise'n crafty in't she? No use making a big deal out of something bound to turn out insignificant. It's not dark or cold enough t'worry. Let'em have theya li'l rebellion... then wail on'em when they show up." Crisply she reminded Balder of his own youth. She could feel his grin coming over the phoneline in response.

"Wait it is! Can I be first t'wail on 'em?"

"I betta do it. You'd be too easy on'em. Leave it t'you to console 'em after."

Hanging up, she recognized her relief. If others can be so easily persuaded that this is normal, maybe it is. She looked at Elda Simon heading for the door. Something needed attending to in the barn. The older woman stopped to smile in her transparent but slightly absent way. She was wearing her usual T-shirt with flannel shirt and dungarees with rolled up cuffs, low sneakers.

"What will you do now, Christy?" She thought to ask it.

"Now?... well, I'm going to thank you f'your kindness." She gave the old woman a grave half smile. "I'm grateful for what you do fah'em. You are a good gran'mother."

Her hand on the knob, Mrs. Simon stopped, embarrassed, surprised. Grateful and guilty over the kind words. "Why-thank-you-Christy." She scooted out the back door.

Shortly after four o'clock they learned what happened. Having spent the afternoon searching and talking to townsfolk, Chrischana came in on

Balder's heels. The smell of the pulp mill was still on him. The three converged in the kitchen as the phone rang, and for an instant they all froze. Then Balder reached for the receiver of the old black wall phone. He twisted its cloth covered cord. "...Yuht.... Uh-oh. Okay. Don't worry, we'll get'em."

He hung up, expelled a breath, and lifted his blue gaze. He looked steadily at Chrischana, saying, "Mystery solved, but it don't look good." Frowning, he would step close and hold her, but instead he stayed by the phone. "That was Olive Lovejoy. Talked to ol'man Kimball's niece. 'Memba ol'man Kimball, Israel Kimball? Was an old man even when we was kids—hermit lives in the tower of the oldest Gothic, up on the side of Crazy Knoll?"

She was quiet, her nod almost imperceptible.

"We knew even then that he looked out that tower fom time to time, seeing all below. Place looks out over the edge of the village waya the railroad runs. Seems he was looking down from theya this morning, saw two kids—one all in blue, long light ponytail—fling theya selves into a moving boxcar. That blue one.... That was Cindabilla."

Her face dim and fallen, Chrischana sagged against the table.

"We gut go downt'police." He said this quickly and started toward the door in an effort both to rouse and keep from going to her. She followed him out and he called back through the screen. "Give them a call, Mutha, let 'em know we're on our way."

Elda, still standing by the door, watched Daniel's parents go around the corner of the house.

They were underground for an hour, hopping first one train and then another in a convoluted attempt to get from Penn Station to Grand Central. The first thing Cindabilla wanted to see was Aunt Sally's Grand Central Station, but she was diverted by the vast subway system itself—transfixed by its screeching tumult, powerfully tunneling disappearing trains and their miraculous charging reappearances. All a steel-dark mystery, the fascinating idea that you could forever ride hundreds of miles beneath the surface of a vast city. Carefully they studied a free subway map, carefully chose their trains, yet missed their stops and connections, bemusedly. And found themselves interminably riding, observing the underground culture of great halls, scurrying passengers, springing train doors, token machines, and musicians with open instrument cases gathering change. The graffiti! Yet, both agreed that the most impressive (and scariest) encounters involved the swiftness of the train doors. The pace and movement of the underground culture awed them, but the speed of those doors, they agreed, might forever separate them if they did not take care.

But at last they stand below the gallery stairs of the great main concourse of Grand Central terminal, staring up and about them, transfixed. Somewhere on the edge of Daniel's consciousness hovers the phrase *sensory overload*. His gaze rises and falls, trying to take in the vast textured movement of rush-hour commuters, briefcases in hand; the early 1980s floor-level glut of vendors and displays which trouble the old elegance of 20th-century New York; the far vaulted ceiling where constellations glimmer, the great *beaux arts* arches letting in light beams where dust motes float in Heaven's light.

The hustle and echoing roar of the busy concourse fills him and dimly he becomes aware of Cindabilla at his elbow murmuring over and over, "Nevah nevah nevah nevah...." Seeing her pale gaze wandering over the scene, Daniel longs only to cover his ears and shut out the overwhelming hustle and roar of Metropolitan commerce; its cacophonous waves crashing without rhythm, its intelligence decayed to babble, with purpose or plan undiscernible from the torrent and might of confused speech.

Long moments he stands by her, acclimating himself, watching others move this way and that. What's it to do with us, except as...? We are overcome in a sea. His gaze fixes on an island, the central information kiosk, crowned with a great cubic clock. One brass face for each of the four sides of the six directions, it stands above the hurrying heads. He stares at the pointing hands of one yellow dial. Five o'clock.

Daniel shivers. They're sitting down to supper now, at *Simons Ledge*, eating together at the kitchen table, finding out what went on all day.... Wondering where he is. But his own day has worn itself away in travels, in this... pursuit. He went after a girl. A girl who goes after—? He looks at her wide eyes again, her open astonished face. Oh yeah. He remembers. Her education. She wants to learn the ways of the world. Well, this is the place to do it. He thought he had learned them in Phoenix.

He thinks of Mother, his duty to her. She's got no idea where he is. None!

And beside him, Cindabilla's still murmuring, *Nevah nevah*. But, suddenly the sea casts a limb at them. No longer just spectators, they must take mindful part. A man materializes, purposely. Disheveled, swart as Daniel. If his eye is a fixed vacancy, his hand is out to them.

Daniel bends to Cindabilla's ear: "Run Cindabilla run." His school books still under his arm, with his free hand he clutches at her. They turn and patter up the marble stairway, brushing the dividing brass rail. Peering out from around the corner, panting, they look down on the swelling sea. With a squeak Cindabilla sneezes and pulls out a wad of lavatory toilet paper, blowing her nose. "Look't that, Daniel," she says, holding out the wad. "Black snot!!"

He pulls back, grimacing.

"Heah," she commands, handing him a clean wad. "Blow into it, see what you get." She looks at her palms. "My fingers is filthy, too." (Pointing down,) "Imagine how many hands touch that brass railing each day. Or how many have held this." She holds up a patterned brass subway token. "Millions! I eat something now, I eat with all theya hands." She thinks a moment. "Daniel! These black boogers ah fom the subway. It's filthy down theya!"

He obliges her by showing her his snot, but he's thinking, Couldn't we have found this out from a book?

Looking around, Cindabilla sees a sign. *Park Avenue*. She opens the map. "Look't. This's East 42nd and Pock Avenue." She points out an intersection on the paper, saying, "Heah's Times Square. All we got do is go out like this" (gesturing). (Counting)... "Four blocks to Times Square! Forget the filthy subway. Let's go."

But Daniel does not move. It's suppertime and they've spent too much of their money on subway tokens. The peanut butter, lettuce and mayonnaise sandwiches, made by Cindabilla before light this morning, are long gone. Dazed Daniel puts a restraining hand on her arm. "I think that was a homeless man that came up to us. Cindabilla, what are we doing!? It's suppertime."

In scorn she looks at him. But thinking a moment and smacking her thigh, she says, "We'll do what *he* done—panhandle." She says it significantly, as though she has studied and knows what to do because of it.

But now Daniel is thinking that he himself was homeless—before Balder became his father. The Twitchell family was homeless on leaving Phoenix. They had to camp everywhere they went. He had seen on TV in Phoenix that homeless panhandlers came out when the President emptied the insane asylums, but he couldn't imagine so many insane people. And he couldn't imagine anyone walking down Front Street with his hand out. No one would have the nerve.... But this is how it's done in the city.

"Cindabilla, I think we should go back to Gott'im—*now*."

"You go. I'm going to Times Square'n see all the lights when the sun goes down." Off she walks.

Daniel stops. Then, troubled, quiet, he follows. He must keep his wits alive, watch out for things. Anything. Anything could happen. Hurry. Don't lose her in this people sea.

Navigating it, he calls after the retreating lithe blue form, its long ponytail swinging. Daniel threads out toward the Park Avenue ramp.

"Cindabilla!"

But he needn't have worried for once outside Cindabilla stops, astonished by her first sight of the great city: staring amazed out through the great notch where buildings stand on either hand, towering up in abstraction of the hills back home. Glass, concrete, brick-and-stone, steel; the endless ranks of great Gotham's façades rearing up like mountains. She is dwarfed, as the mountains at home do not dwarf her. The greatness of it! What masterminds! All straight lines, order and clockwork. Gone the chaos of Sessions' kitchen. Oh the city!

Now the sea of people gives way to the sea of fuming traffic, yellow with taxis converging and diverging, choking the ramp in an effort to deliver commuters for their race to the suburbs. Or to gather suburbanites to the pleasures of the city. Down the Avenue stretches a string of traffic lights, red or green, toward infinity; more cars, lit buildings, banks of gleaming windows, shadows and movement and standstill and hummingness and honking. There are dwarfs and giants here, demons and angels, and mechanical workings undreamed of till now. How in the name of everything that works, can this great city work? How do all the sinks and toilets and lights and stoves and heaters and and and... how! No TV show on Earth could prepare you for it. Place's crammed, compacted of people. People living their lives on top of one another. Doomed to produce neighborliness at a level she would've thought impossible. Block wouldn't stand for the population of Gott'im. Even a building would not.... Maybe just the first two or three floors of that pale monster building over there?

Beneath the monstrous colonnade of Grand Central Terminal, Daniel catches up to her. She does not see the despair in his usually solemn eyes, the dream of desolation troubling his brow. But he says nothing to her, knowing himself powerless to dissuade her. All he can do is watch, as he has done since his day began, since his life began somewhere in the American West when he was born to an unwed mother. He *must* accompany Cindabilla, follow her around until a thought worth thinking, plan worth executing should find him.

"Don't look s'sad," she says. "Look out theya. Didn't choo evah see it like this? In Phoenix?"

Dumbly he shakes his head, aware but scarcely seeing. He wants never to take his eyes off her. She might fly down the stairs, disappear, become a molecule in the polypeptide chains of suburban commuters. And, down there—along 42nd St. was it?—a different type of New Yorker might emerge, one with a more predatory agenda. Can't you tell how desirable innocent *young* you are, he thinks miserably. Can't you see that people here might not have the same sense they have in Gott'im? A sense telling them not to hurt or use other people? They don't even see you here unless they want something from you.

But Cindabilla, map in hand, is heading for Times Square. There is nothing to do but follow.

At 11 o'clock and still alive with the dark shapes of people, the street outside was doubly lit with neon reflecting from puddles laid down by a cold drizzle. She had seen the lights of the Square that did not look like a square. There was nothing to compare with it in Maine, not even that time in Portland.

Their jackets hung down from the stools where they sat, but they'd never be dry before their hamburgers were eaten. Daniel was reminding her that they would have to return to the wet streets and she was saying that they could return to the terminal for shelter. He would have agreed, but it was at cross purposes to his talk which was a constant flow of petitions and reasoning.

Never talked so much before, she thought. If he would just settle down and shut up, maybe sleep in a corner somewhere—then they'd have peace. It had been a long day like a night of partying at home: long, convoluted, full of dangerous thrills, detours, and observations of hard-driving attempts at gratification. But, then again, it was completely different. And now, as though he was Uncle Asher under a mountain of reefer smoke, she couldn't get Daniel to shut up.

He reminded her that it had taken them four hours to get up the courage to try panhandling enough money for supper. He listed the times and circumstances under which they'd been accosted to trade Daniel's leather jacket for heroin or crack. He recounted the propositions they'd had for sex from the "weirdo fucking freaks," as she called the prima-techs and gays. And more he recalled, before ending his recital with the scene of a mother trying to sell her baby. Daniel had yanked her away before she could find out what would become of the little thing.

Once the warm food hit her, Cindabilla could hardly keep her eyes open. She heard her own voice answering his repeated entreaties. "All right, call'em, if that's what you want, Daniel. I give up!" She said it to shut him up, but she was thinking, I'm still gont see the Statue of Liberty, go up the World Trade Center. Aunt Sally said you could see all them pretty buildings lit up from theya, like church steeples all across the city.

They walked back on 42nd St. in the rain, avoiding encounters, a woman railing and ranting at nobody. She seemed to be following them, but maybe it was just a coincidence. Once inside the terminal, Daniel approached the payphone and inserted one of his last quarters.

"Should'o changed that," she reminded him. "Phone only costs a dime." Then she sank to the cold marble, leaned back against the wall and closed her eyes.

"Yuht!" Balder snatched the receiver up, began twisting the cord.

"Father?" He heard the voice saying, *Father*! It was the first time Daniel had called him anything but Balder; no, it was the first time he had called him *anything* directly. Daniel's voice was distant, tentative, tired. Safe! But now he was saying there was but one quarter left.

"Way-you-at-Daniel?" He peppered questions, grateful and full of hope. Now, grinning at Chrischana, Balder forced himself to slow.

She had stood from the table at mention of her son's name. Exhausted and relieved, she wanted to knock Balder into the front room, snatch the receiver, babble and holler at the boy. But, as more of a grimace, she returned Balder's grin and sat down again. Turning her coffee cup, Chrischana leaned into the one-sided conversation, trying to hear Daniel's words.

"Okay," Balder said. "G'me that number." Scribbling, he repeated it. "Okay, stay theya, right by that phone. I'll make arrangements to wire you bus money'n call you right back."

He hung up and immediately began calling Benjamin Biddle, the pharmacist and Western Union provider. "Roust Biddle out, get him to send money to the New York City bus station," he said, looking over at Chrischana.

She jumped up with a squeak of despair. "New York City!"

"Look," he said, dialing the New York City area code after his brief conversation with Biddle, "Just talk to him. You'll feel betta."

The tone of her speaking wavered from stern to soft murmurs and back again as she talked with her son. Her eyes relaxed. Her gaze drifted away from Balder. To Daniel she heaped admonishment, repetitious instruction. Told him how to handle himself in the terminal that night and on the way to the bus station in the morning. Made him promise to stay out of the subway until then. Take no arguments from Cindabilla. Don't look anyone in the eye, get straight on the bus, etc....

Balder held out his hand for the phone. Reluctantly she parted with it, stood near, then wandered into the front room where Elda was slouched in the chair before the flickering television. Sleeping. The box in which the tiny wood mouse nestled was at her side. On the mantelpiece, the Simon's nut-brown clock with gold hands ticked away, drawing Chrischana's attention.

Almost 8 a.m. Was this nightmare really over? Were they really safe, returning home after all that uncertainty? Yes. It looked that way.
They waited down at the lower level, looking for the approach of the train to take them to the Port Authority bus terminal. The long night in Grand Central was over and, hungry, bleary-eyed, they were submerged in the crowd of commuters.

Suddenly came the train, shrieking to a halt. Packed among commuters, they edged forward, Daniel clutching his books, stepping warily into the car lest the swift doors slam. Safely aboard he sought out Cindabilla among the trench coats and suits.

"Cinda," he called, "Cinda!" He pressed through to the glass of the closed doors.

There she stood on the platform, a small slow smile on her face. Even as the train moved, she backed away, her fingers raised above the edge of a denim cuff, wiggling at him.

Boldly Cindabilla waved, dwindling into the distance. Happily triumphant. Then she turned, instantly submerged in the reforming crowd.

Bird Hunting

He felt the lowering day about him, gray and stern, with wind to drive more leaves away. Its cold breath pierced Balder's mackinaw. He stood in the lane looking up through leafless twigs at the turmoil of sky above. *There*, he heard it again, the honking of Canada geese. But he couldn't see them yet. Must be a ways off up the hill. The woodland swept upward, obscuring his view, dense as a shut door against the hillside.

He stood a while, waiting to hear them again. Now his mind went to other things, recalling that Gloria had backed out of supper with the family at *Simons Ledge*. She had to hold her ground. She was holding it, leaving him alone.

Daniel turned the corner from the road to the lane, drawing Balder's gaze. The boy walked the lane toward him, head down, feet scuffing through colored leaves.

"Father," said Daniel, drawing near. "I saw the geese, coming up the road. Like you said we would, come fall." The wind blew back his hair, scrubbed his face, solemn and still. The brown eyes were serious and deeper than before. Balder looked into them, then away. Now he looked back again.

"That li'l girl...." said the man above the wind. "Pray fah her—out theya in the ol'world."

Daniel nodded. He needed more.

"What's the strongest thing on earth?"

Daniel shrugged, turned up his collar.

"Strong to hold the world together. Love."

The two heard honking again, looked up to see the straggling v through the crosshatching of twigs. The birds passed high over the bare branches, sounding.

Balder looked at Daniel's face, still raised in scanning for the geese, quiet, troubled. "Can you do anathin fah Cindabilla? Keep her safe, provide, make her life go right?"

Daniel hesitated, shook his head, kept his gaze high. His eyes still pretended to be after the geese, averted because he could not rest them elsewhere.

"Just recognizing that, you're on the way t'helping her. Maybe praying she'll come back's not it. But that she be safe'n warm, learn what life'd teach her. It'll help, just that prayer. Let the girl go. That's love."

There was no response. Then Daniel nodded, still looking up past the naked twigs and stems. He was glad that Balder had spoken—knew he was hurting.

Balder said, "You coming to the house?"

"Not yet."

Daniel watched Balder wane, going toward the house. It struck him that his father was a lonely figure, not the happy man he seemed. The figure turned the corner, disappeared.

Reaching the back stoop, Balder stood looking into the woods from across the backyard that he had cleared not long ago. He was thinking of Peter Prince. The man was gone. At least Balder had not seen him at work these last—was it a week? Two? Was he out sick, or just in another part of the mill? Maybe he went back to Phoenix. He had never told Chrischana about meeting Peter Prince. Too much going on. But now, is there any need to tell her... if the man's gone? Might drive away her peace. She's almost happy now. Got her own little place, small, but her own. She's busy, contented, goal-oriented.... *Better find out where the man went.*

The wind drove down a flock of leaves, the scent of wood smoke coming with it. Balder stepped out into the yard to look up at the new roof of the children's house. It looked straight and snug now, made to satisfy. But that feeling was temporary. There was still much to do, inside and out. Over the winter he would refurbish its inner rooms. Working on the house was something he could do for everyone, not just Gloria, but especially for her. He never knew what a human being might do.... *On the other hand, you might never see her again.* He might rebuild the entire house and her never set foot in it. But someone will shelter here. Sometime. Something small like this was all anyone could do; and you could pray.

Benaiah crept through the woodland below what he called Monster Rock, as silently as he knew how. He tried to be quiet, expectant, alert. Weeks had passed since seeing the white deer, and the weather had changed. There had been a frost, everything coated in white, like you'd expect. Dark leaves and brown, all trimmed in soft white on the ground. Winter was going to be something, their first *winter*.

He had been working hard against waning hope, hoping to see

Sugarloaf the white deer again. In a few weeks it would be deer season, and Sugarloaf'd be mincemeat. Mother had assured him that the fawn was too young to qualify, but Balder had warned that as a curiosity Sugarloaf might be a temptation for some would-be hunters.

Now it was only October and bird season. But Ben could not rest assured. Some idiot with a bird gun might just as well shoot at the white target. He clenched his fists and dug them deep into his jacket pockets. It wasn't fair that all the rules in the world wouldn't stop the hunter if he wanted that deer. They did what they wanted if they thought they could get away with it. *Is that fair?!* Angry, Ben walked on through fallen leaves.

Then, he saw the orange and was on alert. A hunter in blaze orange hunched several yards away in a clump of evergreen, not moving. Probably a bird hunter waiting to ambush some innocent bird. Ben stood quietly, deciding what to do. He could make a bunch of noise and scare it away, ruin the hunter's chance.... But then he'd have an angry man to deal with, one with a gun. Well, it was worth it. Suppose he was after Sugarloaf?

Yet the hunter did not look very large. His back was to Ben, the feathery branches obscuring most of his form. And there was no gun showing, no telltale barrel cradled in the crook of an arm. Quietly Ben moved closer. Now the tousled head was visible beyond the little clump of evergreens. There was no mistaking that rat's nest. Nathan. But it was no wonder he had not recognized his younger brother. Nathan had never sat so still. Maybe he was sick. Or dead. Or taken over by aliens.

Ben shivered as an eerie feeling came over him, almost as though he were slipping out of his body. He felt hairs rise along the nape of his neck. Suddenly his arms seemed too loose in their sockets. Fidgeting, he suppressed a rising urge to shriek.

Nathan turned his tangled head. Seeing Ben, he raised a finger to his lips then pointed up into the branches above his head. At first Benaiah saw nothing but stems and twigs, a broken branch or two.

Suddenly he saw it. An owl. A tall owl, with two tall tufts on its head that gave it the appearance of a broken branch. Now the tufts looked like horns to him, devilish. He saw that its coloring was textured and tweedy, contributing to its camouflage. It sat on fierce clasping talons, perfectly still. Was it sleeping? Or aware of them, pretending?

He came and knelt softly beside his brother. Together they stared, remembering all they had heard about a great horned owl terrorizing Gottheim. And, before she had healed it and set it free, it had been in grandmother's barn. But now it was here in the wild, uncaged, a fierce bird of prey. Huge. The boys were watching, mesmerized, their minds immersed in its lore. The bird would eat *anything*. It would eat them if it had the chance: an ear at a time, the fingers off their hands. It could puncture them full of holes and they'd stagger bloody from the woods. Or lie rotting, picked apart at its leisure. It was... —Stephen King's owl! Whoever Stephen King was. Nathan and Ben weren't sure. They knew he lived somewhere in Maine, and that this owl had come out of him. "That owl's right out of Steven King," everyone said. The man probably opened his coat, opened his chest cavity, and this owl came flying out to snatch puppies, cats, little kids.

The boys knelt there gaping upward, their muscles taut. Suddenly, from far above, came a startling harsh cry. Their heads jerked back. It came again, a double cry. Falling through the upper branches toward them came a set of wings, black and open, fluted. There came another, behind the first, swooping. The owl's eyes started open, staring at the boys, yellow. Winking once, it turned its tufted head and started up, great wings extending. They beat. Down fell the owl toward the youngsters, and they fell backward, screaming.

Heavy, but quiet as a great moth, the owl swept off as the two great ravens flew like shadows through the upper story. Harrying and harsh, the ravens were after it, crying with protective joy. Out of here! they seemed to say. *Our territory! Beat it!!*

Staring from a thicket in wonder, the Twitchells watched the shadows plying upward through the heights above Monster Rock, passing out of sight. Only the ravens' cries came back to them, distantly.

"Did you *see* that!" shouted Nathan. "They chased that ol'owl right outta here! I thought for sure he was gonna pick our eyes out! Didn't you, Ben'ah?"

"No, I never thought that, you dork." He was still staring toward the heights. Then, satisfied the birds were gone, he sank back, allowing his legs to sprawl. "That was Stephen King's owl, you know."

"Yeah'n we saw it. We saw Stephen King's owl." At school he could tell about it and, at supper tonight, they'd all hear. Ravens had chased the owl away.

On the drive up the river from Guildford to Gottheim, Balder considered. Did he owe something to Peter Prince? Prince was not surly or provoking or cocky or lazy, at least not much cocky. He avoided the idiotic scatological subculture in the mill, men whose brains were from the groin down. If they had brains: Balder wasn't sure. Sometimes you had to work alongside all kinds in a place like Adirondack Paper, but he didn't have to spend break with them. Also, you had to watch yourself, choose the right approach to some people.... They don't stand for display of ego. Some people couldn't help it, though, and wore their foolishness like a brand. Peter Prince wasn't much like that, not a bad guy. You might even feel like tossing back a few beers with him. And here I am, a union brother even, all cozy with Peter Prince's two sons, never saying a word.

But he had terrible suspicions about this likable man. In fact, once he had been *sure*... before actually meeting him. But no one had come right out and said anything to confirm those suspicions. Yet—he must have abused her. To the point where someone as responsible as Chrischana found it necessary to run away. And there was Ithiel Whitman... the likable man who killed his wife.

The highway slid along under the wheels of his pickup, smooth new asphalt lined with high pines. New roadway, courtesy of a ski magnate's connections with state officials. A view of the Arossagunticook opened up, some raindrops speckled his windshield. He went through the radio stations looking for something good. Sultry "Bette Davis Eyes" came on.

Peter Prince was working in the bleachery. Balder had seen him there today. The man was still going through his apprenticeship, spending time in various parts of the mill. He was here, but still keeping away from Chrischana. She did not know that Peter Prince was in Maine.

Balder had avoided dealing with all this till now. Chrischana's reasons for returning had been no business of his. She would have told him if she wanted him to know. Balder hated getting snarled up in emotional revelations, relations. But, also, he wanted to love Gloria with his whole heart, and little moves toward Chrischana would only strengthen the bonds he now had with her. He had one foot in the world of her family, one foot out. You never knew what might destroy the balance and bring you tumbling down slope toward... Chrischana. Even the fact that he saw her nearly every week... while seeing Gloria never.... Distance, placing emotional distance between himself and Daniel's mother, was the only way.

Gloria's great face and eyes, those teasing laughing features, her ways making him light.... Sometimes it all went dim. ...But I want to be faithful to it, to her. How long does love continue? I still love Christy.... and what is Gloria doing now?

Peter Prince got tired of asking himself nearly the same questions about Chrischana. Some subtle inquiries, put to the bartender at Farmingham Royal Tavern late one night, told him what he needed to know. Chrischana Twitchell lived in some sort of camp near an old burned-out farm. He knew what it meant to her, that old place of her childhood.

The old Twitchell Farm crowned the top of Buck Hill, a spur of Blackwell Mountain. Blackwell was low but vast, visible for many miles along the river and highway paralleling it below. With the telltale clear-cut draping its shoulders, it was one of the baldest mountains around (that side), but it was wild, wild as the territorial bear inhabiting it. Moose, fox, bobcat and deer frequented it, he supposed. There were old twitch trails and roads from the days of settlers. Blackwell Mountain was monumental and drear in autumn. Peter thought it might be desolate in winter. How could anyone live here alone? But her family had, generations. Was there even any water up here?

Peter Prince had come up from the dust storms of Phoenix, suburbia edging its desert and provoking those storms. It was an artificial place, sure; totally dependent on precision engineering to bring water to its new sun-loving populations. There were also questions about the water rights of Natives, the depletion of underwater reservoirs, and schemes to divert the Colorado River in order to fill swimming pools. Peter sometimes wondered how long it could last. Even so, he liked Phoenix. He could have lived there the rest of his life. His passion was biking the desert.

But he had traveled cross-country on his Harley-Davidson, towing his tools in a small trailer. It had been necessary to sell Chrischana's vintage Hog in order to make the move, but she had left him no choice. What was he supposed to do—cuddle up to chrome when what he needed was her love? It was all of herself she had left him, but its sale made the necessary traveling money. After all, she had appropriated the family Bonneville for her trip back East.

Now Peter lives in Jericho, Maine. He drives a pickup leased in Waterville, sporting a Maine license plate. His apprenticeship has been served, and this is his week on the night shift, southern schedule. He has not shaken the feeling of disorientation imposed on him by that backwards rotating schedule. And today, a cloudy sere fall day, finds him parked in thorny puckerbrush below the summit of Buck Hill. The surrounding foliage is russet, what's left of it, and he is hidden, waiting for the Bonneville to come wallowing downhill and veer left where the narrow hill road turns on its way down mountain. He watches from the brambles as the rusted old boat lumbers sedately toward the next curve. He sees Nathan's tousled head popping this way and that, jouncing in the backseat—probably irritating the hell out of Benaiah. Daniel is harder to disturb. A slow smile comes up from somewhere, as Peter Prince remembers his sons.

She is taking them down to the school bus stop on Lower Intervale Road. From there she will go on to that job washing dishes at the Inn. He knows a lot about her life here already, though he has been watching only two days. He has yet to see her new home on the hill, however. Today is the day for that.

He starts the engine and pulls out of the brush. Turning up the narrow old settler's road, he wonders how she will get in and out this winter. No way the town crew comes up to plow this dirt road. Maybe she plans to live in town?

Smiling, he recalls following them up as far as the turn yesterday. He stayed far enough back that they would not have recognized the lone person in the pickup coming behind. "Twitchell Twitchell." He says it under his breath. He shakes his head. You can't get away from it like that. You know me better. "Or should I say betta?" He mutters it.

He has tried to joke with Hermann Gottesman over those soft Maine r's. He has a subtle sense of humor but is a hard man to move. Impossible, in fact. The huge man with the tiny voice is solidly immovable and he doesn't think much of... well why *does* Hermann reject the joke? Yeah, yeah. He probably thanks it a slur. He thinks I get sloppy and lack respect. And maybe he's right. Maybe I'm just a wad of useless shit waiting to be flushed down God's toilet. The devil in me would like me to believe that. You cannot joke Hermann off, reason, intellectualize, fake him out. Don't even try wheedling. But there are times you have to rebel. That was how you dealt with inflexibility. Pure rebellion will get you where you want every time. And what I want now is a glimpse into Chrischana's life. And I want to see my own goddamn kids and *that's-what-there-is-to-that*!

Gottesman is full of shit if he thinks these things constitute rebellion. These are goddamn rights. It's not rebellion when it's your god-given right. Ask any patriot. Ask the Founding Fathers. Read it in the Bill of Rights. I'd rather throw the goddamn tea into the goddamn harbor than pay goddamn taxes without my goddamn representation. He smiles.

The hill is steep, the road narrow, deep-ditched on either side. He is coming out of the woods now. The whole clear-cut, draped across the triple summit, is spread out above him. For a moment he gapes at it, stunned by its barrenness and breadth.

They don't fuck around with those trees. When they cut something down, they cut it down. He recalls the pulpwood and chip piles at the mill, understands now how they can be so mountainous; sees again the glut of magazines spread along walls in newsstands and bookstores in Phoenix. There are magazines for every interest except picking your nose. He himself has two subscriptions for motorcycle magazines and knows of half a dozen more. But culture has to thrive, you have to get paper somewhere. Be nice if it grew on trees instead of being trees, but so far, it's the best material they've come up with. Glossy paper is unbeatable for quality, and that sheer seductive look.

The dirt road surfaced on Buck Hill, and curved to the right. It dipped and humped its way through more thickets. He pulled up and got out, following a dwindling track on foot. He passed an opening to an abandoned log yard where skidders had, not long ago, landed pulpwood and saw logs. It was vast as a suburban mall parking lot, empty, with a plain gray floor of weathered tree leavings.

Prince continued rounding the curve, and now he saw through spindly stems. The trees ahead had a withered look. Scorched. He looked up their lengths, surprised. Blackened trunks were crusted in stiff scorched leaves. Leaves that had not changed color and fallen as leaves should.

It's not natural.

Why'd she want to live in this blasted out wilderness? There's nothing up here. If there was water anywhere around he'd eat his saddle bags. At least in Arizona they know how to make a desert bloom. They even make massive aqua reservoirs with wave action so people can play. He shook his head. She's gone out too far to come back. *Gott'im!* You left Phoenix for this?

As he advanced, the scorched trees parted. His gaze grazed an old truck camper to settle on the twisted pile of corrugated roofing. He stepped over the rubble to the great gaping cellarhole, recently purified by fire. In its midst he saw the massive hearth foundation. He looked to the fire-clean stones lining the great hole, pieced together like a jigsaw puzzle, fitted with a skillful hand. He thought, *Whoever built those walls knew what he was doing.* Walking around the cinders along the foundation, he looked down into the jumble of broken bricks.

This is the farmhouse she was raised in. He ran his long mechanic's fingers through his unruly hair. Its strands fell immediately into his eyes. He looked back over his shoulder toward the lane. Nearby stood the camper supported by staging. *That's where she lives now.*

He walked over to it, put his head on its ribbed aluminum side and, hand up to shade, peered into the jalousie window. Covered. He walked around. On this side stood narrow tanks of propane. He shook his head. They all live here?

He stepped around and looked toward the cellarhole. Again he was shaking his head, but his spirit was sinking, his rebellion seeping off.

This is the best we can do? After what, 34 years of living? Is this to be your life? Why don't you come home with me? Can't we do it? Can't we make it work—get rid of the violence somehow? Will there ever be anything good for us?

Peter Prince looked up toward early-morning clouds. His wide shoulders drooped. He sagged a little, realizing that this was all he had given them. A house destroyed, a camper on a clear-cut mountain. Today, it made him very sad. He would go back to Hermann Gottesman now, seeking counsel.

But tomorrow, tomorrow all this would make him very mad.

She was wandering in her dusky dawn garden, stylish and matronly in a soft felt hat and worn tweed jacket with velour trimmed pockets and collar. It was early Sunday morning. Rhetta Bearce had come to terms with herself over the blighting derelict on the south border. She could wait it out, knowing that Lyman Bearce would not keep the grubby old diner out here forever. It might remain a year or two, or even three, but someday it would be gone... whether by his hand or hers. And maybe the peace of their determined coupling would never be disturbed by it. If she possessed herself in patience, blocked pettiness, someday soon it would not mean so much to Bearce to have it outside his back window. She had to take into account his secret sentimentality. No one in all Gottheim knew this about him. No one but Rhetta Bearce.

Stepping around toward the corner of the house, she looked back at the garden, now nothing but a pleasing pattern in neutral hues, with only the perennials remaining inground. She started around the corner where white columns framed the western piazza. Now she noticed the powder blue Saab coming up the drive.

Who's this?

The car pulled around the semicircular drive and stopped before the white steps. Ever composed, Mrs. Bearce moved toward it without hurry. She thought she recognized the flighty manner of the younger person getting out. Theodora Prescott. Calling at, what? She looked at her gold wristwatch. Twenty minutes after six on a Sunday morning. Strange indeed. Even Bearce was still lying in bed.

With staccato footfalls, seeming to agitate the very air of the calm morning, Theodora hurried over. Far below the hill, its tiny roofs visible now that leaves had fled, Gottheim was shadowed and tranquil. Part of the glimmering pond showed. Later, church bells would sound out of the valley of ponds.

"Good morning, Theodora," Rhetta's voice rang out crisply. "Nice to see you out'n'about early." What can the little thing mean by it? But Rhetta kept her curiosity checked. The young woman will reveal the reason for this soon enough.

"Good morning," gasped Theo. She seemed relieved to find the older woman outside. Clearly Theo was agitated. She dropped her gloves, then a silk scarf fell, fluttering. She managed to hang onto her purse, Rhetta noted, and bent to help her pick up the things.

"What is it, deah? You're obviously upset." No use pretending not to notice. The bird-like thing seemed about to fly. The girl looked up suddenly, as though about to seek a perch on one of the mansard dormers.

"Oh Mrs. Bearce, you're a strong person, tell me what to do!" Her hazel eyes were frantic, and the small receding chin quivered.

Mrs. Bearce touched Theo's elbow, concealing her surprise. "Maybe we betta go inside'n have some tea. You must calm down, Theo, if you waunt to communicate. The kettle's already steaming on the back burner." But Theo hung back. "Come on now, I insist."

Looking fearfully up at the long elegant windows, Theo stammered, "Mr., Mr. Bearce—"

"Don't choo worry'bout him. He's still sleeping up in the corner room. Won't heah a thing!" Explaining that the front door was locked, she took Theo determinedly by the elbow, guiding her along the slate walk around to the side. Theo was soon seated in the dining room with the teapot and a plate of raspberry cheese pockets before her. Rhetta poured her a cup of tea and sat down facing her across the fluted curve of the mahogany table.

Meekly, Theo followed her every movement, barely responding to Mrs. Bearce's conversational overtures as she gathered the little repast. Now she fluttered nervous fingers over the cup and saucer, speaking in an undertone, as if fearful that Lyman Bearce would pop up in the doorway, glaring. Whenever she hesitated Rhetta reassured her. It would be another hour before the man got up. Maybe two, she added as one seemed insufficient to calm the girl.

Mrs. Bearce noted with satisfaction that the room's warm and tasteful furnishings seemed calming to Theo. Her gaze wandering from the fabric covered cornices above the windows down along the elegant treatments of rose, seafoam and teal, Theo's eyes relaxed a bit. The marble topped buffet with its groupings of tapered candlesticks above rich dark wood seemed to diffuse a soothing pleasure in her birdlike features. Rhetta did like this sensitive girl. Theodora would come out all right. She always did seem to recover from her upsets... though their financial consequences must often be classified as large embarrassments. At least she could afford it—though it was a wonder how.

Yet, listening, Rhetta Bearce began to be alarmed, though she did not betray her feelings to this daughter of her late peer. What is this girl saying?! The townsfolk, every laborer, has back wages owed—for decades!? Is she out of her mind?—but it's no good being influenced by the child's hysteria. Be calm and try to get at what lies behind this gibberish.

"My deah," she said, taking hold of Theo's wrist. "Eat a bit, and drink your tea. Then I waunt the whole story carefully, a sentence at a time. Rationally. Don't that tea smell good? It's that rich flowery Plymouth Company tea, y'know. I love this tea."

Nibbling the pastry, sipping her tea, Theodora obeyed.

Mrs. Bearce said, "Numba one. Tell me exactly what's this... charge you make?"

Theo gulped. "That the mill owners have been working together to keep wages low. Forever. At least, since I was a little girl."

"How'd you know this, Theodory?"

"Well... I heard them talking. At cards'n such. I was under the table playing, and they'd be smoking, dealing cards, talking. Firming it all up. I heard them several years in a row. I'm not misremembering. It's not one of those fake things. At least I know it was not just one time. They met like that once a year—to confirm it, I think."

Mrs. Bearce looked sharply at her. "You're quite sure you 'memba it truly? Not a dream or anathin?" She held Theo's arm, looked directly into her eyes. "Sure?"

Woebegone, large-eyed, Theodora nodded. "It happened."

"But, what made you come out with it now, afta all these years?"

Theo fidgeted. The cup clacked against the saucer in her trembling fingers. "Something... a friend... said jogged my memory, that's all. I don't even remember what.... Please believe me, Mrs. Bearce."

But doubt hovered, hesitating in Rhetta's thoughts. If it was *anyone* but Theodora Prescott! Suppose she came up with this after some hair-brained session at IICE? Maybe under hypnosis false memories were evoked. And Rhetta could not help remembering all the fiascoes Theo had embroiled herself in. The older woman turned away, just a little, her elbow on the table, her gaze out the window where dark boughs were visible beyond the sheer curtains.

Theo sank back into herself. *Oh what had she done, coming here?*

"Tell you what," said Mrs. Bearce at last, turning to her. "I think now... well, you've told me this, Theodory. So, you can relax because you told someone... connected with this... theory—"

"But it isn't." Her voice was low. "Please don't make it seem— that."

"All right. Yes. I'm sorry, but you must realize that conspiracy is too strong a word. People in Gottheim ah not conspirators, Theodora. And I need time fah this news t'sink in. Can you content yourself with having told me... fah now? You said I was strong, so let me chew this ovah a time'n you rest. Okay? Don't expect me t'jump right up'n stot something." She stopped. "How long you been in this state?"

"Weeks. Only days? A month? It just sort of built up. I couldn't stand it anymore. Can't sleep... feel like I'm being hunted. It's awful, Mrs. Bearce. I haven't even told my boyfriend. He's devout and I'd be too ashamed." She paused and a look of horror came over her. "It would have come out in a session at the Institute if the season weren't over."

"Gracious!" said Mrs. Bearce. That was all they needed—psycho-babbling gossip! At least, she decided, it didn't start with IICE. "And you say a Bearce was there? Lyman or his father?"

"Well, both, I think." She nodded. "The Bearces where there." She said it emphatically. "Most if not all the mill owners were."

Rhetta looked toward the window again. "We're going to... have to consider." She was unable to say more. For, surfacing, came the disturbing suggestion that she herself had suspected something like.... From—long-ago. Theo's tale was jogging her own memories.... Kerosene lit lamps, cigarettes, talk.... She came from an old lumber family in a logging hamlet up the valley into Abenaki Notch... now extinct that hamlet. Nothing there now even to show there'd been such a place. Her father and grandfather had been lumber barons, too. But what possible good would it do to bring all this out now? She tried to picture what it would mean for the town, *for Bearces*. —No. Not just yet. She couldn't.

Rhetta looked at the quiet creature before her. "Feeling any betta now?"

Theodora heaved a slow sigh, then brightened perceptively. "Yes." Her gaze slid away and, with something of exaggeration, she hesitated as though rummaging about in her psyche for evidence. "Oh, I *do* feel better, Mrs. Bearce. *Thank you*."

Gathering her things, she stood to go. Rhetta walked her through the elegant rooms to the front door with its flanking divided lights. Together they walked down and stood in the drive. Rhetta could not feel relieved herself until she extracted a promise of silence from Theo. Then she tucked the young woman into the Saab and watched the car diminish as it passed down the drive and out into the road. She would see Theo again later, at church. Or—no. Theo hadn't been to the Congo Church lately. Rhetta had heard she was dating someone—oh yes, that impertinent Mr. little Fay. The developer with no sense of history or authenticity. He was a Baptist. Theo would worship there today.

Rhetta turned and went toward the steps, half listening, half searching for Canada geese. But, upon reaching the wide steps, her gaze slipped from the sky, startled. In his underwear, Lyman Bearce stood inside the half open door. His great white beard fanned over his undershirt, and above Bearce's eyes glittered.

"Oh-fah-heavens-sake, Bearce. Get on your robe!"

Bearce's glare deepened. Then he said, "She's nuts, y'know."

Rhetta Bearce drew herself up full. "Is she?" She gave him a long cool direct look.

"She will be." Lyman smiled at her, rare treat. "By the way. Howe's moving that dinah. Be sometime this week. I got a spot fah it down by the sawlog mill."

Rhetta grimaced. *You think of this now.* But she said nothing, only turned to walk back along the drive toward the walkway. Upon reaching the back garden, she breathed deeply, taking in her resting autumn garden with hungry eyes. The air refreshing her nostrils, her whole being, she drew a second breath. The morning light was calming. This day, this Sunday, would be calm.

But, come evening, the wind would rise. The pines flanking the grounds would thrash and thunder.

The exchange of roofs was generally made on Saturday, sometimes on Sunday. This week it was Sunday evening. Elda Simon was out in the barn, caring for sick or injured wild animals. Daniel was already up in his room, with school books spread out. Balder had shown Benaiah and Nathan the varying hare, which Elda had been raising, and the two boys were together with it in the yard. In the kitchen Daniel's parents sat at the table, evening coffee in their hands. It was more usual for Chrischana to hurry off for she sensed it made him comfortable: Balder always had an excuse for not taking the time to talk... as in the past, when they began sharing the concerns of parenting. So Chrischana had been intent on dropping the boys and getting away, however—mysteriously—Balder had urged her to stay.

His long fingers, mechanic's fingers she always thought, reminded her of Peter's. They were fidgeting with a spoon. Now they were drumming on the checkered oil-cloth. The familiar furrow hardened between his eyes as he gazed down into his coffee.

He looked up. " 'Fraid theya's something you got know. Christy, Peter Prince is heah. I seen him working in the mill. I—didn't think you knew."

His direct blue gaze startled her. The kitchen light above shone on his yellow-white hair. She felt her jaw drop and quickly closed it.

He said softly, "We don't have t'talk.... but I thought you'd waunt to know."

He watched her gaze drift away, staring off into the darkened front room. "Peter...." She said it a second time, as though trying out his name, then murmured, "I guess it happened then. He came afta me."

She picked up her cup to swallow some coffee. She set the cup down, cocking her head a bit looking at it. As though she had never seen a cup of coffee before. Balder was waiting. Moments passed. She didn't think she should keep him like this, turning them both into statues, trying to make time stop. Make everything stop.

She stood and went to stare out the divided panes of the window. Benaiah and Nathan were out there in the dusk, but reflected light from the kitchen prevented her seeing them. She said, "That's a snowshoe rabbit, in't it?" Continuing to peer out, she put up her arm to shield the glare. "Haven't seen one since.... I 'memba catching one by accident up theya on the mountain as a kid. Hadn't been enough snow on that trap or he wouldn't'o got caught.... You know how they leap atop the snow, hardly sinkin'..."

"Christy...."

Make it easy on this man. Sit down'n talk t'him. He's not trying to get rid of me now. But she could not seem to make herself move.

He stood and went to her, gently turning her by the shoulders. "Okay, Christy?" The look in her eyes was forlorn. She seemed dazed and he wanted to take her in his arms, comfort this sweet wife of his youth.

But she was thinking, bizarrely, Maybe I ought to put a note on the camper... just in case: *killed by bear*. One of her ancestors had written it in his youth, on a handkerchief in his own blood.

She said, "I'm okay, Balder. We can talk now."

When they were seated again, she said, "It's strange. A part o'me is glad. If you met him you know theya's some worthwhile stuff theya. He is worth saving. If anybody can save'em. I can't. I think you guessed.... Peter didn't always treat me s'good.... Or, maybe Daniel told you?"

He shook his head. "Daniel says very li'l—speech-wise."

She nodded then settled back, letting her gaze wander over the horsehair plaster ceiling. There was an old water stain in the shape of Florida up there above the sink. Her gaze drifted back along the expanse, past a few cobwebs, past the grate in the corner where heat from the woodstove lifted to warm the upstairs. Chrischana let her gaze drop back to Balder.

She said, "It's strange to love someone like that. Peter. People would not understand this, but I waunt t'be true to love. And I... didn't do such a good job... first time." She hurried on. "I made up m'mind. I'd be faithful to love."

She looked at him, steadily. He nodded. He was hearing her, while leaving the allusion to himself untouched.

"It's only thing I found give meaning to life. But people think, She's got a death wish. Something's wrong with hah. Well, Balda, we're gonna die. Whether we *wish* it or not. It's not length'o time but how time's spent. Live long, they say. That's best. But it's not. It's what you live'n die *for*. I'd live'n die fah my kids. I'd even live and die fah Petey—if it'd save him. It won't."

Again Chrischana turned her exotic eyes away, toward the darkness of the front room. "It'd be lying to say theya's no fear. I'm awful sorry'n afraid sometimes. And I don't always feel like this... but, who knows? Maybe seeing finally that death is real... that his hands (so good with tools) could really destroy the woman he had to hold.... Maybe it would stop his bent toward destruction."

Balder recoiled inside, but gave no outward sign. Maybe if he waited her sense would reassert itself. If it had been theoretical... he might be nodding his head right along. But it wasn't a principal at stake. It was Chrischana.

"But maybe that would make it worse, too. Anyway, I caunt go that far and it wouldn't save him. I've got the boys t'think of. See," she said smiling, "my faith's not so great. I caunt trust what might become of them.... if Petey murdered me. Even now, with you s'good t'em. Something like that could change the spirit even of Daniel."

She glanced up toward Florida above the sink without seeing it and brought her gaze down again. "If it *did happen*? If theya wasn't a thing I could do to prevent it (like take my kids to Istanbul or someplace)? It would be all right. They would make it through—eventually. My faith's got be like that. But I won't put myself in harm's way or be negligent so long's I can protect 'em fom it."

She was looking at him with grave, beautiful and quiet, Native American eyes. Chrischana had reached, he thought, her full physical and spiritual maturity. He felt the strength of earth in her. That she had stature, dignity, calm. She reminded him of the mountains in morning where he drove along in silence; of the Meguntics glowing at their edges, the sun about to rise. He thought of it: She was Jasper Mary, among the thieves.

Something, not a sound or movement, made him look up from her toward the ceiling grate where a shadow hovered. Behind the crisscrosses of the grate, two eyes glimmered. Balder stared into the eyes of Daniel.

But now, distantly, they heard a passionate sound. All three listened with varying degrees of attention. And Chrischana's most acute. She was on her feet before the sound moved Balder. Still Daniel stared down, his gaze abstracted, yet on the lapsed conversation.

The sound came into the room as though a harbinger of things in the spirit realm. As though from a great distance and through dimensions

misunderstood. The impression upon the man was of a war in a far off
Asian land, or in heaven, and he thought he heard its words coming down on
the wind. Now he realized that a wind had indeed risen outside the house,
rattling the window panes.

"It's Nathan," he heard Chrischana saying. And she was going out
the door.

Two boys played with a rabbit on the edge of the yard. Above them high on
the mountain they heard a wind. It was a benign background to what they
played. Light in the divided windows showed from the kitchen across the
yard; in it they cuddled the hare that Mrs. Simon had been nursing. She
found the hare stunned in a ravine, with both its eyes gouged out. Mystified,
Elda could not guess how this happened, but the snowshoe rabbit was hers
now to care for. A blind rabbit stands no chance in the wild.

Animals have an evocative effect upon Benaiah. With them he
reverts to innocence, playing peaceably with Nathan. He becomes a
younger Ben, tender and thoughtful, concerned with his charge. And, under
this influence, Nathan is more settled, quieter, feeling the delicate softness
of the hare's fur. He enjoys the rabbity twitching of its nose, the humor in
its long ears.

Stroking the soft fur, Ben says, "Fiver needs these ears more than
ever now he's got no eyes. Look how they turn this way'n that, listenin'."

Under Elda's care, the hare has become acclimated to humans. It
seems not to mind the stroking or the soft rise and fall of their voices. "This
rabbit can jump like anything," he said. "Ten, twelve feet if it wants,
because it's really a hare."

Dark has fallen, deepening the woods that stand over them. The
yellow lights of the house show and, when they glance in that direction, the
boys see the shapes of Balder and Mother at the table. Their eyes adjust to
the dark stealing upon them as the great shadow of earth falls in its turning
from the sun. In a related manner the coat of the varying hare beneath their
fingers is changing from dark to light—in reaction to lessening light as the
season wastes. When snow falls in early December the white of the hare
will be hidden in it. Tonight the process is visible in the molting of its coat.

"Fiver don't look bad with his eyes out." Nathan's voice rises a bit,
as the wind of Jasper Mountain dips down. Eddying, it stirs up nearby
leaves. "It just looks like they're closed a while." He spreads the rabbit's
toes with his fingers. "Look how giant his feet are. Guess that's why he can
jump good."

"She." Ben corrects him. "She was a mom, remember. They're
called snowshoe rabbits cause their feet s'big. But guess what. When she

goes into season, a buck'll come around and then there'll be baby rabbits. We'll have rabbits coming out our ears. They're famous reproductors."

"Huh?" Nathan was suspicious. "What's *that*?"

Ben begins explaining his superior knowledge. The hare moves off a bit, nibbling on sparse grass at the edge of the trees. The wind comes down the mountain, blowing and bending firs with its fresh breath. But now an extra breath moves over their heads, falling. A breath with wide wings. The wings cover the varying hare.

Nathan screams. Together they lunge toward the shadow, Ben falling on the great bird. He beats the predator, tossing amid a fury of talons and strong wings. Nathan falls back screaming—a torrent without thought: "Get'em, get'em, get'em, Ben! *Get'em, get'em, get'em.*"

Ben holds on, feeling the owl's mighty scapulas churning, but it will not release the hare.

"Pull-back-his-wing!" Nathan screams the phrase again and again, a singsong. And Ben, struggling, obeys, grasping the wing, jerking, straining his own young shoulders and fingers to keep hold, turning his face this way and that. The talons unclench. Scrambling the rabbit rolls away. With a shrug and waddle, the owl evades the boy's relaxed grasp. Screeching, it moves toward the woods but then turns again, daring them with circular eyes. Its face is split by a horned hissing mouth. The owl spreads its wings in a fierce rotating display. The white feathery feet are spread, its sharp talons splayed. Exhausted, Ben scrambles to his feet. The bird will spring with those talons.

Chrischana runs across the light-slashed yard, her braid flapping. "Get 'em, Mother get'em! Get'em, Balder," hollers Nathan on seeing Balder coming. "The owl wants Fiver for dinner, get'em!"

The owl turns, pushing off with mighty feathery feet. Beating, it reaches into the forest and after a moment of erratic flight is gone among the branches. Gone into the sounding wind on which it had but lately come.

One day before Halloween, Jeffrey Decatur, retired now from the diner named for his father (hauled away by its owner Bearce), finds himself walking quietly through the woods. He wears blaze orange and cradles an Ithaca 20 gauge shotgun, careful not to rustle the leaves in his path. Even before day was stirring, everything as yet indistinct and awaiting a surer form, Decatur got up, as though to prepare for today's labor. As though Monday would again be filled with soup, hamburger, tuna sandwiches, macaroni and cheese, pie. As though the eternal spot on the floor before the grill was waiting... as it had before, for almost the span of his life in Gottheim.

But Decatur donned hunting boots, an ancient pair of canvas trousers, thermal undershirt, flannel shirt and the orange jacket and hunting cap. On his way out he drove past two of the ponds in the valley where the Spirit of the Lord moved upon the face of waters. Already God was saying, Let there be Light. And Decatur saw that the light was good. He saw the little fir-choked island in the midst where Nataluk once threatened Dr. Lapham with captivity. It floated in mist-covered mystery as Decatur passed. God would be busy all week, commanding the appearance of dry land, gathering waters, telling plants and trees what to do, assuring the coming year's abundance of seed. Let there be light in the sky, divide the day from night, give them light on earth: The man Decatur's going to walk in this light.

Partridge supposed to be abundant this fall. Walking alone he wonders about this, for it has been dry. The diets of bird and squirrel overlap and even those rodents are hurting. Now he discovers that the ruffed grouse have spread out instead of grouping in their familiar coves. He flushes one on a new twitch trail and misses it—which he says to himself he ought'n'tove. It's as though the ghost of Father's saying, "Should've used #6 shot, Jeffy. Whad I always tell you'bout that?"

But he has only #8 with him. Aloud, he says as to the ghost, "Good theya ain't no wind this morning. Makes it hard to hear'em fly up."

And Father reminds him, "But it also keeps'em restless unda covah."

"That so?"

"Cuss, listen whad I tell you?"

Decatur chuckles, his glance slipping upward into the spruces. He dropped his gaze back down again, lest he miss something. " 'Memba that year we flushed... what was it? 30, 35 birds? We hit *one* bird that day, Fatha."

"Well, that was the day we learned how smot them birds can be, Jeffy. Wouldn't believe the eyes God give'em. Not like deer. Birds *see* the orange, y'know. They see way betta'n us. He give'em such eyes when he says, Let'em fly above Earth!"

"That's so, Fatha, but they stick to the understory. They don't quite make it t'open sky."

He flushes another one whirring out of the underbrush, straight ahead this time. He catches it with his #8 shot and it falls into the thicket. The faint acrid smell of his firearm wakes in his nostrils. He hurries to search among the leaves and conifer seedlings.

"That'away, Jeffy. It's heah somewhere. Those feathers makes it hard t'find."

Decatur finds the speckled lump among the duff and gingerly picks it up by a wing. The bird opens, unfolding, and he sees the tweed markings of its back, the white and brown stripes of its plump breast. The crested head flops down. Decatur is already thinking how to prepare it for the skillet, but Father stops him saying, "Don't choo think it's time t'say grace, Jeffy?"

Looking on the winged and feathered thing, thinking how its life has fled, Decatur draws a deep cleansing sigh. He gathers and holds the creature to him, respectfully. Looking up toward the firmament, beyond the boughs, he wants to see the partridge continue on its way from where its carcass fell. He thinks, *They must get past the branches after all.*

Won't evah living thing?

Decatur thinks, Bird hunting's worth it, now you showed me how again.

Like God who, once he had created, took his rest, Decatur will not work again.

Gloria left the Jasper Mountain Hotel and hurried along the walk beside to a wing of the building. It was a frosty November 3 a.m., a night as crystalline as topaz, as jasper or white quartz. After the warmth of Phillip's room and bed, the cold penetrated her thin blazer and skirt. She wanted only to get back to the Fay condo she shared with her brother Jimmy and wait for the sun to rise.

She wished for Balder, to speak with him and extinguish her loneliness. She wanted to forget that date with Phillip and subsequent sexual intercourse. Awful, clinical term! She had awakened after a brief sleep with him and then lain in bed, restive, miserable. It had taken 15 minutes to realize that she was perfectly free to get up, dress and leave his unit. Had he roused to see her departure, he would not have realized, until the next time he tried to see her again, that she had wholly abandoned him.

Turning a corner of the building, she came out to face the great heavens straight on. Even with the pinkish glow of resort lights competing, the stars above the mountains shone. Now came the dip in the walk for an intervening ravine. It was darker here, the pattern of stars broken by overhead branches. Away from the building she heard the roar of snow guns high above. Up there intrepid workers positioned and maintained the arteries, veins, and powerful fountains; a network slowly bringing the trails to life again. Certain trails were already open to skiers. For the first time in her life she had the opportunity to watch the silent giant take on its glorious rivers of white. The Goldings were transforming their slopes as they did every year.

Can men own mountains? She wondered it idly.

But tonight she was disturbed, and all this beauty hardly penetrated. She could make neither head nor tail of life. All was in a state of tumbling.

She unlocked the door of her parents' townhouse condominium. Upon entering she followed the pattern cast on the floors by lights in the parking lot, careful not to disturb James. Softly she went to her bedroom. He did not think much of the way she lived her life and the less attention she drew to it the better. It was not enough for him that she had given up Balder—a mechanic. If only he knew, she thought with irony, how alike their sexual mores were. Of course, it took more than that to satisfy James. You had to have position, a life that was worth something; prosperity, authority: It was God's benediction on you.

Beneath the skylights in her room, she cast herself backward on the bed and lay looking up at the stars.

Balder, what is all this—going on here below?

I live in this beautiful place, more beautiful than anyone has a right to—but I can't make sense of it. The days are crammed with this and that, but what does it mean while you're up there and I'm fumbling here below?

She turned on her side and looked at the phone, gleaming faintly with light thrown down from the skylights. I shouldn't be calling you at this hour. Not before dawn, anyway. Probably should not.... Does it provoke you when I call but won't come?

The phone jangled, startling her. She grabbed for it before he could ring again and wake Jimmy. Philip would be wanting some explanation, or simply wondering if she got in all right. She had been clutching the receiver to her blazer, but now raised it slowly to her ear. "Yes, I'm in, Phil," she whispered.

But there was silence on the other end of the line. Then the familiar Maine voice said, "It's me, Gloria. Balda."

She was silent. The line was alive not withering between them, but she felt sorry and shriveled inside. "I—I'm glad.... Balder... I was just... lying here wondering... if it was too early to call—you." It sounded bogus, completely lame. Her voice was tiny, incredulous of her own words.

"Sure?"

"Yes," she answered miserably.

His voice came gently. "What's wrong, Glory?"

"I... can't get it right, Balder."

"Get what right, Glory?"

"I don't know. *Anything*." It was gibberish. She could think of no words to communicate her misery. She collapsed back on the bed, her eyes looking up at the stars. But his gentleness was encouraging, his mute understanding reviving her. Then she thought of something to give shape to the conversation. Still with a small voice, she said, "Um... why did you call me, Balder?"

"Numba one, I missed you." His voice was quiet. "And also to apologize. I misjudged you, Glory."

How can it be? I'm wrong from beginning to end.

Quietly he continued. "It's a sorry thing to admit, Glory. You got a whole lot more perseverance than I... gave y'credit fah. When we first met, y'made me s'happy. Just *glad* the whole time. I maybe thought all that spirit, that joy of yours meant... immaturity. That you couldn't stick at something, anathin. I wish I could think a li'l betta of what you do.... You work so hard, put everything into it. 'N I see now how important it is t'you. Misjudged you'n it's been bothering me. Couldn't sleep till I confessed." His voice was still soft, contrite.

She continued staring at the stars. Venus, is that you? "Oh... that's all right, Balder. Really. I admit I try. It *is* important to me. Most of the time. Not always," she added. She did not admit that sometimes she lost her sense of purpose entirely. But it always reasserted itself again.... Under what circumstances? IICE advised analysis: Could she contrive to bring about the desired balance between professional and emotional life—at will?

"Thank you for the recognition, Balder. I do appreciate it." This was so sweet. His concern, the call and confession.

"You betta, Glory?"

"Much. Much better."

There was silence again, and she said, "Thank you."

More silence. Oh, was the line withering? Why didn't he go on?

Then he said, "Well, that's all I wanted, Glory. G'night."

"—Goodnight...."

And he was gone, leaving her with a dial tone. Surprised, she lay there. Such loneliness in that dead tone. She felt bitter, cut off.

"Immaturity?!" She said aloud, not too loud. She went on her side, curling away from the stars. *Why*, Balder, *why*? Why is it necessary that I give up *everything*! Why why why! Do you require *all* that I am, everything that defines me, the things I *love*? Must I embrace what I *do not* like? What I have no caring or aptitude for?

She was no longer miserable, but Gloria Fay turned toward the wall.

November Waters

"So.... thinking of converting, Hermann?"

In a corner of Hermann Gottesman's *Kids Cafe*, Peter Prince, of medium height and broad-shouldered, stood looking down at the little book lying on the battered circular coffee table before the ratty couch. It was early morning and Prince was just off work. Gottesman was up and bending over the woodstove, huffing as he fed a couple sticks of wood onto the glowing coals.

The door squealed shut. "What?" The big man, straightening, turned. "Oh, the book of Samuel Johnson's prayers." His great forehead glistened, he smiled behind his wire rims. "Not me, Prince, although you might want to consider it. You have that Christian heritage in your background."

"Pummeled into my background." He stopped, his green eyes reluctant, then said, "Ever imagine that everything ever said about God is written down somewhere? I mean," he gestured toward the bookcases, "besides what's in the books in the world?" The room was still cold. Peter kept his jacket on.

"Like in the story of the recording angel?"

Prince nodded. "There's God, or somebody, actually reading the... the transcripts of all these conversations we have about the Higher Power. Maybe Allah, Buddha, Yahweh, Christ, but probably someone lower, like maybe dead people, angels, somebody. Or, maybe they're sitting listening somewhere. But, when you think God (and, hell, you can posit anything in any direction about whatever)—you make God in your own image. Maybe it was women who thought of Mary as the mother of God. That makes her God in their eyes. God has emotion, intellect and will. So he'd be interested in hearing what's said about him." Prince sat down on the cold couch, hoping for a cup of coffee. Hermann's place was always cold in the mornings now—before he had a chance to stoke the fire. And Prince always needed some drink …in his hand.

"I think you meant Muhammad, not Allah. Religions and religious figures are not alike. Not 'equal' by any means, as secularists like to believe or encourage belief about it," answered Gottesmann. He sat in the overstuffed chair at the end of the coffee table. "But going by your premise, I'd say God is more intellectual than emotional, but, having made emotion," he indicated quotes with his fat fingers, "he would have to understand and experience it himself, I … presume."

"But then, your parents and your environment would play a role in your deciding what God was like. He might be a real bastard. Or," Peter sneered, "a bitch."

Gottesman stared at him. "Well, we've already started mixing the imaginary with the true... which makes it all untrue. Is the Higher Power the least bit interested in such imaginings? An egoist? When we are thinking like that it's about us, not God. Your formative experience might contribute to your imagination, but once you're thinking and mature, you can't continue to blame someone else for your concept of God. The roots of these things may go deep, but they can become a form of sadomasochism... an abdication, refusing to refashion the image in the true. Or, I should say, *seek* to learn what is true."

"How's this for an abdication: Why should we believe in God? I mean, look at life. All the betrayal and pain, the way people treat one another, the shit. Maybe I abdicated because God did."

"So what we do to one another is God's fault? Ancient question. And we keep adding more. The way we live, the destruction of species for the sake of consumerism and convenience, the trashiness of our lifestyle, the killing fields and gas chambers, the escalation toward nuclear holocaust...." He shook his head. "A better question would be, Why should God believe in us? Bequeathing us free will (if it is, as I think so), was a tremendous act of faith. Of respect even."

"So you think I'm abdicating because I was beaten and slapped for skipping church to go to the playground, and now I can't stop mistreating Chrischana? My mother knew she was righteous all right, and she made sure I wouldn't forget it." He slouched down, staring fixedly. "I guess you can just thank God you were raised a Jew instead of a Christian."

"You know—it happens in any religion under the pressure of temperament. She acted under an erroneous image of God in child-rearing, inflicting some very unChristlike stuff on you. Bad, even sick, attitudes will cloak themselves in investments. But you don't see it in Christ himself—from what's in your Bible. Therefore can you assume such people are deceived?"

Hermann said this and got up to fix coffee. From the kitchen section of the room at large, he said, "This is from a somewhat disinterested perspective—I didn't suffer like that from my parents. But I have an early acquaintance with great evil. If people are born evil (that's another question), are they definitely responsible for the evil they've done? Or are they making themselves into evil?"

"And God has definitely written it all down, what was done to me?"

"Well, we've talked about this before. It helps to understand how you got the way you are, but, if you're back on the recording angel, shouldn't you be thinking instead of your *own* account?" He set the coffee pot on top of the woodstove with a clank, came back to sit down heavily.

Peter eyed it dubiously. It would be another three hours before that coffee was hot.

Gottesman continued. "You gave the example of God as perceived male. A white, Anglo-Saxon Protestant male? Jesus fits only one of those categories, but we see Christians implying this paradigm and even insisting on it. Reading what his own disciples wrote about him, I can't see him countenancing this. And Moses, whom he quoted, wrote, "Let us make them in our image, male and female.""

Prince smiled. "You think because I call Chrischana little girl I don't respect her."

"No, I think that because you brutalized her." He let that stand by itself.

Prince just smiled and looked away.

"That is a smirk, Peter."

"Do I look female?"

"You're just playing games with the premise." He stood and took the pot to the kitchen stove, turning his massive back on Petey.

"Okay, Hermann," he called. "My mother was not God and neither am I. You want me to get over her 'mistake' in raising me. Well, it's not that easy."

"Have I said it was, implied it?" He waddled back to the low circular table and set mugs and milk beside the book of prayers. He said, "It's not for me to get over it."

"You could acknowledge the difficulty." He got out a cigarette and tamped it against the back of his hand, but did not light it.

Hermann raised one of his big hands, showing his palm in a gesture of acknowledgment. "Okay, Peter, I do. It will get *more* difficult, this process. In fact, it may get impossible."

"This is calculated to make me give up."

"No. You are not relieved of the responsibility to try."

"I am if I say t'hell with you."

Hermann crossed his fat arms and sat back against the dirty upholstery, staring down at the table. The sound of percolation, the smell of coffee lifted toward them. Apparently the fire was hot.

Peter Prince put the cigarette on the table and got up to walk around the room, his fingers jammed into the pockets of his jacket. His gaze wandered, then lighted on the bookshelves. He went to scan the contents. "Martin Buber," he said at last, touching the spine of one book. "What's he got t'say here?"

"That the bigot exchanges the I-thou of some relationship for the I-it. That we turn the subject of our bigotry into an object, something unworthy of our courtesy or attentiveness."

Prince took up his circuit of the room. A ping-pong table, battered pool table, kitchen table and chairs where teenagers could work on homework. Everything helter-skelter with cola cans, comic books, magazines. He came back to the couch and sat down. The chill was off the room. He felt warmth seeping into him and took off his jacket. The coffee would be very welcome. The night had been long but he was too restive to go back to his furnished apartment and bed.

"Okay," he said. "Let's get down to work. Ask me something, Hermann. I'm sorry."

"Tell me about Chrischana. What is she like?"

Peter yawned and stretched. He ran his fingers through his hair, pushing it out of his eyes, but it fell back immediately.

"Stubborn. Head-strong. She's the good one, always right. I'm always wrong. No matter what I say, she's the opposite, always got a better idea. My way of handling the boys is always wrong. I don't budget right, don't care enough, whatever. She's little miss good'n I'm the slob. Hermann, my escapes are warranted. There's got t'be *something* to kick back and relax with. Try to forget you don't measure up. The pressure never stops with her. There's always some way you could be better, think better. I want t'live without always thinking how I could be improved."

"Always is one of those impossible words. *Is* she by chance better than you? Somebody has to be better than you. Do you want to live with someone worse than yourself? If so why?"

There was silence while Peter thought about this. He could not help but smile at Hermann.

"You said you had good times. Rode cycles together, camped out in the desert, did things loving couples do."

"Yeah we did all that stuff. At first partied together all the time.

But she stopped doing that. I know—you're gonna say the partying did me in." He looked at Gottesman's steady gaze. "Okay—the drinking. Dammit, Hermann, you're not the most relaxing guy, either. Maybe you're like her. I can't be that good. Never could. In fact, most times it enrages me."

"That's where the Higher Power comes in, Prince. Recognize It as your help, a comforter. Someone who understands your weakness, with power to help when you're in the throes of anger or temptation. Face the *fact* of your particular flaws and faults and failings as part of your exercise on the planet. They may be a gift. Anyway, they can't be evaded, eluded, escaped from. You can't part with your intestines or any of your internal organs, and didn't make the twists and turns of your nature."

"Them why am I held responsible for them?"

"Because those are the rules."

Peter grimaced. "C'mon, Hermann. You're not one of those blind authoritarians who can think of no reasons but 'I said so.' " He tried the big man with a wry look.

But Gottesman replied, "I don't make the rules. I try to recognize them once I discover what they are. The help I get for obeying comes from somewhere else. Reason is limited in what it can do for us, Prince, but there *is* a kind of grace—the best word I can find. On the other side of some trial, I look back and see that something else, from somewhere else, brought me through. A friend, stranger, turn of events, change in the weather, a piece of pie, a book, a presence of peace.... The last of which by no means the least. The demands of Sinai were obedience to the words on the stone tables. Words impossible to observe entirely—given what we know about human nature. We live a while and learn: even when the will to attempt it is there, the execution is faulty. Simple acknowledgment of the need for help: 'Help me.' Afterward, you turn around and there's another acknowledgment: I was helped. Where'd it come from? But you know. It came from somewhere else. Somewhere outside your own nature or being. Grace."

"... But you're not converting."

"No. I am a Jew. I know who my Higher Power is. But your background is Christian. I don't need to depart from your stories to get my point across."

Peter Prince shook his head. "You're something else, Hermann." He looked away, heard the coffee still perking. "You brewing jet fuel back there or what?"

Hermann heaved his bulk up out of the overstuffed chair, went back to the gas stove, stuck a mitt on his big hand and took the pot. The smell of this brew had suffused the entire room, filling it with invigorating fragrance. Peter Prince could feel it revitalizing him on smell alone. If he drank it now, its strength might carry him away.

The rain began on a dim November morning, a Thursday, and poured all afternoon and evening. The people of Gottheim, of all Western Maine, heard rain sheeting across their roofs on into the night. It was the hard rain for which they had waited, filling their sunken aquifers with water enough to carry them into the following spring, seven months away. But now winter's rest is broken: Without this rain the mountainous land had gone to winter's bed in a covering of dry leaves, dark in the peculiar November dreariness which some hearts found bracing. The store of such folks lay in dreams kindled by the ominous coming of winter with its dissolving darkness, lighted windows, days ending in twilight so dense that only the distant sight of home might split it. In woodland echoed the thunder of hunters. Having risen in the dark, they gutted their fallen prey, counting its polished points with exhilaration. But now... that rain is hammering across the roof, is running in the brook bed empty until yesterday. Streaming downhill in rivulets and runnels, forcing new channels, weakening, widening; disturbing the old footholds of roots and rocks.

  At midnight, one householder on a slight rise hears the crashing of conifer. The fallen tree gathers to itself down-spinning debris, choking the stream flow and forcing it sideways over new territory; making new ditches. Downstream the Arossagunticook takes on the overflow of its many tributaries, rising, filling its empty backwaters and hollows, creating islands and small new floods. Highways will be segmented as sections submerge. Roadbeds and remote notches will churn with new water. People in towns roundabout will be cut off from jobs, their relations and, in some instances, the comfort of their own homes. Some will be in danger of being swept away.

Having been soaked in a scamper from their car to the welcoming door, James Fay and his sister Gloria land in the Bean Corner Restaurant. Still shaken from the ride back down the flooding Copenhagen Road, Gloria Fay is a bit trembly and ready to be comforted. The road runs alongside the now raging Rabbit River, whose rocky sides have had more than they can safely hold. They have seen water spilling over the roadway in foaming brown eddies, frightening and forewarning them against continuing the journey into New Hampshire. Now, in entering the tiny dingy restaurant, they find the room crowded. The little place is chockablock with conversation, full of the hum of people caught up and thrown together. They sit down in the midst of the room at the one empty table.

  Gloria shrugs her navy blue raincoat onto the chair back. James has already hung his London Fog near the door. He takes off his hornrims, picking up the table napkin to rub away condensation produced by the warmth of the room. Ever desiring to create a sense of presence or authority despite his small size, he wears a blue-black Brooks Brothers suit, burgundy tie, and custom-made shoes with lifts.

The door blows opened and in comes a man of medium build, wet hair hanging in his eyes. Seeing that there are but two empty chairs in the place, he approaches the pair to ask if they mind sharing the table with him. James Fay does not like the look of his brown leather jacket, nor the friendly smile in his green eyes. But Gloria smiles, indicating the chair diagonally across from her. "Make yourself comfortable. Some very weird weather we're having!"

James Fay frowns but says nothing as the wet man sits down beside him. His sister is always too ready to befriend the local blue collars.

"You wouldn't believe what it's like up that road," the man says, gesturing away from the highway in the direction of the notch.

"Oh yes we would!" Gloria says it smartly. "We were just up there, had to turn around and come back. It scared the stuffing out of me—seeing that white-water curving into the roadway. All I could think of was flash flood. What if a wall of water came suddenly down?"

"Someone up there did find out what if," answers the stranger. "A van was floating on its side with a woman standing in it, waving out the passenger window. It was trapped by a fallen tree or I wouldn't't've been able to walk out'n yank her out of there. Be gone down the Rabbit by now. That's the name of that River isn't it? She had relatives, a sister or something just up the road. I left her off there and came down t'get something to eat, get warm." He takes up the menu.

James Fay says, "Doesn't seem very hospitable, making you come down here after you saved her life."

"Wasn't like that. They wanted me t'stay, but—didn't feel like it! I'm from away. That's what they call it here, right? If you're not from here there's only one other place you're from—away!" He smiles, scans the menu.

Gloria laughs. "Exactly! The story of my life!"

The waitress has come to take their orders and, hearing the last remark, is a bit stiff. Gloria smiles, gives her order and then makes a joke about asking for water. But the woman merely turns to go get the hot drinks and submit their order.

"See what cha mean!" says the man, smiling, flinging the hair from his eyes. He is buoyant, exhilarated from his recent feat on the Rabbit River. The rescue has sent his spirit soaring and forged a fresh bond with creation. His voice is rapid, a bit above the buzz of the room. The brother and sister quiz him for details and he obliges.

There are a few more words about the freakish weather and its wreckage, then talk fades and silence descends on the strange companions. At last food comes, distracting them. They eat, speaking little, then part on strands of talk and good wishes for the return home. The stranger standing, says, "Go back to Jericho, forget the trip to New Hampshire for that bike part."

"Right." Gloria smiles. "The weather calls the shots, sets the agenda!"

By the door he opens his wallet, pays and goes out into the weather. They watch through the streaming window as he hurries to his pickup.

The noise of people getting up to leave increases as Gloria leans over the table to be heard. "That was nice. Refreshing, don't you think?"

"Yes. You could tell he was glad to save that woman. Had a ... a quality that doesn't exist under regular circumstances. He climbed right out there and got into the struggle. Peril can have that effect...."

He would go on in this vein, inflating, but she can't help interjecting: "Oh why can't we live like that—always?!" Her tone becomes wistful. "So much sorrow—in our, our vagaries of feeling. You find yourself in the middle of some extravagance, acting out something you later regret. But it's done. Then you're filled with the old debris of it, choked."

The place is quieting. A child whines restively at the table across the narrow aisle, as its mother hushes it. Lingering over coffee, the brother and sister try to repair their rained out plans. The scheme to check out a resort on which the Goldings have cast their eye has been diverted by the flood.

"But the water will be gone next weekend," he reminds her. "We can start again then.... So, if you don't mind, I'll just go back and see if I can catch up with Theodora, find out what she's doing today. She told me last night but I don't remember." He looks around for a telephone. "Maybe I'll call her."

"I saw a phone out there." She gestures toward the outdoors, an eyebrow raised dubiously. "It's not enclosed."

They gaze out into the parking lot where gray sheets still fall in gusts. James signals for more coffee. "I guess we got our water," says Gloria. A glint passes into her eye. "Speaking of which, is Theo all set for Sunday?"

Jimmy smiles. "I think she's up for it. She agreed months ago. In fact she brought it up first. But later she was touchy on the subject. Then she gave it up altogether, but in the last couple weeks she's come around again."

Gloria raises an eyebrow. "Is it something she really wants—or is she just pleasing you?"

"Well, dear Gloria, I take exception to that word, just. People who belittle someone's actions on the basis of just. Just because they don't want to hurt someone's feelings.... Just because they want to please someone.... Are these insignificant insecure insincere little motives? Huh? Answer, speak up, defend your flimsy position if you dare."

Gloria flushes, debating whether the embarrassment is worth entangling herself in an argument on hypocrisy and pretense. She decides to let it drop, but she is peeved, seeing his point while remaining opposed. "Okay, I yield. For now. We'll credit her with a good motive. But— beware what they say about the road to hell. Dear James."

"But I happen to believe Theo really *wants* to be baptized. I admit to being doubtful at first, but she's really worked up a fervor. I'm entirely ready to claim that her desire springs from—well, desire. She was pretty brittle for a while but that's past. She's brightened up, smoothed out considerably."

Lucky her. Gloria brushes away crumbs on the cloth. "Well, I wish you both luck." *And I'll reserve judgment. That woman's got a long way to go.* "What I like about her is her lack of meanness. There's not a mean bone there." *All her other bones are cottage cheese.* "Don't see how you can go wrong. She adores, no worships you." *But be warned against reality setting in.*

Reality. Cloud nine is perfect until it slips to cloud eight, cloud seven. Six, five. It can drop to hell in no time. The vision of a god can dim fast in the clouds of life's real problems. Balder wants a commitment to grunt work. He wants me out there turning the soil with him, immersing myself in it up to my armpits. No thank you, Balder. I'll stay where the work is elevating. It's got to be something I *know* I can give myself to without rebellion. Without regret. Let those things stay in the storybooks where they belong. In fairy tales with princesses, knights and heroes, gods and goddesses. I'll be on the mountain, fresh air in my lungs. Ready to ski!

"Think what the rain's done to the mountain! All that perfect base they worked so hard to build!"

"Not to worry, Glory. Storm's an aberration, only a setback. There's plenty of time for them to get it built up again before Christmas. Before Thanksgiving!"

She sips her lukewarm coffee. "I miss those colorful crowds, don't you? The ghost town atmosphere is... I'm a bit bored. But you're all taken up with your house. Haven't got the roof on yet, though, have you? I haven't seen it since—can't remember! They were sheathing the walls."

"I'll get Theo to go. —Go out with us, sis. We'll see how it fares in this rain. They don't have the shingles on yet. It'll leak like a sieve. At least it's on a rise well away from the stream."

"Pretty exciting, this house, Jimmy."

"I could tell you. There's nothing like it. You've got to get started on one, Glory. It'll cheer you immensely."

She nodded. "I'm—considering it."

But the coffee is gone, the rain has slackened. They can see across to the intersection swimming under a pool of murky water. Cars on the highway slow to sail through, trailing wakes.

Cautiously, or recklessly, you drive into the pool, the body of your vehicle testing its depth as you go. Flooding, it inches higher, or, you back away... depending on the degree of your reckoning. You may find yourself committed, in the midst of a lake. Will water cover the floor mats? Will it lift you away? Your trepidation or regrets may be deep, but it's done.

After the flood, the water recedes, leaving debris of rocks and roots, dirt and gravel, or the wreckage of cars. The roads are choked with it—are washed away, barricaded, closed. You remember the flood for hours or years, depending on how well you judged the currents, their depth.

Or, you might have stayed safe and snug in your house or apartment, drinking cocoa, coffee or tea. If your house is secure, well-placed. If the foundation holds.

The pilgrim Chrischana thinks these thoughts, reading the flood today. She is perched high, alone in a camper on the top of Buck Hill, looking out through the distances, misty, obscure. Here she notes rivulets streaming beneath the staging supporting her little home. But her propane is lit, she's here to see to it. She might have chosen to go over the hills with her children to ride out the storm at *Simons Ledge*. She wanted instead to look out for her property. Being here is like being on the summit (instead of the shoulder it is) of some mountain, a summit wasting by rain. This is the place she has been given.

Theodora Prescott stands in the wings, on steps leading down into the baptistery. But for the little girl standing just below her, she is the sole penitent awaiting the call to immersion. Like herself, the little girl is modesty clad in swimsuit beneath a white cotton choir robe. The Rev. Dr. True, up from Portland, stands on the opposite landing above the great basin. He wears a white vestment. They are waiting for the choir and congregation to cease (singing *Shall We Gather at the River?*).

Theo looks down on the little girl. Her hair is the color of a mole's, and straight. At least, Theo imagines that it is the color of a mole. The small oval face and gray eyes are very grave, when she looks this way, as if aware what she is about... standing here above the water, awaiting the washing away of her sins.

Can we really wash our sins away so easily, wonders Theo. Of course this is only a symbolic ritual. It must be a matter of the penitent's intention. You can invest this act with meaning. Is the little girl doing this now? She's not fidgeting.... Does tend to twist the front of her robe. Her fingers are small girl's fingers, twisting and releasing a pucker. She smooths the pucker away.

Theo looks at the top of her head, at her white shoulders, as the girl steps down one step.

Is God doing anything at his end? Investing meaning, as she hopes she herself is doing? It must be so, or baptism wouldn't be in the Bible. John the Baptist wouldn't have bothered. Unconsciously, Theo begins twisting the front of her robe. But she catches herself, strikes at the pucker, grimaces.

The song ends, the organ closing triumphantly. From beyond the wings comes a hush, filled with the rustle of people closing hymnals, sitting. James, even Gloria, is sitting out there, watching. But, when it is her turn to step out and down, Theo will not look toward the congregation. In the hush she hears rain, still pattering distantly on the high roof. Roads out there are still flooded, some of them, parts of Gottheim are isolated. Here in the church they are sheltered, set somewhat apart from other towns till the waters lower.

The woman closes her eyes. A fluttering under her breastbone disturbs her, but the pastor is wading down into the basin now. He motions the little girl forward, and she advances into the water, her robe lifting, spreading out like petals of white. The little girl shivers. Now Dr. True is pronouncing words over her. Gently he takes her arm, covering her mouth and closing her nose with the thumb and forefinger of his great hand. He plunges the girl into the water, her gown and the mole-colored hair spreading. For a moment she is a wavery watery thing, as though made of water and no longer flesh. Gone in abstraction of grace. Then at once she is back again, a girl, flesh and struggling to stand.

The pastor is helping her out of the baptistery, into the hands of an elder who stands on the landing above.

The minister motions Theodora to come. And she obeys, stepping down into the water with a shock, feeling it take her breath. The hand of Dr. True is firm. He has come north to officiate over the two meager baptisms and to deliver the message. Theo looks briefly into his merry eyes. He seems to feel the awkwardness of the water, robes and onlookers; while being aware of the occasion, her commitment: the connection of this act to another and fuller existence. Rejoicing, he knows what she is about. For a moment Theo is glad this pastor is from away. It lends a peculiar pointedness to the ritual, inversely investing it with the spirit of locale.

She closes her eyes, feels his hand over her face, now abandoning herself to his keeping, allowing the sensation of backward falling into water, his firm arm beneath. She is under and weightless. No longer burdened by gravity, care or clothes. Theo relinquishes control, exchanging it for lightness of being.

Up the pastor brings Theo, guiding her toward the outstretched hand of the deacon. The weight of her wet rags is heavy, unbalancing. Staggering, shivering, she grasps the hand held out to her. If the clasp should fail now, she will fall backward into that carefree realm. But it is time to ascend from the baptistery and take on the weight of her new life. For as long as she wears the rags of her flesh, only rarely will Theo taste the freedom of these moments again.

She will put it so in years ahead, retrospectively. But there is only one thing she knows for certain now. God has released her from the turmoil of her guilty conscience over artificially low wages, and nonexistent benefits, at Gottheim Chair. There has been some rearranging during this flood. Some changes will come of it.

Jasper Mountain Breakdown

After the flood it became necessary to hike up and down the final section of the Buck Hill road until persistent request by a woodland owner brought town crew member Ferdinand Sessions out to repair it with the bucket loader. Curious, Ferddy drove up after his work was done to check out the ruins of the old Twitchell Farm. He duly reported on the campsite to town officials, with consequences to follow. In the meantime winter would come, but now its forethought, frost, was doing the work of hardening up the road, so Chrischana was able to negotiate it once more with the Bonneville.

Driving up the steep hill she turned the problem of approaching winter over in her mind. It was now deep November, the land stiffening, life pulling itself inward for rest. Plant tree rock soil duff bacteria: rigid, waiting, all hardening for the great endurance to come. Any day, soon, storm out of Canada would blast the Twitchells. Except for the great triple summit at their backs—southerly, and not in position to protect—they were open and exposed on Buck Hill. Yet, all her worth was in this place, and there was little money to spare for an apartment somewhere. Shelter: the great blessing of God.

Sometimes she felt that her manner of living had always betrayed her nature. Was it true for her to be so unprepared? It was not how she felt inside. Within, she felt provident, wise. It was that initial misstep... that flight into the West, the desert, and away from love and Balder.... It echoed still into the present. That one impulse had forever prevented her pulling effectually on her bootstraps. ...But she was Native, forever dependent on nature and God.

Somehow this encouraged her. Yuht. I like it. An odd kind of wisdom—doesn't need to be a curse. I can still do well with this—fruitful imperfection.

...But, whenever I come into their line of sight.... Like this morning when Sarah Roberts came into the tavern. Chrischana tried to think she exaggerated their notice of her, the town's elite. *She saw me at the dishwasher*. Seemed to forget the homeroom we had in common.

They had never been close, but it hurt to have one your equal in studies consider you a failure. Sarah's manner told her she had not fulfilled her potential. The owner of Farmingham Royal Tavern, Sarah had flown in, harried; the valued member of the Chamber of Commerce, chair of committees, trustee of town institutions. Her hands might rinse out a cup or stray glass after a gathering, but they were never red and cracked from washing a hundred plates and bowls.

So what, she thought as a clear-cut ascended into view above the hill. I *like* the challenge, the person I've become—even if I give myself trouble.

The Bonneville thudded along the dippy track until the camper came into sight. It looked tidier, different. She pulled up, staring and incredulous. Someone had skirted the staging support of the truck camper with plywood while she was at work this morning. In the crisp air she stepped away from the Bonneville and walked around the camper, taking in its new snugness. The plywood had been secured to 2x4 supports with Philips-head screws. There was even a hinged door, beneath the overhead berth, in which things could be stored.

"Caunt have you continuing to burden yourself with this, Balda."

That evening she said it to him, crisply, having dropped in after supper for the purpose. "You're doin'evah thing you should, right here at *Simon's Ledge*. No need to add time and expense to all this. I don't see how you even *had* time. Waunt you at work this morning?"

They were upstairs in the children's house, attached to the old settlers home. He had on gloves tucked into long sleeves and was stuffing the old lathed walls with fiberglass insulation. He glanced over his shoulder at her as he worked. She stood warming herself by the small glass kerosene heater that gave off heat and light. Its light came up around her jeans, throwing shadow and weird gleams over her features. Eerie shadows jutted along the bare walls whenever they moved.

"That's where I was. I plead innocent of all charges." He finished stapling one side and turned around. "Maybe it was Peter."

She stared at him, just as earlier in the day she had stared at the skirting. Chrischana frowned. The room became still, so still that he could hear Nathan downstairs in the kitchen of the settlers house, jabbering, clattering the dishes he washed with his brother, Benaiah. Daniel was in his room in the other part, studying. Mother was out in the barn, tending two wounded deer. She had been distracted lately, fearing death by doe-permit of her favorite, Posey. Posey had not been seen for two weeks.

Her shoulders drooping, Chrischana turned away from him, her brown braid trailing to her generous hips. The sagging shoulders signaled defeat to him, and weariness. Was he just projecting a sense of yearning there, too? She must long for a stable family atmosphere, a real home. He felt a rush of anger. Why couldn't Peter Prince contain himself? Why don't you keep a punching bag, learn to expel your aggression on the air? What are you using for brains—nuts and bolts?... But Balder was not subject to fits of violent rage, not after Vietnam, not ever. He could understand a... a holy frustration great enough for true anger—but not the gross loss of self-control toward those one is responsible for in love.

Her back to him, Chrischana did mourn the loss of what was stable, normal, and *clear*. Deeply she regretted the confusion cast by the bent of Peter's temperament and rage. By his laziness and lack of commitment to conquer his selfishness. In a shriveled voice she said, "It's all these glimpses into his goodness that disturb me, throw me off. They make it impossible fah me t'find my course." Her face crumpling, she turned to him. "The days, weeks, even months and maybe *years* we had of *fun*."

She glanced back in longing on their good times and shared eroticism. "He holds this promise out to me, then crushes it. Theya's so much confusion here! Is he stalking me? Is he caring f'me? All this pattern of crazy weather! He's like the weather. Don't like it?—wait a minute, it'll change. Balda, what's this man gont do?... See, that's the thing. What's this man gont do?"

The sounds below, Nathan's sounds, had shifted from the kitchen to the front room. The boys had finished the dishes and were roughhousing in the front parlor.

"One thing's fah certain," she said. "Substance abuse is a big factor. If he could avoid that, we'd be a lot closer home."

They delighted in the sprawling Simon house. Here, as no place before, they were happy, completely occupied in scampering along corridors, climbing any of three staircases, poking around the shed, hiding in cubbyholes or snooping through attics. They could do nothing more satisfying than to hurry along passages or through dark rooms trying to ambush one another. The game was always spontaneous, breathless, spooky, subtle and sublime. Its best feature was suspense. Is he squatting around the corner, ready to spring? Or is he clean out in the ell shed?

Breath bated, tense to his toes, Benaiah crept up the back stairs of the children's house. The staircase was stale-smelling, cold and dark; too dark to see the vapor of his breath. But nearing the top, along the wall, he saw a faint glow from the little end room. The grownups were up here, Balder was working. Yet, Nathan could come creeping up the stairs any moment.

Or? Maybe he was up here already. Nathan, you puppy. *You've had it if you're in any of these rooms.* Ben would test his skills of approach on the big people first. As he crept toward the glowing room, he heard their murmuring voices.

Then: Among shadows in the doorway opposite the lit room, he saw… *something*.... Dark and very still. Maybe it was an old stack of junk. Or maybe it was a bundle of Nathan.

Quiet, creeping, daring to move but an inch or two at a time, he slumped along the wall toward the glowing open door. Balder was speaking.

"Do you waunt me t'talk to him fah you? He don't seem to know about Daniel'n me. I'm sure he don't know I'm anywhere around you Twitchells. Maybe I betta talk t'him, anyway. He'll be my enemy if I don't'n he finds out elsewhere."

There was silence, and Ben forgot all about Nathan.

Mother said, "It's gone on long enough. The boys prob'ly ought know theya dad's here. One thing they miss, it's Peter. They ask when they'll see him again. Other night Nathan said he was scared Dad would forget what he looked like!" She stopped and Benaiah heard her walk about, restively. "Wish I knew if he's staying out o'the bottle...."

"I could find that out easy enough."

With caution Ben peered into the glowing room. The tall swaying shadows of big people who ruled their lives jutted into its corners and over its ceiling. Balder was kneeling to cut a strip of insulation. Mother stood looking down on him, her back turned. Benaiah stole across the hall into the cold and dark. A slash of light from the room opposite fell across to the window. By it he saw Nathan sitting in shadow against the wall, his knees up. Ben slid in beside him, quietly. No word was said, but he had seen the sheen of his brother's eyes.

In the dark they huddled together, listening and intent. The mist of remembrance settled on the older boy, his recollection of Dad.

He felt his little brother's shoulder lightly touching his arm, testing to see what Ben would allow. Benaiah gave a sign by not moving away. Then he felt Nathan lean into him. Just a little. They sat close together, listening to the conversation about their father.

Dad was somewhere near Gott'im. Somewhere very close. They would see Dad again, and he would not forget them. The adults, who ruled their lives and took them here and there and told them what to do, would see to it. They would remember Dad, and he would remember them, after all.

Outside and across from the little end room, light from Daniel's window gleamed. Deep in the intricacies of nucleic acids, he was completely absorbed in his studies. Daniel did not hear the intermittent pattering at his window. Then he heard it, called it sleet and became lost again. The sound ceased. He made another note and the sound returned, louder, like hail against the pane. Something familiar about it woke him from his work. Just so Cindabilla used to call for his attention. She never knocked at the door below but went around to see if his light was on.

He jumped up to look out, but the lamp's reflection blocked his view. He lifted the sash and looked down. Faintly, his eyes adjusting to the dark without, he saw the gleam of her uplifted face.

He hissed that he would be down. He let the window fall. He was out the door.

Hunched into their jackets they walked the frozen lane. She was laughing at him, her high thin laugh. "Thought I'd come back an addict, din'choo! Thought I'd come back pregnant! A pothead at the v'least. Admit it, Daniel."

No, I thought you'd die. That you wouldn't come back. He said, "We could've been killed hopping that freight or had our legs chopped off... and you know it. Things happen, Cindabilla. What *should* I think—afta Times Square?"

She was silent.

"I told you I only wanted t'see the Statue of Liberty, and I done that. I wanted to see the Empire State Building, World Trade—n' I done that. I saw Greenwich Village. I did not go theya t'get hooked on drugs! Daniel I got no money, but I can still be a tourist. All it takes is a thumb—and feet." She hopped three times, squeaking, "Feet feet feet!"

"It took three months to see Greenwich Village?"

"It was only two months, Daniel." They were out on the road now, heading downhill. She turned and began walking backwards facing him, her pale ponytail swinging. Her breath was all clouds. She wiped her nose on the back of her cuff. "The best part is—you won't b'lieve it!" Her face was lit with a Cindabilla grin. "I been—guess!—Florida! Palm trees! Beaches. 'N scraggly trees like papah birches. You nevah seen such houses—all spanking clean, pretty colors. The sea down theya's like bathwater. Alligators with skin like white pine. Orange juice is evah where. Fountains of it!"

She went on, talking about hitchhiking to Naples and Fort Myers

Beach. Of the kindness of strangers.

"Saw these sad white birds with round heads, looking at bulldozers bringing down trees. Just watching all bewildered as theya homes disappeared. Either that or because they stirred up insects f'them to eat."

On and on she went and Daniel let her, satisfied solely to see her, hear her squeaky voice again. He waited for her first vulgarity, relieved when he heard it. Happy again. They tripped down the frosty hill through clouds of breath. Around the curve, the lights of the distant village showed.

Cindabilla was back in Gott'im, safely, of her own accord. Accord. He thought of the dual meaning of the word. Accord was everywhere. He was ready for Thanksgiving now.

"So why'd you come back?"

Wickedly she grinned. "Pigs is in shot supply down theya. Nevah saw *one* whole time I was gone."

He stood by the back door of the Farmingham Royal Tavern at the end of breakfast shift, like a small mountain, apparently waiting for her. She had seen him through the window earlier sitting in his car. A massive man, he stood there now, huge as any Belgian draft horse or Clydesdale, great-legged.

"Chrischana Twitchell?" He backed off some as she opened the door. His voice was smaller than she had anticipated, higher and lighter.

She nodded, barely.

"My name is Hermann Gottesman, a friend of Peter Prince, a counselor, actually." He paused to let this settle. "May I talk with you?"

"...Yuht,... she said. "...Caunt think waya'd be a good place...." She looked around absently, mystified. ...Not here in the parking lot? His car?

He said, "Maybe we could walk around the Common, find a bench."

"Okay. Meet choo theya?" He didn't look like much for walking. They would *need* a bench. She looked over at his car, a silver sedan with bad shocks.

He nodded. "In a few minutes, then. Down by the gazebo?"

She finished up, got in the Bonneville and started out the parking lot ahead of Gottesman. His fat and bespeckled face in the rearview mirror made her recall that first impression of him, not slobby, quiet, intellectual, faintly ravaged. He had a high bald forehead, receding salt-and-pepper hair pulled back in a ponytail. He did not seem to have a neck under that beard.

Peter, you're blowing my mind.

He had been here at least two months, probably three, and she had not seen him once. It was either incredible cunning or remarkable self-restraint. Yes, he had found out her place and doings. He must have seen her. Wasn't that stalking? Yes.

At the moment, seeing this big man, she did not feel much threatened. She tried to recall the fun, love and intimacy of former days.... was there anything else on the side of stability... besides this (possible) demonstrated restraint?

What about that letter of thanks in *The Voter*, from someone who had been caught in the flood?... But that heroic act was something she knew Peter capable of without special effort. Caunt take it into account. After all, the woman was a stranger to him. He only has problems being kind to one woman. The one he lives with. The woman he's supposed to love.

He huffs, breath in clouds, waddling beside her on the diagonal path through the Common. Gottesman is needing that park bench. He sits down ponderously, relieved. In seating herself on the cold bench, she brushes him and it's like brushing against a monolith, no give to him. Briefly she wonders how this immensity perceives the physical world. What's it like having earth pushing so hard against the flat soles of his feet? Do his bones feel as though they'll collapse under this mountain of weight? Is there more friction with the atmosphere, are his internal organs deformed?

She thinks about Petey, waiting for Gottesman to speak. His gaze is on the old red brick block across the way. Above them great stiff branches of an old elm are lifted in a fountain of leafless limbs. He turns to her, massive arms the size of other men's thighs clasped crossed his abdomen.

"Ms. Twitchell, Peter has asked me to talk with you. Did you know he's in the area?"

"I knew it before I saw the skirting around the camper, Mr. Gottesman."

"Hermann."

' "N you call me Chrischana. How'd you come to know him?"

"I'm a substance abuse counselor in Jericho, where he lives. And I'm an alcoholic associated with Alcoholics Anonymous, where I first met him. I work by referral and meet people through that program, as well. Peter... is taking his Twelve Steps. You know about that? You are familiar with his temperament, dysfunction and lack of self-control—of course. He has confessed these things to me. He's been hard at it... the commitment. I don't think he's trying to put one over on me because he... forthrightly declares his ambivalence. His instability."

She thinks about this. "That's a good sign. He wouldn't do that before.... Just say he's sorry and then do it over again." *But he's a stranger... caunt know Petey yet.*

It is her turn to stare off across the Common. She murmurs, "It's been seven months since I saw him...—I had a horrifying letter fom him this past summer—"

He waits. When she persists in abstraction, he softly says, "Yes."
She sits still, silent.

"Chris—chana. Is there anything in your mind to... give you hope in your relationship with this man?"

There is a pause then she says, "Well, he sent you. Instead of coming himself. Couldn't've stood that." These words are said low, as though to herself. "But... I don't trust him. I *shouldn't* trust him. So I won't.... That word you use, hope. Hope for our relationship. What hope I have—if any—comes from myself. Not Peter Prince."

Hermann had not expected this answer. He thinks it a very good one.

"I know what *I* will do. Not what Petey'll do." She chews her lip, thoughtfully. "I'm concerned'bout what ah kids is exposed to. On the other hand, they love'n miss him."

A group of children, laughing, breaths wreathing, accompanied by a few adults, have come onto the lower end of the Common to gather around a young blue spruce. The pair watch as the group begins decorating the tree. Piping voices drift across the drab expanse. But for that glad group the whole day is drab and colorless. Hermann Gottesman glances back at Chrischana, but she keeps her gaze across the Common on the children.

"The truth, Hermann—I get along fine without'em. Life heah makes me—alive. He's nevah been interested, always made fun of me'n this place. He must love'n need me more'n I do him. But he don't know *how* to love. *I* know how to love.... is that right? Am I being fair?" She takes her gaze off the children, looking at him.

"Think about it," says the big man. "There is a certain amount of faithfulness in him—right now. He's not drinking. I know because I see him every day. You can't hide it on that basis. At the moment our fellowship replaces his reliance on the bottle, and he sees me because I understand what it takes to stay sober daily. So the effort is there. You are the catalyst. He knows it's what he needs to do, but I doubt he'd do it except for the hope (if you will) of Chrischana and his family. He's full of what it's like without you all.... Knows too that destruction is waiting for him. I think caring for you is a better motive than any he could have, even though it goes against current social thinking. We *should* depend on one another; it's right to be dependable. We need family, community.... But still I would not guide you."

"But that's why I came back here."

He had stopped short of saying that self-righteousness may be here but thought she sensed it anyway. He nods. "Yes your need was desperate, you were saving your family, your life. But can you also see what he has accomplished? It is hard to accept when the past has been so difficult. A prolonged pattern was established, but the question now is... has it been broken. Or broken enough to encourage you?"

She turns away toward the children again. "Why'd you come?"

"Because he wants to see you."

The course of the conversation should have prepared her for it.

"I'm sorry, Ms. Twitchell. It's a difficult part I'm playing but he was wise to approach you in this way as you've admitted, and I'm sorry for the intrusion." He looks off toward the library again.

And suddenly she is aware of his discomfort. She almost places her fingers on one of his big dimpled hands resting on his fat knee. "Please, I am grateful for this."

The man is an oddity. Later, when she has time to muse over this moment, she will think of his likeness to some old prophet: strange, and standing in the gap where repentance and a yearning for connectedness must merge. Maybe... maybe only by this strange man will the merging, or union, come. And, by some ... grace will the two be joined again. But only in peace can it happen. And it will be hard. Very hard.

But, today Chrischana is unready. Sitting here beside this immovable mountain, she realizes that even her own feelings are unstable, changeable. Yesterday she may have thought, acted, only with longing. But today when it is asked of her she dreads the thought of seeing Petey again.

Firmly, deliberately, she says it. "I'll consider this. I will, Hermann. He did do something right by sending you, instead of coming himself. *That* would be the intrusion."

Sensing that something more is needed she hesitates. It's a difficult task—the actual reaching through this large man to Peter. Connecting with Peter by these words: "Tell him.... Said I'd consider it."

Again he thought it a very good answer. "How he reacts to that will be—telling. May I give you my number?"

She nods, barely.

He reaches inside his jacket and pulls out a small white card.

Dusk. From his pickup in the parking lot of the restaurant, Balder can look out on clouds pouring off the paper machines from within the mill just beyond town. The complex of great boxy mill buildings, pulp-log piles, conveyors and steam, is lit with the eerie orange glow of sodium vapor lamps. He sits idling outside Wilbur's Bar and Grille, a haunt of Adirondack Paper workers. Maybe he'll catch up with Peter Prince here. From this space he has a good view of the grille's back door. But, Prince might park on the street and go in the front door. Or, maybe he never comes here. Balder shakes his head. More likely Prince is out of the Guildford click. As he is himself.

There he is, pulling in in that leased pickup he drives. Balder climbs out, dashes across the parking lot before the other can reach the door. "Got eat, like evah one else, Prince?" He is almost jocular, the Balder Simon everyone thinks he knows.

"Nah," the other smiles, tossing the hair out of his eyes. "I come for the entertainment. Fun watching the little grill man drop buns on the floor and then brown 'em on the grill. That touch of grit really spices up the burgers."

Balder chuckles and follows him into the clatter and chatter of the bar. Together they walk through the grille and grab stools, the hot toasty smell of french fries just beyond the counter coming up at them from a basket set to drain. Sizzle and steam pour up as the grill man lays frozen patties down. Talk and cigarette smoke fill the air, waitresses go to and fro with trays, coffee cups, beers. Balder says, "Can I buy you a beer?"

"No. —Thanks, Simon."

"Something a li'l stronger, maybe?"

Prince shakes his head. "Think I'll just have what I do when I come in, the sizzler. Good steak."

His beard waggling up and down, Balder nods. "Let's get a booth, though. More relaxing—afta work."

The two men thread through the crowd, finding a booth near the telephone. Jukebox displays are fixed to the wall, above every table, featuring some very old tunes. Sometimes you'll here "Your Cheating Heart" while you eat.

Seating himself, Prince says, "I usually sit at the counter, there being only one of me."

"Not so much in the G'fid crowd."

"Nah. I work with'em, that's enough. You?"

"Same." Balder grins. "We could talk'bout that, but we waunt get out alive."

The waitress comes to take their orders. She walks away and comes back with coffee for Peter, a beer for Balder. A small brunette in her late forties, she's ready to kid. "I made this coffee special f'you. Brewed this here beer, too."

"S'pose you'd like us t'member that when it's time to leave the tip," replies Prince.

"Nope. When you make out your will."

The two men grin and watch her walk away. Balder's grin fades. A frown puckers his brow. He says, "Gut something important to tell you."

"Me?" Prince looks at him, aware of a drastic mood change. "Something personal?"

"Real. Do you know what I'm talking about?" His tone is stern.

"I have no idea."

Balder is giving him the creeps. Prince has never seen a look like this on his face. Simon's expression is transformed. As though he were another man. The black beard and white head always pose an amazing contrast, and now this fierce face. He looks like a pirate in an old B-movie, the kind they showed on TV after midnight when Prince was a teenager. "What the hell is this?"

"Petah, I don't know how to tell you except to tell you. I know Chrischana Twitchell."

"You do?"

"Her son Daniel is my son."

Peter Prince stares at Balder through the brown tendrils hanging in his eyes. A rush of rage, of disbelief, floods him. Of course! It's why she came back! He stands, searching for the waitress, goes to her fumbling in his wallet for money which he stuffs in her hand. He is through the crowd and out the door.

Out the window Balder sees him pass beneath a street light and out of sight. He ponders a moment. His food comes and he eats absently, thinking of Peter, of Daniel. And of ice fishing coming up in a little more than a month. Of buying sheetrock from Beecham's Lumber and Home. Before his meal is done, Prince is back, striding toward him down the aisle. He slides into the booth, running fingers through his wayward hair, curtly saying, "You really ran me up the jack ladder." It was a reference to the log conveyor in the wood room at Adirondack.

"Yuht, but no need t'go through th'debarking drum. You knew Daniel was another man's son. Now you know whose, that's all. He's been staying with me every other week. So've Nathan'n Benaiah."

Deflated, Prince sits back. Walking around outside he occupied himself trying to remember what, when, she had told him about Daniel's conception. Had she ever said a name? A place, even. From somewhere he had the idea that Daniel was tied up in her travels, not her hometown. Whether she lied or not, he should have known. Maybe unconsciously he did know it was Gottheim. Maybe that was why her talk of Gottheim irritated him.

Prince glances at Simon. In the recent sporadic spying on Chrischana he missed it all. He has missed so much in all his responses, his relations with her. His gaze drops back to the table. He glares at Balder's half-finished beer. His second beer. Still glaring, he looks up. "And Christy? Have you been makin'it with her?"

"No." It is all he is willing to say about that. Trying to convince him would only raise more suspicion. "She's got her own place, which you know.... But... I'll say this: she sees no man, Prince. Not that way."

"You know why she left."

"You? Do now. She wouldn't've left without that."

"Without my abuse. My hurting her."

Balder draws back, surprised. He has known men who bully and hurt their wives, girlfriends. Never heard one admit it straightforward like that.

"No more avoidance, evasions, Simon. Open confession. It's what they teach at AA. I'm an alcoholic and a wife-beater. I've got a lot to be responsible for and tell myself not to forget it. Because I do not know if I can restrain myself under pressure. Under the influence. Now let's talk about something else."

The waitress comes back and sets coffee down for Prince. Without speaking she goes away.

Prince draws the cup to himself, muttering. "Planned. This was planned."

Balder swallows his beer, eyes the other seriously. "Chrischana waunts to know if you're still drinking'n I volunteered to find out. And... I thought you should know'bout the boys."

"I sent Gottesmann to talk to her!"

"Know nothing bout that."

The urge to lash out seizes Prince, but he steals himself to consider: We both sent go-betweens. He swallows his coffee, wanting to ask about the boys, but his pride and pain prevent it. Instead, he asks, "How long'd you know—that I was—that it was me?"

"Couple months, maybe. I guessed you hurt her, but I kept quiet. Alert though. And we didn't know about AA."

"She knows now. If Gottesmann met her this morning like I asked. My counselor, Hermann. I wanted him to find out if she'd see me. Simon, I don't want her living up there this winter. They have to stay with me. Jesus, can you imagine! North wind'll pick their bones clean up on that hill. If they can get up that hill after the snow comes. The boys can't handle that, neither can she."

Balder frowns. "Betta be careful, Prince. She loves that place. Waunts to build a house up theya someday."

His jawline tightening, Peter bristles. It galls to hear Simon advising him on Chrischana and defending her joys to him. He brings his cup to his lips, looking away. But then he sets it down, hard, unwilling to swallow the indignity along with the brew. "Do you know how it feels for you to tell me that, dammit! Are you her—anything, now?!"

"Don't plan to be. Wait back a bit, Peter. We all got interests t'be discussed. We're all just talking heah, okay?"

"Stay out of advising me, Simon. I won't stand it. Have you got a wife, girlfriend? Can I give you advice?"

Balder falls silent, holding his beer, avoiding the other's stressed glance. At last he says, "Guess I'm all done." He stands, puts on his jacket and pulls out bills for the woman who served them. "I'm around. Come by the house, *Simons Ledge*. That li'l road above the pond outside Gott'im village. Mailbox out front has ah name on it."

Peter Prince does not look up. He mumbles. "Thanks, Simon."

He does not turn to watch Balder make his way past the booths toward the cash register.

The smell of gasoline mingling with that of roast turkey drifted into the front room. Balder was in the kitchen dismantling the carburetor of the snow machine. Elda Simon was hiding out in the barn.

"Dad's coming! Dad's coming! It's Thanksgiving! Dad's coming!" Nathan bounced up and down on the couch beside Benaiah. The TV was on and between commercials they wrestled and punched one another, alternately glancing at the screen; avidly they watched commercials, and always Nathan's mouth ran.

Daniel sat quietly in the Morris chair, absorbed in his thoughts, a textbook open on his lap. The flickering blue glow of the TV bathed the room until he leaned over and turned on the lamp. There was a chapter on the Middle East to look over for Monday's quiz. There was the Ayatollah and the Marine barracks blown up. The light showed bookcases at the edges of the dim room, showed the rag rugs and coffee table, the afghans and old quilts draping worn furniture; the glass cabinet where decades old whatnots were displayed. The sleek old walnut clock sat on the mantelpiece but he did not hear its ticking.

Daniel jigged his pencil up and down. He was thinking that Dad had always known they were not related. And he had never said a word about it... even when he was drunk. Nobody had said it to Daniel.... Mother said he was different now. He had changed back to more what he was at first—when Daniel and the boys were younger; when he was most of the time sober. Is it true? How does she know? Was it Balder found out?

He looked at the clock. Mother was coming, and Dad was on his way also. Their first meeting since April.

Just up from the pond under the street lamp she recognizes the pickup as the one they saw a couple of times that autumn on Buck Hill. She is glad now that they did not know who it was. Seeing him up ahead her armpits gush. Why am I doing this? It's not too late to turn around. Turn in the lane and go back. *Don't go looking into green eyes.* But her foot on the accelerator leads her, following Peter up the hill beneath Jasper Mountain.

Remember the first time you saw those eyes. On the playground in Phoenix. Talking with Sabrina while the toddlers, Daniel and Felix, were busy tasting sand. Daniel had just started walking. Juan Bacca and friends were there, Sabrina introduced her. Peter was one of two white guys. His Harley pleased her and so did the eyes. She would not have minded if the entire world, all the constituents of her life, could be in those eyes. God things change!

She turns and follows the pickup down the lane. Nerves. Tripping up and down, back-and-forth, thrilling her sickeningly as she shuts off the engine. She yanks the door handle to steady her shaking. She is really doing this, walking slowly toward him where he stands by the pickup. Light streams from tall windows, but he hangs back in shadows. Waiting for her.

If the boys heard the engines, car doors close, they'd be out here. Better that way. Let this meeting be mediated, dear God. But the boys do not come. She has to be firm, Quicken her pace, greet him.

"Hello, Petah. Peter." Her Maine voice, God.

"Christy...." He doesn't notice the accent. He stays by the pickup, waiting for her to come as close as she cares. Does she expect the glib contrition, played as usual after his violent episodes? Times when she stayed in the boys' room, bruised and aching the morning after? He pled then for forgiveness, believed himself absolved. A changed man.

She draws near, not too near. *Be remote from this.* "Nice night, Peter, stars'n all."

"Yes." He looks southward through the trees and up beyond their limbs. "It's like the trees are wearing lights." He looks back at her, wanting to say she is beautiful. But now it would offend her. She'll see it as facile. Words come too easily, a part of his charm. She sounded like Maine a minute ago, almost as she did when they met. Her life in Maine pleased him as exotica then. But it lost its look, became a form of frumpery to him. Now he remembers his merciless mockery, and how he tried to change her, make her into the image of someone to excite and arouse him. Weren't the beatings a part of that? Didn't it excite him to see her frightened and submissive, desperate to soothe. That horseshit drove her away, lost every bit of it for him. Now she must hate the lard of charm that covered the shit.

"Boys here?" He asks.

"Should be."

"Daniel knows?"

"I think maybe he always did."

This piece of insight begins a baptism of shame for him, triggering thoughts of how the boys must have seen him. How could he think they belong to him? Even Nathan and Benaiah. Like they were all motorcycle tools to be thrown in a fit when the obstinate part wouldn't yield.

"Christy... I—" He puts his hand on the door handle, yanking it open. "I think I'll come back—later."

She steps forward, putting her hand on the door. "Theya waiting, Petah." Her hand stays on the door. "Theya ecstatic t'see you. Well Nathan is. Daniel's looking forward to riding with you. Ben'll be bashful at first."

"It's not that." There is an outpouring of shame, and the desire to escape, a powerful thirst. His Higher Power is rejecting him. Peter will not tolerate this shame very long. Even now he feels the rage of it possessing him. *Rage*!

Rage against God's self-possessed purity!

Tricked out in an errant gleam from the windows of the house, his jawline tightens and seeing it Chrischana backs away.

"Goddamn it, Christy!" He yanks wide the door, scrambles in, guns the engine, slams the door.

Chrischana has already hurried to the house through its swatches of light. In the safety of its shadow, she turns to see him back, then swing around the Bonneville. Reckless. Leaving the protection of the house, she steps back into the lane to see his red taillights wane away. He turns right, heading up the hill. She can hear the screeching of his ascent, the gunning engine. Now diminishing. The faint squealing of his tires drifts down. But Peter is ascending on the lower parts of Jasper Mountain, climbing to a higher place.

Bounded with trees, the road curving—in a passion, his tires whistling, he remains alert for the gleam of any oncoming beam. The temptation is to curse God and plunge the pickup down some ravine. Let all this steel and speed and the trees of this mountain combine to pulp me! The ease with which he can mangle himself on these reckless reaches! The pangs of this evil demon!—God deliver me! He hears himself screaming it. "Deliver me! Goddamn it! Deliver me from evil!" Screaming like a maniac, he twists the wheel at every curve.

Suddenly at the turning of the wheel he finds himself on a new road.

There are houses up here, newly minted but vacant, not a light gleams out through the trees. He plows on till the road ends on a cul-de-sac. Peter's foot mashes the brake and he stops, gets out, still breathing and now kicking his passion. Working blindly around the circle of sand and gravel, stomping and kicking, eyes glancing toward stars, his mind is well enough to tell him something. And, staring at the almost circular wall of trees surrounding him he realizes that he has been shouting at God. Shouting for deliverance out of this rage. Purposely he slows his breathing and watches the passion of his rage weaken. *This is not the way to do it.* You can't choke God's help out of him. You've got to stop and whisper for it. Kneel down, make your voice small.

He glances about quickly, then goes in among the trees... to kneel; sheltered, hidden. The ground is hard and cold, studded with granite. But the discomfort to his knees rouses him.

"God...." He says it but finds his voice hesitating, false. "Jesus...." he whispers it, hesitant. "I know you're there. Help me." He stops, his mind working. It's not natural, right, but he tries it again, whispering and troubled. "Could you help me?"

Peter sighs deeply, leaning into the tree. The grip of passion falls from him. The feel of bark on his cheek is cool and smooth. He puts his arm around this tree, closing his eyes; sighing again, leaning on the tree. Cooling peace comes out of the beech tree into his spirit. Joining him, creating a comforting union. Gently this spirit moves, even so it is almost wholly still. A living stillness, hidden in the heart of everything good. And, in this moment, it comes into the heart of Peter Prince.

Christmas in Gottheim

It was late afternoon with snow gently falling as Asa Bartlett trudged along Front Street toward the clock tower in the Congregational Church. Sidewalks had not yet begun to collect these flakes. He liked the way they speckled the dim air; sparsely and sedately, as though December were thinking of snow, spilling flakes hopefully a bit at a time. Shouts of children, skating out on the pond, drifted in from alleyways and gaps in Gottheim's buildings as he passed the storefronts. He guessed the gentle snowfall invigorated the children, maybe getting them thinking of Christmas. Christmases come rare enough in childhood. *I've had a grip full of Christmases, I guess*. He tried to remember what it felt like to have only seven Christmases instead of nine times that number.

He had a 50-year-old image of Mother, calmly moving through the house as though alone, dressing the mirrors, the sideboard in the parlor, festooning the mantelpiece and hearth with ropes of pine. There were long fragrant boughs looped with cranberries patiently strung by his own fingers as he listened to *The Adventures of the Lone Ranger* on the radio. How he loved those old radio plays! Nothing like them now... except maybe the *Prairie Home Companion*. His mother would set up the Nativity with ceramic figures of Joseph, Mary, and a babe in a manger. Shepherds and stable animals. He had seen the significance of the manger early on because of his chores throwing down summer's hay for their own beasts in winter.

Fifty Christmases later he now felt the heft of them weighty upon him: He would be spending his first with Olive. They were married now. All her kids and two of his, and their children, uniting this year in a celebration wholly new. Asa didn't know if he could take it, and he wondered what the dynamics of it would mean. But Olive had said, "Oh, we'll all be togetha, eating, watching the kids open presents, reminiscing, singing carols—"

"Singing!"

"Singing carols round the piano." Olive had said this with a smile.

Asa came out on School Street looking toward the Common. Through falling snow he saw people setting up for the Living Nativity not far from the lighted spruce. Children would be dressed for their parts, including wise men bearing gifts. And there would be live animals, a cow, horse, goat, maybe sheep, to add that spice of the unpredictable. All the historic and mythic participants of the First Christmas Story would be in attendance upon the miraculous appearance of a single child delivered in agony. Asa hoped there would be no cold snap, nothing like zero with wind. Good*ness* don't let it rain!

He came up the walk to the tall white church and entered below the ticking tower clock. It struck the half-hour and he began to climb.

Everywhere, in the village and hamlets outlying, preparations for the season were ongoing. In each Christian house tradition would be preparing. When the day came, the child would be welcomed according to some beloved but trifling custom. In God's House and in each home. Israel Kimball, who was already an old man when Balder was still a child, looks down upon the village from his turret, high in an old mansion on Crazy Knoll. He was headmaster when Asa was in school at Gottheim Academy. To his somewhat dim eyes, the storefronts, churches, backs of houses and schools of Gottheim are tiny, the Christmas toys of the Giant whose hands are far larger than the hotel-in-planning, or the wood mill near the outlet of Ben Hutchins Pond. Israel Kimball is the son of the daughter of a Gottheim lumber baron, Oliver Mason. He was the giant who commissioned the building of this storied mansion now decayed. Oliver Mason became wealthy off the products, made by local workers, from the forests of Gottheim in the 19th century—but now he is earth in the churchyard behind the Congo Church on School Street. Oliver's children are earth, who once wore crinoline and flounces, and took singing lessons and owned stables and racehorses in the Fairgrounds outside the village. The Fairgrounds had been demolished and the runway put in. The Goldings and skiers land their planes there now. Israel Kimball thinks of these things, looking on the village through bleared and aged eyes. His thoughts on death and dirt notwithstanding, he looks on the snowfall and feels its gentleness and purity.

His frame is as frail and uncertain as his vague-seeming watery eyes. The way of his flesh, this tentative bag of bones, is what all come to if they live long enough. But, seeing the snow, he smiles. He too prepares for

Christmas, awaiting the Christ Child, anticipating the birth pangs of its mother. However, these preparations are not apparent—no one sees them. The old man merely prepares his heart, hoping to catch a glimpse. But it has been decades since he has seen a baby closer than half a hundred yards. Once, last summer, a mother walked her baby on the street below.

What's that? He turns from the speckled scene outside his window. That was a noise outside the tower room door. A knock comes, briskly, but he waits several minutes before shuffling, bent and stiff, toward the door. Slowly he negotiates a way around the worn table filled with the remains of lunch, morning papers, books stacked in teetery piles. His old turkey gobbler head and neck project between hunched shoulders as he leans into motion of opening the door. The knob rattling in his freckled claw of a hand, Israel opens the door tentatively.

Perfect timing. No one there. The supper tray sits on the little table of the landing outside the door. He should have put the dinner things on the tray for her, but he forgot. Are there any messages with supper? Not in evidence. Sometimes his niece Regina leaves a note for him about one thing or another, sometimes the odd letter, document or bit of news; perhaps some new joy or hardship in the town. In September it had been the lost children, in November news of extensive flooding and attendant dangers. Last spring he had seen someone sitting in her Bonneville looking out toward Mount Will. He finds less pressing news in *The Village Voter*. Israel Kimball knows what goes on in Gottheim, though he has not been out of the tower in decades. And he takes *The Sun*, *The Journal*, and the *Portland Press Herald*, learning what happens in Maine and the world.

He grasps the tray with long stiff hands, turning gingerly to make his slow way back into the warm room. The stairwell is chilly, but in winter he has a good fire in the little stove from morning till late night. In the cold of morning he can scarcely move, but his fear of creosote fire in the pipe makes it necessary to let the hot fire burn out. Regina keeps the junk box opposite the table on the landing supplied.

His hermitage is companionable enough. He reads the Bible, the Saints, the thoughts and histories of good men and women, the classics, medieval works and philosophies; keeping a diary, jotting down his own insight. There are bookcases under the window sills and piles of his notebooks scattered about the room. Regina brings up texts from the library and stores the old journals in the old study. He also gets air and exercise, climbing the stairwell. The door on the lower-level opens into a bath he had built long ago. She keeps it clean for him. In milder seasons, through open windows, he hears birdsong and observes their activities. His face is sometimes seen by passersby below. They may have the horrors seeing it, he knows. Usually he keeps it hidden behind the lace curtain.

The mansion itself is now a boarding house for students at the Gottheim Academy, which his ancestors helped found. Israel was once a scholar, then a teacher, then headmaster, there. In term now, eight or ten students make for Regina's living; and they are usually present only at night and sometimes on Sundays. Their days are handsomely structured with computer classes, hands-on science and biology, performance and fine arts, the rigors of math physics chemistry; with skiing hiking lacrosse and other sports; with travel and charitable works. The mansion below is usually quiet, but late at night sometimes he hears their manic music, remotely.

Israel's real concern is not reading or writing, nor even thinking. His real concern is praying. Sometimes Israel Kimball prays all day and night. He has hidden himself away like this for a very long time, ever since coming to terms with his own temperament. No—it was the conjunction of this with the loss of Ellie. His wife died more than 30 years ago. But he has always been quiet, shy, inept with people. Abrupt, even irascible. In their early decades, even Ellie did not understand his sense of separation. Yet, their last 10 years together were heavenly. These vanished like the once gracious forms of everything loved. All have vanished, but this house and its view. That will be gone one day, too.

Faith remains. And Christmas.

Israel sets his supper tray on the narrow table before the south window to eat his meal looking out through swirling snow. It's the view beyond the tracks with expanses of farmland reaching to mountains; a few straggling roofs of the Village. There the glow of street lamps is visible through snow. Anyone within and without Gottheim might be the subject of Israel Kimball's prayers—though he knows hardly anyone personally now. Like him, those he knew have aged. Some have gone to nursing homes in other towns and many are in graves along the river or behind the Congregational Church. All were rosy noisy babies once, but since have mutated beyond recognition. Like himself. But Israel does not need to know people personally in order to care and pray for them. He needs only hear about them from Regina's notes or read of them in the paper. If his prayers are feeble, he asks the Holy Ghost to blow on them. He prays continually for devotion. Even after many decades of worship he finds the prayers are always in need of help.

Israel Kimball's custom is to share the Christmas season in a familial spirit with the whole community. Birth notices, obituaries, wedding announcements, neighborhood and town columns, letters to the editor, articles, club bulletins, police reports: he learns from all. Very little escapes his notice. The prayers extend out past the notches and river valley, over mountains, into vast upcountry, down to the sea. They reach across borders, go down into Times Square, up to Alaska, and deep into the Arctic circle darkness. They run to California head-lands and, down the gullet of Central America, or into the stomach of the Southern Hemisphere. His prayers go deep into the ocean, see its creatures, cross fire and water to the continent eastward, and beyond the lonely islands of seas. Anywhere there is pain or abuse, the cry for healing, the hatred of what once was Lucifer. Israel Kimball's prayers are there. If there were need, they would take to the solar system of the next galaxy, but the stars do not need his little prayers. So far as he knows, the birth pangs of the Kingdom do not extend there. He leaves them to the devices of their stellar astounding mechanisms.

No one in little Gottheim knows what the hermit is doing up here in his tower attic. Even Regina little knows. They all have their suspicions and opinions—in which, he supposes, whatever it is doesn't amount to much. Everyone knows that Israel Kimball's life has been wasted the last thirty years. They perhaps surmise that he gave up the ghost long ago, only haunting his old body now and awaiting its withering, disintegration.

How right they are, he thinks. An old man, isolated, keeping up on what goes on in the House of God? He is the most provincial of provincials. Looking to become a stream of molecules, destined for a breakdown of the nucleic acids. He will leave it all behind for the babies, become a broken line of atoms and molecules, mulch for the children of the future. He was a baby once. But you'd never know it to look at him.

Looking out the steamy window of the camper, Chrischana rejoiced. "It's here. Boys! It's here! Get up! Balda's gut the evaporator! Get up!"

"It's here! Christmas's coming!" Nathan scrambled over Daniel with whom he shared the over-the-cab bunk. Snuggling close to mother, standing on tiptoe, he peered out. Balder had pulled out of sight, and the boy saw only the standing scorched trees, now coated with frost. Yet he catapulted back into his bunk to rout about for his clothes. Next, hopping about on one foot while trying to get into his jeans, he hustled Benaiah. "Maple syrup, maple syrup! Ben'ah, gonna make maple syrup!"

"Shut up, you grub," said his brother sleepily from his bunk beside Chrischana's knees. "We can't make it now."

"Right you ah, Ben," said his mother, prodding him to get up. His bed had to be converted into the table so that they could eat. "Tail end o'winta, almost March. "That's when sap stots flowing. "We're just gont'get the evaporator set up. Then, when time comes, we'll be ready." She lit a burner on the stove, took eggs from the tiny gas refrigerator, and began happily cracking them into the skillet.

The last day here would not be sad, now that she had this to look forward to. Maybe the tiny apartment in the village wouldn't be so bad if they could think about the evaporator sitting up here, waiting. Just two months, tops. Then they could climb up here, on snowshoes if need be, and start gathering, boiling the sap mother nature would send.

Balder was at the door, and Nathan reached around mother to open it. "Come in, Balder," he cried, as cold air fell into the camper.

"Don't know's I ought," said the man with a grin. He wore a black wool watch cap and looked, as Elda would think, like a sailor from the North Sea. "Don't think theya's enough room for me in theya, Nate." To Chrischana he said, "Think I'll stot down the trail with this. You can show me just waya when you get done in here."

"No y'don't, Balda." We waunt go down theya with the evaporator. It's the... joy of ushering it down—"

"Okay," he grinned. "But I'll wait outside. Not enough room in theya fah ants."

Ben looked out at the truck with its iron and steel treasure visible in the bed. "That thing got four-wheel drive?"

"Doaw: Don't need it. Once we get down, I'll go back out that ol' twitch trail down theya. Ground's like concrete'neath this dusting, anaway."

Chrischana shoveled the eggs, saying over her shoulder, "We'll hurry. Come on, boys."

Balder closed the door. While still in the bunk, Daniel turned to watch the man through the window. He was walking around the great burnt-out Twitchell Farm cellarhole. Daniel reached for his clothes. That was cool, the way Mother said, "usher it down," like it was the King Jesus riding on an ass. The peculiar phrasing and its context pleased him. Something like that could get you thinking. The placement of words could be pleasing.

Today they were going to go live down in Gottheim village. What will it be like in an apartment, Daniel wondered squirming into his jeans. He pulled on his sweatshirt and lay on his side to put on socks. Easier to get home from an evening's work at *The Voter*. Closer to Cindabilla's. He could walk to school if need be instead of taking the bus. The Gott'im Library and library at Hazel Newell will both be more accessible. Cool. Doing schoolwork there will be easier, research a breeze. He swung down, knocking into Benaiah. He looked under the table for his shoes.

Benaiah elbowed him hard. "You did that on purpose," he charged.

"Did not," said Daniel still stooping but elbowing back.

"Won't have it!" said Mother. She reached around Ben with plates of scrambled eggs and grilled toast, setting them on the table. There will be advantages to apartment living. Two-bedrooms, a living room, kitchen, bathroom with running water. Lights. Take a bath whenever you want! Peter might even visit there, but she did not count on it. Didn't hope for it either. She had not seen him since that Thanksgiving night when he took off from *Simons Ledge* without even seeing the boys. Maybe he was gone for good. Maybe he'd be back. She ought to know him better after all this time.... Running water. Room for the kids to fight.... But, if you had to keep quiet for the neighbors.... Practically only have to step outside to get to work. Life would be more expensive in Gottheim on top of the cost of the evaporator.... But there will be openings on the mountain, too. Maybe a chance and more money? Gut to have more.

"Balda's waiting," she said, sitting down next to Ben to eat her eggs. The savings that had come to Chrischana Twitchell from Balder had made it possible for her to purchase a small acreage from the original Twitchell Farm, plus secondhand evaporator and firebox to provide her first farm income. Made of cast iron topped with a hundred gallon stainless steel reservoir, the evaporator would reduce sap from Twitchell sugar maples. The same maples which surrounded them now as they descended the hill with great joy. The sap would pass where they were now passing with shouts, flowing through a network of carefully laid tubing. It would stream into a holding tank and then into the reservoir where it would heat, bubble and steam, sweetening the air about the family of workers who will tend it. Just so, their shouts now sweetened December's frigid air where they skipped and bounded beside the laden pickup as its driver slowly bumped down the steep grade. Twigs and briars plucked at their clothing as they passed, and their hands sometimes touched the cold sides of the truck. They could not have kept silent if all the sour tongues in town had called them foolish to think this old farm would yield a living again.

Twitchell Farm had never been a convenient place to dwell. There had never been power lines up here. And they would be lucky to build a sap house, let alone a homestead. But this joy did not care. It did not doubt, nor shake its head, warn itself of absurdity and failure. This joy shouted out, the Twitchells providing it tongue. One day those tongues would taste sweetness. A taste that would not come easily, required much work. It would be no glib accomplishment, but when it came: That would be true sweet.

Alone, late in the day, Chrischana. Chrischana came back to camp one last time. She had coils of tubing, spigots, spouts, and galvanized buckets for the few trees downhill from the evaporator; putting all in store in the camper. And she would take down to Gott'im the remainder of their meager possessions. Last night snow had been light, but enough to give them warning. Bumping in past the abandoned logging yard, she thought, Soon this hill will be locked tight in bitter winter, accessible only to snow shoes, snow machines, cross-country skis.

She might get back up here a few times. Maybe. It would be glorious, pure and clean and white. Maybe Peter would come around to share it. Maybe not. Peter was leaving her alone and she thought it a good sign. It showed restraint. Wasn't that a good omen for a relationship?

She pulled to a stop, yanked on the handle. Squealing, the big door protested the cold. The Bonneville might make it through winter, might not. What with rent, utilities, and plans for the future.... If the car could just get her past winter.

Walking beyond the cellarhole, she looked through stiff branches of the winter-sleeping trees to the view. Time to say goodbye to the somber sight, drear and lightly dusted with snow. The near mountains were charcoal colored, bristling with naked stems. Looking around she breathed in her deep gratitude, her sense of arrival and peace. Once an exile, she had come home. Through fire and storm to this place she loved. Chrischana had come back to God's House, to her home in Gottheim, Maine.

Adirondack Paper, in Guildford Maine, will ship 528 tons of coated paper today from #17 machine, but one of more than a dozen operating paper machines in the mill. The specialty paper will be used to make glossy magazines, filled with advertising. To be flipped through by people stuck in doctors' offices, in airplanes and laundromats, subways, beauty parlors—any place where boredom, that small kingdom in Time, must be kept at bay. The dumps and landfills of the nation are filled with the off-scourings of boredom. Insatiable boredom devours the forests whole. Boredom processes woodlands, cutting debarking chipping cooking bleaching, mixing with river water and chemicals; woodlands spraying across the wire, draining, being pressed dried wound-up coated polished slit and rewound. Boredom: spinning the woodlands of Québec, Maine, New Hampshire, and Vermont into tight rolls. Pressed, gleaming and spooled, the forests will be shipped in freight cars to wherever they print glossy magazines. Provision for the kingdom of boredom, thought Peter Prince idly when he trudged from his car to the mill. *You could live and die in a state of suspended animation among the living dead.*

Today, in the midst of the Christmas Season, Peter Prince is supposed to trouble-shoot the flow box of #17 machine. Electricians have already tagged out the breakers and, since the kingdom of boredom can't recognize the season, impatience blooms in management as millwrights test out the mechanisms at the wet end of the machine.

Is the problem in the plate adjustment, plate pivot, nozzle blade adjustment, or adjusting rods? The size of a football field, the building that houses #17 is shockingly silent as the men tinker. This is the stressed silence of managers hovering, white shirts, neckties, wingtips and pressed trousers, hovering. Anxious to let the grease goons know they are anxious. This ubiquitous presence of whiteness and neckties reminds the millwrights that $50,000 an hour is at stake. The machine will lose that amount in downtime, 1980s currency, if they don't come up with an answer. The function of this monstrous machine is to produce enough finished paper in one hour to reach from Guildford to Farmington, a distance of sixty miles.

In the midst of this back pressure of boredom, Peter Prince is strangely relieved. Remorse has vanished under it. For the first time in a month he thinks of something besides damnation. *There's emotional cowardice urging suicide. There's stark physical cowardice checking it.*

It seemed right that he feel the pangs of hell for the abuse heaped undeserved on his common-law wife. He should be annihilated. The demented members of his being should be smoke. He has wasted this careful creation on alcohol and rage. Now it is time to be wasted in return.

Yet at the moment he thinks only of perforated plates and flow elements, hot metal and hydraulics, of adjustments to make this machine yield its reams. Gross slice adjustment, slice roof adjustment, tube bank: get the white shirts out of your peripheral vision. His attention is focused on the mechanism of this plate adjustment, while the other mechanics put away their tools, stand around bull-shitting.

Now he is done, climbing down from the flow box.

After start up, everyone relaxes, the white shirts are back in their soundproof offices. Peter opens the tiny packet and pushes its yellow earplugs into his ears. The shout of this machine starting into its purpose is destruction to the delicate organic mechanisms of ears. In this building it's impossible to hear yourself scream. The force and roar of #17 goes through the soles of his feet into the cords of his body, feasting on Peter's enfeebled senses. Easily the machine absorbs him as he walks past its great length. When in proximity to #17, he becomes #17. On these premises the coated-paper machine tolerates no identity but its own.

Gradually, now that he has finished replacing the front plate adjustment, Peter Prince is beginning to think again. They could be his own but maybe they are really the thoughts of the paper machine he is drifting past... the massive *Fourdrinier* wire, loaded with paperstock draining as it moves toward the presses and dryers. His vacant glance shifts from his reflection through the glass at the great sheet winding endlessly up-and-down, over and under and out the dryer toward the calenders. Maddening, the great sheet makes its everlasting way through coaters and winders, and over gaps in the floor where broken paper can be shoved down out of sight into broke-chests below. Blades in the basement swiftly beat it once more into pulp.

Drifting past, the uproar beating through his frame, Peter Prince is thinking. That's the place for me. His hardhat towering, his eyes encased in plastic and ears packed with foam rubber.... Step into that gap and instantly pulped. One with the ruined forest. Down there the forest is in better shape than that clear-cut above Chrischana's place, with its dry and broken leavings. The paper stock below will be stained with Peter Prince. They could make paper out of his remains but he will be gone to his maker and then cast into hell.

Eloise Patadoe might have guessed. She is deep in Abenaki Notch, gathering spruce and balsam fir tips with which to make wreaths. Eloise got a late start this year owing to that gouache series on formations in Grafton Notch. Neighbors cared for the goats in her absence. She went south for the series and camped, carrying art supplies with her, enduring frost, rain and flood, but it was worth it. Now she is back home and longing to be part of the season, do her bit to make it colorful, lively, bright. To that end she will howl down the sun, howl up the moon, anything to be different. Eloise is sometimes consistently different even from herself. She rarely knows where she will be tomorrow, no matter how thoroughly she plans. In fact, the more she plans the more likely it is she will not be where she had supposed.

Twilight is falling and so is snow, clouding the air with its thick languor. Her eyes are adjusting to catch the loved dimness of dusk. All she has to do is stick to the trail, keep the burlap sack—heavy with prickliness and fragrance—from listing too far. Get those trail intersections right and there'll be no trouble reaching the Quarry Dog Road, no matter how snowy and dark. There's always a little light, right? She asks this of herself.

Can barely see it, but stuff's thickening. Big as saucers now and intricate. She imagines seeing into the structure of each plate passing her eye, winking. *If only I could get this in paint! The gradations of shadow and light throughout the microscopic intricacy. The feel of tiptoeing through the hallways of the snowflake.* The flakes, wet and soft on her face, cake her hair above her wool headband. To keep it from getting soggy, she gives her head a shake. Again, the sack lists on her back.

"Patadoe Patadoe Patadoe," she chides herself aloud. "When you gonna learn?"

Problem is, my schedule's too full. You can't go squeezing the big things into the least dribbles of time like you do. "Won't do won't do won't do." When alone, she sometimes says things in triplicate. Tonight is practice for the solstice celebration at the old Quaker meeting house. Meguntic Mountain Arts has rented it for the purpose. Every year Eloise coordinates the event. She laughs at herself for having hoped her wreaths would be ready in time to decorate the hall tonight. No way I get even one done at this rate.... Maybe if I gulp down some of that broccoli soup. Just one wreath'll make the evening. One small seasonal thing... with... maybe a sprig of cranberries! Some cones! Maybe another with braided ribbon....

Laden with the fragrant bundle, she jogs on through the snow. The intersection! Her path diverges right. Elated, she lifts her face to the feathery breath, howling like a bitch wolf. The sack shifts precariously, Eloise stumbling. Quickly she rights herself. "Hah!" She mutters. "Someday you won't be so agile. Can you imagine doing this at 45, 50? Someday you'll be old, girl, *old old old*."

She stops a moment, listening. There it is again, a coy-dog answering her howl. "Hah!" Eloise howls again.

But Eloise Patadoe *can* imagine herself old. Old and diseased, hurting. And she can imagine herself struggling to endure. She can imagine herself doing anything, especially when it first occurs to her. Out of this imagination have come some killer paintings. And some of the best schemes ever devised by woman. Life is *awesome*! "*Tsk tsk*. Must stop using that word. Heard *two* teenagers use it yesterday. It's becoming a commonplace and no longer your own. You're famous!—it's passed into the vernacular! It will live abused in infamy.... But, someday it'll be history. *Then* you can use it again. *Ahoooo*...." Watch it, El. When this howling thing catches on you will have to stop that, too. All becomes passé with use. In our perception: even belief in God. But it all comes back again. Who knows, maybe I'll be a practicing Catholic again one day.

From a greater distance comes the dim wild return. "Friends of the wild!" Hope I don't run into a moose in this dark. That'll break your kneecaps!... all the way to the top of your head. One more right onto the pale road. No problem after that, Gertie.

A few hundred yards on the Quarry Dog Road will bring her home. Not much in the way of human settlement there, though once farmers coaxed a subsistence living from the rugged country. Back there, in the willy-wacks, streams wandered away from bogs, beaver bogs in the narrow valley steep-sided with walls of rocks and trees. Few now are willing to study over how to get this ground to yield, sprout produce or forage for milk production. What we need is a cooperative. A funky place where you can unload your leaf motif butter and maple sugar, organic veggies, goats milk

cheese. My neighbors—heck, the whole community—would benefit....
Something like that down in Farmington, elsewhere in the state, too.

Goats! "Oh poop!" Is it tonight I'm supposed to have Hetty up to
the Common? But the flush of worry passes, leaving her jogging still,
slower, puffing, weary. She remembers now, its next night. The show must
go on with you aboard, Hetty. You will be a living Nativity.

She turns on the pale road, leaving the thickets behind. Walking
backwards on the road, dimly she sees the imprint of her tracks. But it's
coming down thick, quickly filling the pattern. She turns back, hurries on.
Yes. She is relieved to have found the road.

Once, was it three winters ago? She did lose her way coming out of
Abenaki Notch. Snowing like this but darker, colder. Eloise was a bit
crazed with panic. How grateful, at last, to stumble unexpectedly out of the
puckerbrush onto the Quarry Dog Road. She was shaky with fierce
laughter, like a loon. She found it was only an hour, but had seemed like
five.

That was a time of personal upheaval: the loss of male
companionship. She was uncovering the course of her life in those days,
and it frightened her. Having to adjust to the one thing she had been unable
to imagine: She would be living her life alone. And trying to tell herself
that she liked it, that Eloise could get out of the woods without manly
support. For two years it frightened her, that wide loneliness. The radical
schemes she considered in those days! taking on more domestic animals
than could be properly cared for, even starting proceedings for foreign
adoption. Thank God she learned enough about herself before the child
could arrive. It would have meant an even larger curtailment and
adjustment of her life... as living with a man had not been. But, in the end,
she saved the child. Saved it for that couple who truly cared and had *time* to
care.

Eloise Patadoe, would-be mother.

Well, is it really too late after all? Are you positive you can't
adjust?

Patadoe Patadoe Patadoe. Get a grip. You will do all that you love
(if you continue in health), but you will *not* be somebody's mother. Or
lover.

They are waiting at the meeting hall. The solstice celebration is
your baby. You and your fellow participants are grateful and glad, coming
from miles around. We'll worship together what makes it all work. The
Season comes into us and we embody it. The season with the longest night
happens to be the brightest. The days are darkest and I'm alone, but still the
light finds you, comes into your precarious existence. Go in joy, the joy

found in faces of others in this community.

Even now she spies the yellow light of her own house. In winter she leaves the lamp burning for herself. Eloise Patadoe, artist, homesteader, coordinator of celebrations extraordinaire. Sometimes, and in this season particularly, she can be the saddest, loneliest, even the *emptiest* person she knows. But she has friends here in Quaker, and down there in Gottheim, Maine.

"Hermann, I figure our work's about done. Winter's here. Time to head south. Gonna miss you. You've accomplished a hell of a lot."

They sat across from one another in Wilbur's Bar and Grille shortly before Christmas. The place was strung with red tinsel garlands. Someone was feeding the jukebox to produce a string of moldering carols. Bing was here, Brenda Lee, the Carpenters, Dolly Parton, one after another. Except that Hermann had ordered another grilled sticky bun and more coffee, the two friends were just about done eating. Peter Prince got out a cigarette, tamped it on the table. "You mind?"

"Go ahead with your smoke." Hermann pushed down with his ham-dimpled hand, slicing off a forkful of the gooey bun. Tonight he would be lighting seven candles on the menorah, but now he chewed thoughtfully before suddenly asking, "Do you think Christians remember the birth pangs in that stable, Prince?"

Peter smiled. "I never do."

"Maybe the women think of it."

"Maybe."

"Is there significance in those pains—as part of the story, I mean?"

"You wouldn't be asking me." He smiled some, even to his wide set green eyes. "There's significance in everything else, the shepherds, wise men, the baby, the star. Everything both real and symbols for something. That what you're getting at?"

"Have you ever heard of birth with no pain without drugs? Without dilation, stretching, tearing—a doctor's scissors? A woman literally splits herself open to bring out that life." Again Hermann looked at him with serious brown eyes behind glasses.

"Is there anything worthwhile comes without pain, Prince? For instance, should people get married without going through labor first?"

Flicking his cigarette ash into the ashtray, Prince laughed. "Would they?"

"It would be dearer to them." He said nothing more in that almost treble voice of his. Just took another bite and watched Prince drag on his cigarette.

Peter Prince turned his head, exhaling a stream of blue smoke. He looked up at Gottesmann through locks of hair. "So what's your point?"

Hermann went on eating the bun. "You know."

"C'mon. Are you equating remorse with labor pains?" He smiled. "Have you talked with any women about this, Hermann?"

"I equate all kinds of pain with labor. I don't think women would mind so much the trope—mythic application of the term. It has a kind of heroic stature."

"I could remind you how commonplace birth is."

"Yes, it happens every moment: No one comes here without those pains. Isn't it one reason why each human, or any creature, is... costly. Consider this, Prince: You said I accomplished something. If your remorse is that something, it's mainly *your* accomplishment.... Should you be throwing away something that dear by walking away from here? You've been given another chance with your family. Few would have such chances after such misdeeds. Why not embrace the pain as a good thing... considering what it bought you?"

Prince drew on his cigarette, exhaled, thinking about the other's use of the word bought. "I'm not a romantic, Hermann."

"Romance is not a light, lying thing. There's no romance without pain. Are the people in your family worth this pain, this assault on your pride? Are they the kind of people whose good opinion is worth striving for? Don't let your fear of pain stop you from delivering this child."

He pushed his plate aside to concentrate on coffee.

Prince watched a family settle into the booth across the aisle. Brenda was belting out her *Jingle Bell Rock*. Peter said slowly, "Too bad you don't celebrate Christmas, Hermann. Maybe I could've spent it with you."

"It won't be Christmas, but you're welcome to come over."

Alvin and the chipmunks got off the juke box, arguing. Then Bing sang. Peter Prince said, "Sometimes I wonder about Judas. Announcing his betrayal, it says Jesus was troubled in spirit. Why was that? Was it selfish? Was he troubled for himself—that he was betrayed? Or for Judas harming his own self? Or maybe for the whole great ... play, or whatever, of existence that it could be so...—like this? That *we* could be so—like this?"

"I don't know, Prince, he's not my Messiah, but I recognize the questions, their types. They have the feel of answers disguised as questions."

Peter thought about this.

"Thanks. I may—or maybe not—be over on the 25th."

One of the longest nights of the year is in full moon, the slopes of Jasper Mountain cleared of the day's skiers, all gone below to the bistros, restaurants and pubs under the mountain and down in Gottheim village. As the week wears, crowds will swell in offhand celebration of God's mysterious birth. Two thousand years ago in the earthy world of struggle, far removed from the glitter-shine-allure of the resort, the baby plunged forth bloody wet tethered to its mother; a feeble unskilled thing, incapable of feeding bathing clothing itself against drafts in the sheltering rocks; unable even to turn over or lift its sorry head.

Tonight's celebrants include members of the Golding family and personal friends, guests. The brand new rapid-quad ski lift whisks them high above the hothouse vacation bustle toward a mountain staging area for holiday feasting. Gloria Fay, seated between her father and mother, looks back over her shoulder toward the lighted, diminishing complex below. Looking back on the wee lodges and living particles moving in the glow of the skating rink far below, her heart heaves tenderly. Night is fallen there, lit in the fair glow of all their accomplishments. She looks beyond them, even to the mountains having lost their glow and turned now to somber coals, lonely, vast and dim.

In the chair far ahead above their own, ride Jimmy and Theo, their skis dangling in silhouette. Beyond them ride the governor and her immediate family. The elder Fays, on either side of Gloria, have delayed their holiday trip to St. Lucia where they will spend Christmas with their oldest and the grands. Afterward, between the 25th and the 30th, they plan to attend a Bible conference for business executives. At the moment, Mom is murmuring over the silvery glow in the northeast where the moon hides, promising certain ascent. Dad is detailing for Gloria the fascinations of insect lives, something about hyper-metabolism expanding their sense of time. But, though attending peripherally to each, Gloria is aware of the surrounding stillness—vast, simple, yet shot with echoing chatter and glee coming to them from remoter members of the party. On the shadowed slope ahead, she sees glinting fire and the cheerful glow of parti-colored lights. Things will be roasting there for the delectation of all: glazed chickens, marinated beef, the pink flesh of Atlantic salmon. Higher still, the great dome of Jasper recedes, its snow mantle already catching silver from the promised moon.

"Just look at that happy glow up there, dear," Mom is saying. Still caught in her reverie, Gloria murmurs assent. "Now look," nudges Mom. "There, on the shoulder—the moving gems of the snow groomers. Oh, I just love seeing them ascend like that in tandem, don't you? Like angels moving on the mountains." At last Gloria turns to her mother in agreement. Mom's face is lit by Jasper's reflecting snows: a thin face, aging and fine-boned; gracious when seen above evening wear; pixieish now, being framed by an alpine cap. "It's good to see that smile," Mom says. "It's been... eclipsed... lately?"

But Gloria turns back toward the gleaming mountain. She does not want to talk with Mom about things. Does not want to bring up things insurmountable, the hash she is making of desire. The anger kindling at Balder. The fantasies she feeds on, concerning how they might, might not, live together. Even the mere fact of Balder would not be appreciated, so she says nothing... to anyone.

Balder, you are there, just beyond the white monolith.

Down and down and down among slopes and trees on the further side.... Getting ready to spend the holidays with your new family. The family that came between us and turned life away. How can you stand to live so messily, so all over the map? Embracing that squalor, which—I admit—I once found so interesting. From a distance. Is it so wrong to understand myself? To know that I'm good in certain situations and *so* out of my depth in others?

...I thought, believed, nothing was impossible to me.... That I would do whatever I set my mind to. I am tough, have dexterity in life, self-discipline for godsakes. I am goal-oriented. I attack!

No, she cannot bring herself to call squalor depth, to call french fries under the bed and the dirty clothes of five people a challenging way to live. Extended families and baby talk and diapers—deep? Deep all right. Deep doo-doo. And what if someone becomes really really ill, or has other problems you can't cope with?

... But he said he'd be in it with you. You wouldn't be doing it alone.

No. It's weak to think you can't do it alone. And I'm strong, have been since a child. My will is strong.

You could get your own family, on your terms! One child anyway. Harry is impressed with my education and communication skills—Jimmy said so. If I show interest, he'll consider me to head the ski school. Or, there's the New Hampshire Mountain, its wide-open. With a steady position I can have and raise my own child. Balder's child, too, if I decide. On my own terms, in a beautiful home of my own. God—where do these idiot thoughts come from?

The feast, fire and lights are fast approaching on their right. She sees smoke ascending in moonlight, smells its wafting aromas. The moon has risen, and she looks to it, quickly, then turns to take the ramp with her parents. Together they glide toward the straggling knots of people removing their skis, queuing up for drinks and charbroil on the platform. But Gloria hangs back suddenly, calling for them to go ahead: She just wants to take the view alone. (Before immersing herself in gaiety, babble, schmooze. Brother Jimmy will be pushing his pompous opinions. Theo will mindlessly mistake herself in every turn of the conversation. Dad will get into it with the anti-greens, and Mom will be looking at me all evening—is there anything wrong, dear?)

She watches her parents push toward the party, two black silhouettes against a gathering lit with lanterns. With painful suddenness all she wants is to go up to the snowy summit. Gloria glances toward the private lift with its tall poles and cables gleaming with reflected moonlight, standing silent, the chairs lined up beneath. Can't start it on my own. I could dare the climb, though. Up there the wind would nip her bones.

She might warm herself by climbing. Drag up the skis, glide down through the slopes, thickets, and hills on the other side. Right up to Balder's door, and declare. *I'm here to make babies, Balder. I'm ready!*

But the breath of Jasper comes down to her, holy and cold. Her mood falls to the fact of his wind whipping the snow high above. There is no snow on the lower southern slopes, she knows. The north side has snow because Harry Golding's snow guns put it here. The Golding's make their own conditions. He says: Let there be twenty feet of base, and twenty appear.

Looking toward the distant glimmering summit, she sighs. What are these thoughts? Am I up to any good? Could I love Balder if he *were* willing to come work for his girlfriend's father? If he suddenly got a business degree? He doesn't fit anything I imagine for him.... Maybe he doesn't fit because he *won't*.

... But he expects me to come after him, to change willy-nilly. Or maybe he wants me as I am, inadequate to the vocation. Willing to forsake all other options. Maybe he wants my imperfection to wrestle with itself in some alien environment.... Forcing me to embrace the life *he* chooses—or I can't have him at all. –Or is this another idiot thought?

ξ

Even so, up here, the summit shines like silver, like moon in a cloud. Below, Gloria the fay turns to face the great white disk, now well risen above the quiet Meguntics. There she sees the moonlight, queenly, calm. Dignity is in its appearance, say I, Jasper Mountain. I am Jasper Mountain, and I say Moon's appearance owes to the sun.

ξ

Christmas Eve, with snow falling over the northland where Gott'im's people gather within. Lamplighted windows glow distantly but any walker may approach easily enough. There are travelers, too, on streets and lanes leading to churches. Choirs stand to sing of Angels, of the nature and compassion of God, and of the Fear we are prone to.

Come closer. Windows are inviting, more so than doors for all their wreaths and decorations: A shut door may yield no light. Look within through the panes, walk around the house watching folks at the supper table or enjoying a seasonal TV show, taking sugar cookies soft and hot from the oven, or singing carols around the piano like they do at Olive Lovejoy Bartlett's house.

You could climb a tree beside the Simon house, peer into an upstairs window. In light beyond the falling snow, Daniel and Cindabilla are visible lounging around the radio with the bedroom door open to allay adult suspicions. The lamp on Daniel's desk casts a deeply yellow glow: He put a bug light in it for the occasion. If, by some means, the conversation within those windowpanes were audible, the tale of Cindabilla's family gatherings would be overheard. Christmas at the Sessions' house is hateful to her for its drunks damning one another and calling up abuse and accusation of wrong. But the aunts, uncles, cousins and grandparents would begin happily enough, descending into the nether regions only as the drink increases. Our eavesdropper without is soon made uncomfortable, turning away to descend the tree and steal around the corner toward the front window. These are tall windows, catching snow against divided lights. The crackling fire in a Franklin style woodstove with pipe up the chimney hearth glows appealingly. The mantelpiece is laden with evergreens and tiny lights among their needles. The hand of Balder Simon closes the stove door and adjusts the vent. Now the crunch of tires is heard in the snow blown wind. The stealthy watcher hurries away toward the edges of woodland, still within earshot of the dooryard.

A pickup stops short of the house in the falling snow and two people step down from either door. Waiting for the woman to come around, the man hesitates. She speaks kind words to him of which the watcher catches only their reassuring tone. Together they approach the door, now flung wide and streaming with light, and piping of a young voice.

"Dad! Dad's here!! It's Christmas Eve! You're here! I knew you'd look like that!"

The couple is taken inside. The door closes quickly on the falling snow and the watcher without.

Supper is served, glazed ham, piping baked potatoes, butternut squash with spices, salad greens with thin purple onion rings, a side of cranberry relish. For dessert there will be pumpkin pie with true whipped cream sprinkled with cinnamon. The Simons, Twitchells, and Peter Prince are here, along with one Sessions. Tentatively talking (tentative all but Nathan), they sit down. They wait. Chrischana gives the youngest a warning look as he reaches for a roll. Withdrawing his hand he looks expectantly at Balder.

"Word o'grace," says the bearded man with a subdued grin.

They bow their heads, Elda refraining a gaze wanting to slip toward the stranger Prince.

"Fatha! Thank you fah this food'n this Christmas gathering. Thanks specially f'your son, who came as a child t'be with us'n die with us. Help us dearly love him. In his name amen."

"Amen," says Elda unexpectedly. A blush passes on her thin white face.

Now, his hair sticking every which way, and with an eye on mother, Nathan reaches out his hand.

"It would be nice if you pass that t'Mrs. Simon."

Smiling Nathan hands over the plate.

Elda receives the rolls. "Thanks, Nate."

"Nice t'have your Dad heah, in't it?" Balder says this to the table in general. "Glad you made it, Prince."

"Good t'be here, thanks." He passes the bowl full of squash to Benaiah.

"Guess Chrischana had told you," says Balder, gesturing toward that end of the kitchen where a door stands open beside the refrigerator.

"Theya's a room up theya fah you t'stay in tonight. Save you having to come back in the morning. Got to get t'those presents under the tree early!"

Prince nodded noncommittally. Chrischana had told him of the offer. And he knew she would be going back to the little family's apartment down in the village. Jericho, where he lived, was a good thirty miles away.

"You *see* all those presents in there, Dad!" yells Nathan. "Ben'ah musta put a hundred presents under there for you. Wait'll you see what I gave you. Don't shake it or cover up the breathing holes, though."

"Nathan, you nerd," says Ben. He looks shyly at his father and Peter gives him a wink.

"Did you say you went to Florida, Cindabilla?" Chrischana wants to know. "You go to Disney World?"

The pale eyes of Cindabilla smile. "Couldn't get past the pockin'lot. Couldn't stand O'lando. Awful place, hot. Streets laid out in long straight lines, endless blocks. But Everglades is free. Just walk off the road, you're in! Wouldn't go fah, though. I like my leg too much."

Daniel smiles.

Chrischana turns toward Balder at the head of the table. "Thought Gloria'd be here. Din't choo invite her?"

"Cuss I did. Thought she might make it, too." There is no more to say.

Something stirs along the periphery of Prince's vision, and he glances toward the corner where the refrigerator abuts the wall. Two tiny mice sit nearby, nibbling crumbs. He shifts his gaze back to his children. "Hear you might go snowmobiling this winter." He says it to Daniel. He has noticed that his oldest boy drops his r's now, like any Mainer, and that he calls Balder father.

"You might give it a try, Dad," Daniel returns.

"Might." He is relieved to hear Daniel call him Dad. Maybe this can work out. He could get a Yamaha. Peter smiles, thinking how the guys at MMI in Phoenix would laugh. A hog-head on a rice-burner.

Talk swirls around the table, Nathan's happy warble punctuating. His Christmas present to Dad is under the table at his feet, eating crumbles of roll and baked potato. And there's going to be pumpkin pie!

Without, the snow continues falling, softly filling woodland and hollow. The lane leading to the house was once an old settlers' country road. Now it appears to dead-end at the family home. But, hidden and somewhat overgrown, it continues off through the backyard and woods, downhill where it winds back down toward the pond. On the USGS topographic map, the trail shows as a dotted line and is designated a Jeep trail. Balder uses this trail as a snow machine shortcut to the pond. Gloria noticed it on the topo map as she studied the Gottheim sector and saw the dot indicating the position of Balder's house, *Simons Ledge*.

On this Christmas eve, while others are home or at church, Gloria Fay tracks up the trail through snowfall and woods on slim cross-country skis. Soon she is sweating, puffing, unzipping her jacket and doffing her alpine cap. The snow, itself scarcely visible in the night, dims her sight. She searches for the Simon lights. Sometime later she stands resting on her poles at the top of the trail, looking toward the window-lit house. Laid out stem to stern like a many-angled ship, it seems anchored in a storm of white. Snow falls heavily into the dooryard. The windows send out yellow beams. Inside people sit at the table, tiny people, eating, presumably laughing and speaking to one another. Celebrating Christendom's big day.

Watching, Gloria realizes she is in the midst of deciding. Coming here has been a spontaneous act, decisive at the onset. She was accepting

Balder's glad invitation. Yet here she waits, still leaning on her poles, undecided. If she crosses, knocks at the kitchen door, she will be warmly welcomed. Should she enter the household, join the celebration... or turn around and ski back down to her car?

But there is too much here beneath the ledge on this side of the mountain. Too much standing in the way of how my life should look. Life should have a pleasing symmetrical aspect. It should be pleasant to bear—at least as much as one can manage. It should not be limited by strictures of duty. Life must be what one loves at the moment, and from moment to moment, always. That is the nature of life. Is it an unreasonable expectation? Is it unreasonable to expect fidelity in the face of obstacles, unpleasantness, straining and stress? These are pressures I should reasonably *flee*. If this kind of pressure is what God or somebody wants for us... isn't it right to rebel? Or would God even grant this joy—*life feeling will*—and then expect everyone to abdicate? To bend and bow and say, *yes sir*?

In her agony of ripe emotion she searches toward the snowy skies: emotion searing, heartfelt, proud.

She slumps exhausted on her poles, head down and waiting. *Why why why*!! Her tired mind cries out.

An earnest cry, it reaches upward through the snow, though her head and heart are down. Up surges the cry toward the dim heart of the blizzard. And beyond—toward the vast bright blizzard of elemental galaxies swirling through great gray regions of space and time. But one cry out of a tight little heart of one small creature longing for nothing more than to try her faculties and, above all, *to have fun*.

She leans on these poles, leans into this question, snow falling and soaking her sleek hair.

But only the snow comes, covering everything. Covering Gloria Fay where she slumps. Covering the nearby pile of leftover building scraps, castoffs from Balder's spurt of construction.

Comes a brief undefined noise, not close, to Gloria's ears. She does not look up. A sound, muted by falling snow, seems to come from the far end of the dwelling... in the direction of the barn. Now she hears and recognizes the shrieking of metal on metal. Still leaning on the ski poles she peers through her spilled hair.

A boy stands at the barn door in a swath of light, looking toward the dim snowy shadows of woodland beyond the far side of the barn. Gloria lifts her head to watch, straining toward those shadows. Now the patches of white, of snow against the barn, are looking bunched and fuller. This fullness moves toward the boy, and as it reaches the light, she sees the shape of a deer.

The white deer! She had thought she would never see it again.

The kitchen door opens, siphoning off her attention. There stands Mrs. Simon, Chrischana behind her. Chrischana. And Chrischana is calling through the snowfall. Her voice is muted, remote but distinct enough. "Benaiah! Come here, Benaiah!"

He comes toward her, pleading in his voice. Hearing his bemusement through the falling snow, Gloria's heart softens. She watches as Chrischana's middle son comes to his mother, his voice chastened and low but still pleading.

Then, with a shock she sees what she saw last summer, Elda Simon with that awful gun in her hands.

Mother and son enter the house, close the door, as Mrs. Simon steps away. She points the gun in the direction of the deer, but high. The deer has grown since Gloria saw it in summer. It now resembles a delicate long-legged dog. Alone. The larger reddish deer of summer, its mother, is nowhere to be seen.

The old woman sends out the weapon's invisible charge with a powerful bang. The deer leaps away, gone back into the storm.

Banished!

It's a bitter thought. Like *a scapegoat for somebody's sins!*

The little woman goes to the barn to turn off the light, tug the door closed. She seems to stand a long time, looking off through the snow where the deer disappeared. Is she sagging against the barn? But the light is gone, it's too dim to tell.

Exhausted, Gloria has had enough. Won't wait for that old woman to go. I can't stand this, stand here any longer.

The young woman turns on her skis, careless of whether Mrs. Simon might see or hear her.

She gives a push with her poles that sends her skimming back down the trail. Gloria Fay has had enough for one night. She needs to think again. It is time to go home and shut her windowless wreathed condominium door behind her.

God, I just want to go to bed.

— In Winter —

"Winter deepens behind us…. The heights away north are whiter than they were; snow is lying far down their shoulders. Tonight we shall be on our way high up towards the Redhorn Gate. We may well be seen by watchers on that narrow path, and waylaid by some evil; but the weather may prove a more deadly enemy than any. What do you think of your course now, Aragorn?"

—The Fellowship of the Ring

Layer of Life

On a slope above a white lake the pine stands among a tall grove of white pine. Resting lightly in winter, the pine reports once like a gunshot in the deep settled cold. Then, quiet is here, snow-filled silence. But next, from far upslope near the road, the distant *buzz* of the chipper drifts down through snowy woodland. Passing through trees comes the jingling of winch chains and great chain-dressed wheels, mixed with the gunning of a skidder. Jingling on this twitch trail cut by loggers late last week, the big skidder rumbles right down to the pine. Halting, wafting blue smoke and fumes, the skidder looses a logger.

Alvin and Ansell Robichaud have come to take pines. Their father, Robbie, has contracted with the developer to harvest these trees selectively. Wearing hard-hat and visor, chest and leg protection and steel-toed boots, Alvin steps up to this Eastern white pine and lightly lays his gloved hand on it. He looks up, admiring its straight length. His cascading breath becomes a last bit of carbon dioxide drifting upward to mingle among the needles above. *Good money tree*, thinks Alvin. But there is something more in his thought, an unconscious gratitude, reaching up to gather the pine's own clean-breathing patience.

He rips the starter cord and stoops to notch the trunk. The saw's speeding teeth deftly cuts a neat wedge. Alvin smells Christmas, fragrance released from resin. The pine shudders almost imperceptibly along its great length.

The great bole's bark is chunky, fissured, having guarded its inner bark and a fragile layer of hidden cells. The life of this white pine is in this slim satiny smooth layer. For all its mass girth height age, here only, and in this present moment, does this tree renew itself. The rest of the tree is its history. Outer and inner bark, sapwood, heart and pith: Each layer, itself once risen from *cambium*, lively, now serves but to support the pine and preserve its identity. *Cambium*, this fine cell layer, is present life, conveying vitality to the whole. It is life in very light wood, a soft wood. And its uses in these 1980s are many.

Spot clearing for the developer, these two loggers will not cut here many days. Mr. Fay will show up later when the mercury rises above zero; a blond bespeckled representative of investors. Fay likes the lay of this wooded slope. He will wade about through the snow, talking rapidly at Alvin and Ansell, pointing out trees already earmarked for cutting, wanting to make sure they don't take the wrong ones or too many. It's supposed to be a wooded subdivision with some views of the pond below. He'll think, *If only I can get the speechless loggers to take off some of this hemlock.*

The old pine groans. Alvin pulls the saw away. The tree shudders visibly, shifting on its fresh stump. It comes down with the swiftness of a shadow falling across its neighbors; cracking and thundering. The tree lies prone, covering more earth in this separation than in its hundred upright years. A hush lingers around the severed trunk but, heedless, Alvin jumps aboard, running along its length to the branches. Easily he limbs them with his *awwing* saw. Brother Ansell backs the skidder up to the massive butt and jumps down, exclaiming over its great size. Alvin must cut the trunk to length on the spot, making the climb to the yard easier for the old skidder. Sixteen-foot lengths is right for Bearce's sawmill. Father will have a time loading them onto his truck. The size of these will spark Robbie Robichaud's imagination. Such great old trees are rarer these days, seems, than blue tourmaline.

Alvin removes his hardhat and safety glasses, and the twin brothers stop for a smoke. Lighting up, Ansell looks around peaceably, saying, "Too bad we caunt just mow'em all down." The other takes a long drag, looks up, exhales, agrees.

The skidder is idling, the chainsaw sitting silent on the big white stump. From a distance comes a new noise. "What's that?" Their square dimpled faces turn, listening in the cold air.

Ansell reaches up, absently fingering a blunt spike on the chains of the skidder wheel. Got to find money to replace the chains. Lately they've been slipping on the steep icy grades. Staring through trees across and down the slope, he answers the joint query, "Sounds like a team'o new skiddas. Who'd have s'many in the woods?"

"S'go check it out," returns Alvin. Still clutching their half-smoked cigarettes, they wade down through snow toward the wide expanse of the pond.

On the opposite shore above the cove, the big red machine roars. It is new all right, a mechanical feller-buncher, rocking and roaring, three trees clenched tight in a hydraulic fist at the end of its steel arm. The whole machine pivots on its tracks, laying the trees off to the side. Incredulous, the two watch as the red machine snips more standing trees—like so much grass—laying them aside to turn and grasp more trees.

Ansell stares at the sea of debris forming around it. Two other machines work the cut as well, one to twitch them, another to top and delimb. Only three men to clear the entire stumpage, taking everything at the rate of two or three every five-ten seconds. Fascinated, the twins watch the tiny trio sweeping the forest away. At last Alvin nudges his brother. "Fatha's not gont like this. You know what it means."

"Means we out of work. Ah days is numbered. Caunt afford those machines. One of em's worth half of Gott'im."

"The half without Jaspa Mountain."

Ansell nods. "Father's gont be pissed. Thinks theya's nothing betta'n what we got."

"Ain't no betta, li'l brother," says Alvin, who is nine minutes older. "Woods all be down in no time. Bet theya won't be enough left t'cut till our kids' kids." He looks back at the tree eater. "Think of a logger throwin'way his chainsaw!"

"Must cut down on comp payments, though. Won't no one get hurt inside that thing."

"What'll we need comp for, when we out of work?"

"Speaking of which—"

The two men toss away their cigarette butts and trudge back up through the trees and snow. Alvin's back is suddenly weary and his legs leaden. What's the point—just one tree at a time? And now there'll be none for their sons. It will be a glum week working the shore selectively for the developer, no matter how good the trees, watching the activity on the ridge opposite. And who's gont tell Fatha?

"In't nothing new in this," declares Robbie Robichaud at supper.

"When I started in the early '40s, it took three t'do what one Alvin does today, using crosscut saws, axes'n peavys. You twitched'em with hosses, o'course. I heard those new fella-bunchas'll do the work of six, seven Alvins. Before you stotted, maybe a quarter of your class bought chainsaws and dropped out early. 'Memba that? But I made you stay in school—like I didn't. That machine'll drop a thousand trees a day, but we caunt afford it."

The men and children sit around the supper table, Alvin and Ansell's wives serving. The twins' mother, Esmeralda, stands at the steaming stove, dishing up. There are three dwellings sitting small below the steep ledge, which rises darkly over the property of these descendents of French-

Canadians. Two are single-wide mobile homes, the other an old connected farmhouse. Sometimes the family comes together for the evening meal, filling Robbie and Esmeralda's house with the talk and tumble of but a part of their offspring and grandchildren. This jumble of relations, clatter of cookware and tussling of children pleases Robbie. He is one of sixteen siblings and the father of twelve. Ezzy gave birth to the last few in the hospital but raised all in this helter-skelter farmhouse.

"How many cords you cut today, Alvin," asks Father.

Alvin is patiently chewing a bite of cube steak. "Ten."

"And I'll be paying $260 for it, which you two split. Not bad money—if you was both in Enan Pale's mill over theya. (He'll nevah pay it.) But you'n I know you got equipment t'keep up, payments and such. And *I* pay good. May be because you're my sons. Someone else wouldn't be s'kind."

He winks at Emma, Alvin's auburn-haired wife, who just got her chance to sit down. She spent a half-day at the Headstart then shared the cooking with Ansell's wife Joanna and their mother-in-law. Joanna has her own half-day at the Headstart, sharing the job with Emma. That way there is always someone to watch the toddlers and babies not ready for school.

"Some o'that wood'll go to Bearce's. What I give you for a whole cord will be what Bearce gets fah one 16 ft. board of select wood." Seeing the shock on their faces, he chuckles. "Cuss, he's got overhead."

"You taking this a lot betta'n I thought," says Ansell, swallowing that last bite of meat. He has been hearing bitter complaint ever since he can remember. It once made him think of going into the mills. But Father's temper overflows like that. It doesn't always signify his heart or mind.

Robbie takes a heap of steaming potatoes, passing the bowl to his gray-eyed granddaughter. "Things's coming to a point, Ansell, a big change. Look at that budworm. Takes decades to come back up fom that. That, the big machine, clearcutting—woods'll be a different place in twenty years. But lookit Bearce. He's holding his high-grade in reserve because he knows that once the century turns, depletion will increase demand. We might be looking at the bottom of the barrel. George'n Jim's chances is slim," he says referring to his son's twins.

"Now, Bearce is a smot man. A bastid, but a smart one. What's worse though is the paper maker—cunning like the devil. Paper mill's run the same way the devil runs hell. Knows my cost t'the half cent, and sets his price to squeeze me. They know we won't organize. If one of us has t'dropout, theya's always someone to step in and take his turn getting squeezed." He shakes his head, jowls flushing. "And we think we work for ourselves! We're working fah them without benefits! Doing everything at their rates, n'the way they waunt! How much we make last year, Ezzy?" He stops chewing and turns to his man-dressed wife.

Esmeralda wears overalls and flannel shirts. She has short steel-gray hair and the fullest heart-shaped lips Robbie has ever seen. It was those lips made him fall for a Yankee like her. Ezzy keeps the books and handles the contracts for Robichaud Logging. "Twenty-five thousand," she duly answers. It's what they make as a team.

"If Ezzy'n I each had a job somewheres we'd make more, maybe. Let them take care o'the overhead." He stops to point his fork at his sons. "Prepare yourselves. 21st-century's the land of less wood."

Behind the house soars the steep tree-clotted ledge. Across the street sits one of the area's prosperous sawmills, a competitor of Lyman Bearce. At night the Robichauds sleep to the sound of the running sawmill: rumbling conveyors, humming blowers, whining chippers, the *yumm* of the saws. Some of Robbie's many relations work there. Mornings, on his way to the day's work site, he heads into Gottheim for a second cup of coffee and gossip, but not before first looking up along the ledge back of the house, sometimes in moonlight. Before climbing into his rig he checks up there for the flag. Everything on that high ledge looks tiny, tiny pines, tiny flag. Still, it is a surprisingly noticeable slip of flying white, precariously placed, heroically hard to reach. Who ever put it up there had to climb the ledge, then climb the tree clinging to the ledge, straddle a long bristling limb and hang on.

"That flag's a story," says Robbie if someone mentions it. But he never tells it. Robbie figures the flag tells its own story.

The ledge is named for early settlers, who came here from New Hampshire. They lived here awhile, worked every kind of job, did some farming. Then they packed up and went back to New Hampshire, leaving the mountain their name. It soars above the Robichaud House, above the mill yard of Bearce's competitor, Enan Pale. Before he enters the door next to the trimmer's table, Robbie's cousin can look out and see the tiny flag high on the somber hillside. Flags have appeared there over the decades since this extended family of French-speakers moved here from Québec. But, for all its small fragile and fluttering appearance high up there, the Robichaud flag is actually a sheet for a double bed. Every so often it gets swapped for a fresh one. The wind up there is fierce enough to rip it to ribbons within the year.

After the kids are put to bed, Emma and Joanna join Alvin and Ansell on the deck of Ansell's trailer, where the two are smoking sweetfern picked by Ansell last July. He hung the plants in the attic of the old house to dry in the dark. They still had the deep green color when he went up to roll them into crisp little cigarettes. Ansell was fed up from losing his license and getting sick on coffee brandies so, having heard from an old-timer that the leaves are relaxing, he decided to give them a try. Sweetfern grows in sandy soil in the half-shade between the roadside and woods. And its legal.

Tonight is cold and white, gleaming with the moon. The two couples stand in this silverness, taking hits off the shared herbal cigarettes. High on the ledge the flag is visible, riffling, visually echoing the white of snowy outcrops between the dark pines.

After the manner of identical twins, Alvin and Ansell are thinking alike, recollecting father's grievances of mill owners, and his fiery condemnation of environmentalists. "They hate loggers'n logging s'bad it'll injure or kill you. Inspect evah tree for signs of it. Say they love trees! Who'd spike a tree, leave it wounded, open to attack by bugs'n rot? If the paper maker's a devil, they're the devil's mother."

Alvin exhales slowly, looking up at the ledge. "Flag's in sad shape."

"Thing's in tatters," Joanna agrees.

Emma doesn't want to think about it. She shivers in her old parka. Sweetfern smoke dribbles through her chattering teeth. There must be some other subject to get on.

"It's your turn," says Ansell.

Alvin says nothing. He shakes his head and passes the joint to Joanna. He looks away from the ledge toward the sawmill across the road. The buzz of the headsaw floats over to them, punctuating the drone of the separators.

My turn. But Alvin is tired of negotiating that ledge, weary of climbing the tree that seems no bigger than when he was a kid. He remembers the feel of the branch lying beneath as he reaches, trembling, to knot the sheet tight. He would tell himself not to look down, that he should be less afraid than he was last time. Even now he can smell that old pine pitch sticking to his clothes, caught in his hair. After all the cutting he's done—he still can't get used to it.

"I d'know," he says at last. "I think that flag's good f'another six, eight months. August, maybe."

Or maybe we just won't change it. He does not say this aloud.

The wind is brutal. The hood of his insulated coveralls is up; Robbie sits hunched above the cab of his pulptruck. Off his shoulder overhead— outside the reach of the hydraulic loader—naked branches creak and crack.

The loader *hums* and *haws* as he works it back-and-forth, lifting the logs his sons have cut and hauled to the landing.

A half hour ago he was warm in the cab, eating chicken sandwiches made by Ezzy early this morning; washing them down with lukewarm coffee from a thermos topped off at 4:30 a.m.. Then he glanced out at the thermometer by the sideview mirror, reading five below. But just now, in the seat above the cab with wind-chill added, it aches like -40. His coveralls feel like something Ezzy might wear to bed. Even with the hood up, the fine bones of his ears hurt.

But Robbie can finesse that loader. In wind that could peel his scalp he loads ten cords an hour. He might curse it when it breaks down, but after sixteen years this loader is still his prize. Broken, this rig has taught him how to fabricate almost any part he might need. Operating the levers has so honed his touch that he could pick up a soda in its great steel claw without breaking the bottle or spilling a drop.

He sits pushing pedals, shifting levers, swiveling in the seat, setting logs between the vertical steel bars of the truck bed. And he thinks of the old days when he had to load with hooks and rolls, his youthful strength muscling those great logs up that pile. Now he's grateful for every drop of compressed hydraulic fluid ramming the loader, lifting these logs. He recalls the day he started with Father, being the rhythm end of a two-man saw with brother Louis, cutting trees girthier than these today. Father twitched them to the river with Claude and Claudette, his sleek Belgian draft horses. Together they saw the last decades of the great drives on the Arossagunticook.

Don't make woodsman like that n'more. But his thought snags on the sight of his father lying in mud, his back broken by the butt of a Norway pine. He shies at it, shivering and setting a log on the stack building below.

Saddened, he takes his attention to the talk he had with his neighbor last night when they stood by the woodshed laughing over the idea of bringing a $400,000 machine into the woods. Seriously then to Albert he said, "But they'll save three, four dollars a cord, even time you reckon their interest'n payments, over expenses for hiring reg'lar cutters. Bogs my mind, Albert. Weah kissing the woods g'bye. Won't be enough for ah sons to finish with."

Albert Clough looked down on bits of bark at his feet, his laughter gone. A long sigh came soughing where they stood by the shed.

Now Robbie recalls that sigh. He can hear it, sense it... even with this wind piercing him. Piercing where he sits hunched, loading logs at the landing.

—

Bearces' Mills sprawl along Oak River valley where old Beatitude Bearce started his operation early in the century. Led by Lyman, his sons have souped-up the operation with the latest 1980s technology. In the sawlog mill they can turn James Fay's white pine into a stack of boards almost before you can think of it. Gottheimites count themselves lucky that this white pine isn't shipped to Europe or Japan or someplace, instead of being debarked sliced edged trimmed planed graded stacked and dried by their husbands wives fathers daughters or sons. Asa Bartlett, amateur historian and wood-turning worker at the local spool mill, was stunned when he heard that Oregon had begun sending unmilled logs across the Pacific.

Bearce Mill sawlog workers go at it nonstop, hustling the heavy sap-saturated boards. Five thousand boards a shift is a very sweet thing: this being the mid-1980s, they get a penny for every board over 4000. Yet, 3600 is the limit a trimmer is physically apt to turn in an eight hour shift. After that he's trimming into those last few years at the end of his life, the years he is turning and trimming these extra boards for in the first place: Bearces' retirement plan consists of arthritis and air.

The several lengths of James Fay's pine tree have been hauled to the mill by Robbie Robichaud after Ansell and Alvin are done with it. Here these lengths are scaled in the yard and piled, after the unusual girth is exclaimed over. Hoisted with difficulty to the debarker, they are then stripped with blades and conveyed, patchy and bare, to the carriage of the headsaw. Sitting in the climate controlled cab above, pushing buttons, Thankful Thurston will roll one denuded log off the conveyor with a mighty slam. The machine takes the log in its hydraulic embrace, steel "dogs" nipping it tight, a line of laser red falling along its mottled length. The great girth forces Thankful to depress a foot pedal, bringing down the hammerdog to hold it in place. The carriage hurries the great log into the headsaw, a bandsaw with 900+ teeth vanishing in the speed of its fury. The blade rips the pine's fibers end to end along the red line, spraying wood dust across the cab like snow. These first mottled slices are junk, falling to the conveyor beneath, sent to the chipper blades at the far end of the mill. All this junk wood will be minced and used in the new generating system. Some of the more poorly run, smaller, wood-turning mills in Gottheim survive by selling their waste to Adirondack Paper in Guildford downriver.

When Thankful gets done with this massive pine log, it will be a squared-off cant; its visual identity as white pine tree done. The history of this life, told over more than a hundred years span of chromosomal replication and cell differentiation, will be reshaped into something else. Wages will change hands, human life being nourished and supported, but the life of this tree has already fled. The saw buzzed but no words were said over it. Where did this life go, now that its history has come to the blades of the resaw?

The cold of winter on him, Lyman Bearce stands in the doorway near the circuit of the resaw, surveying his operation. Winter's breath gives way to a sticky-sweet smell of ripped pine. This is the day on which the great Eastern white pine, taken off the subdivision under James Fay's supervision, is in progress of being turned into lumber; lumber, building material for sideboards or sashes or paneling—anything for sheltering, comforting, making convenient, decorating the lives of humans.

They are instantly aware of him, those whose posts permit a peripheral view of outdoor light slashing through the dim recesses of the mill. The mill sounds roar, whine, vibrate into Lyman Bearce. He pulls his ear covers from where they are buried in his vastly bearded neck, clapping them in place. Bearce likes coming into his mill; feeling this ruckus, watching the men work, seeing the blocked cant go its rounds in the resaw circuit... each time a little slimmer as its boards flop off. He likes everything about the place, even the noise: The screaming headsaw makes talk nearly impossible, a boon to productivity. The saws also isolate, encouraging contemplation of improvements. He can design for economy in the men's movements, test the function of each machine—think it all through to determine the shape of the future.

The place is snowy with sawdust—sills, corners, floor, machinery. Old brown piles of it are everywhere heaped with fresher white—wood dust from whatever happens to be passing through on a given day. Today it is pine from a ski resort development, though Bearce is unaware of its origin. The creamy white cant going by is a monster, the girth of which he considers would have disallowed it in the days of the King George navy. It would've been branded with the broad arrow in token of this. Today it is Lyman Bearce's bole.

It almost makes him smile, this clear light-hued limb gliding past; knotless and straight, and slimmer than when he first step through the door. Lyman watches the steel hands of the cant turners heave it toward the sawyer as he depresses one of five petals beneath the conveyor. The turners cradle the cant, rocking it like a baby as the operator draws it into the screaming saw. Aware of Bearce's presence, he is more awake now than a moment before when daylight poured in. And his boss is aware of his refreshed wakefulness, another reason why it is useful to visit the sawlog mill.

His workers are the best, and best paid, within a 25-mile radius. Only Jasper Mountain Ski Resort and, lately, Theodora Prescott's Gottheim

Chair, come anywhere near Lyman Bearce's great wage of nearly one third above minimum. His workers know they have the best jobs around and are properly loyal and grateful. Like Bob Hastings over there on the edger. Bob is one of the best, if not the best; has been faithful 40 years, seeing all kinds of innovation. His job—hell! All their jobs have gotten easier, safer, over the years. Look at Hastings' hands, those twisted fingers, where he grabs those heavy boards.

Pleased, Lyman Bearce watches the edger heave a 16-foot board onto the table, aligning it between laser lines, sending it through with his enlarged arthritic hands. Comes another board and another and another.... Won't stop for hours, not till quitting time or some unforeseen breakdown. Then, maybe even reluctantly, Bob will stop ramming those boards through to the trimmer. Lyman shakes his secretly sentimental head in admiration. The man has been with Bearces since Lyman himself was a teenager getting ready to go off to college. Bob knows how lucky he is, having a decent job at the same place all his life. These men would give their lives for anybody. They saved the mill from burning to the ground last year, really put their backs into snuffing that generator fire.

Why does Rhetta keep on at me, anyway? The old thing just doesn't seem to understand any more what Bearces have done for this town, keeping it afloat all these years. Her!—married for decades into the best, the helpingest business in town. And born into one of the first operations in the area, too! Old Swann, her own father, was one of the originators of wage security!

Yet she's on Lyman day and night to own up to his sins. Sins?! Hell. Without those so-called sins her position would be less lofty, and Gottheim would not have fared so well. That mutual agreement on wages, even the blackball arrangement—it's where employment stability came from. She ought to go down to the Arossagunticook River, smell that: She'd know what *sin* is. Besides, they discontinued those meetings ten years ago.

That widget head Theodora Prescott. Lyman Bearce is deeply offended. Peewee Prescott died and left Gottheim Chair in the hands of his idiot daughter. Now she's upsetting the balance of business in the whole town (hardly to mention what it's doing to life at home).

But.... Maybe it's not that bad, her setting wages up almost even with his. She'll go under any day now. Have to. Her ramshackle ways will bring down that ramshackle place. That disgrace of a mill should be pulled to the ground before it collapses under its weight and someone gets killed. Let its shoddy remains be plowed under to rise in some tolerable form. There's development potential—God no. He'd rather buy the place himself than let the stripping of Gottheim continue. The skiers are uglifying the town at a rate swift enough. *At least Rhetta and I agree on that.*

At waist level the sawmill really moves. Boards whiz by, a stream of white gleaming in channels between headsaw and trimmer. Bearce steps onto the catwalk bridging the chipper conveyor. Below waist level his sawlog mill has a different pace. The creeping lower regions—where gears turn, chains snake slowly and conveyors move byproducts—cannot compete with the speed of higher regions where screaming saws, fast handwork, and the rock-and-rolling of the upper body prevail. Crossing the catwalk, Bearce glances into the chipper conveyor as a matter of course. A metal detector under the walk is a last check for debris before waste wood leaves the mill for the knives of the chipper.

The trimmer's table stretches to the mill wall, just this side of a door leading out to the grader and the yard below. Approaching, Lyman Bearce senses refreshed alertness in the rhythms of Moses Merrill. Merrill's job is to increase the worth of a board by cutting it to length. A good trimmer can shove the price of a board two, three, even four grades higher, depending on how he trims it. Always looking for that select board, Moses is quick. He can spot the face of the next board while cutting the end off the one he is releasing, eliminating as much as four feet to bump that board up to clear select.

Bearce stands back of the stocky trimmer, eyeing the perfect lumber coming through, watching as Merrill turns and trims in a smooth repetitive motion. This wood! Even demanding Lyman Bearce is impressed. Board after board of flawless pine. So broad that other mills would not be able to process it. So broad that Moses can hardly turn it.

"Some wood!" Merrill tosses the observation over his shoulder loud enough to be heard above the whine of the 16-foot saw.

"Not a knot anawaya!" Seeing it, Bearce can hardly keep a smile off. Board after 16-foot board, select. The world can't be as bad as they say, not with this kind of wood still around. Almost he feels like clapping Merrill on the back. As though the boy had prayed and pronounced over it when a seedling, saying, *Thy wood shall be select*! It's the purity they have waited for. All that cutting, edging, trimming, and seldom seeing such wood. The sight of it coming should lift the boy's heart; *it does mine.*

But when Bearce turns away Moses grits his teeth, turning a heavy board, cursing under his breath. When the boss has gone he can coast. No use turning these boards. There ain't no knots in this wood. Won't slip my discs over the old man's lumber. And, at night, when Moses gets back to his house—cold as a back house in January—he'll recall before reaching the lane that Lydia is gone. That the kids live in Lewiston with another man, one with wealthy Bath Ironworks wages. Moses will feel like walking around the frozen woods with his head chopped off. Wondering what there is to live for but those fucking sombreros.

From the corner of his eye he catches Bearce leaning over the conveyor. Now the old man straightens, hurries back to flip a toggle switch on the wall behind the trimmer. At the conveyor again he climbs over the catwalk and comes up with a bit of something his hand. Moses keeps flipping boards, punching buttons. Turning again he sees the boss heading back toward the headsaw. Merrill stops flipping the killer boards.

Through a door near the headsaw Bearce enters the dingy dim maintenance shop. Elmer Robbins, mill manager, and Artemis Kimball a mechanic, are bent over the bench conferring on a piece of machinery. Halting, Bearce holds up a bolt, reflecting fluorescent light back at the pair. They look up from the helter-skelter of the workbench where vices, tools, solder, a welding mask, etc... are spread. The smell of hot metal and scorched bench are stronger than sawn pine.

"Found this in the chippa conveya." His tone is curt.

"Metal detector must be down," says Robbins.

"Guess maybe," Bearce barks.

"Right on it!" Elmer brushes past while Kimball drops the piece he is working on to grab his tool belt and ear protection.

Lyman Bearce leaves the shop speculating about the bolt in his calloused hand. Maybe it fell off the headsaw. He yanks open the door of the cab and steps up, closing it to shut out the noise. Thankful Thurston is pushing buttons, playing the pedal, slamming down on the last of James Fay's white pines.

In the relative quiet it is as if Thankful, sitting high and setting pace for the entire mill, is somehow removed, above it all. Momentarily mesmerized, Bearce stops as the last great log is gripped in the dogs; mesmerized, as though by the last virgin pine in the state. He cannot believe the immensity of this tree. His only wish is that it came off one of his lots. Should look into that. He thought he knew their 35,000 acres... but maybe not. He watches as Thankful draws off its patchy flanks, the last remnants of *cambium* with inner and outer bark; the life, that which formally nourished and protected this great tree. A blizzard of wood dust passes and Lyman sees the tree, naked and light, scarcely touched with a delicate reddish tinge. Now the great blocked cant goes its way to the resaw, on a path to becoming a stack of new boards.

Bearce understands. It has to go. It was perfect, not a speck of rot, but it has to go. It gives place to seedlings, to saplings, to the whole of its spawn—at first sheltering them but ultimately blocking the necessary light of life. The young trees beneath would otherwise stunt, die out, in its towering competition. Woodsmen understood this. He felt it well expressed in the poetry of one of Gottheim's daughters, the master smart child of the mill scion now dead. Rot would surely have come to this tree. No way to keep rot out of living things. No way at all. Better this wood should go now... into cabinets or paneling or planking. Like in the poem: medium and light construction. Useful.

Lyman Bearce's hand on Thankful's shoulder brings the carriage to a standstill.

This is the moment of Life, the present moment. The only moment currently available to Gottheimites. The next moment is but a suggestion, the last is already hardened in history. For all the mass girth weight of the town's unchangeable history, only now is it alive, renewable. In this moment can Gottheim take heed to what it is doing, think, as it proceeds to its finished destiny. Last day comes, everyone "gets done," each looking back through time to discern the rings; sap, hardwood, and pith, formed in these moments when *now* is what we have. When we get done, all *this* will be monumental. An identity, fully fashioned and formed.

These are the translated thoughts of Asa Bartlett, amateur village historian, things he thinks of while walking twice-weekly to wind the tower clock in Gottheim. But he does not consider this metaphor in *cambium*, the living cell layer: No, he thinks of present moments as a tick of the clock, a single stroke of time's hands. Even so, Asa knows wood. He works with it every day. Turning birch into dowel rods at the village wood-turning mill, he handles wood constantly. The blades of the machine hone each rod, cleanly, as Asa feeds them through. One rod at a time.

Daniel and Balder

Some days, getting up from the chair by his window after a night of non-sleep, Balder Simon gives thanks for Lyman Bearce. He gives thanks for the sawlog mills, the little wood-turning mills in all these communities around Gottheim. Some days he even considers making a gesture toward Jasper Mountain with its ski trails running down the north slopes like white wounds: the ownership is nominally local, at least as of this moment. Balder would rather the owners around here had names like Bearce, Carter, Kimball, Chase, Corriveau, Hebert, Ouellette, Clark. He needs Yankee and French names to make him feel stable and whole. You never know. Someday the tree farms might be called Mitsubishi, Yamamoto, Honda. Maybe they'd be clone farms, or deformed berry farms or sludge farms creeping with chemical and miasmic mists. Not that Japan, particularly, is going to take over the world. At this late date, the last fifth of the last century of the millennium, it looks to him like multinational corporations are moving to grasp that distinction. Maybe junk-bond speculators in the cocaine casinos of Wall Street will trigger the metastasizing of greed. He is convinced of the speed of its malignancy, that it will astound everyone in the year 2001. As if he were in heaven, looking down through the ozone hole, watching corporate gluttons gobble up companies and land, vacuuming their way across continents. One day, he says, international trade legislation will supersede local laws protecting the community and its surroundings. "One day," (he said last week to Daniel after a night helping to install computer regulation of pulp and paper production in the mill) "Big Brother will jump his Communist ship to take the helm of capitalism. Forget the lack of privacy in government, we'll be too busy trying to escape the corporations' KGB."

This morning, his mouth foaming as he rinses his toothbrush in the sink, he says, "Gott'im's the residue. The iron monster's gont stomp on us in its furious fulminations. Free market caunt take ana value into account not measured immediately in money."

Peeling paint hangs off the bathroom door. His teenage son Daniel hears him saying this as he comes down the hall in his underwear. Balder nearly knocks him over, clipping through the door on his way to the staircase.

"What's it mean?" Daniel asked this, rubbing his eyes against the glare of the bathroom light.

"What? Who?"

"That. About iron monsters'n money."

Balder raises his bearded chain, eyeing the questionable ceiling. "Well, take borrowing. If a company has to rebuy the equivalent of itself evah few years, they'll decrease worker's'n make'em work harder fah less." He looks down at Daniel. "And have t'use creation down to the nub. How do they know what to do with Gott'im if they don't live here and be fond of it? And, all that shipping stuff around—you can only take out the amount of oil God put in the ground to begin with. Unless theya's some way to siphon it out o'the sky where we been flinging it. Think we can do that anatime soon?"

"But—we don't really *need* to, do we?"

The inarticulate Balder taps Daniel's tangled head with his comb. "I'd advise you to stot separating yourself from your deplorable dependence on consumerism."

He stuffs the comb into his back pocket and heads down stairs. "Stot today!" He shouts, trouncing down the stair. "Start yestadee!"

"How much land we gut heah?" asks Balder.

"100 acres?"

They are painting drywall in the children's house, upstairs. Daniel knows the history. The children's house is an extension of the pioneer's dwelling, added in the prosperous 1880s. Beneath the protective north wall of Jasper Mountain, farming was life. Skiing was something you read about in books. Every scholar in the schoolhouse at the foot of the hill knew that you couldn't get around Norway or Switzerland unless you had skis. Daniel's father wants the whole house prepared in case he ever has a bride to bring to it. He must want a wife pretty bad.

And Daniel thinks he knows which one, too. She's a beautiful blonde with startling eyes and a jutting dimpled chin. Whenever he sees it, he thinks of a man's chin. But Gloria is sweet and nice. Fresh lightly powdered donuts come to mind when she strolls into The Village Voter, where he works setting type for Mr. Nutting after school. She comes in with items on conferences and meetings, things pertaining to town development. She works, somehow, with the resort, which wants to change the town around.

"Daow. Way way back, when Simons was settlers, they had a few lots, hundreds o'acres. Hevn't near that now, maybe near 25."

Dabbing with paintbrush, Daniel nods. He is edging around the window trim. Balder lays long even ivory strokes on the drywall, stooping once in awhile to load the roller. Even with the window cracked, the smell of fresh latex fills the room. "Know what we could do with it?"

Solemn, Daniel shakes his head, waiting for the answer. He knows better than to say develop it.

"Put it to wuk. Theya's the woodland... and we got the barn. We might hire us a bandsaw, stot harvesting bad trees."

"Market bad wood?"

"Good wood, but we take the worst trees. Cull the injured and diseased from the woods, leave a few of 'em for critters, woodpeckers, like that. Coons, bears'n such'll eat the bugs right out of trees. Wood ants taste like cranberries to'em. Decayed wood goes to make soil.... We mill some of the trees, making room for healthy ones t'come. But theya's more going on in the woods we could profit fom. Edible mushrooms, balsam'n spruce tips for making wreaths. We could make weather sticks to sell to tourists." He grins. "Got to get ah li'l piece of the tourists."

This is too much for Daniel. He has enough to do without playing medicine man: working at the The Voter, helping out here, and school on top of that. Mother's been prodding him to do maple syrup maybe next month. He can't stand the thought of all this *work*, but he says only, "Mother says roots'n stuff make good medicine."

"Theya y'go! S'pose she'll find all kinds o' stuff in that woods up theya on Blackwell. What we need, though, is markets for all this. Where'n how t'sell. Got do a li'l research, see. That's where you come in—with those budding reporter skills you been learning at The Voter. If we caunt sell stuff heah, we gut look elsewhere."

More work. *Wuk wuk wuk.* It's all that goes on here. Mother works two jobs and all she talks about is that farm up on Blackwell Mountain. He is supposed to help with that. There isn't even a house up there yet, just an old camper six sizes too small.

"Uh, Fatha?... does this have anything to do with what you was saying the other morning? Deplorable dependence'n all that?" And now he slips in the dig: "Cause I was wondering about that job you got in the paper mill." *Your thoughts are holy but what about your hands?* Look what Adirondack Paper is doing to the Arossagunticook River. The mill's a massive stinking inhaler of trees. The mill yard is a boneyard concentration camp for trees. You're always telling tales of how wasteful they are, how they make workers work unnatural hours, use evil chemicals, demonic machinery.

The man stops painting. "It looks hypocritical...." Slowly he begins laying a white swath with the roller. The grin he usually wears when caught in some ludicrous act is missing. Some act like that of the other day, when he overshot the bog trail in the Skidoo and landed in a beaver pool that wasn't quite frozen. They were up to their necks in ice water, and it took fifteen minutes to hike-jog out of there. And the snow machine is sitting there still, now probably locked in ice.

"But I'm thinking about that job all the time, thinking of ways to t'get loose. If I 'memba right, I took that job to have money to fix up this house. Guess I got kinda bogged down." Here he does grin. "But you're right, Daniel. It is hypocritical. I'm working on it, though. Anything else bothering you?"

"Well... what about Grandmother's animals? Waya'll she stash 'em if you use the barn fah farm animals?"

Balder half turns to the boy and Daniel sees speckles of ivory paint in Balder's short black beard. The speckles just about match his towhead. "Haven't got that fah in my calculations yet either. Interfering with her critters'd be a formidable exercise I don't doubt."

Balder grins and Daniel almost smiles. Elda was as small as an elf and a pushover in just about any area one might intrude on. Balder thinks how she gave up her habitual privacy without a peep when he was surprised by fatherhood and suggested she make room for three boys every other week. Now that Peter is in the area Nathan and Ben don't come as often, but, still, it's not easy for her. Even considering Elda's seemingly pliant nature, Balder is wary of testing her limits concerning the animals in the barn. He suspects an awful surprise.

"What else? Can I take these questions t'mean I'm out heah on a limb by myself? We might *could* act out a living in this place, if we don't get greedy. *Simons Ledge* might sustain itself again."

Daniel isn't about to bring it up, but the "what else" he is thinking of is Gloria Fay. Father is gooey over her. Daniel can't picture her cleaning house, let alone mucking out the barn. She might clean the toilet of her condo, but Daniel can't picture it. He stoops to pick up the paint can and take it to the next window. Time to change the subject.

"Evah see that white flag over theya, other side o'the valley? Across the road fom the big sawmill, Pale's Mill, I think it is. Flag flies on a pine, way up on the ledge?"

Rolling on the paint with vigor, Balder says, "Theya's nevah been a time I in't seen that flag up theya. Been flying over Robichaud's since I was a kid, maybe 'fore that, even."

"Why's it theya?"

Still laying the paint, Father says, "Thought you was the reporter. Find out, tell me'n we'll both know."

Turning eggs in the pan one morning, Balder says to Daniel, "What we need's a way to market what we'll have t'sell."

They are in the woodpaneled kitchen, fixing breakfast. Sunlight reflecting snow-light comes in through divided windows, whitening the wooden cupboards with rectangles. This is Sunday. They are up late with the sun.

Not this, thinks Daniel, dropping whole-wheat slices into the toaster. The slots insides begin to glow red. He smells the wheat toasting, thinking of an assignment Mr. Hebert has given the freshman English class. They are supposed to start keeping a journal. Daniel isn't sure he wants a record of his days. Writing about real-life sounds like a big thing, but he's tried it before and knows better. It's all little things. Lots of little things. Things you aren't even excited about doing, let alone writing about. Things like fixing and eating breakfast, making your bed, riding the noisy school bus, talking about little things with your friends. Or having to listen to your Father make boring plans for your future. Father seems hands off about after graduation, but Daniel is certain to have his life niggled away in the meantime. Mr. Hebert is usually in absolute brick—as they say in England. He makes English interesting. Like that reading he gave of Tolkien's "Leaf by Niggle." Hebert is an *Anglophile*. He gave that word to the class along with *Anglophobe*. Daniel relates to Niggle, a little man whose life is being niggled away by the claims of others.

Still he says nothing, getting the butter out of the refrigerator. The toast pops.

Balder does not seem to notice Daniel's lack of response. His rangy muscular frame leans happily to the task of shoveling up eggs, his talk continuing right along. From the way he moves about, flipping eggs onto plates, talking, Daniel could not know that he spent half the night reliving explosive and bloody scenes which took place on the other side of the planet well over a decade ago. He spent the other half scheming to break off daily association with deafening noise, toxic fumes, obscene and idiotic conversation, and a profound waste of trees. Here and there, tucked in at the edges of all these thoughts, came a healthy merry face, stunning blue eyes, gold hair, and a cleft chin just a bit too pronounced: It was the sun, peeping through chinks in his sometimes dim life.

That is all the sun will do: peep through chinks. Even so, Balder will not scheme to bring it live into his house.

"'N that's waya you come in," he says hopefully to his son. "You can research what markets we got."

Is that all? All I got to do is research markets, help you fix up this house, work at the newspaper, get straight A's, help Mutha collect sap, build her a house out of nothing, babysit my brothers, collect mushrooms in the woods, plant a garden in spring, saw trees, and write it all down in a journal? No sweat.

Daniel edges the plates with buttered toast and carries them to the table. "How do I find these markets?"

Hot dog! The boy has acknowledged his request. Balder pulls out his chair and sits, looking over at his serious son. The man grins. "I d'know. That's why I give the job t'you."

Daniel dips his toast in the gooey yolk, inwardly mouthing the words as Balder says them aloud: "You're the reporter."

The boy thinks, I liked you better that first time, when we went bass fishing. They were just getting started on the relationship.

Balder sat in that boat and worked harder at getting Daniel to like him than he had worked at anything since the Asian war. But Daniel knows little about the war, except that Balder got scarred by Agent Orange. Daniel once heard Balder say he was glad he got into that Agent Orange. Adults can be pretty mysterious, when they aren't being dull as dirt.

Daniel thinks Agent Orange sounds like a name for a rock group. There *should* be a rock group named Agent Orange. Maybe there is.

"Take black birch," Balder is saying.

It's as though his father has been reading his mind, because immediately Daniel thinks that Black Birch would be a good name for a band. He looks blindly at Balder's face, awaiting further information. But, seeing yellow goo rimming his father's mustache, he suppresses a smile. *Yellow Goo.* He can see its drummer wail.

Grinning, Balder takes a napkin to his mustache, to his beard. "Have ana idea how well sap flows outta black birch? Betta'n maple sap. 'N' you don't have t'gather it in the cold. We could extend the sapping that way. When maple gets done'n leaves start on black birches—there y'go, a premium syrup! What a market theya'd be fah that! Takes twice as much sap as with maple, though. And then there's black birch tea. You might be interested: Indians made it."

This was a reference to Daniel's heritage through his mother, who is part Native. Chrischana's own mother, Hattie Trueman, was descended from Abenaki Indians who frequented the Arossagunticook River. They belonged to the same clan as Jasper Mary, Native storyteller of history and legend, who lent her identity to Gottheim and surrounding towns. *Murdered by thieves out to steal my treasure, I crossed over the dark river in the late 1700s. It is believed that no one ever found my peculiar treasure—some think it may have been found by some ordinary pioneer seeking it diligently in the earth without telling a soul. But know, oh reader, my greatest treasure came out of the storehouse of stories I told.*

"Try that book I got out o'the library. The old one on the table in the front room. It says black birch tea was used to wash out sore mouths, and helps diarrhea and rheumatism."

Bound to be a market for that, thinks Daniel.

"It's loaded with vitamins A, B1, B2, C and E. They made wintergreen out of it in the old days."

Wow. But Daniel refrains from rolling his eyes, saying only, "Nevah saw black birch. Seen papah birch and yellow birch, though. And theya's one looks like papah but don't peel like it."

"Gray birch," says Balder nodding. "Don't know if we even have black birch around here anamore. Look at bark on black cherry saplings, it's easy to mistake, they looked s'much alike."

But Daniel is not interested in black birch tea. He mops up the yolk on his plate with a piece of limp toast, saying thoughtfully, "You're always looking to make a living off the land... why can't we look for gems? People say theya's gemstones'n minerals in the woods. That's what I'd like to look for."

Balder looks at him. Now they are back in the boat. He is teaching Daniel how to cast for bass. Daniel has asked him for something, something maybe worthwhile.

"We could. Evah since the Hamlin boys down to Mt. Mica found gem tourmaline tangled in the roots of a blowdown, folks have been poking around, digging out the woods'n blasting out the sides of mountains. The Simons nevah did." He grins. "Now might be the exception. If evah theya was anathin in these woods—still theya! We can take it long's we don't disturb things too much. Valuable things like ginseng'n certain mushrooms should be preserved unless weah sure something's down theya, okay?"

"How'll I recognize those things?"

"Books! We'll learn what t'look fah from them this winter—plants and minerals. Theya's clues, what they call indicators."

They have finished eating, but no one moves to clear. In pauses between conversation, Daniel can hear the dripping of the faucet, the ticking of the clock in the next room.

"I been out a few times with friends, looking for minerals," Balder continues. "'N' we find gemstones by minerals not so rare being nearby. When we get done heah we'll go out to the shed'n see some of the dusty samples up in the loft."

" 'Simons nevah did?' "

"Maybe black tourmaline, feldspar, not rare. Don't know how we come by it. Indicators, though. We got books in the front room. They might help."

Daniel stands, beginning to clear the table. Balder grabs dish liquid from under the sink, sets the plug, turns on the faucet. Sunday is going to be a day absorbed. Later they will be ice fishing on the pond. *My people are still hunting my treasure.*

Old Tires

Legends of Jasper Mary have always abounded in Gottheim and surrounding towns. A part of her story is set in one stretch of backwoods, in neighboring Quaker Plantation also known as Quakertown. This tale tells of her hunts for medicinal herbs in a place called Medicine Mile, and of how she marked the stretch with pouches of deerskin decorated in porcupine quills. Gemstones, it was said, could be found there in clay and rock not far under the surface of woodland earth. Why did she never unearth her trove or carry it away to make her rich? The tales do not explain, but for nearly two hundred years folks have searched the stretch deep into the woods. Pits were dug, trees chopped; and people farmed it, breaking the soil with harrows. Nevertheless, nothing shiny was ever discovered between root or rock. The treasure eludes, its secret keeps, and myth abounds; yet the uses of Medicine Mile have changed.

One old son of settlers, Ceylon Segar (pronounced Ceylon Cigar by townsfolk), has a business "storing" used tires. Set back from the old dirt road, millions of tires are piled in mammoth mountains behind a curtain of trees on Medicine Mile.

The trees where Jasper Mary once tied her medicine pouches are long gone and others have grown in their place. Through their branches one can hear the clanking of gears and rumbling of engines as truckloads come through each week... even as the fear of Quaker's scattered residents builds. What if one of those monstrous piles catches fire? They wonder it aloud among themselves and in desperate letters to the editor. They complain about "environmental terrorism," study the composition of tires, and wonder what kind of pitch, in what quantities would fill the sky around the communities of Gottheim if, say, a dry season with forest fire should set these dense lots ablaze.

One such writer of letters dreams of falling through clouds, bright and dark with flaming imagery. Through layers of expanding consciousness, she falls through the hellish halls. On other nights she dreams of little but trees, of white pine with arms outstretched, praising and resigned. They tower toward heaven, collecting birds, gathering songs from the sky; yielding up fragrance. They harbor weak bobbing heads and pointed gaping mouth. The dreamer's name? Eloise Patadoe. Of course. She is an artist. She keeps goats.

Having ascended on the Golding's private lift, Julius Golding looks out from the summit of snowy Jasper Mountain, a pair of black binoculars in his gloved hand. The round bulks of the Meguntics stretch away, mottled light and dark with conifer and snow. Southward the sun is far, white, diffuse. Beside him stands his niece Amanda, in ski mask and goggles, daughter of his late sister. The little girl stands patiently, strands of white hair escaping her patterned knit alpine cap. She is hooded and bundled in insulated jumpsuit, longing to ask for a turn with the binoculars. She hopes he will remember her standing by, and offer the glasses. The fierce breath of Jasper blows over them, fierce as the Arctic, quickly unbearable.

Below the summit sits the lift shack, a lonely little house at the end of the world. Skiers leap to its ramp under the bullwheel, before gliding away back down the mountain. Billy Glover sits in the insulated lift shack between the two lifts where a heater keeps him warm. He looks down the shining lines of cables and suspended seats, vigilant as skiers ascend. Sometimes they knock at his door and ask to ride to the summit. He just shakes his head, explaining that it's a private lift. Amanda knows Billy. Sometimes she visits him briefly at the shack on her way up or down. Her uncle only nods at him through the window, or raises his voice to ask how it's going when he opens the door for her. He doesn't let Amanda stay in there too long.

Billy operates both lifts from the shack. When any of the family ascend to the summit, he has to keep one eye up and the other down. It's really a job for a two-headed person, but Billy doesn't mind. Actually, he's kind of proud to be serving the Golding's like this. They are some of the most powerful people in the state. Harry Golding has brought celebrities to the summit. Billy has seen Stephen King up here with his own eyes, and the horror king is awesome all the way home. But Billy's wife thinks the writer should go back to the dry cleaners. That night he came up there was no end of glory for Billy and Rayona at the Muzzleloader. They needed a designated driver to get home. Since then he has read up and become an expert on King. "Did you know he once worked in a laundry? He could o'been a lift operator!"

Pierced through with Jasper's severe whole breath, Julius Golding stands looking out across the Meguntics. Shivering, stamping, Amanda slips her mittened hand in his gloved one, hoping to remind him of her presence. If she had been any other Golding offspring she would be jumping around, tugging at him, begging for the glasses. But she is only Amanda, she doesn't whine.

There are no trees here. Not as Amanda thinks of trees. There are some wizened crooked small bushes that Uncle Julie calls krumholz. She thinks them cute shrubbery, permanently bent as though kneeling. The wind seems to move them hardly at all and sometimes they are buried in snow. She has seen them in rime. They are little, but Uncle Julie says they are actually very old, much older than he is. Krumholz isn't handsome or vital-looking like the tall trees on the slopes below but she heard him say they survive here better than a great white pine could.

The wind is pointed, piercing through her coveralls like darts. Amanda is beginning to numb up and bend like krumholz. In a moment she will crumble. Trembling, her hand jerks in Uncle Julie's. Still he looks through the binoculars. At last she cries in her high-pitched voice. "What are you looking at?"

Golding looks down on her suddenly through his ski mask, surprised concern in his eyes. He stoops to hand her the glasses, saying close in her ear, "I wanted to see the tire piles in Quakertown. Sometimes heat from them prevent snow buildup, but it's too late. I think they're covered for the winter."

Below wooded Mount Marriott, 60 million tires are thought to be stored. The exact number is in question. Three years ago there were 20 million, documented. Current estimates set it much higher. Amanda pulls down her goggles and looks through binoculars in the direction he points, seeing only a patch of pure white snow. "Where there's no trees?" She yells, pointing.

"Exactly!"

Amanda is very concerned about the tires. Last autumn she heard Uncle Julie express anger over them and wondered aloud why he didn't call someone to take them away. He and Uncle Harry were always calling people to do important things. Her class studied about Jasper Mary and Medicine Mile on local history day. In science they learned about pollution and recycling and other ecological concerns. She was glad Uncle Julie was indignant, but, when she asked him to call to have the tires removed he smiled faintly and said, "It's not that easy."

"But it's not harder than building a condominium or a ski lift is it?" Moving tires must be easier than most things she saw happening at the resort where strong detailed structures were put together. But Uncle Julie said that things like rights and policies got in the way. He said someone must figure out how to use the tires. Then she came home from school one day to tell them the class had it all solved for him. The paper mill in Guildford was putting in a generator to burn things like tires and produce electricity at the same time. The high smokestack would burn them very clean. Now, if he called, the tires would have some place to go.

But he said the tires were not his, the land wasn't his, and he could not tell the paper company to come take the tires away. The Maine DEP said the tires had to stay, and that was that.

"What's the DEP?"

"The Department of Environmental Protection."

This was beyond Amanda's understanding.

The conversation about tires took place during the drought last fall, when Amanda was afraid the tires would catch fire. It was one of Julius Golding's big fears. There'd be no stopping a fire like that any time soon. He knew how a fine resort with a hoped-for international clientele would fare if shrouded in a volcanic and enduring cloud of soot. The prevailing winter wind would blow its desolate load upon them, the fair white slopes becoming a pall in rains of ash. And skiers would head for Goldings' competitors. The best he was able to do was get the governor to consider the problem of tire dumps statewide. Together they learned that Maine has more tires than Michigan, 60 times more, with a population statewide roughly equal that of Detroit.—One more ironic and idiosyncratic snafu of American life.

Here on the summit of Jasper, in polar wind fierce as an ancient deity, the Goldings lives are hazarded. Up here Julius sees how casually human control is negated. A man may take precautions, pay heed to safety but, ultimately, vicissitudes shall prevail. Below, when he is skiing on Jasper's pristine flanks, or driving along on the thread of highway and looking up at its massive bulks, its almost perfect rounded head, Golding forgets what he has learned up here about his own lack of power. Being on the summit can give you insight, even as you turn your back, fight for breath, feel your heat leave. Julius knows he should get Amanda down from here, shelter her away from these mighty elements but, if he waits maybe a moment more, something may come. One clear thought to guide. It sometimes happens.

But, waiting, no thought comes save the urgency for shelter. Shelter *now*. With his pole he urges her to the slope, gesturing that she precede him. The wind burning his face, he watches her red suit whittle away in the distance. Now he slips down after her, clipping through his turns. She waves to him from a clump of spruce opposite the bullwheel. He stops before her in a spray of white, crisply saying, "Good to get out of the wind. Ready for cocoa?"

She nods, a little red ridinghood in goggles, but Amanda does not turn immediately. "Uncle Julie? When I was up there I had a thought. Don't those little old trees look like little old men? One of them remind me of Mr. Cigar. In class, we saw his picture in *The Voter* when Mrs. Gravalos was getting us to think of him as our neighbor. She said he was—uh—a man making a living, so why couldn't we, you and me, write him a letter about the tires? Or call him on the phone? And talk nicely to him? Couldn't we, Uncle Julie?"

His hesitation is frowning and long. Julius does not want anything to do with talking to Ceylon Segar, nicely or otherwise. Ceylon Segar is thick-headed, vulgar, filthy. He generally sits in his trailer office and watches the trucks from all over the country pile in. Mr. Cigar feels himself a going concern. However, the problem for the little unincorporated township of Quaker is that the used tire business is sedentary. The tires sit there, going nowhere. At the moment this did not concern Mr. Segar. He had the famous land of his ancestors, and people from away were falling all over themselves, spewing money, to get their tires-by-the-ton moved onto his property in rural Maine. Truckloads came, sometimes almost hourly, and Ceylon, who once probably delighted to count them and the piles they made, most likely gave up keeping track long ago. He probably has no idea how many millions are piled on his property. He would know nothing about compromise, diplomacy, courtesy, or how to get along in any way shape or form. It's all there in *The Voter*. He is all ego, a prickly old fart. Julius once saw the old man drive past Janine's ski boutique, flipping it the bird. He probably couldn't read a contract if shown one. And Amanda wants to make friends! A picture of their meeting flashes on him: self crisply attired, smelling of aftershave, cuff links glinting; Segar smelly in grubby hunting jacket, hands and fingernails lined and caked in dirt. Not in a decade of diplomatic negotiation would it work.

"Well," he says to the little red-framed face. "It can't do me any harm to think about it. But I've got to warn you not to get your hopes up. I don't think it'll work." He gestures, saying, "Let's go get that cocoa."

Amanda starts down and is soon a red dot amidst the swirling throng of color. Julius Golding follows. He follows Amanda down.

She is on her way to sign up for a course in carpentry at the Adult Education office, when a rear tire on her 14-year-old Bonneville blows. Chrischana Twitchell is due at Farmingham Royal Tavern to wash luncheon dishes before the hour is out. Now she will have to change the tire and come back another time to apply for a course she hopes will help her in building a house on Blackwell Mountain... someday. It is first lunch period as she limps into the parking lot of Hazel Newell high school/middle school. Spitting snow at 20° and the wind blows, making it feel more like 0. Chrischana sighs, shoves open the door.

Won't be easy, the shape this car's in. She looks from the flat tire to the distant row of cafeteria windows. Sure hope Daniel's not in lunch, or Benaiah. This could be embarrassing for them.

The wind riffles her secondhand parka, bought at a hospital sale in Guildford a month ago—her first real winter coat since living with father as a teenager here in Maine. Until last spring she was living in the metropolitan desert southwest, ever since Daniel's birth out of wedlock almost for fifteen years ago. Now she is back, struggling on her own to make a life for herself and her sons.

Standing at the trunk she looks bleakly at the clothesline holding one end of the bumper to the frame of her car. It will have to come off if she wants to get at the spare in the trunk. Fingers rapidly numbing, she begins working the knot. Swearing but once under her breath, she loosens it and begins unwinding the rope. With a *clunk*, that end of the bumper hits the icy pavement. Chrischana looks over her shoulder at the row of windows. A few kids look out at her through descending snow. *Maybe it's not them. Can't tell.*

She opens wide the lid, heaves out the spare. It's a rummage through the gaping trunk full of junk: tattered sleeping bags, a broken toaster, kids' holey sneakers, newspapers, the livetrap Benaiah got for Christmas, some scattered tools. She can see ice on the pavement through a hole near the wheel well. Where is the jack?

She finds it shoved toward the back under their tangled tent, pulls out its pieces and tosses them onto the gritty ice beside the spare. Where's the hammer? Might take a pounding to get that wheel off.

More rummaging. Doaw. No hammer.

Chrischana stands back, searching for a place beneath the rust-eaten car to set up the jack. The body around the wheelwells is disintegrating. Rust holes lace the old fenders of the dull gold frame. If she sets the jack beneath the door and it breaks through the chrome they won't be able to close the door.

It's all standard procedure. This is how you live.

She could be under Peter's wing, maybe get a good used-car on the wealthy wages he now earns from Adirondack Paper. The pattern of violence seems to be broken, or maybe just abated. She isn't ready—*they* aren't ready. *Got to give it more time to make sure he won't be drinking, won't be hurting me again.*

When she and the kids ran away and came back here to what she knew growing up, Peter sobered up and came looking for them. He got counseling and seems to be recovering. And ever, except for that awful example of intermittent drunken brutality, he has been a pretty good father. She will admit that. Now he wants to be a good husband and she can't deny that he is working at it. But she's been working too. A lot of effort has gone into living without him, into ridding herself of the pain caused by their common-law marriage. Instead of giving the relationship a chance she's out here by herself, working at being independent. Being alone.

Snow thickens the air. The air is white, her clothes are whitening, the spare lying on the ground is already coated in white. She gets down on her knees, looks under the car. There's the axle, use that.

Daniel is calling her. She turns her head, sees him coming through the flying snow. He wears his leather jacket, the one Peter gave him Christmas before last. He has outgrown it and his wrists showing a good three inches of shirt sleeve. No one is thinking to get him a coat. Not Petey, not his biological father, not Chrischana herself.

She stands, rubbing her palms, trying to get rid of the grit. "Sorry fah embarrassing you."

"No problem. But, if you do this in front of English class—with no way fah me to escape?—" (He smacks his knuckles into his palm).

It's a joke but he does not grin like his father Balder would. His face is grave with Native American features, features like Chrischana's own, and that of her deceased mother.

Watching out the window with other kids in his freshman class, he realized that being out here helping was preferable to listening to them mock-direct the operation. Most were unaware that it was Daniel's mother out here. He might have slipped into the hall, escaping without notice. But it doesn't really matter much to him. Breakdowns happen. Embarrassment will come later, when some cop pulls them over for that bumper. Tying up bumpers with clothesline *has* to be illegal. The whole car is illegal. No way it will ever pass inspection. She's been putting off Maine registration for that reason.

Mother is always complaining about overregulation. According to her it should be legal to drive down the road in whatever you can afford. "But no!" She goes on: "Theya's got be expensive restrictions only yuppies can afford. Got be x amount o'sound metal in relation to rust—and now they want t'make it impossible t'drive without insurance! They want all the bumps smoothed out. Think theya entitled to risk-free life! Don't even *see* the rest of us down heah, struggling just to stay operable on theya rules. Imagine working in a place like rural Maine'n not being able t'drive? Caunt they see if you caunt get to work the next stop's welfare? And what would ah forefathers say bout these regulations taking away ah freedom? *They* took food'n shelter, medicine fom the woods. The settlers'd roll in theya graves." Mother's ancestors on her father's side were Yankees, the first to settle Gottheim she sometimes reminds Daniel.

After a teenage requisite roll of the eyeballs, Daniel can see her point. Rich people with computer jobs and skis will be coming in, forcing land up, then wanting to write codes to protect property values and make the place look less junky. Even Balder saves useless everything, saying it saves on parts. But, so what if codes make things more difficult? Both Dad and Father have good paying jobs. Mother complains but won't accept help from anyone. It's like she enjoys hardship. She just likes to pick the system apart.

Saying little, Daniel blinks snow out of his eyes and stoops to pick up two pieces of the jack. "Won't work," he says, trying to fit them together. "You've got parts of two different jacks."

"Figures." She goes to the trunk, rummages, comes back with a different stand. "Try this."

They squat beside the flat and he puts the jack together. Chrischana sets it behind the wheel under the axle, some precarious, but at least the handle reaches. Pumping, she begins jacking up the car.

"Hold it!" warns Daniel. "Car's rolling!"

She lets it down as he runs to the trunk to grab a piece of leftover firewood. He moves quickly to shove it under the front tire. "Try now!"

As she pumps the car holds. Cranking with the lug wrench, she begins loosening the lug nuts and handing them to him one at a time.

If he puts them on the ground they will be lost in gathering snow, but they are too cold to hold so he lays them flat on the snowy car roof.

Chrischana is pulling on the tire, jerking hard, but it won't budge.

"I'll get a hammer." He says this heading for the trunk.

"We don't have one!"

Mother is getting pissed. Daniel turns and runs toward the back of the school calling something over his shoulder.

He is gone in the obliterating snow, taking his explanation with him. Chrischana yanks viciously on the tire. Having been checked by her son's appearance, her anger now flows in his absence. She grinds her teeth, barking out a curse while tugging on the wheel. Standing she barks three quick curses in succession and kicks the tire after each.

How the fallen are mighty, she thinks ruefully, recalling her gentleness of last spring when she was escaping, hurting and vulnerable. Oh well. Best to get it out before he returns. Can't have him thinking it's okay to go profane ballistic. He saw enough of that elsewhere.

The tire and its corroded bolts have fused together. She sinks to the snowy pavement, weary, letting January ice seep into her bones. If she sits long enough her own joints will fuse and then she can stop worrying. She will become sculpture, a work of art: "Woman in Winter, with Flat."

Why is it we're better when things are tragic, and worse when circumstances merely irritate?

Appropriate that my destiny is one with this piece of junk. They found the car in Phoenix, cheap. For $250 the Chrischana Twitchell/Peter Prince alliance gained an ancient luxury sedan that had ferried drivers from Chicago to the desert Southwest, a shuttle. "Those winter city streets." The salesman had exclaimed: "All that sand and salt and weather. But how else could you get something for so little?" Seeing its spottty fenders made her nostalgic for Maine. And Peter was always there to keep it running. But this winter... this first Maine winter—without him.... clothesline kept it together. Chicago, the desert, and Maine have combined to corrode this car to lacework. Untrusty, rusty metal, held together with very iffy attractions. The car is ready to drop. The Bonneville will shred its own weight back into the earth. If she plants it in the woods below the farm on Blackwell Mountain she will see trees nourishing themselves from it within a year.

Daniel is back, thrusting a sledgehammer in her glazed face. "From shop class." She does not respond. Her joints have fused. Chrischana raises her gaze to him. "Maybe y'betta." She says it slowly. Stiffly she stands to move out of the way.

She heads for the trunk and hoists the spare off the ground, resting a moment with it wedged between her parka and the lip of the trunk. Now, for the first time, she notices bits of wire protruding from bald spots in the tire. Disgusted, defeated, she heaves the tire into the open maw. Rust particles sift to the ground on impact. Rust from the holes around the wheelwells is printing the icy pavement. Ahead, Daniel beats on the tire, shaking the car.

"Stop!!" She screams it, fearful less the car fall on him. "Shitting thing's not coming! Tighten the lugs'n let it down!"

But Daniel merely moves out a bit, beginning to beat it all over with the sledgehammer.

A red Chevette rolls by through pouring snow. The pimply driver leans out, saying something obscure. Grinning he rolls past and keeps going. Chrischana grins back. She yanks happily on the fallen bumper, manic and trying to wrest it free. Nights with father, lit by kerosene in the crumbling farmhouse, come back to her: hand pumping water into the kitchen sink, hacking deer meat from the frozen carcass hanging in the shed, chopping wood in the dooryard. Laughing, she runs around to Daniel. "I'll get that tire off!" She grabs the hammer out of his hand and throws it at the jack. The car falls in a shower of tinkling rust. The lug nuts fly off the roof, but the tire holds.

"It's my life." She throws up her hands. Snow pours down the cuffs of her parka, melting on her wrists. "It's Maine. Why else would anyone live like this?" She scrabbles about, picking up the scattered lug nuts, maniacally twirling them back into place.

Daniel stands watching and distressed. It troubles him to see any of his adults acting antsy. Chrischana reaches under the car for the wrench. "Can I tighten them up for you?" He steps close.

But now she is stripping the nuts off again. "Not necessary. I'll just drive around the parking lot till it falls off."

Daniel takes hold of her arm and she stops to look at him, still smiling.

"Mother, you gont embarrass me in front o'the whole school?"

The smile fades. Empty, she looks at him, arms drooping in defeat. She mumbles something, resisting the urge to reach out and brush the layer of snow off her son. It makes her ache to see him standing there, his cuffs hanging out.

She must look pretty dejected herself, because Daniel smiles. A smile from him is rare enough to bring back her characteristic half-smile in return. The false grin is gone and he finds himself comforted: the half-smile is what he knows. She hands him the lug wrench.

He squats to load the nuts and begins tightening them. Standing he offers, "Want me t'call Balder or Dad? They both at work now?"

She has retrieved the jack parts. Together they move toward the trunk and she tosses them in. "Help me tie up this bumpa?" She lowers the lid. "I'm late fah the tavern. It'll be okay till Petey gets off." She says this to give the impression that she plans to call him. Maybe she will. Maybe not. He would be glad if she does, but the feeling is not hers to reciprocate. Her numb fingers fumble with this rope, with this knot being tied with difficulty. She feels sick in her soul, very low. Chrischana always feel so after behaving badly. Briefly, for the first time, she wonders if Peter ever felt this—truly—after his raging. If he did, he didn't admit it, just played his self-deceiving sorry little role. Chrischana is depleted and sick. He must have been too. Beating up on his own soul while he beat up on her.

Mother and son stand together. He points to the flat. "You sure about driving on that?"

"Gont work, Daniel. But... thanks...." She wants to lean toward him, kiss him, but refrains. "Need a note fah class?"

Still looking at the flat and worried, he shakes his head. He watches her climb into the cavernous car and start the rough engine. The exhaust will go next, he supposes; the muffler.

She pulls slowly from the lot, hazard flashers winking red through falling snow. He watches until they disappear over the rise. How long will she be able to drive that car? Gottheim will never register it. And someday, soon, insurance will be required. He has heard her exclaim over this time and again. Shivering he turns, heads toward the cafeteria door. His feet feel like needles and pins. Heat has seeped out his legs right through his jeans. Daniel is snow all over.

Thumping down the highway at nine miles an hour, Chrischana smells rubber burning. Must be the flapping of my tire, tearing apart. Obscuring snow worries her as she tenses for some hit from behind. Awful smell! It reminds her of those rusting industrial cities they passed through on their way here. What was that stinky place where tires were made? They stopped for dinner and learned that two out of three rubber mills had closed. But you smell them like they were twenty.

The Bonneville 500 limps on, and the white buildings of Gottheim village materialize through the snow. Chrischana glances over at the white envelope on the dashboard. Its return addresses the town office. She picked it up this morning at the post office after breakfast dishes at the tavern. The car clock is broken; no watch to check the time. Late for work.

It will be evening before she gets around to reading the letter, a notice that their camper on the mountain is off code for a dwelling. She will look at Daniel and exclaim, "Our ancestors helped found this place. They laid out lots, surveyed the whole town. Their first cabins had no windows. People pooped in a hole in the ground!

Daniel will recall that those same pioneer ancestors usurped the land from Abenaki natives... from whom they are also descended. But he won't remind her that land changes hands, that the yuppies are bound to succeed them. Instead he will just roll his eyes.

Known variously as Quakertown, Quakerton, Quaker Plantation, population 600, the entity has a problem it is not equipped to deal with. When Dr. Goodrich opened his plucky little rubber works for other purposes and products, in 19th-century Akron Ohio, it was primed to originate the vast work of filling the nation with tires. The great heroes and builders of a burgeoning industrial economy believed in latex, and iron, and coal. One thing led to another, and they came to believe in rubber tires and steel automobiles. Akron became the unofficial capital of West Virginia when young people from the mountain state filed north to fill the rubber shops of the formerly sleepy canal town. The place boomed with the clank screech roar stench of tire production. Goodrich, Siberling, Firestone and others had adapted the refinement of latex, using a process that combined sulfur, heat and pressure, to produce a substance durable enough to package compressed air. It made for a fast smooth ride when combined with the urgency of an internal combustion engine. The nation was on the move.

Where was it headed? Doesn't the word *progress* suggest some sort of destination? Living in a little handbuilt homestead with goats, acrylics and gouaches, Eloise Patadoe think she knows the answer to that. She thinks it whenever she walks past the dippy road leading to Jasper Mary's Medicine Mile. *We the people want to move. We want to keep going, don't want to stop. We need the illusion of movement in order to avoid recognizing self at a standoff.*

Ooo, I'm into it now.

She is pulling Hetty's milk down, steaming, into the galvanized bucket between her feet. The goaty smell of the Toggenburg nanny pervades her nostrils here in the small house cum barn, but Eloise scarcely notices. She is used to the variegated odor of goats, manure, mash, hay. Lately, her thoughts during such moments of domestic communion have been occupied with the process and marketing of goats' milk, but tonight she's thinking of tires. Having researched rubber and petroleum based tire-making, she is trying to come to terms with the mountainous pile of Ceylon Segar's lot. She keeps her eye on that once tiny patch, spreading now like cancer over terrain once devoted to medicine, cropland, and trees. She keeps her eye on the truckloads that lumber and growl past the corner pasture.

Movement progress industry revolt. It all stems from the desire to maintain comfort, security. Self cannot trust anything else with that job. "See, Hetty," she lectures, "It's because... when we're moving around in cars and dependent on the revolt of the Industrial Revolution for jobs, food, products—that's it! we're codependent!—we can forget that we're going nowhere but smack into the ground. People just don't believe we can grow vegetables! There is no faith in seeds unless they're produced and put to use in factories. Industry is big-busy-noisy-urgent-smelly and important. Something with that kind of heft, movement, and production convinces us that someone is watching out for us. Any big systematic monster— Adirondack Paper! with its network of trucking and trains booming along corpuscles of concrete and steel—any big system is worthy of faith by virtue of movement. *Yahoo*!!" Eloise tilts back to let the word fly.

Free of her load, Hetty skitters to one side, knocking the bucket, but Eloise grabs it before it can spill. The goat turns back her silly ear-winged face, saying, "Na-na na-a-a!"

"You sound like my sister!" It spooks Eloise, hearing Lisa's voice coming from the goat. She shakes her ponytail, smiles her horsey smile, laughing with a noise not unlike the goat's.

The goat barn, which keeps her tiny herd sheltered, is the shell of an old house that once sat a hundred yards up the road. Eloise had it moved when she was building her place in this sloping valley. "Goats live in houses," Eloise likes to say. Her herd numbers eight, with three in gestation. Come spring there'll be kids hopping and bounding. Eloise will laugh continually, watching them bounce. Kids are hilarious: They spring! (And that's why it's called spring).

The Toggenburg goats are rare because they aren't a product of commercial manipulation. We thrive without artificial hormones, vaccines, or extra amino acids to boost protein production. Eloise tells anyone who will listen. Helping to maintain genetic diversity interests her. "I'm one of those sickos who obsess on insignificant concerns like, Are we going to be able to eat in the next century?" (Forgetting her argument against security of a minute ago.)

Her bag painfully full, Marsha sidles up to Eloise who begins pulling milk down into the bucket. When it is full, she sets it on the sideboard where the kitchen used to be. She climbs upstairs in her insulated barn boots to a former bedroom, throws down two bales, clomps down, clasps her hands with finality and says, "That oughta hold ya!"

She turns, opens the door, picks up the milk buckets, steps into the rigid January night: cold with stars, cold with the unknowable vastness of deep heaven. She sets down the bucket and closes the door. "Inhospitable!" She calls to it, looking up. Searching the clarity of the cold multitudes, her eyes widened. Eloise is always surprised by them. "You outnumber the tires!"

She crunches toward the house, a moving shadow on the star-reflecting white; crushing the snow beneath her boots, shivering for lack of her goats' warmth. With her breath frosting her face she wonders about the virtually everlasting fire of stars. "If only we could get Ceylon Segar's tires to you! To the sun! 'Our God is an everlasting fire!' Away with you to a black hole. Turn those smelly black molecules inside-out. Vaporize 'em! Compact 'em to infinity!"

If that patch of Quaker were to come in contact with God.... The only thing to emerge would be Ceylon Segar, maybe unconsumed, but greatly altered. She loves Ceylon Segar—from a distance. She likes to see him gimping along, an animated set of grime with bits of clothes and boots holding it altogether. In small doses she can even take him in proximity: hear him talk, see his malicious yellow holey grin; hear him snicker, snarl and bark. In small doses only. If she had to live with someone like him or read an entire book about him... she would hitchhike to Cuba first. He's got buddies in high places, has ol'Ceylon. They wear suits and live in large gleaming houses and take fact-finding trips at taxpayer expense. They get invited to doings in Washington and eat under crystal chandeliers. And there are *no* tire dumps in their neighborhoods. They have assured the residents of Quaker that their department will make Ceylon told the line. "Our granting him a license will make it easier to control what goes on at the tire dump."

Eloise laughs like Hetty *bah-bah*ing. "Heck, you couldn't even get him to take a bath!"

Eloise admires Ceylon for having his own junkyard dogs in high places. They think they got him on a leash. But Eloise thinks, as does all Quaker and Ceylon himself, that it's the other way around.

Julius Golding was mad as hell. Yet the hell of his imagination is not a fiery place but ice cold. So cold its captive souls can scarcely move. Inert they sit, frozen mad at absolute zero. Not a molecule moving anywhere. Even the atoms stop their dance. Then slowly, ever so slowly, they begin to move again. A... Something, from Somewhere, reaches down. Down to absolute zero. Some... form of warmth, sent by the Absolute in infinite understanding of zero. It penetrates Julius Golding, and he begins to move again. Lately the hand of this warmth has been that of his niece. Amanda's touch has found a crevice somewhere for the sheltering of her warmth to get him moving again. Today he is less mad than yesterday but mad enough, still, at finding himself seated in Wilbur's Bar and Grille, in smelly Guildford, waiting on smelly Ceylon Segar.

This is not Julius Golding's way. His way is to delegate the disagreeable. He considers briefly that the hand of this new warmth, while enlivening him from his standstill, is the same hand that triggered his cold fury in the first place—by asking him to do something that he does not want to do.

Little golden Amanda kneels beside him in the booth, sipping a tall cherry Coke through twin straws. After the initial distaste of their entrance into Wilbur's—greasy smells and armpit odors mingling with those of stale pulp—Julius has been surprised to discover that fountain cherry Cokes still exist. Kids in a mill town in the 1980s can still get soda and syrup from a fountain. She is eating fishwich and fries. Her presence in the place is all that keeps him in the booth, stiff inside but for the presence of Amanda.

He considered his options before agreeing to this. 1. Invite Segar to Jasper Mountain or some other upscale setting in the village. 2. Invite himself to Segar's trailer office at the tire dump. 3. Meet him here—a good twenty-five miles from the resort. No one he knew would frequent this grille. But it is noon; Wilbur's is packed with mill workers—not Golding's favorite crowd. And Segar is keeping him waiting.

Julius has to admit he's not used to it. He has to give the old fart credit for pulling this. Sipping his coffee (the only thing he can bring himself to order), he thinks about that obnoxious term, old fart. Julius has always held it in contempt as undignified and insulting to anyone no matter the circumstance. Yet, it *is* the definitive description of Ceylon Segar. He can summon no other, and now must remind himself to use *mister Cigar* before Amanda. The offending term slipped out once during one of their conversations about the tire dump owner. He has prepared his niece for her first sight of the old man. Or, *is* he old? How does one tell? His eyes have that rheumy look; he's not young by any means, but his age is anyone's guess. Some of the townspeople could tell him but, now that he has surrogates to act for him, Julius no longer has many dealings with them.

Amanda stops sucking her cherry Coke in order to turn toward the back door of Wilbur's. Her gaze points down the hall past the phone. Uncle Julie's eyes have been on the front door but now, her eyes big, his niece whispers, "I think Mr. Cigar's here." He turns to see the old so-and-so coming.

Grinning. A disheveled colorless bundle, lightly iced in snow, its bewhiskered face framed with scraggly colorless hair sticking out beneath a grimy hunting cap. The grin is darkened by deep scary holes. Julius is seeing him with Amanda's dainty sensibilities. The sight of Segar must awe her small experience. Repulse it. She will probably dream about it all night.

He can guess by the man's grizzled grin that he is enjoying himself. He's hit the big time. Doing a power lunch with Julius Golding, an owner of Jasper Mountain Resort. The event will rumor around Gottheim when Ceylon Segar gets through hitting the big time.

Ceylon Segar comes out of the passage, gimping, threading his unsavory way through Wilbur's noon traffic: waitresses with trayloads, people entering or just sliding out of the plastic booths. He looks to either side before focusing on.... *Theya's Mr. Big, fom away, all shiny'n clean. Thinks he's gont make an impression. Thinks he owns Gott'im now. Hell, he don't even own Jaspa Mountain, thinks he does*! Ceylon squints, thinking, what's that he got with 'em? Li'l gul! Jezuz, she's pretty. Like a flower, a buddacup. I get sit across fom her?!

He slides in uninvited across from Amanda, grinning at her, tossing a nod in Golding's direction. The thaw is on: Segar is so ripe that he has changed the temperature around him. Julius Golding smells old tires, old body bacteria.

"This is my niece, Amanda. Amanda, Mr. Segar."

Ceylon guffaws at Golding's glacial decorum, his use of the term Mr. "Just call me Uncle Ceylon, li'l gully!" He lisps slightly. "Amanda? That's a pert name. You put your Uncle Golding up to this, did choo?"

Amanda nods, her eyes like secret pools veiled in ferns and light. Until now Segar has scarcely thought of the niece mentioned over the phone. His thoughts were fused on this good-time opportunity, with a better time to come on its heels. A chance to roll a Golding over the edge has kept him in spirits since the call came. Anticipation kept him awake nights... but now that Amanda is here... things are different.

He looks a question at her. "You that li'l gul walked off Mount Will after that plane crash, year o'two back?"

Again she nods, her eyes silent, round.

"Said an angel walked y'down?"

A nod.

"Whad it look like?"

"Mr. Segar," warns Golding, frowning.

But she replies in a soft voice. "I don't remember." At the time she was concussed, bruised, picking her way down mountain in the aftermath: her mother dead in the crash. There was the light of a lone house near the bottom. It wasn't that far from Medicine Mile and the tire dump. "My sister says I told her it was an Indian."

A skinny redhead comes up for his order. Segar asks for the Hamburg plate and coffee, scarcely noticing the waitress where once he would have chewed her ears off with his pathetic jokes. She walks away scribbling on the pad, wondering whether to be miffed or relieved.

Segar says to Amanda, "If you don't 'member an angel, how do you say theya was one?"

For the first time Amanda moves her gaze off him. Taking her lips from the straw, she rolls her eyes sideways. "Well, you see... first I told my sister on the phone and *then* I forgot."

"She'd hit her head," said Julius.

The waitress is back with hot coffee. Amanda munches her fries, looks at Mr. Segar. She is thinking about the term "old fart." Every part of Mr. Segar looks brown. Even his teeth. "Where do you get your tires?"

Slurping, he smiles at her over the rim of his cup. He likes that piping voice. He has not been this close to a little girl, to talk to, since he was a young man too busy and smart to bother with little girls. He has been a hunter, fisherman , farmhand, woodcutter, mill hand, and treasure hunter. Then his old man left him this land. This time spent with a little girl is like a treasure, a sight from another world. A world where buttercups peek through in January.

"Tires just come. Someone stopped in once, says have a go." He lisps. "Now they don't stop coming. They call me fom all over. Or just show up—with money." He grins slyly at Golding.

Julius feels it time to facilitate the conversation. He has been more than courteous, observing the custom of small talk, avoiding the direct approach. Segar might have closed the conversation on that technicality alone, disappointing his niece. "Amanda is interested in seeing what can be done about the amount of tires on your property, Mr. Seger."

"Zat so?" He is asking Amanda. "How'd you get interested in my tires?"

"Well, we been studying pollution at school. We talk about recycling, paper mill rivers, sludge... stuff like that."

"They talk bout me in school?"

Happy as a child, thinks Golding with disgust. Pleased with the idea of such attention!

"Yes. We saw your picture in the paper. How many tires to you have?"

"Couple billion." He flicked gaze at Golding.

Uncle Julie looked incredulous then incensed.

"Whad they say bout me in class?"

"We wanted to know why you keep tires since it's bad for the earth."

"Whad teacher say?"

"That you did it to make a living."

"Guess maybe!" He cackles, smacking the tabletop with his palm. "Some of us knows how t'make money off land round heah." Again he shoots the look at Golding.

The muscles tighten along the other's jawline. He quells a sudden urge to take Amanda and leave.

From the corner of his eye Segar sees the twitch while his gaze remains on the girl. He cackles more. "Some of us can understand that— having the chance t'make money."

Julius is ready to leave but Amanda is piping, "Uncle Julie'n Uncle Harry understand. They own the ski resort'n make money, haw, Uncle Julie." She turns to him. "That's how you and Uncle Harry do it?"

Julius looks levelly at Ceylon Segar. "That's right, Amanda. We do."

Segar's grin grows. He lisps. "We're businessmen."

It is pointed, perfectly true: They each own land and use it to make money. I've let a trusting little girl lead me into this, with all its potential for humiliation; sitting in a bar and grille in Guildford Maine, the butt of an old fart's fun. Aloud he says, "There's a difference in the service we provide the community." His chin is up, he looks dryly away. He wouldn't have bothered to comment but Amanda has to see the truth.

Segar snorts. "The community? Skiers, fom away—same's my tires. Gott'im gets your taxes, 'sall. State gets mine."

He shouldn't answer, he shouldn't. "We hire hundreds of people from towns around here." Warmth seeps into him. Anger can warm him after all. He looks to see the waitress coming with Segar's hamburger plate, takes a sip of coffee, looks at his watch.

Segar notes these cues without taking his eyes off Amanda. When the woman sets the order down he stabs three french fries sopping them with gravy. He is now ready to tweak Golding with those notorious seasonal service wages... but refrains, recollecting what he pays his own part-time assistant. He has been bitter his lifelong over the low wages he got for mill work, farm work, logging. With this chance to make money on that cutover parcel of his family's he has found it easier to forgive and understand the tightfisted ways of others. He swallows, grinning his dirty yellow grin at Amanda, saying, "Goldings is good bosses."

The jawline of the man sitting across from him rolls again. *I need this old fart's pat on the back, his singing my praise to Amanda.*

The tire dump man continues. "Goldings fit in, if they do be from away. Us businessmen stick together, Mandy. Understand one another, we do. We can talk'n I'd be glad t'heah what pointers your uncle has fah me— t'get my tires unda control. Try's I might, caunt find no markets. Even with that monsta mill sitting out theya." He gestures with his fork toward the window although the paper mill is cut off from view by Guildford's brick blocks. "Theya online t'stot suckin' in tires for that fancy generator... like they suck in the woods to make papah." Ceylon is sore. He has called and visited in an attempt to get them interested, but not a tire dump in the state can sell to Adirondack. Instead, clean chipped tires will come from out-of-state by the trainload. "Think they do business with a 'memba the local community—help us out? They won't even talk't me. Mandy, I got tires enough to keep that generator going donkey's days."

"They're not *part* of the community." Golding says it quickly before Amanda can chirp in with some unthinkable collaboration. "Their headquarters are somewhere in the Carolinas now. They don't care about the quality of life here. Only one mill in the state is even locally owned anymore. If you went to Adirondack corporate headquarters you would see lush landscaping and open, glass interiors. The community there is proud to have the company among them."

A flicker goes through Ceylon's rheumy eyes, as he shifts his gaze from the girl to Golding and back again. He was humbled himself in asking Julius Golding for help and is accorded this compliment of a respectful response. God knows he needs help. He has tried getting a shredder to transform those tires into something marketable but no bank around Gottheim will lend money for fear of liability. What good's a shredder without markets anyway? Ceylon knows next to nothing about researching markets for used tires. He heard there was a market in Saudi Arabia or Africa. Did you just get on the phone to information Jerusalem? Ceylon Segar squirts ketchup over the remains of his gravy slathered plate.

Julius Golding winces but Amanda is delighted. She wipes her mouth on a crumpled napkin, then dusts french fry salt and grease from her small fingers. In silence Golding curses the DEP for licensing someone so ignorant of business, for sanctioning his storage operation before marketing mechanisms were established. Golding takes out a gold filled pen from an inner breast pocket and begins writing on one of Wilbur's napkins. He slides it toward Ceylon's plate but, on an intake of regret, he recollects that Segar might not be able to read. —Yet, the man must be adept at covering it if he can't. He will say something about leaving his reading glasses at home. "Here are the names of two local parties who might be able to steer you in the direction of specific markets. One is a fledgling consultant; the other a group of retired business leaders at the county seat. They volunteer expertise in such matters."

"Gloria Fay," reads Ceylon Segar. "The pipsqueak's family?"

A smile twitches at the corners of Golding's mouth. "She is the developer's sister."

"Gloria is nice," pipes Amanda. "She helped me wrap my Christmas presents."

"Zat so?" Ceylon is mopping the plate with his last fry. He wants to prolong the conversation, sit a while with Amanda but.... They aren't going to speak anymore, pressure him about the tires. They're going to say goodbye nicely and leave him here in Wilbur's without a fight. How does

Golding get anything done this way? Pure money, that's how, but you'd expect more arrogance, impatience, a sense of command.

"Tell you what, Mandy. You'n Uncle Julie come out'n see my ol'tires anytime. Give y'my personal tour. Like that?"

Amanda nods. She looks up at her uncle. "Could we?"

Julius looks down on her open expression. There is ketchup on both corners of her mouth. He takes his napkin and wipes it away. "Maybe when the snow melts in spring." He will regret this when the time comes. Neither Amanda nor Segar is likely to forget. But this meeting has been a way of trying.... Those tires are a menace. God help the old fart.

Time on Jasper Mountain

"How's it going?"

Billy was watching along the line of chairs coming up through shadow cast by Jasper Mountain now that the sun was slipping below the mountain's blue white crown. Billy thought he heard a voice, coming from outside the lift shack and reached over to turn the radio down. He spit a mouthful of tobacco juice into a Coke can, expecting one of the Goldings to pop his head in. Maybe Amanda was here for a chat. But the door opened and there stood a kid he had never seen before. The cold came in with the adolescent—maybe 14 years old, and a blue cinch-waist parka, his ski mask and goggles pushed up under his hood; eyes curiously searching the shack. He shut the door. Billy saw that his skin was clear and crisp, red from the mountain's breath. He looked like a kid newly minted. Like he had never seen a day of trouble, never a night of worry. That his father didn't scramble for a living. His car never broke down at midnight and 30 below.

"How much to ride to the top?" He was sleek and sure as a 40-year-old in a suit.

"Sorry, it's a private lift. Owners don't waunt no one up theya." His cheek was loading with juice again. He reached for the handle to open the door again, but the kid was quick to block it a bit and Billy stepped back. Had to respect the customers. The artist Prince was on the radio, moaning about his pocketful of horses. Billy's lip was full. He reached for the Coke can. Then switching his wad to the opposite cheek said, "What can I do f'you?"

The kid fumbled for the wallet inside his parka. "I want a ride to the top. Doesn't matter what it costs."

"Sorry," said Billy, all patience. His ponytail swished below his ball cap as he shook his head. "Can't."

"Just want to see what's up there." He was thumbing through the wallet, muttering, "Cut through this.... Here." He showed Billy what looked like a new hundred dollar bill. Billy couldn't tell for sure. He had never seen one before.

"Sure," he said pityingly. "Your father must have his own Xerox machine."

"Never mind," said the kid sticking the bill back, thumbing some more. His cheeks had already faded. The shack is the coziest place on earth—phone, heater, radio, insulation, paneling. A view across the Meguntics that won't quit. Billy swore once he saw God's backside up here. His wife Rayona accuses him of imagination. He reads too many books on the supernatural, spends too much time sitting up here chewing on Kodiak. He can get pretty meditative over that grotty Coke can.

The kid was fanning out five worn twenties. "These look real enough, don't they?"

Now he had the man's attention though Billy did figure himself a good and loyal employee. He stuck to the rules of the smooth running resort, but he had other obligations as well. Got to be a good loyal husband and father. In that hand is shoes for the whole family! Shoes and socks for everyone. What about that bill for Sam'n Kelly's mumps? Pay the health clinic, there'd be enough left for a night at the Muzzleloader. *Magnum PI* and the *A-team* were good shows, but he needed more sometimes. *Rayona needs more*.

Billy said, "Once is all y'get." He stuffed the twenties into his jeans pocket, picked up the binoculars to check the lift below. The long blue shadow of Jasper was deepening as the sun sunk rapidly behind. But the seats of the lift continued carrying skiers, emptying one after the other outside under the bullwheel. No sign of ski patrol anywhere. He opened the door for the kid, watched through the window as the boy seated himself on the upper lift.

Aren't the Goldings in Vermont now anyway? It was all hush-hush, rumors always are. He would read about it in *The Voter* any day. Sometime soon he'd transfer out of Gottheim—if he could. Rayona would kick his butt good—too much family here—but Billy liked to daydream of other places, other mountain tops.

Jason ascends Jasper Mountain on the private lift, feeling himself the last man on earth. Looking back at surrounding hills he feels they are his own. He looks down. Any tracks on that snow? None that he could see.

Having a bank account is good for something! Changes have come, I've made changes too. With money you can control destiny. You look into your future and see it all going exactly as you planned. I'm not going anywhere without my bills again. Dad is so guilty he'll see to it. God, guilt

is good! All my life it's been used against me. Now I can use it myself.
Divorce has its advantages. It's not *all* pain and confusion. Let Mom get
hold of this for her support group: Pain is a paying industry.

He is suspended above it all, ascending the bald white head of the
best Mountain in the East. *Gnarly!* Imagine owning your own ski resort,
your own private lift. The summit is yours any day of the week, the tracks
you make might always be *first* tracks. Ascending, the chairlift takes him
out of the shadow and now he sees the sun as though rising. He glances
back to watch the dark ants sliding down slope in cold blue shadow. The
sun has gone down on the other skiers as Jason prepares to take to the
summit. With this deepening bright breath of Jasper in his nostrils, he
adjusts his goggles and mask. The cable above is silver in sunlight, the
ramp comes up, he's off!

He plans to allow himself plenty of time for experiencing the
summit before heading back... when it's about dark. That should give
Brandon and Mom something to think about. He skates long strokes into
the wind, pushing; poking at snowy stiff krumholz where exposed with his
skis and poles; looking off across the expanse of surrounding summits. The
wind here is unreal! Like knives. Feels like I'm wearing nothing! Is that
Mount Washington out there? This summer Dad will have to take me
hiking in the White Mountains. Jason had read that there was a network of
trails with huts running along those summits out there. This is what divorce
is good for: Dad now puts me right into his schedule. We are going to do
all the things we couldn't when Dad was too busy. *The office, airports, hotel
rooms have seen more of him than I have.*

And it's so good jerking loose Brandon. Can you imagine a grown
man named Brandon? Jason had lost his mother's boyfriend on Blissful
when he hid in the woods below that second knoll: The man, intent on
keeping up, was unaware that the boy had snapped him loose. It was like
cracking the whip, sliding into the woods on that curve. Slipping onto the
utility trail, one quick stop and Brandon was history. Can she really think
I'm going to be buddies with dad's replacement? Work this out in support
group, Mom. Be your own woman, just don't expect me to adjust. I don't fit
into your meaningless little recreation of a family. You like Brandon so
much, *you* babysit him. Total stranger! Total fucking *stranger*!

Jason turns to be pushed back along the pate of the mountain by the
wind. Relieved somewhat of its brutality he glides south toward the sun.
He has always wanted to see the wild side of Jasper, the mysterious slopes
covered in trees, not cut with wide white trails. The trails on the North Side
were awesome, but he knows them all now. The great round solitary head
has fascinated him from the moment he saw it, riding with Mom and Dad as

a little kid. Solid, white, almost perfectly round, rearing above the lesser summits. All the others are low and dark with timber, but Jasper is aloof, ascendant, bright. Like a mountain from ancient history. And I'm here! Right on the lid of the fucking world!

Even so, he is intimidated by the unexpected force and fierceness, the freezing of summit's wind. It is a presence, pushing him, prevailing on him to leave. Up here is no shelter, no place to hide. God he has to get down! He looks at his watch—hard to believe! He's been here only four minutes!

It feels like five too many, but I just can't join that little party Mom has cooked up for me. I'm here to ski, goddamn it! Not bond with some banana. Going to ski all night if I have to. The hills on the south slope.... They're crisscrossed with logging roads, aren't they? Plenty of light once the moon's up, right? Gottheim is just down there back of some ridges. Logging roads lead to the highway. No restaurant is going to have a problem with that hundred. Enough for a room for the night even. He thinks about Billy in the lift shack. Yokel blue-collar was actually chewing tobacco!

Jason stands poised above the steep slope, pierced by the wind, digging in with his poles. The sun sinks toward the hills as he seeks out a likely route down the steep smooth bald slope. *Got to get into some trees fast.* But before he can scope it out the wind sweeps the boy off the summit. Speeding, struggling for control, he goes down, feeling the mass looming over him; rising monolithically as he shifts through his turns over the clean ungroomed powder. The great head gleams on his periphery, golden, now quickly fading to rosy cold. The swift hand of the summit wind has sent him packing without a map.

Jason is glad to be going, going through freshness and the joy of these wading turns. He speeds, blindly now, into the steep intrigue of the mountain's unfamiliar backside, knowing nothing of its territory. This is the adventure of his young life. That bribe of limp twenties has assured him of this absolutely. Here Jason will work through the turmoil and anger of bewildered relation his parents have called down on him. He did not let them tell him go here or there; that he had to accept this or that person in response to their desires. Her only reason is, "This is what I want." Well, Mom, likewise. I will not adjust to him! He will not have to adjust to me.

No way those owners can keep the summit, and the slopes, to themselves, once I tell everyone about this awesome adventure. No way. The clientele demands the whole experience. Southern slopes will provide the next thrill for skiers at this resort.

Down through trackless snow hurtles the boy with these thoughts—but now! There are no turns! It's a straight descent.

—

But in the beginning God spoke. There shall be Time, said God. Time and becoming. After and before. Pastpresentfuture, my riddle being Time. I will clothe Time with things—with particles, elements, creatures, events. Thought and emotion shall fill Time. In Time living things germinate, differentiate, grow. Time will expand and contract according to the movement, size, placement of its bodies and to the measure or interests of its occupying activities.

In Time things will fall and rise; minerals salts gases moisture; species and intelligence, dominions. All things cycle, cycling upward, drifting, falling. But light shall flow straight; yet here and there under certain conditions Time will see light bend. See it sneak around corners, shiver to colors, fall sleightly through cracks. Memory and light shall salt the darkness of Time, overtake Time, turning backward and forward. But light shall see Time bend: as great celestial bodies turn, gravity will work out the course of Time. In earth time will be humbled. Forced to creep, weigh and sigh, shudder and weep. But it will pursue with implacable persistence.

In Me Time shall stop altogether.

I let my spheres loose in Time to keep and change its measures. Let gravity layer these spheres; and in some come a layer of life. Earth has magnetosphere, our radiant veil of star-particles; a veil of gas beneath for the protection of Life. Within, we set the veil of our breath. All exchange breath with me in the veil.

But Earth's pith is molten, full of the great power of melting... sulfurous, fulminating, inflamed. The great mantle above moves the crust about, thrusting up from below with tension and verve. Making mountains. Mantle crushes and cramps the earth, forcing edges under again, humbling, fusing and refusing the crust we call earth. Grinding, shaking with terrible violence, the continents heave and slide. Molten heads rise. Rounded, ballooning upward, these Plutons warp and compress the crust.

The energy of the command rises, shaking foundations. At our Word arise the plutons, ascending through layers and bearing unspeakable treasure. Monstrous with bending and folding, burning and pressure, the plutons form forth an array of gemstones, minerals, a catalog of Crystal: Chalcedony Jasper Agate and Beryl; tourmaline amethyst topaz and manifold quartz: there are myriad minerals here.

This! Say the Plutons, *This our treasure and glory! This, our implacable power!*

But these giants lay hidden inside the mountains, in warped, tilted or downturned layers of metamorphism and sediment; guarded and shielded in rock. And Jasper was one of these, a hidden giant, secure. Jasper Mountain patient in waiting.

But without... without move fast climatic currents. In the veil of Breath float a tumult, extremes of hot and cold; down falling, uprising vapors of moisture and air. Cyclic, these powers, whirling and twisting. Hot and cold blowing, drying and drenching, freezing and thawing; great Powers play over crustal surfaces, shaking these faces with Weathers.

Composing tiny crystals, water condensed around specks in the veil. Floating and falling they fill the bright veil; ecstatic innumerable; falling in lightness and blizzard. The Earth darkened, snow fell. Snow fell. Snow fell. Snowfall arched over mountains, sinking them under the burden of white. Ice and earth overlaid what was hidden but the grinding of glaciers wore their covering away.

Time wore, uncovering the hidden. Naked, the Meguntic Mountains emerged. Naked stood Jasper, crystalline and exposed. Bald in his beauty, he was polished and running with rain.

In his cracks seeds gathered, the gymnosperms dying then sprouting, stitching themselves together. Dark evergreen, their lacework gathered on the mighty flanks. They sifted their load of hard seeds. In Time came other plants, less hardy yet enduring on lower slopes, those whose seeds were wrapped in soft fruity ovaries. For the veil moderated to yield a Southern influence. Jasper's great features were fringed and garlanded, softened and green. Leaves sprouted, swaying, glimmering.

From south and westward came many manner of animals insects worms spiders; birds, the fingers of which are filled with feathers. People came, having faces, arms and legs, torsos and hands and imaginings. They gathered hereabouts clustering, clinging together; or sprinkled themselves sparsely. The People lived beneath Jasper. In winter they hunted, sheltering families. In summer they climbed and ate Jasper's blueberries. The People encouraged the berry's seed for its sweet ripe blue fruit, burning patches to renew springing growth. Later came people of another kind to Jasper Mountain, climbing Jasper's knees to set permanent dwellings. They falled his trees, building cabins. They gathered his rocks and turned earth that had collected in the feet of the gymnosperms. These people toiled and stored. Following a period of mutual stress, the two peoples dwelt together; but the first people were thrust to its margins. Yet, in Time, some of each came to share a common descent.

Above them all stood great Jasper Mountain, quiet for the most part, but not ever so. He might gather water from the veil in abundance, flooding them. He might bring snow. He brought aweful wind. Jasper collects storm. The Weather and Mountain colluded, holding their counsel in common. Sometimes they kept the water away.

Even so, over and around People of this great creation was the blessing of God in time. For God said, *Let there be Time!*

And the People answered, "Ever so! (Will it be ever so?)"

There are people who wonder if the trees on the mountain are as glorious as the catalog of its minerals. Beech, popple, hackmatack, four kinds of birch, many of maples; oaks, ash, spruces, four kinds of pine, Eastern white cedar. Robbie Robichaud has purchased stumpage above Gottheim Village on the southerly slope. Alvin and Ansell are up cutting wood, twitching it to the landing. Robbie's gone off down mountain with a truckload of pulpwood, heading toward Guildford. Slowly the landing begins filling with wood again. It is late afternoon. The sun is off behind a ridge, but, in woods above, Alvin thinks he can take a tree or two before Ansell gets back with the skidder.

They'll twitch these back to the yard, jump in the pickup and head down to supper. A long cold day, the woods full of snow, and he can taste Emma's pork chops and mashed potatoes already. Or will they be eating at mother's? He rubs a sore shoulder inside his flannel lined jacket then stoops to pick up the saw, yanks on the starter. Bawling, the blade sprays sawdust as it bites into the base of the tree.

Alvin is just laying out a tall spruce, cracking and thudding, when Ansell arrives with the skidder. They stop for a smoke in the dimming light. Dangling his legs from the cab of the skidder, Ansell gestures. "Who's that coming?" Alvin turns to look up the icy track, still glimmering in the dusk.

Keeping to the crusty side of the track, a dark shape descends, led by a stick. It nears and they make out an old woman in hunting clothes, boots, hat. The pack on her back jostles as though alive.

Alvin says, "Balda's mutha, in't it? She prowls the slopes. Probably got an animal in that pack."

"What she doing with that stick?" Ansell hops down from the cab, calling out, "Gettin'dock ain't it, Miz Simon!"

While still above in the woods coming down, Elda Simon heard the hawing of the saw, the cracking of trees, the rumble of the skidder. She cants her head toward Ansell's call, lets the stick lie still at her side. "Gettin'that wood out'susual, boys?"

"Gut keep up with demand," says Ansell, his square dimpled face breaking into a smile. The ash on the end of his cigarette glows as he drags on it.

"I'd say light's about gone," she says. "Best get on home. Caunt do n'more today, guess."

"I'd say."

The twins agree as one and Elda grins shyly, turning away. The union of their voices has told her exactly who they are.

The brothers watch her disappear into the dusk. "What you suppose she's doing with that stick? It's too long for hiking."

"Looks like she's feeling hah way with it, but it ain't that dock."

"Nevah saw anaone s'wussy'n strong."

Ansell agreed. He knew what was meant. He thought the same of himself sometimes.

They finish their smokes, snap the glowing ends into the snow. Ansell goes to snub up the butt of the spruce with the winch chains. Alvin climbs aboard the burbling skidder, and when his twin returns to the cab it's a tight fit but they ride down together.

Elda stands by the track, careful to give the heavy trailing spruce berth as they pass. Enduring the roar and jingling of chains she feels the length slide by. The sound of the diesel recedes in the distance and she is left alone. Elda Simon depends on her ears more and more. One morning, she woke up to realize that the dark spot in the exact center of her vision was not going away. But, if you have to get by on peripheral vision.... You do, that's all. It wasn't that hard to hide the fear, to panic and mourn secretly in the barn with her wounded and ailing wild animals. She can cry all she wants in the now-not-so-familiar woods. You get used to doing everything patiently and subtly, with secret care. Can't have just everyone knowing that she is legally blind. In fact, she'd like to avoid admitting it to herself so there's no sense bothering anyone else with it. They might try to—Balder has enough to do learning to be a father, trying to get the house shaped up. Caunt stand to have that kind of attention anyway, don't want'em looking at me, thinking about me, wondering what in the world he will do with a blind mother. Maybe I can even continue getting by with driving in daylight if I need to.

She wishes now that she had paid better attention to that reading she did last summer on diseases of the eye. Or remember it better. Did it say that macular degeneration took the whole of sight eventually? Maybe she can use a magnifying glass to help her in reviewing the material?

Geez Louise! Being able to pick up a book and just read! She mourns that loss terribly. Try as she might—how precious that fine, precise, detailed concentrated sight! It was hers all her life... till now. She failed to recognize how sublime good vision is. Not until it fled back to heaven, leaving her dimmer. God gave it for a span of time, taking it back before her own span is done. Light and time—not given for ever.

Elda feels her way down with the stick. She guesses, if time and vision don't coincide... you just do what you can. Gory! *It's dark.*

Many lights glitter on Jasper's northern knees, like tiny gold stars fallen in darkness. Condominiums cluster below his strong glimmering flanks, their lights a'shimmer, twinkling here and there among black boughs as though some of his glory has been unearthed. Within the scattered glow, many lives advance through time.

In one of the tasteful townhouses, a pretty white and auburn woman makes up her face while, remotely, on the other side of the mountain, a teenager is lost on its subarctic margins. But Time is not ripe yet for his mother's concern. She thinks that Jason is due in with Brandon after hitting the slopes this afternoon. The slopes, she notes, are expensive this year. With painstaking care she studies her face in the dressing room mirror lined with special lights. With a flick of the switch its lighting can be changed depending on what type she plans to be seen in, whether daylight, office, or evening. It's early still, but evening is preparing. The romance of candleglow waits. The cheekbones can use a touch more blusher. She picks up the brush.

Is that the tinkling of a key in the lock downstairs? They must be returning now. Jason will be more than happy to stay here and watch TV, maybe order pizza, ask a friend. He won't want to go to the Gemstone Restaurant with them. Adult conversation in candlelight bores him. Everything bores him now... so silent lately, sullen. Brandon certainly doesn't please him. Must face it, deal with it. Give it the attention it deserves.

...Maybe the afternoon on the slopes did something?

Brandon calls from the living room. She'll find out now. Her fingers crossed, Jason's mother stands up, surveying herself in the brown satin slip. She dips a bit to check that the highlights are just about right.

Gottheim Village has gathered close about the mountain's feet, so close that Jasper's cold bald head is cut off from its view. Slopes of conifer-covered rock rise darkly in mystery above the little New England village. The eyes of the village glow in its houses gathered below. Lights in the schoolhouse are lit for night classes. They glow also in the back room of the fire station where Boy Scouts are scheduled to meet, and in the hall of the Knights of Pythias, and inside village churches where prayer meetings and Bible studies take place. The village points heavenward its steeples, glows with street lamps, treads carefully where its sidewalks glare ice.

Here tonight Chrischana Twitchell will reaffirm her particular faith—which a more secular tongue might call life-style. She slinks into a back pew of the bare little church, just as the last bong of the tower clock sounds overstreet at the Congregational Church. Seven o'clock, and this little mongrel denominational service promptly begins.

Will you turn in your hymnals, asks the gangly young pastor of her scattered congregation. Holding the book in her confident right hand, she lifts her left and begins waving out three-quarter time. Her body is angular, long, moving unevenly. Pastor's energetic face makes up for the awkwardness of her form. Chrischana takes this in as she watches her from the back pew, singing. She feels for this lost soul, valiantly waving on the plain wooden dais beside the lectern.

What prompted her to attend service tonight? Rising from the supper table, in a moment she decided. "Anaone fah prayer meeting—get ready."

"I'm going to Boy Scouts," proclaimed Benaiah.

"I got rehearsal tonight!" chimed Nathan.

"Mr. Nutting's gut proofreading on the Linotype for me," Daniel reminds her.

"Well, let's get these dishes done." It's a command. "We can all meet at The Voter when we get done—if you think you'll be more'n an hour o'two, Daniel." That said, they got to work in their little apartment on the second floor of a large subdivided Victorian Gothic not far from the village center.

Chrischana has not been to church since the funeral of her mother, Hattie Trueman Twitchell, an Abenaki Native who died in the early 1960s when Chrischana was an adolescent. Prior to that they would bump down the mountain together, leaving father to his westerns and police shows. Reception up there was the best in town, and father had his own battery-operated television which he kept in juice by driving around with the 12-volt in his pickup. Besides the gossip and occasional bickering, the only complaint mother had about church was that the ministers from seminary were continually reassigned. New ministers of the Gospel were rotated fresh out of school, enthusiastic, but lacking a long intimacy and deep commitment to a single parish. Thus there was no possibility of a long-term emotional investment in Gottheim. They came, ministered, and left the community just as parishioners were beginning to feel a bond, exhibit budding trust. The loss was painful and somewhat humiliating. Mother said people couldn't shake the sense that they were being practiced on; that they were just a link in the chain of advancing careers.

The hymn ends and pastor is saying, *Please turn with me to Mark 14:3*, where she begins reading and interpreting in strong contralto: A woman comes in where Jesus is eating to break an alabaster box of spikenard over his desert-dry head. She proceeds to work it into his scalp with her fingertips. Why was this waste of such substance made!? It could have been sold for 300 denarii to support the poor!... But.... *She has come beforehand to anoint my body for the burying*. He says she will be remembered for this.

Sitting on a hard pew in the bare, plainest of the little churches beneath Jasper Mountain, Chrischana thinks, *That is so*. I have remembered her story ever since hearing it as a child.

After the woman wastes her precious ointment on Jesus, the one who objected went out to sell his betrayal. Well, what do you think of this story, this record of Christian experience?

Somewhere a telephone is ringing...in the pastor's office A woman sitting by the doorway slips out.

No one seems to know what to make of the story. Most of the members of the sparse congregation look not at one another nor even into their own minds for the answer. They look at the young Rev., waiting for what she will say about this expense. Why would he want his body anointed while it was still vital, alive? Death's maybe around the corner but it's not here yet. Maybe, says pastor,—did it really have anything to do with a concern for what would happen to his flesh in death? Remember what he had said about the body, the temple.... So, maybe it had more to do with the woman herself. Remember she was distressed.

Chrischana admits to herself it seems likely. She smiles: It certainly wasn't to make herself famous. The ointment stands for everything costly. She might have had a healing massage for herself with it... or used it a little at a time on her lover, or waited for a child to become ill. Maybe she could have sold it to buy a house! Chrischana has been thinking about building her own on the mountain, Blackwell Mountain, considering practical designs, economy of building materials. Something she might build with her two hands.

Jesus was concerned for the woman's well-being, says pastor. Her eternal well-being.

A woman approaches the dais from the doorway, a scrap of white paper in her hand. Pastor walks slowly to one side, takes the note. She looks at it, tucks it into her pocket saying, The woman believed Jesus when he said I won't be here much longer. I may be gone in a few days, Peter.

But the disciples didn't take this seriously. They just didn't get it. *I won't be here*. Anything you do for me is a waste. I'm going to die—Andrew, James, Thomas.

Pastor walks back toward the lectern. Even way back of the hall Chrischana hears her heels clicking on the wooden floor. But now pastor moves beyond the lectern to the opposite side of the dais.

Oh no, Lord. It won't happen. You're not going to die. (Not us either, Lord; we're not going to die.) There's time yet. We don't need to pour ourselves out. We've got important things to do, a kingdom to establish. You can't waste your existence, squander yourself as though time were ending. It's all coming together, they threw down their palms and their cloaks and you're going to rule. See how they adore you? It's your kingdom! Isn't that what you've been telling us?

In the excitement of the disciples' vision, pastor's voice rises. She's been walking back and forth, building to her punchline. Now she stops in her perambulations of the dais, silences the light sound of her heels. Her face glows with the glory of the story she's telling. The thought of it makes her happier than she's been all week. Her angular, animated body, with its ungainly spidery gestures, has focused the little congregation.

Her voice falls.

(Almost whispering.) *No*. Peter, you missed it entirely.

She turns and walks back to the lectern, grips it square in her hands saying, *This woman with her spikenard was just like Jesus*: squandering what was costly, healthful, fragrant. *On someone who is going to die.*

Pastor stops again. She looks at them, quietly. *Who* is going to die?

She steps quietly back, letting the question resonate.

Now she says, "I have just been handed a note, requesting prayer, from the mother of one of the ski patrol. A storm is on its way, and they are out on the mountain after a lost child. People let us pray."

There is always something to learn or rediscover. Tonight some will risk injury, exhaustion, exposure or death in an effort to discover what has been lost.

Away from the village, and along the stretch of back roads silvered in ice and snow, an old meetinghouse is one quarter full of society members meeting to rediscover a piece of the history of Gottheim. They meet once a month to hear lectures, see presentations, and discuss the esoteric and local past. Of course, members are always glad for the attention of people from away provided the setting is formalized and removed from the threat of encroachment. What after all can a stranger do to influence history? Yes, you can bring on the bulldozer and topple a sagging hundred-year-old spool mill, but what can you do to Uncle Ned Robertson's account of the night Amos Twombly burned his ferry on the 'Rossy River? We have memory, written in documents, photographs and mulled in conversation. Remembered. Asa Bartlett thinks of these things when he extends invitations to interested outsiders.

Asa is town historian, one of many. Everyone in Gottheim holds at least a little town history, unconsciously or not, guarding it with sharp eyes and devastating tongues. "What's gossip, anaway, but history?" He said this to Gloria Fay with a straight face when she inquired about the Society.

The young woman has been a Gott'im wannabe most of her life. She's from away, and what you'd call monied. Along with her parents, who are Evangelical Baptist Christians, and brothers and sisters, she has been coming here to ski since before they bought one of the first condominium townhouses on Jasper Mountain. He's in insurance or investments or pawn shops or something, down there somewheres about Boston; the mother, they say, is a study group facilitator for women interested in applying Bible principles to their lives and marriages. Asa's wife, Olive, tells him that she assumed this career once her five children were well on the road to worldly success. Gloria is the baby, and, when she buckled down to the business of living, she began doing very well. However, Olive will soon be avid to report, this new life of Gloria's may not be exactly what her parents would have desired.

Gloria acknowledges to herself and to anyone interested that she is no longer a believing Baptist. The new sources of her power are a little more obscure. The range of her ideas is inspired now by the invigorating belief that she can be or do anything her imagination conceives. There's no stopping this one. Like any missionary, she's determined to inspire her newfound neighbors with the vision. These Gott'imites are in need of her youthful can-do spirit. With her education, talent for organization, and interpersonal skills, Gloria and Gottheim are going places together. She tells herself this in the morning when she looks in the mirror, toothbrush in hand. She nods confidently, grins. And just being with her, seeing her beauty bright, listening to that melodious conversation, you begin to share in her confidence. This go-getter is not going to leave you behind. Even the ghastly grotty Ceylon Segar, with whom she has plans for consultation next week, will benefit from this talent... if she can get Daddy's help. Networking is at its best when it's all in the family.

Seated in their midst and interested, Gloria's presence gratifies the local historians. She is eager to hang onto these words of what happened to who, and when. She is also delighted to be networking with them: just what is needed to cement the influence of her committee for the renewal of

Gottheim. (Once known as the committee for Gottheim's alternative to IICE. The international Institute of Coordinated Experiments was poised to withdraw its regional headquarters last year, but has since been persuaded to remain in Gottheim. Town leaders are, ambivalent but for the most part, relieved.)

Another reason to be here tonight is that suggestion made by the best person in her life, Balder Simon. Long ago, last summer in fact, he suggested she talk to Asa Bartlett about the origin of the town's name.

Asa is now seated behind a table before the little group in the wainscotted meetinghouse, clearing his throat. His crewcut brick red hair glistens in the soft overhead light of electrified wrought iron candelabras. "Now that the business end of the meeting's over, it's time to welcome Gloria Fay. Please stay fah refreshments'n sociability after the meeting, Miss Fay." He looks her in the eye, gesturing toward the refreshment table.

"Tonight we gont hear fom Olive Bahtlett on some local'n Maine history of dowsing; and she's got stories of her own t'tell. Some o'you might know she's got considerable experience with the craft we know as water witching."

Asa and the secretary, Elsie Roberts, stand and move into the audience. His wife, a large woman, sways toward the table with a sheet of yellow legal paper clutched in her red-painted fingertips. She sets the paper on the table beside her, positions it nervously and with care, then with a hesitant smile launches into her talk.

"Some o'you know that I help people find water. I show'em waya to dig that well they might be wanting when they go t'build. 'S'really simple t'do. And how I got stotted was watching someone else—about thirty years o'go—when my brother built his house. Didn't really believe in it at the time. Tried it out as kind of a joke. Fact is, I must o'done it twenty times fah I even stotted t'believe it. After, that well, I recognized I could feel it working. I could find water evah time, and that's why I stotted t'believe."

Hesitating still, she glances down on her paper, straightening it with her polished fingertips. Now Gloria notices the y-shaped stick lying on the table beside Olive.

"People waunt know what I mean when I say—that I recognized the feel of it. Well, I could just feel it—pull. You take a forked stick—like this yellow birch." She picks up the stick, gripping it palm upward, by the forks, in either hand. "You just go along like this till you feel it pull." Olive walks toward the door, holding the stick up, an inverted y. She turns back, walking toward the window. The point of the y starts turning downward. She stops. "When you're just learning, go slow—because you don't know what you're looking fah. After while y'get to recognizing this pull. The closer you get to the vein, the more it pulls down. Theya's a vein right heah. Unda the floor."

She relaxes the stick and sways back to the table where she deposits it in order to resume her talk. Looking at it, Gloria is mystified. Just an ordinary twig?

"People ask what causes it. Nobody knows. It's not the stick itself— cause you can use anything. A coat hanger, two metal rods, a plummet, most any kind o'twig. I think it's in a person's body t'begin with. Not Evahbody can do it. Maybe it's like ESP—only some have more, some less."

Gloria is leaning forward, listening intently to this large plain speaking motherly woman. She imagines her with a houseful of grandchildren, the aroma of cookies wafting through quaint rooms.

Olive continues. "Onct give me the spooks—a couple years ago when I was at a friend's house (this was Brunhild Kenniston on Grover's Pond). She mislaid her wedding rings. I, joking, says, 'want me find them?' And she says,'witch fah my rings?' 'Cuss,' says I (but joking like). Well we went through the house'n long the dooryard with my forked stick—out on the sand by the brook, me thinking about the rings, the stick pulling. When it pointed straight down, she dug that sand away with hah fingers and theya was the rings right in that sand." Olive's smilelines deepen. "She looks at me s'funny. Just stared, putting on those rings. She said, 'You're a witch!' Jezuz, was I spooked! We both were."

Gloria is fascinated, but now sighing and leaning back against her chair. Olive continues, telling about old-time dowsers in Gottheim, and finishes with novelist Kenneth Roberts' curmudgeonly defense of the art.

Olive takes her seat and Asa returns to the table saying, "Anaone waunts see a demonstration of Olive finding water, sign up afterwards'n we'll call you come spring, next time someone wants a well done. If theya's n'questions, we'll have refreshments tonight from Sarah Harrington and Lorna Thibodeau."

Eagerly Gloria waves her hand. "Ms. Bartlett, would you equate this unique talent with the intuitive arts such as musical composition, dramatic arts, painting and so forth? Don't you think they are all somehow related?"

"No, I don't."

The young woman slumps a bit, deflated. Asa looks around for more questions and, seeing none, indicates the refreshments. Conversation begins slowly, as members stretch and stand. Two woman begin uncovering refreshments, Gloria rushes over to Olive, complimenting her talk and promising to signup for a demonstration. She peppers the older woman with questions about the sensation of dowsing and then gets down to what's on her mind. "Have you gone on to widen the variety of things you search out with your stick? Have others come seeking guidance on lost people or things?"

"Oh no. That's not something I'd be interested in. I just look fah water. Theya's nothing betta'n water t'find. That's enough."

"How much do you charge for your service?"

Olive laughs. "Don't. Oh, I get my gas money if it's much out o'town. People just give me whatever they feel. Sometimes I get deer meat, a bag o'something fom the garden, maybe a meal. Occasionally I get maple syrup."

"But you must *do* something with this. You could develop it to benefit all kinds of searches. Think of the pain you could ease. Could you find lost pets, do you think?"

"Gory, no. They'd have t'be dead, wouldn't they?"

"—Mrs. Bartlett, I could put you in touch with a group of women who are interested in developing these kinds of psychic pursuits. They've been sort of feeling their way toward a new worship of—a new kind of worship that's really old. There are ancient rites and the creation of sacred space, and the... invocation of the old goddesses.... I know these women would welcome you and be very supportive in helping you develop—"

But Olive's expression has changed from motherly humor to open horror. "Oh no." She shakes her head emphatically, but then remembering her manners says thank you very stiffly. She turns away, moving quickly toward the coffee urn and doughnuts. Gloria watches her go with regret. *That's pretty clear*! She sighs over the waste of talent. The sting of rebuff evaporates as she considers alternative ways of approaching Olive. At last she discards these, believing that Olive is too old and set in her ways to except new practices.

Spying Asa, she recalls the question of Gottheim's naming. The older bespeckled man is pouring himself a cup of coffee as Gloria approaches. She picks up a styrofoam cup. "Will you leave the spigot open for me, Mr. Bartlett?"

"Cuss!" His eyes are merry behind his horned rims. Olive has hissed Gloria's strange proposal to him just moments ago as they met beside the home-fried doughnuts. He was shocked of course, in a small way, but Asa finds Gloria refreshing. He enjoys the engaging minor false moves she commits from time to time. If she were 55 or 60 and tried these things he would be sour and mocking, telling details all over town. But Gloria is simply glorious; and he loves these morsels to chew on with Melviny or somebody in front of the post office. Gloria dated Balder Simon a while back but nothing came of it. That was interesting because Balder is such a smart boy, good with his hands and a Vietnam vet. Used to be a mechanic at the chair factory and she is this upscale beauty from away, hooked up snug with IICE and the Jasper Mountain resort. "Ain't that odd!" people said. And Asa was curious as hell about that relationship. He could almost feel his ears twitch forward now as she sips at the coffee he has poured for her.

She says brightly, "Balder Simon said *you* were the one to ask: Just *how* did Gottheim get its name? Apparently he thinks you can tell it better than he can. Guess that's why you're the historian!"

Asa's gaze just glows on her. Oh those blue eyes. Lashes all black against good skin. Ain't it a wonder—how her skin stays golden all winter? Interested in local history too!

"Doaw," he says modestly. "But Balda Simon probably don't know it well enough to speak."

"It was Farmingham Royal to begin with, I know that much. What happened?"

They step away from the urn to let others near, Asa finishing his doughnuts, Gloria sipping her coffee. When the meeting first started the room was still a bit stale and cold. Now it is warm and filled with the comforting aroma of coffee and sweets as Asa begins.

"Farmingham Royal came from the French and Indian wars—as the town was granted to descendents o'the veterans o'the battle of Port Royal Canady. The young men out of Farmingham, Mass'chussets took ship'n sailed to Nova Scotia, once called Acadia, which was held by the French at the time. Sacked the place. A few generations later—after badgering the legislature'n still hadn't got paid fah the job—theya descendents finally won a grant o'land in the wilderness of the District of Maine (being a province of Mass.). They called it Farmingham Royal in honor o'that battle'n the place they hailed fom. Gott'im wasn't decided on till come time t'incorporate. That's when they wanted something gut a li'l more sound to it, high sound."

"God's House! Guess that's high enough. But why the German? Why not Hebraic or Hellenic or something? Weren't the Classics big back then?"

"This was more of a popularity contest between two Gott'im fathers. One thought the biblical Luz was the ticket, tother wanted Gott'im in honor of his ancestors' origin. He was town clerk'n his name won out. He turned out to be a rascal. Even five years after, when he done his dirty deed, they'd got so used t'the name, they'd f'got it was him chose it... till the man whose name lost out reminded 'em."

Chuckling, Asa picks up his second doughnut, waiting for her to prompt him. He loves a show of genuine interest.

Her eyes widened over the rim of her cup. "Was he an adulterer, an arsonist? A horse thief—maybe a lunatic!?"

"Worse. He absconded with evah nickel o'tax money."

"God!" She is gratifyingly astonished. "How'd it happen? Did anyone see it coming?"

Asa shakes his head. "Apparently even his wife knew nothing about it. She nevah left, due to straightened circumstances. She did have the fine house, fust house in town t'have real glass panes, but she had t'take in boarders, husband gone t'New Orleans."

"Wow. How'd they find that out?"

"He died aboard ship heading north after three years. Some thought he was on his way home to repent. Others said he was gont New York to hide theya."

"*What* a story!" She crows as if the theft of funds from poor settlers were some sort of entertainment now that it's old stuff. She's visualizing a four seasons resort brochure with blurb of this history in pictorial detail. What luck to be able to add a touch of the rascal and the risqué—New Orleans?—to the otherwise puritanical atmosphere of this New England village. "Mr. Bartlett, you have made my day! I suppose the clerk's house is gone now?"

Highly gratified, Asa nods. "Lost in a fire. Oh we're full o'good stories. Come back'n heah s'more!"

The high beams of Balder's pickup light the icy highway on his way from work to the little village huddled at the snowy feet of Jasper Mountain. A trucker's lights shine impatiently in his rearview. Balder eases up a bit on the gas just to give the trucker something to think about before returning to his bemused thoughts on the divided heart of Gloria. In her ritual of distraction will she be seeing someone new tonight? Her dreary serial sensualism is chilling to him. Will she ever open to the possibilities of the vast mysterious continent of love? He believes in a territory yet to be explored... to which we have no access nor any knowledge of except through the care of children. There is treasure here: the treasure of sexual ecstasy and its offspring. It is what he desires of their union, nothing more nor less.

The glare of his rearview recedes to a glow. Balder pours on a little more gas. Now, into the last curve lights of the Village begin to show.

But he thinks of the nearer problem, of an older lonely woman, bereft of her husband and apparently now losing also her sight. Although...

he's sure she still has sight. He is more worried about Elda than he ever worried about anything except his own sanity. And she thinks she's putting one over on him.... And that Daniel doesn't know, either. She's wrong both places. They've each seen her stumble enough to know the lights are going out. Mother evades their hints like some little old fox but—till now—has not been pressed on the point. She'll do damage in the barn one day, or fall down a cellar hole in the woods, anything. But Balder has a surprise for her after supper. Tonight he's going to take her in hand, literally.

Grabbing hold of her arm he announces it, suddenly, after the meal. "Let's go fah a li'l ride, Mutha!"

Elda was shuffling toward the kitchen with empty plates in her hands, careful as anything. The clock on the mantelpiece chimed 7:30. They've been eating in front of the television, watching the NewsHour. Surprised by his unexpected touch, she veers. "Got dishes," but she's unable to pull away.

"I'll do 'em when we get back." He takes the plates from her hands, goes to the sink to get them soaking.

"Gut check the animals." She heads for the coat rack.

"Hold on theya sweet woman!" He lets loose the dish liquid, stepping to block the door. Light gleams off the darkened pine cupboards. Once this kitchen bustled with the controlled chaos of family interaction in the calling of one another's bluff. On hearing these words, Mother stops dead. She has not heard anyone say *Hold it theya sweet woman*, since Everett used it on her. Try as she might with various subtleties he was not one to be gotten around when confrontation was due. You had to face up to him and make your case. Surprised—hearing these words out of his son. He sounds like Everett! Everett Simon was a man quiet around strangers, a farmer among other things, adapted to the silences of woodland and field. Following the death of his own father it was that full-bodied silence which brought the quiet sense of his sovereignty into the household. Elda never allowed herself to resent it. One body can't be ruled with two heads. She reasoned thus with her own urge to rebel. And in those days the culture agreed with her. Or, maybe, she agreed with it. Consciously seeking not to challenge its assumptions. Either way, their household enjoyed unity and peace in consequence. After a straightening period of adjustment Elda enjoyed this unity herself. She came to enjoy Everett like she enjoyed the use of her own fingers. He was a part of her as though of her own body. The ache of phantom pain, brought on by his loss, has never left her.

Balder's *Hold on theya, sweet woman*, brings it all back. For an instant she looks hard at him but finds only that annoying dark spot where his face should be. Her glance slides away. Elda says, "Well, if you want it that bad...."

She hesitates, off balance and unsure. Is he going to tear into her about this? But suddenly... she is quietly taken with the thought of spending time alone with Balder on the dark road. Having some of his attention without his usual preoccupation. A ride folded in darkness with him might even be nice. Turning her head slightly, she grabs for her coat. The heavy rough feel of it comforts her touch.

Again the unexpected. Balder takes hold of the coat and helps her into it. Now she understands. Balder knows. But then again maybe she's wrong here, too. —Wrong about so many things. Always has been and only lately understanding it.

"Well... okay, Sarge." She grins mischievously, letting herself be handed out the door. He was a Sergeant—impossibly young Sergeant—in Vietnam; leading men to safety, leading men to death.

But Balder gives no sign that he has received this as a thrust. She does such things unconsciously, only recognizing the implication once the damage is done. She makes her criticisms inadvertently. But surely just the same.

The front end of the pickup is heavy with the plow he packs in winter. Balder picks up extra money plowing out driveways. At night the lights can trouble and confuse her, yet she keeps her gaze ahead, sensing Balder is looking her way. As the truck turns out from the Village onto the highway, he exclaims: "Look't that! Lights on Jaspa Mountain!"

"What, where?!" She turns toward the dark giant, dark as usual but with glimmerings faint and high above.

"Those lights up theya y'nevah see lights on Jasper—less someone's lost.—Oops, gone now." (The lights.)

"So cold out! Imagine being up theya on a night like t'night. suppose'd storm, too. No night t'be up theya."

"Deadly night." He shifts into third, shifting conversational course as well. "Mutha."

"Yuht."

He hesitates, uncharacteristically. He will seldom hesitate in speech once he has made up his mind to speak of something. He states all, plain and directly as possible. Now he starts again and goes right to it. "Mutha, I'm taking you to the health clinic. You ah going blind—stumbling and looking at things cockeyed. I don't think you should be driving, d'you?— and I'm not letting you go on like this. I got an appointment fah you."

The Gottheim health clinic is open some evenings to allow appointments for those who can't get off work other times. They also have sliding fees based on income. There are meetings for substance and domestic abuse, a room with therapeutic equipment, even a babysitter for the children of patients. Two doctors, physician's assistant, nurses and a counselor provide professional services. But Elda has always resisted setting foot over that threshold.

The pickup is silent except for the steady sound of its engine, the whispering growl of tires switching from pavement to icy patch and back again. Balder begins thinking maybe he's got her now. That just maybe she will submit. He has made his point and stance impossible to resist.

Comes a small voice from the huddled bundle in a corner of the cab. "I'm not going," it says.

"Yes you ah."

"No."

"You ah! We'll be in the pocking lot."

"No." The voice has retained its small steadiness.

"Why not?"

"It won't do no good."

Balder is tired. He was in the bleachery today. Head to foot in protective plastic, soaked in sweat—January. Four hours he was there, working on valves in that suit.

His lapse allows her to continue, slowly. "I read about this disease. Theya in't no rebuilding those cones at the back o'my retinas, Balda. Theya's a hole in the middle of my sight'n no amount o'knitting's going to put them back together. I can see t'get around a'foot, but I'll give up driving... if you say."

Balder is considering. "You sure about this—caunt be treated?"

"Certain. 'N I already faced it. You can too. Just caunt see cranking all that machinery they got in them offices today. I can see—it's called legal blindness. The worst is over now, I'm used to it." This is not quite true, but it is true enough. It will have to do. She will let him ask around if he wants—find out for sure for himself that the damage is limited to direct sight... and then she'll know it too. But she will be no invalid, not occupied by this ailment any more than she must be. Its gods twilight—like in the stories. She will find life, now, in the moving mist. She will live this tale.

Balder has been driving around, wanting to break the bad news to her with his talk before going straight to the clinic. Now they keep on though the road is icy and dark and steep walled with towering pines. The cold of January seeps in more than the heater can handle. The cracking cold of winter dark is with them in the Western Maine mountains. The man's thoughts are now on those searchers, roaming the awful heights with powerful beams of light. Someone is lost. No one would be up there if it weren't so. No one brings light where it's not needed. Light goes where it will help.

The boy made his blind leap into the screaming breath: airborne in sudden terror of the white wall beneath, a headwall already dimming in earth's shadow beneath his flying skis. The awful height of this headwall in taking off its pluming brow—surprised him. The approaching slope was no mere slope but the great white wall of a cirque carved in the wasting of the last glacier. Yet Jason had no thought for the formation of mountains. The cirque was an almost vertical drop, taken with reckless but wrenching skill. Afloat in taking it, *Jason The Defiant* found himself schussing the headwall, streaking the holy white veil a gash from top to bottom. He screamed. And the breath of Jasper screamed back: Like an aggrieved old woman, or squaw (he thought), burning through the ski mask and swallowing his own scream out of his face. The initial terrifying moments of his long descent expanded to hours. The thews of his legs felt as though they were ripping to ribbons in the scarcely controlled glissade down the mountain. What seemed hours compressed to a moment as the basin of the cirque came up to meet him, forcing Jason relentlessly toward a dark crust of trees. At the last moment he whirled away, tracking northward, fiercely flailing with skis and poles.

  The small grade slows him and Jason stops. He leans on his poles, stunned with relief, with the weakness of a great gratitude. He slips backward a bit, his legs trembly, exhausted.

  Made it!

  He looks up at it, thinking, *I made that fucking headwall!* Joyfully the words replay themselves, cleansing him of terror.

  I'm alive on the backside of Jasper Mountain!

  Looking at the scarcely glimmering height, he is thrilled. Shadow surrounds him but the headwall soars monolithic and crystal white.... Pure, he thinks.... Holy! The high top of the great curving wall, maybe 500 ft. in height, shows plumes of snow lifting like swirling veils off its mysterious rim. Listening he hears these winds conversing, speaking with the mountain, roaring. This is the fierce face of God. Never will you forget its awful aspect.

  Its appearance is sublimely remote and disinterested but its impression upon him is personal. Digging in with his poles, Jason is filled with the thought of it... yet...vaguely aware that the great headwall thinks nothing at all of him. He is tiny—minute—beneath the vast purity of this mighty circular wall.

Where did you come from? Why didn't anyone tell me you were here?

But this immanent place will give him no answers. He feels the cold here as a burning and lets his gaze fall. Now he looks around. Shadow is deepening, light fading fast, seeping out of the great encircling snowy bowl.

He turns his back on it, facing the long dark arms of the woodland, set there as though a bar to his escape. Conifers, scattered nearby, seem to cower in this piercing wind. They are ancient, scrawny and bent. Jason glides down toward the dark ranks and finds the wall of conifers breaking. He enters into their shelter. Now he stops briefly to turn and glance backward at the great sudden source of his awe and predicament. He turns back, glides on.

Slowly, finding his way, he skis deeper into the wind-breaking arms of bent spruce. He finds deepening dimness and shoves his mask and goggles up under the hood of his parka in remedy. It seems an age since he handed those limp twenties to the tobacco chewing lift-shack man. The eerie wind roaring high above upon the headwall sounds. He shivers, moving slowly among the trees, the sweat of his turmoil chilling him. Shivering, shivering he seeks a way down.

Find a good logging trail... something white, smooth.... Then it wouldn't take long to ski down into Gottheim. There's bound to be a light from some chalet or other. Something will show when I get past this scrub. *God! it's cold!*

He stops among the close branches to take off a glove and feel inside his parka for something to eat. Before leaving the condo after lunch he slipped a few fruit rollups into his pockets. Now he rips at the wrapper with numbing fingers, fumbling; tears at the cellophane with his teeth. The dried fruit will sugar him slowly, restoring warmth and encouragement.

Night has fallen, his eyes acclimating. The temperature on the slope is dropping even as stars appear in branches above him. Chewing, he moves on, his skis turning through the narrow crooked ways. The boughs up here are heavy with smoothly sculpted snow forms. Some other time he would be fascinated but now he cares only for the twisting trail on which he finds himself. Maybe it's a trail the deer make in summer. Or maybe it's no trail. He must keep moving, moving, following gravity's lead. The roar of the headwall is muted now but still pursuing. Their thunder erupts at the tips of his skis as, startled, wild wings graze past. He slips; but snowy arms of spruce keep him upright. Wild himself, he hurries on.

After a bit, on second thoughts, the presence of the gamebird has reassured him. Jason admits to himself that being up here alone is stressing. If even Brandon were here now! The guy's not such a jerk, really. Just an intrusion. *Maybe he can't even help it.*

Knowledge that there are creatures on the mountain with him comforts, but in the dark he misses much: the three-footed track of the varying hare, the lacework of the deer mouse's threading tail under his long artificial feet. Coyote and bobcat tracks cross, telling the tale of animal interaction.

After a long struggle among the trees he finds.... The problem with this deer track...or whatever—it's not going anywhere! The trees are closer than ever. Crowding. He can no longer turn or even move much. It's hopeless!

Panicking, nearly entangled, he looks wildly round. Wait—that looks promising there on his left... an opening. Now he can descend.... But... after a hundred yards this game trail also disappears and he is left amazed again among the boles. His only comfort is that the trees are taller. A good sign, says half his thought. *But it's darker and there are too many and you are trapped like a rat*, says the other half.

The cold of night has seeped into him, sucking on his marrow. Already his feet are aflame with pain. *Your face is almost tire rubber. Touch it to make sure you have live skin.*

But too quickly he brings his gloved hand to his face, accidentally punching himself in the eye with a ski pole. Pain and fear leap up, throttling.

Jason stands very still.

It's happening. I'm here on a mountain in Maine. At night. In January. Am I going to die?

Grandmother- Wind and-Weather shrilled out to her grandson Jasper Mountain. *That ignorant arrogant child on your head!*

But strong Jasper answered, approving him.

Wind-and-Weather bent fiercely over the round white head of her grandson, replying, blowing the boy off the summit.

While the light from the little moon still gleamed off his head, Jasper said, *Contend!*

Then Grandmother-Wind and-Weather lifted great plumes on the mighty brow pouring cold fury upon Jasper. In winter, wind is wedded to mountains. She would compass surrounding mountains in her thick blankets. But their summits remained low before great Jasper. His is the one crowned

in krumholz, his decked most in the glory of crystals, his the shape of
perfection.

And he confirmed, saying, *Then he will acknowledge he knows not
what keeps him alive.*

But Wind-and-Weather screamed over his summit, bringing down
clouds with her out of the North. The night long she would contend with the
mountain over the mortal. Vapors drift now past the glimmering face of
stars.

Jasper Mountain is submerged in storm.

Wind beats upon the trees above Jason where at first he founders
then, arising, flounders along its alien flanks. Overhead branches creak and
crack. Here the trees are high and deep in old and new snow. So the skis
are his allies. If he loses them now he will die on the mountain; sink in deep
snow, struggle and wade then collapse from exhaustion and cold. Keep my
wits, keep my skis, not go casting them off in a panic. Use hop-turns around
trees and my skis will bring me down into Gottheim, at least to the highway,
some house where I can call Mom.

He is grateful for the downslope of Jasper: The way in which he
finds guidance simply in continuing down. But sometimes the downslope
way is compromised, blocked; his progress routed by tangles, deceptive
dips, ridges, sudden ravines. The storm engulfs him; the blindness and
horrifyingly pure smell of snow. He fights the desire to curl up and sleep
against the trunk of some tree, burrow himself into the snow.

The skis on his feet become alien appendages, his boots concrete
castes he should molt and leave behind. Briefly, at moments, Jason feels
himself still schussing the great headwall. Coming to himself once,
squatting amid the flying leaves of the beech thicket and clinging to the
slender twigs: These are the autumn leaves of some other life. A warm life
on the far side of some distant planet. Jason clasps the frail stems of these
trees with fingers unfeeling, struggling up and still—miraculously—locked
to his skis. Crying in anguish he pulls through the thicket, helping himself
along on their outstretched hands. His poles are gone—lost among the
thicket through which he struggles, or lost in the fir wood he happened
through some time before. Experience is shattered, marked not by time but
by passage through stages of woodland—phases of forestation characterized
by the hand of man, or of God. Height, density, blowdown, cutover....
Terrain makes all the difference. Once he traversed acres of open territory,
what he hoped would be smooth skiing, only to be checked in his crossing
by the treachery of hidden debris. Had he known that these snags were but
the leavings of loggers, he might have been encouraged to search out a

skidder trail, something plain to lead him out of the woods and down to the road. But ignorance, and storm-panic, prevent this; leaving Jason open to exposure, laying him bare to the torment of wind driven snow.

The young skier, gasping, keeps moving, moving when he might stop in some hollow beside upturned roots of a downed pine—willing his feet move on the hated skis. Only as one can they make it together downmountain into the recognizable land. A mythic land of safety, sanity, kindness and health. There was such a place once, when he was a kid. Jason feels sure he will never be that kid again. He will be blessed to arrive with arms, hands, legs, with a face.

The trees around him creak and clash, reporting like gunfire. Fiercely the weather of Jasper Mountain plucks at him, reaching its apex of fury. Now blind, unaware, the boy stumbles forward.

Grazing his forearm, something startles him, and he shies away. *What is it? Did I imagine it?*

But again the thing comes at him, now brushing his leg. Stopping, he feels for it, grasping feebly with his numb hand.

Here it is again. A dog?

The creature has come to him, halting his progress. Jason allows himself to be checked by this scarcely touching animal, and squats on his skis, feeling for its pointed face and large moist nose. Too gentle and silent for a dog, its face is slender and quieting. Can this be a deer?—but it's almost invisibly white.

The deer allows him to hold its warm neck in his arms, to sag some against it. It hardens its small body to stand against Jason's sagging weight.

This is death. *I'm gonna die.*

The deer has come for him out of that strange place of stories and dreams. *Is that where people go... when they die?* Dying would account for the creature's odd hue and behavior.

Is he leading me there?

Nerveless and weak, Jason cannot speak. Go... go on to the place you're bringing me. *I'm ready to go with you now.*

Aching and cold he trembles against the deer in the storm.

And the deer turns, Jason still leaning upon it but pulling himself up out of the snow. Floundering and wallowing, the deer leads on as Jason takes courage and, again, to his skis.

The creature leads him along the lip of a precipice unknown, on through the beating and keening of the storm. Here Jason finds thickets on patches of rocks cleansed by the wind. And, as they go, he becomes aware of the drop-off beside them and of naked treetops bristling in the flying dimness beyond. *Wouldn't death would have led me that way?*

Together they descend as the ledge lowers itself gently, merging into the forest floor below. Jason has glided past his helper but now returns to him over the snow. The skis set the boy above this wallowing creature but he finds himself stooping to stay with it, accepting what guidance it may give. Now, with relief, the boy feels the strong presence of sheltering rock above. Where once it would cast him to his death it now stands over him, protectively, a monstrous rock.

The deer stops. And Jason rests, leaning shoulder and side against the great rock. The deer stands near, its warm side against his shivery leg. Out of the wind now, Jason dozes off, drifting in vacancy. Soon he is traveling again through images in some terrifying dream. A noise, a limb falling perhaps, wakes him with a jerk. He comes to himself, finding his shoulder against the rock, the deer by his side.

As if its terrible fury and fire were slaking, a change is felt in the blast high above. As though the storm has had enough of him and begins passing away. The change is perceptible to Jason, who has lived in it almost from before its onset. He has been beaten, made to believe in death, but now begins believing in life again. Will he make it out of this dimness and thrashing? Will he yet come to tell her of this night? He pictures her lovely face full of rejoicing, relief.

But this is the backside of a January snow storm in the mountains of Maine and Jason is still lost in the woods. He looks down at the deer, at its pale back. Pale, as though the storm has seeped into it. Strange strange deer. *Where have you come from? Why hasn't anyone told me of you?* Gently his awe suffuses him with gratitude and peace.

As these thoughts occur to him Jason lifts his gaze and finds himself staring at something familiar. In a moment he recognizes it. A light. Through dim creaking woodland a tiny light shines. Fitfully. Jason looks away from it, hopeful. He looks back. It is. A light.

He says this aloud, but softly, to the deer. Yet the deer has already moved a little toward the light. Now it stops, as though pointing with its pale muzzle.

Did you mean me to see it?

Jason cannot bear to break the spell of his peace with skepticism. After all that has happened. ...To do so would be—*I'm grateful*. Maybe the deer *did* bring him here. But could it, really? He saved me from falling. What's so hard about him showing me a light?

He can scarcely command his legs but, with great effort, he turns his skis. The strength of the deer still seems hardy, sinewy. *Please, little deer take me to the light?...*

—

The great world beyond his control was filled, suffused, peopled with caring. He lay on an old couch in the bearded man's dim kitchen, heaped in quilts, hearing the quiet rustle of the fire in the stove, the comforting smell of wood smoke in his nostrils. He heard the stove door squeal shut but did not open his eyes.

Jason had not known that some people have gifts of caring for others: that it could be an art form like rock-and-roll or photography and requiring skill, precision, like that used in shooting moguls or carving through the turns of the slalom. They knew exactly what to do when they saw someone hurting, went through the necessary steps with agility, as though in a tender ballet. Coming in off the mountain he learned this; coming down from heights where he escaped being destroyed. Caring permeated creation... in the form of people just doing what they were supposed to do.

His shaking and shivering were abating, but his cheeks and nose seemed to be missing, sheared off by the wind. Yet, with broth and warmth penetrating him he might go home soon, even with this face-firing pain. The man said an ambulance would be coming. The man said he would be going to the hospital.

The man had believed him when he told of the deer, though at first Jason thought him pretending; just to be kind. The deer was gone when he opened the door and saw the boy collapsing there. Swift and sure the man's foot released Jason from the impossible lengths of his skis. The arms were strong in lifting him into the shadowy kitchen, the long hands tender in releasing numb feet from the bondage of their boots. His humor was quiet in telling gentle jokes on himself and on Jason: about the lack of service, the poor accommodations and nonexistent lift lines on this side of the mountain.

"The white deer... real?..." Jason murmured it more than once while the wind roamed under the eaves and roared on the mountain above. "A white deer?"

The man came near. "Yuht. Real as you or me. Been roaming Jaspa Mountain since he dropped fom his mother's womb last summer. We call 'em Sugarloaf cause he's so white. Pure white."

The man stopped then, thoughtfully fingering his dark beard. Light from the living room beyond threw a gleam on his white-blond hair. He went to the counter to get Jason cocoa. When he came back he said, "You could do something fah Sugarloaf."

"How?" His voice was a whisper.

"Don't tell."

"Don't tell he saved my life?"

"Lots'a people'd love t'bag that deer. ...If word got round. Caunt you see him stuffed and mounted in the lobby ovah theya at the resort?"

Jason lay silent.

Whether to give Jason space to think or on some errand, the man went into the next room. Maybe he was getting ready to go to work. It must be morning. The sun would be coming up. Jason sipped the cocoa, thinking about what the man said of the deer.

All he would ever want to think of for the rest of his life was the white deer. He wished he could be here with him now. He wanted to lay his hand on its bony head, feel its thin furred ears between his painful fingers. He wanted the deer to lead him through the rest of his life. His heart filled at the thought of the deer walking with him from class to class at school, the deer going down to the hockey rink for practice, the deer kneeling beside his desk in the bedroom while he studied chemistry.

—It would never work, never. Jason would leave the woods, leave Maine. Already the distant wail of the ambulance told him. The deer would stay here, and he would be gone to a bright place bustling with noise and people in white, caring for him. The little deer would remain quiet, anonymous, safe. Here. This house would be here, and the man... in the middle of the deer's range: this man, this kind man, regular blue-collar man. And all Jason could do was be in suburbia where he came from... but now looking after, always thinking of what he had seen. The deer will always be... and what had really happened. That was memory now, it couldn't change.

The man returned saying, "Theya almost heah. Y'folks'll be glad t'see you. Police called 'em."

Jason scarcely acknowledged these words. He was thinking... but now drifting off again. Had he been sleeping just now? Was there a storm... I dreamed?

The shadow of the man loomed over him still. Looking up, Jason whispered. "Was there a deer?"

"A white deah, Sugarloaf. But don't tell anaone. Keep that deah safe."

God's Creatures in Winter

James Fay, a developer at Jasper Mountain, sat across from Theodora Prescott in her snow-bright kitchen in the village. He was full of plans for Mason's Mills, already under construction in the wilds of the borderlands of Quaker and Gottheim; having financial backing from resort owner Harry Golding. James was looking forward to moving into his own home, being built in the development, come spring when the budding leaves would enhance its beauty. The old settlers' mill had flourished during the last century and its foundation stones, near his unfinished house, lent it a solidity and security which added to its appeal.

James had other plans as well, plans for himself and Theodora. He wanted to marry her this spring or early summer when the house was complete.

Theo's own home, in this historic residential heart of Gottheim showed her taste for the fine old things. James called regularly on his fiancé to set him straight about arcana for historic simulation. He admired her antique pot rack hanging above the butcher block from the pale stamped tin ceiling. Even its utensils were authentic, both iron and brass. Under one window stood a slate sink with splashguard of pink marble, flanked by sideboards of wormwood. The windows above were divided lights; snow cover without reflected soft light into the room. Theodora also contributed valuable guidance on his business attire, for instance, convincing him to import linen handkerchiefs to wear in his breast pocket.

James Fay was still smarting over Rhetta Bearce's polite but pointed attacks in editorial letters to *The Village Voter*. The old girl had accused him of lacking authenticity in his design for an extension of Gottheim's traditional village and, in part because of her, he continued a target of anyone angry over the plan. They accused him of tasteless architectural eclecticism, of backpedaling and reneging on his promise of authenticity. He needed Theo's help to avoid similar impugning of his recent project.

Mason's Mills was now the one he wanted to be remembered for. His greatest hope always lay in the latest effort.

Now, over midmorning coffee with her, he said, "Think of it, Theo. This is aimed especially at people who care most for family life. The life *we* like. The planning board, especially that notable but overly vocal Mrs. Bearce, will *have* to sail this through. No possible way they can find it objectionable. I followed every ordinance to the letter and on time!"

Theo sipped her coffee, daintily. "Well, it certainly helps that you were the one to dream up this concept in the first place." She beamed. She was always beaming at James and believing high things of him. Every night she thanked God for sending him. His love and presence in her life imparted stability that she had not dreamed of even six or eight months ago. Being loved was the most wonderful feeling in the world—and James the most wonderful person to bestow it. He had come, bringing God with him, and now she knew with certainty that God is love.

James smiled his shiny indulgent bespeckled smile. Cluster development had been pivotal in his relations with the townsfolk. Of course, Harry Golding had been the one to present it to them. The virulent resistance of these people to Fay's charm had surprised him. He was good with people from away. He could sell upscale strangers garages for elephants, being a master at mining images dear to the heart of yuppies. But it had taken a Golding to break through to Gottheim's leading citizens. They were every bit as tough as any old Mainer.

"The sweetest part," he said, "may have been my proposal to deed all the natural areas, horse paths, hiking and cross-country ski trails to the town. That way *they* can be responsible to the DEP. Now if only that misguided New Age hippie would leave me alone, Mason's Mills will be ready for the summer building spree." He frowned, remembering too late as he always did that Eloise Patadoe might be related to Theo. "She's not an old friend... or anything?" But—it might also be advantageous if she *is* related to Theo.

Theodora's eye had been caught by some movement in the bright yard outside. Vaguely distracted she turned back to him, laughing. "Goodness no, James! *She's* not from here. *She's* been in Gott'im less time than it takes to be born here!" Theodora was fond of putting it this way, indicating the premium placed on having ancestors who settled the town— or, at least, were around to contribute something in the previous century. Eloise Patadoe dated only since the back-to-the-land movement of the late '60s and '70s. But Theo knew that in colleges across the state the newer tradition was heralded as an active demographic phenomenon.

She pushed her chair back and went to the window. "That awful squirrel, James—at it again! I've tried everything to keep those gray squirrels away from the feeders!" She gave a disgusted wail and rapped sharply on the pane, but the huge rodent simply turned its fat backside and bushy tail to her, ignoring the sight of her threatening white knuckles. "I do *not* want those things eating the birds' food! Look at him! He's practically inhaling that seed!"

James helped himself to a sliver of the almond spice pastry which, along with coffee, scented the table. He wished she would stop going on about that creature. Her behavior bored and irritated him. Sometimes it made him consider forgoing these midmorning get-togethers. Why she tended to these obsessive fixations. ... She was a bit bonkers. Originally this trait had attracted him, but lately its charm eluded him. If only she would settle down and not let little things bother her. *Lay off, Theo*, he wanted to say. But he gave his response a soothing quality instead. "You want squirrels to make it through winter, too, don't you?"

"Well... yes. I guess I never thought of it that way. Thank you." Theo came back and sat across from Fay. She leaned over her coffee toward him. "James there's something... well, I'd like to confess something. You might... remember last fall... when I was, well, distracted about something?"

She paused and he nodded adding, "Yes, but you seemed to straighten out all right after your baptism...." He gave her a quizzical look.

She hurried on. "I-I've been somewhat concerned...—because you're a religious man." Her gaze slid away. "You might—you know... be offended. But James, you did say confession—and repentance—is what God wants."

James felt his pulse quicken. He looked at her fearing a sordid confession. Was she about to tell of former (and probably botched) affairs? Things had been going so well! She had made a beautiful confession of faith at the altar following that poignant baptism. And he was looking forward to a wedding solemnized in church and honeymoon bed that was as clean and fresh as—himself. James Fay had managed to keep his virginity despite temptation and hoped she had to. God knew it wasn't easy in such times! But it *was* possible—and completely desirable to him.

Although it was a cold January day in a drafty old house, he felt a faint sweat forming on his brow and above his upper lip. He kept the dread from his voice, feeling a reluctance he could not cover. "Yes, Theo. We are to confess.... If we must."

"Well...." She dropped her gaze. "The wages—" She swallowed and looked out the windows. The squirrel had gone but she didn't notice. "The wages—at Gottheim Chair—?" She missed seeing Fay's shoulders relax, his brow smooth out. "...For a long time, decades even, they weren't as high as maybe they should have been." The last was said all in a rush, and then she stopped and turned toward him, a part of her auburn hair falling across her eye.

Never had she appealed to him more. Tenderly James prompted her, leaning toward her to take up her hand. "Theo, I don't know what you're talking about but it can't be as bad as this."

"But it is." She allowed him to continue caressing the back of her hand. "For years there was a sort of... arrangement... to set mill wages—by the owners. Even... even Father and Gramps. They all agreed on exactly how much workers would make. And on workers being blackballed if they quit one place and... so forth. The sawmills paid highest and the smaller wood mills would keep a wage agreed on.... That was until the national minimum wage was instituted, I think. Then that was the minimum. That way," she went on as if he did not understand, "owners were assured of maximum profits and almost no competition for workers. You see how advantageous it was."

"But was it wrong, really? How was it immoral? Was there a law against it?" Gently he let go her hand.

"I never consulted my lawyer.... Just been— uncomfortable. Look at industrial wages in other parts of the country and what about rates and paper companies? Those mills started out just like the lumber and wood-turning mills."

"Yes, and look at the quality of the workplace in Gottheim Chair. No toxic chemicals to worry about, no unhealthy atmosphere like you find down the highway in Guildford. Theo, these workers of yours have had a job they could count on for most of their lives. Maybe that arrangement ensured this."

"But James, those wages have never been enough to support a family."

"Yes—the families here have had *two* breadwinners... and well before people were doing so in other parts. They've been out in front with equal pay for equal work. Don't people stay married here better than on the national average? They do all right, believe me, Theo. They do."

He had picked up both her hands again and bent his head to look encouragement into her downcast eyes. Such concern lifted her gaze and she smiled a tentative if vulnerable smile.

"James.... It's wonderful of you to be so understanding." She had expected a shock to his sense of fitness and conscience. Yet, even as she spoke, she felt unconvinced, maybe even a bit disturbed. Was James' lack of censure his charity shining through? His forgiveness for error seems full and complete. Can it be right to think it too easy? He says these things because of his love. Yes, she saw it now. She should be relieved.

She squeezed his hands. "I'm trying to make it up to them, really I am. Now they're wages are nearly as high as Bearces'!"

"But I'm sure it isn't necessary, Theo." (How *does* that tumbledown place stay in business?! Should not ask, however. Just keep my mitts off. Leave it alone.)

"No, James. I want to do what's right. If at all possible. Your faith and concern for what's right was—has encouraged me!" Her smile beamed out on him.

James smiled and returned the pressure of her hands.

Stamping snow from her secondhand L.L. Bean hunting boots, Eloise Patadoe steps into the office of *The Village Voter*. She strides up to the battered pumpkin pine counter, declaring, "Here's the ad for my wholesome delicious goats milk cheese!"

Seated at his desk, James Nutting looks up from under his green visor at her horsey face, saying dryly, "I don't eat goats milk cheese. It's not me you have to sell."

"I'm merely hinting at the content of the ad." She digs in her old leather zipper case, pulling out a typewritten sheet. "Also, I want you to consider this letter to the editor. Can I get your reaction right now?"

"Ms. Patadoe, does it occur to you that I might be busy working?" But he rolls back his squawking desk chair and comes to the counter.

"This *is* work." She says it boldly. Everything Eloise does is bold. She may go flat and weak inside at times, but nothing of that leaks into her expressions.

Her gaze wanders to the huge press in the back while Nutting reads. The monster sleeps, she says to herself. In an age trending electronic, the vintage machine shakes this turn-of-the-century building whenever an edition goes to press. When the building stops moving, Rozelle Wight, an attorney on the second floor, comes down to pick up a fresh copy of the week's paper.

Dear Editor,

I see we have our good times in store from Mr. Fay & Co. as they plan another big addition to this formally humble town. The Gottheim Theme Park and Brewing Co. is set to specialize in New England Family Fare and Landscaping. Mason's Mills, that once hidden gem of Gottheim town history, is to be excavated and prettified with clusters of imitation capes, gingerbread villas, sanctified saltboxes, and Georgian ticky-tacky. I was hoping to avoid being pressed into service as the Grinch who sabotaged the entertainment industry, but Mr. Fay's plans for my backyard, specifically my side yard, precipitate this. I refer to his attempt at establishing his point of egress (such would no doubt be his term for it) beside my hitherto secluded goat pasture and breeding area in the bordering township. (These properties abut).

I'd like to suggest that Mr. Fay take his clusters and arrange them in another point of egress—one located in a part of the human anatomy not generally associated with parks and amusements. He is not going to finish this project without a fight from the hippie element of the more remote, but vocal, town next-door. Sincerely, Eloise Patadoe, Quaker Plantation.

The letter provokes little more than a sheen in the brown eyes of Mr. Nutting's gaunt face. He looks up from the type script saying, "We can use all but the second from the last sentence."

"Poop! That was my best line. You should've seen the goats' reaction to it."

Nutting gives her his dry steady look.

"All right, all right, Mr. First Amendment." She shakes her blond ponytail, grins like a horse, and says, "Does that remark about cheese mean you won't except a brick in trade for the ad?"

Elda Simon had been in the barn since 3 a.m. nursing a wounded raccoon, a raven with a broken wing and an older fawn who had stepped into a trap. At daybreak, stooping with weariness and pain, she came into the kitchen through the back door bringing January cold and the smell of musk. The red kerchief on her head was askew, a pucker of worry between her brows. She did not notice her grandson Daniel sitting on the couch near the woodstove quietly feeding peanuts to a red squirrel.

After shutting the door on the emerging sun and snowlight, she heard the chattering of the critter shucking its peanut. Yet Elda was startled when she heard Daniel say, "How's things in the barn, Gra'mutha?" He never called her Grandma or, especially, Grammy as other Mainers would. *Grammy* just seemed too familiar to him, and though she was shy and sometimes awkward in conversation Daniel perceived her, rather, as withdrawn and stiff.

Elda straightened, her expression of worry smoothing itself out. Her voice, while not exactly light, was not unpleasant. "Thought you'd gone b'now, Daniel." He had come to stay for the week, as usual, but he should be gone on the school bus by now, headed for ninth grade homeroom at Hazel Newell High School.

"Teacher's conference's day today. No school. I can work in the barn. If y'waunt."

The frown returned. "Well... it's s'nice of you to offer."

She said it slowly, trying for a grandmother's courtesy. Elda was about to brush him off, dreading the obligation to crank up social coping mechanisms. Think of the awkwardness and trouble. A wild stumble through verbal minefields. Her natural mistrust; involuntary concerns over missteps in caring for the wild ones, doing of chores as they ought to be done. She lacked natural grace in giving directions tending to nitpick... whether internally or out loud. Her instructions would come out halting, confused, or sounding like an insult to her helper's intelligence. She might suddenly bark some idiotic command. But—aside from all this piddling aggravation there was a profound worry she wanted to conceal. Once— Lord such a short time ago!—she had got on fairly. Now she was failing, the barn getting away from her. Just how bad... she didn't even know. How well are the animals being cared for?—now that she could scarcely see to do the work as it should be done.

Her careful manners and nice if labored way of speaking told Daniel a deflection was coming. With a plea he cut off her rejection. "I can do it. I need something t'do." Not true. Daniel had plenty to do—too much in fact. But he could no longer let this weird troubled grandmother walk in and out of his presence without some form of personal contact. The mute sorrow of this situation troubled him. Even father was quiet now, more like Daniel than Daniel had suspected he could be. His father was more silent distracted remote. The boy recalled that even glorious Gloria Fay's neglect of his father's love had not so silenced him... as did this twilight of grandmother's. Besides, Daniel liked being in the barn with the animals. As the squirrel turned the peanut over and over, he looked at its hyper heaving sides and almost smiled.

"Got to eat," Elda declared. "Had any breakfast?" She turned to hang up her coat.

Handing the squirrel another peanut, Daniel shook his head. "Just got up."

"Okay, we can have it togetha. Waunt do toast?"

"Can I do the eggs?" There was only discomfort in watching her cook. He wanted to broach the subject, get past the awkwardness of letting her know that he knew. —What if talking only increased the awkwardness?

"Okay," conceded Elda, heading for the bread box. In a case like this she was a pushover. "Toast is mine." She thought, *If I can't talk—toast*!

Daniel washed his hands at the sink then went to the refrigerator and got out eggs. "Like 'em ovah easy, scrambled?"

"Whatever is easy." She got out bread, waiting for Daniel to finish seasoning the pan and start the eggs before starting toast. The smell of hot oil filled the kitchen. She went and got juice from the icebox, heard eggs crackling and sputtering the pan, and pushed down the toast.

Just for something to say Daniel dug into his own curiosity. "How'd you s'pose that Jason guy missed those big houses up theya that night?" Daniel had been with his mother and brothers last week when a teenager from away got lost all night on Jasper Mountain in a storm. He wished he had been here to see the survivor firsthand. He could have reported on it for *The Voter*. His first opportunity to break into print. He itched to get out of his gopher rut at the newspaper.

"Caunt say. Sugarloaf brought 'em down."

Daniel was skeptical. Balder had told him of the white deer's part in the rescue, leaving Daniel to ponder what it meant. Not that he disbelieved... exactly. "The guy never mentioned it to Libby," he said. The reporter at *The Voter* had gathered Jason's story from the ski patrol, from Balder, and from Jason before he left the hospital in Guildford for home in Massachusetts.

Elda made no answer. She had tried everything to keep Sugarloaf away from humans; away, even, from herself. Depriving herself of his company had been the hardest part—that, and the way it made her feel to shoo him away. She continued to pine for his dainty mother, Posey. Having to frighten him and miss getting to know the doe's offspring—. Sugarloaf would have replaced what the hunter took away. Sadness and purblindness where her companions now. But there was comfort in recalling the conversation she had overheard, while sitting in the front room, that dark early morning when the lost boy showed up at their door. She blessed Balder continually for inviting Jason to "keep that deer safe."

Daniel shoveled beneath the eggs, breaking one accidentally. He decided to scrambled them. Soon he was scooping them onto their plates. Elda added toast and they sat down to eat.

"Gran'mutha, ever seen that flag ovah tother side o'the valley... way up on a ledge. White flag?"

Taking a bite of toast, she nodded. "Robichaud's flag. Been theya years. Don't suppose it's the same flag all the time. They must change it. But I caunt 'memba a time it waunt theya.... Maybe when I was a girl. No, I

think even then. Cuss that family waunt theya so long as others around....
people whose ancestors settled the place. French, y'know."

"So?"

"Used to be a big difference—not so much now. Lots of bigotry
against the French. People used make jokes, I spect. Maybe you heard
'em." She shied her small smile at him.

Daniel reached for his juice. He could see her relaxing. "That have
anathin t'do with the flag, you think?"

"I would." She stopped as though considering. "That flag... always
made me feel...." She shook her head. "Something."

He waited for her response, wondering if she was really thinking of
this for the first time. Maybe it was something people were just used to.
Maybe they don't even see the flag anymore. Would he be like that one
day? Would the flag just stop impressing him with its spirit of.... He said it
aloud: "Victory? Defeat?"

"That's it. Victory."

"Like they came here from away, and it took 'em so long,
struggling, but they made it."

So'll you, she thought. But she said, "I don't think—when they first
put it up theya, they still had a way t'go. And, it's not like it's ovah yet.
They're still working on it. Those ah Robbie Robichaud's boys cutting up on
that stumpage up theya on Parsons Knoll above us, east. They got trailers
on Robbie's land, so one of them prob'ly put it up on the ledge."

"We saw 'em cutting up theya last week, Cindabilla'n me." He
didn't say Cindabilla had gone up there to smoke reefer, that he went with
her to try talking her out of it. He was going to have to give up that girl.
But how could he? It wasn't like she was just anybody.

He finished his eggs and toast. Grandmother had got up to take the
kettle off the woodstove. He took the plates to the sink and went to the
refrigerator for more orange juice. He sat at the table again and began idly
brushing crumbs on the checkered oilcloth into a little pile. Grandmother
had come back with her steaming cup. The smell of instant coffee perked
them both up. He tried not to be obvious about it but he had been watching
her since she came in the door. At the moment it appeared she was looking
off in the direction of the coat rack, but he had the feeling that she watched
him, carefully, on the sly of her vision. Balder had described macular
degeneration to him.

"Gran'mutha," he began. "What is legally blind?" There. It was out
in the open now.

She made an involuntary movement and was quiet again, looking quickly away. "Is that what Balda said?" She still had not got used to saying, "your father."

Daniel nodded, then wondered if she caught it, so he said, "Yes."

"Well for me it means seeing light and shapes. And having to pay attention. Details sometimes get away. A stump might be a rock'n vice versa. I look at you and see maybe a—something—your head, maybe no face."

Just talking she had given him a lot. And he understood a little better what she was up against. Daniel flattened the tiny pile of crumbs with his palm still damp from holding the juice glass. He scraped them up again with his thumbnail, saying, "There's a blank spot in the middle—most every where y'turn?"

"Yuht!" She came down quick on that affirmative, swung it straightahead like a sword.

There was silence in the room. Then to dispel it they spoke each at the same time. Together they stopped but each began again. Grinning she said, "You go first."

"I was just gont say... I could tell you what things look like... when we're in the barn. Like, if a deer's got something wrong with its eye —I could describe it."

Elda hesitated. Carefully, her instinct being to repulse this kind advance. Yet, hearing the earnest spirit of his voice and for the first time recognizing something of Balder's childhood speech, she delayed her parry. Some sacrifice was called for. Somehow, Daniel must have his caring acknowledged, not be treated as though he had just come in off the road. Why was everything so difficult? Lord all these nagging concerns. But he's not from away. He's from here, from her. How could she ever find anything genuine—if she did not take Daniel's offer seriously?

Hers was an inward sigh. She said, "Well... sounds like a good plan. That might help. Yes."

"Good. What was that you stotted telling me?"

"Which?"

"You stotted telling me?..."

"Oh. Most forgot! Theya's something we could do—maybe this spring." She had intended saying something *you* could do, but now Elda could maybe see herself working with Daniel—if the impulse did not wear itself away in regret when the weather changed.

"You saw those loons last year? They been having a hard time lately, what with more people coming, new houses'n all. Gott'im's busier, ponds is more crowded. Something's wrong with their eggs, too. They're not sturdy. Loons need help raising theya young. We could build floating nests for 'em." She waited for some hint of interest, turning the coffee cup around in her hands.

"Cool," he said. "How?"

"With narrow logs, little longer'n pulp logs, to make a square frame. Then we put screen on the bottom, fill it with dirt, leaves, weeds, twigs, stuff. Then anchor it in a cove'n leave some slack in the line in case of changing watah levels. Did you know they hardly walk on land? Caunt get away from predators except by deep diving."

He nodded. "Fatha told me theya bones are solid. Making 'em good divers. Maybe wintah vacation we could build one in the shed."

Elda could not catch the light of interest in his eyes, but speed and lift in his voice were unmistakable. She smiled and, for an instant, he saw her white wrinkly face glow transparently. She finished her coffee and stood. The kitchen was cooling a bit. Should put on more wood. Daniel had come out of his chair too and for a moment they moved as one toward the wood box.

Shyly smiling, she turned aside, letting him tend to the fire. "Be back in a minute'n we can go out to the barn." She scuffed into the next room and began climbing the stairs to the bathroom, too embarrassed to use the one off the kitchen.

But, an adjustment had been made in the relationship. Elda would continue in her little hesitancies, her stumblings; never quite getting the hang of dealing with Daniel... or anyone. Despite her self-consciousness she carried on, more or less attentive to others, even sometimes deeply enjoying their company. With her it was continually like a Maine winter evolving toward spring: stop and start, surge and sink. One day budding, the next wintry again. The spring will come someday. And summer, full of fruit. But not for Elda. *Not*, she thought.

She took the stairs slowly, wondering over Daniel. Where did this boy come from? How had this happen to them, Balder and her? It would not occur her that Daniel was the result of seed spilled passionately over the ready walls of the womb. She would not try to answer the question posed by her wonderment. No answer would be worthy enough, nor contain the whole story.

This was rare. A weeknight when both Rhetta and Lyman Bearce were home. Both occupants were descended from Gottheim area lumber barons, tough ambitious men who had come into Gottheim with axes, crosscut saws and portable mills; men who knew how to organize and put people to work. Rhetta and Lyman each exhibited the toughness and organization of this joint heritage. They were fearless, stubborn, aggressive in what interested them. And each could be belligerent or beneficent in pursuit of some goal. For them to be at cross purposes was something anyone in Gottheim would pay to see. Now that the kids were gone to America's corners, fierce displays of puffed feathers, of beaks and talons, might electrify the house for hours, even days. Hissing and snapping and separate beds were not uncommon when Bearces were in their frays.

On the north side of the house, pine woods sent near a bristling wedge. Lately, a pair of great horned owls cohabited there. Although sharing the territorial woods, the owls lived separate lives much of the year, but occasionally meeting in provoked attack. The female is notorious in Gottheim, having made the front page of the weekly with her predatory escapades of the previous spring when domestic animals and pets had come under her taloned onslaught. Asa Bartlett still had a scar on his temple to prove the formidable character of this owl. And Elda Simon had mended its wings twice—for assault by bullet and birdshot. But now it was mid-January, and the strange chemistry of creaturely sexuality had begun making inroads. At night the two Bearces, lying awake in separate rooms over some spat, could hear the gutturals of predators in love.

Week nights were busy nights for Bearces. Lyman had selectmen's meetings, the Knights of Pythias, Academy Board of Trustees, Rotary and Maine Timber Growers, and others all spread out over the course of a month. Sometimes he would attend the historical society or other meetings, if the speakers were addressing something in which he had a direct interest. Rhetta worked on a number of committees, besides the Planning Board. She was interested in Chamber of Commerce, the Birches Cemetery Association, legion auxiliary, the library, historic preservation, etc., many included meetings of a seasonal nature. An evening home together was rare, and the nature of these found times was seldom predictable. The pair could be as sociable and affectionate as a couple of old lions greeting one another after a dry season apart; or, as on this night, going at each other like mated great horns in July.

They were in the corner (master) bedroom which, in daylight in summer, overlooked on one side a long curve of the drive with its flowering rhododendron planted twenty-five years before by Rhetta's own hand. Outside tonight starlight and moonglow shown coldly on snow but, inside, Bearces were arguing and heedless of moon and snow. Rhetta stood tall and formidable in a silk wrapper, her hair half in curlers and face scrubbed of makeup. Eyes sparkling and jowls trembling, she had come out of the bath to continue "this discussion" as Lyman tried to sneak in and retrieve clean nightclothes. She faced him squarely across the great fourposter, telling him what she thought he owed the workers of the Bearce family's mills. As yet, no one in town understood why Theodora Prescott had raised the wages of her own furniture mill. As she spoke, Mrs. Bearce emphasized each point with a jab of her hair brush in his direction.

But white-bearded Bearce, almost as tall and somewhat portly, was not going to stand meekly under her know-so-much manner. There was no way he would agree to this. He stood coldly eyeing her, reflecting back her fire off his steely white front; as though he were a block of ice reflecting a blaze, unaffected by its heat. He let his partner sputter herself out, then said was cool precision, "Owe? Talk about owing.... Look what the town, hell, the whole region owes Bearce's. You know so much about heritage, New England heritage. What would it be without New England mills? 'N' waya would the mills be without a surer hand to set a solid economic strategy? We provided culture a'plenty, have these mills, fah the people of Gott'im. You, an arbiter of culture, ought to know this. Any money made on checking wage escalation has gone back into the community. You know it. I know it."

She switched tone and tactics on him, adopting his coldness. "Do I?" She would not let him appear the cool client, the reasonable one trying to undercut a hysterical opponent with calm logic. She swept the room with her hand. "Does the rest of the community live like this? Doesn't it occur to you that working people might be trusted to spend theya own earnings, and determine its use and benefit to the community?"

"Doaw. Does not!" He thrust his big hands into his pockets and leaned forward, hooting. "What would they do with it?—drink it away. They'd come to work worse'n they do now. Workmen's comp'd go up. Think of the time Octavius Peabody came in pissed'n got sliced up good'n propa? *We* end up paying fah that, Rhetta."

"Lyman Bearce, they're not all like that! You know it."

"Do I." This was a mockery of her choice response, and his eye upon her was cold.

Mrs. Bearce thought of all the hard-working mill wives she had known over the years; women who had come into the smaller wood-turning mills in order to eke out their husbands' wages. Some decades gone, while traveling elsewhere in the country, Rhetta found that blue-collar mothers did not work much outside the home, as traditionally they did in Maine. Now she wondered if the setting of wages occurred elsewhere in the state. Were workers who quit a mill elsewhere punished with the blackball? In any case, she could not well answer his accusations about local drunkenness. Alcoholism seemed endemic. The police log published in *The Voter* yielded proof every week of Lyman's accusations. There was so much abuse on these back roads. She bit her lip and dropped her gaze in the face of his challenge.

Her honesty quelled his distemper. The fragrance of victory almost brought a smile to Lyman's lips. Quiet came into the room, and he saw that the old girl was his.

Into the silence came the staccato *hoo-oo*ing of the great horned owl, muted by the pine woods and panes of glass. The female responded to the male's more distant, deeper and prolonged, call. The call spoke of cold and the dark, of thick pine boughs. Of January snow, of ice and sleet and moon. Of silver light on ponds. The calls echoed the fierce ardor of great owls. Those brutal birds were suited to the rigors of winter mating, laying and brooding. Fearless they were, building not their own nests but usurping the large nests of squirrels, raptors, even of the eagles themselves.

"Hear those owls?" asked Lyman Bearce in a low voice. He had stepped to the window, head cocked to receive the eerie cries. He reached to turn off the lamp by the bed. As a young man set over a logging crew in the deep woods, Bearce had seen such a pair. In response to her mate's song, and gift of a mouse, the large female had lowered herself urgently, leaning forward on the branch before the smaller male. Spreading her tail feathers, like a cooped fowl, in ardor she humiliated her dignity. To the young Bearce, it had appeared an act undignified to both partners: a joint bundle of feathers rhythmically humping, fulfilling the ecstatic urgency of instinct. Later had come the long cold nights of patient watchfulness, the sexual ardor of both replaced by the vigilance of brooding and nurture.

He said, "I read in a book once.... The author called them saturnine, savage...." He said this softly, as a tentative offering from Lyman to Rhetta.

"I'm not surprised." She said it low. "They seem—like that." She had been retreating to the bathroom to finish rolling her hair for the night, but something in Bearce's manner made her stop. She had long trained herself to stand and reach for any straight drop of Bearce's honey. It was rare enough, but—the old woodsman could still drop sweet when he wanted. Silently she moved around the fourposter and came to his side, listening to the owls. Their shoulders touched, his arm went around her broad hips. They might listen at the window awhile, they could end up listening from the big bed.

Hannah Sessions was Cindabilla's grandmother and she was slowly losing her mind. Like the mountains around her farm—slowly shedding grains of granite, eroding away in streams and creating sandbars along the shoreline of the pond—Hannah Sessions' mind was losing vital grains of thought. In this simple process of weathering, concepts sometimes came in pieces triggered by the spoken phrases of others. Words might elude her, faces appear and pass but their names just don't come.

Outside Hannah's decaying old cape, the young apple trees she planted three springs ago were being secretly girdled by mice. Mice passed one another on tiny trails beneath the snow, nuzzling furred sides with sensitive whiskers as if to say, *food's up ahead*. All but two of the little trees in the orchard would dry up and pass away this coming summer because Hannah forgot her precautions to prevent winter's rodents from nibbling strips of bark around the circumference of each stripling. Outer bark, succulent inner bark, including the precious living cambia, would all be eaten away. Round and round the mice were eating. Fattening beneath safe snow cover, while great storms came down over Jasper, roaring. All this circular dining would forever break the finely tuned communication between hidden nourishing roots and the slender canopy of its outer visible form.

Sometimes Daniel Twitchell actually worries: How do all the creatures make it through winter? Daniel himself is a somewhat unusual creature, a worried and helpful teenager. Or is that so unusual? He grew up in a household slowly rendered dysfunctional by alcohol. There is hope now that the situation has altered—just maybe.... Yet Daniel has not altered with it. He is still fraught with the urge to watch over situations, alert to cues of developing extremes. It's part of his attraction to Cindabilla, part of the reason his fellow teenage traveler is dear to him. Cindabilla lives with her grandmother and her Uncle Ferddy and his girlfriend, Babette. Sometimes Cindabilla's messed up mother stays with them in the sway-backed cape of the ruined farm.

At a far end of the property, in a nook between mountains, a bunch of beavers live in a bog. They have a great stout dam and a winter's lodge full of edible trees. There they spend the season in an upper chamber, munching away on popple. During their first summer as friends, Daniel and Cindabilla spent some time there watching the critters on the sly. This stealthy exercise taught them patience and how to stay awake in trees and avoid falling into the pool. The beavers worked incessantly, never stopping except to eat and sleep. Once Daniel and Cinda saw the dam break and the water drop. Immediately the huge rodents waded in and swam over to repair it. "Like little buck-toothed Mainers," whispered Daniel to her. She said, "They waddle'n flap like um, too."

Daniel forgets those summer evenings when worrying how creatures will make it through winter. He thinks instead of the short January afternoon spent in the woods with Elda Simon, sawing down cedars for deer. Watching the trees fall he thought that just chopping them down would be enough to help deer survive, but Grandmother, having lugged up a snow shovel, busied herself clearing a path to the deer yard several rods away. There the herd had trodden and fouled the yard and were ragged, sickly and thin. When he asked why the shovel, she replied, "Deah's so stupid, they starve without an easy way out the yard."

"Caunt they just look over here, see the cedar'n come get it?" Can they be so dumb as to starve with food only a hundred feet away!

But, shoveling, Elda just shook her head.

Sitting in the hayloft with Cindabilla, Daniel thinks of this. Uncle Ferddy's wolf hybrid, named Demon, lies at their feet. It's late afternoon and dark out. The dim barn beneath them is lit with a few pathetic hanging bulbs. Looking down they can see the breath of cows filling their stalls with vapor. Half wolf, half dog, Demon stares at the cattle, speculatively.

The two adolescents sit on bales of hay, glancing at Daniel's history notes and trying not to move around. You can ruin good hay by playing on it, roughhousing; but it hurts nothing to sit quietly leaning back against the bales, smelling the fragrance and warmth of summer in the bundles. Cindabilla has known forever that being careless with the bales can ruin fodder. Even so, to Daniel's disgust, she is lighting up more reefer. Calmly, he mentions again that this is a lame thing to do in a barn full of hay. She responds by calling him names beginning with the letter *w* and prefixed with the word worry: worry-wart, worry-wasp, worry-walrus, worry-wrapping— paper. The cleverness of this cracks her up.

She falls off the bales giggling, clutching the burning joint while cupping it protectively in her palm. The boy, in his leather jacket and stocking cap, grabs the notebook they were holding between them. Water sloshes out of the bucket by his foot, the bucket he made her bring up in case of fire. He notes to himself that the sweet-burning smell of the drug is like burning hay. Watching her pull straws from her ginger ponytail, he considers that the drug heightens her sense of humor. He has seen this level of idiocy before—in his own home in Phoenix.

It was a sight, the combination of reefer and alcohol at those parties Petey and Mother used to throw. Daniel cannot square the inconsistency of Cinda's marijuana use with her urge to break coffee-brandy bottles over Uncle Ferddy's drunken head. He'd like to drop her stash into the bucket. Everything they've been reading about land speculators of the previous century is hilarious to her, but when he asks what's funny she stops laughing, thinks a moment, says she can't remember, and starts laughing again.

Ferddy's wolf hybrid continues staring at the cattle below. Two are black calves, born last spring but still unsold, though now stolid and strong.

Also among the herd are two old cows that don't look particularly healthy to Daniel. He sees that Demon's gaze goes most often to them.

Demon is Uncle Ferddy's idea of a pet... bought last summer after Cindabilla accidentally shot him in the rear. No one could prove she shot him, but Uncle Ferddy knows. He enjoys the idea of Demon insuring that nothing like that ever happens again. For insurance of her own, Cindabilla has taken time and the skim of farm produce and slaughter—on the sly—to befriend Demon. Now it's a tossup whose "dog" it is.

Of course this demon dog makes Daniel uneasy. The boy likes the idea of *wolf*—wild, pack-living creatures living on the fringe of things. They are hunters, hierarchical, howlers, mysterious, untamed. He likes the idea of *dog*—people-specific, family friend, tame, semi-trained, rascally, lovable. Two good concepts, domestic and wild. Why try to splice them and throw it all out of balance? What makes him extra uneasy is an Uncle Ferddy owning one. The experiment with these natures has brought Demon willy-nilly into existence—nothing you can do about it now—but what you don't want is this "pet" in the hands of a man with no grip on the reality of warped instincts. It's more like vice versa, so don't go letting him own and operate one.

"Look at'im," whispers Cindabilla, seeing Demon so attentive. "Ferddy prides himself on 'em—drunken ol'Babette-beater. Thinks he can identify with him. No way! It don't do Demon justice!"

"Maybe he's *just* like him."

"No way. Is not."

"Is too."

"Is not."

Daniel stares at her sucking on the reefer.

She says, "Is not."

"Is."

"Snot!" The girl rolls away, giggling. Daniel grabs the notebook again.

He says, "Don't choo think Demon misses the pack?"

"Who'd you think we ah—Gram, Ferddy, Aunt Nellie, Babs'n me?"

"Who's the lead wolf, then?"

"It sure ain't Babette. Ferddy's reduced her to blubber. Once Gram was lead, but now it's me'n Uncle Drunkman."

"Which means Demon submits to neither. Wouldn't want a baby around him. How you keep chickens'n pigs I d'know."

"He did get over the fence once. Ate a Piglet."

Daniel is getting nowhere with his notes on land control in Maine. The focus in history this grading period is regional. For a while he shuts up, letting his eyes scan the page, leaving Cindabilla to her pot-induced giggling.

"Evah notice," he says at last. "Maine's map is different than other New England states? Look." He has flipped to his laminated map of the region in the back of the notebook. He shows her. "No roads up theya. No towns, anathin."

Her eyes tearing from the smoke, she squints at it in the bad light. "S'all woods up theya."

"But how'd it happen." Should he even bother trying to get her involved?

"Papah companies."

"'N' how'd *they* get that land?"

"Won it in the lottery."

"Mrs. Mason says it's a result of state legislators being land'n railroad owners in the last century. They made laws to suit, paid hardly any taxes."

"Like my answer betta."

"Guess what, you're partly right. Theya *was* a lottery fah land in Maine. Didn't work, though. Before the land grab the Massachusetts legislature tried everything to get rid of land."

"Now people'd *kill* fah some. Fact, somebody did, last year."

Daniel lets it pass as reefer imaginings. "What about Gram's land, though. She'd get rich selling to developers."

"Don't think Ferddy hadn't thought of it. Gram wouldn't hear of it."

There is silence. Cindabilla drops the last of her reefer roach, sizzling, into the bucket. She reaches out to tickle Demon's nose with a piece of straw. He sneezes and licks his chops. The girl giggles. "What was we saying?"

"About Gram not letting Ferddy sell off."

"Oh.... Time'll come, though, she caunt do anathin 'bout it. You said something about land grabbing?—he's one t'do it."

"What would happen t'you then?"

"Whad y'mean?" She is stroking Demon's coarse hair.

"Won't he kick you out—if Gram's not... quite there?"

Her hands stop stroking and she glances quizzically at Daniel. "Why would he do that?"

He looks at her wide soft eyes. Her dilated pupils. Cindabilla is stoned.

"He shrugs. "Ferddy don't exactly *like* you."

"What's that got do with it? He's my Uncle. Might kill me, but he'd never kick me out."

Right, thinks Daniel remembering the wolf pack. A wolf might dominate and chastise, but would it kick another wolf out of the pack? He has never studied wolves but, one day, he might get the chance.

Loki

When it came time to hear of it, Chrischana would decide that her intuitive procrastination had been a good thing: Petey Prince was never going to make it. He *would* come back and start pounding on her again: he would he would he would.

Petey Prince found his way back to alcohol in Gottheim, falling in with Ferdinand Sessions and Alvin Robichaud. Of late, when it came to socializing, the Robichaud twins were pretty much split up and gone their separate ways. What the hell, thought Alvin, it was January and you could only stay sober as long as the saw was in your hands. Or, according to Petey, while in the fucking paper mill. He thought he had a better excuse than whatever Ferddy's was (Ferddy didn't need one), or Alvin's. But then, he did not know about the tattered flag flying on the cold ledge above Robichaud's, or that Alvin could not get it out of his mind. Peter could not get his wife to come back, his counselor Hermann Gottesman was on his case to think about being useful to others and the God-awful paper mill was getting to him. Get out the violins, get out the sombreros.

Evidently he had forgotten that alcohol made him insane. That it made him hate her with pretended impunity.

I'm a changed man, he thought sentimentally. "You shouldn't be doing that," Peter said to Ferddy after the other slugged Babette on that blistering January night. Babette had run into the bathroom and locked the door.

"Shit," said Ferddy. "I'll bust you instead, flatlanda!"

The words they spoke resembled mere sounds, muddled and slurry like the sodden brains in their heads. Sitting at the kitchen table beneath a single glaring bulb, gentle Alvin looked on, slobber-eyed but pitying, as the brawl erupted in Hannah Sessions' kitchen. She came clumping down from upstairs to see what the matter was. Hannah had pretty much kept her nose out of her son's petulant brawls, but now that she was losing her mind she would come clumping down, her long gray hair wild and nightgown flapping... and she always misunderstood. Tonight she thought Ferddy was her long dead husband, Brazelia, horsing around with his brothers, Barbour and Absalom. Brazelia was deceased fifteen years, and Barbour and Absalom never came around anymore.

"Brazelia! You boys just watch the crock'ry, heah?" She croaked this and Petey turned to see what was talking. Ferddy cracked him a good one—a perfect sucker punch that sent them both sprawling. Together in a clatter of chairs they fell back against the porcelain sink, ripping its curtain and exposing the plumbing, a couple cans of scouring powder that had been used up a decade ago, and two cases of empties covered in dust. "Fucking asshole," Ferddy slurred, trying to pull himself up by the curtain, which tore the rest of the way. He hit his head against the box of empties, cursing. As Petey rolled away with his hand to his eye, Ferddy lay there, uttering unintelligible threats.

Sitting there still, Alvin thought he heard the word *Demon*, and decided it was time to go back to Emma. He slipped out the gable end door into the brutal wind, wondering if his pickup would start.

The gale was roaring through the valley, waking his slobber eyes. "Holy fucking funeral march!" He pulled the door of his truck closed after him, fumbling for the keys.

"Keys keys, fucking keys...." He said it under his out-pouring breath, searching one pocket after another. He felt the ignition with his finger, searched his pockets again. The wind blew a spray of snow from the field across the hood. Again he searched his pockets, mumbling. "Just lay down a minute," he said, resting his head on the seat. "Find the keys in a minute...."

The door of the Cape Cod house slammed, but Alvin never heard it.

Petey Prince left the sagging snow-caked house, hurrying to his own pickup parked behind Alvin's in the dooryard. For an instant he wondered why Alvin's truck was still here. Then, forgetting that Babette was holed up in there, he thought maybe the logger had gone to the can instead of slipping out the door as he had first supposed.

Well leave 'em to the madhouse, then, he thought. *Jeezus Crowbar!* Where'd this fucked up wind come from! He hurried to close the door and turn the key in the ignition, gunning the engine. For a minute he sat there, trying to clear his head, staring out at Jasper Mountain where it blocked the stars and showed itself faintly white. The wind had chilled and waked him. Now it buffeted, rattling the truck. Jeezus, I'm drunk. Got to go see what's his name, the big man in Jericho. Whad'll I do?—can't live with drinking, can't live without it. Why did that bitch leave me? Are you gonna start blaming her again? She did nothing but live right. God help me.... Lord Jesus, I'm fucked up again!

Peter threw the truck in reverse and turned the wheel, backing. At first he did not see the wolf-hybrid come bounding around the corner through blinding snow. Snarling and snapping, it charged the truck. Peter looked out the window at the pale working jaws. Demon leaped onto the hood, growling, challenging him through the glass. The screaming wind gusted, as the dog's claws scraped the hood and frosty glass. Peter put the pedal to the floor, flew a dozen yards and stomped the brakes. Demon kept going and hit the lane, but he scrambled up on the gritty ice. Peter turn the wheel and drove across the snowy yard and into the road. Off his shoulder he saw the demon dog, hurtling through the snow fields to intercept him. But the pickup was faster, leaving the wolf loping behind. Peter Prince drove off, with a glance in the rearview mirror. The black speck that was Demon moved behind in the shimmery snow-gusting night.

Cindabilla went to school in a daze, seeing little, hearing nothing. *Why couldn't it o'been Uncle Ferddy? Should'o'been a skier, at least, why?"*

At dinnertime, Daniel noticed her silence. The cafeteria hustle and clatter was a sea of sound in which they floated together isolated, as the lunch line snaked along. *What's the matter, Cindabilla?* He wanted to ask.

Then, finding conscious comfort in his attentive silence, at last she murmured, "Why'd it have t'be Alvin?" Her pale eyes turned toward him, questioning, before turning away again.

"Why? What happened?"

But she only stared past him, silent again.

After school he went as usual to *The Voter* office to start sweeping the floor. Mr. Nutting in his green visor stooped over the stone, setting type for the week's edition.

Daniel scanned the backward letters, reading the lead upside down.

An area logger was found frozen in his pickup truck, Monday. Hannah Sessions' teenage granddaughter discovered the body before school, outside her house. Alvin Robichaud was thought to have lost consciousness in his vehicle, and it is believed that alcohol played a role in the ....

Today was Monday. Daniel looked away.

"Loki's beating one of his children." Small explosions of boiling pitch popped onto the hearthstone. Watching the fire crackle, Gloria Fay said it dreamily. She sighed.

"Who's Loki?" asked Theodora Prescott, Gloria's future sister-in-law. "And why would he beat his children?"

Staring into the fire, Gloria made no answer. Her irritated brother James answered for her. "Loki is one of her heathen gods." Lounging beside Theo, he pursed his lips and cocked his gaze toward the ceiling.

From a comfortable chair Gloria looked over at the flames reflected in his glasses. The niche in which they sat, above the Great Room, was glowing and shadowed by the play of firelight from the hearth. It was intimate space with its own small fireplace. She said tartly, "He's not my God. He, big brother, is the Norse counterpart of your Lucifer. I just happen to enjoy reading about the gods—Teutonic or otherwise. Is that so bad? I find it intellectually stimulating." Again she turned her eyes toward the living flames.

The nook, in which they relaxed after dinner so intimately, was dark. The diaphanous blaze across from them was set in the midst of weeping stonework. It gave the setting a somber medieval cast.

Idly pinpointing the source of James's irritation, Gloria became aware that she had been ignoring his fiancée again. "I'm sorry, Theo," she said. "What would you like to know about 'my' Loki?" She shot James another glance.

Theo understood that she lacked Gloria's approval and could never be admired by her. She felt, even while striving for the other's respect, that she was merely tolerated, the object of recollected kindness. Almost in her mid-thirties and a few years older than her betrothed, Theo had learned that she was never going to be the wise, poised, cool, undisturbed and dignified thing that she longed to be. She wished only that she did not care. If only she might stop trying to work herself into some elusive but desired form. She said, "Well, I just wondered why he would beat his children, but, if he's a devil, I guess that explains it."

Golden Gloria hid her impatience behind a smile. "It's part of the story of Loki the Mischievous. Whenever the fire crackled, old wives would say Loki was beating his children."

Theo smiled back, her prominent teeth and receding chin tucked beneath her bird-like nose. Dainty and refined in posture and bearing, she was dressed with taste and care. Theo often reminded James of fragile spring flowers. It helped that she worshiped him, made him feel admirable and wise.

"We can learn a lot from the tales of old gods and goddesses," argued Gloria. She was thinking of Balder the Radiant, who was destroyed by the treachery of Loki. In the tale, this active jealous malice became Loki's undoing, for the gods could never forgive Balder's loss. Gloria continued. "Loki married Glut, whose name meant glow. She gave birth to two children, Ember and Ash, who were regularly beaten by Loki. Apparently Loki was the god of fire who corrupted himself for the sake of his own glee."

"Oh. I remember you saying once that these stories originated in Iceland? That makes sense because Iceland is built on fire? They'd just about have to have gods who could come from a volcanic region. We've all heard about that trench in the Atlantic terminating there —or something— right?"

"Yes, but they didn't know about that then," said Gloria. "It was just to show the dual nature of fire: They made Loki and had him turn bad."

"Before Christianity came along and made more sense to them," breezed James. Dryly he said, "Then later people from a totally unrelated and secularized culture would throw Christianity over for that senseless stuff again."

But Gloria was too tired and dreamy from a day on the slopes to snap at his bait. Let the little hot air balloon float itself to the ceiling on its little superior hot airs. No need to look, she could see the self-satisfied smile her wiry blond brother would wear. He was *sooo* good at what he did: He merely pointed at a piece of prime property, said the word *condominium*, and (with a maximum of grief from the planning board) a condominium would appear. He huffed and he puffed and all their strictures fell down. The huffing and puffing made him the butt of jokes, but Gloria noticed that he frequently got what he wanted. Harry Golding thought he was a gem of a salesman because James could sell off those condos and ski hauses before they were piled together. He was good at evoking them for prospective buyers. She knew she was no match for his rhetoric or insistence, yet she kept her own counsel, answering him back. But generally not out loud.

Even so they were close as siblings, if not so friendly of late. Staying together at their parents' condo, each worked toward a firm financial foothold in Gottheim, with a certain amount of recognition thrown in. It cast a necessary zest into their lives. They were earnest, hard-working, talented, and believed or at least tried to believe that these other things were subordinate to what was truly valuable: a basic underlying decency. Their closeness clued James Fay that Gloria persisted in thoughts of the mechanic, someone named Balder, long after denying interest in him. But she denied it because she was getting nowhere and thought it best to give up and move on. Or try to move on.

Gloria stared into the fire and thought of Loki plotting to use the god Balder's blind brother against him. Why does her Balder insist on traditional values and children? She has answered him back several times but he remains intractable to the point of seeming not to care if she wrecks her life on inconsequential trysts with others. Maybe these thoughts are worthless, but he certainly needs no help from Loki in plotting against himself. Does he feel the pain he should be going through? Every time she saw him he seemed as cheerful and unperturbed as the time before.... With absolutely no sign that he knew she has been to other beds.... That she was in no way, shape, or form true to his impossible conception of love.

But it wasn't like they had a commitment... yet what *was* it like? They had feelings... feelings that would grow stale and dissipate over time... if left unattended. She wanted to prevent this with a living arrangement. One that would safeguard her status and career. She must be adamant, true to herself. How could she compromise by joining with the man who found her dreams fantastic and futile. The man talked of living in what he called the real world, but his "real" looked like fantasy to her. Having adjourned to The Coffee Story after bumping into one another in the store, Balder had proceeded to fill her ears with plans to make *Simons Ledge* yield what he described as its wild "commercial" bounty. Mushrooms, roots, berries! If that wasn't fantastic and futile, what was? With humor she reminded him of the highly efficient network in place all over the globe which saw to it that more people were being fed than ever before. He had chuckled and said it was better for its people to be made out of what grows in Gottheim because that's where they live. Fantastic! "The place is made of them and they should be made of it. People here would be better off not being made out of Mexico or South America." She had laughed of course, asking if he planned to do without coffee. At least he enjoyed her wit.

But her dreams of a consulting career in Gottheim and the prospect of a beautiful new home for herself—he thought these indulgent. He did not say so or accuse her in any way, but his wisecracks showed plainly enough what he thought of any plan connected with the ski company. Did he think people had no business exercising talent, know-how, or capital? The social and psychological professional agreed that work in the service sector is *not* unhealthy or degrading. Providing work in Gottheim, clean, nontoxic, non-industrial work, was not something to be ashamed of. Gloria sat by the fire, meditating this. A sputter of sparks from the hearth scarcely roused her.

Vaguely disappointed, James saw that his sister would not be provoked into engaging him in religious debate. That extra cup of coffee at dinner had primed him to expound, but it would be no fun if she continued to slouch there gazing mindlessly at the fire. Its yellow gaze reflected from the dark pupils of her eyes but her expression was in no way kindled by it. The antique owl andirons, standing tall before the flames, showed fire in their yellow gaze. He had always admired those owls for the glow passing through their glass eyes.

He sighed. *Well, Theodora, it's you then.* He turned to the lady who made him feel wise. "I saw a bumper sticker that cracked me up today. 'Keep Maine Green,' it said: 'Shoot a developer.'" He laughed his popcorn laugh, a sputter of little explosions like the popping of corn. "It was on a brand new four-wheel-drive pickup, as shiny as the day it came off a lot—even with all the snow, sand and salt we've had. Like the guy had something to complain about.... That's the kind of guy I'd like to convert to our clusters. It's such a great concept, the cluster.... You won't be sorry you invested, Dory."

"I never could be sorry, James." She brightened at his attention, eager to please and be pleased. He had not needed to ask if she was interested in supporting his project. But she had another reason for investing, as well, something of which he had no inkling. The mountain was the real future of Gottheim these days: The woods could not last forever, she thought. She had reasoned it all out—forgetting her laughter of only weeks before when someone mentioned the decline of the woods. Gottheim Chair's own decline was derided among area business people and attributed to her mismanagement. In her low moments she had to agree with them. Then she came upon the verses of scripture that led her to believe her ineptitude was predestined by the sins of her ancestors. In spite of her fear of other mill owners' possible retaliation, Theo had raised employee wages. She shrank whenever she saw Lyman Bearce... which wasn't all that often now that she had changed churches, but he always stared at her keenly and did not speak if they happened to meet.

"Know what I've been thinking lately, James?... That Jasper Mountain coming into my life this way might be the signal for me to go ahead... with something I've been planning... ever since...." She did not finish the thought aloud. James already knew about the sins, but he *loved* her. She could not quite bring herself to confide these things to Gloria. Gloria was a flaming liberal, always championing the little people... but this she would like.

James leaned toward her intently and there was an eager interest visible just behind his fire-bright glasses. He felt sure she was about to do more.

Triumphantly, she burst, "I want to give Gottheim Chair to its employees!"

His gaze drifted away. He had to consider and turned back to the fire. Gloria sat up suddenly in her upholstered chair. This was just *too much* instability. She stared at the back of Theo's head in disbelief. What in the wild world was this woman onto now? At once Theo's harebrained idiocies became swiftly charged with import unseen until now. Everything she had ever said or done now gathered to itself presentiment. James turned just a bit, sending his sister a flickering gaze, a slight frown of warning.

But Theo saw the signal. Although she had perceived movement she did not see Gloria's expression. Yet, it was not necessary to see her fiancé's sister. From the changing expression of James's face, from the change perceived in Gloria's posture, a change of attitude was betrayed. Theodora waited anxiously for James to compose himself. He always did. He was wonderful at covering any disturbance, at changing an awkward situation with loving assurance. Swiftly and surely he would put her at ease with but a few words of comfort. He could coax both himself and her into comfortable compromise on an instant's notice.

But the expression of comfort does not come. James looks away. He stands quietly and walks to the fireplace, staring down. If only she could see through his back into his face.

His sister comes forward in her chair, with a look of disbelief ripening to scorn. Fidgeting, impatient, she bores a look into James's backside. Why doesn't he speak? Gentle the situation?

But James is staring down at a crusty dark char of wood, its undersides glowing. The fire needs fresh wood. Even the tall owls' eyes have stopped glowing.

A stack of birch and pine nearby suggests itself. He stoops to gather three sticks. Theo begins twisting her hands together. Now she laces and unlaces her fingers.

"Theo," says Fay. He lays a log with curly bark on the live coals. Quickly its curls catch. Flames roll themselves around the wood, a firm sure hand of fire. "Theo, you shouldn't do that to the legacy left you by your father."

His back toward her, he lets the statement hang in the air.

Now softly, "Think of it, Theo. The beautiful chair factory, maker of fine shaker-style furniture, your great-grandfather started it. Remember that heritage, how those elegant chairs furnished the finest resorts in New England and upstate New York. You can still find those chairs in the old resorts in the Berkshires and the Adirondacks. He was an upright man, beginning with the best motives: to make beautiful furniture that would last, chairs to hand down to one's descendents. There is no way you can even know if he was involved in—that... other business. No way at all. How would he feel, knowing you gave away what he worked so hard to achieve?"

Mute, a pathetic dejected look sank into Theo's features. The slight sagging of age, just beginning in her face, was hung with the sadness he kindled in her.

"Look at that factory now, Theo... what it's become in Vernon's hands, your hands... in this last generation of Phineas Prescott's descent. You two cousins have let the place deteriorate to the point of collapse. Your series of... erroneous investments... that elaborate generating system you bought.... These things have contributed to the factory's decline. What your workers need, if you want to help them, is a steady and knowledgeable hand at the helm. You can't just throw the place to them—to the winds."

Gloria has sunk back, resuming her lax self possession. Momently she feels sorry for Theo. But her gaze rests dreamily again in the fire as she contemplates the renewed images of her thoughts.

Turning from the hearth to his fiancée with a tentative look, softly he says, "You understand what I'm saying?"

With sad eyes she looks at him, her chin sunk into her neck. She bows her auburn head meekly before him, tears glistening, slowly shaking her head. "Oh James...."

Now he came to her. "Dory." It was tenderly said. His hands reaching for hers, he kneels on one knee. "Dory, don't worry. It's the last thing I want. Please. We'll work it out. Now that I see how real your concern is. A conscientious concern for your workers. We'll work something out—you, Vernon and me." He lifted her woebegone chin with two fingers, tilting it upward and catching her eye in a pleading look.

Hopeful eyes turned up to his. Things *will* be okay. James will bring her through. He had not left her comfortless, shut out. He was bringing her back with his great understanding.

She sat back, looking over at dreamy-eyed Gloria. James' sister glanced back an abstracted smile. Theo turned toward the fire again. The room was warm, but she shivered. Already, outside the lodge, January's cold had put on a sudden warming trend. But James had placed two more sticks, of pine, on the fire. He stood back, looking with disgust at pitch stuck to his hands. Flames took hold of the logs. Orange fire leapt up playing over the wood, strong. Soon they would sputter and pop, a tiny fireworks exploding in sparky showers. Loki, beating his children.

James drove Theo back into Gottheim, waiting to see her safely into the house on tree-shadowed Swann Street. He kissed her on the threshold, holding her some moments. Again he kissed her, saying good night as she stepped inside. He turned and walked into the surprising evening air. January had softened. A thaw was on. Snow beneath his boots in the drive had turned to slush and rivulets ran into the street. He loosened the buttons of his overcoat then surprised himself by taking it off. Think of it! Wasn't it just a day or two ago that one of those loggers he hired froze in his truck? Shy man. Quiet. Good worker.

Fay stamped the slush, salt and sand from his boots, and climbed into his gleaming BMW. The street lamp shown onto the dash as he flipped through his keys. He started the car and rolled down Swann Street. He now had his doubts about the best way to handle Theo's—idea. James always tried to be particular and conscientious. She should not be encouraged to do such a thing to herself. Gottheim Chair should be made a viable company or else sold for scrap. It had an expensive generating system, and a prime location on the highway between the resort and village. This incident had confirmed that Theo needed him desperately. She was fragile and screwy and lovely and loving, and he was completely happy in her. This would be a good Christian marriage. Theo would be a kind submissive wife. The Scripture and common sense would prevail in their union, and Theo would be safe knowing that he would look out for her interests.

... Even so, he wasn't quite comfortable. You had to look out for the one you loved, but you also had to be careful of that element of self-interest. *Always seem to have a problem with that.* It's tricky, trying to come along in the world. But it can be done, carefully and without corruption. His personal income was growing (unlike his sister's—who seemed content to bestow her professional energies for very little compensation). His fiscal equality with Theo will quiet his conscience. Then they will be one in every way: Theo Prescott will be Theo Fay. The date will be set. They will arrive in the same place at the same time.

The slushy turnings of Gottheim brought Fay to the highway. He turned north, heading for the mountain resort and his parent's condo which he currently shared with his sister. His own home at Mason's Mills would be ready by late spring, summer. If only Gloria would find what James had found. He worried about her, suspecting that she was becoming promiscuous (although she would never use that term). James could not believe that what she did with her own body didn't matter. That is a disastrous supposition, he thought, its potential great for harm. But if that fact eludes her (by some fantastic notion that evil can't happen to her), then the sheer *ugliness* of bedhopping should deter her. She has such a sense of beauty, of elegance and charm—of the fitness of things.... Why can't she see its application in this? She would never confess to anything specific, of course, but when she says things like "It's just sex, Jimmy," what can he think? As though intimacy were something to be used and carelessly tossed aside. He himself was looking forward to sex with Theo, but it will be a sacrament—as well as fulfilling and fun. He had succeeded in repressing the gift of God, and now he planned to enjoy it. *And I don't think Gloria is really enjoying herself. She seems downright miserable to me.*

Gloria sits on the sofa staring at the night-blackened glass of the living room windows. The lamp on a corner table shines, reflecting her back to herself off the otherwise darkened panes. She has flicked off the television following a report on a hideous new social disease. *Incurable.* One that has been haunting the homosexual community—but now they say it can be heterosexually transmitted. This mere information has evoked sudden panic and she cannot rest her mind on a thing without feeling the fear of this report. Her intrauterine device can prevent pregnancy, not disease. Gloria clutches at the arm of the sofa, picturing submicroscopic bodies busily infiltrating her cell surfaces... reducing... even destroying their capacity to produce antibodies. A tingling sensation sends ticklings through her arms. She sits momently paralyzed. Suddenly Gloria jumps up, rubbing her arms, runs to close the drapery. Stop that! She tells herself. You're being hysterical!

An abstracted glance into the parking lot below shows the high beams of her brother's BMW cutting through the pink glow of parking lot lights. Yanking the cord she closes the drapes and scampers across the room to shut off the light. For a moment she stands, torn between a desire for mute safety in his company and the dread of exposure. Yet at the sound of his step outside the door she flees to her room, swiftly shutting the door. She does not turn on the light but sits tensely, taut as a night before storm.

The night softens into a mild subtropical mood. Daytime brings a ripening through the mountains as the next night approaches, threatening to turn summer out of the atmosphere and down onto the slopes. Summer settles to warm the stiff limbs and thin twigs of the trees toward incipient budding. Thickets, soaking up moisture from this thaw, begin reddening. In the morning people will marvel, coming out to greet the next disturbing phase of their lives. They will wonder over the electrical storms that passed well before dawn. They will even take an acrid whiff of the passing age.

Not long after Alvin Robichaud froze to death in his pickup (his chainsaw and protective gear in the back), the weather turned wicked freakish. So warm is the night that a few vehicles loaded with teenagers head out toward Quaker Town in search of a place to party before the weather hardens up again. This is no Gott'im January, that's sure. A thaw is usual, but this one is balmy enough to make summer hearts kick and call. Tonight just has to turn out awesome!

The international cross-border tire dump of Ceylon Segar will make an exceptional party place. Imagine the freedom of bouncing—bombed, bonkers—off the top of some pile of rubber. No punishment!

Daniel and Cindabilla are crushed into the backseat of Jenna York's powder blue '74 Plymouth Volaré. Jenna worked evenings washing dishes at the Pennywhistle Pub in order to buy this car. She found it in a rural used-car lot in Copenhagen and fell for its soft color and low feminine lines. It had dingy white bucket seats so she scrubbed that vinyl for hours trying and failing to bring back its marshmallow whiteness. She plans to write Heloise for tips.

Some kids have already begun partying, tilting back bottles of Budweiser in the back of Buster Boone's pickup ahead of them. They dash empties against rocks along the edges of the wooded road, reveling in the crash of broken glass, yelling.

The vehicles turn off their headlights as they slide into the exit at the far end of the tire dump. Ceylon Segar's office is in a secondhand trailer, at the opposite end, beside the shed housing an old combination backhoe/bucket loader next a huge pile of sand. Their plan is to stay away from that end of the dump in case Mr. Segar (pronounced Cigar) shows up unannounced. Jenna pulls up behind Buster's beat-up Ford truck. The vehicles vomit kids in all directions. With exaggeration they try to keep the noise down as the teenagers regroup, some of them scattering over one immense pile of tires.

"Mr. Nutting, there's no way to contain sound in a group of hormone saturated bodies. There was more energy there than the headsaw at Pale's sawlog mill. Think what a carload of that kind of energy could accomplish if it wasn't intent on partying. Visualize it helping at a natural disaster. Picture 'em filling sandbags beside the flooding Mississippi." Eloise Patadoe will say these things later, when she tries to help reconstruct the night's events for the editor, corroborating what Daniel Twitchell himself will finally have an opportunity to report.

Their eyes adjust to the dark on the drive out to the multi-million tire dump. The air the adolescents tumble into is fresh and mild. Dampness comes on wings as it lifts the hair of these children of Gott'im. Their vehicles are parked in a puddled lane between two mountainous piles. Tires are scattered about on patches of rotten ice and in muddy puddles. The puddles throw back dim reflected light from a few tall lampposts. The atmosphere is so saturated that it too seems to give back the light. The tire mounds rise around the kids in massive smelly walls, some draped in melting snow. The dripping and dampness is over everything. These huge piles remind Daniel of the great wood-chip and pulp piles at Adirondack Paper where his father works. Except there the smell is of butchered wood overlaid with the toxic stench of pulp digesters.

The party split into three, more or less distinct, groups; with a quiet couple or two drifting away from the more social center. The groups drape themselves across lower tiers of one monstrous pile. Three conversations are brewing, three elements in the variegated dialogue abroad in the last decades of the 20th century since the first advent of Christ.

Weasel Whitman's group sits highest atop the pile, alternately smoking pot and downing Budweiser, searching for the best buzz; taking loose sometimes headlong leaps onto the bald castoffs of a gluttonous and spendthrift society. Tonight Weasel's group jokes loudly about dumb Frenchmen and, from time to time, calling out mockery on the second group below. This bunch sits a bit isolated on a lower tier, talking philosophically and pronouncing on the fate of the world: quieter and not quite solemnly led by Simon Perkins and John Brown. Daniel and Cindabilla are in the third group which stays more or less on the puddled ground talking of many things. The conversation ranges a wide and desultory course, including substance abuse, the size of the tire dump, the latest gossip, records, the new compact disks and VCRs, TV shows, *Flashdance*.

At some point the conversations of these three groups will converge and an angel of the air (now lying in a large mud puddle) will lift itself and hover in Snotty Cob's lurid face, grinning like hell. Eloise Patadoe will show up then, casting her unique brand of weirdness into the gathering of this strange January night.

Cindabilla opens her blue denim pouch to take out, with a flourish, her long-stemmed clay pipe. She packs it loosely with home-cured marijuana leaves from her stash. The pungent smell of burning grass mingles with the moist air and stink of vulcanized rubber. Some of the kids stare at the pipe in amazement. "Found this in the dump next the old cellah hole in the woods back o'the farm... when I was little. Really had'd dig, they picked ovah that dump s'much. Come direct from China... when it... fell through a crevice on tother side o'the world." She grins. "Worked its way down through earth'n come up tother side till it reached the ol'settlers' dump. Frost upheaves"

"You're full of it," says Daniel. "It was brought d'Portland by a sailing master and sold to a potato farmer."

"My version's betta. You want upgrade yours a li'l just take a puff." She points the stem of the pipe in his direction.

"No thanks. Don't need no head full o'dope to heighten my memory loss."

Jenna breaks in. "Daniel's right, Cindabilly. Weed expands your mind, and then, being too big fah your head, it drifts out your ear holes'n floats into the air." She points to the misty low skies. "Look. I can see your leaking mind drifting up theya now."

Involuntarily Cindabilla looks up, her eyes wide. She drops her gaze, glaring at the other girl. "*Shut* fuckin'up, Jenna!"

"But Cinda it happened to m'Uncle Benny when I was in seventh grade'n now look at'em! He's over to 'Gusty till his paranoia goes down." She says it all with a level face.

The other grimaces then grins back at them, turning her back to scramble up the pile.

Daniel looks admiration at the dark-haired Jenna, her mouth firm, attractive eyes full of humor. Suddenly he decides that her tactics are cruel and he follows Cindabilla up the pile until they are ten feet above the kids on the ground. Jenna takes a pull on her bottle of Bud and smiles up at them.

"My brains might be leaking," quips Cindabilla "but that stuff'll *pickle* your brains! Uncle Benny, Uncle Ferddy—what's the difference? Ain't neither what we gont be, right?" She rolls her eyes.

Jenna screeched. "No way! That slob-eyed brute! I'll never be that bad." Her tone is solid with confidence. "The way he goes bout it's all wrong. I just get t'the place waya I feel nice'n happy, then stop. Stop right theya. But not them." She throws her hand in the direction of Weasel Whitman's group. "Drunks like that keep going till they fall down. Look at them!"

They looked to see Weasel up there, tottering. Down he tumbles, like a bag of disjointed bones. He lies in a heap, one arm and one leg partly submerged in a mud puddle. Rolling over with a groan, he pushes himself back up, heedless of ridicule shouting, laughing, filling the air. The remaining boys up top follow with copycat tumbles. Then they all climb up the pile to their sixpacks again. They upend cans, wobble about, and start the process all over again.

Weasel wears an innocent blithered face. To Farty, Burpy and Snotty—his target audience—he yells out, "What's smotter'n a French kid in Headstart?"

No one is bothering to answer. Burpy is entertaining himself with the pastime that earned him his nickname. Farty upends his can. Snotty just grins and waits for Weasel to provide the answer.

"Two Frenchmen in med school!"

His friends laugh, sleepy-eyed, shaking their heads and having heard this one time too many. Snotty grins, waiting to hear another.

"What's scarier'n a grammy's ghost?"

Farty, Burpy and Snotty just grin.

"A naked dumb French grandmother's ghost!"

"No no," objects Farty. "A dumb French grammy ghost dressed t'look like Stephen King's grammy."

"What's cold'n harder'n skier's snot?" Weasel yells, looking around to make sure of his audience. He's got the attention of everyone, including the group to one side pronouncing on the fates of the world. Jigging on his tire, Weasel says, "A Frenchman taking a nap in his pickup—at 20 below— while his keys sit on the dashboard."

Silence. A movement of the skies draws off their attention. All look toward a faint flashing in the southwest. Remotely thunder sounds. Farty and Burpy decide to laugh. They laugh so hard... they roll into Weasel, taking him down with them. Snotty just grins and clambers down to where John Brown and Simon Perkins sit shaking their heads. The philosophers begin buzzing over Weasel's tasteless joke.

Nearer the ground, Cindabilla says, "His brain's so pickled he clean f'got his father married a Frenchwoman. We all got French in our families some waya. Weaz, you shithead, your own mother's French!"

Weasel is sprawled on the ground in a puddle, his eyes closed. It looks like he has stopped breathing. But he moans and turns onto his stomach, the side of his face all muddy and wet.

"In't dead yet, anaway," says Cindabilla, sucking on the narrow stem of her pipe. A little above, Daniel and Jenna watch its contents glow.

"Somebody ought do something bout these tires, says Jenna's boyfriend, Almon Ouellette. He's a gangling basketball player, and not generally known for environmental concern. He has been casting an astonished gaze across the piles ever since Jenna pulled her Volaré into the fantastic setting. Under the influence of Cindabilla's pot it feels like something out of the movies, some sort of science fiction or horror show.

Simon Perkins calls out from the little group above: "You know who's gont have do something bout it, don't choo? Us, that's who. Those friggin'yuppie baby boomers is making messes like this all over the planet— expecting *us* t'clean up after 'em!"

Cindabilla laughed her squeaky laugh. "Ceylon Cigar—a fuckin'baby boomer?"

Someone says, "What's a yuppie?"

"S'a inside out hippie give birth to a puppy."

Something comes around the base of the tire mountain, turning all eyes. The party freezes, staring at Eloise Patadoe with her horsey face and awkward walk. She is wearing a tie-dyed T-shirt and denim overalls.

"Well don't stop on my account. It's just me, an errant baby boomer... but you can treat me as a figment of your imagination, if you want."

Her sudden appearance, coupled with the faintly charged atmosphere, suits the fantastic frame of mind that has taken possession of them. Almon Ouellette stares at her like she is the Holy Mother come down to bid them good night.

She says, "Glad to see others are concerned to keep an eye out for Jasper Mary's treasure ground. Indian treasure *is* buried around here somewhere isn't it?"

"Shit," slurs Weasel from his puddle. "There's no treasure in this mud."

"Evidently," says Eloise, eyeing him pointedly.

Tentatively, a couple kids laugh. She is after all an adult. Sort of. And they *are* trespassing. Was the reminder about the treasure sarcasm?

Then, as if to emphasize her statement about him, Weasel retches. He wallows to his knees, vomiting.

Everyone groans. Jenna moves away.

Crossing the puddled lane, Eloise keeps walking, rounding the corner between monstrous piles and passing out of sight. They stare into the dim direction where she has vanished. "Was that f'real?" whispers Almon Ouellette.

"Real as the six fingers on the ends o'your hands," retorts Cindabilla. "Anybody else got puke?"

Laughter erupts through the group, breaking the spell.

Their former vigor dissipated, still Farty and Burpy recommence wobbling on tires. The party's interlude with Eloise has started the night in a new direction. Softly, a sort of depression settles. The couples who initially wandered away now drift back. Nothing much is said until Buster Boone notices that the gas cap on his beat-up pickup is missing. He circulates, asking who took it, but no one seems to know. A flash lights the distance, and a tiny rumble of thunder is heard. At last someone says, "What's that smell?" They all start sniffing the air. "It's ozone," says one. "Storm's coming."

Another says, "That's not ozone... it's..." (*sniff*) ... "rubber burning."

"Rubber burning?! You shittin'me!" exclaims Cindabilla.

"Tires is burning!" Yells Daniel.

But they stop where they stand, listening, as a distant bleating approaches, followed by the pounding of quick feet. Snotty rounds a corner of the great pile. "Help!" He cries. "Tires is burning! Whad'm I gont do?!"

Galvanized, the kids come to him, leaping across scattered tires, splashing through puddles and slipping on patches of ice. As Snotty turns, they follow him around the mountainous pile. Across the lane, ahead, an intermittent glow of fire shows through heavy black smoke billowing down toward them. Cascading, it mingles with the saturated air. The black breath of burning rubber and flakes of ash fill the lane, as panicky teenagers hurry toward the fire—then scatter back from the snapping, hissing and popping of the blaze.

John Brown, whose father owns an excavating business in Gottheim, scrambles off toward the opposite end of the dump were Ceylon Segar has his office and shed. Seeing his plan, Jenna York runs after, calling him as she heads to her car. The others stand back, talking at once or staring wild-eyed over their shoulders, everyone wondering what to do. As Jenna catches up, John Brown jumps into her car and they speed off. "Waya they going?" Someone wonders, and Daniel answers, "Prob'ly gone to call the fire department."

Everyone talking excitedly, the kids head back to the pickup. Someone says, "Snotty, what the hell'd you do?"

But weak and white Snotty merely blinks. He stammered, "S-simon said it was up t'us t'do something bout those tires. I done something!" He flings his arms up across his eyes. "The wrong thing!" Trembling, blubbering, he leans against the grill of Buster's pickup.

"Shit, Snotty," says Cinda, tempted to put her arm around him. But Snotty's name is apt, and she can't quite bring herself to do it.

"Whad Snotty do now?" It's a sleepy slurred voice. They look over to see Weasel still in the mud but now lolling against the tire pile.

"Nothing! Just set twelve million tires on fire."

"That what I smell?"

"Doaw. Just marijuana burning. Go back t'sleep."

Daniel steps away, listening for the distant wail of fire engines. The others grow silent as well, leaning toward the direction of Gottheim, hoping for the faint whoop of the volunteer call. But Weasel is saying, " We betta get in that pickup'n get.... Big trouble heah...." He continues lolling there, still unable to move.

But the sound…hooking the group's attention…is the sound of an engine approaching from the far end of the dump. Then through the dimness and murk a dark shape looms out, roaring. Its bucket high and full, the loader lumbers toward them. A cheer goes up. John Brown is coming with a load of sand, Segar's makeshift provision for such an emergency. Snotty lifts his ragged head, snuffling, wiping snot. He follows the hollering stampede toward the fire.

Waste is a terrible thing to mind.

Daniel Twitchell reported the evening's events to James Nutting as accurately as some veteran reporting an incident witnessed in war-torn Lebanon. Eloise Patadoe came in to tell what she had seen, for, after smelling the fire upon entering her goat pasture, she returned in time to watch John Brown manhandle burning tires with the backhoe and bucket loader. He had succeeded in isolating and smothering the fire that snotty had started with gasoline soaked rags from Buster Bean's pickup truck. No one left the scene until certain that the fire was out. By then a storm had blown in with its reassuring load of fitful rain. The teenagers crammed themselves back into the vehicles and departed for Gottheim. Eloise stayed behind long enough to satisfy herself that the fire was well and truly history.

Two days later, booted and bundled, the editor of *The Village Voter* stood on the dismal summit of Jasper Mountain with Julius Golding and his niece, Amanda. Having taken aerial shots from there for the paper, Nutting held the camera in his gloved hands. The scene, both above and below the summit, was like a living Hendrich canvas inspired by Norse mythology; as though an old storyteller of early Icelandic epic poetry had breathed upon the mountainous white landscape of Gottheim to create the mythic picture surrounding them. Fantastic black billows churned up out of the low place that had once been primeval woodland, since vanished along with its aboriginal personification. Ceylon Segar's own treasure, of steel belts and rubber, and oil from under the earth was on fire down there. Though they were hard at it, nothing could be done by the good people of Gottheim to stop that fire.

Tires. Tires made somewhere in the Midwest, down South and elsewhere in the world; tires driven on the nation-wide network of highways and streets until they were worthless: These tires poured particles and ash and smoke down on the village. These tires, aflame, were busy making their own weather.

James Nutting had spent most of the past 48 hours trying to unravel the story of how it happened. That the story had come to him was no surprise. He had been reporting and editorializing the ins and outs of this DEP sanctioned tire dump ever since Ceylon Segar opened it with no discernible plan for recycling the tires. Nutting thought now that the only question had been when. When would this story of disaster be written?

The three on a mountaintop were aware of the changing shape and drift of the fire cloud. According to weather and wind direction, it would change. Today the billowing black went up, gathering in an anvil-shape, trailing and falling upon the wind. The white landscape of the surrounding fair Meguntics contrasted sharply with this apocalyptic fall of cloud and ash. For the moment, the slopes and vicinity of Jasper were spared the indignities of this baptism of filth. But shortly, as Julius Golding was now thinking, the winds would swivel and return to lay the burden of this burning upon the white dome where he now stood. James Nutting said something to him and he turned, noting Amanda standing a little apart and gazing raptly off into the dark cloud. But, helpless, Golding would attend to Nutting instead. He would submit to the newsman's questions. He had a certain amount of respect for the village editor's background. Hadn't he been a journalist in Montréal—or was it Toronto?

Nutting raised his voice to repeat himself. "From I've managed to piece together, contrary to gossip and early reports, the fire was not set by kids. A witness, that goatherd in Quaker, came around last night and said she had seen the kids after the original fire was set by one of them. She watched them extinguish it, she says." Nutting looked squarely at the resort owner. "She also told me she saw lightning go down into the dump— several times—from the upper window of her goat barn. The dump itself was out of sight beyond the puckerbrush. But it was quite a display, according to her. She didn't think much beyond that until she woke in the morning to—this." His eyes swept the scene. "Now she's convinced those strokes brought on the disaster. According to the state fire marshal's office, ignition was scattered, not localized. One of my employees was there that night, a trustworthy young man. He says the first fire was started by a loose cannon but was dead out when they left. The three accounts agree. I'm just not prepared to blame the children—although at the moment the authorities seem to. They were very stupid: drinking, driving, trespassing."

He hesitated. "In print I will not be calling this a freak accident. That interpretation is sure to be put forth if the children are cleared. This state, powerful people in the state, have known about this accident-waiting-to-happen.... Allowances might be made if these tires had been used on Maine roads by our residents." Nutting continued looking at Golding's eagle-like face, the wind blowing stray wisps of dark hair from his hood. His voice fell a bit, beneath the wind. "Maybe we've all been less than good stewards."

He had spoken in earnest, trying to be heard above the breeze, but he said these things with immense sadness. Golding thought the voice of the editor made audible the look in Amanda's great eyes. He watched his niece as Nutting continued, "So here we are, Golding. Our readers are going to want to hear from you and your brother. What will this mean to Jasper Mountain? To the Town of Gottheim?" The pages of his little notebook rustled in the wind. Golding was an impeccable man and, to the recurring surprise of the editor who had interviewed him before, a somewhat diffident man. Yet at times Nutting judged him arrogant.

The resort owner lifted his gaze from Amanda. "I'll give you something, of course, but you may want to ask Amanda some questions. You may want to ask her entire class. They've all been working on the tire problem—at least until now."

Once more he looked out toward the great cloud of ash and smoke. "We've heard from those with condos or timeshares who have family members with respiratory problems. They'll stay away. We have our well-wishers who are taking a wait-and-see attitude. Some people are excited by this disaster, waiting for the inevitable wind shift like a pack of hyenas: people with no financial or emotional stake here. As for the town, you'll have to ask them, but it doesn't look good for our plans to extend the commercial center. I can hear our investors trying to tiptoe away. As for the jobs, we'll have to wait and see. We'll have our losses, no doubt, and must deal with them as best we can. I hope it won't last long."

He scribbled some, then Nutting said, "You still have other resorts, more recently acquired, some deals still pending. How will this affect that? Will you be able to fold your tents and quietly make your way west?" There was a dry challenge in his question.

Golding suppressed a grimace, his eyes still on the smoke churning, lifting across the valley. He made a brusque retort. "It's not that easy." He was not where he wanted to be at this moment. He would have preferred the solitude of the office, calls outgoing on business. What could he do? When he got down from this apocalyptic summit the Portland reporters would be waiting to aim their cameras at his face. He tried softening his answer. "I just don't know yet, Nutting. I've got business associates to talk with."

The editor rephrased the question, but Golding remained intractable. Nutting looked down at Amanda, who moved near her uncle to slip her hand in his. Her features were soft, framed with strands of escaping hair. "What do *you* think, young lady?" He left the question open for any type of answer she might feel led to give. She was part of the generation on which these things... were already falling.

Amanda hesitated, at last replying in her small voice, "I don't know."

"Are you worried?" He asked it gently.

"Yes."

"Shall I come to your class?"

"Ask my teacher please." She was not comfortable with the way the editor spoke to Uncle Julie.

"And who is your teacher?"

"Mrs. Carter."

He wrote it in his notebook. "Thank you." He closed the pad.

He turned to take one long look. *The scene is set.* It will stay this way a while. He greatly hoped that something could be done and he would spend his days trying to find out what, but his doubts were entrenched. He had discovered, when he began reporting on Ceylon Segar's dump, that no officials were working on contingencies.

They Suffer in Gottheim

On the first day of February, Chrischana finds herself crunching up Blackwell Mountain, toward the top of a knoll once owned by generations of Twitchells, now in her hands again—thanks to Balder. She has borrowed the man's snowshoes for the trek, helps herself along with old ski poles, and follows the long-tailed track laid by her youngest, Nathan, son of Peter Prince. Fueled by a burst of child's energy, Nathan has gone ahead on his pair of Balder's childhood snowshoes. At times she sees the track here, or spies his tousled head behind a stump. Or she might see an eye peeping at her around a beech or birch. He likes to pretend he's a hobbit, accustomed to vanishing when big folk are near.

They are on their way to see what winter has done to their camper, and to check on the equipment for sapping. When the weather changes they will commence making maple syrup. Today the air is crisp and bracing, full of winter's freshness and appeal. All is covered in cool, clear snow. The sheen of it comes through naked trees on the hillside both above and below. Here and there she has a view of Mount Howe with its white bristling slope across the valley. The smell in her nostrils is refreshing, so clean in contrast to the nasty air of late.

Her thoughts are full as she climbs the rise on the winding snowy road. The lower parts of the hill have been easy enough even for Nathan, a snow machine having been through to break the trail. But here and there she can see a dismal black underlayer, laid by Ceylon Segar's spewing tire fire. Successive layers of filth have been poured out on Gottheim and surrounding areas. But there is no mind for it, such as she has daily in the village. Her thoughts now are on other things, things she has some control over. Tire fires are the domain of others involved in its problems and resolution. She may think again of the fire, near the end of her climb, when woodland and Mount Howe no longer stand between her and views of that great plume, shedding its dark load in the distance. The descendant of pioneers thinks now of her syrup-making venture.

She pictures herself toward the middle or end of the month, possibly the beginning of the next, clanking along distributing galvanized buckets to outlying trees; lugging coils of tubing, snowshoeing from tree to tree; tapping, laying lines along the hillside to funnel all the incipient sweetness. Sweetness looking and tasting and feeling like water, going straight down into the holding tank and evaporator where, by means of fire, it thickens to rich consistency, heavy with godly taste. She can see sweet vapor ascend and drift away. She's picturing syrup bottled and beribboned in the exhibition hall at the Fairgrounds next summer's end in neighboring Blisville. She will walk into the white-washed barn—a barn brim full with home-crafted goodness from neighboring farmsteads and townlots—the place where people still delight to see what their hands can do. Tables and shelves and walls full of fancy quilts, needlework, hand-knits; everything imaginable pickled, canned, bottled—home-brew and mincemeat, forty kinds of vegetables, home baked pies and candies, saltwater taffy and fudge. And among that outlay, golden and glowing, a mason jar, quart jar of Twitchell Farm maple syrup. The jarful will remind everyone of Gottheim's first paying industry, and of a time when people eked out their livings by boiling down sap—something that the tree itself thinks of each year.

Chrischana pictures the bustling white barn at Blisville Fair: a shrine, the jeweled fastness of the exhibition hall, top to bottom with brightly colored things in glass. The thought makes her winter weary soul sweet to think of it, refreshing her own little hall of thought. Coming up to the camper in winter, getting away from dishwashing in the restaurant or cleaning others' houses; getting out of the apartment—someone else's property, which she shares with her three sons; getting out like this reminds her of how much she has. What if camp is entangled in town regulation, or locked away up here in winter? What if it is made of tin and 6 x 10? *Up here I'm free awhile.*

She is about to round the corner leading onto Buck Hill Road. Straight ahead the track branches, reaching toward the top of Blackwell and cleaving woodland, then clearcut, toward a wooded crown. Somewhere up there, curving out of sight, the white path leads to the sky. Nathan's long-tailed track starts up that way, but veering abruptly into a thicket of hemlock on the right. Chrischana stops to take a breath and look again at the high snowy trail. The noise of her crunching snowshoes goes still, as silence comes.

The sky up here is holy blue, not a trace of boiling filth from the poor little town next-door. Sky up ahead holds its promising mystery, a majesty and power in its occasional cloud. *But no home to me*, she thinks.

Just an old Mainer, me, needing homely comforts... the woodstove, funky sauna, snugness in weathertight walls.

Still... the sky.... *It makes you think.* She leans on the ski poles, still catching her breath at this crossroads in the puckies. She is tired after all, climbing the hill. Sometimes... nature, family, industry... aren't enough. You want trusty arms, deep rest.

She thinks of Balder—and then thrusts the thoughts away. Life has *gone on.* And on and on. Balder belongs to Gloria, heart and head, and I'm.... just about to reach out to Peter. Again. (Reluctant as she feels.)

She has always had a strong sense of the fitness of things, a feeling for what is appropriate and interlocking. There is an orderliness to life, a pattern. When she can find and accept it. Often she does. *The right pattern comes before what I think or feel.* Thoughts and feelings change; impermanent. Thinking and feeling come best in the pattern. I do best there.

Tears well in her eyes. Didn't I learn it in the Hard School of Rejecting Balder? Rejecting the wise pattern once... you go forward in it when you find it again. You don't go groping back, rummaging bitterly through memory, dreaming of things no longer there.

Chrischana turns, starting along the Buck Hill Road, away from the low summit of blue and white. But now to her ears comes a disappointed squeak.

Nathan pokes his head from the thicket to see her disappear into mixed woodland along the track. "Ain't cha gonna look for hobbits?!" He hates the thought that she would even pretend to leave him behind. Scudding along he comes up behind her, worried, wishing to grab hold of her coat but the snowshoes prevent him.

She wades on, wrapped in her thought, but aware of his quick clumsy steps behind. She knows these thickets, the woods sloping upward on their right, downward on the left. The snow cover makes crosses of white on the dark furry fingers of conifers among the naked popple and beech on either hand. Above her runs the ribbon of blue, for the trees are young, immature. You see through the part in their ranks.... That's what's so irksome about Gloria. A woman who does not know how to engage life. She's still a girl—at twenty-four? Five? She seems bent on throwing away one of the best human beings ever to pick up a wrench. "Doesn't see the consequences—like me back when."

"Huh?" The voice squeaks behind her.

"I just walk in that office o'hers! That'd get her attention. I could tell her what's what."

"Why?"

Doaw. *Caunt just manhandle life's stubborn customers.* I'd've stood no one man-handling me. Day dreaming. Got no business meddling there. Got to be clearheaded, fair. But that girl's got problems. Life's got be glamorous, exciting. Timid, partway, self-involved. Everything carefully controlled, Gloria-controlled. Thinks it's either/or. Either Gloria controls the course of life or Balder will. No one controls life. We only collaborate with it. Who could make her see it?

"Not me." She smiles. I can't even stop myself thinking how other people should live.

I can collaborate. I can go back to Peter. Not tonight. Not tomorrow.... Next day? (Have t'see bout that!) But not for Peter's sake... nor even the boys'... or even because it fits the pattern. No. Because it will engage me. It's *my* life. The rough and tumble, give and take.

Yes, they all knew those sweet days, in the beginning. Maybe if we try... he is trying after that botch-up. Showing something, at least. That he had... he has parted with the idea that he has the *right*... should be able to manhandle, dominate. He *knows* now it in't right. Bless that Hermann Gottesman! Got to acknowledge with some act. One that will lock together all the pieces: Nathan, Benaiah, Daniel, Peter, herself. Peter. He'll have family again, a committed lover for his reward. It... wasn't easy for him either.... When will it happen? How?

Nathan has been surprisingly quiet trudging beside her. No whining, no complaints. Climb's not easy for a kid. She turns, looking down on the small pointed face. "Keeping up okay, Frodo?"

He smiles up on her.

The road takes a turn, coming clean of mixed thickets. It starts up the last leg through tall hardwoods. This last track goes through sinking powder. The machine trail has departed and they are on their own, working harder. Nathan needs help... but at last they come out on the hilltop below the clearcut summit. They look out on the valley opening below.

Beyond Mt. Howe the smoke of burning goes up. Black, and contrasting like an evil vision in the snowy hill-land, it pours into the sky, sifting out its filthy burden. Just outside Gottheim, there is burning. How long will it affect their lives? Even on a day like today, when she desires to think of her own industry and engagement, Chrischana would embrace all Gottheim. Thinking with gratitude of being here in Maine, she embraces the whole worried community. All are engaged with making do—either overseeing community concerns or small family tasks. In the city she knew almost no one and could scarcely care. Now, standing here, gazing out on that smoke, she recovers the memory of an ancestor. A young man wounded and treed on Puzzle Mountain with an agitated bear roaming and restive below.

"Kilt by bear." The boy had written on his handkerchief with his own blood. A band of neighbors, with torches and trumpets, went into the woods looking for him. They found him after dark, alive, still clinging to the tree.

Sitting in The Coffee Story, cup in hand, Gloria waits for Chloe and Eveladore: a pre-meeting meeting with coffee and conversation, a fun way to start on that emergency campaign for the beleaguered Chamber of Commerce. The Coffee Story is a good little place, full of framed artwork on white walls and the smell of freshly roasted coffee beans. In the rear of the wide open Italianate house stands an antique brass roasting machine. Gloria sits musing in the fragrance of the morning's roast. The conversation she had with brother Jimmy over breakfast plays again through her mind: She will have to... to rethink her take on Theo. Only out of courtesy, or a sense of discretion, has Gloria kept her patience with the other intact. Theo lives in her on very scary dreamtime. The things she comes up with can scarcely resemble reality sometimes. There's been no substance to her, just a wild career from point to point, zigzagging like a token in a pinball machine; certainly lacking even the control of Pacman. But—at last—here's something to make you stop and think: Real reason. Theo has grasped an important truth—in her latest spectacle.

Over his eggs benedict James again spoke of trying to keep Theo on track. "She's been slipping back into that restiveness she was troubled with—before that wild announcement about giving away Gott'im Chair. I thought she was all straightened out, but now—"

"—What *is* her problem? James, you *know* sarcasm and irony aren't my way, but Theo manages to push my boundaries." She could not conceal her annoyance from him. Lately, he doesn't seem to mind irritation where Theo's concerned.

"Just some idea that she owes it to them. Thinks they've been exploited—in the past. Of course, I disagree. Completely." He emphasized the last point with a tap of the side of his hand on the tabletop: "These people had jobs (*tap*), make a living (*tap*); something that would not have happened without these mills and the owners looking out for them. Somehow she's lost perspective. But she doesn't talk about it anymore. Not since I let her know what I thought. —But, disturbed all over again. Let's see if we can keep her thinking straight."

"What does she mean, exploited?"

"Oh, just some notion that her father was involved in some sort of plan to fix wages. Long time ago." He gestured dismissively.

"You mean—conspiracy theories? She has those?"

He stopped to look at her. "Theo's not crazy, Glory."

"But what does she base it on?" Gloria stopped eating her granola and yogurt and set down her spoon.

"Things she overheard as a child. Apparently they met occasionally to reaffirm their agreement, an old-time blackballing and wage setting thing. It's ancient history now. She even says maybe the meetings stopped years ago. Boy, is she afraid of Lyman Bearce on the subject. She walks out of her way to avoid him."

"James Fay, those kinds of backroom agreements are despicable! Don't treat this so lightly." She leaned over the table suddenly, hissing at him.

"*Backroom*! Gloria, for someone so big on the taint of labels, you should know better. We just disagree. I could debate it with you but you'll only see it as cloak-and-dagger and smoking guns. I've got more important things on my mind." It was time to short-circuit this time wasting: "Have you forgotten about Ceylon Segar's bombing of our project in the Village?— or what's happening to Mason's Mills? Of the soot hill this place is becoming? Eat up—if you can. I've got a strategy session later this morning and have to prepare. If there is such a thing." His gaze gripped hers through his glasses. "This is ruination, Gloria. Forget archaic practices that no longer apply. What do you think will become of it all? All our hard work, the plans? Please don't talk to me about those workers. Half of'em are dead! We've got living workers to think of, the young people in this town who make a living off this resort. I'm afraid to look out the window this morning!"

They looked reflexively toward the great windows across the room. The once pristine view of ski slopes was now filthy with ash.

Gloria looked back at him, dropping her gaze. Plainly he was scared. She herself was not so upset over the fire. Fear had not hit her like that. His face made her want to shrink for guilt. And to comfort him. But how? All her words on the subject seemed too little. Her talk would seem glib, but she could not help the remoteness she felt. The magnitude and intractability of the situation numbed her. She had an odd urge to suggest he pray. But Gloria kept quiet. After her own standoff with faith it would be just more words. And, with the way things were between them lately, he might even think she was mocking him. At last she said, "I'm sorry James." She pushed her half-empty bowl of granola away. Maybe that would convince him of her sympathy.

Eloise and Sherla Simon come over with coffee to sit at a neighboring table. The Coffee Story is filling up but, absorbed in her thoughts, Gloria scarcely notices. The two talkers at the next table are on break from running errands, come in to enjoy a spot of gossip and commiserate over the disaster. The conversation started after a chance meeting in the grocers'.

"So... it was the devil that started the fire in the tire dump... you say." Sherla jogs Eloise into continuing. The former has a nice round face and twin dark braids, a certain comfortable fullness stuffed into her jeans and blue flannel shirt. Her barn-mucking coat, faintly redolent, is draped over the back of the dainty soda fountain-type chair. The paper cup warms her pudgy hands and she possesses the happiness one might think of while looking at apples hanging from full boughs. At home she bakes bread of coarse grains for her family; also makes and sells white butter with a raised design.

"Eloise, you were born off-the-wall." It's a compliment, a complaint. "Where do you come up with these things?"

"Shouldn't conjure up those images about birth and walls," says Eloise. "Mama wouldn't like it."

Sherla spills tendrils of laughter. "You were the one who told the town it was lightning. Now you think the devil is lightning? Or the devil controls lightning, maybe."

"The devil *wishes* he controlled lightning. And as everyone knows (smiles) he fell like lightning from heaven."

"He?" Sherla arches an eyebrow, smiling.

"The-devil-wishes-he-or-she-controlled-lightning." Eloise rolls her eyes, the glasses on her nose reflecting rectangles of light from the windows. "Let us assess the devil's sex. Like with the wish to control lightning, the devil wishes the devil had a sex, wishes it *could* have sex (otherwise we would not see the devil trying so hard for it in our all-out culture)."

"So how did the devil start the fire? By rubbing two sticks together up there in the clouds?"

"The devil is not a Native American." It's a dry retort. "Maybe at one time, but not today. Today the devil is a three-piece suit and carries a briefcase. Yesterday he wore a conquistador's metal bonnet, bloomers and tights."

"So you saw him sneaking around the tire dump with a blow torch in his briefcase, and, deciding no one would believe you, said it was lightning."

Eloise gives a mischievous grin, shakes her dirty-blond ponytail and says, "It *wasn't* lightning that started the fire. The tires started the fire. Lightning hits all over the globe, continually—something like 100 times a second. The lightning belonged there. The tires did not. Someone in a suit and tie—coulda been a woman!—decided useless tires belong in little Quaker township, Maine. Several someones in suits and ties. Yes, I'm bigoted, but not that bad. The identifying feature of the devil is not clothes or vocation or sex but a foolish reliance on one's own machinations. I mean, night and day, there's no end to the vulcanization of rubber, and endless glut of tire manufacturing. Where are we supposed to put it all?"

"The Ayatollah is right, then? Corporate America—we *are* the Great Satan?"

"Maybe it takes one to know one.... What could be more devilish then fanaticism? Look at peer pressure. What's more Puritan than kids pressuring each other to do drugs, smoke, or perform some dangerous feat? The undoers of repression can snake the most devastating oppression throughout society. Ever see *Twelfth Night*? Sir Toby is as correct as Malvolio, and probably a lot more potent and hurtful. Repression is the 20th-century sin that psychiatry tried to bludgeon us with."

"Oh come on. If it takes one to know one, what does that make you?"

"Well, I do keep goats." She smiles toothily.

The other sits back, thoughtfully chewing her muffin. At last she says, "Who's the devil around Gott'im?" Lowering her voice she leans forward. "No, don't tell me: remember that time we worked in Copenhagen, turning out brush handles?" She hisses. "They turned off the heat during second shift because the bosses and office workers went home."

Is it the hissing or mention of millwork that wakes Gloria from her reverie? How long the two women have been sitting here talking she does not know, but she recognizes Eloise by her reputation and the fact that she is a foe of James on the Mason Mills project.

"They really get away with it," Eloise is saying. The other answers, "People still work all night in this terrible cold.... Minimum-wage and chilblains—in this day'n age!"

Gloria glances at her, looks away. Boldly she eavesdrops on their talk under pretense of staring out the window.

Says Eloise, "You think we have it tough, you should hear the old-timers talk. Sometimes they worked twelve, fifteen hours and got paid for ten. Their sandwiches froze. No coffee breaks. And some of these mills are still owned and operated by the same people—or their descendants."

"At least now, people can get compensated if injured on-the-job."

"If they can keep workers compensation going. Politics is trying to overturn it every day from too many abuses, they say, but what's the incentive for policing conditions without it? Do you ever see OSHA going into these little places?"

Agreeing and congratulating themselves on their insight, the two women stand, pick up their cups and napkins and head for the door as Gloria looks after.

"Hah!" Eveledore yelps, spying her while coming in with the cold behind the departing hippies. The girl has a killer overbite and her great grin is like a shiny wall coming at Gloria. "Thought I was gonna be late!" Manner breezy and broad, Eveledore with pixieish haircut above the wide sexy smile; her features bright as brass with the power of her confidence: She's got unstoppable personality and knows how to keep you right up there with her, even in the midst of disaster. Vel is ready for the long haul, up for this adventure of Gott'im's volcano, or "apocalypse" as she refers to it... being not so glib as to use the term holocaust. Yet many agree that the scope, smell and sound of the thing suggests a biblical idiom. "I want to stay and watch the unfolding," she said yesterday. "Think of the stresses it will put on the townspeople. We are in the right place to study the impact of catastrophe." Her interest in the social aspect of Ceylon Segar's aborted attempt to earn an industrial living off the land of his ancestors signifies with her association in the International Institute of Coordinated Experiments.

"Right up IICE's alley," Gloria had observed agreeably. IICE meets informally only in summer but, as with her own situation, some members with second homes in Gottheim have an emotional stake in the community. Skiing has always been a bonus.

The third member of their party, the intense, dark, pensive and angular Chloe, comes in behind Eveledore. Together the two step up to the counter for coffee and croissants, returning to Gloria's table with the fresh scent of coffee and pastry, the rustling of napkins.

Eveledore is saying, "We don't hear complaints about snow from the locals anymore. It's all about ash. The sky is snowing ash and flakes of unburnt tire. Complaint is a sort of mitigator for the helpless."

Chloe's response, between bites, is somewhat dry. "In the same way that disaster mitigates our focus sessions?" She looks directly at Vel. "You forgot to tip the counter folks."

"I didn't forget. You tip too much and it evens things out. Too much breeds unrealistic expectations and spoilage."

Chloe picks up her cup, sits silently, but her dark eyes do not turn away. Eveledore, with clear green gaze, just smiles at her. She shrugs her coat onto the back of the chair. "Have either of you heard about Gwendolyn Bella—institutionalized by her sister two weeks ago?"

Gloria grimaces. "I knew it! The sessions last summer were too much for a... a fragile psyche like hers."

"I agree," says Chloe. "She had this genuine sweet air, very refreshing. Why would they want to change that? It was a mistake—trying to instill assertive values and attitude in someone like her."

"It was what she wanted," counters Vel. "She was sick of being the weak one. In any encounter. She *wanted* to be more aggressive."

Chloe shakes her head. "Would she, though? Maybe she was just being true to what she is—by caving to the influences in that session. The whole program was geared to consciousness-raising... and it became an irresistible atmosphere for someone like her. After all, she happened into the sessions as a diversion—advertised in *The Voter*. ...She was just another tourist or summer—"

" So you're saying—" interrupts the other.

But Chloe's look is piercing: "That atmosphere overwhelmed her, crushed her! That episode in her last session should have told you something."

"Sometimes an episode is necessary if you want a breakthrough." She puts pearly fingertips up to loosen her tie. The room is warm and Eveledore is insistent, giving no ground on this.

"Don't you mean break*down*?" Gloria has been sitting with an empty face but now she speaks. Recalling Bella's hysteria makes her unhappy. The heat of her feeling rushes out in flippant irony. "Like if you want to make an omelet, you have to break some eggs."

"Couldn't've put it better," says the other with a touch of hauteur.

Gloria's answering silence is neither hostile nor friendly. She looks thoughtfully at the bold young woman across from her.

Chloe has finished with Eveledore on the subject. She blots her lips with a napkin. "Looks like we got an omelet in Gott'im. And what are we going to do about it besides take notes? Will we just poke and probe or is there some action we can take to alleviate the pain? Do we know what civic leaders are doing; or Augusta?"

"To find the answers to these and other burning questions, let us adjourn, copies of *The Village Voter* in hand, to our own fact-finding meeting." It is smartly said, Eveledore swirling the last of the coffee in the bottom of her cup. "Let's hope that sourpot Nutting sends someone to report on it. Better destroy the croissants and go." She puts the last bite into her wide mouth and stands, picks up her suit coat and turns toward the door, leaving the table littered. With a wave of her hand, she turns back to cut Chloe off. "Don't say it, Chlo. It's what you stuffed that tip jar for, deah." She smiles her killer smile and breezes out the door.

The moon is up but its light, fitfully fringed with pine, is alternately blocked by ashfall. Ansell Robichaud is climbing the ledge among the thick trees: a difficult climb through ice and snow, grabbing at branches and scrabbling up icy rock. He has no crampons or ice-climbing equipment like that worn by those who climb for sport. He wears steel-toed boots—good protection if a limb should fall, but in February they freeze the feet fast. Shivering with cold when he first came out, his limbs warm as he climbs.

     Nothing would prevent him from climbing this ledge tonight, nothing prevent his communing with Alvin. Or, to put it in his own terms, Ansell is thinking: *Gont climb the ledge'n put up the flag*. It's something he has to do, what this piece of time is for. He has to put up the flag tonight.

     Trees around him are mighty with age. White Pine here is girthy and tall, its once smooth youthful bark now crusted in thick ridges of age. On the side of this cliff they catch the light. So, if hazardous, climbing is not impossible. Yet Ansell has to make sure of his flag tree. Hell! If he climbs the wrong one now.

     For the trees and the night he cannot see it coming over the mountain behind him—ash from the tire fire falling on the breeze. He smells it, feels it fitfully sifting across the bridge of his nose. He winks it loose from his eye. Ash *plinks* on the sleeves of his nylon jacket.

     The new replacement flag, dark, is neatly coiled and wrapped around his neck, tied under his arms. He feels it bunched around his shoulders and under his armpits, the breeze tugging at its edges. The first thing will be to get the old ragged, sun-bleached flag off the limb. It was supposed to be Alvin's turn to change the flag. Now it's up to Ansell.

     Searching among the high dark boughs he remembers the first time they made the climb as kids: serious, intent on getting that flag up. It was what a Robichaud could do in life, get that flag up. Since they could remember the flag has flown: tiny, white, high in the pines. As kids they talked of it, the twins, and of how one day they'd be the ones to put up the flag. Great Uncle Pierre Auguste, who spoke only French, told them one day they would. What a feat it turned out to be for them! Even tonight Ansell recalls the way his little heart thumped among his ribs as they climbed. It was the first time he noticed he had a heart. Breaths came in gasps, his legs trembling, feet scarcely touching each limb. Hand-over-hand, together they ascended, neither speaking. Never, since, has the intensity of the experience been duplicated. Never until now. Because Alvin was found outside Sessions' in his truck. Now life is intense again, but Ansell no longer craves intensity. He wants only to see Alvin alive. The thrill of life can go to hell.

High up there in the halfmoon light he catches a glimpse of gray. Pinkish gray moving among feathered shadows. And off aways the stars are snared, though every once in awhile their lights are snuffed. From the ash and burning tires, he guesses. Ansell sets his hand to the branch to get a leg up.

Because his feet are so heavy with years, the branch feels sure in his instep. The wind has knocked out the snow. He grips each branch hand-over-hand, smelling pitch. Through leather work gloves he feels the coldness and strength of each limb.

Slowly the logger ascends, sometimes climbing, sometimes clinging. Clinging he feels a stuporous life in the great tree. Even in winter evergreen manages to live in its secret layer of life. Ansell is jealous of it, thinking of Alvin, but then he relents for his realization that the tree's life takes nothing away which his brother might've used. It breathes with its own kind of life and they have always made a living from wood. There's nothing here on which to blame Alvin's death. He must look elsewhere for that.

Starlight and moonlight are spreading now, the tree's great branches parting. He leaves the closeness of needles, emerging into falling soot and pinkish night. He thinks the soot is proper to this night: The sky should be raining such sorrow. But in daylight he wishes it would go—for Emma's sake, for Mother's. The children. Let the dreariness of the ash fall off them onto him, remain in his own heart good'n proper.

High in the branches now, the tree swaying, Ansell sways with it. He's near. Where'd the flag get to? He leans out, one hand holding the branch above. There. The flag swishes, fluttering listlessly among furry boughs. Now it flaps high in a sudden gust.

Ansell climbs. Now, slowly, he hauls himself out; slowly, lying along its length, clutching the branch. The replacement flag, specially dyed by Alvin's wife Emma, lifts at its edges, still wrapped around him. They always used the white sheet, but now Ansell and Emma agree: black. "Don't think it'll show up much fom down heah," she said. Ansell only nodded his head but he thought the flag's meaning was different now. It stood not for triumph for the town to see but as a memorial, unspoken, for Alvin. That was all Ansell wanted to see. Black was the color of his grief.

The bough sways and Ansell with it. The whole treetop sways. The heavens sway, bending back and forth. The halfmoon and stars go up and down. Soot comes poring over him in a swift gust. Ansell squeezes his eyes then blinks. The earth is far, a long way down. There is Pale's sawmill spread out in the valley, glowing pinkish dark. Now that he is out in the open, the buzz-and-growl of the saws and separators comes up to him from that distance. His family's house below shows like a toy across from it, lights in its windows. The slope blocks his view of the two trailers, one for each twin, tucked beneath the ledge. Again the vapor lights and sound of the sawmill draw his gaze. The mill is one of many belonging to a family in Portland. Uncle Anseller worked there. Once. ...Didn't sober up properly before coming in one morning. Fell into a trimmer blade. Sliced into his lung, his breath and blood seeming to pour out of him. That was how he told the tale. "Thought I was all done. Wadn't though. Kep'right on living but not the same."

Swaying high on the pine above the valley, Ansell hears those words again. Swaying in the cold and needles, lit by moon and stars, blown about in smoke and ash. Clutching the limb, his dark flag flapping, wind-whipped, unfurling; the swift scent of pine pitch pierces him. He hears the words: Kept right on living, but not the same.

Winter and night in Jericho, and the conversation was desultory in Hermann Gottesman's *Kids Cafe*. Some teens were bent to their homework at a battered oak table with massive legs. Others played ping-pong while a few watched, swallowing sodas, snapping gum, jibing. There was an old pool table in the big room, and the gentle knocking of balls was heard from time to time. Hermann had a stereo playing a stack of scratchy platters that teenagers hadn't listen to for twenty years. Few listened to Elvis and Buddy anymore. The kids complained about this music to him. They wanted heavy metal or Prince, John Cougar, and The Gloved One. Hermann was deaf to it all.

He sat on the sagging couch, one massive hand seemingly always in a great bowl of freshly popped corn. Hermann was like a minor mountain, great in the knees, a mass of flesh, topped with dark curly receded hair in a tail, and beard. Peter Prince sat nearby in a dirty old wing chair. Though the popcorn on the table between them was tempting with its hot fresh smell, Peter never ventured a hand toward it. He drank coffee instead—as though his life depended on it. Considering what had happened to Alvin, he thought maybe it did. But if coffee were rescuing him from the temptations of alcohol, it made sleep harder to come by. And he was on southern schedule.

Peter Prince was friendly, compactly built, and green eyed through unruly brown hair. One eye was still bruised from Ferddy's suckerpunch.

Sometimes he was desperate with hankering for Chrischana. If only he could straighten up, quit listing like an old shed.... Was there *any* chance they'd be back together? No. No chances, only desperation. Desperation from now on. Sometimes Peter Prince believed in God and Jesus. Frequently he did not.

He watched the teenagers playing table tennis, shooting stick. He liked looking at the girls with their French braids, crimped bangs and straight-leg jeans. Girls didn't look like that when he was a teenager. They wore bellbottoms and ironed their hair or let it billow out like Brillo pads. But the boys in Hermann's Cafe reminded him of himself at that age, except for the jeans. They talked big, snuck outside to smoke, drink, get high. Hermann wouldn't let them back in when they did this.

Tonight was a school night so the kids began to drift out in twos and threes at about ten o'clock. By 10:30 it was quiet, the pinging and clinking of balls gone with the teenagers. The tobacco haze, which the big man permitted, was thinning out. Hermann had replenished the popcorn twice. He was drinking orange juice by the half gallon, pouring it over ice cubes in a tall plastic cup. Peter had made a fresh pot of coffee. It was time to get down to business.

"Know what that fire they got up there reminds me of?" Prince was asking. "Know that opening scene in the *Blues Brothers*?"

Hermann shook his head. "Never saw the movie."

"Aerial shots showing the God awful murk and smoke of some industrial section, East Chicago, I think. Stacks, fires, foundries, just pouring this filth into the air. Like the Flats in Cleveland where I grew up. Pollution so thick y'could swim through it. Honest-to-God. Half expected t'see a frogman with flippers'n mask bubbling his way through it. 'N'there were glowing spots in the darkness—like looking down into hell through a blow-hole. That tire fire makes me think the whole planet's turning into one big crematorium. No wonder they talk about a greenhouse effect."

"What you're describing reminds me of something more horrific." Hermann responds as though from a distance, sadly. "...Although... people are probably on to something with that term. We may live to find out how bad the warming trend can get, especially since we do nothing but fund studies. Science can frequently find things out but knowledge rarely moves anyone. Warnings are out there, we do know enough now to push for legislation but policymakers don't move until the agonizing pictures start rolling in. Take *Uncle Tom's Cabin*—not that I could get through Stowe's novel but, back then, it was able to emote truth people couldn't help but see. Feel. An imaginative depiction can kindle action but a dearth of images or strong books... that's why slavery continued, why Jews kept being gassed and burned. People could not grasp—really believe in the death camps until they saw pictures. They weren't moved until it was too late. The two wars—Civil and World War II were precipitated by agendas not specifically aimed at the evils of slavery and anti-Semitism but, if man's intention differed from God's, in the end they collaborated."

"That's another thing, Hermann. This question of free will we talked about... and how God won't prove his existence because that would violate free will... meaning we'd have no choice but to believe in that case. There's free will and yet—my question: Is this really free will? Why give us free will if the end result is we must capitulate?"

"That's good, Prince. Maybe it's just God liking a good story. Would you want to read a story where everything moved along just as you thought it should? What would keep you reading in that case? (Leaving out the question of omniscience.) But he would like it to be worth his while. If you believe that's God in chains, red with the lash, gassed. In your throttling hands."

Knocking a pack of Viceroys against his forefinger, the other dislodged a cigarette, smiling, thinking of God's reading material. "Think he's that simpleminded, though?" He snapped his lighter shut and looked around for an ashtray. He glanced up at the ceiling. "Just kidding."

Peter Prince blew smoke into the air, but sensing a lack of savor in his flippancy, he said, "I'm not superstitious, Hermann, but I swear d'God that tire fire gives me the creeps. Hadda see it up close—just once. Never again. The stench! Melting'n heat... besides the richest looking smoke you ever saw. No end to it either. Looks like it'll keep burning till it burns its way to hell. Make a good pathway for demons to climb out on. They're probably putting up signs down there now: 'This way to Gott'im,' or, 'Five more miles t'Gott'im.' My kids live there, y'know."

Hermann looked right at him. "Haven't your kids already seen the devil?"

Peter dropped his gaze. *He's really going to work.* Prince was silent, then quietly he said, "So you keep reminding me."

"Is it something you should forget?"

"Here we go with the probing questions. No. I don't think I should forget it." But his face hardened. "You know, if it weren't for— everything—I'd tell you to go fuck yourself."

"You just told me anyway."

Peter snapped, "You know what Hermann, you tenacious irreligious Jew? I'm never gonna get rid of this anger. Not in a hundred million light- years. According to this, I'm *never* gonna have Chrischana. Not to hold again. I'll never be fit to live with. One more smack on'er and I'm out!

"I'm out anyway." It was a mutter.

He went quiet again then said, very low, "Shoulda taken a bite outta Sessions' dog. I should have got out of the truck'n let the fucking thing tear me apart."

"This is doing any good, Prince?"

"What *will* do me any good?"

Hermann Gottesman drank his orange juice. In silence he let the question—a very good question—say itself again. He filled the tall cup once more. "I'll ask something designed to get you remembering the answer to that. But first tell me what all these things we've been talking about have in common?"

Prince stood, ceramic cup in hand though his coffee had cooled. He walked between two littered game tables, set the cup down and picked up a pool cue. Deftly he dropped the seven solid into a side pocket. He set down the stick, picked up the cup and walked around again, thoughtfully, resigned to these questions. "Let's see. Slavery, the Holocaust, smoke from thirty million tires, global warming—anything else?" At the bookcases he turned and came back toward the couch where Hermann sat like a mountain.

"Battering."

With a sidelong dip of his tousled head, Prince acknowledged the word. "Battering." He sat down, took another swallow of coffee and said, "Domination. They are all about domination."

"People dominate because?" Hermann was urging the answer toward greater precision.

Peter looked at him, then away. "Because they are powerless." He turned his back, shoulders slumping. "Because sometimes they can't control even themselves. Especially themselves. Can't accept what they are, what they've been given. Because they despise the weakness they live in... or see in others." He continued with his back toward the big man, slouching against the grubby wing chair.

Gently the other said, "What's despicable about weakness? About weakness or humility? Or harmlessness?"

Peter sighed. A long grief-struck sigh. He sat up a little, saying, "Nothing. I guess. There's nothing wrong with certain kinds of weakness. I mean, I like Nathan and he's weak—harmless. His being young'n innocent kind of appeals to me. It makes me sorry that someone stronger could come along and harm him. Someone tricky or mean.... Someone who might treat him the way I treated Chrischana.

"For years she came back to me after I hurt her." He looked seriously at Hermann n. "I used to wonder how the Jews could allow themselves to be herded away like that. But it never occurred to me to wonder how people could herd'em away. That's what I should've been wondering. But when I think of it—maybe I do know. It was like with Chrischana. She was the kind of person who could not believe that someone would really *want* to hurt someone else."

Hermann sat silent, intently. Prince was coming to it now, and speaking as though these things were written in some high calm airy place. Gottesman listened carefully, feeling as though the two of them were up there together.

"Goodness was so strong in her that she couldn't believe in that evil. She thought I would change or get the message or something. It took a long time and a lot of pain for her to be convinced of what I was. Am. And then she left." He leaned forward. "Hermann, there's hope. She *might* come back. Not because I'm worth it, but because she's good."

He stopped and leaned back, looking at the ceiling tiles.... "But there's still the problem of how to change. Where's help for that?" And he fell into quiet thinking. Hermann too was silent.

Then Peter Prince said, "Never mind, Hermann. I remember."

Hermann smiled. Not that rare a thing. He could smile over small happiness, instances of thought, pieces of conversation. But he did not smile without reason. Now he smiled again at Peter. "I eat a lot, Prince."

"Yeah, Hermann. I noticed." Then, in a mischievous play on probing questions and also because he was curious, he said, "Why'd you suppose that is?"

"It may be because I have a faint but entrenched memory of being hungry. It's always here."

"You, Hermann ? When were you ever hungry?"

"Long ago. I was very young." His mouth continued to smile but there was a fragrance of sadness in his eyes. "My father tried escaping by taking us to Romania. To Hungary. It didn't work. At Birkenau I was hungry."

Quakertown was so called by second-generation Gott'imites. The little group of people who settled the wild town next-door never actually used that appellation themselves. Shortly after Jasper Mary ceased roaming the byways and tributaries of the Arossagunticook, the strange little sect came, purchasing land from absentee grantees or their heirs. They made stranger worship in the woods beyond Gottheim and the mountain. Although the predecessor to *The Village Voter* was still a generation or two away, many Gottheimites were well read, exchanging books, periodicals and outdated newspapers from Portland and Boston, so they knew about Quakers and Shakers. Since it was known that dancing was part of the newcomers' ritual, the name Quaker seemed apt enough to townsfolk. For these strangers' name was unknown to them.

According to Dr. Kimball, the 19th-century Gottheim historian, the people who settled Quaker were virgins, their men and women celebrating celibacy. Describing their form of worship at secondhand he wrote of its slow beginning, measured and sedate, consisting of a kind of locomotive dancing and oral devotion. As though nothing in particular were going on. Men on the right, women to the left, they faced each other in groups. A rhythm and rhyme where soon perceived, a pattern of increasing complexity. Like a boiler burbling, it built to a particular and a peculiar pressure. With increasing speed came a release from caution, a casting off of the former pattern. Worshipers whirled and wailed unto the Lord, spinning off singly in ecstasy of devotion. As though each were now coupled with the Lord alone. The fully energized locomotive—of Dr. Kimball 's metaphor—had jumped the tracks, as though to head out of the mountains on a mission of its own.

The townsfolk of Gottheim longed to accuse the Quakerites of being no earthly good, but the industry of the sect precluded this. It seemed there was nothing these people could not accomplish. Each member was *master*, no less, of half a dozen trades, and could perform to satisfaction any other necessary job. Tailoring, metalwork, woodworking, invention, husbandry, all manner of needlework cookery beekeeping herb-doctoring and more: all done with artistry and perfection. In a little more than a dozen years, the tiny community had a prosperous commercial seed business and were disseminating a multitude of northern fruit and vegetables throughout the known world. They had a brisk export of blueberry blossom honey and maple syrup.

This shaking quaking sect of Believers in Christ's Second Coming had their peculiar secrets, one of which concerned a Sacred Stone. The Stone was boldly inscribed and stood in what Gottheimites whispered was an unholy hollow. Shadowed by hemlocks and ringed about by woodland, this setting suggested the rumor that these odd people actually worshiped that piece of rock. Rumors flew about this Stone. People said it was solid quartz. Others said imported marble, some said it was rubbed red with the blood of chickens or deer. No one actually believed about the blood of course (except children, who listened big-eyed to everything). "What was written on the Stone?" The children would ask. And certain fathers and mothers would reprove them for listening to outlandish tales. But others, as eager of voice as the children, would close their eyes and darkly intone: "The God, who has caused His Word to dwell here, destroy who shall put forth their hand to alter or destroy this house of God." Still others declared it said no such thing but only, "THE WORD OF THE LORD"; adding, "But folks oughtn't to set up worshipful objects anaway. Ain't propa."

The history of rumor recorded by Dr. Kimball states that the sect's members broke the Stone apart and buried its pieces in secret diverse places in an apparent attempt to stop the communitywide misunderstanding of the Stone's purpose. But no one actually knows what became of the so-called sacred Stone.... If there was one to begin with.

Few in Gottheim even remember that sect now, though it comes up at the Historical Society from time to time. Making her home in Quaker, and curious as she is, Eloise Patadoe has read Doc Kimball's history of it. Asa Bartlett and the faithful of the aforementioned society know the various peculiar histories of the little township. But, of late, Quaker is just a logged over sparsely occupied tire storage area, with a remote outback leading to vast wilderness—lakey, mountainous, filled with game. The whirling religious have long since departed. Celibacy carries its own peculiar and unspectacular form of extinction. The neighboring community of Gottheim is the poorer for it; just as they suffer from the departure of Jasper Mary and her clan. They would suffer if the hippies and back-to-the-landers in Quaker disappeared. But, largely, Gottheimites remain ignorant of this. Prosperous townsfolk feel reverent for remembering the Yankee pioneers and benevolent for, at last, allowing the French their place.

Another culturally important resident of Quaker, the most ancient, pervasive and enduring, is nonhuman. Regardless of natives or colonials or the republic, insect and animal populations have settled and moved at will here since the wasting of glaciers. Their pathways to food and water were secure and inalienable until the human invasion. Humans have paved the trails over with logs, gravel, asphalt and concrete. Humans have intersected and paralleled animal trails, but the innocent and ignorant continue to travel woodland, water and field by the only pathways they know, maintaining their ancient routes surprisingly well; the mothers of various species teaching the next generation, faithful to the point of slaughter.

A week passed since the tire dump began what Peter Prince called its continuing descent into hell. Then the numerous rodent population of Ceylon Segar's burning rubber and oil mountains began entering the village and the resort on the other side of the mountain. At night, as people slept in their snow and cinder covered houses, or dreamed in their condos, rats that had harbored in Quaker tires came looking for refuge and food. Some few old people, and some mothers, were awakened in darkness by the persistent gnawing of rodent incisors. They gnawed cellar bulkheads or on floor plates to gain entrance. They gnawed at convenient cracks in restaurants and trendy shops. Upon entering the grocers on Front Street, they gnawed their way into what seemed like rat heaven. Morning came and people awoke in quiet households where sleek guests had discreetly hidden themselves away for a cozy winter's day nap. Outdoors a few keen observers spotted what looked like giant mice trails inscribed in the sooty snow cover. The rats were so numerous in their role of hidden guests that household pets emulated a passage from Harriet Beecher Stowe and "gazed on the rats with respectful curiosity and ran no imprudent risks."

Elda, Balder, and Daniel have taken on the crusade for creatures. Balder is on nights at the paper mill so in daylight they come into the wood surrounding the fulminating dump to look for suffering or disoriented birds and animals. Through swiftly changing cloud of smoke and soot, sometimes laden with snow, they poke and prod the dirty cover of woodland, of puckerbrush, of former clearcuts. They venture into high woods where the saw has not been in decades. Working together or apart the little family gathers the sickly or fraidy-eyed creatures, bringing them home to *Simons Ledge* in cages in the back of Balder's pickup. The barn, into which the man had planned to bring a team of draft horses to help on his proposed farmstead, is now full of wild animals, mostly small. Daniel and his brothers busy themselves helping the legally blind Elda clean fur and feathers. They feed and otherwise help restore heart-breath-strength to the wounded population of wilderness surrounding Ceylon Segar's dump.

Today Balder is alone, wandering the southeast quadrant off the dump, searching the underbrush for frightened creatures that may have been left behind. The smoke and cinders come over him in waves when he reaches the high point of some knoll. There he looks out on the rapid upsurge of darkness trimmed low in flame and surrounded by a dense living atmosphere. Popping, cracking, and blowing. The filthy mass moves and breathes, heaving its breastful of fire in upwhirling, writhing flame. At intervals a blaze bursts up in dirty drafts, forming an undulant glowing face. It invokes that vision of fire, projecting across the low heavens and earth, in the red days when he was a warrior in the forest surrounding some unofficial enemy's hometown. That such a fiery face could come near Gottheim, spit and rain on the quiet streets of his familiar village, makes unspeakable sadness in him. When he looks on the downturned faces of neighbors, friends, acquaintances walking the dim streets, the wounds of Vietnam awake. When they look up to speak to one another conversation is of difficulties breathing or disruption of lives, the sorrow and darkness upon the white New England face of Gottheim. One or two have died of exacerbated respiratory disease on account of this.

But the punishment of this fire has reminded Gott'imites of tender relations too much neglected. Of love too seldom surfacing in healthier air. Seeing Asa Bartlett overtown, Balder would think, Why'd I never see the faithful way he has of going twice a week to wind the town clock? Year in, year out, no vacation, no honeymoon since—before I was born? Winding it evah week, twice a week, while I was lost in Vietnam.

Now, while he looks out on the great smoke of burning, the rumbling and blowing of its devouring fills his ears. Then some other sound, tiny and thin, comes up, its faint mewing waking him from his reverie. An animal is crying somewhere. Intermittently, the call comes a bit more distinctly now. From below the knoll behind him comes the sound of his name. Thinly, fine, the voice sends on the winter breeze. Turning, he looks down through tall trunks at the tiny figure in blue, toiling up toward him.

Who is wading through deep snow, following his snowshoe tracks, calling his name?

The joy of recognition and desire rushes into him whole. Gloria! And Gloria's voice. Here comes the creature he sought for, in soot, in ice and snow. Climbing toward him, growing in perspective, she rejoices him more than he can say. His great wish is for her to climb up this knoll, telling him that she comes to return his love. With the smoke of Gottheim's spoiling rising behind, the remedy for his aching heart is to see her face... come grave, smiling, saying, "I will. I will return your love."

But, for the moment, Balder will stay. Stay quietly waiting as she struggles up to him... so obviously ill-shod for the venture. Even now the disappointment of her rejection burns into him... deeply... as would her love. If only it would come.

Her day a dreary mix of snowfall and ash, she drove the back roads of Gottheim, disconsolate. Crusted in ice and ash, the wipers screeched back and forth across the messy glass. Gloria's hands clenched at the wheel as she hit an icy patch sidelong. A tiny yelp escaped her lips, but the car righted itself as she turned the wheel into the slide. Everywhere fell a dense mingling of snow and smoke, making visible the sadness and her inward distress. All that heady limitless opportunity for her talents, which she had so enjoyed in Gottheim—convulsing away, upward, into a sky of billowing filth.

How did it happen? How could something so far on the edge of her consciousness as a pile of old tires become invested with such power? Could a few bolts of lightning really transform this beautiful happy place into the media's next disaster? For weeks it is burning, never ceasing. They say this fire may take years to extinguish. Oh why hadn't she done more for Ceylon Segar!

Her field of reality had turned on end, spinning her plans away. At first unreal and almost peripheral to her, the fire had assumed absolute authority over everything. Jimmy was even talking as though they must leave. As though Gottheim and its dreams could just be thrown away. A nuisance he must extricate himself from at great cost and aggravation. He wants to salvage the future by moving west or north to one of Goldings' emerging acquisitions.

Can't *something* be done with the fire? Isn't there *any*thing, some contingency, some government bureau, disaster coping mechanism... but God knows they are trying them all.

Her mind sank lower, thoughts thickening and quickening toward chaos. Incipient until this mess came along, depression forced its inroads, pushing down on her: a heavy hand, mighty and enervating. Powerful panic swept through, carrying off her wits. Terrorized, she must stop the car before a loss of control bore her away.

"Are you with us?" It was a whisper, expecting no answer. Again she spoke it low, and again; parked there beside banks of snow. Curious comfort came merely in saying it, draining off some of the desperation. Gloria's religious upbringing had made this turning toward comfort familiar to her with its quiet associations of childhood. Again she asked this question aloud, maintaining the same low intensity. Driving slowly, saying the question, she became aware of the grace in these sounds. She was leaning softly into the wholeness of these whisperings. Nothing now but this faintest whisper of words.

The mereness of it balanced her. She felt it supporting her, lending its sure arm. Her own arm resting lightly on the wheel, she sighed. Having come to what seemed the extreme end of her wits all she found there was this question.

I wish I had sense enough to remember it. Had sense enough not to be upset over this fire. I... I'd like a lot of good things I don't have.

Tall and dark in this dismal fall, a wall of conifer curved just ahead from where she stopped. There she saw the pickup, its fenders mended, patches of spotty dull primer. Balder's pickup. *Let not your heart be troubled*, she thought.

She thought of this man with the white-blond hair and contrasting stern black beard—comforting. ... His Norwegian blue eyes that flickered with humor and irony, his sure voice sounding the pattern of the happiest old Mainer. His arms were what she longed for in dreams and out. Balder Simon. He loved her.

In spite of confusion and suffering—or, she thought, because of it?—she saw this. Gone are doubts and resentments that plagued her. Balder Simon loved her. No matter what. No amount of distrust would stop his love. Gloria pulled the red car up behind the pickup and got out.

Stepping carefully in the ice and grime, she walked past it. Looking up the roadway and off into the woodland she wondered which way to go. The road had been plowed, maybe early this morning, but new soot and snow had been laid since, covering the dirty plowbank lining the curve. There she saw the tailed track of snowshoes, climbing over the row. It led off into dark woods on an old discontinued twitch trail.

Snowfall wet her cheeks and lashes. Her breath came in clouds, mingling with the acrid smell of ash in her nostrils. She looked at the dark speckles on the arm of her down filled jacket, the match of her blue ski pants. Her stylish boots of Moroccan leather were wet, pelted with it. She looked again at the trail. *Should not wear such boots through deep snow.*

She longed for Balder. If only his track doesn't take me far. She thought she could do it... if the way were not long. It was February but not bitter: A fool would tackle a track like this under harsher conditions. She nibbled at her lip, chiding herself. You'd do it in a moment on skis. Still, she equivocated. Don't go too far. Not onto an uncertain terrain. The boots are just wrong.

Gloria clambered over the plowbank, following Balder's track. It was work wading through the snow. Layered in crusts of soot and frozen rain, the snow did not bear her weight well. Many steps were taken on top of the cover but often she fell through. Sometimes she floundered, wallowing. And with each awkward step, frustration mounted. But she had come into the walled woodland and was now committed. To lay here wallowing or turn back would disappoint the momentum of her quest. And of her longing love.

At first the way wound through high evergreens later yielding to hardwoods. Now she saw the trail mounting toward a steep knoll. Through naked trunks and snowy limbs above she saw the black cloud of burning rubbish, billowing, and edged in a fitful glow. She ceased from her struggling to gaze on it fascinated, but again dismay clouded her. Then she saw the red- and black-checked back of Balder in his mackinaw, tiny and high, backed by the flame wreathed in billows. From the distance she heard the fire's speech, screeching, rumbling and cracking. Erupting often with power.

Balder! She wanted to call but the name would not come. "Balder." She whispered it holding it under her breath.

Evoked by the surging mythic cloud, the Norse god of beauty, of purity and light, came lightening to mind. Frigga's son, slain at Loki's urging, by Hodur the blind. Balder the god, slain with mere mistletoe, a parasite. Everything in great creation, save this parasite, had taken an oath not to harm this gladsome son of Odin, lord of all gods. The great fire swelling behind, she thought of the god Balder's funeral pyre. The body of the god was set to burn aboard ship but, so laden with precious things was it, only a giantess could send it down the ways.

The awful spell and horrific stench of this place now mingled with that of the myth and, kindled by the mighty sight, she struggled on, up the steep knoll, calling to Balder as she went. He seemed not to hear.

The rumbling of the fire increased as she clambered up, its speaking in flames and burning swelled. Its roaring cast a reverie of awe upon her, and still she cried his name.

She saw his steps exaggerated by the snowshoes, and slowly he turned. Balder looked down through tall trunks, his stance above her one of waiting. Oh why doesn't he call out to me, answer? A darkening loss of confidence checks her. But she wallows on, slipping and sinking, wading through deep snow.

At last he called out to her, using her name. "Gloria! Atta girl! Come up heah d'me, Gloria. You're making it fine!"

He opened his arms and she came to him.

Oh couldn't you comfort me better. Why didn't you come down to me, she wanted to say. But now she was in his arms, weeping.

The man held her, feeling her slenderness against him. He felt her soft gold hair with his hand, gently smoothing it. Her hat had come off and he found her hair soft as rabbit's fur. "What's a matter, Glory? Anyone hurt? Anyone lost?"

"No, Balder." She said it against his rough mackinaw. "Just me. I'm hurt and I'm lost."

He hugged her to him, gently, strong and sexual, still smoothing her hair. She looked up at him, whispering. "I'm happy to be here, comforted by you."

He had to duck his head to catch it, listening thoughtfully. Again he hugged her, felt her deep sigh. "'N' I'm happy t'comfort." For a long moment they stayed so, together. Then he pulled back, looking down on her, eyes grave. But he smiled. "Think we could do this f'evah?"

Together in the embrace, they turned a bit, making smoke and tumult the background to the grace of this moment. The dismal drizzling had ceased and the wind increased, fanning the fire in Quakertown. It held her gaze and he saw it reflected in her eyes. Troubled, entranced, she said,

"What's going to happen? Will we be all right? Will the mountain go under?"

"Doubt it. Caunt possibly, not in this age. The resort might have t'go, though."

Her voice became excited, pitched. "But the skiers, the investors, the jobs!... the local economy of Gott'im! The pawithin. I... if only I'd worked harder with Mr. Segar!... we're ruined!"

"The pain." He said it gravely. "The whole place suffers." He shook his head. Gott'im'll go on... unda the cloud."

She understood him and wailed. "The resort! The investors, the project in Gott'im.... Balder!"

"Don't mean a thing, Glory."

She pulled back, looking at his fire bright eyes. Incredulous, she shook her head slowly. "Don't you care? The ones that *could* backed out. And Jimmy's responsible. There are debts to Savings and Loans in Massachusetts, in New York."

But Balder said, "Ask carefully. What kind of harm will it do to his spirit t'be troubled this way?" He shook his head. "I caunt lie t'you, Glory. The loss o'the projects don't mean a thing. The hurt'n your eyes means something. The *pain* of folks who lost money.... That means something. The other could safely be in the fire. Should I lie'n say it ain't so?"

"But it's my *life*." She pulled back, but would not loose herself from the embrace.

"No it's not, Glory. It's just something to do."

"You've no right to say that...." But, she wondered. *Let not your heart be troubled.* She leaned against the rough of his woolen jacket and said it low: "My life *is* mine. Isn't its meaning mine to decide?..." She stopped a moment, thinking. Again she pulled back, looking up. Seeing the irony in his eyes she recalled the conversation they shared once in which he had seemed to doubt her expressions of love.

"Oh Balder. I do! I *do* love you. Why won't you believe me? Can you see? Can't you see how I love you?"

He loosened his arm, letting her fall back more, but holding her still. He said, "Yuht. I do... as far as you're able.... Glory, I know the watchers in town've beat you bout the ears for what you tried to do f'this place. I'd be honest to say I don't always care much for the ways you had in mind to help'n encourage us. But I never doubted you cared—care now. You care as much about Gott'im as any soul here. Thank you f'that."

It was salving. She smiled some, eased. Gloria rested her arms upon his, and their legs adhered, cold thighs pressed together. The fire, visible through the woodland below, was forgotten in the kindling of this moment. Sexuality pervaded their embrace, tender and aching-sweet. They stood together like a sheaf of wheat, sensuous and bound, supported by its own rich golden weight.

"Balder," (she sweetly asked) "how is it that your love is better than mine? You don't give up your dreams... yet you expect me to give up mine."

Again he smiled that maddening smile. "We both care about this place. Maybe it's the difference in the way they're expressed." The irony of his expression deepened but his arm tightened about her. Her ski suit rustled against him, sexy and sweet. Like the rustling of sun-drying green leaves, ripening toward a full warmth. He said, "Evah heard the story—how the man'n woman fell fom grace? She fell fom ambition; he from desire o'her. They had a simple life, live together, enjoy all fruits but one...." He shook his head. "Wadn't enough fah her."

She smiled up at him, kindly. "Okay. True!—it's *not* enough. But... —let's look at this desire thing."

He grinned. "Wait a minute. Story's got lots'o points to it but another is, two heads to the family. Like Siamese twins—two heads, one body. No agreement but lots'o misery."

"But why's it the man's choice? To be only misery for one, then?" It was not even a halfhearted challenge. She was completely happy here with Balder on this knoll among tall trunks, the fires of hell just off their shoulders.

He grinned more. "I'd'know. May because ambition is inferior to this kind o'desire." He jigged her in his arms, grinning. Balder's sex came alive. God! He was happy with her! Gloria felt it through her suit and grew happier, too. A melting moved among her limbs, sweet tendrils twisting into every part. She was breathless, rustling wheat.

"But if that's so, why won't your desire let you fall—as Adam's did. Yours must not be as strong." Barely she spoke it, smiling. All this sweet teasing—too much to bear. How could he stand it—oh!

"Ah," he said and let her go. Their embrace was broken, they came apart. Beyond, the smoke and fire surged, rumbling. It boomed and roared. They turned toward its fresh speaking, hand in hand. Together they watched and were lit by it.

"I'll tell you, Glory." He said it as they came away down the hill. She was in his arms and disappointed once again. Carrying her, his snowshoes sank deep beneath their combined weight.

"Adam's dead. He didn't love enough. Should'o been willing t'walk through fires solely fah the sight of her."

He looked down on her gravely there in his arms. She was a sweet person, good, very good. But she did not love him. Yet.

Going downhill with Balder on his alien feet is not as awkward as she supposed. She is happy in this present moment, nestled in his embrace. Comfortable as a child in his father's arms, except for the top of her head itching against his scratchy short beard. Sign of his fatherhood, she remembers. This is how he cares, as protective and sure as a father. Could I love him like that? No. I can't mother anyone. Too careless; with my heart like a little stone. She sighs. Let this go on. Carry me home, Balder....

But at the base of the hill the man stops, his gaze on a twitching thicket. Something's astir in the hemlock seedlings edging the twitch trail. He sets her down, reaches into the dingy snow needles and comes out—like a magician—with a very lean patchy white hare. It squirms and beats with impossibly large feet. Then quickly it subsides, as though exhausted.

"Oh, Balder... so helpless. Is it in shock?"

"Don't look too chippa. Li'l snowshoe rabbit."

Opening his mackinaw he sets it inside, buttoning it snugly but not enough to smother. She smiles at its pink rabbity nose poking out, twitching.

"C'mere," he says hoisting her up again. "Take y'both to mother at *Simons Ledge*."

Through dingy snow and woods they go, the varying hare a little lump, scarcely felt between them.

"So small," she says. "A snowshoe, you said?"

He nods, scratching her temple with his beard. "They change color, spring'n fall, depending on the light. Brown to white'n back again. So they call 'em varying."

But Gloria has stopped listening. She thinks of Balder's mother, Balder's house. No, she cannot go there, not to *Simons Ledge*. That rambling old place, last century's farmstead. The barn full of wild animals and other people's children. Happiness will not go that far. It ends when this traipse in his arms is over. She will get into her little red Caprice, not his patched pickup. Return to the resort warmed and, in some measure, healed by his embrace. She will dream of this many nights and stay out of other men's beds. The *loneliness of other men's beds* is how she thinks of it now. Balder's nurturing, chaste embrace inspires her with better desire. She is more secure and, at night when she drifts off she will sometimes feel him there with her, loving and strong. But her dreams will try to work themselves into some semblance of her preferred reality... and that's when they will stop. Dreams of him stop when she tries to borrow his form for her purposes. For Gloria cannot picture herself in *Simons Ledge* and she cannot picture him anywhere else.

He is carrying her from the woods and she is busy with these thoughts. Tears come silently, roll down her cheeks.

He sees them fall, knowing she will not come. There is sorrow in the silence of those tears. But he does not kiss them away. He does not dare kiss the tears away.

The Village in Twilight

Weeks passed as changes became apparent in the village. At first skiers from Massachusetts poured in to see the spectacle, but poor conditions ensured that these visits would not repeat. Skiers stayed away and investment stopped, reversed, vacated the area. Ground would remain unbroken, new building stopped in mid-construction leaving their standing white skeletons. Back at the mountain, streaked and strewn like dreary tenements across Jasper's dingy knees, condominiums were abandoned. Dispirited, many of their owners tried to sell. Others held out hope of recouping, maybe next year. The tires will all be consumed some day, won't they? Going to the initial spectacular display, business scarcely dipped in the village. Restaurants, clubs, bed-and-breakfast establishments were all busy, domestics, cooks, waitpersons, clerks kept their jobs as news of the show spread before the inevitable slowdown. The locals, depressed by the intermittent atmosphere of darkness felt the call of their ancestral blood to make do. The old, asthmatic and ill, the young with developing lungs continued to suffer: on bad days they stayed indoors. Eight fire departments from surrounding towns moved several lots of tires which had been strewn in the woods to a new dump site in Copenhagen, one proposed by another would-be magnate. Loggers were employed to cut a buffer in the woods surrounding the fire. Experts from away came to study and suggest ways of extinguishing the hapless fulminations. Augusta appealed to federal agencies for help. But it was new, this aberrant variety of industrial terrorism; new from what went before, and answers would be slow in coming.

One bright spot in the gloom was the revival of Decatur's Diner. Secretly sentimental and reluctant, Lyman Bearce had not secured the buyer for his plum spot. He resurrected the grubby silver and maroon dining car, an authentic piece of history from the old Atlantic and St. Lawrence Railway. He had it hauled out of storage, set on a new foundation, slightly altered. A new kitchen was added to suit. Nancy's Neatniks in the village came in to clean and paint the diner's tin ceiling, strip the wax off its linoleum countertops, table and floor. Grease everywhere, thick with the dirt of decades, was washed away. Bearce even had some of the plastic booths recovered in vinyl. Of course he didn't smile, but Lyman Bearce was pleased that the diner was back and better than before. Since he had made some money on the deal in that failed ski apparel boutique proposal, things were sweeter than ever because the Goldings were taking hits. That fire was no doubt a terrible price to pay for things to be sorted back into their proper order, but it *was* entertaining to contemplate what would become of them.

The first day of the diner's reopening people came in early. Some were tentative and hushed, looking around. They sat themselves down before Melvinia, Chrischana, and one other new waitperson, all crisply attired in new aprons and perky little hats. Melvinia, ear rings tinkling, submitted to the hat because she did not want to discourage Decatur's niece, who came up from Mass to run the place. Gildy is young, a business graduate missing the friendliness of her hometown. The anonymous cubicle in the giant insurance company in Boston was getting to her in a way she had not foreseen. Despite his declining constitution, Decatur himself was quietly happy, content to sit on the stool next nearest the kitchen window, sipping cocoa and reminiscing with anyone who happened to plunk down beside him.

The Goldings of Jasper Mountain moved to Québec, leaving staff behind to run "the freak show," as Eloise Potadoe dubbed it. Even James Fay, once considered a top associate, was left behind. As Harry Golding put it, "I have every confidence that you, with your golden touch and gifted entrepreneurial sense, will soon sort out the various ventures in Gottheim. And there will be ample opportunity, before long, for us to work closely together again. Keep in touch."

Lyman Bearce and Jeffy Decatur are having breakfast side-by-side on their stools in Decatur's Diner. Chewing contemplatively, Decatur looks through the opening beside the coffee urn to see Gildy's capped but frizzy gold-red head and determined shoulders, where she stands at the grill carefully turning eggs and flipping pancakes. Happily inhaling the fragrance of homefries and spattering bacon, Decatur washes down his fluffy eggs and toast with a swig of Melvinia's coffee. "Y'see," he says to white-bearded Bearce, "having that MBA is nothing but a help t'her in running this business. Wouldn't be surprised if she does it even betta'n I did."

Jasper Mary does not say what Lyman Bearce thinks of that. He just grunts, eating his plate full of sausage and eggs over medium.

In a corner by a front window sits brick-redheaded Asa across from his wife Olive, a largish brunette; he with his plate full of eggs over easy, she with a stack of blueberry pancakes. Gildy has gone overboard with the blueberries, making the flapjacks darker and slightly unappetizing, but Olive is forgiving. She piles excess berries to one side of her plate with her fork in hopes that Chrischana will scrape and load it into the dishwasher before Gildy can see it.

Shaking his head, the fastidious Asa says, "I'd tell her about it, f'I was you. She ought see'em so's to learn." He looks over as Willie Kimball sits down in what was once Asa's regular stool in the elbow of the counter. Asa has given it up for the occasional breakfast out with his wife. The faintest look of regret surfaces briefly in his face.

Olive shakes her head. "Don't do to discourage hah, Asa."

"She ought learn it right."

Olive shakes her head vigorously. Her fingernails flash ice blue, waving her fork.

That was another thing. Asa wishes she would go back to the smashing red she wore when he courted her. He looks out the window, a bit dejected. Outside Abner Chapman walks along in his camouflage fatigues, head down, eyes on the puddled ground. To Asa he seems the embodiment of gloom, the gloom of a dark Gott'im morning. When's somebody gont do something fah that boy? For the first time, a bit of grace slips into the older man's thoughts concerning Abner... where once he had judged the other self pitying. Does the boy still wander some tortured and unceasing scene of fire and blood there in that steamy faraway Mekong Delta, or waya evah it was?

Willie Kimball has stood to move to the opposite end of the diner as Robbie Robichaud comes in the door. Asa pops his head up to shoot a wave at the logging contractor. Robbie gives a reverse nod without his customary bounce and smile. He sits down on Asa's stool across from the booth, within easy speaking distance. Nothing much is said, however. In his continuing grief over Alvin's death, Robbie is sober, inconsolable, lacking the alertness to sense his melancholy influence on those around him. He lives in a constant smear of gray. The weather of Gottheim perfectly suits his mourning, however. He continues working, bringing truckloads of pulp and saw logs out of the grim woodland, day by day. His nephew, Hiram, now works in the woods with Ansell, but it is a slog all the way. Ansell had always been a quiet worker, and now, bereft of his twin, is just no use in telling Hi what and what not to do. He gives the boy directions but if it doesn't take the first time that's the end of it as far as Ansell is concerned. Robbie has been loading pulp logs nowhere near the uniform 4 ft. length. They are either too long or too short. And a Robichaud teenager ought t've been born knowing how to lay a pine down. Robbie has seen Hiram notching his trees: It's a wonder he hasn't killed himself.

The steamy, hot-oil-biscuit-bacon-coffee atmosphere of the diner suddenly gives place to a more concentrated, a foul now-familiar, odor: the smell of burning tires comes among the regulars in bodily form. Ceylon Segar scuffs up to the stool that Lyman Bearce vacated moments before.

The spell of his rumination broken by the stench, Decatur starts back, a look of amazement spread over his bald bespeckled face. But for the fragrant clinking of flatware, diner life stops. Everyone stares at the grimy dishevelment that is Ceylon Segar.

In his first appearance in public since the disaster.

In a booth by the window behind him, Simeon Sanborn is thinking hard. For weeks he has been mourning the awful atmosphere permeating the village... but just yesterday he got a piece of good news. It siphoned off some of the impotence that has been gnawing at him since Goldings' resorts sent the price of property out of sight. Simeon has four children, all young adults, none of whom have been able to afford a loan for a place of their own. They were like sad-eyed Robichauds—trailers on their lot. Even the cost of an apartment in an old house in the village was heading beyond reach: Landlords could get more renting to weekend skiers over the course of a single season than they got renting to local people year round. Robbie's twins had dealt with the problem by setting trailers on the home place, but there was no option for Simeon's kids, his place being in the village on Livery Street. Everyone understood that development pushed Gott'im property into the realm of impossible. Until now. Yesterday Simeon's eldest gave him the news: A loan and house have finally come together. Gerta is going to own her own home. And it has just occurred to Simeon Sanborn that the smelly article, sitting right in front of him, is the reason why. A slow smile coming, Simeon stares at Ceylon's filthy backside a moment or two more. Looking around, he sees something akin to his own feeling emerge on the faces around him.

Once... twice... three times, Simeon claps his hands together. He keeps it up, deliberately, a few more claps echoing—one on his right, the other at the far end of the diner where Elvy and Ernest Sessions sit with their three little kids. They are having cereal together, a rare treat before its off to the dowel mill for Mother and Father, day care and school for the kids.

Clap clap clap clap. A chorus begins. Someone is banging a sugar dispenser to the rhythm of this slow applause. Salt and pepper shakers in hand, flatware bouncing adding a tinkling echo. Everyone in Decatur's is clapping or pounding the table. (Everyone but the contractor Evan Bean. He thinks ruefully of the boys he's had to lay off.)

Now Decatur is standing beside Ceylon Segar, pouring him a cup of coffee. Grinning, Gildy has abandoned the grill in the kitchen, to take the old fart's order herself.

Down in the elbow of the counter, Robbie Robichaud is smiling with his eyes for the first time since Alvin froze to death in his pickup six weeks ago. Across from him, Asa looks with resignation at Olive. Their fledgling bed-and-breakfast may not survive the ashes of this fire, but Olive is smiling, thinking of her children and grandchildren. She runs a blue fingernail along Asa's freckled hand. He sighs, saying, "Still got m'job, anaway. Mill's not hurt ana by burning tires." Olive nods her brown head, smiling faintly.

Ceylon Segar's smile is nine miles wide on his grizzled face. He looks around smugly, it suddenly occurring to him that he just might be bigger in Gott'im then either of the Goldings. For a few moments it is worth it to lose all that money in escrow and have his property attached for defraying of fire fighting and cleanup. And Gildy has just informed him that breakfast is on the house.

While he eats, talk in the diner heats up. Now that Lyman Bearce has gone back to one of his mills, it focuses on how gleeful he must be since Julius and Harry Golding have vacated town for whiter pastures. The sour

The sour apples over Bearces' handprints being all over Gott'im were shelved temporarily in favor of picking over the Goldings while they prospered here. The townsfolk have grown tired of this: of telling back and forth all the Goldings' peccadillos, describing in exaggerated and often erroneous satirical detail how they treat their children, employees, associates and spouses. Now they are free once again to concentrate on the latest piece of dirt picked up in the laundromat or grocery aisle concerning their own local homegrown and related elite. Eloise Patadoe, transplanted West Virginia artist and goat queen, calls it bloodsport.

The door opens and in comes Nellie Sessions, the frizz-headed aunt of Cindabilla. She is an amateur archaeologist who works in the local dowell mill at the outlet of the village pond, along with Asa and other locals. With *The Village Voter* under her arm, she looks around and sees the jubilee set lose by the stinking presence of Ceylon Segar. She is thinking, *Not a soul here's read this week's Bellyache.* Walking straight to the left end of the diner, she unfurls the rag, flashing the headline before Elvy and Ernest's surprised eyes. "LOCAL DOWEL MAKERS AND NAME SOLD TO CHICAGO COMPANY: <u>Mill building and equipment to go at auction</u>." Ernest whistles softly, reading the first paragraph, saying, "Says heah 58 families gont feel this. That's us, El."

"Chicago?! What's Chicago got do with it?"

—

"The King and all his company sat on their horses, marveling, perceiving that the power of Saruman was overthrown; but how they could not guess. And now they turned their eyes towards the archway and the ruined gates. There they saw close beside them a great rubbleheap; and suddenly they were aware of two small figures lying on it at their ease, grey-clad, hardly to be seen among the stones. There were bottles and bowls and platters laid beside them, as if they had just eaten well, and now rested from their labour." (*The Two Towers*, 207)

The three sat together in the cramped second-floor furnished apartment of a Victorian Gothic house on Kimball Street. Paperback in hand, Daniel sat reading aloud between his brothers on the scratchy woolen couch. His hair sticking every which way, Nathan leaned into Daniel's side like the disciple John leaning on Jesus' bosom at the Last Supper. The smaller boy's eyes looked unblinking upon the page; yet he saw, not the curlicues of the words printed there, but images conjured by Tolkien. Beside the two, sitting against the arm of the couch with the soles of his feet pressed against Daniel's leg, Benaiah stared at the book in his big brother's hand. He too saw the ruins of Isengard and the hobbits lounging here, peaceably smoking their pipes.

At the table across from the three boys sat Chrischana and Peter, also listening to Daniel read aloud from *The Two Towers*. It had been Chrischana's idea, late last year, to begin reading the trilogy aloud. Shortly before Thanksgiving, together they had tested the waters, discovering that Nathan was now old enough to receive the great story of the One Ring. Benaiah had encountered *The Hobbit* in school, and Daniel had long since devoured the three volumes concerned with the last war of the Third Age. Lately they had discovered that reading it aloud made Peter's visits a little easier, every family member being engaged by those events leading to the advent of Men's rule in Middle-earth. The three boys were quietly happy to see their parents harmlessly together again if only for occasional evening visits when neither had to work. They were reassured seeing Peter drink coffee. Mother having on her good blouse and mascara also made them hopeful. Now and then she would bustle about the tiny efficiency kitchen, fixing him a meal. Life in these moments was merely what it should be, yet to them it was keenly lived... as though a living good story.

"'You do not know your danger, Theoden,' interrupted Gandalf. 'These hobbits will sit on the edge of ruin and discuss the pleasures of the table, or the small doings of their fathers, grandfathers, and great-grandfathers, and remoter cousins to the ninth degree, if you encourage them with undue patience.'" (208)

But as the words came off his tongue, Daniel was dreaming up images of his own. While absorbed in the story before him, he yet kept in some part of his imagination an idea that came to him time and again. Daniel wanted somehow to reenter as though for the first time the subcreated world of Middle-earth, on a creative impetus of his own. For months he had hoped to start his own series of hobbit adventures, even making several attempts in notebooks when he could snatch time. But something always interrupted to ruin his momentum. Half-finished adventures were the result. With Benaiah digging his toenails into his calf, Daniel sighed but kept reading.

Across the room, Peter Prince heard little of the tale. He sat looking at Chrischana, hoping she would notice. If she would only give him her gaze. He wanted to look straight into her solemn Native eyes, drink from that well of patience and kindness. He longed to take her large and generous sexuality in his deft mechanic's fingers. He wanted her to want him again.

Then suddenly, as though rewarding his hope, she did turn her gaze. Slowly she smiled, letting him look into her eyes. She was coming to him now, full of attention... something he had not seen for a very long time. Her dimpled hand was fastened to her coffee cup but she opened her fingers, pushing the cup aside. Now her hand lay open on the table before him. Again she smiled that slow smile.

Slowly Peter Prince reached out for the brown fingers, covering them with his palm. Her flesh was warm and strong against it. Gently he held the hand, gently smiled. Her eyes warmed toward a faint suggestiveness. Then slowly she turned her gaze away.

Her face was turned toward the boys on the couch but she held Peter's hand across the table. It was not that he would never hurt her again. He might. *Probably would.* But now she had knowledge about him crucial to her security. This and only this made her secure: Peter had understanding. He still had the power to hurt her but understood now that he had no right. So together they sat at the table, leaning like bookends toward one another. When one or another of the boys looked up, he saw his parents clasping hands, leaning on their elbows and silently sipping coffee.

God was in the household with them. Everyone thought so whether consciously or not, and no one said anything.

Elda Simon holds a guided belief that she lives in eternity. She tries to live all her time each day. Knowing something of the metabolism of insects and animals, she thinks time is as elastic as need be for whatever creature inhabiting it. She gets a kick out of the fact that humans lumber and slur in comparison with damselflies. On the other hand, houseflies as a species have a long history and humans have not yet begun to live. The generations of flies out distance our own like the swift edge of the universe fleeing beyond remnants of light left in the dust of the original cosmos. Sometimes she wonders: Will the universe curve back to meet itself falling toward its own core?

Here is Elda's (and all our) descent into decay. The substance of her form mutates, deteriorating. For lack of seeing the fresh scribblings of ravens' wings where they have washed themselves in snowcover, she sorrows. Crossing on snowshoes she looks down on her hand in some patch of snowlight among the hardwoods but, where the blue-veined thin white parchment of her fingers should be, she sees darkness. The wiggling of her fingers hardly registers until she waves her hand into the peripheral light of her eyes. She has heard of the darkening of Gottheim and by it her darkness has deepened. Her nostrils smell burning, her hands help the animals harmed by it. She knows what the twilight of gods entails.

The world would think of her story (and ours) as ending in sorrow. But Elda thinks she knows something, dimly, about this bewildering house of life. To her, coming down mountain on Everett's ancient snowshoes, the fire is like macular degeneration. Because of this disease she stumbles over snags, watches for fallen trees out the corners of her eyes. Trying to stay with the twitch trails she largely succeeds. The snow is awful cold on her legs when she falls, joints ache, the pain dipping even to the core within her skeleton. On her side in the snow she wallows helplessly like a beached whale. Elda stops moving. She rests. Snow begins melting against her cheek.

Balder has described it for her, telling the fire as glimpsed in the distance, snagging the gaze, becoming a hole in the vision. Everything surrounding it becomes peripheral. Only marginally present, the village, the mountains, the river or intervale farms. But, if you look directly at the village, little and lighted and hopeful, the damage becomes peripheral.

Better, by loosing the bonds of fixation, you can scan the scene to take in all.

Lying here in the snow, Elda thinks Balder has experienced the three ways of seeing. As a child growing in Gottheim he lived like the second. From Vietnam he found a hole so black he thought he would never see light again. He went sightless a while... until he discovered Love sitting there in the darkness with him.

Elda remembers her little sisters—still rascally and sweet in memory—crossing into the darkness. And Everett also crossed over the dark river. She is crossing now, a too lengthy crossing. They married when she knew little, consciously, of love. All she knew of life—well it wasn't much. Just some intuitive stuff about animals. Knew nothing of Everett or mothering!... By time he died... she was looking for him everywhere. She saw his box lowered and covered in earth. Earth, earth he knew and worked intimately. When her sisters died she sought them; later she sought him more. Seeking and seeking... until he turned up in her half-wakeful, half-dreaming, sleep. He was attached to her and she to him. With the snow melting under her, she remembers: They were attached at the ear, her ribs to his upper rib, her cheek in his so close they were one. He was a limb of her being, and she of his. But of course in waking life he was gone, leaving only the ache of phantom pain.

Oddest things drop into your mind! The taste of semen, sour like frog eggs—or was it dragonfly foam?

A tiny gravelly sound escapes Elda, laughing at herself lying here. Ooo—her body is saturated with pain. *Well, your arthritis is worse, you nut, 'cause your lying in the snow!*

But she makes no move to extricate herself from this wallow.

Just some intuitive stuff about the critters.... God just must enjoy half-making His creatures. He gives us a body and environment, interests... some abilities... and leaves out the important stuff. Then, when He thinks you can handle the inability to handle things, he sticks them in on the sly: commitments, children, chores, blindness. You can't handle it, any of it, but it's too late. Look at sheep. So stupid he uses them as a metaphor for people. Now you've got no choice but to handle things, trying to make it all work.

"If only I'd see Sugarloaf." She says it aloud. She has never even had a good look at him. Always too busy scaring him off... and now with this black hole—can't even find a cup of coffee directly!—oh why'd they go'n shoot Posey? *Never* get used to that killing. God could come and explain it to her and still she wouldn't get it.... But... again... she can't quite believe in death, either. Everything dies, yes, but Posey is around somewhere. Little sisters'n Everett. "Just too blind d'see'em!" Everybody, *blind blind blind!*

Elda squirms around and blunders up, dusting off snow. She continues on until coming to an old deadfall. Leaning there, she hoists snowshoe feet over the prone trunk. Why not sit another spell?

People ought to have kids. World needs more kids, not less. What's wrong is theya's too many old people. Don't die off as fast as we used to. Refrigeration, sanitation, modern medicine, technology, keep us alive too long. What do we want to live for when kids are grown anaway? So don't I know Balder has Daniel, Glory'n all. He's safe now. Don't need me. I'm ready to go, huh, Sugarloaf. Her old fingers stroke his ear while the little deer nudges her.

Sugarloaf!

Her old face pushes into a grin. She has no idea when she first began stroking the pilar side of the white deer. Somehow he stole to her as she sat there on the deadfall. Her hands feel his knobby head. Soon he will be a button buck. She faces front, tilting her head, and can see his pink features on the edge of sight. Posey's fawn.

There is no thought of chasing him off. And Elda is very glad. Relieved. *Glad glad glad!*

Here they are, leaning together in the House of Life. Simple and soaking up the grace that was urged, patiently waiting for them to unite.

Decidedly, James Fay is not curious about Balder, knowing this mechanic inside out. It has been months since she spoke of him, now suddenly Gloria is talking about the blue-collar like he's Olympian or something. James Fay sighed when she insisted on the meeting. Just no success in wishing the millwright away. No success in a lot of his wishing away. He is surfacing in their lives again with a vengeance. At least he will be able to report back something to Dad.

He never met the man, but Balder read all the episodes and escapades of James Fay in *The Village Voter*. Today they will meet... if the man shows. In spite of himself, Balder is curious. Fay. The Golding go-getter who, until recently, ate whole tracks of Gott'im for dinner. For reasons of her own, Gloria is now big on this meeting. Balder takes it as a good sign. Once she was big on their *not* meeting.

Sitting at the bottom of Buck Hill, Balder is waiting to take them up to the sugaring-off party. He has just come back downhill on Artie Osgood's snow machine, having borrowed the sled to take them all up. A toboggan in tow, and Chrischana, Peter and the boys already on the hill where the evaporator steams its sweetness into the cool air: She's got the firebox stoked with ashwood, sap has been running for a week, snow falling every night. The woods are dense and dingy with it. Like the mill down in Guildford, the tire fire makes its own atmosphere. It can be clear as an icicle out in Luz, but hereabouts it will snow. Sometimes you have to turn on headlights to drive through. Luckily, for the sugaring-off today, the sun shines.

Mother's up there, too. Sometimes she sorrows him with those pathetic timid eyes of hers. He has read up on macular degeneration and talked to the doctor about her symptoms. Apparently nothing's to be done except the vitamins, but he has been urged to bring her for an exam to check the eyes for other signs of ill health. Sitting here on the snowmobile, he thinks maybe he bout has her to the point of consenting. Or maybe it's Daniel who's bringing her around. Balder grins. No way Mother'd say no to Daniel. Hey, they might even get her to take an entire physical exam.

But, standing now and shaking his head, he reconsiders it: Doaw. Don't do t'get carried away. Anyway, maybe he should consider carefully her hopes and dreams about dying. She *will* die someday. Betta get used to it. Again he grins. All get used to death—or die trying.

Theodora's custom-painted powder blue Saab 900 shoots down the plowed road toward him. It zips past, slides to a stop and begins backing toward him on the opposite side of the road.

"Balder!" Theo calls out, happily waving.

Balder is surprised to see her driving instead of Fay. She pulls over onto the shoulder across from him, turning off the ignition. Three people step from the car into the grimy road. The sun is shining on them, a strengthening sun shedding a larger light as the earth trails slowly back from its apogee along the ecliptic: This northland will lean again toward its own star.

Balder grins at Theodora. Gloria gets out behind, but his eyes now are all for the homely yet dainty Theo. In nature she has not changed. He feels sure she is still the same fragile person she was born to be. Like some ghost who isn't quite sure of its own reality. Even so *something* is different. Something.... she has done one right thing in giving Gott'im Chair Company to its employees. But why she did it, he has no idea. Unlike others in Gott'im, he does not think of this as just another of her harebrained stunts. To the village elite it is a nutsy act, in a long list of Theodora nuttiness. Balder would have liked to see James Fay get the news: His grin widens. *Probably did it first, told him after.*

Gloria hurries up to him, shining in the sun. Softly, lightly, she kisses his mustache. "Balder Simon, this is my brother, Jimmy Fay." She steps back.

The two men reach, shake hands. Balder grins his greeting, the short bespeckled Fay nodding. (As though their locally cultural positions and characters were reversed: Balder being from away and Fay with East Anglian ancestors living here nine generations.)

Balder says, "So..." and there is a slight awkward pause. "So, who's first? Here's the sled, anaone fah snowshoes?" All are dressed for a trek in the woods, ski pants and boots for the snow, nylon jackets for the sun. "Sugar's just waitin'fah us up theya. How'bout it, Fay. Snowshoes or sled? Theo, you remember how the machine works."

"Let James do it, show him how, Balder."

Gloria exclaims brightly. "I'm for the shoes!"

Balder shows the other man how to start the machine, give it gas, how to stop. The developer is not what he expected. Fay is not eager, forthcoming, or much of a personality... monosyllabic, taciturn. His sister stands looking on, unhappy, anxious.

Theo knows where the old Twitchell Farm once stood. The nearly deserted hilltop has been a favorite berrying spot, party destination, picnic and trek place for off-roading. She asks only about the last turn and location of the evaporator. In a moment they are off in a whining two-stroke cloud.

Standing alone with Gloria, Balder says, "He's glad d'be heah!" It's cheerfully said. "Why'd he come? Have to threaten him much?"

The unhappy look stays about her eyes but she returns his grin. "Said I'd marry you tomorrow if he didn't come."

She looks off up the trail. "No, I don't know why he came. Don't know why I insisted, either." She shakes her head, still looking the other way. "Guess I'm just... groping."

He takes her hand, begins examining her fingers. Lightly caresses them.

"Groping is not such a bad thing. Sometimes it's betta'n charging ahead. Most times. What's bad about being unsure? Shows a li'l humility."

Her look is dubious. "Humility's good—I know.... But it can be... painful. Why do we value it in others... but mostly never consider it? What's its real purpose, y'suppose?"

He does not respond right off, just stands gently regarding her. He says, "What a good girl—fah wantin'to know."

Gloria's smile is wistful as she says, "Maybe that would've been demeaning to me—once. Your little compliment there. Now I feel like you've given me a small piece of amethyst, of jasper or something. Thanks, Balder."

He moves closer, holding her. They lean together and Balder holds her to him, lovingly.

485

— Mystery Gottheim —

"The heroes of old romance, who went about smiting
dragons, lopping giants' heads, and otherwise pleasantly
diverting themselves, scarcely deserve mention in
comparison with our New England champions, who,
trusting not to carnal sword and lance, in a contest with
principalities and powers... encountered their enemies with
weapons forged by the stern spiritual armorer of Geneva.
The life of Cotton Mather is as full of romance.... All about
him was enchanted ground – devils glared on him in his
'closet wrestlings'...."

—Supernaturalism of New England
John Greenleaf Whittier

Mystery Gottheim

"We don't know why."
    "We don't know why it happened in one night."

~~~~~~~~~~~~~~~

Burly Lyman Bearce walked down in the moonlight from one of the Bearces' family timberland parcels, checking on damage to the new logging road—washed out in a torrential onslaught. As always on a mountainous downhill the backs and caps of his damaged knees ached, hobbling him. *Old age. God damn buckets of fun.*

    It was cold spring in the early 1980s, wet and leafless. Mud season. There was no one around but the spirits of his yankee ancestors to see him come limping down over the washout of rocks and gravel and sand; no one maybe but them to witness the dark-haired old lumberman in his jacket and hunting cap, his canvas pants and caulked boots, great white beard gleaming on his chest like the moon it reflected. The treetops just off the edge of the road were great pines shadowing the uneven surface here and there, but Lyman Bearce managed to take the view off across the valley where the Arossagunticook gleamed, the flank of great Jasper Mountain showing darkly above with its unready stands of spruce, fir, hemlock and white pine. Even with the painful knees, the late hour, the ravaged road surface, Lyman Bearce was strong and ready enough on his legs to pay but scant heed to how he went. Instead he looked off at the great things of God reflected in the moonlight of another blesséd Gott'im evening, now well into night. And so it was that he saw there across the river valley a road he'd never seen before, cut like a thin white scar in the conifer wood on the lower west side of the mountain.

    And Lyman Bearce stopped. *What in hell—a road?*

    He was a local lumber baron, almost bigger than anybody: He had forty thousand acres if he had a foot of timberland. At the moment he was not even sure exactly just how much he had, that's-how-much-he-had. And Lyman Bearce knew this part, he knew this county. He would have said he
~~~~~~~~~~~~~~~

knew every road in every mountain between here and Lord's Hill to the southwest, in New Hampshire.

The first thing he thought was *Liquidation Leo*, Leonard Guerette. He was gobbling up land—not just stumpage—from the paper companies the last few years, and was beginning to encroach into Western Maine. Bearce did not stop long in his hobbling descent, but he was busy over who owned that parcel. His mind just wasn't working now. *Old age. Buckets of goddamn fun.*

He came to the next opening and, sure enough, the cut was still visible, gleaming like a thread he could reach out to grasp and follow. Wonder where it would lead? That timber's not ready, he thought.

Champion, Woodland, Great Northern, Scott. He ticked them off on his fingers, not bothering to ask himself why the name Guerette was the first thing in his mind. Adirondack Paper was sure to be next. Yes, he thought that section over there belonged to them. Guerette was the next big enemy—an independent contractor! *Hell.* Lyman Bearce ate logging contractors in this county, and halfway to the middle of the state, for breakfast. But here was Liquidation Leo taking advantage of the state of the industry, the unlooked for passing of the great companies into other, less considerate, hands. Great out-of-staters and internationalists who cared nothing about—about—about how to *do* a thing!

Guerette would turn that side of the mountain into a melt down— timbers flowing like milk from a cow. Jasper Mountain—cash cow! He was clambering down the washout apace now, fists clenched, shoulders fixed, as he searched out his footfalls to get below to the Blazer. What was he going to do when he got there? Hop in and drive along the river ten miles to the bridge, backtrack ten miles, search out some obscure gate from any of the many miscellaneous deadend lanes going up the side of the mountain? It was impossible. What was he going to do, roll in at 3:00 a.m. and have the old girl asking him where in hell he'd been? *Old age. You go crazy too. God damn buckets of fun.*

~~~~~~~~~~~

"The intellectual are different to I and you," paraphrased Eloise Patadoe out loud where she lay prone overlooking the edge of a cliff. In the same moments when Lyman Bearce began fuming over the apparition of a thin white line on Jasper Mountain, she had cast off her pack and was high above on the same mountainside, chuckling gleefully over the opening line in her proposed illustrated comic novel. "They suffer a low threshold of boredom, catching on quickly and conserving their skins."
~~~~~~~~~~~

....It needed work. Maybe it should be businessmen... or entrepreneurs. Or high school principals... or – It can't be the rich because that's been done. She could see it needed work but not with clarity, being too easily enamored of her creativity. Scarcely regarding the rocks, twigs and spongy lichen, she rolled over onto her back and looked up at the washed out stars. There was too much moonshine to see and feel the grip of their wonder this night, too much wash to make much interest.

Ah, she sighed, it's nice to be back from New York City, back in Gott'im where the emperor is forced to wear clothes or have a sense of humor about himself. She could feel her lanky ponytail hanging over the edge of rock collecting bits of this and that, the rock supporting her neck, the lichen cushioning her head. She recalled briefly how the village had failed to appear immediately she hit the curve of the highway where you first catch a glimpse of it. After being all night on the road, she had found only a thick black mist in the morning. The village had been disposed of— again. Ever since Ceylon Segar's tire fire, the village had drifted in and out of apparent existence. She had heard tales of people just missing it, bypassing an invisible Gottheim all together on their way to ... wherever. A couple of her artist friends had failed to materialize for a visit once on account of this.

She inched backwards a bit, letting her head lay over the edge of the precipice, her ponytail hanging down its face. Mouth agape, her bespeckled eyes rolling back, she looked across at the mountain, the same flank that had so irritated Lyman Bearce who was well below her now, hobbling down the washed out road.

Ah, Jasper Mountain. You're upside down.

She could not see its rounded summit from here but she scrutinized with the alert observant eye of an artist the dark conifer flank across the way, spotting here and there the glint of mica or pegmatite in its outcroppings. Do you know, she said to it, there is a zany movement afoot by the local neo-witches to begin some sort of worship of you? She sighed. An exaggerated sigh. All of Eloise's sighs are exaggerated. *Why can't people just treat you like the normal great being you are?* You've got your Goldings and your paper companies treating you like a gold mine (let alone the actual miners mining you for beryl, topaz and tourmaline); skiers using you like a playground, jumping on you like a trampoline; now the silly believers are thinking you're some kind of god (it's not like they're Native Americans or anything). The only people who use you normally (besides my own gracious self) are the descendants of settlers who live on you. ... But you are upside-down more and more, aren't you? ... You look strangely so, with your head in the stars of earth and your feet in the heaven of the river rapids.

Eloise heard a faint scratching and inched backwards towards the woods. Now she lolled over onto her side, staring into the mysterious shadowed tangle.

"Here, Sheila," she said. A black goat came out of the shade and puckerbrush and began licking her cheek and glasses, knocking them askew with her cross-shaped dark pointed face. One of her small polished horns was perilously close to gouging out her owner's eye as she went on licking.

Eloise and Sheila were up on the ledge ostensibly to scout out the townline, but it was rare that Eloise bypassed an opportunity to see anything from a new perspective. She had spent most of the day hiking through puckerbrush and swamps and over beaver dams, slogging the occasional small bog and hunting through woodland, trying to decipher the true boundary line, shared with Quaker and Gottheim. Not that Eloise had much land, but she had gotten curious about the land beyond. This led to curiosity about the boundary of the two towns. With her were compass and topographical map and lunch and a goat. Sheila could be a pretty good companion if the coy dogs were on the other side of the mountain.

Now Eloise sat up and began rubbing her lenses with the tail of her shirt. Then she stood, stuffed it back into her overalls and jacket, and brushed herself off; now carefully scrutinizing shoes, socks and the cuffs of her overalls. "Let me check you, too," she said to Sheila. "We don't want to go swapping bodily fluids with ticks, do we?"

It was time to wander back home into Quaker from the margin of Gottheim. She thought she had seen a logging road down below somewhere. Eloise and Sheila went back into the woods, never having seen any sign of a cut, the line of silver indicating a road on the opposite flank that had so infuriated Lyman Bearce.

Moonlight in the woods is her undoing—as an artist and as a person. She tries to capture her experience on canvas, on paper, in collage, gouache, charcoal pencil pen and ink. The shadows are blackly evocative, rich, slanting back below the white of trees dressed in moonshine. The quality of black and white is all you get, what you perceive even if shades of gray and silver and selenium toning do reside in these colorations. *It should be so easy, but I fail.*

Eloise sighed. And I can never get enough of this, the haunting overwhelming mystery of moonlight woods: it needs forever, an infinity of experience—no time out. *At the full moon I have to be here.* Have to creep around, get renewed by this mystery.

Everything was damp, and fragrant of duff and earth. Sheila meandered through the blowdown and puckerbrush and beneath twisted dead limbs of cedar, her mistress always a little before her. That strange woman who never took time to munch on lichen or nibble arborvitae. The goat looked like a wandering black misshapen shadow following in the wake of the white lady in white-seeming jacket and overalls.

Eloise clambered over deadfall and then the descent began asserting itself. The wet leaves were slick and treacherous. She took handholds on branches and saplings and the rough trunks of ash, the smooth of beech or knobby birch. In the mystery of moonlight she'd gotten away from the ledge and now the woods deepened and she felt she had lost the opportunity of the road. At least Sheila seemed to be enjoying herself on the downhill, her nimble cloven hooves grasping hold of rocks and roots, while Eloise had to concentrate on how she went through the trying mystery of woodland descent.

It gentled some and then she saw the deer, one of which was small and white. They followed deer, but at a distance until the deer startled and leapt away. All but the white one. It led them on. Later Eloise found it leading to rocks that had a straight-edged human-made look to them. She realized that she was looking at gravestones akilter: narrow rectangular slabs, some still standing crookedly, others flat on their backs or faces among the stems of seedlings and the duff of leaves and pine needles. And on all sides the woodland had grown up around this settlers' and descendants of settlers' graveyard, overcome by the growth of a century, washed but not righted in the mystery of moonlight, the frightening white moonlight. "This is the best ... Sheila," she whispered. The white deer was gone.

~~~~~~~~~~~~

She let it all in: the blacks and whites of the moony boneyard with the bare trees overhead weaving their stark limbs in the moonlight that was broken and darkened here and there by shadows of conifers. Many of the slabs were blackened by decades of lichen and mold, but some were still clean and white, upstanding and hardly weathered: the slate ones, she supposed. The ground was somewhat springy beneath her feet, surprising her, for one mostly feels the rock of New England, the hard bones of the country wherever one walks. In the rear hunched a large dark form. Backed by tall thickets of shading fir. At first she thought it was an erratic, the ponderous leaving of glaciers from lands far to the north. But as she neared and her eyes adjusted to the gloom, she saw it was a vault of hewn unmortared granite, its great lintel large and heavy beneath the stone roof deep with duff and sprouted seedlings. Approaching it she was shocked by a sudden jolt to
~~~~~~~~~~~~

the shin and, glancing down, saw what at first sight looked like a human tibia beneath the old leaves. At that moment Sheila nudged her from behind and Eloise shrieked.

She knelt on one knee and put her arm around the goat's neck, hugging it and burying her face in the soft wool.

"Sheila, I thought it was a leg bone .... I really did."

Rummaging around in an old New England graveyard will do that if you must go creeping through woods in the moonlight.

She sat back on her haunches still leaning against the goat and looked again at the thing. Mesmerized, she picked it up.

I'm holding in my hand the leg bone of a human being. I'm holding in my hand the leg bone of a human. I'm holding in my hand.... Then she thought about the laws of physics and wondered what had made it jump up and hit her. She held its knobby end out into a shaft of moonlight, surmising that she had leveraged it into her shin as she went. *The leg bone's connected to ...* went running through her mind and she started to her feet—feeling the creaking of her knees and creep of fear play through her nerves—wondering what else she might find.

At first she nudged at the duff with her foot, but then she picked up a stick and started stirring through it slowly; like a woman with a metal detector looking for gold. Stirring the dank ground made her sneeze and cough. Her finds were scattered but various: large and small finger bones (some misshapen from arthritis, others tiny and delicate as a baby's); a jaw without teeth, a broken calcified shoulder bone. Granting their strange beauty, she liked the look of them all lined up neatly in a swatch of moonlight upon one face-down gravestone.

It was a trail of bones leading to the door of the vault: which was slightly ajar. She stopped stirring the duff upon realizing this trend.

Sheila was dining on the edges of the graveyard beneath the ghostly white oaks, but it was a narrow burying ground, and Eloise said to her across its crazy dishevelment, "I'm not going in there.

"This is a boneyard, now, is it not? A yard where bones are piled and stacked, but they are supposed to be kept out of sight of our delicate eyes, letting the worms do their worst in private, as becometh the pathetic creatures, woman and man."

Sheila said nothing. She chewed cud from one of her stomachs. Eloise was not sure which stomach, never having learned the exact anatomy of the creatures under her care. "Maybe I should sit here like Shakespeare and muse aloud upon these things, chewing the coughed up cud of the intellect, seeing what's below in my helter-skelter unconscious." But then it came into her mind, *The intellectuals are different than you and I ... catching on quick and preserving their skins.*

Leaving most of the beautiful white pieces, she walked over to the goat to lead her away. Together they walked on through the silent rich configuration of moonlight and woodland shadow, the human murmuring, "... Why couldn't they keep their skins?"

Eloise had a long way to go that night through the black and white of the rising full moon and deep woodland; on and on toward the Quarry Dog Road where she lived with her goats and her paints. She had a lot to occupy her mind which moved from one thought to the next, thoughts changing hands like partners in an old-time dance. There was an old-time dance coming up she hoped to attend; in what had once been the Quaker Plantation townhall. After tonight's experience Eloise realized she would be changing hands in the dance with skins full of finger bones.

Besides the bones in the boneyard Eloise thought of the upcoming straw poll, to be held in the same hall, meant to decide on a move to turn back the township's legal status to that of Plantation. This was preparatory to preventing a backer of Native Americans, at the other end of the state, from building a high-stakes bingo parlor in their midst. She thought then of her other discovery, made during the early evening; one that suggested an error in the boundary between the Town of Gottheim and Quaker township. With increasing weariness in dismay, again and again as she worked her way toward what she hoped was the direction of her little homestead, failing to find and take Lyman Bearce's new logging road back down to Quarry Dog Road. How simple the night would have been. How lacking in bothersome complexity, how restful. After all the multifarious twists and turns of New York City, with its intense and troublesome physical exertion of mounting a show in some almost nameless gallery, she had craved the uncomplicated quiet of Quaker and Gottheim.

No, unlike her friends from away, she would not have missed Gottheim even shrouded in a pall. What a euphonious name, she thought: spelled S-E-G-A-R, but pronounced cigar. Ceylon Cigar. The burning of Ceylon Segar's tire fire continued apace, mingling its soot, oil fumes blackness and stench with rain and mists. It dampened all the excitement of the ski resort and its accompanying development. The little great grubby Ceylon Segar with his pathetic great grubby machinations had inadvertently managed to best the great shining, decidedly ungrubby Goldings by converting the treasure ground of Jasper Mary into a tire dump for millions of America's castoffs.

"Could anything be worse for the legend of Jasper Mary than a monumental tire dump with millions of tires?"

Locals had opined it before freak lightning extended the inquiry to include natural disaster. Could anything be worse for Eloise Patadoe than to discover the bones of a dead person on top of a grueling and complicated week? How about discovering the bones of dead *people*? Would that be enough to agitate and discompose a deceptively phlegmatic personality?

While down below, riding off in his car, another soul wondered. Could anything be worse this night for Lyman Bearce, besides bad knees and a washed out road than an apparent new cut in the side of Jasper Mountain? How about that plus a wife confronting you at 3:00 a.m. with irritating questions?

But all these things are merely troublesome and soon able to be comforted away with hot baths and whiskey with a beer chaser, or a cup of herbal tea with a bite of goat milk cheese followed by a sound night's sleep. It's not quite enough for a savoury story featuring at least one descendant of the old settlers who routed the Indians and drove them, crowding, into remote corners. It's not enough for a woman from away who was essentially meant to live on the edge. There is no real challenge in this. It needs more. It needs the writing finger of a storyteller who knows much about mystery, human nature, and hidden treasure. It needs the writing finger of a Jesus of Nazareth, the stylus of a Virgil, or tongue of a Jasper Mary: It needs a shifting and sifting of the winds.

The Village of Gottheim glowed faintly, fitfully, in a dark fold of the old hills. From one of the new houses perched on a ledge overlooking it beneath the faded stars, the village looked sinister. Like some volcano crusted over in colder lava and moving with its furnace hidden beneath. Its line of street lamps on Front Street could be faintly guessed, and most of its houses and all of its stores were dark— if a couple of its nightspots *were* open underground. But there was one light on its edge unobscured by the moving cloud of soot and mist hovering over Gottheim's ponds and treetops and byways.

Descend from the ledge where the new house stands, to the field and railroad tracks at the edge of the village, there to see a light high against the moving dark upon a knoll. Crazy Knoll it was called, filled with old and in some cases rundown Victorian mansions and houses. Here was a lane which twisted this way and that without apparent rhyme or reason, ultimately twisting back upon itself to exit from the same point of its entrance in the village proper. Tonight Crazy Knoll, as on many other nights, was mercifully spared the pall which frequented other parts (troubling the respiratory systems of certain sufferers and clinging obscurely to the exhaling pond waters). High in a tower upon the edge of things was that one light, the light of the village eccentric and hermit. His name was Israel Kimball.

Israel Kimball was the town's biggest busybody and know-it-all, though nobody knew it. Anybody would have laughed at the idea and ridiculed his informant into the ground. "That old recluse? Nobody's heard so much as two peeps out of him in three decades at least. Unless his niece is going around under cover of darkness listening beneath windows and at keyholes, he can't know a thing what's going on in Gott'im—but what he might read in the bellyache if he had a mind to. Which he wouldn't. How do we even know he's still alive? Maybe he's been dead the last decade and no one knows it. Maybe his niece goes up into the tower and turns on the light every night to make everyone think he's still up there. Maybe he's really down in the cellar, or the subcellar might we say? Not that she'd do away with him or anything but he's in his 90s if he's a day—maybe even his 100s! A person could die in that condition."

Though not so old as Israel Kimball, these would be the old timers talking, those of his niece's generation. Most people in Gottheim knew little enough of Israel Kimball. A few of them knew that his shabby old mansion was home to some students at the academy, the poorer variety, those on scholarship. Housing them was how his niece earned a living. That and a few other odds and ends of jobs she had, like taking in laundry, sewing, things like that. Israel Kimball used to teach at the academy himself. In his day he was thought very learned if quiet, imparting his learning only to the scholars.

And up there, in that six-sided tower, high above everything else in the village—that's where the one light glowed. And there Israel Kimball was reading the bellyache and praying after every few paragraphs. And there Israel Kimball was stopping to meditate upon the great tire fire of Ceylon Segar; and there too, he mused upon that one's grubby old soul. And then when he got done doing that, he began to give thanks for the disaster that had brought death and plague, and blighted the entire quality of life in the beautiful white New England village of Gottheim in the beautiful Western Mountains of Maine. After that he gave thanks for the rats.

<p style="text-align:center">~~~~~~~~~~~~</p>

Before his mind turned to the subject of rodents, Daniel Twitchell had been walking along the Lower Intervale Road in the light of the fabulous full moon. It was one of his favorite things to do, though he was more rarely conscious of the fact. There had been an impromptu party down by the river at the Old Ferry Landing near a deserted farmhouse, the site long disused and abandoned but still relevant as part of the town's history. He had seen swaths of the gleaming river in passing along the road that was interspersed with one small working farm or another and thick dark clumps of woodland. But now he turned off into the rich suggestive shade of the forest on the long dirt track winding up toward the beat-up old truck camper he shared with his family: Mother, stepfather, and brothers Nathan and Benaiah. He thought maybe the rats were busy sneaking back into the household. He did not know if Peter would be with them much longer.

Of course Daniel was not drunk, though there had been drinking and reefer at the party. He did not drink or smoke pot but, if he had been so inclined, it would have been disastrous to show up with even the faintest sniff of alcohol on his breath. They were all probably asleep anyway, he thought; but then his mind took another turn, for the moonlit woods would have its influence upon him. How alive with blacks and whites and dark mysterious shapes, with a webwork of light and shade arcing the gray track on either side as he began to climb. It was spooky.... It was *sinister*....

Daniel was thinking about that word sinister. He had to think about words, he was going to be a writer, maybe a journalist, maybe a poet. He did not know which but he did work after school at the local print shop of *The Village Voter* for Mr. Nutting, the editor. And he had been thinking a lot about words because he had to set up words for the press, so letters were always before him in some form or other. He was a reader as well. But that word *sinister*: it was meant for these woods. And now Daniel thought it was weird that the word had originally stemmed from left-handedness. No other 15-year-olds in his class would know this about *sinister*, he thought. They would not know that he knew this oddity about that word. To them his job at the local weekly was just an after-school job, a way to earn money. To Daniel it was a way to get out of Gott'im some day. I am left-handed, thought Daniel. Does that mean I'm sinister? He almost half-smiled.

Now, as he climbed through the overarching tunnel of woven branches with its patterns of light and dark, he thought again about rodents. Not about the rats that had taken up residence wherever they might in fleeing the tire fire, but about Mr. Mason's survey of the local ground hog population. This interested Daniel enough to want to try and sell Mr. Nutting on the idea of a feature story about it. Of course Daniel had never done anything like it before and this was rightfully Libby's job; he might be considered to be undercutting her if he suggested it in connection with himself. But at least he could suggest it and hope that Mr. Nutting might take the hint, grant him the opportunity.... Especially if he fleshed out a presentation.

...Which would go something like.... "Remember I told you about our biology class working on that groundhog survey? Well, it turns out we may even be turning in our data to the Department of Environmental Sciences at the University of Maine.... Mr. Mason says not to count on its being used before its quality is assessed.... The students are helping a behavioral ecologist determine what makes them solitary—the groundhogs, I mean. She's working on her doctorate, I guess. I mean she is. She *is* working on her doctorate."

He tried rehearsing it, placing emphasis, even memorizing it, but then realized this was no good. Such strategies never worked for him. He would just have to wing it and *hope* it was good enough.

The woods kept distracting him from these plans anyway. He had come up the track many times after dark but it had a stark romantic luster tonight and he realized that every night the walk had been somehow different; that nothing was ever the same. Its shapes, so familiar in the morning when they came down to get the school bus, seemed to morph through night's changing atmosphere, its variety of darkness and light .... Spooky.... Sinister... but not with evil; more with... what?—expectancy? Here is that old logging track he had meant to follow one day just to see if any changes had occurred since last summer. Not that he expected any. From here all looked completely unchanged, covered in leaves and pine needles, starting to grow over.

On impulse he decided to cut away with it. He might end up in the puckies, but at least he would be below camp and able to work his way up past the sapping ground were the evaporator sat under wraps after serving its first great sugaring-off—to the profit, Mother said, of the entire family. Here the trees on either hand had not grown up so thick as on the main track. The night above was bright, its stars barely visible, but the clear disc of the moon was cut off by a shoulder of Blackwell Mountain.

He went deeper and deeper along the bright track. Up ahead was a big old stump, probably a mossy old stub, lopped off long ago, not in the more recent cut that was only a decade or two old. But, as he approached, he saw what looked to be a manmade shape on the stump. The stump was not out in the moonlight, but under the shade of some evergreens; yet he recognized that here was either a block of wood— or a book. Yes, a book it was.

Sinister .... "Presaging trouble; ominous." He almost half smiled.

Daniel Twitchell approached and picked up the old book with a tentative gentle hand. He could see right off that was not in the best condition. Even though it was somewhat watermarked it was now dry, which surprised him. The weather had been rainy or misty. Without taking his eyes off its cover he walked out into the light of the night and opened the book, softly flipping its pages to test its condition. The leaves held to the spine and he closed it and read its title and author: <u>Phantastes</u> by George MacDonald.

Phantastes, he thought. Related to fantasy.

Suddenly there was more light and he looked up to see the moon apparently slipping from behind the shoulder of Blackwell and now shining through the webwork of the trees. There was enough light to read its text if he cared to, even as he walked along the track. He had often whiled away the long climb up Blackwell Mountain toward Buck Hill with a book, beating back his small boredom with it, but he was not of a mind to do any such thing now. He did, however, stand there a moment to sample it. He was certainly going to keep the book. You don't just find something like this on a stump every day and walk past leaving it for the mice to eat. He knew from time spent at his grandmother's house that mice would nibble the thing to bits and probably enjoy its glue for a treat.

The book was open at random, and Daniel read:

> *All this time, as I went through the wood, I was haunted with the feeling that other shapes, more like my own size and mien, were moving about at a little distance on all sides of me. But as yet I could discern none of them, although the moon was high enough to send a great many of her rays down between the trees, notwithstanding she was only a half-moon. I constantly imagined, however, that forms were visible in all directions except that to which my gaze was turned; and that they only became invisible, or resolved themselves into other woodland shapes, the moment my looks were directed towards them. However this may have been, except for this feeling of presence, the woods seemed utterly bare of anything like human companionship; for I soon found that I was quite deceived; as, the moment I fixed my regard on it, some form showed plainly that it was a bush, or a tree, or a rock.*

Daniel looked up from the page in his hand at the bright track now barred and detailed with shadows laid down by the trees before the moon. He looked off on either side, noticing the shapes of bushes or trees or rocks or blowdown. He grimaced and closed the book with a snap of finality in his two hands.

Suddenly he was aware of the sounds. He had not been noticing noises since leaving the cheeping of peepers behind sometime before on the road below: His own thoughts had been too loud. But now the atmosphere of the moony woodland overtook him. Whispers threading through the pines above him on his left hand sounded almost too suggestive to bear. He looked at his hand holding the book and switched hands, shoving the offending left hand into his pocket.

He held the book to the light again, reading its faded curlicue lettering. *Phantastes: A Faerie Romance for Men and Women.*

What in heck is this book doing out here?

It had not occurred to him to wonder this even when he first saw it on the stump.

He started on again, this time aware of passing woodland shapes and the sounds of night: from the owl way off in the woods below, gently questioning, to the persistent lonely muted chirping in the shadows on his right: nebulous rustlings, rhythmic creakings, faint crackings and droppings, as though the woods had nothing better to do than let things down from above. Random noises in the woods intensified until he felt himself one big ear to receive it all. He was also an all-eye to receive the dark suggestive richness of the woodlands' Being, the great bright Being of the Moon through teeming black branches—nothing had ever been so evident as this mountainside in the night. Its mounting nonhuman intensity seemed about to reft his identity.

A disembodied enchantment began setting him apart from it all, even as he looked down and saw his strange sneakered feet moving rapidly over the duff and twigs and debris of the track. Were they his feet?

~~~~~~~~~~~~

Earlier in the same evening, Asa Bartlett and his wife, Olive Lovejoy Bartlett (who once had the keeping of a few mentally disabled), were on their way back from the old meetinghouse where the Gottheim Historical Society usually met. There was a nice full moon —and so they had ridden to the white meetinghouse, with the his-and-her doors, on a pair of Asa's great old bays. They were now *clip-clopping* single file back home on the shoulder of the road along the river between the old hills. Everything was silvered over with moonlight: the intermittent fields and woodlands, the occasional house or farmstead with extended dwelling—house-ell-barn. Sometimes the river was visible in the distance, pouring back moony reflection into their eyes or a dark surface untouched with direct light. Once
~~~~~~~~~~~~

they moseyed through a deep tunnel of trees where a lane intersected leading through deep dark down to the river, and then they heard the remote sound of frenetic music driving itself up to their ears from some boombox down at the hidden Old Ferry Landing.

"Kids is havin' a party down theya," observed Olive over her shoulder to Asa.

He saw her plump profile beneath her battered fedora. She looked more stylish than usual in a belted trench coat. He said, "Wish they'd choose some otha place. Those kids'll end up burning down history one o'these days."

"If wishes were horses ...."

He knew she would answer him thus. They hadn't been married a year, but of their nearly sixty as friends, he knew pretty much what she was bound to say.

Things didn't change that much, he knew. There was a pattern to personality, to relation, to history, to the generations and how they were bound together; a pattern, just like there were patterns of seasons or weather or a fine piece of workmanship or a song. Human nature, he believed, was stuck in one God awful pattern, for sure. No force but God's own could change that. Kids were bound to either burn down or overturn history, make that pendulum swing, because that's what kids were bound to do. He still didn't know but what they hadn't set that tire fire, though that crackpot artist from away swore up one face of Jasper Mountain and down its backside that they didn't do it. He had no evidence her word wasn't trustworthy, but then he didn't know her well enough to know otherwise, either. She was just too talky smiley, what they call flaky, and know-it-all to be trusted. Asa was not going to share these ruminations with Olive. That too was predictable— as he already knew she liked Eloise Patadoe, which counted the same as approval with Olive.

He looked at his wife's large back on the large bay, both almost as plain as day in the moonlight. Together they went moseying up the spine of the road and into the trees again. But as they were coming out to the open at the top of the hill, by the intersection with Quakertown Road which ran back into the hills, they heard what sounded like the rumble of iron-bound wheels... from a great distance. They heard the remote thundering of hooves on hard-pan, and a far off panting of horses. And they looked down there and they saw.

It was one sight they neither of them had seen before, and when it got done with them they neither of them hoped they would see it again, though they always would ever after.

Later Asa thought that the seeing and the hearing were not put together right. It was as though what they *heard* was coming to them over a great distance or through tunnels under the earth or maybe from some distant star. But what they *saw* was coming like an avalanche tumbling rocks and trees and the great side of a mountain down on them. It was a pair of great Belgians with what looked to be a stagecoach or freight carrier tearing down a rise toward them as they stood stupefied at the intersection of the Lower Intervale and the Quakertown roads.

Their bays were old and they were old horsemen themselves; instinctively they gripped their great mounts and held them steady. For, in their spookery, even the horses acknowledged the apparition. Apparition it had to be though it looked to Asa as solid and convincing as Olive herself coming toward them. If driver it was—all bundled together in the shape of a man topped with a bowler—at the last moment, he geed his Belgians away toward Gottheim, and they heard him imploring, but again as though from that distant star, *Gee! gee! lay 'em away! Lay 'em away my townsmen!* The lips muffled beneath the bowler may have been moving, but the adjuration came not from the driver before the box. And then it was gone, that great long box of a carriage with its lathered and furious steeds. Stupefied still, Olive and Asa watched its backside receding, now but a dark rectangle between the thin lines of its wheels, two lights barely showing high upon either side in the light of the moon.

Suddenly they were alone and awake on the Lower Intervale Road.

"…You saw that, I s'pose," said Olive, whose bay was ponderously dancing beside his.

"What? Oh that. Yuht, I saw it."

"Ever seen it before?"

"I don't think so."

They moved on up the road together, side-by-side, slowly, toward Gottheim in the wake of they knew not ... —*what* to call it?

"Ever seen such a long carriage in any of your books on such things?" She wondered aloud. "Or in person?"

"How would *you* describe it?"

"Kinda like a traveling medicine show ... or ... something. Except granda."

"Could'o been fah a medicine show—except fah the driver's elevated seat ... and that glass paneling ... and the gilding and was it red?—drapery."

"Guess you saw it good enough....Way too fine."

Asa and Olive went on clopping along the road toward Gottheim.

"Whad you s'pose he was saying?" wondered Olive.

"Was that him saying it?"

"Well, I don't know but I s'pose maybe."

"—It couldn't 'o been a.... 'twas all too solid fah a ghost, that. ...Wouldn't you say?"

Olive didn't answer right off. Then she said, "What else could it'o been? Not makin' a sound like that?... Not that I know much about... ghosts. Firsthand. D'you?"

They were both feeling their way along the road back to Gottheim. Feeling their way with their words, not really looking at the hot-top or the moon or the trees or fields or each other, just feeling their way with their words.

"Would I say if I did?"

Now she did look at him sidelong. "I b'lieve you would, Asa. If I 'memba right you gave a pretty good talk on the subject, complete with stories, last summer."

"Not my stories. And they mostly came out of the old books and papers. Hardly anyone around here owns such sights anamore .... But this wasn't anathin I've heard anywhere. —You know there was something familiar about it...."

Olive sighed and they moseyed on. After a bit, she said, "Should we tell anaone?"

Asa could have predicted the question. He might have asked it himself. Some things are predictable, he guessed; most things aren't. He would not have predicted that he would soil himself riding Elmer on his way home tonight, for instance.

No need to tell Olive, he thought. She might find out soon enough.

But not if he can help it.

~~~~~~~~~~~~~

Daniel has come back into his body, recovered his senses, recognizes his own feet again. He finds himself breathing heavily, slowing down, still on the track bright and wide in the moonlight, full of small growing things. It's going to take a jog up ahead, he reminds himself, and he'll have to go on straight into the puckies. It should be no problem ... just keep alert, pay attention to the lay of the land. It's all uphill after that. No sweat.

He looked again at the book in his hand, at the shadows of the woodland, the great shining moon. Now the moon reassured him and he felt foolish over his momentary imaginative lapse. He reminded himself that he likes walking alone at night in the moonlight far from the city. Sometimes when the woods encroached, he missed the desert outside Phoenix: There was the place to be warmed by the moon! He liked the desert better than the
~~~~~~~~~~~~~

Maine woods, but it was Mother's choice and there was nothing he could do about it. Besides, it was not a choice between the city and the desert: Mother and Petey never would have been able to afford a place in the desert. Now they were here and that was that....

Or was it?

Sometimes he wondered if Peter Prince was going to be able to stand living here. Sometimes he thought maybe his stepfather would blow again as he used to in the old days. If he did he would start drinking, start treating Mother bad all over again, and then what would they do? Was there any place to run after Gottheim? The good Peter, led by the bad Petey, would probably find them again wherever they went. Or was it the other way around: the good Peter leading? Daniel had not figured it out yet. He didn't like to just consign Peter to Hell. He had been good to them most of their lives. Have to recognize that. He can make life hell, and he can make it normal. It amazed him that people had such power over the quality of everyone's life.

He looked again at the book, <u>Phantastes</u>. What a way to spell it. It made him think of the oddity that was language and how it could make you see things differently, make you feel things you didn't know you felt.

He opened the book again at random and read,

> *Meantime, how fared Cosmo? As might be expected in one of his temperament, his interests had blossomed into love, and his love—shall I call it <u>ripened</u>, or—<u>withered</u> into passion? But, alas! he loved a shadow.*

... Must be a metaphor. Nobody would love a shadow.

He read on, trying to get a glimpse of what the writer was talking about.

> *Nay, how many who love never come nearer than to behold each other as in a mirror; seem to know and yet never know the inward life; never enter the other soul; and part at last with but the vaguest notion of the universe on the borders of which they have been hovering for years?*

Maybe marriage is meant to do something about this (yeah common-law marriage). But watching Mother and Peter together Daniel had yet to see much sign of it.... Either they did not know each other, or were no good at communicating what they did know. ...Although he thought maybe Mother was closer to understanding Peter. In a way it was kind of like the way Mr. Mills understood the weather—because he was a farmer and had to know how to get around it. Daniel did not think he knew what made Peter tick, but he did know when weather was coming. — Ticking was too much like clockwork to describe Petey, anyway.

Daniel slid back into the book again at random and began reading about the Ash-tree and its shadow. The first-person narrator seemed to be somehow menaced by it.

There were plenty kinds of trees in the woods, he knew: he was sure Mother had mentioned ash trees before, something about using them to make baskets. She was going to try getting into her Native American heritage. Daniel was indifferent to it; he was indifferent to kinds of trees. Trees are trees, rocks are rocks and puckerbrush is puckerbrush, that's all .... But now he wonders about ash trees.

He scanned the hardwoods to see if he recognized anything there. The woods were taller, scarcely any budding branches up there. He noticed different kinds of bark in the moonlight. Some of it smooth, some ragged, some knotted, some ridged. All kinds of trees, and of course he recognized the birches but could not tell the gray from the paper birch. *I'm not going to know which of these trees is an ash tree. If there is one.*

He realised now that he didn't know much of anything about the woods yet. Maybe this book, however fantastic, would help him get more familiar with it. Already he felt like paying more attention when Mother might say things about the woods. He looked around again on the moony richness of it. He did, however, know something about its shadows. He had been through these woods in all kinds of light and had never got turned around in them.

He had also been through his own young life in all kinds of dark and light and, if he got turned around in it occasionally, he always found his way back out into what was recognizable as wholesome and good and right. You don't live in all kinds of weather very long before you can recognize a healthy atmosphere. ...And he did not think conditions right in the truck camper they were calling home. Not anymore. There just wasn't enough room in there to contain a blow. He closed the book and walked on.

<div style="text-align:center">~~~~~~~~~~~</div>

Below the moon-struck triple summit of Blackwell Mountain juts Buck Hill, with its burned out clearing and the truck camper housing the Twitchell-Prince union. Peter Prince climbed out of the camper and walked across to the cellar hole full of charred timbers. He was going to go nuts if he had to stay in there much longer. Place wasn't big enough for a gnat's ass.

He dug in his crumpled pack of Viceroys, pulled out a half flattened cigarette and lit it. Peter Prince drew deeply and exhaled, watching the smoke drift out into the bright night. He looked right off across the valley toward great Jasper Mountain, the Gott'im town mountain, domed and shining in the night. The murmur of Nathan's voice jabbering away sounded almost pleasant from here. Peter was glad to be removed from its proximity, let the beauty of the night absorb it.

How that kid can talk so much when he's poring over the homework, that stubble of pencil gripped tight in his grubby hand as it spurted across the page. And Benaiah—always scowling and letting his little brother get to him. If they fought one more time he was going to clobber them for sure. Either that or Chrischana. And he knew where that would lead. Daniel does right to get out of here every night. ... He must be doing his homework at school, or the library. Kid gets good grades.

He looked down into the wide pit at his feet, at the moonlight gleaming off charred bubbles of the Twitchell farmhouse timbers.

He thought of the vandals who had destroyed the abandoned and rotting farmhouse. Probably partying, and, who knows, maybe they didn't mean to do it. Things happen when you're having a good time.... Which I'm not. *Not now.*

It was getting harder to tell if any of them were having a good time now that sugaring-off was over. It's crazy to live like this ... and there's so much work to be done. The Town was not going to allow them to continue either, so they had to apply for permits and build another house and drill a new well and put in a septic system and.... Chrischana wants to plant trees! An orchard for crying out loud. They'd had a great life in Phoenix where he was a motorcycle mechanic just about set to go into business for himself— and she had to throw in the monkey wrench by coming back to this place to do these kinds of things.

And to get away from you, he reminded himself. Yeah, Hermann would like that. Maybe you ought to keep reminding yourself, Peter, since you're so apt to forget. Remind yourself of her mildness and patience, firmness and toughness. (No Hermann, don't remind myself of my dissatisfaction, even my despair.)

Peter kept steadily dragging on his cigarette until it went out and then he lit another off it, tossing the butt into the cellar hole.

The wind seems to be shifting, the smoke drifting back now into his eyes. He moves along to one side of the pit. "You don't want to do the work," his counselor, Hermann Gottesman, keeps reminding him.

Well, Hermann, you try doing it. You're sitting there in Jericho doing exactly what you want with your books and your *Kids Cafe* and your substance abuse counseling. You're doing your work and it all seems pretty manageable and you don't feel hopeless but I feel hopeless. I'll tell you what won't work. *This* won't work. Be honest, be honest. How goddamn honest do you want me to be. *This* is honest, Hermann.

He looked bitterly over at the beat-up camper, the glow of gaslight within faint and somehow romantic. Weather was coming, he saw, from the direction of Gottheim. It would probably move up the mountain and maybe even engulf them. It had done this before. The moon still gleamed off the fenders of his Harley beside the camper in front of Chrischana's new secondhand truck. He ought to go to the utility shed and get out his bike cover—keep the acid-soot from that goddamn tire fire off its leather and finish.

But he stood there, smoking.

He heard the camper door open, Nathan's jabbering still going, louder; saw his common-law wife climb out, her long braid swinging off her shoulder. She looked off toward Gottheim. She looked back at him. She went over to the beat-up metal shed and he saw the play of the flashlight beam as she rummaged in there and came out with the cover. Did she have ESP? Did he have her trained? Or was she just too good for him? He thought these thoughts bitterly. She's always got to make me feel guilty.

She covered the bike and came over to him, saying, "They'll be done soon." She stood by him and he looked at her face in the moonlight. It was calm and full, with the slightly exotic Native American features that came to her through her mother. He scarcely noticed, so full was he of recrimination. She stepped back, seeming to sense it.

Chrischana looked off again in the direction of Gottheim.

"Don't tell me you sensed a change in the weather?" He said with a nod toward the bike.

She merely nodded. This minimizing was a shelter she went into when she felt a change in his mood.

She was silent, looking back at the camper. They heard Nathan emit a loud "*Ow!*" They both knew it was bound to escalate, this provocation, this tit-for-tat.

The breeze was strengthening and again she looked in the direction of Gottheim and the view of approaching weather now dimming the mountain slopes and woodland out across from them. "Daniel's still out," she said without looking at him. The moon behind him still shone and he saw the contour of her full cheeks and high cheekbones and lashes, turned away from him. "Maybe I should go look fah'em."

She waited.

"Yeah?"

The faint sneer in his voice reached into her, and she said nothing. Then he relented and said, sulking, "I'll go."

He moved past her toward the cycle. It was in her mouth to suggest that he walk down in case Daniel was coming up through the woods some way other than the dirt road. Without the bike they'd hear one another, maybe. She watched as he removed the cover, restraining everything pushing out to speak through her.

But the camper was erupting in squabbles and the Harley already exploding to life beside it. He wheeled around and without even a nod in her direction, took off through the thickets bordering the track on either side.

Just as well, she thought. He better get out of here. But the thought of Daniel came back to her. They are going to miss one another, sure. She chewed a bit on her lower lip.... He'll find his way back.... They both will. She walked back to the camper and peered inside, saying, "Quit fighting and get into bed! It's too late fah anathin else now. And shut down that light."

Nathan started protesting and she shut the door on him. If that light wasn't out in two minutes he'd be sorry and he knew it. Chrischana walked back to the cellarhole to look out at the weather coming as a black mist, dissolving her view of the Meguntics as it came on from the direction of Quaker and Gottheim. Ceylon Segar's tire fire was still mingling its toxic vapors with the weather of the mountains after all these weeks. When would they get that thing extinguished and make the place livable again? When would the asthmatics and others with breathing problems, the old, be able to stop suffering? Bronchitis, sinusitis, depression, sadness. Stuff was in all the houses, curtains, carpets, floorboards, couches, air ducts. When would the woodland be safe from its fires? They better get that thing taken care of before the dry season gets here. All they needed to complete the devastation were underground fires, fire leaping from root to root, pine pitch burning, exploding out the tops of trees ....

She was starting to rage herself—and no Harley to roar off on either.

Still gazing out there, she murmured, "Why don't *You* do something?"

It's work, I know. You've got work to do, I've got work to do. All God's children got work to do. It was a thought halfway between bitter and flippant, but she let it go. She wasn't going to be like Petey.

She looked over at the camper. It was dark. It even seemed quiet. "Thank you," she said still looking at it. She could see the metal of its frame gleaming in moonlight. She smiled. She could actually back the truck up under there and haul the thing away, if she wanted to. She could do it while Peter was at work. Should. Before he starts on me again.

....You could go insane.

But God wouldn't like it. He doesn't like the tire fire either. He doesn't like the flabby system that unleashed it. She sighed and went back to the camper. She would tuck them in and open her own bed. Hers and Peter's. But she would not sleep.

Chrischana Twitchell lay a long time thinking and looking up through the narrow jalousie-glass at the bright sky. She lay planning the heirloom orchard, turning over in her mind the various varieties, considering what to choose. Baldwins were good winter keepers but the Westfield-seek-no-further and the Northern Spy had narrower crowns requiring less space. She liked their names.

Then the sky darkened. She heard the pinging of soot on metal, and she could no longer restrain her real thoughts pushing to speak through her. It was dark as pitch inside the camper. She thought the phrase apt. Daniel would like it. The even breathing of her other two sons reassured her. So. Still dressed in shirt and jeans and the jacket she had worn to alert Peter, Chrischana climbed back out into the night. A world and night so different from its beginning as to be a discredit to its Creator. Yes, she thought, standing there in a baptism of soot and acid mist, You've got work. Looks like Your day of rest is ovah.

She flicked on the flashlight to find the reach of its beam quenched in the drizzling dark mist, reflecting it. Nevermind. She would feel her way down the mountain. She would call Daniel. It couldn't quench the sound of her prayers.

~~~~~~~~~~~

Peter Prince had wound down through moonlight still streaming with leafless tree shadows; down, down on stretches of the mountain road deep in the shadow of conifer. His stepson Daniel was so deep in the woods that he had not heard the far-off purring of the Harley as it drifted down behind a distant shoulder of the mountain. Peter watched along the road, expecting to see the dark shape of Daniel at any moment in the beam of his headlamp. But he was thinking, Why am I supposed to be doing what *she* wants? An orchard!

Peter chewed over such thoughts all the way down the side of the mountain until he slid neatly out into the wide light of the moon on the Lower Intervale Road. It seemed to him that he had been chewing on these things and swallowing and regurgitating and chewing again ever since they moved out of the apartment in Gottheim, when the roads were clear again.

On the smooth white road he was tempted to ramp it up but thought he had better keep the pace if he wasn't going to miss Daniel.
~~~~~~~~~~~

Daniel would make it back all right, but would *he*? God! It was so tempting to turn the bike around and float off into the night on the back road to Guildford!

He could always save himself at the last minute by turning off to Jericho and flopping down on Hermann's beat up old couch. The obese giant was always ready to listen to him .... Though he could get disgusted, Peter remembered wryly.

He remembered the story Gottesman had told him that time in Jericho when the power was off. About how far he had had to fall, how deep, in order to climb back up again—Hermann Gottesman. Clearly he was trying to scare me! Well it won't work, Hermann. You can scare infants into behaving well but you can't help full-grown men that way. It's got to come from something more genuine than fear and trembling. Go back to the counseling books and learn how to help me, for God's sake. And please don't bring up the "necessary" work again. I need relief, not more pressure.

~~~~~~~~~~~~~

The night of Hermann's story had been cloudy and dim but lit by a few neon signs. He had swung off his bike on Main Street in Jericho, stepped across the sidewalk and up the stoop. The cool elegance of "Kind of Blue" came drifting out of Hermann Gottesman's *Kids Cafe*. He had just stepped over the threshold when darkness overcame him. The horn trailed on a long deflating note and stopped. He looked down the street and saw darkness and a few dim shapes of buildings.

"You in there, Hermann?"

The voice characteristically treble and soft came to him. "C'mon in Prince." It still amazed him that such a big man could speak with such a small voice. "It's dark on the street, I suppose?"

Peter came in, his hand on the loose old doorknob, feeling his way with his feet. He felt for the pool table and let it guide him to the couch where he knew Hermann would be sitting, probably holding onto a full liter of Coke with his huge dimpled fleshy hand. "Kids all got somewhere else to be tonight, Hermann?" The silence of the whole town seemed invoked by the dark. Then a set of headlights brightened the street, passing, and another.

"No. I told them to leave."

"But it's early, ain't it. We weren't supposed to get down to work for another half hour."

"I told them to leave."

He heard Hermann take a swig from the plastic bottle. Prince found the ratty old chair beside the couch and sank into it. He could feel the bare
~~~~~~~~~~~~~

greasy spots of its arms where the wool had worn off from years of use. "I'm not deaf, Hermann. Why did you tell them to leave?"

"... I knew it was going to get dark."

"So you're a prophet now." He thought, if I was Jewish like you, I would've put a question mark on the end of that. "My eyes aren't adjusting ... or it's *really* dark. Maybe beavers took down a tree across a power line, like they did in Gott'im that time." There's something spooky about this. *Hermann* is spooky tonight.

"What've you been doing, Peter?"

"Not drinking, Herr Mentor." But he knew he was not going to jostle Hermann out of this. "Not drinking, Hermann."

"But you will be, Peter."

"So you *are* a prophet now, Hermann?"

There was silence. There was darkness.

"Did I ever tell you how far it took me?"

Peter was silent sitting in the dark. He would welcome the sound of the refrigerator coming back on, the music beginning again. The occasional beams passed out on the street, visible through the streaked plate glass. There were some barely discernible shapes now in the long narrow room. Some sort of texture to the interior darkness. He fumbled in a shirt pocket for cigarettes, found his lighter in the pocket of his jeans. He lit up and the yellow flare showed forth the room and Hermann's great bespeckled dark solemn eyes on him, as though they had been there all the time in the dark and seeing Peter as though it were day. He snapped the lighter shut and shoved it back into his pocket. He drew on the cigarette. Prince exhaled the invisible smoke, but it was as though he had not even touched that nicotine craving nor tasted the cigarette.

He resigned himself. "Maybe you better tell me, then."

And Hermann Gottesman had begun by telling him the story of his plan for the long sabbatical to write that great philosophical/psychological treatise. He had decided to head for the coast of Maine first for a little rest and relaxation away from his friends who meant so well. And away from his two drinking buddies who maybe meant not so well, but he had to get away from them anyway. Because that's all they were: drinking buddies. There was nothing else going on, intellectually, emotionally, or otherwise. Worse, what was left of his family were urging the observances on him as a duty to the memory of the gassed and burned. And he had never seen the coast of Maine.

He found himself in Guildford at that old hotel down by the tracks.

Peter had been incredulous at this: Guildford is almost two hundred miles by winding roads from the coast, smack in the mountains surrounded by woods. But he spoke no sign; Hermann was ongoing with the tale.

He finds himself, next, standing on the bridge spanning the river and staring out at the hellish glow of the paper mill, its pink vapor lights playing off steam rolling in great sheets and billows off the driers and into the night-dark miasma of the Guildford/Spain valley air. The glow even plays off the rapids churning, tumbling and foaming with hellish spite among the rocks in the river far below. He is standing here thinking, Wasn't I going to be on the Gulf of Maine?—Casco Bay?

Fearful, Gottesman went back to the bar in the barren hotel to continue drinking. Then he must've gone up to his room to lie down because that's where he woke and heard it again. The same voice he heard while standing on the bridge. The one that earlier spoke each word distinctly, scaring him back into the bar.

"*You.. have.. left.. your.. friend.. to.. burn.. in.. the.. house.*" Each word is spoken as though it is the only word, by a calm voice right beside him. "*The.. officers.. are.. looking.. for.. you.*" Hermann sits up and looks about him but, as on the bridge, there is no one. Yet he begins to consider: the voice is kind, maybe it's true. Maybe it happened. Maybe I don't remember it. He thrills with fear.

"Follow me. I will help you."

It must be an illusion. I'm going insane. I will distrust it. But, thrilling, he jumps from the bed and goes to the windows staring out at the pink glowing sky over the rooftops of Guildford. Again the voice says, "Follow.. me, I.. will ..help.. you.. escape."

"It was a hoarse kindly voice, Prince. Something of a whisper; but not particularly ghostly. That of a friend. I did follow it in the dark, out of the room, along the hall, down the stairs, to the lobby, and then into the kitchen where there was a door. By light thrown in from the alley window I saw that it was a dark paneled door. It had a rattling knob, and following the voice I turned that handle and there were more stairs, going down."

Then two turns and Hermann stands in the darkness at the bottom of the stairs, trying to feel his way with his hands; the kindly firm voice attending him: "Follow me."

But he cannot quite trust. He feels with his feet, finds a stair to mount, feels for the second stair but it is empty space. Gently he kneels his great weight down upon the basement floor and feels with his hand. The dankness of a well comes up into his face and nostrils, speaking through cold water about how far Hermann Gottesman had been taken by it.

The house, with its semicircular drive, seemed more or less a museum, a three-story mansion with mansard roof and dormers. Complete with cupola and gilded weather vane; painted paneling, columns, piazzas with balustrades, even porte-cochere side entrance. Rhetta Bearce was walking around the dormant gardens of what some people in Gottheim referred to as the mansion, as yet the only one for miles around. It had always been so. Until the Harry and Julius Goldings' ... what would you call it?—extravaganza?—*rustic* extravaganza-in-progress.

Well, she thought, it had *been* in progress before all those tires caught fire. The ski business being interrupted, they've all taken off and are waiting elsewhere for the soot to settle.

It was late but at last the horrible atmosphere was lifting. She had seen the bright disk of the moon shining through and decided it was time to come out and touch up the mulch and maybe refurbish the landscape fabric for one or two of the beds. Of course there would be another month at least of night frosts but she thought the dangers were over for the perennials she had put in last October. She got down on her knees and began piling together the wet soot-covered straw of that corner where she had neglected use of the fabric.

Wearing one of Lyman's old woolen shirts Rhetta gathered an armload to her broad but aging bosom and took it off to the compost heap. She dumped it into the first bin and thought, *Better go get the wheelbarrow.* She was about to go to the shed behind the summer house when she looked up at the moon and saw that it was almost clear. Everything she looked upon was coming cleaner in its light. She looked off down toward the village, but could barely perceive a glow in that direction. Oh well. The weather is taking itself off from here, anyway.

... Wonder where Lyman is?

He has possibly managed to avoid the terrible brew that Ceylon Segar has cooked up for us here in the valley today ... if he went off to one or another of his far-flung tree farms, possibly that tract up in Somerset County. It may be raining up there but she doubted it would be sooting. He never has trouble avoiding the discomfiting. ...But to be fair he won't hesitate to confront it in his interest either.

Why should she worry? Lyman was as hardened as a bag of old rocks. If anybody could take care of himself it was Lyman Bearce: He had seen to it that every one of his enemies had been taken care of. ... All but that new one, what did they call him, Liquidation Leonard? ... And then there was poor little Theodora Prescott. She almost chuckled over her husband's failure there. The town scatterbrain, as he referred to the girl, had done something no one would have foreseen —in giving the chair factory to the employees. He had not got over that yet! (Neither had Theo's fiancee, James Fay.) She almost smiled.

... And yet she was worried. Rhetta Bearce could not really put her finger on it, but she had lived with Bearce long enough to ... to know him. And what she was seeing now she did not quite know. There was something new, but what was it? She had not even been aware of any difference, she was sure—not consciously anyway—until now in these thoughts. As she removed the rocks from its corners and tugged away at the fabric shielding clumps of ornamental grasses, she thought, This is going to be more work than I wanted just now.

She raised herself slowly from stooping, a hand to the small of her back, releasing a soft puff of air. Well! That's enough of that. And she thought, staring off towards Gottheim again, *It's enough of those strange thoughts about Lyman, as well.* He's no different, and I'm not going to start looking at him differently now. Wouldn't it be sweet if I started in on mothering the old bag of rocks after all these years of wrangling with him? Neither of us needs that!

Lyman Bearce needing a mother!? She laughed out loud, she almost cackled. She could not begin to picture Bearce being mothered, being six years old, in any need of TLC, in need of ... of anything whatever. It's absurd! He was the kind of man that wouldn't tell you if his leg was broken. The kind of man who wouldn't mention it if he fell down three flights of stairs. If he had Alzheimer's you wouldn't know it. He was the kind of man who would be walking around the woods barking orders on his two-way three weeks after he was dead—and no one would know it. It's absurd!

A very strange image of her husband's bones, a skeleton walking beneath tall woods—a two-way radio to his grinning teeth—came into her mind. Suddenly shivering, she backed away from the shadows of blue spruce by the drive where she had set monkshood and European ginger last year. Then she heard it. Distantly.

She would have sworn there were horses on the other side of the hill, coming up the road out of Gottheim and driven at an alarming rate, screaming and neighing and snorting. How very strange. No.... It wasn't that way but over there, far more distant, as though from the top of Jasper Mountain or way over in Madrid or some place. Rhetta Bearce turned around and saw a team of wild Belgians barreling straight toward her on that curve of the drive smack in front of the house. With a great box of a carriage overshadowing—it was huge, it was monstrous, it was going to run her over!

But at the last moment it swerved aside, keeping with the curve, heading back out toward the road. Looking stunned at the squared back of the box carriage with its sidelights and wheels flinging gravel, disappearing through the grove by the road, she heard distinctly these distant words:

Haw, haw, lay'em away! Lay'em away, my townswoman!

Rhetta Bearce had stumbled backward into the trees, the spruces upholding and cradling her. Now she tumbled to her feet and into the white gravel of the drive, staring in the direction of that passing apparition. Yes, it was gone. It had probably never been there to begin with. Rhetta held out her trembling hand and stared at it. *Me, trembling.*

Dazed and distracted, she started in the direction of its vanishment without any thought for the reality of the thing. Without any thought for her movements stepping deliberately toward the darkness at the end of the drive. She was thinking instead, very carefully, about how she was never going to mention this to anybody, about how she was going to hope fervently for the rest of her life that she never saw or heard anything like again. And she thought carefully about how she understood it all now:

Lyman is all right. There is nothing different about Lyman Bearce. It's you there's something wrong with! It's you... — all wrong!

She was standing in the shade of the trees staring vacantly out on the white road in the moonlight. There came the cracking of a twig behind. Rhetta Bearce emitted a shriek. She hopped. She looked backward, gaping and wild, wide-eyed, on Elda Simon coming white and kerchiefed out of the trees. In the light of the moon she was ghostly, her clothing looked white, all but her pale sneakers and jeans.

"Elda Simon—! You scared the jee-*zus* out'o me. What ah you doing way ovah heah in the dark?!" And it was out of her mouth before she knew it. "—You didn't see—anything." She went quiet, looking off toward the direction of the village.

The slight woman peers at her, shyly smiling. Even in her distraction Rhetta Bearce notes, with her habitual surprise over the fact, the grin is like that of Elda's son Balder Simon.

"I saw ... something." It was a small speech, and Elda Simon is also silent now.

"Elda ... did you—what did you see?" And Rhetta thinks, in my own way I'm as bad as Bearce. Elda persists in silence, and she decides to wait her out.

Ask yourself, say I, the hermit who lives on Crazy Knoll. Are things always what you think they are? Are you what you think you are? Are people what you are thinking of them? Do you know what is happening in the cells of the membrane lining your colon right now? Do you know what is working its way toward you through the air as you read these words? I am ninety-three years old, and I might answer yes to the last question. I'd be very surprised if I knew anything else for sure. However I do know the answer to the first three questions: The answer to the first three questions is no. Elda would not know the answers either.

You may or may not know about Elda Simon's macular degeneration. (Nevertheless there are times when she can see better in the dark than in daylight. It has something to do with the difference between the cones and rods of the retina, the kind of light available, and what she is looking at. She has adapted to accommodate her perambulations.) Contrary to what Rhetta was thinking, she was not hesitant to admit she had seen an apparition: Elda was hesitant to admit that she had not been able to see it *clearly*.

Well, thinks Rhetta, *If you're not going to mention it, neither am I.*

Elda is looking off down the road but then she turns and says, "What I don't understand is the steam. Theya was vapor pouring out of their nostrils, even the driver's. ... Like 'twas the middle of wintah. In't so cold as all that now."

Relief fills Rhetta, but she says merely, "...Yes ... I hadn't noticed that detail then, but now that you mention it .... "

Again they are silent, speculatively.

Rhetta said, "But what was it, do you think? It wasn't a carriage—not really.... It had columns and panels, maybe carved drapery with a glass window in the center. It went by so fast I didn't think I'd remember such detail ... I don't think I even noticed then."

Elda was silent.

"Something antique, of course, but beautifully preserved. The driver even looked ... well, antique. He was bundled up, but still there was something antique about him. Maybe it was the bowler."

Elda said nothing. We don't know that much about Elda anymore. No one would know what she was doing out there that night. Likely some errand: There was that pack on her back.

Rhetta ventured, "... I *heard* something. Did you?"

" ...Sounded like 'twas further 'way."

This lacked the kind of detail Rhetta Bearce was after. "I heard a voice way off in the distance."

Elda nodded.

Rhetta was ready to give up, but then she said, "Wondah what he meant by it?"

Elda said she did not know.

"I almost think I saw some scrollwork or something arabesque. Maybe leaves or flowers ... something."

Elda was silent.

It was that unwieldy moment when one or the other would start with the excuses; time for some awkward verbal device used when either, having nothing to say, said (in essence), we will part now. What more could be said about it? But who would want to replay the apparition again alone in thought—which was surely what would occur if they parted now.

"... Have you ever noticed how many flowers, flower parts, look male?" wondered Elda aloud.

"Oh yes. I notice it especially in the roadside wildflowers: mullein, plantain, not to mention lady-slippers, which look like gonads to me."

"And then there are the bugbanes in the woods."

"Pickerelweed in the ponds, and white bog orchis in the bogs."

What in the State of Maine are we doing? Rhetta wondered as they stood in conversation. ...Standing here in the dark talking about similarities between plants and male sex organs. It's crazy. The whole night from beginning to end. Absurd.

~~~~~~~~~~

The Naiad was intimately connected to her body of water and her very existence seems to have depended on it. If a stream dried up, its Naiad expired. The waters over which Naiades presided were thought to be endowed with inspirational, medicinal, or prophetic powers. Thus the Naiades were frequently worshipped by the ancient Greeks in association with divinities of healing, fertility and growth. —Bulfinch's Mythology

Approaching over the rutted road with Balder Simon in his patched pickup Gloria Fay saw the glimmer of golden lights through the tree stems. It was the opening season for gathering smelts. It was also the season when smelts gathered one another in fertility. The night air was cool but they were traveling slow over the ruts the windows were down. It would be maybe more than a month before the bugs showed. But the ice was out now and smelts were running. Gloria was happier than anything, being out like this in the mysterious night with her boyfriend Balder.

They passed a gap in the trees near shore and she looked out upon the wide dark pond, its shoreline half-strung with the gems of the lanterns of fishermen out with their great nets after the smelts. The lights shone above
~~~~~~~~~~

and below the encircling shoreline, reflecting. "You know what this reminds me of?"

"Something pagan?" His answer was fast on the heels of her query and she saw the flash of a grin he aimed at her before turning back to the sight himself. "Something about the equinox or the Maypole or Easter."

She jabbed him in the arm with her fist. "How'd you know about Easter?"

"I d'know. Just a lucky guess. I told you about my grandmother. All that information passes through the placenta from generation to generation."

"I guess that explains why I have to read up on the stuff if I want to learn anything. It seems everything that crossed my placenta's all Baptist related." She smiled.

"I wouldn't be so quick t' get rid o'that stuff if I was you. What do you want to go and be a pagan for, anyway?"

"Somebody's got to undo all the hardship placed on us by Christianity."

"Like having all our sins took away? What hardship you talkin' bout? Seems to me you've had it pretty good with all that you was raised with, master's degrees, two homes and brand new skis every year." He flashed her another grin.

"You know what I mean—psychological hardship. All the guilt trips, and having to do everything just so or lose God's favor ... go to hell, stuff like that." It was her turn to grin. "Besides, I don't see you going to church."

"I would." He looked at her, grinning more. "If I could stand it."
"Hah! See, we are agreed."

He looked over at glorious Glory's even features, shadowed in the cab of the truck, but her sleek blond pageboy still held its light. He wanted to say, *But that's about all we ah agreed on.* Then, slowly, he did say it. Balder gave a slow smile.

On the last curve the track had turned away from the lights and they were in the moony shaded woodland, Gloria staring out the window upon the mysterious crosshatching of shadows. They were deep in the woods several miles from Gottheim and on what was possibly one of the best dates of her life. She sighed. It was true about their disagreements: she was a confirmed consumer, he a traditionalist. She bought everything; he made and repaired things, was going to start growing his food. He wanted children. She... didn't think so... didn't know.

He turned his attention to the track in his high beams but picked up the thread of the conversation again. "So you ah throwing out what you call the mahden tradition with all its hyper industrial support—I guess I take back what I said, we do agree on something else. But with that pagan stuff you still got gods getting mad and needing propitiation n'manipulations and all that stuff. Plus, you don't know who your friends ah. Who's the Lord Jesus if not that?"

"Well, he should not have let himself get attached to all that other stuff, that's all."

"How many masters' degrees d'you say you had?"

"—Just the one," she said dryly. But then she could not resist adding, "And I'm going to go after another one in classical Greek literature, too, if I can."

The track had widened out and the truck's beams revealed either side lined with pickups and old Broncos, a new Blazer or two. They got out and he reached in back for the gear: a propane lantern, long green waders, the great smelt net. He handed her a cooking pot: "Handy place to put 'em once theya caught! L'me get these on, and we'll just go get'em."

"Aren't they just a teeny bit ridiculous?" She couldn't help but arch an eyebrow over the waders.

Balder loved it when she did that. "I'll be the envy of evah body theya! Ones without will all be losing their legs fah I do, n'hev to give up fore they get their two quarts."

He shrugged into the suspenders, grinning as big and bright as the lantern he had lit. She burst out laughing.

"You look like a blond, black-bearded frog from outer space—after it's jumped! Oh Balder, you should see yourself!"

"I'm seeing myself right now." He indicated her ridicule with a gesture. He might have said that he wanted to go on seeing it for the rest of his life. He did not say it. Balder Simon did not think he needed to.

They followed over a beaten uneven path, the light of their propane lantern moving through the woods between them, seething. After passing a few others coming or going, Balder said he wanted to see the brook black with smelts.

"But aren't smelts silver? I saw some in the fish display at the supermarket."

"Black just means packed with smelts."

They came to the stream and he shone the lantern onto the excited milling strands of mating life. They reminded her of water weeds drifting in the current. Balder walked on, the great net on a long pole projecting off his shoulder. She caught up with him. "Aren't you going to get the smelt?"

"We don't dip the brook. Wouldn't be fair, gettin'em while theya in the act. You got to get 'em in the pond where they circle round its outer edges. Wouldn't be none left fah us if we dip where they drop n'fertilize their eggs. See, they'll be looking fah that stream n'then we'll get 'em when they go past us on the shore. You'll be on the shore. I'll be in the water. Those lights all round the pond is like a lure to the fish when they school past. Here, turn that down a dite. This looks like a good spot."

She lowered the flame, stood on one rock staring down into the water. He waded between rocks with a net and submerged it. Her eyes were still dark from the light of the lantern, but sensing Balder's suppressed excitement, she looked harder. Then she exclaimed in a fervent whisper: "There!!" But he had already seen and was lifting the net, fish wriggling in the bottom. Popping like corn. He grabbed a fistful and tossed them into the pot she held out to him. She watched him lay the net on the water and let it settle where, edging the shallows, flecks of lights flickered through the waters. Now he dipped again and lifted against the drag. He stuck in his hand and threw her another fistful. Each time he lifted she watched his muscles flex before allowing her eye to be drawn back to the fish.

Gloria Fay was wholly alive, coming out after a long long winter and a cold, ash-strewn spring. All her dreams for earning a living by investment and wit in Gottheim had been covered in smoke and ash, but now she was alive again. And here with Balder in the water again, this time in the pond not far from some mountain stream pouring out into the wide experience of moon-gleaming life. He held out the net to her, she plunged her hand into the cold squirming fishes, she popped them into the pot.

~~~~~~~~~~

They were sitting on shore under the shadows, resting even as some of the lights began to dim and move away into the trees. There was cold lake water covering the fish in the pot where they still moved, but sluggishly. Gloria leaned against Balder, dreamily, happy in the reflected gleam of the water, now that Balder's lantern was out.

Balder was going to say something, she thought. Yes, Balder spoke.

"Since you stotted mooning ovah Jaspa Mountain like it was some sort o'deity ... and since I'm named fah that there Norse god y'studied, when ah you going to stot worshiping me?"

Gloria said nothing. It was going to take her a moment to come up with it. Then,

"...God of gladness and light, meet Gloria Fay. She is a naiad."

~~~~~~~~~~

*"And when I did look around, there on the bridge, within a
few paces of me, a huge black dog was sitting, with the face*

of a man—a human face, if ever I saw one, turned full up to the moonlight. It remained just long enough to give me a clear view of it, and then vanished; and ever since, when I think of Satan, I call to mind the dog-man on the bridge."
—Supernaturalism of New England, John Greenleaf Whittier

Prone, fifteen-year-old Cindabilla lifted a heavy head at the sound of an engine purring past. She tried to focus her eyes on the moving object – maybe a motorcycle. She thought she saw the gleam of something but couldn't be sure. Cindabilla rolled over and glanced up at the moon, seeing its circle through a thick shroud. There were two of them—two moons. She tried to move again. She felt a groan or maybe an upchuck coming on but decided to keep still in case the engine was something she didn't want to face. She was finding that it wasn't too comfortable lying here in the roots or rocks or whatever it was on the shore of the Old Ferry Landing. Then she was on her elbow, quietly vomiting.

She lay back on a sharp rock then moved aside a little, trying to nestle down into the earth. *Ah ... feels better ....* But the two moons were still whirling.... She sat up, leaning against a big rock. *Oh, why dint I listen to Daniel Twitchell?* Cindabilla considered taking off his jacket and throwing herself into the filthy river. *That'll get me out of this.* But she sat there. The moon faded into the dirty mist.

The engine, she noticed, had stopped. She looked over her shoulder to see a form walking near the fire pit, embers still giving off a faint glow. What was it doing?

The dark someone stooped and came up with something in its hand. She saw it was a man, someone she was familiar with. ...Daniel's stepfather .... Probably came to give him a lift home—way too late. He was holding up one of the bottles and shaking it. She heard it clink as he threw it back down and picked up another. She wanted to say, What are you doing, why don't you listen to Daniel? But her mouth didn't feel like speaking, her body didn't feel like moving. Petey Prince? Ah you going to get like Uncle Ferddy again? Are you going to turn everything inside out and make Daniel go away fom me?

Peter Prince put the bottle to his lips and drank what was left of it straight down. Then he went rummaging through the other bottles, and the case clinking with empties. She heard him swearing. He held up a bottle but then he stopped.

They both felt it.

A sudden yet vague sensation of horror, welling up like an intuition.

They both heard it. A muted growling, a snarling, a snapping. As though from a hundred. The sound came from far away but when they both looked toward it they saw something on a rock by the misty dim shore. It was only a few feet from Petey and as large as Uncle Ferddy's wolf-dog. But it had the face of a man. Oh yes, they saw. It was the face of a man. Staring at them.

No one said anything, not Cindabilla, not Petey, not the dog-man. A great Presence of Evil, and loathing and madness enveloped them almost to bursting. Cindabilla thought it was more than anything she could bear. "*Daniel!!*" she screamed. "*Daniel!!*"

And then it was gone. And all the hatred and loathing and cursing and damnation had gone off with it.

But now the storm had come on.

~~~~~~~~~~~~~

At first it is nothing but a vague mist, scarcely discernible from any midnight mist on a seeming all but moonless night. All is suffused in clammy darkness. It's a netherworld. You are not yet divorced from your surroundings of vague dissolving shapes. You look at your hand held out with a certain sense that it is your hand. Somehow you can tell if anything big is blocking your way. You move around it with a faint sense of reality. But that sense is rapidly slipping, dissolving like everything else in the darkness of night and ashen mist surrounding you.

There's weather, drizzling a strange mixture of moisture and metal and what seems pumice or talc. You can't see to say what it is but it gives you a feeling of all this. If it were not for the drizzle driving it downward you wouldn't be able to breathe. It is not a driving rain even so. It's more nebulous than that, creating a world within a world unlike that first or outer world. You are alone there. It seeming only you. There is nothing but you and the panicking atmosphere you inhabit. You cannot really differentiate between the two. It is a oneness of almost uncreated being, frightful and reft of innocence.

The spiritual horror that overcame the representatives of two generations had vanished with Cindabilla's fierce cry after Daniel. Following the vacuum of his initial relief, to Peter Prince it seemed a cry *for* Daniel, his son. He looked at the bottle he still held in his hand and could barely see it. He threw it down in disgust. Self disgust. Self-loathing came over him but he said merely, "That you, Cindabilla? Where is he?"

"Didn't you see that shit-awful thing!!?" she screeched.

He could just barely see her skinny shade stumble up and weave through the rocks toward him. At first he answered nothing but then he
~~~~~~~~~~~~~

said, "To tell you the truth I'm glad to hear you say it. Thought I was seeing things, feeling things."

"Asshole, we *were* seeing and feeling things!"

It was Cindabilla, after all, and he could see that she was drunk. She did not regularly call him an asshole so he let it go by. Perceiving her start up the lane he called after her, "Where's Daniel?!"

But Cindabilla made no answer. Recollection of the thing came back into his mind and he shuddered involuntarily. Worse, Cindabilla was already gone, leaving him alone with —it. He found his bike and climbed on, kicking up the stand, igniting it. He tried the high beam then lowered it and started feeling his way up from the river, looking for her. Was that Daniel's leather jacket she was wearing?

He tried the length of the lane slowly all the way back to the Lower Intervale Road, calling her as he went. He didn't think it was possible to be any darker than it had been by the shore but it was in this tunnel of firs, with that sinister ash-falling mist. It was definitely falling now, and no longer merely an atmosphere.

Though he went calling for Cindabilla, his thoughts were on Daniel and he realized that his stepson had been gone from the landing and the party a long time. Peter had been attracted to the site on seeing a car full of drunken joyriders depart out the Landing Road. He cursed himself impotently for seven kinds of fool in having started off on the bike in the first place. No doubt Daniel had come through the woods and the puckerbrush. Either that, or he had just missed him some other way, some way that he could not think of now. The dog-man with its hundreds still snarling distantly through his thoughts, Peter Prince decided to go back down the Lower Intervale Road and find his way again up to the camper on Blackwell Mountain. Possibly Daniel, whom he felt for as his own son, was home safe again. Concern for his safety kept the panic at bay. Cinda was something else, but if she was anything it was tough, and he was not going to worry about her. She never seemed to worry about herself.

~~~~~~~~~~~~~~~

Cindabilla is many chilly wet miles from home. Cindabilla is drunk. Cindabilla is staggering along the lane in a thick darkness. She has been scared by something that lingers, powerfully.

If only the dog-man would get out of her head. If only the darkness would get out of her eyes. If only Ceylon Segar's tires would stop falling. It feels like they're falling straight on her head without being burnt up first. No, it feels like she's wearing the whole tire dump on her head. Cindabilla wobbles a bit, she giggles. ...Ohhh, Daniel. Oh Daniel.
~~~~~~~~~~~~~~~

"... Didn't theya used to be ... wasn't theya an ol' tumbledown on the field lane through th'woods? ... Old field lane ... old field lane .... Corn down by th'river?"

She had been walking roughly the middle of the lane but now she teetered to the shoulder, trying to feel for an intersection she remembered seeing on the way down. She heard the cycle coming up on its way toward the Lower Intervale Road and, looking over her shoulder, saw the dark misted light of its beam passing into the woods on a curve. She almost fell over. Cindabilla let herself fall hidden into the woods, just as the beam went ghosting past. She couldn't believe it: Peter Prince was still calling her. He's an asshole, she thought, but I wish I'd a father like'um.

She rose on her elbow and puked again. Then she felt better. Maybe that was the intersection she glimpsed in the beam of his headlamp a moment ago—or was it an hour? She was lying on her back in the damp shoulder full of seedlings. She climbed to her feet and wobbled on. (Cindabilla finds the shed and goes in to sleep away the filthy storm.)

<div align="center">~~~~~~~~~~~~</div>

On a lower flank of Jasper Mountain the paths of two men are about to converge. Lyman Bearce has let his obsession overpower his usually canny common sense, that which has contributed much to his sound forestry and business practices. In the moments when Cindabilla looks up to see two dimly circled moons in the dark of developing weather, Bearce is coolly searching for the mysterious new road he saw from the other side of the river, slowly nosing his Blazer up the only deadend that the road could have been cut from. ...Unless ... could it have been cut into that knoll and upward —beyond the backside of the gravel pit?

The mist has not yet begun to fall when he sees lights in the rearview. Who-the-hell...? Well, maybe he'll get some answers now. Bearce pulls over to wait for the vehicle to pull alongside him. It seems to be taking its time—almost, he judges, from reticence. Maybe he had surprised whoever it was. They hadn't expected his tail-lights after rounding that curve. Hell, he is taking his time!

Moving slowly up behind him, James Fay is doing a nervous tattoo on the steering wheel of his BMW, trying to make up his mind whether or not to proceed. He has turned off the late-night Christian broadcast, considering: *There's no turnout here, but I could back up till I come to one:* He thought he had seen an overgrown track probably leading to an old log yard a couple hundred feet back down the road. ...Don't think I've been up here before. Probably it deadends at one of those old connected farmhouses ... but I doubt this guy, whoever he is, is going home to it.

This associate (—Fay does not like the way the term is being degraded—) this associate of Julius Golding, ski magnate, is also on the track of a mysterious road he thought he saw earlier gleaming on the side of Jasper Mountain in the moonlight. On the face of it, his reasons for doing so varied from those of Lyman Bearce; but if one were to scratch those various surfaces, he or she might find much the same thing. At last he decides to close with the other vehicle, discovering that its driver is none other than Lyman Bearce, selectman and foe of many projects of James Fay, developer. Projects that do not necessarily coincide with benefit to Bearce's own.

Soon there are two sets of lights aiming up the dark road, a road in fact long used by the descendants of a single proprietary settler of Lot 32 on Jasper Mountain. The recent deluge has not defaced its long-settled and compacted surface, but the many decades have dwindled the parcel of the original inhabitants' descendants to almost nothing.

The Twerp, thought the old lumber baron as a pale car cruised to a cool stop beside him, its window gently lowering with a hum.

"Mr. Bearce," acknowledged James Fay with a nod—as this Massachusetts transplant's sister Gloria had taught him to do with these truculent old Mainers. Fay's head for business does respect the man enough to notify his social soul to be on best behavior. The other looks him in the eye and nods slightly, a reverse nod, barely discernible. His arm on the open window frame, Lyman Bearce waits for the bespeckled young man in the plush driver's seat of the other car to continue the conversation—if there is to be one. It is dark here below the trees, but the great white beard of Lyman Bearce glows faintly on his chest. James Fay represses his cool impatience and tries to focus on that beard. *Facial hair.*

The two men sit in their respective little caves, sending pounds of carbon and other toxins into the air for every half cupful of fuel they expend: each hoping the other will give some reasonable sign however slight for his presence. The lumberman could sit there like a glacier, appearing immovable while slowly grinding away the earth beneath him, for a millennium. In contrast, the dynamo salesman of Jasper Mountain ski resort feels the length of each half second as though it were glacier upon his soul; and so he speaks. "Nice night." It was an uncharacteristically brief conversational gambit. He was learning.

Bearce considers this observation with contempt. He would say nothing to the Masshole ... but for that thing that is on his own mind. Instead he says, "It was." It was not going to be to any advantage to treat James Fay the way he would as a matter of course. He thought he had learned all he needed to know to deal with James Fay.

"One good thing," said Fay, smoothly choosing to ignore what might be construed as an insult, "Ceylon Segar's business dealings won't do any harm to your trees—with them being such big carbon absorbers." It was maybe meant to insinuate camaraderie in superior management technique.

The response was typically hasteless. "If it don't turn dry enough fah the fire to creep through th'roots and turn 'em back into carbon."

Fay felt the relief of his new advantage: Bearce was making conversation. It was a refreshing moment ...of an almost friendly leisure. It was not a middle of the night's seeking after...? There was a new road, certainly, ahead somewhere; the possibility of a new way opening, and perhaps here was the man who was making it happen. There had been talk of the Bearces' beginning to consider opening up some of their land to the purpose ... the only purpose, really, for Jimmy Fay to even be in Gottheim. (He sometimes thought this now that things were not going so smoothly with Theodora; of course the tire fire was eventually going to go the way of all flesh. Then development would pick up again.)

"There's that." He said nothing more. He was getting the hang of it. Soon he would be as taciturn as any Bearce or Kimball or Sessions or Howe.

But still Bearce said nothing. He had only to wait. What he wanted to know was bound to come out soon if he did. The Twerp would never be able to out intimidate someone whose ancestors were not from away. (Because of the extent of Bearces' holdings and his father's longevity in the business, Lyman had forgotten that his own forebears did not help settle this area.)

There was silence, each man looking at the other.

Facial hair, thought James Fay. "Yes," he said, "Just thought I'd come up and take a look at the new road."

It was not quite enough to let Lyman Bearce know what, if anything, was on his mind. Or that Fay was peeved at himself for stumbling into the open....

Or *possibly* into the open...? No, maybe there was no harm in what he had just said. He stared straight ahead into what had become the wet dust of the headlamps and tried to think of the beard. Then he said, "It's reached us."

The light of their beams was bouncing back into their eyes now, Bearce saw. He was not going to find that goddamn road tonight. Not with this ash fall. Not unless Fay led him to it. With that almost imperceptible reverse nod, he rolled up his window. But he did not leave. James Fay activated the passenger window, and he also sat there. What do you do now? He drummed his fingers on the wheel, wondering what Bearce was up to with this parcel. And who was its owner if not him? He turned the radio back on.

~~~~~~~~~~~~

Eloise is caught out in it again. If she had a nickel for every time she'd been caught in a snowstorm, freezing rain, sleet or lightning-and-thunder ! Wouldn't you know it: Ceylon Segar's tire fire has caught up with her on unfamiliar ground! If she were at least on an unfamiliar *road*, a lane, a cut or three-wheeler trail—but the willy-wacks! How were they supposed to get out of the woods?

She felt for the small polished horns and ears of Sheila, comforting herself in the feel of soft hair covering the bony head of her goat.

They were fumbling through thickets and under the high rustling boughs of pine through a dense black mist, a drizzle. It was no use trying to sit it out somewhere: There *was* no where. No, it would be better at least to keep fumbling downhill. Not like West Virginia, with its roads on the ridges of mountains. Here if you fumbled downhill long enough and then resisted the urge to go up another hill you were bound to run onto a track, or at the very least a stream ... which would have to empty into something. That was one good thing about being in the mountains. Down East in the flatland—in the real Willy-Wacks—you could go all night in nothing but circles and come—again—nowhere.

Hmm ... let me see ... where was I? Oh yes. The inhabitants of Goatham were all rabidly discussing the misfortunes of those exalted members of the exalted order who had been inexplicably and surreptitiously poisoned by ground rhubarb placed in a coffee urn at the Grange Hall.

She tried to block out the illustration in her mind: There was the counter at D'catter's Diner with its black baldheaded proprietor sitting on his stool eating Yorkshire pudding and beyond him, visible through the order window, his Eurasian niece flipping tostados. [Show outsized tostadas with falling toppings.] Standing behind the counter gossiping her head off was Alabama Persimmons, her huge dangling circular earrings flopping back and forth with every yak.

"Just like Decatur's, isn't it, Sheila?" Eloise tried to crack herself up.

It was no use. Her formerly white jacket was now black and nearly soaked through, her hair straggling into her eyes, her glasses hopelessly blackened and fogged. She kept taking them off to wipe on the insides of her overalls pocket, but it was no use. She tried to make herself *walk straight* —through the brushing understory, over the blowdown, over boulders and feeling for ledges. But it was no use. She tried to make believe that they were not coming to any ledges to freefall off, any ravines
~~~~~~~~~~~~

to tumble into, any stone walls to...! A stone wall! Yes! She tried to make herself believe that she was going to find a stone wall and follow it out along some old settler's property line into the open. But it was no use. Then she felt for Sheila's head again. The lanolin comforting her fingertips: This was useful.

"See, what it needs is a tavern of some sort—like Farmingham Royal Inn—to be called ... Fatham! Yeah! *Fatham Inn and Tenpin.* And the landlord keeps pet rats in the basement to entertain the customers.

... Because ...he doesn't really *want* any customers. He's not like these new small business owners that have come in trying to make the place quaint: He is like the locals—doesn't really want any customers—can't stand to see 'em coming—is cold, stony, just stares at 'em—and his wife— his wife is Irish and she is sick of not having customers and she's drinking up the bar and she wants to go back to Ireland!

But it was no use.

She was shivering now. If she were going uphill she would want to trend toward higher ground on the finger bones of the hill—avoiding the innards, the small ravines. But now a small ravine would be good to creep into, follow along down to—somewhere. She had been here long enough to learn something of how to get along in the woods. Not like when she first came and got herself lost, got herself scared, got herself turned around in the woods. And that was when the sun was shining! Of course now, all these years later, you've got weather, you've got a tire fire, you've got a black night. You've got shivering, you've got.... She sniffs, sniffs again. You've got bear. ...Smells like bear.

"Now don't go getting scared, Sheila. It could just be rotting vegetation. You know that happens this time of year—you get that smell, almost as big as pig—bear smell. Sometimes even bigger. Maybe it's stinkbugs."

The goat seemed uneasy now. Eloise went down on her knees and stroked and stroked the bony head. She sat back on her haunches and began telling herself a joke in her loudest deepest voice. She did this for a while and the smell did not disappear and the wet rock she was sitting on got colder, wetter, and harder and Eloise decided it was time to get up and move on again despite the horror filling her nostrils. "Sheila," She said at the top of her voice, "That is the largest most frightening smell I have ever smelled!" But the heavy black drizzle closed these words in on her. Shivering, Eloise and the goat moved on.

Down and down they went, and they brushed through some saplings and seedlings, and there was a bare spot and then more seedlings, thickets and trees again. And Eloise thought, There was a bare spot ....

She retraced her steps as best she could and found a hard bare spot again. She got down on her knees and stretched, and felt this way and that, and realized that here was a path. Eloise got up and felt for Sheila and walked along the path, testing to see which way it inclined: gravity would be her guide now.

God is the ultimate hard-to-get player, she thinks, feeling her way over the bones of the path, feeling for the polished horn of her goat.

~~~~~~~~~~~~

Daniel Twitchell is moving through the greasy dark, feeling his way through blowdown and puckerbrush and over the occasional outcropping, trying to make his way up the mountain. Oh man would he welcome that camper just now, the camper he had been beginning to hate—how long ago was that; just one or two, maybe three hours? If only he had stayed at the party until someone else had been ready to leave and willing to give him a lift. Right now he would give anything to have his leather jacket on and be the designated driver of a passel of drunks—puking and peeing themselves and passing out in someone's car.

Or the desert! The desert with no rain. He hasn't been in the Maine woods long enough to know: How was he supposed to find his way in this stuff?

Shivering, shivering.

If he keeps on the uphill he won't fall off a ledge, right? Just keep going up: don't be tempted by an easy down slope. No matter what. Thickets, blowdown, just keep going up. Stay on the high dry ground, stay upright. Stop shivering. —No, keep shivering—that's how you keep from getting hypothermia.

But, shivering in shirtsleeves, Daniel knew. He knew that just going up hill was no guarantee of finding the camper. Blackwell Mountain was too big for that. The sides of its slopes were vast and long, its top was nothing but a series of long ridges, mile on mile. And there was no way to keep on a straight line, like he had been able to do down below when he first got off the track. When the moon had been shining, the black tree shadows suggestive, its light shining on the pages, and the book was in his hand, Phantastes.

> *At length, when the course of the moon no longer permitted*
> *her beams to touch me, the night was dreary as the day.*
> *When I slept, I was somewhat consoled by my dreams; but*
> *all the time I dreamed, I knew that I was only dreaming.*
> *But one night, at length, the moon, a mere shred of pallor,*
~~~~~~~~~~~~

scattered a few thin ghostly rays upon me; and I think I fell asleep and dreamed. I sat in an autumn night before the vintage, on a hill overlooking my own castle. My heart sprang with joy. Oh, to be a child again, innocent, fearless, without shame or desire! — George MacDonald

The stories she told were those of her travels along the river, of her adventures among the wildlife, of odd backwoods characters from her forays into deep wilderness. She liked also to tell the tales of her hero Culuscap, the mythic Dawnlander who had some characteristics in common with her Lord. Culuscap was the human embodiment of heaven and earth. He was, if not actually born of his grandmother, then raised by her. He had a mischievous or evil brother, was always ready to accept and meet challenges, responsible for creatures, and helpful in forming the surface of the earth. This mythic Dawnlander, while full of a sinewy temperament, was also capable of being temporarily deceived. There was a persistent, lingering belief among the natives that Culuscap would return once more to help restore all things. The English scoffed at this, asking when his dust would rebuild itself into skin and muscle and bone; when would it grow eyes and see again? —Jasper Mary

"Daniel! Daniel!"

Chrischana was in the maple thicket on the downslope of Buck Hill, below that tiny clearing where the evaporator sat covered until it should be needed again in the sweet sapping season of next late-winter. She had taken the trail down past it and was now in the pathless thickets of the black storm, calling out for her son.

She was a normally calm phlegmatic person, silent even in the throes of violence, the violence of another, rarely of herself. She knew how to have the inner conversation, but in silence. She could weep with grief or regret in her closet, her closet which had become the out-of-doors when she worked there. She knew how to wrestle with God. Peter Prince, she knew, wrestled with God too, but Peter Prince would get bent out of shape by it. When Chrischana Twitchell got sick in looking around on the world she would say things like, "When I say come, I mean stay, don't leave me." She wrestles forthrightly with God. "This is Your great creation, Yours," she would say. "Don't You sometimes feel just a little bit ashamed of letting your creatures get into the shape theya in?" But still, Chrischana Twitchell was not bent out of shape. She had been pummeled by all kinds of grief and had seen terrible things ongoing, but still she kept her posture, gave up no ground. She knew what she believed in, and who.

"*Daniel! Daniel!*"

The ground she was walking on had been absorbing the soot and carbons and toxins of millions of American and Canadian tires, off and on, for the past three months. This little accident had convinced her for all time that there were no policy-making stewards concerned enough to love and care for the earth and creation the way God commanded in the Bible. There were no stewards but her, and all the little people who were trying to plant things and grow things and nurture beings, and just—just do their jobs. ...Without compensation but a living. Why should we ever have anything more than a living, she wondered before God.

"*Daniel! Daniel!*"

Don't leave us. It's your creation. When are you going to come and judge us?

He doesn't know how to get along in the woods yet. He can maybe get along in the desert when it's dry and cold. He knows how to start a fire with shavings. No one can make shavings in this, she thought, trying to wipe her eyes on the inner breast front of her jacket. "*Daniel! Daniel!*" She stopped to listen for an answering cry.

The sky, your sky, is raining down filth on the creatures of Gott'im, making 'em all sick and ruining their habitat, and losing themselves in your storm. The storm that you and the Devil and your creatures collaborated in making. When are you going to come and judge us? Don't you see how much better that is than just letting us go on and on until the blood is up to the stirrups?

Oh please bring back Daniel. Oh please keep Daniel safe. Oh please bring back Peter and Daniel ... and me ... back safe to the camper, Lord. You are the God of all creation and all creatures, and all the-good-and-evil-doing people and all evil doing devils: You are the God. And the great angels and all the planets and suns and constellations and galaxies and molecules and atoms are yours and your making, oh God.

"*Daniel! Daniel!*"

Stopping her movements, she has silence. Only the sound of the drizzling grease hitting the dead pine needles and leaves at her feet, plinking off the needled boughs and bare limbs above her head.

She whispers, "But I'm not your judge, you are mine."

He is a shivering vessel of grime, misty grime, saturated; a vessel of darkness and sharp things in search of his eyes. He had no eyes he supposes, only trembling fingertips, hands and arms held up to protect his theoretically more valuable members. He might need them some day ... if he ever gets out of this. Daniel is fallen timbers, is legs to negotiate them. He is rocks, piles of rocks to wrestle over. Like some other fourteen or fifteen year-old before him, he is lost on a mountain in Maine.

And he could not see his way through the thick darkness. He came through a patch of seedlings and a bare spot; and thickets of seedlings and a thicket of saplings and a forest of trees. He stepped in something big and soft and stooped to his shoes and came up, himself now a pile of bear dung. Daniel was a vessel of thrills and he was the smell of excreted carrion. And Daniel was the well-loved son of three people in Gott'im, and he was lost in the woods.

If only he knew where he was. Then he would have no trouble finding his way out. No, he thought, it would do me no good: you only think you know where you are when you're lost in the woods.

Daniel's father is Balder Simon, Vietnam veteran and lover of Gloria Fay. They would have made it back to the truck okay, if, after stashing their gear and smelts in the pickup, he had not been intent on pursuing a moonlight view of the pond from the ledge for Gloria. It would have been the perfection of the evening had the off-pouring of the tire fire not caught up with them. But now they were out in it, her hand in his.

She did not want to, but she was crying, trying not to let go of his hand, wiping futilely at her nose with her free hand when it was not needed to fend off branches and twigs. If they had not been on the steep side of a small mountain she would have sworn they were in an old cedar swamp, full of those hideous spike-like dead limbs that are bound to put out your eye. If she had known that her guide was flashing back on his war experience, reliving the tropical ash laden mist of the jungle, the sound of a mother weeping for her napalmed child, she would have been horrified.

Polystyrene, benzene, gasoline; incendiary bombs. Flaming jellied gasoline, its targets atomized and falling in the mist. He wanted to let loose the hand and break heedlessly through the jungle, stopping his ears, but simultaneously he was aware that it was Gloria's hand he was holding, and that they were feeling their way through the atomized products of chemical warfare brought down on the house of God. "This stuff came up fom the pit," he was telling her. "Now you see, Glory, why we gut to grow our own food.... Everything the devil brings up fom the pit is uncontrollable by mankind. He's just too good at ducking back into his hiding holes to be caught'n held accountable ana moah."

"Ceylon Segar should be held accountable for this mess," she said, sniffling, dragging the sleeve of her jacket across her nose as she tried to keep her footing on the slippery downhill.

"That ol' fart?—what's he gont do, pay damages out o'the sale of his burning tires, his burning prop'ty? No, it be betta to hold the gov'ment responsible. It give him permission to have all them tires trucked in and stored there. —See what I mean about the devil? That's why he's called lord of flies. We ah the government, we ah a democracy. Who is going to take responsibility for it?"

"Well—they will. —You wait and see, disaster relief, clean up, everything. They'll do it." (*Sniff sniff.*)

He took her hand and kissed it, thinking of the weeping mother. He was kissing Gloria's hand, and he felt he was shedding Gloria's tears and kissing the hand of the weeping mother. Washing Jesus' feet with the two women's tears.

They were dark, blind. Trying to get down a steep face of rock safely.   Testing each tree for its foothold in the cracks of rock, something to take hold of and let themselves down. Some places there were drifts of pine needles and dead leaves, the leaves of years piled in the crannies. Everywhere were trees acting as though they were actually going to maintain a long life, hold and grow in these rocks; but many were loose, barely holding, and many more were dead and ready to fall down the mountain. At length they came to one giant too large to get their arms around, and Balder felt along its length, thick ridges of bark, hoary and strong. A giant white pine with massive roots, tenacious in the rock. Its great roots reaching out in every direction on the downslope, like the massive tentacles of a giant squid. High overhead its boughs of thin pointed leaves seethed gently in the foul breath of the falling mist.

"Let's rest here on these big legs, Glory, and see if we get ah bearings."

This seemed doubtful to Gloria, but she was too depleted and discouraged to do anything but settle down on one of the great limbs and lean back against Balder. No, they were not yet lovers in the intimate sense of the word. They were not going to have children. ... Maybe some day.... But not now.

<div align="center">~~~~~~~~~~</div>

In the camper atop Buck Hill below the summit of Blackwell Mountain two boys had awakened in a familial vacuum. It was their sense of this that woke them, not the tinkling of cinders on the roof, not the wash of ash upon the windows, not even the closing of the camper door. But somehow they knew they were alone together in the world. Of course Nathan and Benaiah did not sleep together, rather Nathan slept with Daniel because Daniel had the required quantity of patience, and because he would never let Nathan provoke him (which perhaps amounted to the same thing).

"I don't like it," said Benaiah from the dark of the bunk below.

This was unusual because as a rule Benaiah would not initiate a conversation with his irritant of a little brother.

"I know what you mean."

This response, with its quiet, even intelligent tenor, was also unusual.

Nothing more was said.

This itself was another aberration. And, for Ben, especially disquieting.

"... Aren't you gonna say anything more?" he asked. This was asked very tentatively.

"I ... think I'm scared."

The incessant tinkling of soot, the speaking of trees on the mountain, the parental vacuum in all this loneliness of the great immane bulk of Blackwell ....

"... Maybe we better sleep together," said Ben.

He felt Nathan clambering out of the overhead. "Bring your own blanket, though."

"Right. You might have cooties."

~~~~~~~~~~~

Asa was standing in the barn looking at the ancient farm wagon with its wide seasoned planking and old ironbound wooden wheels. It was still half full of bales, the overflow stored here from last season. About half the spokes were missing, he saw. There wasn't much light, just what fell in from the now indifferent moon through low windows and that high one up there in the gable over the loft. He could smell last summer coming off the sweet, almost-green bricks of hay he had put up last year. The bays were over in their stalls pulling in some of it right now. It wouldn't be too much longer before they would be done with that and out there cropping grass on the hillside full time again. Get rid of those hay bellies, he thought.

Looking at the old wagon he was thinking of the coach apparition. He kept wanting to place it, sure he had seen it or something like it,
~~~~~~~~~~~

somewhere before. History seems to take ahold of a man, me especially, he thought. And don't waunt let go. Now he had a strange and uncharacteristic notion: What if the apparition *chose* us ... because we know local history ... or thought we did, anaway. He just could not piece this one together. Although he would like to see if it rang bells elsewhere, Asa Bartlett was reluctant to tell any of the other buffs about what he and Olive had seen.

Just then the bell on the tower clock down in Gottheim struck the hour and he listened to it bonging. Tomorrow he would have to go down there and wind it. Time again. But now the bonging got him to thinking about the Village of Gottheim and what all was there, his mind traveling like a ghost over the rooftops and down on the village streets, through the backyards and alleyways.

"Lay 'em away! Townsmen!"

And now he was walking on The Knoll, Crazy Knoll, and looking up at the rundown mansion, the old Victorian Gothic, with its tower and light in the higher-most window. The hermit teacher was up there, probably reading musty old books and murmuring inwardly to himself.... If he wasn't lying on the floor. Asa wondered: Can you keep your wits up when you're that old? Israel Kimball had taught him as a boy in the Gottheim Academy. Maybe he ought to take a walk over there to the school and look around. ...But, no. Instead he went over and peered through the window of the carriage house, two stone's-throw away from the mansion proper. Of course all kinds of houses had been put in or around the mansion since it was first installed over a hundred years ago. And the carriage house had been converted to a garage long since. But now there it was, just as he had remembered seeing it when a boy. Through the dusty dark he saw a big long boxy thing with filthy tattered and gaping covering and stuff piled on it. But there were ironbound wheels leaning against the wall at one end of it. In the light of the moon shafting through an upper window he saw their spokes. And Asa had seen what was under that cover, maybe fifty years ago. From the stone floor underneath its chassis.

Jesus, he thought, coming to himself. What am I doing! ...This is like them kids being on drugs or something. He shook his head and walked out of the big barn into the night. Just seeing Olive again would bring him back down to earth.... He hoped.

But it was enough. Asa had remembered seeing what was underneath that cover from the ground up. He had seen the thing's undercarriage, and it was starting to make sense. Something was. But what sense was it making?

~~~~~~~~~~
~~~~~~~~~~

Meanwhile, up in the tower, Israel Kimball was peering through age-bleared eyes at those dry little meaningful symbols on an aged page of some old fairy romance from a day gone by. He was reading *Undine*, in French, and smiling to himself. He looked up at the black glass of the window, staring the ancient skeletal teacher of classics in the face. He said, in a voice like a rubble of stones rolling slowly and surely down the drive of the mansion to the lane below: "And I like what they're doing today in books with their characters. Like us, not one of them knows much what he's talking about. ... Nobody knows—except maybe a Prophet of God. He asks us for eggs and we give Him serpents. 'Command these stones be made bread,' we say to God."

~~~~~~~~~~~~~

The two men sat in their respective vehicles moments after the dingy downfall began. Bearded Lyman Bearce, in his Chevy Blazer alongside Fay's BMW, was almost ready to conclude that the evening's opportunities were at an end. Trying to find the new road in this stuff would be a chore, and, unless he were willing to turn his personality inside out and invite James Fay over for a talk, they were not going to have a profitable exchange. The filth was coating his windshield and running down in dark trails. He flicked on the wipers, and gazed into the dingy backwash of the two vehicles' lights. What was the twerp listening to on the radio, anaway? Talk radio ... with music.... Was that a hymn?

Idly, almost without seeing, he kept his gaze straight ahead while his mind worked. Then he saw that something was in their dirty beams of light. At first he thought it was a deer though he knew that deer might not step intentionally into light.

The old lumber baron kept his steady gaze on the creature, carefully scrutinizing it in the dingy disturbing light. It was a dog, probably a coy dog. Ears pricked, its head was turned away and its tail hung out stiff, waving slightly. But then the creature turned, and he saw something he had never seen before, something impossible. Bearce continued to stare. A dog, with the face of a man, was moving slowly toward him where he sat invisibly thrilling. Then Lyman Bearce trembled. He started to fumble with the shift lever, but his great trembling hand was like another creature and he could not make it do as he wanted.

In the pale car alongside him, James Fay was seeing the same through a miasmal mist.

No, it cannot be. It cannot be. These words kept playing themselves over in Fay's mind, and in his working throat, but they would not come out his mouth. The creature looked casually toward him as any alert
~~~~~~~~~~~~~

dog in comfortable surroundings might, its tail waving slightly. But that face—so human despite its pricked ears, its visibly canine ears, cupping this way and that as though listening.

And now James Fay was listening, too. For, beneath the radio hymn, he was hearing remote sounds ... of confusion and chaos. Sounds like the subterranean squalor of insects or formless feeding hordes .... He was not consciously parsing their sounds, but James Fay was aware of them, distantly—as an atmosphere or background of the *mutant* coming toward him. God! How can anything be part human, part dog? He may have been appealing to Jesus, whom he had talked to in prayer many times, sometimes in public at church functions. He was good at public speaking and prayer, sometimes it was mentioned in the paper in Gottheim.

The dog-man seemed to disappear as it moved around the front of the Blazer. For a blessed moment, James thought he had imagined it only. But then, in the apparition's absence, the sounds increased. As a cacophonous background of the hymn playing from the speakers, he recognized the noise: It was almost as though—as though he were about to enter upon the floor of the great New York Stock Exchange.

He felt it before he turned and saw the bland face of a man directly adjacent his own out the window. The sound of the floor came up into his face overpowering the hymnal joy that had surrounded him. But he could not see the face with definition, its shade remaining more a fantastic suggestion than a concrete affront. Dimly, thrilling powerfully with fear, he was aware that the Blazer was leaving him, slowly pulling ahead until it had cleared his bumper, now moving rapidly up the dirt road. The vehicle took off, gravel flying, its red lights swiftly disappearing through the bleak drizzle.

James Fay was left alone with the creature, but the creature had disappeared. No, there it was just beyond the hood ornament, its mangy mantle and stiff tail moving through the lights. Its awful head had vanished downward. *Get out now.*

It stopped, intent on something. Suddenly its—some part of it was erect on the right; and over his shoulder James Fay discerned its movement. Then it was down again. And though the paralyzed Fay could not see what it was doing, it occurred to him dimly in the wilderness of his thought that the creature was leaving its sign on his car.

As suddenly as it had shown itself, it was gone.

Dear Lord, I hope it's gone.

His limbs shaking, James Fay moved the car ahead. It stalled. He turned the key and pushed the gas. It stalled again. He turned the key and did not push the gas. It started. He followed up the road, in wake of the red lights that had long disappeared. Until he came to a ditch the town crew had cut to handle runoff. Trembling he backed into it. Trembling he tried to go forward and the car stalled again. Trembling, trembling. James was able to start and move back down the road again.

Out on the highway he did not know how he got there. Could not remember any of it except the man-dog, its darksome man's face next his own. And Lyman Bearce alongside him. Lyman Bearce pulling away. The roar and turmoil of the stock exchange floor. It seemed to surge again in the beating of his own heart.

Oh Lord Jesus. Why can't I be light like a balloon?

~~~~~~~~~~~~

The Fatham Tavern was dim, pointless, and dark. The bottles under the counter and beneath the mirror behind the bar were dim, pointless, and dark. The clientele were dim, pointless, and dark. The proprietor behind the bar was dim, etc.… The intellectual are different than I and you. This is my story. I am Eloise Patadoe, dramatist and illustrator.

The dim pointless proprietor glared at the dim pointless clientele, of which there were two, so they plunked down their money and beat a retreat into the dim night; mounting up, and riding off from the quaintly hospitable Town of Goatham without so much as knocking the dust from their jingling boots. *I was sitting in the corner with my sketch pad, the one that's delivering these well crafted scenes to you now, and I saw the whole thing.* The dim etc. proprietor would be glaring at me, so that I too would beat a hasty retreat, but he can't see me. I'm invisible, except—perhaps—for my bones. He may be seeing my bones, but he's not letting on. He's an old Yankee and nothing scares him. [Turn page; see picture of skeleton dimly sitting with drawing pad at the corner table. Note its engaging toothy smile.]

There are two kerosene lamps, one on either side of the mirror behind the bar. This is the only light except for what comes through the door when it opens. Moonlight can't stray through the two windows because they are so pointless and dark. Enter proprietor's wife, a thin threadbare downtrodden woman with eyes all over the dim pointless bottles. She struggles to prevent a hundred rats (just up from the basement) escaping into the main parlor with her. With thin hapless hands she thrusts the door shut behind (eyes still all over the bottles). [Dim drawing with round white eyeballs plastered all over bottles.]

"Sure and me darling, you're a sight for sore eyes," she says, ostensibly to her husband, but he's a Maine Yankee, he's not fooled, he knows its for the bottles. He glares at her. This is not one of your middle
~~~~~~~~~~~~

America hot glares. It is a stone cold non change of expression. He's a Mainer, or did I tell you this already? [Blue painted face on blue granite stone, wearing glasses.]

"Where are the girls?" He asks, referring to their two Irish daughters. "We've got guests, treasure seekers, and I don't waunt'em to be a bother."

Now this may seem like a contradiction—what with him scaring off all his customers with his cold demeanor *on purpose*—but it's like I told you, I'm no intellectual, I haven't got that figured out yet. I'll work on it, because he does definitely scare off all the customers, intentionally, as you can tell by the rats. He refuses to keep a cat for the purpose of ridding them out. [Multitudes of rats creeping all over the bar, peeking out from behind the bottles, and nibbling on the eyes.]

Enter customers, strangers from Oklahoma, who come in talking and laughing and jingling their spurs, and walk up to the bar to say *howdy*. Bartender glares, they turn and walk back out the door, jingling, no dust shaking off. They ride away. [Brown and black drawing of dust sticking to their chaps and boots.]

During the distraction, wife has found a nearby bottle and, scraping off the eyes, tipples some into a shot glass. The remainder she pours down her thin gullet.

The proprietor stares at her, stonily. Of course his expression has not changed one iota since the beginning of the story which is why I can get away with using the same color and ink drawing over and over. [See above.]

"Ah, sure'n that treasure of Jasper Mary's." The slattern no longer notices the stare. She looks hungrily at the shot glass. "Now won't that be a happy day when 'tis discovered. Betther days are cohmin', I tell ye."

"There is no treasure," barked the innkeeper, peering at her intently through the gloom. "The Indian is making fun of us. How many times do I have to tell you."

"Did you want to be saying that so loud, then?" She is cunning enough in this return. "Ah, but there is a betther day cohming sure."

At these words, as though on a signal, unearthly sounds begin emanating from.... Well it's hard to tell just where the unearthly sounds are emanating from. *I'm having a difficult time sketching these sounds. My bony fingers are all a-fumble. Are they coming from the dim plank ceiling, under the floorboards, or from the night-dark outside?* That's the problem with wandering in the woods with a goat on a blighted night while simultaneously sitting as a skeleton in an imaginary historic tavern. I can see the eyes all over the bottles, but can't locate the source of the weird sounds. [Jagged creepy pale letters forming eerie ghostly and shrill onomatopoeia, rippling from every angle.]

The wife's eyes roll toward the ceiling. All the eyes on the bottles look up too.

"The tourists is out looking fah the treasure," he snaps. Naturally the tavern keeper does not acknowledge the strange sounds, preferring instead to interpret his wife's gesture as a hint about the guests. Did I tell you he's a Mainer?

Meanwhile, out in the woods the treasure seekers, with the aid of a Massachusetts clairvoyant, are seeking for treasure. Did I mention they're Massachusetts treasure seekers? Aside from little bells and incense, they've got a dousing rod, presumably one that's familiar with.... Well ... all it's got to be is familiar, right? So far they've dug fifty-nine holes in the woods and what they've got to show for it is a bunch of dug wells. [Drawing of woods with tall trees and fifty-nine wishing wells, charcoal and ink.]

<center>~~~~~~~~~~</center>

"Where are they?"

"How am I supposed to know?"

"What are they doing it for?"

"I don't know. Now shut up."

"Should we turn on the stove?"

"No."

"Why not?"

"Because we could suffocate or blow ourselves up."

"I'm cold."

"Go get all the blankets off the bunks and bring em here."

Silence. The dark fills up with sound, the incessant plinking of soot and ash on the metal of the camper. Then there is the sound of movement as Nathan climbs out in search of blankets. Now he can be heard and felt piling them on the bunk, pulling out corners here and there to tidy, covering up his brother. He climbs back in with Benaiah.

Soon they are warm and sleeping.

<center>~~~~~~~~~~</center>

Here is one whose body has become a hindrance to the work of finding its own. It picks its way through the thorny, the dark, the cold and damp. The body is buxom with a long braid that keeps getting tangled in the prickly covering of the mountain. Finally the braid is tucked into its own covering, the jacket on her back. It's a mother, struggling through the wet and dark, looking for one who gives her role meaning. She comes from a line of such possessed of the role. She would not be here doing this otherwise. No one has come here except as Fruit of Coupling. The role fulfillment—or nonfulfillment—is where the pain comes from.

This one happens to be the result of coupling two lineages, Yankee (East Anglian) and Abenaki (Native American), both of whom knew this mountain left and right, up and down. The descendants of the grantee proprietors knew it as Blackwell Mountain, the native proprietors as *Three Faces*. Chrischana Twitchell is the result of seed passed along from the original town father of Gottheim and Abenaki natives, seeded in the mysterious loins of Time. One of her Abenaki fathers actually lived, earning his keep for a time, with the family of the grantee proprietor's son. But Chrischana, if she ever knew, has forgotten this. She cares now only for the living seed. She is representative of her ancestors who ate of the mountain and were in their turn consumed by it.

Away off in a Farmington history class they discussed, in less specific and personal terms, this strange inheritance—some of it pieced together from bits of bones, piles of shell fragments, shards and flakes of stone, and musty traveled documents. They will be mulling over the clash of cultures, of enemies who became relatives, became friends; or regard one another warily.

But listen! The words are crying forth, even as the besmirched creation cries forth its burden of failure and sin.

"Oh Culuscap!" *If such insipid tears can charm you, be welcome to them....*

Her weeping stops. Chrischana Twitchell wonders, *What did I just say?*

Yes, she was praying to that mythic hero of the Dawnland Natives. He who formed the body of the mountain.

<div align="center">~~~~~~~~~~~~</div>

The spookiest thing in the woods around Gottheim (usually) is Elda Simon. She is silent, shy, ghostlike, and an animal rehabilitator. Her ghostliness is a suggestion of both her slight stature and the way she moves through the forest, looking for creatures to repair. You may happen on her for a passing interlude and notice in parting some movement of her backpack. She's not likely to say much, but she will never be intentionally rude. Jasper Mountain is her more usual territory, of course, because her old crumbling homestead is above Hutchins Pond on a hillside of that vast monolith.

The wind has been freshening favorably, the weather passing to the great town mountain's hinder quarters, and she is out in the moonlight now, searching for any who may be in distress after the recent day in the dark and ashfall. It's thus that she happens upon the dog-man in the woods on a spur of the mountain above her home.

He sits back on his haunches regarding her beneath the boles of a tall leafless thicket, much as any canid might, who was wild and yet unafraid. The difference is that this one has not taken cover. At first sight he shocks her.

After that start she cocks her kerchiefed head and looks at the creature again out of the corner of her eye. His face is white and gleams in the moonlight, yes, a human face ... with dog's body and ears.

Poor creature.

What can be done?

They continue to regard one another, Elda more carefully than the dog-man. In fact, the dog-man is already bored. Rump in the air, he goes down on his fours, rear high to stretch every muscle and tendon including those in his paws. He trots off deeper into the thickets above, its human face turning this way and that.

He is lost to her vision, and she turns away, convinced that she would have been able to do nothing for him. He is a mutant, plain and simple, and there is no helping the dog part of him, which would have been her sole concern.

"I've gut to tell Balda bout this," she muses, peering into the bushes at her feet. It would be a good way to get a conversation going. Better, she thought, than the thing she'd seen at Rhetta Bearce's.

James was more irritable and nervous than was usual for him. Of course ever since the tire fire, he had not been very happy ... what with the Goldings practically abandoning him to the scourge of the market ...until ... just until the air should clear (so to speak). Theodora sighed and watched him pace about the darkened parlor, touching things here and there, an antique knickknack, a picture frame (ostensibly to straighten it), the half-full glass of buttermilk upon the doily on a small round mahogany table at her elbow. He did not pick it up to finish it off.

She had not helped matters by giving her family's heirloom chair factory to the employees. ...That had been very hard. She sighed again. She just did not know how to help him. Theodora prayed, but it didn't seem to do any good. ...Except ... it helped *her*. Yes, it helped her to pray for him.

It was something she wanted to suggest he try, but that would've been absurd, of course. Of course James was already praying. Of course. Hadn't he been the one to bring her back to church, to point her in the right direction, to tell her about God? ...But it didn't seem to do him any good. Then she felt ashamed—or was it guilty?—for even thinking this.

It was dark here in the parlor, the only light happening in through the hall from the kitchen where there was a night light. She was wearing her nightie and dressing gown, having been startled awake by his ringing of her bell in the middle of the night. He had something urgent to tell her, she decided upon seeing him there in the porch light, his eyes very uneasy through the sheen of his glasses.

"What is it, James?" Her query had been urgent, full of anxious concern as she stepped back allowing him into the entrance hall.

"...Nothing really, Theo." He had brushed past her into the parlor. "I probably shouldn't have come. It's just—I wanted to see you."

He had looked at the mantelpiece clock then and seemed taken aback. "—And, well, we *are* engaged. It'll be all right."

But it wasn't all right. The allusion to what the neighbors might think was not the point. The man she loved, who was everything to her, was distraught. The competent self-assured James Fay was splitting apart at the seams.

"James...."

He seemed not to hear her tentative verbal approaches.

He said, "I don't know why I came."

"You came ... because you're worried. Won't you please tell me what it is, James? You know I love you." Her tone was as soft as dove's down. He seemed not to notice.

"Theo, I don't know why I came to Gott'im."

She stared at him where he stood in the gloaming, just outside the small glow from the small light down the hall. He stood, slight and nervy, a twilight shade of himself, of James Fay, the strong confident mover and shaker, the salesman. The golden boy of the Golding salesforce. He had made her feel she was everything.... Well, at least not nothing. Not like most everyone else made her feel. And now all she could do was sit here like a dunce, saying his name. James. Such a wonderful name. Such a wonderful man. There must be something more. Oh, let there be something more she could do.

"...Well, you're here to live. You came to Gott'im to make a life. ...You thought maybe you would just be a developer, but then you found me." She said this last hopefully. It was her soul hope to encourage him. She hoped he would not remember about the chair factory.

He seemed to consider her words. But then he began pacing again and touching things. His attention had disintegrated once more. He began to tremble.

Her spirit flowed toward him. She stood and put her arms around him softly saying , "James.... Couldn't we pray? ...I know it helps me when I'm scared...." Her voice dropped softly. It was full of calm.

His arms flew up. She stepped back.

"—I'm sorry, Theo." Nervously he backed toward the hall entrance. "Yes, I'll pray—and you pray."

And then he was going out the door and she was standing there in the lamplight of the doorway watching him where he stood beside the dingy BMW, its passenger side. He was just staring at the car. Or—staring through it. He seemed befuddled. A more definite person would have said he *was* befuddled. Theodora did not know such concreteness. But she knew that James Fay was in trouble.

He stared at the grime all over his car. Even now the urine smell of the inverted man-beast pricked his nostrils. He shook his head. There was so much of it. Otherwise it would have washed off in his travels back down into the pondside village. With this and the filth of the tire fire combining, the beautiful symbol of his hope was besmirched. Idiotically besmirched. He felt like an idiot, a crumbling idiot.

Rhetta Bearce watched her husband narrowly, wondering what he was thinking. She could read Lyman Bearce, her spouse of too many years. What he was usually thinking fell neatly into its few categories. ...Something was different. It was a category unknown to her ... unknown to either of them she supposed.

He was walking around in the large glass enclosed veranda. That was the second time he had filled a shot glass in the last two minutes. It was dark, the only light filtering through from the first of two lengthy well-appointed rooms at the other end of the house. And there was moonlight. Seated in her comfortable chair, Rhetta glanced past him out into the landscaped garden she had been working on earlier in the evening. And over there was the crescent drive upon which she had seen the apparition charge her. She was certainly not going to mention it to Bearce. She had had her own shot of gin, with tonic, earlier. That, coming on the heels of her somewhat absurd yet calming conversation with Elda Simon, had soothed the irritation out of her.

"So waya were you, then?" She said it crisply.

He stopped. He smoothed his great faintly gleaming beard with an imperceptibly tremulous hand. Lyman could not shake the feeling that his hands were but two great paws. He downed the Scotch whiskey and his scattered thoughts seem to resolve themselves into these spoken words: "I had to go up and down the washed out road on tother side of Quaker."

"On those knees? Well, I'm sorry to hear it." But it could not have taken him all evening to do that. "So what did you find out?"

"About what?" He was headed to the portable bar along the wall again. But then he seemed to think better of it and changed course abruptly to go stand looking through the glass at the drive. She had the feeling he was not seeing anything visible to her eyes.

Rhetta betrayed no exasperation, as she might have when Bearce was fitting into his known categories of thought and demeanor. What *is* it?

"... About the proposed cut," she suggested after a moment.

Could it have been a dog? Just a dog?

But then that face came back, the awful bland human face in that awful malevolent light. What was he going to do with it? Would it ever go away?

He turned back toward his wife. He tried to look at Rhetta, tried to absorb her inscrutable steadiness. Absorbed, it could last him but three or four, maybe five seconds, he guessed. The unflappableness of his wife was not going to do one thing for him: For that to happen he would have to tell her. He walked to the other side of the veranda pretending to look out on the back garden. ...He could not.... He could *just* bring himself short of it ... but it would never come out. Never. No.

He had driven every village street several times. Fay could see the grime coating everything in the quiet avenues, neighboring houses filthy in the moonlight. Every house, parked car, storefront, the shrubbery, the Common, its gazebo where the Community Band played. The Village of Gottheim, archetypal New England village, a mess. He does not know how he was able to focus enough to recognize, but, rounding the corner again, he saw the Chevy Blazer of Lyman Bearce parked in the street before the Farmingham Royal Tavern and Inn. The discovery startled him. The companion of his distress. The Blazer, Lyman Bearce. Lyman Bearce must be in there.

The age of the man struck him as he approached, through the dim light of this old cellar tavern to the bar where Bearce sat, elbows on the bar. James had never been in the tavern or any bar in the village before. The thick stale tobacco smell almost gagged him. A TV above the bar was on, slanting its light down onto the few patrons' faces. Fay was too distraught to notice anyone but Bearce. The old lumberman was staring into the shot glass in his hand. He did not look powerful. He did not look like Lyman Bearce. He looked old.

But again the dog's human face was intruding upon James's observations. He had to stop this. Somehow. Prayers in the car he had made while driving the village had not seemed like prayers to him. Not real prayers. ...Not even real words. They were flaccid verbal constructions masquerading as meaningful words. James Fay might not have put it like this. He might have said, *My prayers are pointless.*

James Fay sat down beside Lyman Bearce at the L-shaped bar and ordered a glass of Schweppes ginger ale. Hearing him speak, the older man looked up sharply.

"Mr. Bearce," nodded Fay.

The other dropped his gaze back to the glass and grunted.

The ginger ale was set before James and he took a swallow then pushed it back toward the edge of the bar.

"You're going to need something stronger," said the old lumberman.

"I don't. —Drink." Fidgeting, Fay cleared his throat. "You did see it then?"

Bearce said nothing. He finished his shot and ordered a beer.

Suddenly another voice, higher in pitch, intruded itself. "See what? Whad you see?"

They both looked across the bar through the haze of cigarette smoke. There sat the king of used tires, Ceylon Segar. In the ghostly light James Fay looked at him through a decimated expression. He had never seen the singular grubby individual he would have designated "gentleman"—being at a loss for any other term to use on him. But he knew instantly that this grizzled thing was the personage responsible for everything that was wrong with Gottheim.

The small unshaven pinched face that looked as though it were ready to spew a jawful of Kodiak cola was split by a yellow grin, aimed at both men.

The disgust of Lyman Bearce began to reassert itself as he looked at that grin.... There was a comparison to be made between James Fay and Ceylon Segar, he was sure. Both were small and compactly built men: grasping, looking for the deal. Maybe their abilities weren't that dissimilar either, he mused. If you cleaned up Segar (everyone pronounced it Cigar) and gave him a few more brains, a little more class, took off twenty or thirty years, you'd have James Fay from away.

... Except that he knew Ceylon Segar's forebears had been here even before Bearce's own. That the land he owned had been in the family for generations.

Then he remembered the dog-man and its face, and how he had taken off when the creature went behind his Blazer; off up the road, winding, winding until it deadended at the old homestead of one of his own mill hands, Hastings. Hastings, the competent edger with the arthritic hands who had been with them forty years. Bearce had circled in the yard, his beams passing over the dismal dark front of the house and back into the blackened rain. The sight of the house had surprised him. How had he forgotten that Hastings lived up there? It had come into his mind to hop out of the Blazer and knock on the door but just as suddenly he remembered that thing he was usually able to forget or discount. Lyman Bearces' father had cheated some of the Hastings out of a large piece of prime timberland. God, he was going to have to see Hastings again tomorrow in the lumber mill.

It might even have occurred to him to knock on the door, ask for a drink, confess a theft, the theft of his father. But no, there was too much pride for that. Too much pride even to consider the possibility. It was his father's deal.... No sense in bringing it up now. No sense. No sense.

The dog-man with its human face: no sense.

He looked away. Lyman Bearce ordered another whiskey.

~~~~~~~~~~~~~~

Nathan was whispering into Benaiah's ear. "Dad's coming!" It was not his usual volume of response to the remote thunder of the Harley coming up the mountain road. Usually he was on his feet in a moment, crowing, turning out to greet him. At the sound of the Harley purring through the undergrowth on the lane toward the camper both boys were relieved enough to take up the usual tussle, but now in an uncharacteristic and muted manner.

Nathan tumbled over Benaiah, inadvertently punching his elbow into the other's abdomen before landing in a heap on the floor. Benaiah stayed put, relaxing into his relief, while his brother hopped up and began crashing for joy into things. Two pans that had been stacked on a stove burner fell to the floor with a clatter.

Peter Prince called. "What's going on in there?" Through closed jalousie windows they could hear him pull the cover onto his bike.

"Dad's home!" crowed Nathan. He opened the door and stuck out his head. "It's raining clinkers again!" He had been hearing them on the roof all night, but now he felt their greasy wash on his face. "Dad, get in here out of the clinkers." He thrust the tin door wide. "Nobody's here but Benaiah'n me."

"Nate, this isn't home, it's a holding tank, remember?" He climbed into the dark camper and sat down on the table-made-bed he normally
~~~~~~~~~~~~~~

shared with Chrischana. Nathan stood to one side of his knees between him and Ben's bunk. "What happened to your mother?" He circled the boy's skinny hips with his arm.

"We don't know. We don't know where Daniel is, either."

Into the dark he said, "You there, Ben?"

"Yeah."

"She's looking for Daniel." He tousled Nathan's hair. "He's on his way home and it's probably too dark for him to see through the clinkers."

"I thought you went to look for him."

"I did, but I couldn't find him on the motorcycle. You know what it's like when you go into the woods? My bike doesn't go in there, does it?"

Nathan's thought for a moment, then said, "That's bad, that being in the woods in the clickers."

"Now they're clickers," muttered Ben from the darkness of the bunk.

Peter shrugged out of his greasy leather jacket and tried to figure out where to put it. It was a larger version of Daniel's own that he had given the boy two Christmases ago. Didn't he see it on Cindabilla tonight? ... It might keep her from getting hypothermia, he thought. He put his arm around Nathan again and thought of the dog-man. *Wherever you are, buddy*, he thought, *it's home*. Then he began to think of leaving these two and going out into the woods to look for the others.

"Maybe I better go look for 'em."

Neither boy spoke but they were thinking *don't*. Nathan said, "Maybe. What can you tell us, first?"

"God, you don't mean a story—*now*—do you?"

Ben liked it but he said nothing. This was one of those times when he hoped much from Nathan and his nattering, as Dad called it. Often he just had to wait and soon Nathan would speak his own feeling. It was a secret thing he seldom if ever acknowledged to himself.

"Yes yes," said Nathan.

"Did I tell you the one about the man with the dog's face before?"

"I don't think so. Do you, Benaiah?" Nathan turned toward the hole where his brother was lying, silent and still. "Do we want to hear that one—?"

"C'mon, now. I'm here. There's nothing to be scared of. I won't tell you a story to scare you. You boys are good and I don't want you scared, so don't be."

Nathan was jigging on his feet. "Yeah, but Dad—. Didn't you say you weren't gonna be here in a minute?"

"...Trust me. You know in Europe they are afraid of them and call them werewolves. But this one isn't a wolf or a wolf face. He looks just like a man but he's got the face of a Pekingese. Remember that dog that lived two trailers over in Phoenix?"

"You mean Mrs. Marquez's little dog that was so funny? His face looked like a brown hand had flattened it."

"Well it was a flat brown face, anyway. Now that dog was smart. Member how smart his eyes looked? If it wanted to bite you, which I don't think he really did, he'd only be able to reach your kneecaps."

"He chased me once. I shouldn't've teased him."

"Yes, we know," said Benaiah from the bunk.

Peter grabbed Nathan's arm as it flung out toward the source of provocation. He held firm and put it by his son's side.

"This man had a flat smugged-up face like that Pekingese, and no one loved him for it and this made him mad, of course, but *that* made everyone laugh which made him even madder. So you can see, it was a vicious cycle."

"Kinda like a dog chasing his tail," said Nathan.

"Exactly. The harder he ran after that tail, the madder he got. What he needed to do was stop and realize that he was getting mad, and that he didn't wanna be mad anymore. So then he asked God to help him live with the Pekingese face and said, I won't ask you to change my face, but will you at least help me not be mad anymore?"

"And God said yes," said Nathan.

"Of course. But it didn't happen overnight. Sometimes he had to ask for help again, and then one day he didn't need to ask any more.

"Now get in bed and say your prayers, and if you wake up and I'm gone you'll know what I'm doing, okay? Maybe Nathan better sleep on top?"

"He can sleep here if he doesn't bother me," said Benaiah.

"Are you going to bother him?"

"No."

"Okay then."

Peter took out a cigarette and started smoking in the dark. In the dark the boys watched the light of its ash move from his knee to his mouth and back again. Soon they were asleep to the sound of the clinkers.

It sounded to Peter like one of them was wheezing. That was new. He went to check who. It was Nathan.

~~~~~~~~~~~~~~

Demon got loose and was prowling through the woods looking for deer to harass and destroy. This worked best when other dogs got loose and joined in. Of course demon was top dog and any other encountered would, after
~~~~~~~~~~~~~~

the ritual sizing up, be invited on prowl with a mere glance over the shoulder. He was bristle-haired and black, with long white teeth in a grin accenting his almost slant-looking eyes. With regard to ownership, Demon was a strange combination of Cindabilla's and her Uncle Ferddy.

The latter was a brutal sot who made tolerable his days by making them as intolerable he could for others. It was not too long after Cindabilla accidently shot him in the butt (with his own bird gun) that he purchased this awful hybrid of a doberman and wolf. He had felt the need to arrogate a little top-dogging in the household so that his niece might see what's what. He needed, he thought, more respect from her.

But she was nothing if not contrary to him and soon had Demon eating out of her hand and answering her call before that of Uncle Ferddy— who had never been quite able to divest himself of the fear he felt for the hybrid. Demon had not come to the household as a pup, but as the nuisance castoff of an apartment dweller in Lewiston. It happens that Ferddy can read—a little—enough to spy something unusual in the classifieds when a notion seizes him.

But Demon was the terror of the neighborhood. He had attacked a girl who had known no better than to tease him when he was tied to the dilapidated shed of the dilapidated farmhouse the Sessions lived in. Naturally when he got loose and saw her again he went and took a bite out of her. Her folks had thought that since it was her own fault there was nothing they could do in the matter. They would not have been inclined to call the police, or animal control officer, to complain of their neighbors' failure to control. Besides, they were drinking buddies.

Here's Demon on the scent of deer on the wooded hillside in the gleaming night above his house. He's alert and excited and already tasting the whole flesh of deer molecules lodged in his brain via direct connection to his snout. Suddenly he's checked by another, stranger, scent; one he has never encountered ... or has he?... It is either a man or a dog. Or —? It is a senseless commingling of smells making the hackles of Demon rise. He keeps trotting straight ahead but now his ears turn this way and that, alert for any clue to the forthcoming encounter.

He sees it stepping through the moonlit trees, the crosshatching of shadows and light on the hillside; its own ears visibly cupping. And that face, the face of a man unperturbed by his presence.

Demon is not prepared. He slows his pace but advances, tail at a slightly uncertain angle, his ears as high as he can get them—not all that high. It is not a time for hostility but caution. The other dog—was it?—also advances but without checking itself first. Its tail is high and its neck arced. All this confidence Demon recognizes for having experienced it in himself.

But it is that other part put together with it, much as his own has been put together, hybrid that he is.

If he ever thought about such things he would realize that he is rattled. He would recognize in himself the signs he has witnessed in the other dogs, the underdogs. He is the dog that tried to attack Petey Prince right through the windshield of his pickup in subzero weather, the dog that sent him back to substance abuse counseling the night Alvin Robichaud froze to death in his own truck parked next to Petey's. If he has feared not man nor beast why fear the combination? Is there something more here?

Demon must stop and let the other come. The stranger approaches, swift and stiff.

They are opposed, neck by neck, hackles raised. Ears low, Demon inquires, looking directly into the human face whose eyes are averted. Demon turns slightly away. Tentatively, he lowers his snout to sniff the other's groin and is frustrated by a sideways hop. The other's tail is high and his strange head continuing averted. His interest in Demon appears small.

Suddenly, at no apparent sign of aggression, the stranger knocks Demon's haunch with his own, casting him momently off balance. The wolf-hybrid's tail goes down and he turns to watch his mangy superior tear uphill through the barred moonlight. The human face looks back once over his shoulder and Demon follows, his tail, though a bit higher, still drooping.

Already Demon senses where they are headed for he knows the lying down place of deer; he knows their trails and frequents and slaking pools, much like you know where your neighbors live and work. He has harried deer from these places before. He does not need to be an opportunist. And he does not wonder that the new top dog knows where to go.

Up the side of this mountain and, rounding, down the dogs go. And there they are, not a little way up from a drinking pool, resting and chewing their small cuds. In a moment the deer are all gone off, but one.

The stance of the top dog checks the flight of the undisciplined Demon after them. A sudden, if remote, sound of a thousand growling, coupled with an almost casual glance is enough to stay him. So he looks on the one left behind, the white deer he has glimpsed once or twice before. It may be that this whiteness is an indication of illness. Or it may be a sign of injury. Not yet a yearling, it seems not so wise as the others who have scattered even as they tempted chase.

See it standing there: so brightly reflecting moonlight in the midst of a chill unleafed woodland of mud-season Maine. Its shoulder twitches faintly, but otherwise the deer seems to have reverted to that trancelike protective feint of its early months. The animal rehabilitator, Elda Simon, had once seen such a youngster in a tug-of-war between two coyotes. She knew they were coyotes and not coy-dogs as was commonly supposed in the region. Coyotes had made recent incursions into the state, perhaps from Canada or even New Hampshire. She had seen firsthand what such wildness will do. But she had also seen the pets of her neighbors so destroy deer. They would tear open a fawn and stupidly watch its life sink, agonizing, out through that brokenness.

The white deer will be easy prey. Delicate and fine as enameled porcelain, it stands— not ten feet away as they watch.

But this is *not* the instinctive eyeless trance of innocence. This is a true *look*—complete. And unlike what Demon knows of young deer. Yet there is no actual expression beyond that which says, *I am deer*. Here is the language of a body completely without fear.

Demon glances at the dog-man, who moves to circle with lowered head, it's chin leading as though a snout. Demon licks his chops, gulps, and starts opposite.

The deer leaps up and moves away, the others in surprised pursuit.

Through thickets and stands gleaming with bars of heavenly light the chase carries up and over the slopes of the mountain above Cindabilla's house. On and on the deer leads them, mile upon mile and the dog-man's thousands howling ... over deadfall and down ledge, up the sides of ravines. On and on the sheen of the white deer leads, on and on until they are passing together into the raining atmosphere of ash and black night where its gleaming hide is almost extinguished, and still they pursue like a horde.

Comes a flickering break in the darkness, though dog-man's howling continues as ahead a new rumbling threatens to overcome it —the breaking and bursting and blowing; the roaring of fire pots from melting cast-off tires, its hellish glow firing distantly through the fall of its up-sending fury.

Straight through dense black downpour the white deer leads them, still leaping over and through the grimy wreck of woodland. The dogs' splayed paws tear up the leaf mold in their panting pursuit. Excited Demon feels no bounds. He adds his snarling and snapping to that of invisible hordes, even as the fire mushrooms before them.

At the top of a knoll, scrambling, they see the fiery skirts of the billowing black crust, taste it in their nostrils, follow toward it furiously. Having not once overlooked its shoulder: Down the white deer plunges before the moving volcanic semblance, its white hocks, forearms and hooves working without stop. Leaping the dike installed by firemen to contain both runoff and the conflagration, straight into the fire it goes.

Translucent, aethereal, the white deer stands amid the heat, flames and thunder, only now stopping to look back upon the hounds of hell.

Demon stops in his descent, tumbling end-over-end in his already scorched and frantic withdrawal. With canine flexibility he scrambles to his feet, drooping, quaking; bristling, swerving away.

The dog-man follows the white deer over the ditch and dike into the fire.

Demon has gone back through the blistering heat, the drizzling oil and soot; circling back the way he has come toward Sessions'. Had he stayed to glance back from the hilltop upon the outpouring of hell below, he would have seen two tiny creatures, one in flames.

Igniting in foreground, and from deep within, explosions send jets blazing upward, momently parting the dense moving cloud. Had he stayed to listen Demon would hear multitudes of men screaming, scorched and cursing, their filthy blasphemies rising in toxins, not distantly nor remotely, but pandemoniac loud. The cries are extinguished in a burst of flame and the dog-man is gone. Only the deer remains in the fire and fulmination, testament to God's own spirit of repentance, purity, goodness, and grace.

~~~~~~~~~~~~

When the all-volunteer firefighters of the rural towns surrounding Gottheim first arrived on the scene in little Quaker Plantation weeks before, they, with all their trucks and equipment, were together for the first time since the Jasper Mary Day parade last summer. (On that day they came gleaming and screaming along Front Street to the delight of the assembled children, their elders grimacing.) The scene before them on Jasper Mary's legendary treasure ground, now tire dump, was unlike anything they had ever seen either live or on TV. In a rush of adrenaline that would have powered the creation of the earth itself, they set to work with backhoes, hoses and ladders, pumps and lines leading up from surrounding streams and the River Birch. They knew there was nothing they could do to extinguish the hellfire that was spreading before them. This was a stopgap from which they would be lucky to escape with their lives.

Men and equipment came up from Guildford and even Lewiston, and still they were stop-gapping this fire. It was winter and cold, sometimes with subzero weather, and where there were not explosions and conflagration, there was misting ice. Some places both men (and equipment) could scarcely operate, and some places they were in danger of heat prostration.

In company with the state fire marshal's office, the suits from the Department of Environmental Protection came up from Augusta to oversee
~~~~~~~~~~~~

the work. Initially, when they had seen what Ceylon Segar was up to, and slapped him with a pile of fines for illegal tire dumping, on second thoughts they reasoned that the tires had to be someplace, and, under their tutelage, decided to license him. They showed him proper pile size, fire lanes, etc., made sure his bucket loader and other equipment were safe and inspected, and before you knew it Ceylon Segar was a proper businessman and quasi pillar of the community, though he still smelled bad. If he did not do everything to the letter—and some of those piles got to be big as mountains, big as a ridge of mountains—he would be more than happy to explain why.

Lightning *will* strike. If anything can go wrong....

Foam retardant, by the tankload, was tried with no result except an increase of toxins to the flaming brew, surrounding aquifers, and streams. That's when they brought in the pump panels, deluge guns and firefighters from as far away as Bangor. Also the EPA, FEMA, DHS, LURC and the Guildford Salvation Army. By the second day, when it was clear weather (in the north), the black smoke from the fire could be seen on the edge of sight from Portland. People donned their snow gear and climbed to the tops of mountains to look out on a distant funnel cloud, pitch black, as though touching down from a massive thunderhead. Booms to absorb yet more runoff contaminants were set around the original moat and dike.

We will not speak much of the devastation to animals handmade by God and breathed alive with His breath. We will not speak much of the destruction to surrounding woodlands woven out of the particles and elements of God's elegant imagination. Or of the pollution of breath which was meant for the health of the children. The rats We know about.

We have spoken to the stewards of all these things. We are tired of speaking and of their ill response.

We saw the heart of the volunteers and others who came to quell the fire of nature's rebounding wrath. We saw the fertile response of those who care, the Caregivers. And we saw the others, the stewards, behind their desks, on their networking fairways, working away in their fast craft. To the first I say, Watch, guard against influences coming and harmful to your community, strengthen what remains though it's already dying. To the last I say, buy repentance of Me if you can. There are no more words We speak to encourage you.

~~~~~~~~~~~~

"And the rats have all left their cozy homes in the tire dump to make their abode in the hamlets and the village of Goatham. God is the ultimate hard-to-get-player," murmurs Eloise stumbling through the damp and dark, its acrid bitter downfall on her lips. "....Absurd for the self to believe it the
~~~~~~~~~~~~

owner of the human being with which it's associated, the soul to which it attaches, Sheila. They've studied the Self, you know, but don't know beans about where it comes from. They know how it operates, and believing it to be prime mover of humankind, have elevated its status to ultimate *raison d'etre*. I mean, here I am walking in the shivering dark in tire drizzle, with you for company, and I've found this path and will cling to it no matter who or what tries to get me off. Is there anybody else here with us? There's you, me, God, and Self. Remember, you can't get away from God no matter what. We are living walking bones and, make no bones, the rats are also with us in Goatham.

"We need to get back to the Fatham Tavern for shelter or we might not make it home tonight. We've got to save the Irish lady, and all those rats in the basement, because ... because.... Well anyway we just have to. If we keep working along at it enough, it'll show us how those bones got loose in the woods. That's my plan for making it back to the house and the other goats, got it?

"....Those bones had a definite body language, don't you think? What can you tell from it: them being scattered all over the graveyard and that gaping door of the vault.... Like maybe they were in there first and somebody forgot to bury 'em—? Or maybe they were "interred" there and got dug up by critters. —Or maybe they decided to go out and walk around, quite forgetting they had no skins to hold'em together. Maybe they were family and had a brawl in the graveyard."

Her grimy glasses had long since been stowed in a pocket of her overalls. Sheila's bell tinkled faintly beside her. Eloise held onto her horn alternately stroking her silky bony head. She shoved a stringy piece of hair behind her ear.   She jammed her hand back into the pocket of her jacket and trudged along the bony spine of the path.

"Do you think we'll ever find that graveyard again?" Do you think they've been dead long, or were they mass-murdered last year? Have you ever noticed that it's hard to talk through chattering teeth? I'd be warmer if I were sitting in that tavern and these teeth were nothing but a grin in a skull instead of a chattering skull grin in a tire fire rain."

She had been stolid and silent then talkative by turns, and now it was time to be stolid and silent again as she willed her legs along the path.

~~~~~~~~~~~~~

Daniel Twitchell cannot stop his teeth chattering nor his limbs shivering, violently shivering, as he stumbles through the woods. His shirt and jeans are plastered to his skin by a fine rain of not forty degrees. Maybe it is time to turn around and try going down the mountain instead. It is all beginning
~~~~~~~~~~~~~

to seem one to him, but he has a recurring idea that he will keep warmer through uphill exertion.

The name of Donn Fendler has long since gone out of his mind. Earlier he felt the ghost of the lost boy walking with him; probably, he then reasoned, because he had read Donn's story. Whatever became of him after that, Daniel had wondered; after he wandered the slopes of Katahdin, lost in the Maine woods, for so many days—or was it weeks? Did you grow up and have a career, get married, have kids? Did you become a policeman or game warden? Did you ever go into the woods again? .... No, you didn't find a book named <u>Phantastes</u> and get scared out of your mind while walking along reading in the moonlight. There was too much else on the mountain slopes to scare you. Things like thinking your knees are hinges. But aren't knees really hinges of some kind? Something to enable you to open and close your leg, lengthen and retract your legs as you walk? Could knees ever rust shut?

But all that careful reasoning is over for Daniel now. He knows himself to be lost beyond recall. Even such fatal certainty fades as heat and health sink out of his lithe body into the night. The requital of nature slowly absorbs the essence of his being upwards into its gritty diffusion. His mind is withdrawn into its own center, softly sleepwalking and inchoate.

Daniel rouses in the falling snow. The blowdown that he climbs over are wet and white with it. It pelts like sleet down his lashes and into his eyes, its formerly bitter taste turning to salt on his tongue. He has climbed into a white clearing and, Look, it's a man and boy! He tries to call out to them across the way where they are sloughing through the snow on snowshoes. They look over at him briefly before turning back on the way with their weapons. The boy has a gun and his father bow and arrows. On their backs are an ash-splint basket for the boy and basswood carrying bag for his father. Daniel does not know how he can tell they are father and son, nor why the polliwog style snowshoes seem familiar. But didn't he see something like that hanging in the shed next to Balder's everyday snowshoes? They are the kind Indians make and use. ...But I am an Indian, thinks Daniel. Why don't they come here and help me?

The boy and his father are gone in the thickly falling snow, dissolving into it as though they had never been. His hope sinks within him and he begins to cry, quiet tears falling, mingling with the smear of his face. He lies down in the wet tangle, folding together shivering as though he would shake apart. "Jesus, Jesus," he whispers through clattering teeth. The teeth in his jaw, clashing together, seem to have outgrown his body, their clashing is like the pitching of great limbs in a storm overhead. Daniel heaves himself up to continue his wandering.

But something is standing there in the drizzly snow not far off; standing beneath the boughs of white pine: sifting in and out of the snowfall. At last he sees that it is a tall Abenaki, robed and mantled in blue with a hood of worked blue and white draping his head and shoulders. In his hand are tall bow and arrows and he stands regarding Daniel through the pouring snow.

"W-w-will you—?" whispers Daniel.

But softly, thoughtfully the Dawnland Native regards him before fading back into the snow.

Now Daniel stands with his back against a rock wall, cold, damp and furred; a rock with barnacle bumps along its surface. It's a ship with wooden hull.

He feels with his hand, trying to pluck plates of lichen from it. A rasping voice startles him and he looks up into the great face of a man with raven-like beak staring down on him.

"You are pulling on my plumage," the voice croaks. "Maybe you better stop now."

"Sorry." This is a sullen mutter from the mouth of a child who has been greatly wronged. "You don't look like a real person, anyway." *I should be taken away from here in an ambulance. They should give me warm cloths and hot chicken soup. At least give me some stinky quilts or a pile of dry leaves to crawl under.* He is silent, indignant and grumpy in these unvoiced thoughts.

"But I *am* a real person. I'm a folk of the forest, with the same body parts as yourself ... but perhaps made out of other materials. For instance, parts of my hands and arms, unlike yours, are delicately hollowly boned— many such delicate bones—my scapulars far stronger than your own. And my long fingers, unlike your own, are feathered. The cartilage of my nose is without skin, and horny, while yours is bulbous and soft. We are like the People who thought of us—arboreal creatures. Did you know you are going to die?

Daniel began to cry again, softly. "Yes, yes. We're all going to die. The Lord made us this way."

There was grave silence. Everything stopped except the snowfall and the heedless tears.

Said the queer man quietly, "Why d'you s'pose he did this?"

"So we wouldn't get swelled heads like the devil. It's prob'ly why he does everything."

The Forest Folk gave what seemed an involuntary gurgle. Daniel was a moment deciding it softly raucous laughter. He had taken a step back when the rock spoke to him, but now looked fascination at its wings. "I'm desperate," he said. "Can I get under there?"

Anyone who knew Daniel would have been surprised at this forwardness.

The Folk opened his wing and Daniel entered into its shelter, surprised by the soft thick dry down of its interior, and pleasurably grateful. He stayed there a while, standing beneath the sheltering wing, shivering, before poking his head out to say "How do you keep it so dry and cozy in here?" He drew his head back in and leaned into the thick down against the man's warm side.

The folk's voice seemed both muffled and as though it came vibrating through the upper part of his body next to Daniel's head. "Of course you know that without my outer feathers the down inside would be saturated and of no insulating value. In fact it would be the worse for me. Maybe in the first draft of me it was such, the same as it is for baby birds, but then seeing so many dinosaurs and birds and forest folk walking around plastered and dying, God probably decided another draft was in order, so he evolved these structures over the down in my arms and hands. You can feel along them with your fingers if you like. Notice the lattice-like structure and how the contour feathers are covered over by flight feathers, which shed water like one of your raincoats. Of course I can't really fly with them—yet. I'm waiting for the resurrection, I suppose. When the Lord will descend from heaven with a shout and I will rise up to meet him in the air."

"Are Indians suppose to be believing that?" Daniel assumed his own voice to be muffled, as he felt the comforting pressure of the other's wing in a momentary hug.

"They don't have to. Nobody has to. But then look at Culuscap. Didn't he help to form, or formed, these mountains and the way they are dressed? And wasn't he sort of attacked by his evil brother, and supposed to be coming again? Of course, I don't know about that up in the air part regarding him —myself.

"This conversation is making too much sense," murmured Daniel.

~~~~~~~~~~~~

"The vocabulary of Mainers' body language is a small one," seethed Eloise through chattering teeth.

"You take those bones up there somewhere in the lost graveyard. Their body language is all over the place, they could be saying any one of a number of things now that they're dead. But when they were alive? Very limited body-language vocabulary. In fact, they only know how to say one thing: 'Go away.' But it's probably a good thing they can say even this much
~~~~~~~~~~~~

in body language because they're too taciturn to say it with speech. Take our tavern owner over there at the bar. He can be as talky as he needs with everyone that's not from away, but look how he's dealing with those treasure hunters from Massachusetts.

"[Lots of crosshatching, chiaroscuro, more light localized around the bar where stone-glaring innkeep is making tea for the abstemious treasure seekers.]

"In thickly crosshatched shadows the plain little group dressed in typical nineteenth century garb cowers beneath the stony gaze of the barkeep. They of course have long since lost their own native Bostonian suspecting and puritanical outlook on the rest of the world. The garrulous great-hearted high spirited Irish have seen to that. Up here, in their grant-fostered independent and unconscious solidarity, Mainers would not allow the minority Irish or French to make a dent in their so carefully placed rock walls. But I digress.

"They drink their tea in silence at the circular table usually reserved for card-playing loggers and river men when they aren't getting wood down to the mill. (Yes, I am trying to get a little history in here, nevermind that Maine was a dry state during this period long before Prohibition. Some of you will overlook the fact if you want to have a good story. For authenticity's sake we should go down into the cellar, where the rats are, to dip into the cider barrel, but instead we will have our California folks belly up to the bar.)

"[Open door reveals white moonlight illuminating strangers therein. Enter the Californians with big smiles and good hair. Tavern owner stares stonily as they approach talking rapidly and eying his skinny wife who is still trying to scrape her eyeballs off the shot glass in her hand. Big rippling onomatopoeia of scary sounds emanating every which way.]

" 'Fascinating atmosphere you've got here, sir,' flashes one set of big teeth in the direction of the owner. [Talking balloon in the shape of a megaphone.] 'This would make a tremendous setting for one of Mr. Edison's moving picture shows. The West would have nothing on you!'

"Barkeep looks at him.

"Unfazed, the Californian talks on: 'But what we really have in mind for this area is *bingo*, you guessed it! Yes, high stakes bingo, that is—once you get this tire fire business cleaned up, that is. But it's never too early to plan: that is, plan BIG! Naturally we're here to do the talking for the Native Americans. Just between you and me, we know they're not much better at talking with outsiders than you Yankees, right? (*wink wink*.)'

"[Collection of big hair and teeth, with sharp eyes looking around at strange noises emanating from every which way.] 'You really should have that plumbing looked at. Here's my card. Don't worry we'll be in touch.'

"[The teeth, eyes, and hair throw a last glance at the tattered Irish lady and depart back into the moonlight, voices trailing.] ...'Did you see that skeleton in the corner taking notes? What do you suppose is holding her bones together like that, what keeps her femurs attached? And what about those bony fingers holding that pen! We have got to tell them about this in Hollywood ....'

" 'Rich-bastids,' says the tavern owner, shoving the card across the bar to his wife. 'You can't trust 'em. Says here theya fom Nevada.'

"She picks up the card and, squinting, pretends to read it in the light of the guttering lamp. 'Aye, hoosband. Sure'n didn't I tell ye betther days were a'cohming?' "

~~~~~~~~~~~~

Engine running, Balder and Gloria are sitting grateful and warm in the old pickup. The heater is roaring and they are wrapped bare together on the bench seat in an old Indian blanket Balder normally keeps draped over the seat-back. It is black night under the pines and raining soot, their breath steaming the windows. They are happy and snug in their own little Balder and Gloria world.

"Now what was that you were saying to me about that dismal guy last summer? The one said food growing couldn't keep pace with population." Balder stops kissing the top of her dirty wet head long enough to murmur this.

The kisses and murmurings are making Gloria weak in the thighs. She misunderstands what meaning there may be—if any—in the words. She asks a question to stop the weakness from spreading. "—Dismal— who?"

"You know: the reason we caunt make babies." It is still but kisses and murmuring, soft as gently falling surf.

"Malthus," she said. "The dismal theorem. ...Yes. ...He had it all figured out ... mathematically."

"Then it's a math problem ... we caunt make babies."

Gloria chuckles, happily.

"Don't worry, Glory. God's got the problem figured out. ...He's good at math." Balder tightened his hold on the blanket, tightened his arms around Gloria.

"...But if you look at Ethiopia...? ...Look at Africa. ...People are starving. Malthus was right."
~~~~~~~~~~~~

"So God doesn't have it figured out ... doesn't know how to care for the people we make." He kisses the greasy shell-like ears on either side of her head.

"Well ... I won't blame it all on him. I mean ... humanity hasn't done such a great job of keeping the planet stress—less ...." The last syllable is said after a sharp intake, on a sigh.

"...I like a sweet woman who thinks." He bends his head gently to her responsive lips.

But it is no patronizing verbal trick, these words. She has just made a profound concession. It is their first time.

Afterward, they snuggled together speaking softly about this and that. "You've been happy ever since you discovered your son Daniel, haven't you Balder?"

"I was getting happy when I found you, and then he came ... and that made it pretty set." It was yankee understatement, she knew. She would never get it but she wasn't sure she didn't like it.

"The most solemn kid. You should've seen him helping me on the house last summer. I could tell he didn't want to. He's generous, he nevah said a word. Volunteered to help Mutha build her loon nesting islands. Ah, he's a great kid, Glory."

"You think we'll have one of those, you and me?" She did not want to say that she wouldn't know what to do with one, but Gloria could not help thinking it. She sighed again. She would think all about that ... if there ever came a time.

"If weah lucky ...."

What did it matter if they were naked and in love and never imagining the tedium and turmoil, the mysterious deep magic, of long life as one? They drifted off to sleep in the mythic Balder and Gloria world.

Asa and Olive were lying in bed beneath a big sheet of divided-light moonlight. They too had had their connubial embrace, but now lay back together under warm handmade quilts, wakeful. The bed, with their combined slightly porky weight, was sagging; soon Asa would be leaving for his own room. Easier on the backs of both that way.

He was saying, "I think I figured out where 'twas I saw that thing before." They had seen the great apparition and heard its distant echoing cries together on the Lower Intervale Road earlier, yet Asa was not about to reveal his extraordinary—hallucination—was it?—in the barn. That was just too much sharing for him. Maybe he was coming down with Alzheimer's, and if so it wouldn't do to let Olive know. She'd find out soon enough.

"You were bound to," she said. "I read somewaya that answers come fom the subconscious when you're not looking."

That was some comfort. Not much. They were both staring out at the big bright moon.

"Don't it seem funny. We ah looking at sunlight shining on us fom that," he said.

"Evah thing's weird if you think about it too much," said Olive tersely.

That's why I'm telling you this, he thought. So's I can stop thinking about it.

"So where did you see it?"

"Must've been fifty years ago, but .... In the carriage house of the Gothic mansion on Crazy Knoll waya our old schoolmaster Israel Kimball still lives. Don't know if it's still there, but 'twas under a canvas tarp that I lifted and saw the carved pillars and glass panels, then I crawled underneath and looked up and saw stamped on the bottom: Grable & Sons. When I was a teenager I read up and found out they made hearses, this one being of the mosque deck style. But when I saw it there as a kid it was on top of an automobile chassis. Evidently, early in the century it had been used to that other purpose, but I nevah found out show-a." He turned his head slightly to look at her, noting the marble-like quality of her eyes.

She let her gaze slide from the moon to his face, noticing the same quality in his eyes. Must be something to do with the moonlight. ... Pupils reflecting moonlight reflecting sunlight.... Too much thinking. "Wouldn't it be fun to go visit ah old schoolmaster? Think o'all the stuff he could tell us about the old days."

Asa turned back toward the moon. Gawd, what Israel Kimball wouldn't be able to tell about this place fom the last part of the previous and the early parts of this century, thought Asa. Wicked smot schoolmaster like that. He didn't say much, but back then he knew what was going on as well as what went on in Greece two thousand years ago. Still gazing at the high silver disc, he said "Jeezus, his mind's gone by this time. He won't know a thing. Prob'ly in diapers by now." He said this last ruefully, thinking of how he had ditched his underwear in the middle of the compost heap by the garden before he even got the horses bedded down for the night. He'd be strapped into a wheelchair in no time.

"Well," she said, "what would it hurt to see? Yuht, he's been a hermit all these years. But you nevah know. He might waunt to see us. He was a good teacher, waunt he?"

"Daow, I misdoubt his marbles is scattered all ovah the top floor of his tower."

"...So it's a coffin carrier 'stead of a circus wagon?... Was he—or whatevah it was—saying he wanted to put his cargo in the ground, think maybe? Whad it have to do with us, wondah?"

"Nothing," said Asa. "That's the way ghosts is. They got theya own business to mind. If we just happen to see 'em while doing it...."

"That's not what you said during your talk last summer after collecting all those regional ghost stories, Asa. Sometimes it's got something to do with the one who sees it."

Asa thought then of the story about the young girl at an evening's musical in the last century, seeing that dead infant at the window and crying out 'twas hers, she'd done away with it. ...But the others present said it was her own reflection.

~~~~~~~~~~~~

She could not see a blamed thing. Oddly, she was thinking of the state social worker she had had a conversation with in the grocery, a person the size of a small office, who thought there was something wrong with a neighbor who gave birth to twelve kids. *You have to woo God. God is the one who conceived the personal. It is impossible to approach God in any way but personally. One-on-one.*

She was blesséd. She was alive. She had come down the dark mountain through the tangled greasy wet woodland and out onto the hottop. Eloise wobbled down the center of the blessed road, still feeling her way with her feet, her hand yet reaching down every so often to touch Sheila, her goat. She had no idea what road she was on, it was still dark and drizzly, and she was shivering, but she was alive. Alive. It was a real road, and going to take her home.

She was thinking doggedly. I don't care if we get hit by a car, Sheila, I am not budging from the center of this road. Dying by automobile is better than hypothermia. At least then they would have to take us to the hospital. I would shoot them with their own hypodermics if they did not take you with me.

Already the lurid glow of hell surrounded her, its whining demons coming for pathetic Eloise Patadoe. She was not even going to make it to Gott'im or Quaker or wherever this road was taking her. They were squealing and screeching and swerving onto the gravel behind her, heavy fat
~~~~~~~~~~~~

things. Who would have thought that demons could be so big. She kept walking.

A car door opened. "You! What are you doing in the road?"

She recognized the dry glooming voice of the bellyache's editor. Eloise turned back, facing into the grizzled misty headlights angling for her. *You are in hell, too, Mr. Nutting?* She wanted to ask, through chattering teeth, but could not make herself. She had to get home, she turned back again.

The hands caught up with her and turned her around. She stood her ground; faced into the gaunt sidelit sallow features and nut-like eyes of the editor, scarcely recognizing him without his green visor. "D-d-don't you feel naked?" she asked him.

"Ms. Patadoe," he said. "You and your goat had better get in." Hand and arm were held out toward the light firmly, an ushering gesture. He saw her disheveled features in the greasy light, the lank strands of hair, the tips of her ears peeking out. He saw she was obstinate, numb.

The touch of his grip was surprisingly gentle if firm. Eloise allowed herself to be guided to the car. She watched as Nutting opened the rear door and suggested she put Sheila in back. "In the backseat of your car?" she asked. "I don't think she'll go in there."

"She will if we make her."

"Yes, that's right."

She was never able to remember afterward just how they did it, but soon she was strapped into the front seat of Mr. Nutting's car, with Sheila's dark head between them. "It smells just like wet goat in your car. She ought to be at home in here."

"Yes," said the editor dryly.

The head withdrew itself, the bell tinkling wildly, as small hooves behind them began thumping and clattering restively.

"Take hold of her collar or whatever you've got for her," he commanded.

"You don't have to get huffy," said Eloise, huffing.

They rode several miles with the heater blasting, Eloise alternately aimlessly speaking or silent, shivering. Nutting was on his way back from a long day in Augusta, where editors of Maine local weeklies annually convened, and now he was glad of the distraction to help him keep awake on the road. At last they pulled up in the yard of Eloise's dark house on the Quarry Dog Road.

"You know w-where I live!"

"I know where practically everyone in and around Gott'im lives." He reached a hand across and opened the door, got out and swung wide the

back door for Sheila. He came around and helped Eloise to her shaky feet.
"Where's your keys?"

She dug in her pockets and came up with her smeared glasses. She put them on, took them off, dug around some more and came up with the keys. He gently pried them from her slow bewildered hands, quickly took the steps in the filthy diffused light of his highbeams, and inserted the key. Eloise followed, smelly, hangdog. Tinkling faintly, Sheila followed them both. Nutting flicked on the light by the door and Eloise stood in it, blinking, amazed.

There it was, just as she had left it, the kitchen still full of unsold paintings in crates, but otherwise neat except for a few utensils and crumbs on the counter where she had made the snack she brought with her on what was to have been a short hike. Jim Nutting was already in the next room. She heard the squeal of the woodstove door, the scrape of a match coming from the next room. She walked like a sleepwalker toward the sound.

"Good you had the fire laid. Maybe you want to get out of those wet things—a hot bath." Numbly, she unzipped her jacket and he helped her peel it away. He went to hang it on the peg by the front door and turned to see her fumbling with the buckles on her overalls. "Maybe you better do that in the next room, or upstairs—maybe the bedroom where you keep your dry clothes." He does not, after all, know where most everyone's bedrooms are.

Eloise went up the stairs between the two rooms and before long he thought he heard water running. He checked the stove to make certain the fire was going — the draft was good but not perfect — and went back to the kitchen to peer into the cupboards and come out with a can of soup. When Eloise came back down in pajamas and robe the front room and kitchen were warm, there was soup bubbling on the stove, a pot full of steeping fragrant herb tea, and what looked like buttered bread; yes, it was buttered bread—bread from the freezer she had made before going to New York. Soon it was all on a tray, and he was bringing it into the parlor in his purple-stained hands. She backed into the rocker he had pushed toward the stove and sank down into it, gratefully. The light in the room was that of the stove, what came through from the kitchen, and a small dark-shaded table lamp behind her. He set the tray on the arms of the rocker and said, "Don't rock."

Eloise was no longer shivering but her normal ebullience was flattened. Because he didn't care for it much in anyone from away, Jim Nutting was some grateful for this, but on second thoughts, he thought it a bad sign. Eloise ate, staring into the fire. At last she looked around, saying, "I thought Sheila was in here."

"She's eating. I took the goat out to the—barn." Eloise had another old house outside that had been moved there from down the road specifically to serve as both barn and roost for her goats and guinea fowl.

Eloise was silent. She munched the stale bread. She took a swallow of tea. "They all get fed?" No old Mainer could have been more terse. She was not from away now. She had lived here five generations and was beat down by it.

"Yuht. You okay now?"

She looked up at him standing there to one side of the stove near the kitchen doorway. Eloise noticed that his head did not look as bald as it usually did when he was wearing the green visor. He had sandy hair and a now invisible bald spot. "I guess that means you'll be going. Want to take some goat milk cheese with you?"

"I don't like goat milk cheese."

"So you've told me." He had never been willing to barter ads for cheese. She took another swallow of tea and thanked him for bringing her home and for taking care of Sheila, making the fire and the food. "You don't seem like a Mr. Nutting anymore," she said. She studied him lounging against the doorframe, hands in his pockets, regarding her levelly through his glasses.... *You've added to your body language. It doesn't say, Go away.*

"Jim, call me Jim."

"...I discovered a discrepancy in the townline between Quaker and Gott'im." She was handing him a scoop. As an afterthought she added, "I found a bunch of loose bones in an old graveyard. Humans."

~~~~~~~~~~~~

Damn tire fire, thought the editor of *The Village Voter* as he drove back through the falling filth toward Gottheim. He was now thinking of the nutcase goatherd artist from away.

~~~~~~~~~~~~

The chrome lines of Decatur's Diner gleamed in the moonlight, its front also dimly lit by the one streetlight at this end of the road before the loop to the highway. Early morning dark. Unusually, one of the fluorescent lights inside was also lit, dully flickering. Bald-headed Jeffy Decatur sat at the counter on the edge of darkness. In the haphazard light next to the opening where the waitresses could stop at the kitchen window to pick up an order. The place had been closed since 3:00 p.m. yesterday, and he was talking away as though to himself but in reality to his niece Gildy who was in the kitchen doing prep work. Gildy Hart was getting a jump on it because she was not going to be there to see to things today. Decatur was going to substitute in his old place at the grill. Thinking to spare him the early rising, she came in to ready tuna salad, chowder, gelatin, and puddings, but he had insisted on keeping her company. Suddenly the glass door opened and he turned, shocked to see Rhetta Bearce enter.

"Turned out to be a nice evening after all," she said, seating herself on the stool next to him. She gave him a moment to get over it before turning to say, "Don't you think, Mr. Decatur?"

"Who's that out theya with you, Uncle Jeffrey?"

"It's just me, Gilda. Rhetta Bearce," she called. "I saw your light on and thought I'd step in for a bit of conversation. I'm not after coffee or anything."

Gildy Hart, a net covering her auburn ponytail, looked dumbfounded through the order window beside the coffee urn. She did not think she had ever seen Mrs. Bearce except in the broad light of day when the older woman might be enroute to some volunteer organization or club meeting; more rarely grocery shopping or going into the post office. Never in the middle of the night.

"That was a nasty batch of it we had, earlier; I was just mentioning to Mr. Decatur." The older woman was dressed in a tweed jacket and felt hat with speckled feather cocked at a stylish angle. Her hands were clasped in front of her on the counter, a small gold wristwatch peeking out from the velour cuff.

"Yuht." It was all the young woman could think to say. To compound the surprise, she was recalling all the old gossip about how much Mrs. Bearce secretly hated the diner where her husband frequently conducted business, in his apparent scorn of the suite in the fine old office block on Front Street. Yes, she was quite sure she had never seen the dignified matronly figure in here before, though Lyman Bearce owned the old dining car and lot it sat on. She looked at her uncle, as though for help.

But Decatur was never any sort of help in such surprises, and was always the worse for it. His pasty Anglo-French face stared drop-jawed at his landlord's wife a full five seconds. Then he remembered to shut his mouth and look away.

"But maybe you'd like a nice cup of tea, or instant coffee—?" Gildy was able to get this much out. "—Yuht, guess we got dirty again." Her glance slid furtively to the big round fluorescent clock on the wall.

Mrs. Bearce hesitated. Gildy did not think she had ever seen her do this, either. "... A cup of tea would be nice—if water is already on the boil and it's not too much trouble."

"Got it right heah," the other said, her head disappearing from the window.

Rhetta Bearce slid from the stool and moved past Decatur around the counter to the order window, saying, "No need to bring it out, Gilda."

As Rhetta brought cup and saucer back to her place, Decatur thought he heard the faint rattle of ceramic and looked to see a slight trembling of her hand. She sat, removed the tea bag after a moment, blew on the surface and took a sip, then turned to smile benignly at him.

"It's been awhile since I seen you in here," he said. From anyone else it might have been a sly or leading statement, but from this gentle puddinghead it was an innocent recognition of things as they are. Yet, he was trying to figure it up and he reckoned never. —No he misdoubted he saw her in here when she was a teenager several years his junior. His father had had the place then, and Lyman Bearce's father was the landlord.

"That so?" It was a typical response from anybody hereabouts, little more than a tacit ascent. But it could lead one to go on. Decatur realized he had nowhere else to go with it.

Rhetta Bearce was thinking, *But I was in this place last summer.* When it was sitting in our backyard behind the garden. She had had some sort of victory then. Not victory over Lyman Bearce, exactly; over herself. Yet she was not thinking of this any longer but of her husband's Blazer parked in front of the tavern. More, about how troubled he'd been earlier. Probably still was. She had never seen him troubled like that before. For some odd reason this was comforting ... to sit here drinking this tea. This was where Jeffy usually sat now, she knew, next to Lyman when he was at the counter with the mail, sitting where Jeffrey is now. It was the only way she could think to act out solidarity with Lyman.

~~~~~~~~~~~~~

Theodora Prescott heard the car come to a stop in front of the house, and looked up. It was silvery dark in the bedroom, the moon's light and streetlight fallen in predictable pattern, adding drama and even mystery to the room's pretty tasteful furnishings. She rose from her knees beside the bed and went to peer out the front window. There was the roof of James's BMW gleaming dully up at her. She waited for its door to open, but it didn't.

She stood there some moments, looking down,waiting. Then she sat on the cushioned window seat, gaze fickering off across the Common toward the shadowing gazebo, and then back at the car roof.

Down in the car he sat with his arm on the rest, gazing off down the street, seeing not parked cars and empty sidewalks but *the dog.* The dog that was a man, or the man that was a dog, or whatever it was—that awful thing he had seen while looking for possible development properties. He
~~~~~~~~~~~~~

was still seeing it. His time in the tavern with Mr. Bearce and Ceylon Segar had not helped beyond showing him that he was not going crazy. It had shown him too that he was not going to join some cozy fraternity with Lyman Bearce. He had failed to grasp—they three being each be of the brotherhood of businessmen, it could not make them anything but enemies, for such is the ultimate nature of a fraternity based solely on its profession. Though he had seen the same creature, the lumber baron was not going to acknowledge a mutual—anything. As far as James Fay was concerned, Ceylon Segar belonged to the same misbegotten race as the dog.

.... But man was supposed to be God's crowning creation....

The ungodly are not so, but are like the chaff which the wind drives away. Without are sorcerers and dogs.

"But you're my savior: 'Its leaf also shall not wither; and whatsoever he doeth shall prosper.' "

Silence.

He raised a tremulous hand and looked at it.

Again he tried to pray. His mind formed words but they tasted of dust and ash.

For the Lord knows the way of the righteous; but the way of the ungodly shall perish.

He thought he glimpsed something ... however slight: Yes, the *way* shall perish. ... Don't let me be on it. He whispered, "Don't let me be on that way." *Please. I do need You. I do. I am that sinner, I know I am. I keep shouldering You ... aside.*

He thought, if I have to see the dog-man, at least don't let me be *with* the dog-man.

Please. He was shivering all over. He clutched at the door handle and pulled it, climbed out. There was the Common, mottled with shadow and light. He crossed the street and walked into the Common, wandering, restive. I can't possibly be .... I am not like Ceylon Segar.

The Pharisee stood and prayed thus with himself, God, I thank thee that I am not as other men are.... I give tithes of all that I possess.

Wretched on the Common, he circled the somber silence of the mostly early spring leafless giants, a few tall red pines with shapely needled limbs. He had to take off his glasses and stow them in the inner breast pocket of his blazer, for salt tears kept running down his cheeks as he wondered for the first time that he might not be saved after all. The roar of the stock exchange floor rang relentlessly in his mind, that awful bland dog-man face was stuck in front of his own.

"Let me just stand near You, then. No matter what. I know you came for sinners. "You won't stand off from me like that Pharisee."

He was standing in the shade of a Norway pine, murmuring. If he had been asked, he would've said it was an evergreen. He leaned against it, wiping his face, heedless of getting resin on his coat; its smell like Christmas in his nostrils. He felt some relief. He lounged against the pine, much as Jim Nutting had lounged against the doorpost, between the kitchen and front room of the artist, wooing her. "I know you won't desert me, though I am a sinner. I know you won't. I know you won't."

It was not as the psychologists say, "Methinks thou dost protest too much." A true lover cannot protest too much. Not when his or her attention is undivided.

And there was Peter Prince walking down the mountain road in the ugly falling ash and mists. He too had seen the dog-man, he too was seeing the dog-man. He thought maybe he had seen the dog-man every day of his life. Even though James Fay had only seen it once to recognize it, there were comparisons to be made between the two men. Although one grew up in the Midwest and the other in New England, both were children and entered adolescence in the same evangelical denomination. Both had mothers who were and still are pillars in their respective churches, their fathers only nominally so. They are of the same generation, the Vietnam generation (Fay being five years younger than Prince), and know something of the cultural pressures of revolt and subsequent assimilation into the established order. Both men are likable, willing to extend friendliness. There, seemingly, the similarities end. Fay has a graduate degree in business administration, and is proficient in sales technique and interpersonal communication, when working. Peter Prince is prone to violence and he is a college dropout with technical training, a skilled blue-collar worker. He works in the paper mill. He knows he is in trouble nearly every day of his life, and so tries to live them one at a time. He does lean on the Christ, much as James Fay is doing at this moment under the pine tree on the Common. Unlike James Fay, he knows himself enough to know that, for all this true sweet leaning, his nature remains unchanged. It is not yet time to be changed.

Peter Prince was smoking one cigarette after the other as, occasionally stumbling—especially on the upper track—he felt his way down mountain in the dark and falling mist, calling as he went. The tiny glow of his cigarette was comforting to him and he thought it might help anyone close enough to see, but it gave him no satisfaction to smoke for it was too dark to see the toxins parting from his bronchia and lungs on the exhale. Once he got below the highest leg before their camp, the going was easier for the road was packed and crowned and comparatively wide. His calling was interspersed with coughing, hacking, and spitting. The dog-man was still visible and sounding in his soul and he remembered to pray, if feebly. Peter Prince was discouraged, his heart was low because of his sins. He'd been the cause of the abortive search, the turmoil of the night, and the loss of Daniel. Why would God want to bother with him?

But it's them. It's Daniel and Chrischana, and I know they are good enough to bother with. You're good enough to bother with, good enough to trust.

He thought he heard a tiny distant voice in response to his own, calling. He stopped. Yes. It was too remote to tell, but he thought maybe it was Chrischana's voice. He called again. Cigarette still between his fingers, he cupped his hands around his mouth and gave several shouts. He stood still, listening. The voice was on the left, far off in the woods. That would mean she had crossed over the road at some point, for the direction was not below camp but more towards Gottheim. There were still several miles between the village and their part of Blackwell Mountain.

For many minutes Peter stood; smoking, calling, listening, as gradually the sound of her voice grew distinct and he knew she would find him in the road. Now he was hearing her movements in the brush, twigs snapping and cracking. He called again and puffed harder on his smoke. She would be standing beside him out of the thickets in a minute or two.

He waited to hear her speak and, as she stepped out into the road and brushed herself off, he came near and held up the cigarette to look into her face. It was dirty and solemn and, as ever, he could not tell if she had been crying.

"You didn't find him." Her syllables were hard, clipped, tense. "I didn't either. What ah we going to do? Do you know what time it is? I don't know how long we've been at this, d'you?"

The first thing Peter thought of was his training under Herman Gottesman. "Chrischana, I left you in a foul mood and disregarded some good advice from you." He did not say he was sorry, for those were words he had spoken often in the past, falsely, though at the moment of utterance he believed them true. Instead he made a mere confession.

"I know." She was not interested in confessions now.

He suppressed a self righteous urge and suggested the thing he had been thinking of all the way down the hill. "We need help with this. More people searching."

"But it takes so long. One of us will have to go back up to get the truck and go make the call. Balder will come right off, and know others to get. We could call the police, rescue workers, the Maine Warden Service, evah body."

"What about that nearest farm down there on the Lower Intervale Road?"

"Betta. You keep walking up and down this road calling. I'll go down to Roebuck's and make the call." She started off and was gone in the darkness before he could speak.

Remotely hearing its hundreds howling, he resisted the urge to go after, grab her and make his own suggestions, hand out the orders. He was afraid, but not in the same way as James Fay. Both men were in the throes of seduction: For James Fay the uncovering of his own purposes in their true nature was frightening to him. But Prince was drawn by the dog-man's naked corruption, seduced with a strange hunger to consume himself and others in his own anger—leap from its sides straight into the pit.

Walking back up the mountain in the dark he thought about Balder in the war. Balder had to have encountered the dog-man in Vietnam. He could not have escaped doing so, Prince reasoned. He wondered how Balder did it. There was a lot of shit under there, had to be. Sometimes he thought he could see it. Highly controlled shit, but you never got a whiff of it. How could the man be so damn good? He was a walking grin-machine. Petey was sometimes glad to sense Daniel's annoyance over that grin. *He* didn't have a predisposition to addiction; he wouldn't allow it.

Time to be ashamed of myself, he thought. I am ashamed. He flicked the still-glowing butt away. What did you make us for?

Blessed are all they that put their trust in him.

James stood outside the glowing pool of light cast by one of the decorative streetlamps that had been placed around the Common by the benevolence of the ski magnate Goldings. He had been walking in shame, but now stood looking out across the street toward Theo's house with its spacious bow windows and the otherwise straight clean lines of its front. He thought he detected a faint glow coming through from the back where the kitchen light was still on. Faintly, he remembered her conversation from earlier. It had been all but consumed by the apparition that was no apparition ... except in its continuance in his thoughts. Slowly her quiet conversation surfaced with more strength in his mind.

How brief it had been, how kind, tender even. She was so often tender and kind. He thought of this now, displacing his recent irritation over what he had considered her foolishness and weakness. She was without harm, he thought. This usually meant he thought her harmless, but briefly now he recognized the difference in tone between the words harmless and without harm. For the first time it occurred to him that being without harm was a great strength and probably difficult to achieve. Even so, he did not think it would be honest to tell himself that this was an achievement on Theo's part. ...But he had to be careful now: This shame. He was just too dismissive of her. Hers was a gentle soul. And she had been right.

He looked up toward her bedroom window, and there she was. He saw what seemed the whiteness of face and shoulders, bodice. She must be in the window seat. He thought he should let her know he was all right. He should not let his unshakable shame deter him in this. A living presence, it weighted him like a depression. He stepped into the light and held up his face. He waved. The figure moved. Its gesture an answering.

A kind of call and response; not entirely unlike that between Peter Prince and Chrischana Twitchell in the woods and on the road of the mountain, dark with shame.

Lyman Bearce was on his way home from the tavern, his senses not yet extinguished by the quantities of Scotch whiskey he had consumed. He was smart enough to leave the Blazer behind and do the legwork necessary to stave off the stupor he was going to fall into. Coming up out of the night shadows of great trees on Front Street he spied his wife's Buick in the lot at Decatur's and stopped dead. He wiped an arm across his eyes and saw it there still. He stood a little straighter, smoothing his great beard with his hand, a woodsman's hand still.

He did not leave the shadows but stood gazing out toward the highway loop, then back at the lot, and the old dining car of the Atlantic and St. Lawrence railway. Drifting down came the distant sound of an eighteen-wheeler floating on its engine breaks, riding large on the night.

What are you doing, he wondered, his thought directed toward the tiny figure of his wife, seated next to that of Decatur in the yellowish fluorescent light on the edge of darkness in the old dining car. It must be Decatur, and he has my stool. Of course.

He stood there, stolid, his hands shoved in his pockets. It was hard to get Lyman Bearce drunk, and he was not there yet. He could still think, steely as ever, but he was chastened tonight (for reasons already mentioned). Lyman Bearce in chastened form is not like you or I. In appearance of manner or action he remains unchanged. As Rhetta has discovered, it *is* possible for something to be working away in him other than pet projects, town politics, business and what's going on in the woods.

He thought, This is the oddest damn night I *evah* had.

He recollected it with due diligence: coming down the washed out road below the lots on these damn bad knees. *Seeing that road I nevah seen before—nor since (ain't that odd), seeing the twerp'n....* In spite of the alcohol, he trembled. And now her sitting in Decatur's, waya she nevah sits—in the middle of the night!

What time is it? He looked hard at his watch. Hell.

Then he stopped and thought again.

It had been years since he thought of it, the cheating of the Hastings. *It had nothing to do with me.*

He stood there thinking.

Lyman Bearce started walking again. By the time he got to the parking lot he knew just how it was going to be. Nothing would ever be said. Nothing would ever be known. There was nothing to acknowledge in any other way but what he was going to do.

It was the old man.

He went and sat in the front seat, passenger side, of the Buick.

~~~~~~~~~~~

He was sitting at the battered, golden-yellow oak desk going over his notes beneath the glare of a naked light bulb. Of course he had on his green visor. The behemoth press, the old Miehle, stood silent in the center of the room like some heavy ancient iron monster waiting to be charmed awake. Then it would thrash the floor and shake the whole building in its monstrous agony to get out the word. The printed word. Jim Nutting rolled back on his squawking chair and thrust his legs up on the desk. The notes were neat on his clipboard and yellow pad, as complete as he could make them for now. Tomorrow late he would send Libby back to the artist's house in Quaker to get the whole story again.

He reached up a moment to turn off the light, then settled back into the complaining chair, his feet again on the desk. Light from the street fell with its strange orange-pinky glow through the windows. His eyes adjusted to the gloom around him, as he stared out into the almost empty street. Oddly, there was Lyman Bearce stolidly striding with his hands in his pockets, his great white beard spread across his equally great chest above the now-stout middle. He hadn't always looked like that. Nutting remembered when he was handsome, clean shaven, lean—if just as impassively sure of himself.

What a crazy tale. He had been thinking right up until this minute that it was a figment, a product of Eloise Patadoe's ordeal. Even the town line thing he could hardly bring himself to believe. She was from away, after all. What was she going to know about it? ...But then ... he had
~~~~~~~~~~~

believed her about the lightning starting the tire fire. How long has she been here? He knew for certain she was here when he came back from Toronto to take over his father and grandfather's enterprise, the village newspaper. It was probably the Nearings ... inspiring her to come here. What a crazy quilt of a place, too, that farmstead.

Everyone who's ever been down the Quarry Dog Road recognized the individuality of: in summer sunflowers and snapdragons and hollyhocks everywhere in clumps; fencing woven out of wire and blowdown from the woods; the house painted worse than a coat-of-many-colors out of perhaps a dozen shades. Someone said it was paint left over from the dump. She ought to fit right in, but she doesn't. She'll never fit in. Hopeless. He smiled faintly.

He thought of her sitting there, deflated, in the front room, spooky front room. A whole shelf full of dolls' heads. One full of glazed pots, several with oversize colorful books. An old Victrola. A large loom with something in progress, probably made out of goat's hair. He looked back over his shoulder and thought the loom reminded him a bit of the Miehle, but wooden. Did it smell like goat's hair in there? It was probably his shirt: He was still smelling goat.

Scattered with bones, an old cemetery. Leg bones. Finger bones.... She did not bring any bones back with her. Claims she had one but lost it. Doesn't know where the graveyard is but thinks she can find it again. He started thinking about the town line once more, stood up, stretched and yawned, and went over to the old wooden file cabinet, which was a match to the desk. ... Well, he might have to go upstairs to the morgue, though.

On second thought he wove his way through the crowded, darkened printshop to the back door, and stepped out into the night. What was left of it. There was the pond with its wide peculiar light. He got into the car beside the building. He would be driving like a drunk if he didn't take care.

The phone at his house several blocks away had stopped ringing. It was ringing now in the office. Jim Nutting drives away. The call received would have been one of desperation. But the editor, old as he was, would have been no use to Chrischana after the night he had put in.

<center>~~~~~~~~~~~~</center>

"It was right heah," said Rhetta pulling up on the drive in front of the mansion. The moon still shone broad on the steep stately white length with its verandas at either end and porte-chochere side entrance. "And I was right theya." She gestured toward the ragged, ghostly, mud-season garden opposite the curve of the drive.

Beside her Lyman Bearce grunted. "So what'd Elda Simon say about it?"

She responded tartly. "I *did* say she saw the same thing, exactly .... Although she was a little vague about it. But we both had the b-Jeezus scared out of us. Theya's no doubt."

He grunted again, and climbed out of the car.

~~~~~~~~~~~~~~~

The drizzle has stopped but the particulate falls in waves, fitfully. Peter Prince is still on the mountain road in the dark, smoking. He's on his last cigarette and thinks maybe it's time to head back up to camp. He's calling, he's calling. There is no answering. On his way up the mountain he is calling yet, but he is also having a recollected conversation with Hermann Gottesman.

"You want to keep it, the very best you have, the whole wad? Throw it away," Hermann was saying.

"But what if it's like pearls before swine? You know, they turn and trample them under their feet. Hooves."

"No, that's what happens when we think the swine are noblemen. We want the attention of the noblemen, so we give them our very best and that's what they do with it. Because underneath… maybe they're actually pigs."

"Let me get this straight: You're saying give the best away to the worst?"

"To the ones we love. We know they are not the worst. But give to them too. Sometimes the worst is just what appears a blind alley. Someday it'll open out into ... what? That's what the Messiah is all about. You believe in the Messiah, don't you, Prince?"

"Do you really think they're different messiahs, Hermann?"

"What am I a prophet?"

And now Peter Prince is hearing an answering to his calls, and there are some moments of call and response, before he realizes that Benaiah is running down toward him in the dark and falling soot. And then it sounds like he has fallen, and he is crying harder and now he is running again. And his voice grows in volume and in sorrow, desperation.

"Dad! Nathan's choking! He can't breathe!!"

Seems the crying he has been hearing is some eerie distant wailing of a siren, for now, having rounded a bend down on the Lower Intervale Road, its sound drifts upward.

He held his crying son a moment, trying to calm him, and heard the siren's wail drift away. There was a strange glowing, coming from
~~~~~~~~~~~~~~~

somewhere back down the mountain, yet Ben would not be quieted, but kept tugging upon Peter with the insistent desperation of someone not big who would be heard, trying to drag him by frantic force, back up the mountain. Peter encouraged his perseverance, but kept looking back toward the strange source of light, pulsing dirty orange light, he now saw through the stems. As they took the last corner he saw the pulse and glow of light refracting through the falling waves of ash before them, and in a moment a pickup truck with flasher pulled to a roaring stop behind them.

He went over to the driver's side, Benaiah standing by, hopping, anxious and inarticulate. The driver had rolled down his window, letting the ashen air drift in. Peter did not know him in the light of the dash.

It was Moses Merrill, who worked in the Bearces' sawlog mill on the trimmer where, with thoughtful skill, he was able to get the worth for Bearces out of every board. He had been on the way home from his shift when he heard a call on the CB, and being a volunteer fireman, decided to respond. It wasn't that far along the road from where he was at the time. It would be a better thing to do, he thought, than to go home and start pounding back the beers. ... Which was just about the only thing left for him to do now that Lydia and the kids were living with someone else. Knocking around the woods was always fun, and at least he might see if he could save someone else's kid.

"You the one that called in?—Twitchell?"

"Prince. Peter Prince. Daniel Twitchell's my son. But I think something's wrong with the littlest kid—up at camp."

"He's choking!" It was a quivering wail.

"Get in."

They rattled and bounced over the ruts and rocks, threatening to shake the truck and themselves apart as they climbed. After what seemed a lifetime to Ben, they pulled through the bushes, their beams lighting the small taut form lying not far from the truck camper in the now abating fall of ash.

"That's an asthma attack," said Moses, kneeling beside him. "My wife's gut this. Gut get to the hospital!" He was putting the gasping boy into his father's arms.

"I thought I heard an ambulance down below before you got here," said Prince to Merrill as they rattled to the base of the mountain. Moses had reached into the glove box, as they started down the mountain, coming out with an inhaler for Nathan, trying to instruct Peter in its use as they went. Attempts to get the struggling boy to use it were ineffectual. Now they sped at a high rate along the river valley route, the yellow light flashing across the trees and fields as they passed. It flashed reassurance to Peter, on their way south to Guildford.

But back in the bed of the truck Benaiah was holding on tightly to the ring where Moses sometimes secured his dog's chain. The wind blew by him, tossing wildly his hair as he turned this way and that, trying to discover what was going on through the dark glass of the rear window, trying to breathe on his own account, letting the wind flap away his tears.

Meanwhile, up in the tower of his Gothic mansion, old Israel Kimball spied suddenly the view out his window. Looking up from his book, he had expected to see his own reflection cast on the black night of the pane, but he found himself looking in the eyes of his great uncle, the one who always wore the bowler.

"Lay them away," said Uncle Hezekiah, his long friendly face— how young!—looking at him matter-of-factly. "It was me, but.... No it wasn't you. T'was me, but anaway....

From the fragments of his physical dissolution Daniel thought, But I'm a kid ... I shouldn't have to. *It's cold, so cold....*

.... He was warm, as though for the first time. Real warmth, as had only ever suggested itself on earth ... and in grateful Gottheim. The Bright Man of Creation was talking to him and showing him His wounds.

He looked into the fierce glowing eyes, the Locus of all warmth and light, the extreme melting of love.

What happened to the Forest Folk who helped me? Daniel asked.

He said, *I'm He. I made them.*

Chrischana was toiling back up the mountain in the thick dark woods. Above, through many stems, spread the ghostly flat suggestion of light to come. "You did the right thing, bringing us back to Gott'im, Mother," said Daniel climbing over deadfall with her. "It was the best thing that could happen to Ben. The best for all of us."

"I know that," she said. "Thank you, Daniel."

She felt him turn and walk back down the mountain.

The flat ghostly light reflected as from pewter off the still surface of the otherwise dim river behind him. He turned back. He might have gone through the wall but he stood flush with it, his head one with the small divided panes of the window, his frame stretched out flush with that of the weather beaten side of the tumbledown shed. He was grinning like Balder on the sleeping form of Cindabilla. All the dark solemnity Daniel had ever felt in what we call life was still in him, but now it was as bright as an iridescent blimp.

"Told ya you shouldn't drink like that, Cinda."

For a while (or was it an eternity?), protectively he looked down on Cindabilla, skinny in his leather jacket, her ginger ponytail spread out and lightly frizzing. Then, without turning, he recognized the Bright Man of Creation on the other side of the dark river and, still gazing on Cindabilla, went backward toward Him across the flow again. He turned then toward the glowing eyes of the Man's bright face and said, "Okay." He was melting in gratitude, awe and love, for the Man and His wounds.

They were gone together before they even got there.

"Ma Mere!" said Robbie Robichaud under his breath, coffee from his steaming cup burning his fingers without notice.

He was idling at the landing in the cab of his pulp truck, waiting for Ansell, his son, to come up on the skidder. He had just loaded every log that was in the yard from yesterday, but still there was room for more.

The landing was deep in the woods but that did not stop the apparition of Israel Kimball's great uncle with his elegant state-of-the-art mahogany and glass paneled hearse, led by a matched set of great Belgians, pulling soundlessly through the stems on the old track that had once been a county road, a main artery leading directly to the county seat. Gaping, he saw it through the windshield charging soundlessly past. He heard the bowler man's admonition, as though all the way from France on what was here but a suggestion of light from the noonday sun of Reims.

He set the cup on the dash and sucked on his fingers, muttering, "What does he mean, 'Put 'em away'?"

Back down the track a quarter mile into the woods, Ansell had just turned off the rumbling skidder and hopped down to have a few words with Balder. In what had been a vacuum of pale, slow, eerily brightening silence, they conversed, Ansell answering all Balder's questions in the negative.

Ansell's cousin Hiram had set the chainsaw on the clean pale stump he had just made, and the two loggers stood there, the smoke of their cigarettes mingling with the remnants of diesel and small engine fumes;

quietly talking with Daniel's father. Then they watched him walk back up the track down which he had come from a remoter reach of the mountain. Watching him disappear—slowly—slumping, his towhead faintly gleaming, Ansell recollected into himself the grief of his twin brother's passing several weeks before. Froze to death in his pickup outside Sessions' house. He pulled out a grubby notebook and stubble pencil and wrote something, fast, to set on the seat of the skidder for his father.

C'mon," he said to Hiram. Silent, flicking their still glowing smokes away, they followed up the track after Balder.

Such light as this made hardly any difference to Elda Simon, for whom twilight was not transition. Her days and nights were something like twilight now. She was in the woods on Jasper Mountain looking, not for her grandson Daniel, but for Sugarloaf the deer, son of Posey. White. An albino deer. The sides of the mountain were steep. She made her arthritic way over deadfall and carefully past the piercing limbs of the standing dead trees, soon to be deadfall like the rest.

"Waunt he something good, though, Sugarloaf? ...Why don't choo find him, like you did that other boy, bring him home? In't it only right?"

Daniel, Daniel. You just got heah. It don't make sense—you go now. He just stotted getting to know you. Don't leave. What would he do, without you?—still carrying Vietnam n'all. ... back spaceWe was gont set those loon islands we made together in the ponds. It was going to be what we would do, just you and me.

She leaned her head deep into the side of the white deer, quietly, gratefully absorbing his musky scent, letting the tears soak his hide.

Sugarloaf would come at times. He was a whitetail deer. But he was wild. Untamable. Not like his brown mother Posey who used to come into the house, eat pancakes, and sometimes slept on Elda's bed.

The atmospheric cursing of the tire fire had moved off the slopes of Jasper Mountain and the Lower Intervale and Blackwell Mountain. And, somewhere, not far from that point high above the river on which Lyman Bearce had stood to survey in the moonlit night, finding....

Liquidation Leo stood on the soot and ash and mud of the Bearce lots road spying out that corner of Jasper Mountain where he could swear he had never seen a road before. But there it was. And yet ... was it quite there? In the twilight of this morning, the morning that had not yet fully come. Thank God he had brought his four-wheel-drive beater and had time to check it out before his first appointment.

<center>~~~~~~~~~~~~</center>

Below and a few miles to the west, Cindabilla was waking up in the tumbledown shed beneath the orange glow of the divided lights window where Daniel had stood gazing down on her. She looked up at them, thinking, Your arms were out, stood like a cross, I dreamed you was *there*.

She lay still, not quite chilled but not warm either, thinking about her dream. And the bright man. ...Yes. She had gone over the dark river after Daniel and stood there with them, seeing how well He loved him. And she was glad because the dog-man was not. No dog-man. Not if there was ... Him.

She jumped up brushing off the twigs and straw from her hair, from her jeans and jacket, and pushed open the rickety door.

Daniel, she thought, *You're not gont believe this! None of it.*

Cindabilla hurtled across the field that would be full of small corn in neat green rows in another two months.

But as she reached the Lower Intervale Road, she also thought, Betta not go up theya s'early. Chrischana won't like it. So Cindabilla went the other direction, flapping along the road in her shot sneakers. People would be on their way to work so she might catch a ride back to the chaotic Sessions' household—maybe still asleep.

<center>~~~~~~~~~~~~</center>

What is happening to me, thought Eloise, that I should be thinking of going to charm school?

It was twilight, and, after her ordeal of the previous night and a fairly sound rest today, she was sitting before the fire gazing on the flames and drinking an apple flavored herb tea. She was tired of playing hard-to-get with reality.

Now she looked at her fingers, listening to the regular ticking of the clock in the stillness of her creatively cluttered living room. She was feeling the finger bones she had held last night, hefting them again, like long loose marbles in her hand.

She heard an engine, the crunching of tires on sand and gravel in the yard. She did not get up. Eloise wished that it was Jim Nutting coming back to hear the story again. But she knew it was only Libby.

She heard the doorknob rattle in the kitchen, where the useless still-crated paintings leaned against the sideboard and table. She heard his voice call out.

~~~ Interlude ~~~

And that was one night in the woods and on the mountains and in the village of Gottheim, Maine. And I suppose there will be a coda after this, and that I may or may not write it. It may be that your ultimate purpose is to save the wayward and evil angels through the wounded shattered fragments of your creation. I don't know. It's a mystery to me how you, making everything and yet being incorruptible, have seen corruption into your realm. How is that possible? But it's here, isn't it? The tire fire, murder and mayhem.

And then there's that well opening on the abyss in that tavern cellar in Guildford. How did bottomless destruction come? Out of God? But you are not corruption. There may be something other than me, but how can there be something other than you?

So now I'll have to write James Nutting, my former student, and tell him about the ghostly appearance of Great Uncle, who neglected his job in the winter of ... well, I will have to research it; and left those bodies in the vault that were supposed to be buried after the thaw. Still up there in that vault after all these decades. And who were they, I wonder? Now let me recollect.... That would make a story all on its own, those folks. Better save that.

That old reflection of mine in the window pane. It's fading as the dawn comes round, glowing orange in the light of that smoldering mess out there. It comes around, the dawn. What was it George MacDonald said, in that book Daniel found and was reading?—

> *My spirits rose as I went deeper; into the forest; but I could not regain my former elasticity of mind. I found cheerfulness to be like life itself—not to be created by any argument. Afterwards I learned, that the best way to manage some kinds of painfill thoughts, is to dare them to do their worst; to let them lie and gnaw at your heart till they are tired; and you find you still have a residue of life they cannot kill.*—Chapter VIII

Yes, and James Fay.... And Chrischana, too. Sometimes we just have to go on and find out who and where our enemies are. Who and what our friends. ...I know. *I'm sorry too.*

This is the story I've pieced out from *The Village Voter*; from imagination, hauntings, gossip, rumor, speculation, innuendo, related to me
~~~

through my niece from a chorus that is our townsfolk. And I offer it in this notebook from my recluse's cell. Who will it go to when I'm gone, I wonder? I think I've left different notes here and there about where my papers should be going, but I would like for James Nutting to have this notebook. I'm not sure why.

I have not told the story as well as a Jasper Mary could, but I've done my best. I admit it's somewhat disjointed, but cannot help hoping that the reader of it finds some quality of unity in it. And yes, I was influenced by <u>Undine</u>, and by <u>Phantastes</u> in my telling of it. The brevity of this life is one of its salient features. As Moses said: a vapor, coming and going like the breeze, we know not whither nor how.

Oh yes, and, more obviously, Whittier's sampler: <u>The Supernaturalism of New England</u>.

Asa, the kids did not start that tire fire. It was, as Eloise said, lightning. ...Hmm ... it seems to me you're out-of-body experience and subsequent discovery lets me, somewhat, off the hook. Good. I did not really want to write any letter to James Nutting.

I, Israel Kimball, have told the story of how Gottheim came to the point where they might lay their dead away. Now may the Lord do the same for me. I have been in Gott'im all I want and then some. And what's on the other side of Jasper Mountain, I wonder? Shouldn't it be time I got out of this room?

<center>~~~ Afterward ~~~</center>

The sun was coming up east of the maroon and silver diner with Decatur's name in neon. Its interior was crowded before the start of the solemn parade. The coffee redolent atmosphere was humming with clink and clatter of plates and cups and flatware, the buzzing about Hastings' anonymous windfall.

"It's a reg'la mystery," said Robbie Robichaud who looked over at Asa from his place two stools up from Decatur. He turned back and mopped up some congealed eggyolk with a junk of Texas toast. He took a swallow of coffee.

Asa Bartlett was seated in the elbow of the counter, facing out as usual, Olive at his side. "Maybe .... " This small word from the town's amateur historian, was laden with suggestion, prompting Robbie to look sharply back at him.

"You know something we don't?"

"May be," said Olive on the end stool, her large back to the rest of the diner. She was seriously buttering her cinnamon roll. She looked up smiling at Melvinia, who was topping off Olive's coffee cup.

"Prob'ly,” said Melvinia Sessions, she with the short gray teased hair, dangly earrings and glasses. "Wouldn't believe the stuff he knows. He once sat down and took three hours to tell me exactly how I was related to myself." She stepped around Olive on her round of neighborly visits to the booths with coffee pot.

"His silence must mean he's gont *keep* it a mystery," speculated Robbie around a mouthful of ham.

From his stool beside Decatur with, on his opposite side, the counter interrupted to allow passage into the kitchen, Lyman Bearce took in the conversation as usual, and said nothing.

"Mystery's abounding heah, of late," said Melvinia, pot in hand, standing by the booth next the door. "They going to get that ghost-sighting, one with horses and the driver with a bowler hat, cleared up? Scared bout ten years' growth off me, night I saw it ovah off Littlehale Lane while taking out the trash."

"That the same ten years you took off for the census in '80?" asked Asa. "Or is this a second ten?"

"Wondah what he'll do with all that money?—maybe quit the edger at Bearces?" Robbie raised his voice on purpose to make sure Lyman Bearce caught this. Yes, Robbie had a job, of sorts, as logging contractor for the Bearces, but that was not going to stop him speaking his mind, ever. He didn't get paid enough for that.

"Daow, doubt it," said Asa. "S'lot of money, but you nevah know what'll happen. He could come down with Alzheimer's or some other catastrophic movie-of-the-week thing. He ought to put it in land. Buy a nice tree farm." Asa smiled—a catastrophic occurrence. Robbie did a double take when he saw it.

"Well, aren't you going to say anything about the old hearse-ghost, Asa?" said Melvinia coming up behind the counter to wash out the pot and fill it again from the urn. The bell by the window rang and she picked up the order for Hiram and Ansell that Gildy had set down. Melvinia waited to see if she'd get an answer before trotting down to the other end of the diner with the tray but Asa had turned back and was murmuring something to Olive.

When she came back, he said, "You can read it in this week's *Voter*. Or you can just attend the service this morning on the Common. Not only will we be honoring our veterans, but, if you 'memba that story a few weeks back, bout the lost old cemetery up on Morrill Mountain.... We'll be honoring those dead, too."

She gave him an exasperated look. "Where we thought 'twas murder? —Why don't choo just tell me. I admire your great smart history pieces'n all, but I don't have time."

"Mass murder, you thought 'twas, if I 'memba right. All the time it was those blankety kids, of whatever generation, which we'll never know for sure. They always have to find someplace to party'n frig with something—even the bones of theya ancestors!"

"Speaking of which, one of my li'l cousins (save workin' that relationship out fah another time) been telling everybody how she saw a half dog half man. Or was it half man half dog?" and (Melvinia did a double-take in seeing Lyman Bearce actually turn from his pile of office papers to look at her as she spoke.) "Says it happened when they was partying down at the Old Ferry Landing. ...Believe it was the night that young Twitchell died, Balder and Chrischana's boy. Sad."

"Well what can you expect—her mom was tripping out on acid night she was born." Asa remarked as usual on the subject of Cindabilla.

Beside him Olive said nothing, just sipped on her coffee and gazed past the neighboring booth out the window. She was thinking about her younger friend Chrischana, worrying over her like a mother.

"Cindabilla claims she saw Daniel after he died," said Melvinia.

"Like I said." This was dryly put.

"N' you always claiming historical evidence of ghosts. *You'd* nevah see anathin not made out of something."

"Mind putting some intelligence into that thought? And I did acknowledge seeing that hearse and horse apparition. It needed somebody seeing it that had some sort of knowledge about Gott'im."

This time Olive turned to give him a little attentive (and was it amused?) scrutiny. "And just how did you come by that knowledge?"

He ignored her. He had not been tripping out, no.

Robbie spoke. "Said in *The Voter* he saw the identical of the hearse in the schoolmaster's carriage house."

"You couldn't've said," replied Olive cryptically.

"Well, he finally keeled ovah and died. Left a lot of papers too, I hear. Not much else." He grinned at Asa, showing crooked yellow teeth and a renewed ability to razz his friend. He was coming back, just a bit, in the wake of Alvin's death.

"That's the way it should be," said Asa seriously.

Robbie said, "That was some piece you wrote about him for *The Voter*. Where'd you get all that information? Thought nobody knew anathin about him."

"Daow, that was only after us kids gut through with 'em. It wasn't too long after ah class he turned hermit."

"Talk about kids frigging with people's bones," muttered Olive.

The place was beginning to thin out, many of Decatur's customers drifting down toward Front Street in anticipation of the solemn Decoration Day parade. Asa and Olive stood up. He would be saying a little piece on the Common before the true solemnities began.

~~~~~~~~~~~~

Breathing hard, she had climbed almost to the summit of the hill on which Daniel died in a crevice of the rock. It was not Buck Hill, atop which they lived, but another more distant spur of the great ridge known as Blackwell Mountain. It made Chrischana sick with grief to remember sending out dogs to find the body of her son. It had been she who suggested such a search. She knew he was dead; he'd been with her in spirit even as she searched for him: It was an astonishing but nonetheless subtle memory— but she was dead to astonishment now. She was numb to everything but anger. Hatred.

If she had been more literary she would have said it was tragedy— her hubris, in leaving the abusiveness of Peter in Phoenix; bringing her implacably to the losing of Daniel in Gottheim. ...She could never have come here without Daniel's committed aid. Chrischana received it as an irony. ...I should not have allowed you out walking at night. (But he would have said, *No, Mother. That was one of the best parts*.) She casts her thoughts in her own terms: *We ah in the hands of the monster God.*

...The exact place she had so loved and been drawn to by that love— Daniel gone! He was better far than Peter, better than Balder, better much than Gottheim; better than anybody—certainly far and away better than herself.... And yet it was for *herself* she grieved, *her* loss. No one else had lost anything. Especially not *Monster God*! Monster God has Daniel, everything.

You!

She was reaching for breath. *You ah a big gazillion pound ape. A gorilla.* "Any waya in the theater You waunt You sit." She hissed it.

Turning back to look out toward the village of her homecoming (but it was hidden behind a flank of Jasper Mountain), she was struck through with a great sword of beauty. There the distant slopes; framed by the tender generous spring green of all the trees about her. There. She saw a great
~~~~~~~~~~~~

rainbow, mostly of amethyst, glistening in pure morning air where cloud-mottled slopes of the giant stood. There early morning sunlight cast its heart-breaking shafts.

She screamed. "What good is it!?" Chrischana, who but seldom raised her voice, who had stood much, and moved from defeat to victory. Bereft.

They were all down there, somewhere, in all that great beauty, solemnly marching, some of them, marching to the Memorial Day ceremony she would shun.

It had been more than ten years since the end of the Southeast Asian war, almost 40 since WW II. She did not think of Korea or the First World War. Eloise was following along in the puddled gutter, watching and walking with the parade participants, most in uniforms of one sort or another. Starting from the parking lot of the American Legion hall they strode along Front Street toward the Common. Silent solemnity walked with them over the pavement, the feet only of these participants sounding. There were gently fluttering flags and banners, and Girl Scouts, Boy Scouts, Cub Scouts and Brownies marching in dignified little clusters. There were soldiers old and new, a few from every branch of the service, marching. These were followed by straggling townsfolk of every age and description, some wheeling strollers; gathering more as the parade passed. Eloise watched as quick wiry Libby hurried along ahead of her, then behind her, clicking off pictures with *The Voter's* camera, sometimes with careful attention to framing. Jim Nutting was ahead on the Common, Eloise knew, probably still with his green visor, but possibly not. At least his pencil would be poised. It was something he might have sent the Twitchell boy out to do, but Daniel Twitchell was ... well, Daniel Twitchell was no more.

And then she was thinking of the bunch of bones she had found, and the hidden graveyard, and the black vault, and the night it had all happened. And Eloise was thinking that she'd been saved, and that later there would be a motorcade for the legionnaires and whoever wanted to join; that volunteers would be hiking up to set right the headstones and view the new graves, decorate them with flowers. And with flags: There was at least one veteran in that bony bunch, and more remains, long buried there, from the Civil War. And then Eloise visualized the dust of the Dead rising in bodily form and clothed so bright with new flesh, themselves setting right the headstones, so that there would be nothing to do when the volunteers got there but decorate. Here was love. She thought she was through being the hard-to-get player.

And now the silence was broken again by the drummers, keeping solemn time on the march. They were passing the solid block of Gottheim's churches, white and silent and firm. And now the deep green gem of the Common opened out, its trees a-bud and blossoming, the clean streets of its margins flanked with Gottheim's proper old houses. And Eloise Patadoe tromped along.

~~~~~~~~~~~~~~

Balder Simon had not marched down with the uniformed soldiers from the Legion Hall. He stood on the edge of the Common near the respectful gathering beneath budding branches. He was lithe, his muscular arms folded across his pectorals, wearing the uniform he wore now, flannel shirt and jeans, work boots. His hair was white blond, trimmed as though with a bowl over it, and he had a short but full black beard. Slightly behind, and touching him, stood gold and shining Gloria. She was pregnant with their child, conceived the night Daniel died. She would be telling him soon. She had to do something to console his grief. But was it the right thing? —right for her? One good thing—he had been talking to other Nam vets…lately.

The breeze ran lightly across them; it ran softly through the solemn gathering listening to the sturdy speaker in his WW II uniform. It used to be that Gloria was highly attentive to speakers, but now she scarcely heard the former Army Pfc.

" 'Not long ago I heard a young man ask why people still keep up Decoration Day, and it set me thinking of the answer.' "

The speaker was reading a modified version of Oliver Wendell Holmes Jr.'s "In Our Youth Our Hearts Were Touched With Fire," delivered one hundred years ago at John Sedgwick Post #4, Grand Army of the Republic.

Watching the aged former infantryman as he spoke, Balder could not help seeing and feeling the slippery disintegrating flesh and bones in his hands as he lifted Marine Pfc. Socotomah who had been baptized in the napalm of friendly fire. Tears streamed down his face, the tears he never cried. Not until Daniel. Daniel came and went. And now, heedless, Balder cries.

Gloria felt sure she had never seen a rural Mainer cry before. This was certainly not usual. Certainly not for Balder. She could not even be sure he knew he was crying. Possibly if he did he would stop—? She did not know. She was starting to wonder what she did know. ... *Have to stop thinking now. This is creepy.*

But it was good that Balder had been working on his little farmstead. *Daniel's farm he calls it.* But sometimes he seemed distant to
~~~~~~~~~~~~~~

her now… and more golden-bright. Like the god, she imagined. Once he said there would be another war.

In front of her Balder shifted his stance. He heard the Pfc. quoting,

"The day embodies in the most impressive form our belief that to act with enthusiasm and faith is the condition of acting greatly. To fight a war, you must believe something and want something with all your might. You must do so to carry anything else to an end worth reaching. More than that, you must be willing to commit yourself to a course, perhaps a long and hard one, without being able to foresee exactly where you will come out.... The rest belongs to fate."

This Gloria heard. She was thinking about the child and all her ambivalence. And that she just did not know. ...Fate? Does anyone know what this means today? They used to know...in ...the Middle Ages. But perhaps it was an erroneous construction of the times. *Well they thought they knew a hundred years ago, too.* "Our times'll nevah be erroneous," and "How many master's degrees you got?" In memory she heard Balder say these ironical things, grinning.

Balder wiped his eyes on the shoulder of his shirt, still heedless, but he heard the old Pfc. say, *" 'As surely as this day comes round we are in the presence of our dead.' "*

That's so every day, Balder thought. And sometimes they are dead ... and sometimes alive again. Painfully alive.

Chrischana. To Chrischana Daniel is dead. Everyone in her church thinks her faith has failed. Because she can't look at anybody without glaring, without that smoldering hatred. She says things like, "It's not you, it's Him. It's that monster, God." They look askance at her. But Balder knows. She has more faith than before. More than them all. She is going on with God, wrestling. Balder still believed, after all he had seen and done. It was his descriptive error, he was sure, brought that fire down. Or maybe it was a joint error. He wished it was. They said it was, the investigators but .... If there was a monster it was this life, he felt sure. God's attitude was this: As long as it's here He might as well make use of it, suffering. Suffering. When it's not around anymore He won't.

"On this day when we decorate their graves—the dead come back and live with us. I see them now, more than I can number, as once I saw them on this earth. They are the same bright figures, or their counterparts that come also before your own eyes."

Oliver Wendell Holmes had spoken again, and the people of Gottheim listened attentively. Soon the graceful blossom-scented Common would smell of acrid smoke, it's tranquility shattered by gunfire.

All the heroic deeds of the heroes of Viet Nam. They weren't the scenes that kept returning through time.... Besides, didn't Einstein say the velocity of time is not constant? For the pilots splitting the sky the war is a little bit longer but, yes, he envies them their cool distance from carnage. ...And there were more, by far, heroes ... everyone doing their job. Even the berserkers. ...But he could not count himself among—.

He looked at the soldiers standing attendance at the front of the encircling gathering, focusing on those he knew who'd seen action. *They are the only ones who know.*

"This is where we'll live," says the Marine lieutenant, taking in the linkage of sagging littered bunkers and beyond to the valley of rice paddies and endless jungle, the piled up ridges. "We'll clean it up. Make our own fields of fire. They left us a mess, but we'll fix that."

Those commemorating stood at attention, some enduring some relishing the thrill, the repetitive *bang* of the twenty-one gun salute. The white heads in the group did not flinch, but a baby began to cry. As the seven in their dress uniforms stood straight and fired down the length of the Common toward the opening where Hutchins Pond was glimpsed through a neighboring yard. There distant islands appeared and disappeared in the early fog; the reality of each island with its reflection touching one another and breaking, touching and breaking apart. The hills surrounding this greening valley with their piled up endless ridges echoed the anomalous blasts.

A year ago Gloria had witnessed the same ceremony and heeded its rendering of life in ritual, receiving it with a mind eager to embrace the life and heart of little Gottheim. Now she felt merely bewildered. She gripped Balder's arm and let loose of it to hurry away toward Beck's Bed-and-Breakfast—going to be sick. She had to find a place to vomit.

Balder turned to watch her go, puzzled. She had liked the salute last year; it had stirred her. He watched the smoke of gunfire drift off in the direction of those fields of fire and thought how his youth was truly touched with it, just as Oliver Wendell Holmes had said. And he was never the same after. His name was still Balder Simon. But it should have been something else.

— Balder's Wilderness —

'Consider your origin; you were not born to live like brutes,
but to follow virtue and knowledge.'

—Danté Alighieri

Balder Enters the Enchanted Forest

They walk through the woods, two tall lean men with shoulders sloping, those shoulders once carried so loose and high; and with them goes teenaged Hiram. It is cold wet spring, mid-1980s. Balder Simon and Ansell Robichaud are walking the old tote road ahead of Hiram, Balder's hair sticking out beneath his dark watchcap, that hair the brightest thing going in the woods this time of day. It is drizzling filthy rain, and cold. The younger man, by maybe fifteen years, follows them in the bleak predawn as though Balder's hair is a candle flame of the Advent of Hiram's unreflective Faith, his possession since a boy. He is the only one of the three to notice the distant rumble of the pulp truck far down the track below the mountain where saws put back some of the woods. The skidder has torn up and ground down all the seedlings and puckerbrush growing up on what was once an old settlers' road.

Hiram does not think about the old track that once connected the dwellings of yankee settlers from Massachusetts. His ancestors were from Québec and, in comparison, not that long ago, too. The moldering walls honeycomb these old slopes of Blackwell Mountain where folks once kept a few cows secure behind stones piled, here and there, as thick as half of Jericho's walls that fell when two of the original Israelites, surviving God's wrath in the wilderness, helped knock them down. That would be their trumpets that knocked down those walls. It takes a would-be poet, full of impractical exaggerations, to think of these things. But Hiram himself is practical, a would-be logger.

Hiram is not even thinking of the emotional condition of the two older men. If he does, he thinks first of dimpled unsmiling Ansell who lost his twin brother, Hiram's cousin Alvin, maybe three months before on what must have been the coldest night of the year in these northern Meguntic

Mountains of Western Maine. Drunk on coffee brandies. Froze to death in his pickup right outside Ferddy Sessions' house.

Yet now Hiram considers the terrain more carefully. Here are old rounded eroded ruts full of growing things, made from old wagon wheels, he supposed—still here after hundreds of years. There is an old stone wall going off right. Balder, the paper mill mechanic, is from those old settlers, somehow. He's got a big pressing problem, Hiram knows, but that doesn't stop the younger man studying the old tote road in the odd half-dark. He's never been up this way before. Blackwell must be named for one of the old settlers. It's not the highest mountain in these wooded rural towns they log, but it's almost the most far-reaching. Of course nothing is bigger than Jasper Mountain across the river, and that greatest mountain is so tall and bald it's bit on one side by the glacier once was, said Robbie (whose pulp-loader was idling now far down below). Ansell's father, Uncle Robbie Robichaud, knew lots of strange stuff, including French that he almost never used.

There are massive humps and hills and knobs and wood-grown ravines on this mountain, and seeming dozens of these overgrown tote roads; great rocks pushed here from God-knows-where, though Robbie once claimed they all came from Québec like the Robichauds who couldn't make a living up there, the land was so bad. Why didn't they just log it like they do here, Hiram asked. The answer was that they had to grow food to eat back then. What, no grocery stores in Québec? Hiram grinned. Yes, he does know better. Just but.

Point is, how are they ever going to find someone lost on this monster? Balder's son has been lost all night long somewhere on Blackwell Mountain in the cold and drizzle, and they are going to look for him. The pulp logs won't get cut, the pines for the sawlog mill won't get marked, and Robbie is probably sitting down there telling himself some stuff it might not matter much to know—but at least they'll get to see some of this mountain, thought Hiram.

Balder had put his woolen hat back on. He watched Balder's watchcap and towhead turn this way and that. The woods were showing good now, popping dark out of the twilight like wood grain on a sawlog board. He heard the faint breeze whispering in the long needles high above. He thought how that great pine over there off his right shoulder might yield 100 select boards getting $26 apiece—about like Robbie's take on the whole tree if they took it. He looked down at the dusky pine seedlings, thick here, struggling up out of the wet track. He heard them swishing against his nylon chaps, hoping it wasn't time yet for ticks. He had picked one off his shin last year before he ever came to work steady (when Alvin was still alive). It was swollen like a fall pig with Hiram's blood.

"It's nothin'," said Robbie. "Just a dog tick. You got in the puckerbrush. No sickness in that. Stay out the bog."

Still with the filthy drizzle. Yet Balder's wool mackinaw showed its color some now, big black and red checks. The mechanic hadn't said a word since they left the skidder where he'd come down to them out of the dark: just turned his head left and right. Broad dark-haired Ansell seldom said anything anyways. Balder was always a talker though, always smiling, joking, poking fun in a general way. Hiram never heard him say a ridiculing thing about a particular person, but he might get a laugh out of the situation, an article on the town warrant, or way of doing a thing. His face, looking around now on Hiram, looked blank and gray, bony and drawn; and his beard, particularly, black. That white hair and black beard were startling anyways. But that face. That blankness. It was like someone had put a mask on him.

Balder's breath came in clouds. He pointed high left. "I come down fom theya when I heard the skidda." He said, "F'you don't mind goin' ovah that way." He gestured straight left.

Hi looked. There was no trail by the stone wall. He nodded and left the tote road. Beating the puckerbrush maybe, but at least—unlike the mechanic who'd been up all night—he was fresh for the day's work. And the drizzle thinning a bit. He heard Balder showing Ansell the right, then, "Hi!" Hiram turned back.

"His name's Daniel. Daniel Twitchell. F'you don't mind callin' it time to time."

Hiram nodded and hand-springing leapt aboard the wall, which happened just there to be more level and clear of trees than the forest floor either side. Saplings were thick around it. He walked along it without looking back but the once to see where they went. Soon he was so deep they were gone in the trees. He heard nothing then but the breeze sifting pine needles high above. They seemed a grove of big pines over there and here's some oaks or something: There were no leaves on the trees. He saw the pines as fruitful of money and wondered whose land.

"Show-a you want to?" said Balder to Ansell. "Hi's okay. Maybe you'd rather not?"

"Oh no," said Ansell. He thought, *Maybe I'll see Alvin over there.* "S'no problem. I just go'n circle back down. Wide." He didn't say, We'll find'im.

Balder nodded. He started up mountain.

Ansell struck into the woods. The floor was uneven, covered in last year's sodden leaves. *These leaves were alive when he was*. He jumped a rocky stream, splashing through cobbles, and went up, keeping abreast of the mountainside. He didn't want to double on Balder's trail. He could see his twin's face. It was exactly like his own. Broad, dimpled, fair, long dark hair framing. They used to joke they had given each other those dimples while still in their mother's womb. No, it was Father said they scrunched there together, elbows in each others cheeks until they made those dimples.

He went on over the blowdown, over rocks, through the thickets, thinking of Alvin. Ground's soft enough for interment now. He started to choke. *He's dead. Get used to it*. "Daniel! Daniel Twitchell!" He stopped, cupped his hands, and called.

Meanwhile Balder was high and to the right off the tote road. Here were the remains of an old wagon road. *Jeep trail, they're called on the late 1960s topo maps put out by the US geological survey*. Daniel was a gleam in his eye right about then, Chrischana the best thing he ever saw. Wish the sun'd gleam in here clear out this drizzle, he thought bleakly. It would be coming up about there sometime. In those trees, clearing that flank, maybe. "Daniel! Daniel!" He had been calling it the whole time.

His attitude, his condition, was changing. Up all night. Usually woods-wise and certain, he now walked and half-stumbled about, calling, his voice beginning to soften. Soon he was scarcely speaking. The name of his fifteen-year-old son was a mumble on his slow lips. He tried shaking himself awake: Up all night. If he'd been able to formulate thoughts he might have said it was one of his strangest in Gottheim. There had been many stranger nights in the green jungles of Southeast Asia but such nights were rare in Gott'im.

It had begun with fishing for smelts in Abenaki Pond, him and Gloria Fay and the big net; wading out and dipping, the silver smelts popping up in the lantern light like the living slices of taut life they were in this mating time of year. Later had come the ash-fall and weather from the tire fire, blackening the night; and then getting lost in it and finally finding the pickup and then they made love. He did not know it but they had conceived. Then they drove out and he heard over the scanner that Daniel was lost.

He began to stumble more, tripping over deadfall and rocks and into the thickets. An unease fell deep into him and then the fear. Instead of growing light the forest was darkening. Is the ash-fall coming more this way? He wondered vaguely about the tire fire. (Stored on the historical site of the rumored Jasper Mary treasure grounds, Ceylon Segar's millions of discard tires had had several bolts of lightning thrown into them, setting all afire and precipitating the now too familiar atmosphere in Gott'im.) Yet, instead of that heavy but familiar reality comforting him, he fell deeper into fear. The dark of the woodland on the mountainside troubled him. It seemed that the disc of the world was turning backward into the black-and-white night that had just passed. But this untimely night did not share the moonlight of the other before it. *There's something wrong*, he thought to say to himself. Daylight'sposed to be coming.

Get hold, get hold. He forced himself to slow down, stop stumbling, go quiet. "Charlie's just ovah theya," he said under his breath. *That's why I'm afraid*. He reached back for his weapon, moving without sound over the wet mountainside. It wasn't there, his M-16. He felt for and slipped his knife out of its sheath, opened it without looking down, straining his sight into the darkness of the tall trees. His movements were quiet, slow and deliberate.

Now came a thicket open to the fading pale light. He looked into it and saw a black sow bear, sitting back on her haunches suckling two gray cubs. Her long light nose shone downturned; she was watching her cubs.

Balder slid his gaze down and backed silently away. He moved into the trees and kept going. *There's some mistake*. I'm looking for Daniel. He did not call out for fear of disturbing the sow back there in the clearing. The drizzle fell. He put his knife back in its leather sheath on the belt under his mackinaw jacket. These aren't the hills back of Chu Lai, it's Blackwell Mountain.

Off to his left, high, a bobcat screamed demonically. He went on.

He tried to rouse himself. When's the sun coming up? He searched the dark hillside over, through the dark boles. All was still. The tall black trunks stood high all around him. He set his hand on one. It was wet and smooth. "Some light up theya," he said.

Sure enough. Light shot down through the trees, a white beam of it in the wavering drizzle. He saw the source.... Way off there. *How can that be—in this drizzle?* A light very white, like a great white-shining star just on the top of that big shoulder. It shone down through the trees. Almost, it seemed, as a promise.

Wonder if Daniel's up there somewhere...?

He started to climb. It was a very faint white beam falling through the drizzle. Sometimes the light itself was hidden, but he kept on as much as he could, passing with the beam through the trees. Then it was gone, the drizzle still falling.

This is nuts.

Suddenly two dogs showed thin and pale, white around their lips pulled back, snarling. *Coy dogs!* He grew stern and said a command, very quiet, very low: to go back to the den. They circled widely, heads down, then melted into the puckerbrush. He said, "Those ah coyotes, those ah. Got get it straight." Though he was a competitor, a deer hunter, he felt sorry for them. Their pelts looked mangy. He thought they could have used a big plateful of rabbits.

He was shivering now. *This is a bad sign for Daniel....* Maybe they found him. Should have gone down to check if Robbie Robichaud heard anathin on the scanner. He shook his head side-to-side, brushed the drizzle drops from his beard. He did not consider going back. He kept climbing and calling as though the fat white star were still up there and Daniel was with it upon the mountaintop. Of course that was not necessarily the top. He doubted the top was visible from here even with a light on it. Maybe that was a searcher's light? A great big search beam. Someone could have taken a big light up with them. But why was it stationary so long? Could be Reggie, the Gott'im police? Maybe a volunteer. Or the game warden. Somebody.

He tripped and fell on his face, getting jabbed. It was a piece of blowdown with a small stub of a broken branch, just missed his eye.

He turned over and sat still in the sodden leaves, leaning against the fallen tree. Blinking, rubbing his cheek. Daniel....

Dazed, now he felt more than saw the light behind him. Or maybe he saw its beam falling on his legs, or down below him across the wooded slope. He turned. The star was up there again. But he didn't think long about it because a man was stepping long-legged down toward him, a shadow, a shape. Not Charlie, he knew. Not the right size or shape, that silhouette. Not that of a small man in the black pajamas of the VC, but tall. Now he saw the felt hat and buckskin of a... what? Back-to-the-lander? One of that homesteader woman's friends up from Chesterville way? He carried a long vintage rifle of some sort and spoke out kinda friendly. Normally Balder would have asked about that rifle right off. Maybe, what kind of spin-drift did projectile forces give its ball?

"You the man looking for his lost son?" He said out, no longer just a silhouette and, yes, wearing real buckskin. Needed a shave. Having come down from above, the man stood now below him in the lit drizzle.

He did not offer him a hand. Balder jumped up, nearly losing his footing in his earnestness to stand. He could almost have reached out to touch him; to touch or maybe test his reality. The man slid his rifle to his back, hanging on a leather strap. Maybe it should've been sheathed. Balder wondered vaguely if he had been hunting. That was no bird gun though. It was bird season.

Balder nearly shouted. "They find him?!"

The man had circled swiftly back round him and now stood just above again and backlit, the soft fine slow rain like a nimbus around him, dirty drizzle jumping off him as though he were crystal and not a sopping piece of flesh.

"No!... Well, I mean...."

His voice fell.

" —What?" Balder said it with urgency. "He's—" Balder stopped.

"No-no," the man was quick to say. "That is, I did not find his body... if that worries you."

"His name is Daniel, you heard? Will you keep looking? He's been out too long in this— 'less they found him." His voice dropped. "They might'a." There was no note of hope. Balder's was the most unbelieving voice you could fear to hear. The man's breath fell on Balder in a cloud.

Balder looked up toward the light. "Not finding a body.... That's a good thing." He looked down from there on the shade of the man outlined in dancing wet light. "Is that a searchlight, you think?—You know?"

The man said nothing. Just stood there in a stance to hold onto the hillside, arms akimbo, rifle at his back, regarding him. He seemed almost as though listening for something, poised. Balder gathered the swift impression despite his thoughts for Daniel. He could not really *see* the man. He was almost all shadow.

Balder, at once defeated and determined, stepped around him and mounted, trudging, toward the light. It gleamed out very bright but peculiarly. Not glaring. Not as though shouting, exposing all in its swath. It had the calm white purity of a star but, as said, its light was falling as from the moon over all in its way. Yet it was not moon-cold but soft and wholesome. It made Balder feel better seeing it there.

Daniel, he said to himself. Then the light moved softly away. It seemed to slip off backward, as he moved, through the tree limbs and trunks, to slip down behind the shoulder of the mountainside. It was gone. The drizzle fell coldly, unlit, adding more to the twilight.

He stood contemplating. It was hardly spoken, the thought merely escaping like breath through his lips: "Oh, Daniel." Quietly. Wondering, and not entirely grievous.

He thought about the man below, but stood there. *Why didn't he answer me?* Balder stood there, head bowed.

He was kind of helpful, that man. Didn't say much but it seemed good or comforting that he was there.

Balder turned to go down and find him, but here he is, right at his shoulder. Shoulder to shoulder with Balder, looking off in the direction the light had gone. Balder might have jumped had this been an ordinary night—was it night?— He might have throttled the man and not stopped until he came back to himself in Gottheim. He might swiftly have wrested his weapon away. And God then knows what would have happened.

But this presence made him better than he was.

He said, "I was gont go look fah you. You'll help me?"

"Why I am heah!" This was said, friendly, kindly. For the moment it made Balder feel completely at ease.

"Maybe we go togetha a bit," said Balder. "Ansell and Hi ah lookin'. We split to cover the slope betta.... But if we talked it might help you look betta — help *me* look betta." He smiled a ghost of his old smile.

"Yuht, I've seen Ansell. He'll get on, I think."

"Which way should we go, think?" Balder the woods-wise was asking the stranger.

"Up theya, I guess," the man answered. "Where we saw the light." He gestured and they began.

Strange thing was: they were able to keep much abreast of one another. The Maine woods is no easy woodland walk. Not usually. Logging is not landscaping, after all. Moldering stone, fresh slash (an obstacle and trip hazard), rock crevices hidden in leafmold... waiting for the unwary twist of a leg. The man was light on his feet, as though he barely made contact with anything—He did not even muss the duff as he climbed: shoulder to shoulder with Balder.

"Balder Simon," said he, stopping to shake the man's hand. The man stepped back a bit.

"I'm sorry," the man said. He did not take the proffered hand and Balder did not feel repulsed. He felt normal. It was a relief.

Balder said, "Daniel. He's been gone all night." He stopped, thinking about the night.

The man had a warm voice, said, "A strange night. Still dark. Thought the sun'd be up now?" It was a question.

Balder nodded and went on. He talked of small things occurring to him about his son, some of which he'd said to Gloria in the pickup earlier. How Daniel always did what was asked of him. Always did a little more. He was quiet but had a lurking sense of humor. He loved but without a trace of show; sometimes a quiet anxiety. But he's "there" when you want him to be, taking part. He had his young girlfriend who was trouble. Always has been. It occurred to him now that no one had even thought to ask about hardscrabble Cindabilla, whether *she* was lost. Balder understood Daniel's friendship with her.

"So he's just decent and natural," agreed the man.

"Yeah. —Wait, is that natural?" Balder smiled.

"In some places it is," said the man.

Balder climbed around a giant boulder left by the ancient glacier. It took a few moments to clear this monstrous moldering thing speckled in all kinds of lichen. It had trees growing out of a crack or two, splitting the rock. Might have it apart in another generation, or two or three. The man stayed right with him. "Daniel! Daniel!"

Just to have a bit of conversation, Balder said, "What's yaw place? I don't 'memba seeing you round heah. You fom Chesterville?"

"I'm fom Gott'im."

Balder looked over at him as they climbed. It was drizzling invisibly, vaguely twilight. He could not tell where the light came from, this seeing darkness. Just enough to make out the whiskered face... a vague nonlight.

"Nevah," he said. "You know the homesteader woman fom Copenhagen? Quarry Dog Road?"

"Eloise?... Yes, I'm a friend of hers... a sort of." The man spoke quietly with a matter-of-fact tone that belied his uncertain-seeming qualifications. No Gott'imite Balder had ever seen.

"You must be bout my age, maybe a li'l younger. We'd a seen one another by now."

"I been away," said the man.

"Been away long? We go to school, Gottheim Academy fah they built the SAD combo?"

"I was in the war."

"Nam? You been theya? —I don't envy you." Now he grinned. He actually grinned a Balder grin. "You see action?—of cuss you did. They don't send us just to cook, repair engines!" He looked at him. "Army, Marine Corps, what? Not the Navy, I don't think."

"I fought at Shadagee."

"Shadagee?—that's new to me. Haven't hud o'that. Was that on the coast? On the border with Cambodia? Sounds Frenchified. That happens to place names where the French have been." He grinned again. "Look what we done to Indian names."

He thought a moment. Uncertainly he said, "Shadagee...?" That old neighborhood out by Alcohol Rosy Road?

His voice dropped. He stood a moment, bewildered. "What's your name?" He had not forgotten that a name was not given.

The man turned to receive his regard. He said nothing at first. Then he said, "Bahtlett."

Slowly Balder said, "Lot'o them."

The man nodded.

"You sure you waunt in my class? What's yaw name?"

"Abna Bahtlett."

Balder looked at him. It was dark, cold, drizzling. He brushed the moisture slowly, thoughtfully off his mustache. "It's Daniel died?"

He heard himself say it. He didn't want to have said it but it needed to be said. Just so. Right then. To this man.

"No. Wait. Don't answer—. Who ah you?"

"Just some would-be pioneer poet... like I said, heah t'help."

Balder said, "The only Abnah Bahtlett I know is historical. One Asa Bartlett tells about, his forefather. Caunt be you." He had stepped back from the man but now he reached out to touch him.

Without hurry the man stood off. He said, "We have something to do. You caunt lay hand on me just now."

Silent, Balder looked up the slope and saw the light start into the trees. "Is he up theya? Is that it? That Heaven?" It stood silent and pure in the trees. If he moved his head it stayed where it was, and the mist-limned trunks appeared to move before it.

"Something tells you it is." It was quietly kindly said.

Balder nodded. "Yes."

He said, "I always thought there was something. Even in Vietnam. I knew it was. Maybe especially there. Maybe first time I knew—it was there I knew. Hell, too."

"Yes."

"Then he's all right?"

"You know."

Again Balder nodded. "Yes." He looked up at the light. "Can we go theya? That why yaw heah?"

"May be... and to tell you about Daniel."

"So you're a poet and you can help?"

The man laughed. "Would-be poet. I'm no Virgil, no Homer. I could not have written the *Aeneid*. Or the *Odyssey*."

Balder saw his smile as the man turned his whiskered wet face toward the light.

"Will I see Daniel? I'm not losing my mind.... This doesn't feel like losing my mind."

"No. You have been in a war. Exposed yourself to fire to help your fellow wounded corpsmen: You've been bewildered in fire and chemicals and strange forests. Feel responsible for death. You found, then lost, your son. But you are still sound. You are as near whole as you can be given this life, who you are, what you've experienced."

Balder was silent. Grieving. "But... but I'm gont miss'im."

The man did not hurry to say anything. When at last he spoke he said, "I'm that Abnah Bartlett who was Asa's forefatha. I heard Daniel call upon the LORD, lost in the wilderness. He found him and brought him home. That home." He pointed to the star.

He Meets His Guide

"May be you had betta make a fire." It was a suggestion. The man said this
to him kindly, matter of fact. But at first Balder did not quite comprehend
what he wanted. He stood shivering, troubled, verging on incoherence. In
truth he had edged toward the netherworld Daniel himself had emerged from
into the warmth of Life and Light some hours ago; right before he was taken
into the heavenly city, which sat now somewhere off above them as a purely
shining great star.

"Have you got matches?" The stranger asked. Dressed as he was in
buckskin and other homemade stuffs, and with waxed pouches slung from
his shoulder, he might have flint and a fire-starting kit on him instead of
matches, twould almost seem. "Check your pockets for matches," he
suggested.

Balder did as bidden, patting the pockets of his mackinaw. He
reached inside one and came out with a ziplock containing tinder and
matches. It also had a few sticks of waxed kindling. He looked at it.
Dazed, he held it out by the corner just looking at it. It was a rather old kit
he carried always with him but seldom used. It was for emergencies only.

"That's right," said the man, standing back, looking about him. "See
a place looks dry enough anawaya?"

They both looked around. The woods was a twilight of wet trees,
drizzle, darkness mingling fog; faintly lit by the heavenly city that was a
pure small white-shining thing through the dark trees.

"May be that leaning rock ovah theya." Again, it was but a
suggestion for Balder. The stranger moved up along the duff-and-sapling
crowded slope a bit toward the backlit boulder. "See heah. It's all ready.
Some critta's dug it out fah you."

Balder plodded up to it. The man stood aside. "Get down theya,
maybe. Use some of that game-smelling pine needles and bits and get a fire

going, why not?"

Balder crept under the rock and did as bidden without a word. He was too used-up to speak. Before long he had a small yellow-red blaze going. There were pine bits and other dry twigs. It was good.

"You ah doing a li'l betta," said the man. He stood a bit above where Balder had squatted over the small fire. Balder glanced at the man's lower half standing there, the fire flickering over his pant legs and homemade boots. You might get in here, he wanted to say.

"Have you got anything else on you? A bit of jerked deer meat, some rabbit or squirrel?"

Slowly Balder glanced up past his soft buckskin-legging doubtfully. The man's face showed, whiskered and pockmarked. His hair stuck out around his neck from under his hat. The fire cast a spookery over the friendly mild countenance. His eyes were the kindest Balder had ever seen in a man.

"Whad you say your name was?" It came out a whisper.

"Abnah. Abner Bartlett."

"Like in Asa Bahtlett's story 'bout Gott'im's monster?"

"The same."

Balder wondered how that could be: *Must be some Bartlett descendant I nevah heard of.*

"No," the man said. "The same."

Balder looked at him, those kindly features in the infernally lit face.

"I know it is not easy," he said. Next, the strange Bartlett said cheerfully, "Say, I heard some waya... you want to homestead, do some farming again. Like we used to do, the old settlers. Of course there's a lot of knowledge out for it now, even betta ways o'doing things. But you can learn from the settlers, too. In fact, there's something I noticed right there you might eat. Get the ol' hearthstone fire working in you again." The man pointed to a nearby fir. Balder recognized the tall sapling's needles as distinct from those of spruce or hemlock.

"You might try that for pitch blisters."

Balder, squatting, feeding the fire looked at him. Nice man, he. *Trying to help me.*

"Could help you," he said when Balder did not respond beyond his thought.

Balder stood out into the mist and opened his knife. With as much care as he could muster, he sliced into the smooth bark around the blister, cutting away and lifting out the pitch. He pulled it off the knife with his teeth, resin filling his nostrils. Balder grimaced and the man laughed. They stood in the misty sheen afforded by the Kingdom-city hovering off the mountain's shoulder.

Balder helped himself to more and went back to the fire. After a bit, and chewing on the astringent nasty-tasting pitch, he said, "Drizzle's lifting."

"That wool you're wearing's good, eh? It all beads up on that. You shake it off a bit, you'll dry some. Nice l'il blaze theya."

"Why'n you get in heah, too?"

"Nah. Don't need it. I'm too hard for it to hurt me."

Balder looked at him, chewing, his teeth about stuck shut; but he felt warmer. He took off the mackinaw, shook it out and put it on again. He had been especially glad of the mackinaw when seeking out injured animals for his mother to nurse after the tire fire began: Sparks had landed on his arms and back without harm. Unlike synthetic fabrics, wool is basically fireproof. The rock behind him did not feel so cold, he noticed. He stepped out and lay hold around the needled fir stems, drew down his face a bit and sucked the water off. He went into the rock crevice again.

The man stood still in the pale pure light.

Balder continued slow. He was torn between asking, 1) how long the light would linger; or 2) to say where again he'd seen that action? But he did not feel like talking. He wasn't sure the curiosity was worth his effort.

The man said kindly, "It's not fah certain how long the star'll appear. But it was Shadagee where I fought the—what you'd call guerrillas— mostly *not* the redcoats like my father had fought before me at what you would call Bunker Hill. Shadagee was upon the border with Vermont, New York and Canady. Not your kind of war—conflict they call it now?—But it's war. What is war like anawaya? Any time? With any kind of weapon? What you call high or low tech?—Killing in't? Dying. Great wounding of the man, body and soul. Crushing force.

"Left behind a wife and babe to do it, too.... That would be Asa's, oh, great, maybe great-great-grandfather." He stopped to do them in his head, Balder thought. "Yes, Asa's great-great-grandfather. My son was a baby." He paused.

He did not go on.

Balder said, "Was that story true?"

"Yuht. Theya was a monstah in Gott'im. Well, it's all wrote down. Asa tells it pretty accurate. He *is* a historian.

"Unlike you Marines, we militiamen were not well-trained to fight those Mohawks, those Frenchmen. And the English held, sailed, Lake Champlain. But there were far more of us than of them. We were to prepare for advancing to Montréal but we got lost in the hemlock woods and wetlands. We gave that term *bogged down* its meaning there, I guess. The battle for Chateauguay Woods. You won't find that much in the schoolbooks. Too painful and humiliating to remember, that was. It was not in the newspapers, I discovered on my return.

Balder had about cleaned his teeth, continually running his tongue over them. The wide-awake smell of resin; the taste of pitch lingered in his mouth worse than medicine. "Sounds familiar. The part about painful and humiliating." Balder grinned.

"It was a morass. We fought one another in the confusion, our troops did, that night.... Bad for the young country's morale, that bit in the woods of that war."

"Which war was that?"

"The War of 1812 you call it. Happened in the fall of 1813."

Balder said softly, to himself, "I knew about the pitch... not about Shadagee in 1813."

Said the man, "I am real."

Balder looked at him, quietly. "Then why can't I touch you?"

"As I said. I — we —have something to do first."

Balder was thoughtful again. Drifting.

Suddenly he said, "F'I was up theya... I could touch you then?"

The man was now silent. At once, again, as if listening.

He would not answer.

Balder felt the void emptying him of hope. The star passed away beyond the mountain, and it was dark again. He sat down beside the fire and began once more feeding it, mechanically without thought, until the dry bits of things should run out. He could go get some dry but should he? Daniel was dead somewhere on Blackwell Mountain. Then he thought, "It won't do to leave his body for the wild critters, bears, scavengers." He said it aloud but to himself.

"There's a she-wolf come over the bridge at Guildford Point in the dark of night, evahbuddy sleeping."

Balder heard this and looked up at the man in irritation. "So it's the only thing that'll save me? This puny hope you give me, this awful threat? Why'nt you go back to your den—up theya in those stars? Why not leave me alone? Haven't I got enough problems without your taunting me?"

He frowned up at him. He dropped his gaze back to the fire, hopeless. "That waunt fair. You waunt taun'in.... Just troubling." He looked up again. The frown had not left his blackbearded features beneath his towhead (topped with the watchcap). "Why does it move off like that just when I need it most?"

The man opened out his arms a bit. Balder took him in, still slung about with his pouches and the ancient rifle. He said, "I'm still here. Maybe I can help."

"Can you show me where's Daniel's body?" The frown had taken up its steadfast abode right where all the residue of Vietnam had hunkered; there in his brow between the sad great angry eyes— like whenever he was alone since he'd been again in Gott'im. "What good is that next life now anawaya? In't it only fah that life, not this?"

Angry he said, "Don't tell me. You'll say the opposite: this life is only good, its only purpose, is fah the next. I'm glad Daniel's theya now.... At least *he* is."

He continued, "He did nuthin' wrong'n only waunted t'be a newspaper man, a writer. He could write. Why give him such a desire'n talent and then kill'im in these woods, you know? Why not me who—"

Abner Bartlett said nothing. Just let it finish itself echoing in the other man's heart and mind. All that killing, dying; deafening explosive power, the wounds of one's friends, blood spouting, agonized screams: the awful mistakes, hindrances, sorrows, heroism and uselessness of the war.

Then Abner said, "May be... might be... the purpose, since you seem to believe in it, is not escape but acceptance."

"O'what? Sorrow, sin, suffering? Are these acceptable? Is misery? Emptiness. Is emptiness something to be accepted, embraced? What do you know?" He was about, not quite, shouting.

Not a bad sign, Abner thought.

How do we know Abner's thoughts you ask? I am Abner, that's how. I'm telling you this story. I killed the monster with the help of Jasper Mountain, disease, a firearm, my knife, the Town of Gottheim, and the monster's maker.

"...Well... there was Shadagee. ...There was the monster, I said."

While going through those experiences I had strength enough, courage enough, wit enough, guidance enough. I had love; sometimes felt love, used love to accomplish the monster's destruction. To endure Shadagee and its aftermath. It was never easy, and yet all those qualities and helps I knew in doing it were *given* me, and not out of myself. I experienced the range of being possible to us in extremes: the revelations and extremities of our being we know in such experiences; what Balder knew as he worked with all his might in the toils of the Vietnam War. Yes, he was almost shouting. It would've been better to shout. The ones who cannot be healed are those who won't or cannot express such range. They're closed in with themselves, at times heroically so because they spare others. But it's not the way just now. Could Balder cry? I doubt it. He'd been through just about everything life can bother to do to us. And he had heard from me of his son's death. But he was still the hero Balder. Now, maybe, it was his turn to let that go.

The fire at his feet was drying the rock face and crevice. He stooped and put on more bits: needles, twigs. He left me standing there, my subtle promptings dead off my lips—and went to get dry kindling, what's left when loggers have been through sometime before. There was plenty of that below and from the direction we had not traveled. At a landing, especially, where bolt-wood and logs have been loaded, there are skeletal leavings so deep it's like a battlefield after the battle. Sometimes you'll see it along the skidder trail. All the bones and bits, the cracked skulls and limbs: all of life turned into *things*. This is what force does, brute mechanized force: takes a living creature and makes an object of it. A concrete ground of objects here. Leavings of trees dried in the sun and wind, turned into old bones of treetops and branches, crushed against the rock of the mountain. Trunks, stubs; upended, their roots pointing helplessly toward heaven. These dried out things can be more easily burned in the interval between weathering and rotting, especially the white pine used in lumbering. It takes a long time to rot.

His breath a vapor, Balder came back up through the misty gloom with an armload and dropped it under the great overhanging rock that had formed shelter, almost as a cave, for some coyote or maybe a bear. He mumbled, "Why am I doing this?" But he fed a few sticks to the fire, and then fed it some more.

Balder looked around for the man and seemed almost surprised to see him again. He said, "Whad'bout Daniel's body. *Please*." The last word was tinged with impatience and desperation.

Again, he said, "In fact—maybe you're lyin'. Maybe yaw just in my dream, here. Maybe I should get! Go an' look fah'im."

"The others are seeing to it. His mother Chrischana. Listen."

The Bartlett man stood in that listening posture he had.

Balder stopped. He listened.

"Dogs," he said softly. "West of here."

"They will bring her and their handlers to Daniel's body.... But you can see *Daniel himself* one last time. Alive. As I am alive."

Balder stared at him, the firelight a flame in his eyes. Then, suddenly, Balder felt his face light up of its own accord. He grinned—not the kind he wore to cover himself. It was an innocent grin bespeaking belief. He said, "I know. I won't be able to touch him."

"Let's go!" He started out of the rock crevice.

The man did not move. He stayed looking at the fire now popping and crackling. Then he looked up at the rock face. Then down, his gaze fixed on the glimmers of warped mica at the back. The fire picked mica out, glimmering, now that Balder with his looming dark shadow had moved away.

But Balder did not wait. He went up past the great rock toward the direction, last seen, of the Star. Then, seeing the man stayed, he came back down stepping over some blowdown—blowdown looked a bit like a man lying there, like himself— and stood behind him. The black-powder gun hanging on the man's back caught his eye.

"That thing rifled?" He it said with interest. "A bit long and thin though, in't it?"

The man turned. "It's a Springfield, a musket. They were lighter than the British fire arms. And you couldn't do as much damage. But even our enemies weren't using what you'd call rifles at Shatagee. Might not have done as much good, I don't think, to have those with their long range in the woods that so troubled us. Men were *throwing* even these shorter range .69 caliber beauties, some about straight from the Springfield Armory; throwin'em away in their haste to flee the Forest of Error — as I sometimes call it."

"That's not the flintlock you used on the monstah?"

"No. No, they did not begin manufacturing these until the following year."

"And I can't touch it eitha, I s'pose.... So ah we goin'?" He stepped back down a bit, resisting the temptation. No sense in disobeying the injunction not to touch. Not when he was going to see Daniel. He would have liked to handle that gun. Finger the flint and screw clamp. What a beauty, he thought. You can almost love something so stylish as that firing mechanism. Oh, that long and gently angled line of barrel and butt. He started back up the wet slope. The runoff had settled into the ground since the rain stopped, and walking was not as slick as it had been.

"Yes. We'll go," he called. "But that's not the way!"

Puzzled, Balder came back down again. Hands in his pockets, swaying a bit in his work boots, he stood there looking at the man. Really looking at him. The kind solemn gaze, the whiskers and worn buckskins, and those straps for his kit gear crisscrossing him. At last Balder said, "You look like you really fought in that war. That battle, Shadagee, you said.... we got a Shadagee, you know. Guildford south o'here's got a Shatagee. That waya those names come fom? That battle?"

"Yes."

"Neighborhoods of Gott'im'n Gil'fid. Most folks don't know how they was named."

"Yes. They were forgetting that name well before, even, the Civil War. Those neighborhoods were where Shadagee's local veterans lived."

"Two ways of spelling it I always noticed. Funny how a place name becomes a mystery afta. Something like that, a real telling battle, and no one remembas it."

"Yes."

Balder looked at him, the firelight still lighting him. "Well," he said. "How do we get theya?"

The man turned back toward the fire, his hand on that long barrel. "There," he said, pointing. "We go down theya."

Balder stood as close as he dared and looked over the man's shoulder where the barrel pointed. He saw the fire, the sheen on the rock overhang above. Then he saw. What had not been there a moment or two before... or so it seemed. The fire flame fell back in the draft from a gape in the rock, flattened, fluttering, then it rose higher than before. The rock had opened without a sound. There descended a true cave of blackness. But now there *was* a sound. A faint whooshing or distant roaring as from a place touched with something remote, to trouble a man's soul.

What is a soul?

Balder stood back. He said, "No."

Balder Descending

He backed away. A tree lay behind him. He had been stepping surefooted over it during his ins and outs with the overhanging rock, but now this ancient moss-covered blowdown, as it then seemed to him, sent him sprawling. He lay on his back in the wet duff shivering, the seedlings scratching his bearded cheeks and closed eyelids. He heard the song of a thrush and looked up to see sunlight just touch the bristling mountainside above him. He began to laugh. It was the helpless laughter of a man who momently catches the great chaotic orchestration of life, from the massive incalculable swirling of galaxies down through the infinite interlocking roominess of a protein molecule: the absolute feebleness and inability of the soul to order its way. Tears of laughter streamed from him. He rolled over, pushed himself up out of the tangle and stood swaying helplessly before the man. The man was still there, no phantasm, no dream.

He frowned. "You want me to go down theya now?" He said, "Now that I know Daniel's dead'n Chrischana'll find'im, and the sun is out'n it's morning? The tire fire's blowing its filth away fom heah."

"If you want to see Daniel living one moah time."

Ear cocked to it, Balder stood listening. The distant cavernous wind-howling came up out of the dark descent. He looked away up at the burnished hillside, the morning just beginning to reclaim beauty for the hopeful mud season.

Balder said, "I'm pretty sure I been theya, don't waunt go again... I don't think."

"I'll be theya, too.... Think of something Daniel said about story, about his life."

Balder, his eyes yet on the sunlit trees above, the cavern remotely sounding, thought a moment. He said: "He said it was like being bodily in a story. I memba thinking that's clever, that is. Boy's master smot, he is."

"Think of this venture like that, maybe. Could you do it then?"

"A story I'm in? How's that work? No consequences. Just experience the thoughts and emotions of the story — storyteller?"

"Something like that. You will experience all these things and it will be deep experience as in life, yet something of an escape ... but not in imagination; story experience in your own spirit and soul. I can't guarantee about the consequences but you will almost surely see Daniel *if* we go this way."

Balder looked at him. He looked back at the dying fire. He was doubtful. He looked at the kindly pockmarked face again. "I think Chrischana'll need me."

The man saw that this was a real concern for the veteran. He said, "You should be back in such a time that she will not miss you.... Peter is with her." He spoke of Daniel's brothers' father.

"I will then," said Balder. He stepped past the pioneer 19th-century man, past the fire that man had encouraged him to kindle. He stood peering down into the dark draft of what seemed the abyss. But the descent was wet rock, granite, uneven. The way looked tumbled, jumbled with the pieces of Blackwell Mountain. Then came the narrow dark.

"The abyss?" He asked, looking back. "Kinda narrow-looking fah that."

"I did not call it that. Physically it is not. That was your imagination talking. This; this is better described by the poets as Limbo. Known to the Greeks as Hades."

Balder stepped down, his hands on the rough wet overhang above him. "This the way Christ went?" He asked it into the darkness, the sounding draft a bit louder now coming up at him.

"A different rock wall, maybe. But, yes, the place we descend to is that place."

"So you're a mechanic, you work in the G'fid mill on the 'Rossagunticook?"
Ain't that odd? A ghost is making small talk with me.
"I seen you read my mind. Why ask the question?"
Balder had been many times to the Ice Caves on Uncle Bob Mountain. They were nothing but great holes in the disarrayed rock of the mountain. The glacier had played with its flanks, leaving overhangs and erratics forming pockets where snow kept till July. On first entering, this cave was like one of those. Now they picked their way down through the wet twilight around rocks and over streams, the way was longer than any cavern in New England he'd heard of. It went deeper, lit with perilous dark; showing, with retinal adjustment, that this dark material had maybe some form of reflectivity ...if the eye were but able to receive and interpret. The

thought flitted across his mind and was gone.

"But it is a work of art, that paper mill," said Abner.

Balder was willing to laugh his head off at this but he kept watch over every step, kept his balance on the slippery slope, put up his hands to handle the pegmatite and keep his head from banging. He answered only, "Could use my hardhat about now."

"Not the same kind of poetry they had in Dante's day, nor the same kind of paper mill. Thirteenth Century Bologna had one though. Paper was made by pressing pulp between pieces of felt until all the water ran out. Did you know that your mill was built by Italian stone masons fleeing the crushing taxation of fascism's rich masters – or so I saw. Now the pulp slurry runs about fifty miles an hour along wiremesh and water's sucked out with huge vacuum pumps, that right? But it takes a monstrous structure, monstrous amount of chemicals and machinery to do it. Whole different kind of poetry, that."

Abruptly Balder stopped. The man did not bump into him. He stayed back. The mechanic turned. Abner's face seemed to glow of itself. Not a great light to be sure. The features, especially his eyes, seemed limned ever so faintly in a very pale light so pure it had no yellow, nor any color Balder could discern. *This is where the light comes from?*

"Are you sure you're not Dante's guide?" He said it with a grin but he had that odd feeling again. Who would not feel odd being shut off from all of life known to one every day? Complain of the folks, of the look and feel of the day being like that of any other (as we do); to have all the same folks, the look and feel cast away and to descend through the cavern of shadow as we must.... Will not you, friend, feel so strange? But Balder was not now afraid.

The man smiled. His very faint light did not increase but it shone more pure. "No, I'm just a veteran of a misguided battle upon the French Canadian border... if it was the English and American war.... Think, for a moment, how it was, so many surrogates fighting there: some from the District of Maine, the Indians and French. You notice the parallels to your own struggle. *That's* why I'm here. Not so much because of poetry. It's the likeness of experience, in't?"

Balder's grin shone back at him. "Right in't? —Who'd send me a bigwig like Dante or Virgil. Just a millwright, me."

"Would you feel confidence in someone wasn't fom Gott'im, had no knowledge what it's like all your life?"

"Well, I guess you're almost as good's Asa." He said, "P'rolly betta! Don't know's I could stand Asa's gossiping down here." The two men smiled just a moment; before Abner, with the suggestion of a gesture, turned him back onto the downward trail.

They went down. Down, down. Oddly, there was the vulcanized vegetable smell of the paper mill flowing up out of the passage as down they went: The sound of tumult piled on the draft, increasing. "Why does it flow this way? Cold air falls, not rises. The cavern's s'posed to be colder the deeper we go."

The way down had taken a regular turn, that is, its features were more regular. Now there was a handrail and steps which had at first a more natural aspect and appeal, like that of granite stone steps and rock ledge. But now the handrail became an iron pipe and the stairs pebbled concrete, what was once called cement. "They don't look that old, the steps," said Balder. "Might have been made in the 1930s or '40s. It's getting warmer, too. Look, that's like the glow of sodium vapor lamps. It could almost be coming up from the mill yard."

They were hearing what sounded the roar and racket of a mill yard. The pinkish glow came as though from some deep cavern under the steep stair, around some corner... and Balder stopped.

"Don't tell me," he said. "Looks like I'm goin' t'work t'day afta all. Don't I get a chance to grieve with Chrischana and the boys'n Peter? What is this, Abnah Bahtlett? Am I off my head afta all?"

"No, no, this is Limbo. This is Hades, that place from the mind of antiquity halfway between here and there, between hell and earth, death and birth, between the haves and have-nots of eternity. It's *neither* here nor there... but maybe a last chance to abandon or seize on hope, every hope."

"I waunt hope," said Balder. "Will I have hope?"

"Have you been hopeless so far?"

"Ask mother." He grinned the Balder grin he'd been putting on ever since he got back from 'Nam. "I don't doubt she found me hopeless fom time to time."

Abner smiled and showed the way down with his open hand.

They continued down the stairwell and turned the corner onto a platform, and there was the crowded, sounding river valley; the mill yard and paper mill spread out before them beneath the misted glare of the orangey pinkish lamps that burned on forever, or so it seemed; beneath the night in the valley of the Arossagunticook River where once salmon leapt among the rapids and rocks, on their way to fulfill the mandate of their Creator "way back when."

But wait, thought Balder. *This is different. What's that ferry doing here, and that line of folks flowing alongside the river out of the hills?* He looked out across the filthy river at the mill yard gathered round monstrous mountainous buildings, strung with conveyors, towering smokestacks;

adding filth to the night-mist, clouds of vapor enriching the night-weather; the low thunder, shrieks and screams of its machinery speaking to him. "It's the mill, all right!" He turned to yell this into Abner's face, a face now lit with infernal reflection. In his bewhiskered, pockmarked and untroubled features there showed no scrap of reaction to the debased subcreation before him.

Their voices had to carry the following conversation at a shout. "What ah those folks, teaming out the hills onto that ferry fah? Almost looks like theya going t'work! The mill caunt use s'many's that!"

Abner looked off toward those hills and the souls filing out of them by the millions. His features betrayed nothing but the eyes shone a fierce yet tender sort of... what would Balder have called it? *Compassion.* —Was that it?

He bent his ear a moment to his guide. Low and even Abner said, "Those ah the consumers. Theya to go to theya masters to be made into paypah."

Balder pulled back and looked at him, carefully. A slow grin spread through him shining out of his black beard. "N'what'll theya masters *do* with all that paypah?... Use it t'buy more consumers?"

"Something like that. Avarice turns us humans into habitual consumers. Consumption feeds avarice, which feeds consumerism."

"Where's it end? Must run out o'fuel sometime...."

"In a closed system it's a cycle. Like the water cycle, or the geologic cycle where rock is first molten, pushed up then cooled, crushed, crumbled, dissolved, or forced down to be metamorphosed and remade into other rock. Only difference is, earth's minerals... sort of... don't much mind the cycle. They don't call out to their maker to free them from the rock cycle. The planet's water is content to move up and down and in and out the oceans and the atmosphere and aquifers, also spending time deep in the rocks. Even the carbon cycle, our bodies taking part, will not so cry out. Though these things are mighty goodness, made with care, a human soul was made for better things. The soul cannot know the communion with its maker in such a custom as consumerism. Whereas I don't doubt the rocks do know their maker in such doing: It was what he made them for."

"But do you call this," —Balder gestured toward the mill and millyard, the great moving scene of the living dead— "their master?"

"They are enslaved."

"Isn't God their master?"

"Not if they don't want God's master. That's the difference between them and the water, the earth, the air, the fire. All these elements obey the will of God in which the principle of their life is founded. The lively principle of humanity is freedom of will to ask for, to choose, Life; and to know the extension of that freedom into eternity. In the personal movement of will, which we are granted, sits the sole opportunity for a real response."

"But they obey a principle in this cycle, like the natural cycles."

"They cannot help but obey their master when under its customary compulsion."

"Am I a consumer, then?"

"Didn't you give everything you had saved to Chrischana last summer when you found out about her and Daniel... in their extremity?... Was that a compulsion? Or was it freely given?"

During the course of this conversation they had to call out these things to one another, for the sounds of damnation filled out the whole of the valley without surcease. Now Balder was yelling, "If I'm not one I don't have to get on the ferry'n get made into paypah?"

"Neither had Christ to get on the ferry, but he did. And preached to those souls and some heard and were freed from their chains of avarice or other chains and walked loose, you recollect."

"But he could save'em. I caunt."

"Nevertheless, our road to the heavenly gate, where maybe Daniel waits to see you one last time, makes its progress with that ferry."

"All right," said Balder. "I will."

The platform on which they stood was that of a capacious factory elevator. Even as they held their hollering conversation, forklifts had been loading around them — gigantic bundles of used paper and huge drums of chemicals, the former for recycling, the latter for processing. Now the platform began lowering, the two men leaning on the railing looking downward on the ferry surrounded by the jostling crowd, fast enlarging in the gloom of their descent. The paper stayed on the platform and the two men, one dressed in his 1980s outdoorsman clothing, the other in his early 1800s buckskins, stepped off after the chemical drums.

The crowd at the ferry parted for the drums, which rolled rumbling under gravity's compulsion along a chute onto the deck. Most with shopping bags or shoulderbags, these people waiting to cross looked impatient and aggrieved that these men should get on ahead of them. Some complained with curses, while others smiled and said, "Have a nice day." Everyone sipped at their coffees and the whole surged onto the deck of the barge after the cargo passed and rolled to a halt against the gate opposite. Forklifts operated by the blue-collar workers turned the drums on end. Abner climbed atop the drums and began preaching, his legs spread apart as for balance, one arm resting on the long barrel of the musket slung behind him, the other raised in exhortation.

Balder wondered—was he levitating?—if his feet made real contact with the drums.

Abner pointed out the mill and millyard with its chip piles and toy-looking bulldozers running over the mountainous ridges of chips, sculpting them, pushing all downward toward great chutes. On the further side were mountains of pulp logs. "See how you'll be flumed to the blades of the chippers!" He yelled. "They turn a two-foot diameter log to chips in half a second! Do you want to be fodder for this mill?!"

"We will if Madison Avenue tells us we do!" This, screamed the crowd gathered round them, with gestures; though some merely looked bored and exhausted, while others looked eagerly toward the flumes.

" 'Consider your origin; you were not born to live like brutes, but to follow virtue and knowledge.' My friends," exhorted Abner, "don't you want to go to heaven?"

"This is heaven," said some of those who had wished them a nice day. Others complained that heaven would be boring—full of preachers like the man on the chemical drums, and angels who played bleak hymns by the hour on harps. You could not hear a good guitar riff there, and the only thing to drink was nonalcoholic grape juice. Those furthest from Abner, on the opposite rail paid no attention, gazing down into the filthy water, scummed here and there in riffles of toxic chemicals. The looks their eyes shed were hopeless. Balder was now passing among them. He found one to speak with who looked especially bleak.

But the millwright was silent, looking on him in awe. Then he spoke, "Alvin, what ah you doing? You don't belong heah."

The handsome dimpled face of Alvin Robichaud looked up, hopeless. "But I do, Balda. I caunt live without my sombreros, my coffee brandies. My suitcase of Bud."

Balder stood looking at him, feeling the psychic tug of Alvin's hopelessness. Both their faces were greasy with sweat and the mist, their hair hanging dingy and limp. The poisonous stench of the atmosphere and river assaulted Balder, the dead things in the brownish purple water, the caustic and toxic chemicals; the nauseating smell of chemically cooked pulp saturating the air from the massive digesters, like cauliflower soaked and boiled in white liquor. He recollected the many times he'd seen the logger haplessly plastered. This spirit and mugging air were more than Balder could bear. Then it came to him.

"Alvin," he said with urgency. "Alvin, can you jump? You say you caunt do without. I believe you. Not like this, you caunt. If you caunt control yourself in that, can you at least jump? Look, we'll jump off heah together, me and you! We'll swim back across, come on!"

Alvin had not taken his abject gaze from the river flowing by, the weak wake of the iron barge. But now he did look at Balder again, briefly. "I caunt swim. It's no use."

"I'll swim fah you! I'll get you across. —We got do something to get God's attention. Do something so drastic he'll have to notice. C'mon he's up theya, he'll see! C'mon. Jump!"

Alvin hesitated. He looked back at Balder. Others nearby looked at him. Some in amaze, others looked back in hopeless daze at the foaming filthy water. Came a sudden splashing and they looked to see a head bobbing to the surface—a swimmer now behind the ferry as it moved on. There were a dozen strokes and the swimmer slid from view on the current.

Alvin said low, "Help me," and climbed over the railing. Together they dropped out of the filthy iron barge, one landing in a snow stream, the other feet first with a splash into the slimy foaming river.

Alvin stood up and waded through thick white powder, laughing, breathless. The snow fell crisp and bracing, clean. It sparkled beneath starlight that was itself thick as falling snow. He dipped his hands and threw up clean powder, rubbing fresh snow all over his arms and chest, laughing a breathless delighted quiet song. He looked swiftly round for Balder, joy pouring off his dimpled features, but the mechanic was gone. Alvin was alone on the pure sparkling white river, the bristling hills muscling up on either side beneath the snowing stars.

Stars make snow!

Like an amazed boy, he looked down from the gentle cascading in time to see a sled zip by. It was the quietest engine he'd ever heard, nothing but a soft swooshing sound, and no hint of exhaust. The driver was dressed in sleek darkness, head to foot, and as he vanished down the pale star-snow-lit river Alvin knew it was his twin brother Ansell.

Ansell! He called after him. *Ansell! I'm okay! You can go back to work now Ansell! Hi'll help you! It's okay!*

Oh my God, thought amazed Ansell as he climbed Blackwell Mountain over deadfall and wet leaves. The sun had come and the world shone. *It happened! It did happen! Alvin's okay!*

He stopped and looked around. *Alvin?*

The tall trunks were dark with wet, the world clean and fresh. The quiet morning was profound. As though a shout had cleared away the gloom and smoke and ashfall, the drizzling mist of the tire fire.

Alvin was here, he thought. He was.

God how I love that brother o'mine!

"Daniel Twitchell." He said this softly aloud. "S'posed t'be looking fah Daniel Twitchell."

Alvin never surfaced though Balder dove again and again, searching for his friend with all his might. "It was an accident," whispered Balder. "Alvin didn't mean to freeze himself to death outside Sessions."

He clung to the side of the barge, soaking wet, his watchcap gone, clothes plastered to him; befouled by the innocent river folks must cross on their way to damnation. This is not precisely the "dark river," referred to by the old-timers in Gott'im. That dark river refers to death as seen by those left behind: where loved ones cross over and the earthbound know not what lies on the other side. Here in Gott'im the story of Balder's bewilderment is told; and finds its way into your hands now.

Clinging to the edge of the grimy deck, Balder shivered. The water was warm, the air of the valley was warm, but he shivered. He heard the ferry operator endlessly repeating instructions to the passengers over the PA. He turned back if perchance even now Alvin might appear. In the leap toward faith in God he had lost sight of the logger. And now the barge had stopped. He looked back one more time and… tears streamed down for the first time since leaving Vietnam: down his filthy wet face and into his beard. He climbed aboard over the iron railing and lay down, looking up from the deck, gasping. He saw Abner's legs. And the legs of the crowd. The consumers prepared to debark the barge behind the forklifted drums.

"God makes and knows all things," said Abner. "He hears those words, and all the sentences, ejaculations, prayers, curses flowing out into the air, mighty rivers of words, each loaded with its denial or appeal to his sufferance, every last word. Your friend will see the Lord of Creation, and his own creation, and he will be judged by One Whose standard is both merciful and *just*. Don't think the One Who is Justice itself won't know all pertaining to the logger, down to the last particle of his deed, thought, and heart… *and how he is made*. He knows all in every moment and wills nothing but good for each... though He suffer evil to find it for him."

Balder brushed at the greasy tears and was silent, exhausted. He wanted to say *how?* Who suffers? How does God suffer? Seemed we are doing all his suffering for him. At last, his breathing slowed, he said, "Where is he? He caunt'a drowned, he already froze to death...." His tone was listless, discouraged but not abject. Not like that of Alvin when he was still bound by the spirit of consumption.

"He has gone on," said Abner. "Not like the souls here go on, on and on." He turned slightly to gaze with light-limned eyes at the unrepentant as they pushed and jostled in their haste to fulfill the compulsion of the consuming spirit. "They continue in the cycle of the mandate. *Listen!*"

Over the clanking rumbling roaring screeching of the yard, Balder heard the ferry operator intoning through the amped up PA. "*Woe to you base humans. Don't expect to see the heavens in this place. I carried you here for makings in the eternal round of your base religion!* Step to your immediate left as you exit. And-have-a-nice-day."

At first it sounded a sarcasm but then Balder thought maybe not. He lay against the railing. "What about us? What about Daniel? How can I get to'em fom heah at this rate? Abner Bartlett, why'm I heah?"

"We gut go now," said the other as the crowd thinned. "The ferry will be heading back to the further shore for more of the mill's material."

Balder got slowly to his feet. He looked back across the flow toward the dismal crowded dark queue of folks lining the river beneath sodium vapor lamps, that queue itself filing as though a river slowly poured from the surrounding mountains. *When's it evah end?* It must have some end. What's he mean— closed system?... Why eternal. He turned and followed Abner out into the screaming millyard. He saw the line thick with people filing toward the flumes.

He turned at these words of Abner's: "This is not all there is to Limbo. There's otherwheres the human soul can go to flee its rest."

Suddenly the dark fire-eyed ferryman stuck his head out the little glass-and-iron wheelhouse. Despite the fire-eyes his look was rather numb. "Hey you! Living man! What ah you doing heah? You're not pulp material! You can't go in theya!" Then he said in a colorless undertone, "Not yet anaway."

Balder, wondering, looked at him as he was about to step off behind Abner. He saw the man's empty-looking countenance, but his eyes were flames. The crowd beside the ferry in line for the flumes shouted out, as though the boatman were revealing something they had not realized till now. They began cursing Balder and pointing out his hair. His cap was gone in the river and his hair, cut as though round a bowl, was pale. He was a towhead from birth and now they took it for an irrational sign that he would never join them in their empty pursuits. They cursed him up one side and down the other, including his parents, grandparents, and great-grandparents. Then they forgot him and were carried away in their curses, cursing themselves, their parents, the day they were born, the trees and flowers, the fresh-running streams and every good thing God had made, including again themselves, who had once gurgled and shone forth the face of God in infant form.

Balder looked at Abner, who motioned him off the barge, saying to the ferryman as he did so, "Don't torment yourself. The Power to do this is equal to the Will for it, so be quiet and patient over the irregularity."

The fire of his eyes subsided and, stepping back into the shack, he wished them a great day and began reversing engines as the earthly mechanic stepped off deck over the borderline demarcating Limbo.

"Ah you scared, Abnah," said Balder to him. "You look whiter'n a minute ago." In fact he was looking for reassurance from the old pioneer. This elder quality made for a fluctuating assessment of his guide. Most times Abner seemed in the same age and generation with him: Other times he seemed like something out of a painting, book or movie, some Davy Crockett, Daniel Boone, or Leather-stocking. Something out of an art form conveying deep truths wrapped in "the other." An enigma fast with his imagination of what life was in a time gone by.

Balder looked down at his work boots. *Yuht*, they were his work boots all right. Still on his feet from yesterday, no wonder they felt like concrete. Pulp from the beater-room basement was still stuck to them from those hours spent replacing a motor. Down there paper was chopped to bits to be repulped. You couldn't avoid stepping in it. And *this* was where he went to work every day... but different.

Abner said loudly in Balder's ear, "What seems fearful in me is truly pity. My face is pure-seeming, calling for these curses in perdition, as any pure thought or action might, where it can be envied but not believed. The souls have mistaken jealousy and envy for truths, clothing their custom, and consumptive cynicism, in bitter belief. Their faith, if you will, is in faithlessness. They believe, not in the true, but in their own faithless beliefs."

"Caunt anathin be done?" He looked pitifully on their faces distorted in outraged disgust, but no longer heard their outcries now drowned in the noise and power of the mill.

"Look," said Abner, and Balder turned back to see the barge pass, disappearing into the gently falling snow. It seemed itself breaking into or breaking through myriad white specks of clean flakes or particles, becoming part of the fabric of the falling everlasting purity. The silence of this purity's descent muffled—and finally hushed—the sounds of both the mill and the blasphemy. What remained was solely to be seen. The moving distorted multitudinous face of willful depravity.

"Your friend called out for help and went into that! Rest is but a hand-grab away."

Awed, Balder watched the ferry disappear, the snow descending, and then turned back to his guide. He looked down again at his pulp encrusted work boots. He looked them over, mystified. *Was that yesterday?* Was it only last night he got lost with Gloria on the wooded hillside in the falling tire-fire soot after they caught the smelts? He tried to think what happened to the smelts that had popped so with life and sexuality, small silver arcs of life jumping in his great net. Were they still in the bucket in the pickup?... And Daniel was alive then with his friends.

He turned and looked up as though to search the mill-glow, and saw instead the Aurora Borealis in the north; as though rising pure and bright out of the yard with its mercury and sodium vapor lamps glowing pink and orange beneath. "Look! It's like a storm of light full of hosses'n riders!"

Abner looked closely at him but did not follow his gaze. Then he turned and led him downward, as through a wet cavern, and, but with the feel of the rock beneath Balder's feet to guide him, they crossed behind a great dark fall of water. Roaring, the waterfall sounded the sighs, the roars and cries of great sorrow, exhaling upward on the draft around him even as the dark misty shade engulfed them. Here (if he had but known), much of the greasy filth and toxins attached to the great river were pounded and purged out in great quantities, water droplets rising in dense mists. He could breathe a little easier here.

Balder thought, *Crossing under the river we just crossed?*

Just so, if he could have known of it, did they return to the side of Time. Then he saw the shadow opening beneath him and there a dark mountain trail precipitously hugging the edge of solid darkness. The millyard was gone as though it had never been, nor visited in afterlife by one who still lived. Unlike before, where the passage cut through the rock in narrows and became something of a twisted stair, this was a vast black gulf of darkness full of disembodied human grief sounding with overwhelming sorrow, lamentation, deep remorse. Above and surrounding loomed a mist, a night without moon or stars. Chief among the cries, all whispered fullsome as some wind, sounded a single word, "*Father*." And, *Father, father help me*. Tears poured down Balder's face, baptizing in their falling; so many and unstoppable were all these tears. He heard the sorrow, felt the abandoned psychic suffering, understood in part that his own voice sounded among the grievous sighing and the whispered crying.

In the darkness his hand reached out for Abner but found him not. Oh if only the lit eyes of Abner were near to light this psychic and physical misted horrifying blackness! The mechanic came a little to himself and felt the cold hard wall behind him. He leaned against it, wet face turned toward the unseen rock, watering it with tears. "Why oh why Abnah did you bring me heah," he wondered, whispering. "This is worse than all I saw in Southeast Asia. There leastways we lived at pitch, always what to take away the thinking awful grieving of my errors and all my seeing, doing; my lost and wounded friends… the child's severed hand…. Tim Man Bean's suicide!—latest casualty about ten years since Saigon's fall." He whispered it to the solid bosom of the rock.

"*Oh oh oh.* You said my rest was but a hand-grab away." The tears were falling, watering the dark unseen and unseeing rock, like springs to trickle, wash, erode. "*Oh I am so lonely for you. I am lonely, solely lonely, there's none to feel my pain. Don't linger here. Come out away from everlasting sorrow. Leave your grief and regrets behind. It is meant for an evening and the dark of morning, but then I'll come and wipe your tears away.*"

"You will?" Balder heard his whispers answering his own speaking dejection. "You will not leave me alone? You left alone even the one who did all You asked, took nothing for Himself. How can you help me, wipe away my tears, if even He was not good enough for you?"

He waited. Then, having cried all and said all, slowly Balder reached out his wet hand. He felt the warmth of a human hand come into his. Rather, he felt his hand now within that hand. It was the only answer he could have. The warm hand, holding his, was the answer of his sorrowing.

Gently the hand pulled him away from the cold wet rock. He grasped hand and wrist with both his hands; felt the strong arm lightly furred or feathery with hair, leading him downward, felt the fountain of his grief assuaged. The sighs and cries, still whispering ever, faded even as he went downward along the great headwall of the chasm, until they sounded no more but as the wind in treetops, the whispering of pines above, white pines, red pines, with tops high in the skies of Western Maine where he lived always, except when he knew the fiercest pitch of living — in that other, Southeast Asian, land. So vivid, so near within, and yet so far away.

Mist Limbo

He saw the eyes faintly lit below upon the slope, and looking up at him. With no other signs he knew that they were Abner's. Coming near, his hand still along the ancient cold wet wall, Balder said, "That was your hand was it?" But he looked at Abner's arm, sleeved in buckskin, in the light of his eyes; remembering his injunction against touching. "Holding mine, leading me?" He felt yet the lingering warmth in the left palm, not the right that felt along the chasm wall. Why had his comforter disappeared again?

Again? Yes, again. Intuitively, Balder knew the one whose hand it was had come to him before, sometimes often in one day where he sat on in his room reliving....

"No. No, that was not my hand. Didn't know there was one. So, it was, guess.... —But it wasn't mine."

The eyes were near now, studying him; wondering yet reticent, as though his eagerness for news or insight were modestly restrained.

By the lightened eyes, faintly lighting through the tear-mist, Balder saw quiet gleams — the veins of various kinds of rock not far from his hand. He saw by them what great mineral and crystalline beauty might here be seen, were it not for the sadness pervading as human souls in Limbo. Here their whispers mingled with the sighing: "Have you noticed even beauty is untouching—heah?... But my *thinking* 'bout stuff seems heightened. Like, except sorrow, it's almost all I'm made of. Thoughts. I hate'em, don't choo? I'd be purely happy I could be like one o'mutha's critters. Critters don't think much: Where can I get food? Get warm. Here's the babies. Stuff like that.... So sad heah."

"Yes," said Abner. "It is sad." He turned his eyes away from Balder there beneath the darkling mist and cloud that shrouded all the sky — if any. They could not tell the sky, and the light of the pioneer guide could not penetrate there as he lifted up his gaze. "I hear something," he said.

"So'd I."

They stood together, silent, without moving, with an ear to catch the sound above the general sighing, breathing. Abner closed his eyes to listen, shutting off all light.

"Her soul was here last night," he whispered. "—Last night in the scheme of Time. Your last night 'twas." He now seemed to hear the sound clearly: He opened his eyes and moved down ahead of Balder until they came near a strangely double-figure standing, as though wrapped in gauzy bronze-like mist.

"What *is* that?" Balder whispered in his awe. It was partly woman-shaped but hardly to be seen, and certainly would not be felt were he to go near and reach out his hand to touch it. Whoever she was, her whispering, whimpering laments were joined, and somehow amplified, by the vague and spectral general lamentation; this speaking whispering sorrow of the great courage-defeating chasm.

"Betta, *who*?" answered Abner. His long gun scraped against the wall as he moved, surprising Balder. Evidently he was made of the same stuff as this place and was not, maybe, a ghost. But then, again, Balder thought he was in no position and of no material himself to discern of what substance either things or beings were now, here, made.

"It is Eloise the homesteader," Abner said, answering his own question. "Not her, but her shade."

"Meaning she's dead, think?" asked the other.

"Meaning she was neither here nor there. Neither living nor dead. She was if anything but a visitor to this woebegone dark realm and has gone away again in gratitude... but leaves behind, for now, this specter.... I would call it some kind of psychic likeness or residue of her soul, spent here, lamenting.... Much as you have spent time here in spirit with frequency during and since the war. But with this difference. Her sufferings have mostly been what folks, who see only her outsides, would call imaginary."

"But isn't my own suffering, pure and simple, of my imagination? I keep remembering, is all."

"And suffering, with fresh suffering, in each remembrance."

"Yuh*t*."

"Balda, if your soul was visible like a body it would appear mutilated, crippled; something mutated that healthy people would have to look away from. That is, in part, why you grin so much. It hides what would otherwise suggest grotesquely bulging scar tissue in your benighted expression.

"She has her own manner of hiding what goes on in her soul. But to folks her hiding mechanism is what's grotesque. It is so obnoxious to them, who can only see her outsides, that they think it is the real her."

"Who'd you say this was?"

He looked at the still softly bewailing figure draped in mist, faintly illuminated in the eye-light of his guide. He thought that if he blew upon it the misty figure would vanish, leaving not so much as a figment speck upon his thought, his mind. "Eloise? Who's Eloise?"

Abner didn't answer right off, standing there gazing on her. Balder said, "What's that with hah?"

"One of her goats. I think it saved her last night." They felt its fascination, this odd twosome of brownish mist, a dark faintly copper metallic-seeming cloudiness. "... Eloise is the homesteader. You recall thinking of her when we met. Asked if I was her friend, fom among her back-to-the-land friends. Last night she too was lost on a mountain, one with the border twixt Gott'im and Quakertown. The weather of the tire fire overcame her, disoriented her, chilled, and set her in desperate circumstances.... Unlike your Daniel, she *almost* died.

"I was in the neighborhood. First I thought it was because of her. That it was *she* not meant to die. Which was true, but turns out it was you I was to help. But I may have had just a bit of a hand in her saving. Maybe not. Another story, that. Anaway, she was almost here before her time, and that ghost is the evidence. It'll be gone soon. She found her way safely home and will wake fresh and clean and fairly healthy in her own bed, I think.... And begin to wonder. Right now I suspect she is dreaming of this place... maybe even looking for a way ... out... as she dreams. When she awakes she will find she's in love."

Having greater interest in other things, Balder ignored the last thing he said. "Would we be in hah dream?— ah we?"

"I don't guess so."

They watched, discerning a lessening of darkness in the myst-person, a fading or dissipation. It was a slow passage while there she lingered with her charge, that goat-mist; and they stood musing on these products of the strange night just past. Abner spoke of Eloise having discovered the unburied dead of some local people's ancestors and played with their bones, in a not disrespectful manner. She merely lined up her find on some toppled grave markers and constructed an alternative history for them. Maybe it was this in which Abner Bartlett had had a hand. But, he said, it was Eloise's concern for the nanny-goat in the wild environs that kept her going, stumbling about in the filthy cold woods. That and the passion or desperation of life. Life wants to keep living, keep expressing itself in the form chosen for it, even as that form is degrading. It starts in newness of life, as a babe, whether babe-tree, babe-deer, babe-planet, or babe-person. It develops and extrapolates itself in that form until the form itself is almost extinguished by life and must go into a complete decline. We get just enough of the form to see its worth before that happens: one kind of gift before the expression fades and its host life departs.

"She may never have been so creative, herself, as last night when she knew the greatest of stress on her own form. When at the moment she felt herself most ghostly and disintegrating, that's when her subcreative faculties came searching forth in a very fertile imagining. Between that and her charge, her nanny goat — the three beasts you encountered in the woods made no inroads on them.

"You, friend, ah even more fortunate, because yours was the closest encounter I've witnessed in the enchanted forest—and you have survived in body and soul to this moment."

"I always thought...." Balder had thought that the body hosted life, not the other way around. He was not sure how to take this, nor was he able to receive all this information now. He told the man that a lot of it made small sense except as a sort of story, but not one he would want to tell his kids. This made him stop. *My kids?* He did not continue in that vein conversationally, but held the thought of Daniel, still hopeful, in his mind.

He said, "To someone else coming heah— someone we caunt see?— would we seem as she seems — some pile of loose-knit molecules, all cloudy like that?" He gestured, then quickly set his hand against the chasm wall again. He felt more its sureness and security and did not like much to be here in this depth of darkness without touching it.

"Of what substance ah we made, do you wondah?" asked Abner.

"Yuh*t*, do we hev any?" Balder grinned.

"I do," said Abner. "You have very little, if any. My form is something like the wall you cling to. You ah moah like a mist exhaled of the rock's moisture. You ah like the substance of the weepings and sighings."

Balder nodded. Yes. He knew it. "Why can I touch it and not you?"

"The difference is the degree of content for the likeness. The rock and its elements and constituents overflow with God—no containment; expressing but some aspects of his supra nature. Because I am human I come closer, being most in the image and likeness. The wet, the wall, the rock, each atom and molecule of it are all living expressions, but not completely so. Neither are we of course—but close enough to be an excelling expression. And neither are quite the finished work. It is not time nor place yet for us to touch. Something or someplace must first happen." He smiled, the faint pale light of his eyes increasing but a moment. "In the meantime, you can feel the wall as we go on. Is that enough reassurance for you?"

Balder nodded, thinking, *Makes small sense, though.* "Guess I caunt do nothin'bout it if I'm only half here!" He grinned.

Abner laughed. It was very light laughter, bubbling yet smooth; soothing, unexpected and rekindling. It seemed out of character with the old Mainer. But it made the veteran of the foreign war forget all about Eloise and the sorrow surrounding him in this sad place. Gritty, wet, and enduring, the rock wall beneath his hand did comfort him, but the voice of that laughter, suggesting real substance but too light for the realities he had known was of far greater comfort and value. For the moment everything seemed light and immaterial, brightening with mild mistiness. His soul and spirit were one in it.

The shade of Eloise was gone in light mistiness. The path beneath his feet seemed not so steep, its pitch leveled, as though he were not now descending but walking straight and even. Wasn't he still in the mountains, was this a chasm after all?

Without turning to look, he touched the wall behind him. Balder looked out through lightening mist as though sensing a great field before him, with clumps or varying degrees of denseness suggestive of... of tents. Tents, huts, he thought. Maybe an encampment. The lightness accompanying Abner's laughter had settled softly, turning the mist almost white (or so it seemed to Balder). And Balder felt again the approach of sadness. He longed to escape it. He turned to Abner but again his eyes streamed, his face and beard full of them, tears. He put up his arm to blot the falling of this unwelcome rain. Futile... indestructible iron sadness. Abner's face, he saw, was also wet, his eyes yet lighting the very tear-streams, glistening as they fell down and into his chin whiskers.

Balder, blinking, felt tears congealing in his lashes. He looked back out over the thick mist and saw the encampment shaping itself in firmer delineation, building in the steeping mist of tears. He heard the sorrow, softly slowly, increase; sounding as though the heartbreak of the world were concentrated in this single encampment of—what had the man called it? — Limbo.

"What's this place?" He whispered, his words sighing and soughing like some vagrant flaw of a scarce breeze.

Tents of white, and makeshift huts, were set in rows over the white field. The mist, out of which these faintly showed, was cold. Like the smoking mist of Hutchins Pond on a settled deeply cold morning, it bodied forth the catastrophic comfortless cold. He felt it sink into his very bones and lungs as with the thrust of a bayonet. He felt it bleach his skin with frost, where exposed, biting toward a numbness signifying pain. He could die of this cold. He looked—helpless—at Abner, whose own face, he saw, was masked in frozen tears. Their breaths mingled together in the disastrous cold.

Now the hush of the deep cold seemed to absorb the sighing and soft crying that had before mingled as a mist of sound wedded with sight. Night was again descending but the sense of this place of mist and sorrow remained. The tiny dwellings submerged here stayed visible, if obscurely so, as the whiteness dimmed. Then they heard it: the crunching of solitary footsteps through snow, and the suppressed sorrow of a single soul walking. Walking and stopping. Walking and stopping, and walking on again.

He goes among the tents, and from hut to hut, thought Balder, watching. *What is this place—like iron in the cold? Who is that tall man walking and stopping?* Shivering, shivering, Balder was so cold he could not speak his question to the silent guide beside him.

Then he heard Abner answer the thought as though he had spoken it. As though suppressing his own agony, very low, he said, "General Washington. Walking to and fro, he is. And that is Valley Creek, Pennsylvania, where the iron forge stands. Its stream flows into the Schuylkill." He said no more.

Then Balder understood. As a child sitting nigh the woodstove, he had heard it said by his father that one of the great greats, a Simon, had gone there to stand against the British. It was said he died of dysentery and pneumonia before getting his redcoat or even any Hessian mercenaries, leaving an infant son in backwoods Farmingham Royal before it was renamed Gottheim. So this is what it had been like for them. This faithful immobility, this sorrow, this mute suffering.

Why ah they still heah? In't my old gramp gone on? Is he still lying in a tent theya dying? No picture show: It's real. This cold is The Cold. It's cold like the cold of Gott'im's based on but nevah sunk to. Nevah this cold in Gott'im so fah north in the mountains.

Finally he spoke. "Is it fah-evah?" He said it slowly, with great effort. "Caunt I go get'em, take'em out heah?"

Abner made no answer. The solitary figure walked on through the mist; stopping and walking. Stopping and walking.

At last Abner said, "He is a prayer walking. He is the embodiment of prayer. He is what a prayer moves like, walking and stopping in the withering cold and sightless mist."

The two ghosts stood watching the prayer walk on and on, from hut to hut, and tent to tent. Crunching, crunching, footfalls starting, footfalls stopping. For ever and ever, the continual prayer in the body of a man who has given up but knows not how to express his surrender for the sake of all.

Look, thought Balder. Slowly he raised his arm. *A light.*

Abner, too, had seen it: a small glow coming from the cracks of some dim bark hut. The tall figure, like their gaze, had stopped there. The two Gott'imite phantasms, far off in Time, heard but the murmur of speech in the mist.

Slowly the mist thickened, the light dimmed, and disappeared. The Gott'imites were left alone in the murky mistiness with only the eyes of Abner Bartlett to light them. The awful cold eased off him painfully, and warmth began again in Balder's limbs and chest. He drew a breath and expelled it sadly.

"Ah they like that? In spirit—you say?—fah-evah?"

Abner shook his head, tears yet in his eyes.

"Please. Say theya souls went on somewaya." Balder implored him with a look.

"You rightly discern the difference between soul and spirit in this. Their souls did go on, but the spiritual suffering of each, wedded to that spirit of suffering, remains."

"But why? What *is* a spirit like that? This spirit of suffering?" He wiped his eyes with the rough sleeve of his mackinaw.

Abner was silent. He had returned to the demeanor first seen and felt by his charge—hesitant. As though listening, or waiting. As though searching for a word or act in those woods about Gott'im that might help move his charge to action without forcing his will.

At last he said, "You saw the light."

"In the hut."

"That was the light of the menorah, lit in the encampment of the goyim, the encampment of the suffering and waiting soldiers, soldiers dying for no apparent good reason. There was the lone Jew in the encampment. One of God's own chosen dispersed sufferers sent to suffer—and to hope— with the patriot soldiers who had come to such a pass in order that they might no longer be *called* warriors. That *spirit of suffering* was with them in their waiting because it wanted them. It did not want the soldiers of the Empire. It wanted the ones who were struggling for causes more pure than possession. He wanted to be with those who were willing to lose everything, even their lungs, bones, and hearts for something dear. Back then they called it independence. But it is *freedom*. That suffering spirit is... seemingly ...eternal.... I... don't know that for certain. Truly, Balda, I do not." He was silent again. Thoughtful. "I do not know if Limbo itself is eternal. —We are told the world is founded in suffering. God slain in the effort to make all. And suffering will itself be consumed. —I assume in the fires of love. Maybe when we catch up to the future; and Time, with its memory of sin, shall be no more."

Who tells? Prophets? What does it mean? God suffers? Suffering is part of God? How can someone that devised moving galaxies full of massive stars suffer?... There was Jesus: he suffered. What does it mean?

Balder was about to voice these thoughts, but had only a jumble of words for his deep concern. He might have asked, Is suffering solely part of creation? Are other emotions?... Or are those feelings beyond creation also, as God is.... Or, does God suffer, feel what we feel independent of us, before we ever did. And for what cause? And shares that by imparting it to his made stuff...?—us? Maybe it was suffering to make everything...?

Balder, you may guess, is deeply concerned in suffering. He doesn't much try to escape it but experiences it full force. He does try to make it go away through particular acts. Like the time he gave Chrischana all his money: money he felt rightly belonged to her anyway, because of Daniel. Or the time he saw a ragged man hitchhiking and bought him dinner at the diner. That time suffering was mitigated for both of them.

They had walked on, leaving that part of the suffering behind. Balder kept his hand lightly brushing the rock wall, the gaze of Abner walking beside him faintly lighting his feet. He heard but the sound of his own footfalls as though he were alone, and allowed himself to be led away from his wonderment by this fact. (He is a mechanic, with a mechanic's mind, and with the intelligence to have sought schooling in mechanical engineering but, for some fool reason as some of the townsfolk thought, threw over a scholarship and college exemption in order to join up: as a Marine, at the very moment when the outrage against the Vietnam war was fueling itself. A kid going off to the alien killing fields.)

Abner's not touching... Abner is levitating. He had discarded the idea that the place wasn't real. —But was it material like that of Gott'im? He tried to think if the man had actually stood on the chemical drums— or if he had just hovered there looking as though holding some firm stance with that easy, ready posture while preaching.

"We ah going up," he said to his guide. The road beneath his workboots slightly inclined. It tugged faintly at his physical strength as they walked on toward distant misty light. Balder slowed: There was a bend ahead, and a shining of vaporous light cast the mountain wall ahead of them into relief against a further wall. These walls were far higher than any cleft, cirque, or ravine of even the White Mountains, south over the border in New Hampshire. They towered up into the mist out of sight. This near almost perpendicular wall was limned in the glowing mist beyond it. But the mistiness of the gulf beside Abner, who was walking on Balder's outside, graded away into darkness. On their left hand, just beyond where Abner walked, was a drop-off; the deep misty fall Balder had sensed in descending from the mill yard beneath the waterfall—before they'd come upon Eloise the goatherd and the mysterious encampment of sorrowful Limbo. The wall ahead beyond this wall showed distantly, differentiated by the mist-light. It seemed a gulf extended from this gulf beside them, curving ahead, and separating the two mountain walls. Here and there threads, possibly seams of metals, gleamed faintly or redly, as though the further wall beyond the great chasm held secrets unguessed.

Gradually his eyes adjusted as they walked on. However, Balder was in no way prepared for the green glorious sight his vision framed as he rounded the sheer wall on his right hand—and saw before him, distantly between the dark clefts, a knoll or small castle-mount, topped with a tiny white castle, tiny in its remoteness. Light fell through the surrounding heights, shining off what, at first, he'd taken for a castle amid fairyland, or in the midst of the Alps in summertime, such as he'd seen in old *National Geographic's* or snowy travelogues on public television beamed to the rabbit-ears antenna at *Simons Ledge*. But, as they hiked on toward it, he saw that it more resembled a Georgian colonial mansion-house. It shone like a dollop of sculpted whip cream atop the green mount. To his eyes it looked good enough to eat. He scanned down the green mount rising out of shadowy gloom, gloom like a dark murky lake of lightless mist between the two great mountains whose sides framed the gulf.

The Count of Time

He tried it. He liked it: *That is where Daniel is, and we will meet. At the white mansion we will talk.*

But Balder knew it wasn't so. He couldn't help it though. He had such longing-love, such grave hope. He aimed a look of appeal at his guide—as appealing as someone like Balder can look, which for most anyone else was just a look. But Abner knew his hope was false and merely watched the way ahead.

Saying nothing, he kept to the outside of the trail cut into the mountainside; while Balder, his eyes on the remote green knoll and its beautiful house, no longer set his hand to the sheer rock. They were still gently climbing, the green setting and white jewel slowly enlarging at their far approach. From below the murking gulf, where the celestial light did not penetrate, the jewel and its setting rose like an island supreme, serene and perfect in its midst. It promised a haven between two fearful, even terrible, heights; and was so heart-break beautiful that again tears started in Balder's eyes and began to fall. He considered the tears even as they fell. Were they tears of consolation, tears of relief, of sorrow for all the suffering? Were they tears of joy? He could not tell. Perhaps they commingled all these aspects of deep emotion. Neither could he keep them from falling.

Now he saw the porte-cochere, and thought of the Bearce mansion on its spacious gardened hillside in Gottheim. However this mansion seemed of crisp white stonework, where theirs was painted wood. Both had the spacious grandeur of high iconic columns, but here the columns supported from spacious stairs to roof behind a flower-bordered terrace spread before it. The immaculate green lawn, fringed with elegant shrubbery, was graciously framed. The whole gave welcome to the bleared and weary eyes of suffering. Then he gave his attention to the pale stone bridge spanning the gulf between his own mountainside and the green knoll. He looked to see if there was another bridge, on the further side of the green mount, leading to the mountain beyond the gulf. He thought maybe there was not. He brought his gaze back to the knoll bridge and found it a work of great mastery, combining the science of structural engineering with the grace of classical, elemental form. He thought then of the path where he walked and the easy elegance of the bridge with its curving arches and wondered who had made these things... and if, again, they were of the same material as Gottheim; as America, as the earth, the solar system, the Milky Way, the stars. In other words: Were they real? They felt to him as real as any of these things. He could tread, handle, see, smell, hear. Right now he heard the crying of white birds as they hung, sailed, or wheeled in the ether about them and plied the mountainous drafts. He smelled the fresh air and the growing things of the green knoll, where before he'd had but the mineral smell of rocks and dust, and the smell of the damp that clung to dirt and stone.

They stepped onto the white stone bridge and found it pure as crystal rock sugar, with a grain as of freshly hewn limestone, very rich and appealing to his senses. *Maybe it's even <u>more</u> real than Gott'im!*

As they were crossing he could scarcely take his eyes from the splendor of the white mansion and its green grounds spreading before him. But then he thought, *Might be worthwhile to look below, over this bridgewall at the murky sea of stuff there.* He stopped by the wall, which was waist-high to him, and peered down.

They had not spoken to one another for what seemed hours, hours spent hiking among the Giants... ever since, in fact, Abner had expressed his ignorance, and perhaps bemusement, over the sorrow and suffering spirit of Limbo. Maybe just one or two commonplace observations... and no exclamation whatever about the beautiful house, despite the mechanic's deep thrumming desire to be here: to go to this elegant green glorious place.

But now, eyes on the impenetrable mist, he said, as any mechanic might, "How come the light caunt get rid that thick mist? S'dark'n gloomy-like." He looked up for the light's source and saw, not as expected a Sun-ball of brightness in the vapor above, but a still more diffuse light. As though, while he studied, the vapor itself were the light. As though each droplet, in the general almost moveless slow current of vapor, were itself light, a micron of light so small it held the body of light in concert with its minute fellows. All one in the vapor surrounding the heights, the atmosphere, the breath going in and out of him. It might be said that the Murk went far below, how far he could not say, and that it too seemed of a body and general quality all its own: darkness impenetrable by nothing but itself.

A child might have asked, at the moment of his spying it, about this place on the knoll. But Balder was not yet a child. It is a testament to him, to the kind of person he was, that he asked not but awaited its revelation.

He contented himself with practical questions and did not attack the thing of moment directly with what might in a man be an unseemly curiosity. He had always been interested in the way things work, the peculiar physics of this place now being an example.

Still Abner spoke not. Balder looked at him where he stood by gazing up at the mighty bulk off their right shoulders, around which they had hiked the morning. —Morning? What made him think morning? —Exhaustion?

Sensing his purpose, Balder now also turned to look that way. The mountain they had apparently circumscribed was steep, dark, high and misted. So high he could not discern its true aspect. Was it indeed, as it seemed to him, a mountain? Or was it something *like* a mountain? Something like a monstrous wall? It was of darkly glistening rock, erect fissured flanks, shining in vertical seams reflecting the light of the mist. Abner turned about, his back now to the white stonewall of the bridge, gazing out on the further mountain. It had been beyond the gulf, on their left hand as they came toward the green knoll. Balder had failed much to notice it in his excitement over the white mansion and green great mound and its mist-light The mountain beyond was not much touched — in no way could it be said to be bathed—with the light. Instead it merged with the murkiness of the shadow-mist-lake below. Its rising flanks he now saw were fissured here and there with reddish light: brownish, umbrage, and dark orange. Conversely the flanks of its opposite, around which they had come, faintly glistened with almost vertical fissures, its elements seemingly hardened to crystal. But the mountain on the further side of the green knoll had cracks more horizontal, elemental and alive with their own lurid and burning light.

Whoo—ee, thought Balder. There's a many questions I could ask about this place. *—And Abnah don't seem s'talky just now.*

He gazed his fill and then followed after his guide as that one turned toward the green pleasant mound. To Balder it was very bright and glistering. Walking on the stone bridge toward it he could not help but smile like a child.

Yet he felt a mysterious hush growing within himself. Quiet filled him, brimming. Maybe the mist-light itself was filling him, spilling from his look in a quiet smile very unlike his habitual grin. Abner looked back and saw it. If Balder had but known: The smile was in his eyes spilling a great happiness that had no cause save the green place onto which, with his last footfalls, he was about to step.

The bridgestone carried over onto the mist-shimmering grass. As he stepped off the white stone, laid even with the green lawn, he fell instantly to sleep. Balder dropped to his knees and fell on his side. He lay curled in his red-and-black checked mackinaw, and jeans. His giant steel-toed work boots, so like concrete before, were as soft baby-booties on his feet. Balder lay still, gently breathing.

He woke gently also, turning and stretching. He felt so rested, lying still, his eyes closed. The smile lingered in his features. He felt it, a smile. He opened his eyes. He lay supine looking upward into the serene diffuse light. He saw birds, some high and hovering, some flying. He sensed movement or talk—or was it some *thought?*— and arced his neck, looking upside down at the white mansion. Looked kind of like the White House this way. He saw Abner and some others, women in mobcaps? Slowly he sat up, feeling a bit foolish. He stood, wondering how he would explain it to them, this peculiar untoward rudeness.... Sleeping on the lawn? It did not once enter his mind to call it a yard, what they had at home.

"D'I sleep long?" He came over the grass toward them, too self-conscious to take them in. He did not grin as he would at home over some self-foolishness but came up to them nodding briefly at each in turn, his question directed at Abner, whom he did not much look at either.

"Not long," he thought the other said.

Balder felt so refreshed he wondered. He could not help smiling.

The others smiled too, open smiles. He felt the openness, quietness, the generosity of the smiles. Here were Abner, two ladies, and one gentleman. The mansion rose behind him in solemn splendor, the stately porte-cochere entrance to one side very grand. They stood off the corner at a little distance, the further dark mountains and mist-light above setting forth the elegant white house and green lawn with great clarity. It looked not above four stories high. A half-moon balcony, colonnaded with porch, graced the mansion side. He could not, at first, take his gaze from it. When he turned back to his hosts he was again sorry for his foolish inattention. "Not a bad li'l house." It was the usual Yankee understatement. He felt deeply foolish giving his gaze back to them, but they seemed not to mind.

"Would you like a cup of water?" He thought one of the ladies said this in having turned from the table behind her and now proffering the cup that had been poured out for him from a ewer. She was plain-featured and wore a dress with long blue full skirt and wine-colored bodice, sleeves covering her graceful arms. Her hair, pulled back severely, was covered in a white coif. She wore a big white apron, and curtsied faintly making her offering. But Balder scarcely noticed any of this as he took, but did not yet drink from, the elegant white-gold stemmed cup. Instead he was moved by her face and deep inward beauty which seemed to radiate from her in a light-form more substantial than her outward appearance. The longer he looked at her, returning her quiet smile, the deeper he saw and felt the person coming forth from within.

"Anne Bradstreet," Abner maybe said. "...Phyllis Wheatley." Balder turned to the other woman, whose smooth skin was of a deep rich brown. She wore a frilled cap, tight bodice with high neck, an apron, three-quarter sleeves, and full skirt, leaving vague impression on him of the late Colonial period; of a more recent vintage or fashion than the first woman's garb. She held a quill pen in her brown fingers and moved it lightly, as though playing or writing from time to time. She also shone an inner person forth with more vigor and lightness than her outer form. She was slender and smaller than the other, but pouring forth such lively quiet light that, again, the physical frame was overcome. It was as though she were a picture, whose form was for its framing and was soon almost unseen in the warmth and light of her person.

"...Philip Morin Freneau," said Abner, and Balder turned to the white man with dark hair curling about his ears, wearing a high white lace collar and short black velvet coat with bronze buttons. He wore long pants of the early 19th century, perhaps the Napoleonic years, imperial style. But, again, these impressions were vague: These things dimmed in the light of the man's person within. He nodded attentively but with an enigmatic smile.

"Balder Simon," said Abner.

If it pleases, said Mistress Bradstreet as he looked at Monsieur Freneau. *The water will refresh you.*

Balder smiled on them all, pleasantly. He felt so good, and now relieved of his foolishness. Better than he had felt since.... He could not remember. But he drank the water. In its cool freshness upon his tongue, and as it fell down his throat, he was taken deeper into the refreshment. He felt as though brimming refreshment into his eyes, his head, his whole form. He smiled broadly but was not carried away. Simply refreshed beyond any like experience he'd had in Gottheim. He did not think of ecstasy but solely of pure goodness.

Again Abner's voice spoke. "These are the names they are known by in old New England, and colonial and republican New Jersey. These are the names they have in history. These are God's poetry of the American past."

Thou also, who suffers and slays the monster, said Mistress Bradstreet to Abner. Balder looked at her. Did she speak?

And this is the count of time, said Abner.

Quickly Balder looked to him. No, Abner had not spoken, had not *been* speaking this while. All these things had not been said. No mouth had opened. But meaning had been conveyed — directly to his mind *as thought*. Balder now looked his bemusement.

The Count of Time is the name of this poetry, this place.

Balder found his own voice an instant after, voicing his own thought almost as it came. Maybe a little bit behind: "The house?"

The mount, the house, the folks now tending it— hosting here for the moment, you might say. Poetry is tending the Count of Time. You note how it stands between the two dark Walls of the Worlds... so to speak. The only thing here not a piece of the Count of Time is the mist lighting it.

Balder looked past at the beautiful mansion and saw how it stood so clean and sharp against the shadow of the dark beyond where dark fissures glowed. He wanted to yelp for joy over its great beauty and elegance, its so very clear presence and delineation against the dark. Back home, *the tug of time*... it could weigh or it could speed. But here it stood still and fierce. The Dark of that other World, or of both Worlds even, he thought while turning, set this mount and mansion in such sharp and dear relief.

He looked again at his hosts and felt the same for them. They stood out like colored lights against the dark—sharp and pure and fierce. As he looked steadfastly on them, first each in turn and then as a group, he found that he could read the poetry alive in them. Balder's tastes had been old-fashioned in this regard, his taste for verse savoring more of Whittier, Longfellow, William Cullen Bryant and even Robert Service. How he liked "The Cremation of Sam McGee"! He had not read much poetry contemporary with himself. But now, looking and listening to the poetry these were, he began to feel the worth of a John Berryman or Jane Kenyon, poetry from the deep human interior. He heard the rumor, cadence and lyric of their personal stories solely in gazing on them. And he was astonished most by their suffering on earth; and next by their calm forthright attempts to write upon the great themes of their day and age; or on eternity.

Anne Bradstreet, child bride, mother of eight, pilgrim emigré at the age of 18; she suffered a three-month voyage to sail to the New World in obedience to authority and hope. Swollen with scurvy, nursing others, watching over their deaths. She came to make a New England home and community. She suffered smallpox, consumption, paralysis: but did her duty, being, as she felt, an unprofitable servant: elevated through her learning and social position. She wrote politics, medicine, history, theology and poetry with authority. Watched over the death of her child, the burning of her household so dearly won in a wilderness community, and lost to fire all her worldly goods.

And when I could no longer look,

I blest his grace that gave and took,
That laid my goods now in the dust.
Yea, so it was, and so 'twas just.
It was his own; it was not mine.
Far be it that I should repine.

Balder's awe of her banished the residue of foolishness. Now he had no idea of time, being taken up in this place and these poems of God. He had received only glimpses of beauty in Gottheim but now he was taken in Beauty and forgot himself.

He looked on the slim Phillis Wheatley: captured as a child of seven in Gambia, renamed Phillis for the slave ship in which she was manacled. She was taught in the Wheatley household of her Boston owners. She became fluent in the humanities of her day: the true Classics, religion, geography, history, Latin, the Bible foremost. Because of her blackness she was made to defend and demonstrate her erudition and skill in a court of law, being certified authoress by eminent white man whose attestation was used by the publisher in preface to her poems. She died in childbirth and poverty at the age of 31, having suffered the humiliation of her life, but knowing and acknowledging also in her poems, the dignities bestowed upon poets. She encouraged and was brought before General George Washington and other fighters and founders of the New World republic. Balder saw all this in her, her beauty, honesty and humility, so magnified before him that, had he seen her in Gottheim, he would have fallen before her in worship. But, here on the *Count of Time*, he simply, purely, and gently smiled in his disappearance into her beauty, the poetry of her; and felt or remember himself no more for a time.

He turned to address a pure attention to M. Freneau in whom he saw the persecutions of that one's Huguenot forebears, and his love of the wilderness of the New World as also personified in its Natives, whose lives he championed.

In spite of all the learn'd have said
*   I still my old opinion keep;*
The posture, that we give the dead,
*   Points out the soul's eternal sleep.*

Not so the ancients of these lands —
*   The Indian, when life releas'd,*
Again is seated with his friends,
*   And shares again the joyous feast.*

His imag'd birds, and painted bowl,
And ven'son, for a journey drest,
Bespeak the nature of the soul,
Activity, that wants no rest.

His bow, for action ready bent,
And arrows, with a head of bone,
Can only mean that life is spent,
And not the finer essence gone.

Thou, stranger, that shall come this way,
No fraud upon the dead commit —
Yet, mark the swelling turf, and say
They do not lie, but here they sit.

Balder gazed on the poets, forgetting all save them until Abner spoke... or otherwise drew him from their beauty and their unspoken words, to ...perceive another person seated at the marble table on which the ewer stood with cups. There was something familiar in the reddish head bent over papers, and his hand busily writing; not with quill as Balder might have expected given the company, but with a fountain pen. He looked and saw the crisp blue script freely flowing over the page, not fiercely but with firm strokes and calm. Then Balder felt his gaze drawn to the words the hand was penning. He found he could read them plainly though they were upside down.

As he read he felt the vicarious traumas of his Vietnam experiences arise in him. To his amazement the mighty pictures flowing and punctuating in his memory were now without their fresh actuality but were become as though both a part *of* and yet apart *from* himself. They were as though stories being read and drenching him in all their pathos, might and grandeur; now elevating both himself, and what he'd seen and done, into a place, emotion, and insight unknown before in all his repetitious reliving of them in homely Gott'im. He understood that he had been unmade by all, each and every instance and demand upon his being, and was now flowing back together again remade and whole.

Balder laid his hand upon the hand that was writing. It stopped. The face of the writer turned up to him.

Hi, Balda. How-ow-you?
Good, Dayner. How-ow-you?
Good.

This was the beginning of their conversation as though in words. But it went on in communion not replicatable here. This was Dana, unlike Balder, now young as he was then: Balder's best buddy in the platoon until the day he watched the other's insides open on the green jungle ground in red profusion mingling with the rain. This personal agony had not left Balder's mind's eye but for the briefest moments of time in New England Gott'im. Ever since they built that wall a year or two or three ago, Balder had desired to go to Washington DC and place his fingers in the regular graven wound, upon the black shining surface, that represented the name of this one gone. The one whose Absence was the only Dana-presence left to him. It had been like trying to clasp the void.

Now he and Dana Mills were the words they "spoke" to one another in their solemn glad communion and rejoicing over being reunited in flesh— or was it spirit, or was it *both*? —here on the Count of Time. These two living souls were one as two cannot be upon the earth. How long they talked together is not frameable in words: However firm is the count of time, it cannot fathom eternity.

Balder looked away in what proved to be farewell. Was there a movement on the part of Abner? For there was Abner standing, feet spread, his arms clasping on either side the long slender Springfield musket at his back. For some reason Abner, standing there as though in patient prospect, was all he saw now for some little while. And when he looked back for the Poetry of God, and to see the poets who once stood and walked and suffered upon the earth, they were gone. Yet there stood the monumental, calm, solitary mansion-house in its white colonial, and antebellum as he thought it now, splendor.

Astonished, Balder said, "Waya'd they go? Way's Dayner? *Please.*"

Abner looked at his earnest expression with, *Oh, well. You are not theya sole concern.* Aloud he said, "To explain then in words? Caunt be done: Time and Space. What is that? If you use the word *like*, you will not understand. The *experience* of time-and-space is time-and-space itself. — Wouldn't you resent it if someone took it upon himself to study you, and then said, 'Balder is this this and this?' But no. What is Balder? As nearly as it can be put: Balda is the experience of being Balda. You know *this* dimension, these dimensions, as they are called, in Gottheim. But consider that His Poetry is before the LORD in contemplation of His goodness, faithfulness and purity. And they are also going about His business. They sup, plant, venture, study, explore, learn yet more of Him. No doubt theya making preparations fah the feast within. All these kinds of worship together, RIGHT NOW."

Balder glanced at the great house standing calm and serene. He had suddenly in these words the sense of things happening inside, unknown to him, from which he was excluded.

"You mean... while they are heah... theya also there?"

Balder saw limning his eyes yet the same light as that of the mist. Abner smiled. "Something like that."

Balder considered this… with a momentary smile.

Then he said, "And you, Abner? Ah you theya in wawship?"

Abner spoke not, as Balder looked earnestly on him. The light of the guide's eyes then seemed central: His eyes but slowly intensified in light. They shone as fierce as flames, impersonal and pure. Balder stepped back. He fell upon his knees, gazing, worshipful. Tears flowed. Oh how he melted with love for the monster killer. He loved Abner more than he could ever say.

Abner yanked him fiercely to his feet. *Your worship is received, Balda, but not by me!*

With power scarcely to be conceived he shook the mechanic so hard his teeth rattled and his sinews loosened. His bones were like to come untethered.

And Balder was a big man, powerful and fleet.

"I-I-I'll die Abnah! I'll die!"

He hit the ground of time so hard his life-force flew upward just a bit and fell back quickly, anchored in his body. He lay sprawled upon the lawn, petrified, shaking. Afraid.

He thought, *Gott'im oh Gott'im. I caunt go on!*

Abner knelt beside him, gently saying, *Take the water. I'm not sorry I was so rough.* But it was kindly, oh so kindly communicated, this harsh thought. It was like the softest sweetest thing Mother had ever said to him as a child, learning right from wrong. But so much more gentle, kindly yet. He felt a child lying there. As though he'd done some wrong thing and was now corrected. It would not be thought of anymore, by anyone. His eye at first upon the ewer standing there in the green short grass, silver-golden gleaming, he next took the proffered cup from Abner's hand and drank deep, with gratitude in fine. How good it was. How good the water. So cool and fresh, paradoxically imparting warming health to his shaken form.

He handed the cup to Abner, who set it clinking by the pitcher on the marble tabletop. Abner's eyes were softly lit with kindness. And his smile was kind. He stood and offered the other his hand. Balder took it and slowly stood. He stretched and lightly shook himself, checking round his bodily being for any damage, such as many a'time he'd done in Nam. At once he found himself quite happy. So much he grabbed Abner's hand and shook it. Then he stopped.

Smiling all over he said, "We touched."

Well, said Abner, *so we did. I am not so much of a ghost here, I guess. And here we have crossed over from that place*, he said with a gesture toward the great mountain of Time, *and so are in substance more like than unlike.*

"I don't get it," the other said.

There came a call.

"Did you hear that?" asked the man who had not died.

They both turned in the direction most likely for the source: beyond the corner of the mansion toward the dark. Someone there was remotely calling from the direction of the other mountain—was it also in Time?

Balder turned and looked his question at Abner. Abner shrugged. *I think he wants you.*

Me? Why me?

I think he thinks you will do something for him.

Who? Who is he? Balder was bemused. *What can I do fah someone heah?— or ovah theya? Is that beyond the world?*

I think it's your last C.O. but one.

Balder had been looking toward the perilously high dark and misted wall. The shadowy mist was very thick about the flanks there. Now he looked swiftly back at Abner. He looked down at the table, still some water in the cup. He shrank into himself.

"I need moah water."

The voice had not ceased its calling. It was at first faint but seemed to intensify, increase in volume and verve—if still remote. It was his old commanding officer.

Abner plucked up the cup and gave it to him.

Afraid that the peace of the place was being disturbed, Balder, although deeply reluctant, followed across the grass toward the edge of the green mount. He felt a sense of quiet relief in Abner's following with him once the cup was drained. He felt still as though a child and was half afraid to be left to this obedience on his own. In fact, his reluctance was so entrenched, and Abner so seeming unconcerned about Lt. Noruas, that he had to question his responsibility—*was* he meant now to obey? Had someone spoken with such insistence to him in Gottheim, he would perhaps have ignored it, or evinced but slight attention. The insistent command continued and its recollective power was so sure that he turned again to Abner, desiring, like some kid, to take his hand for reassurance. He

refrained. Abner looked his light at him. Eyes limned in quiet light.
Between that glance and the strengthening water, he felt a slight easing in
his spirit.

They stood upon the steep descending verge of the mount, faces
toward the dark mist, and the voice ceased. Balder strained a look into the
darkness but saw nothing. He felt instead the mist-light at his back and
upon his head, warming. But his face was held toward mist and darkness
and it felt cold. Cold, dank, damp. He looked upon the left, at gaze toward
what must be the precipitate dark slope across the gulf from here. There
were the seams of angry molten lights in sills—more vibrant in proximity,
the night-mist at times passing and obscuring only to move away in brighter
revelation of the fire-seams. He thought perhaps he heard the noise afar of
seams blistering forth, for they seemed anything but steady or consistent
with the terrain, as were the more vertical sheens of hardened mineral
seams, on the other now far side of the *Count of Time*. Below them he
sensed the gulf, and that its sides were fixed, but could determine no bottom
there. The dark mist moved out of it and moved about, wreathing, drifting.
It was thick and impenetrable, as though darkness were its source and
makeup, materials unknown.

The voice began again; this time speaking (not so much calling).
Through the mist and, as he supposed the distance, it spoke in volume above
the norm. Sounding as though falling through a misted cavern, of vast
height and depth, it spoke his name with military precision, using military
appellation. This combined with the awful elemental heights and deeps and
darkness to set Balder quivering within and out.

"Sgt. Simon! I can see you clearly, backlit and silhouetted in the
main, though I think you can't see me. Is that right?!" The voice was
drifting, hollow sounding.

Again Balder felt the full stop of reluctance. At first he made no
answer. Lt. Noruas was dead before he'd made squad sergeant.

Then he said without fervor or hardly force enough to reach across
the misty Gulf, "What choo waunt?"

There was silence. Then, "I want water. Some of that water they
have over there. You've had it."

Balder peered into the black mist. He strained but could see
nothing. His eyeballs were full wet. He turned back to Abner, who was lit
from above. Abner's eyes, in the shadow of his hat brim, had that faint light
of their own.

Abner looked doubtful. He shrugged. "How's he gont get it?" he
said.

The C.O. must have heard, for his voice drifted to them, saying,

"Send Mills over here with it."

Balder cried, "Bull *shit*!" He looked his outrage into the mist. "No wonder they killed ya!" He was seeing that reckless mission again: all the signs were there: the squad should *not* have been. Dana should not have been there! Oh God! Here is the hidden rage he has been eating like a damn cud, coughing it up, chewing, swallowing it back, coughing it up and chewing again.

Hollow, the voice drifted. "You're the shit. Did you do any better?" The voice wandered through the mist, and Balder, having been awakened by the explosion, saw the C.O.'s tent fly up, smoke blowing out in the moonlight.

He said coldly after a moment, "Why dint you listen when they wahned you?"

"Don't you mean 'we'... when 'we'... warned you?"

Balder said nothing to that. He thought he had had no part in the fragging of Noruas. Maybe that was the problem: He had not known *what* to do about the casual conspiracy... and had done nothing. Nothing before or after. He could not plot with them; he could not restrain men who were for it; he certainly could not go higher up—for the red tape, disbelief, recrimination and unit unrest: It would never have saved them all from Noruas's insane and extremely harsh bravado, whose zeal embraced, it was said, the slaughter of innocents. Eighteen years old, did not know what to do, did nothing... and that was the part he had played. Suddenly he saw it again: had seen it off and on over the years. *That* was why it always came back: doing nothing is something after all. Nothing is *active*, not passive. Passivity is only a slower action, the slowest action there is. Action in slow-motion, as in some Twilight Zone episode. Rod Serling, with his nightmares of WWII, might have thought this one up: The consequences of slow motion don't show up until later. Sometimes *much* later. *The Count of Time*. "You cannot escape good-and-evil's struggle you are born into." So said the historical Abenaki Gott'imite, Jasper Mary.

"I'll bring you the wadah—whad'you need it fah? They's plenty mist: Just stick out yaw tongue'n get some."

"You don't know what it's like here. I'm perishing from thirst. You think you are innocent, merciful, but you won't answer that call for a cup of cold water your Jesus is fond of. Weren't you the good one—weren't you the Christian in the bunch?"

Oh shit! Shit! Balder said, "Why'n you jump in, swim that mist— looks thick enough! That'll get God's attention, maybe." He shrugged. Abner had said it worked for Alvin.

He turned back to Abner, who stood stolid, the length of his

Springfield hanging behind him, arms slung around it, hands holding on either side: He would finger the firing mechanism, running a hand over the long barrel and ramrod. Lightly, very lightly, Balder sensed Abner's impatience. But Abner was giving no aid.

"Buddy..." said the voice through the thick mist, "you have no idea what a drop-off that is. Were I to try such a thing I'd fall through the abyss and keep falling. That'd compress me so tight I'd know nothing but me for all eternity. I know you, Simon. You're kinder than that. You might frag me but you will not send my soul to hell."

Balder looked helpless at Abner. I can't be kinder than God, he thought.

I'd be tempted to send'em theya.

So'd I.

"So you waunt me to go to hell getting you wadah?! How's it work? I toss you the cup on my way down?"

Silence.

Then, in a voice firm yet small, "He won't let you go there. You know it."

Balder strained his gaze. He could see nothing. He had been bitter, but now felt the extreme pathos of this tragedy, the wreck of humanity on the opposite shore.

"Abner," he said. "Is he my responsibility?"

Abner spoke.

"If what I read in your thoughts is true he would be having each of the children in turn bring him water, Balda." It was a note of warning.

Balder now thought of My Lai. Why? Because that massacre's brutality approximated what he had heard about Noruas. …Yet he knew from life in Gott'im that most often what is rumored, what is *said*, is in some way untrue. And from what motives is it said?

That is good, Balder. Consider that. If he were unrepentant over such a sin, or any sin, why is he still up here? He seems to believe in mercy.

"I'll take him the blesséd wadah.... If I can."

By this he meant, If I may. Gott'imites of his class did not use *may*. It sounded too spleeny.

It was given to him to take the cup of water. The murky substance he plied, elegant cup in hand, was not itself too unlike water: this thick darkness in which he found himself surprisingly buoyant. It was what he imagined the astronauts felt like weightless in the medium of space. The substance was not too cold, nor was it warm: more like lukewarm, this myst he plied. He thought of it so: myst-mist. It felt as though he inhabited, moved through, a strange mystery. He was treading into darkness.

It would not be correct to say he swam. He had that cup of water, cool in his right hand, and wanted to save it at all cost. Balder dog-paddled, one-handed, into the darkness; like a lobster boat off the Stonington coast feeling its way, engine burbling, through the soup toward the next buoy. The cup with its contents was his sole reason for doing this. That at least must be safe. So he tread the thick darkness as one might Hutchins Pond, while holding a beer, to the middle of the cove for a jaw with some friends. Only this was no friend over there, calling. The man's precision and drive were familiar to him in that voice.

"I think you are coming out of it toward the ledge now."

Cup tight in his hand, the mechanic turned about to see the *Count of Time* more distant than he had supposed. It was mist-framed and heart-turning, green like a setting, white with its jewel. The myst had yielded him strange buoyancy, and he felt, as he neared the voice, a lightening of spirit and even a strangely freeing sense of adventure. He had known something like it several times during his tour. He wondered what he looked like to either man from their respective shores. Then he remembered that Abner would not be able to see him. This gave him a turn. But he kept going, slowly crawling toward the clipped and determined voice. He could not see into the cup he clutched with upright care in his sure mechanic's hand.

"There is ledge when you get here," said the voice from the shore, above him. "Speak to let me know where you are. It might be that the thickest mists aren't high enough to support your weight to the shore where I am: Height varies, like with the tide on earth. You will not be able to take hold. It's very sheer."

"That's nice," said Balder almost under his breath, struggling slowly toward the sounding.

"I'm here. Lying on the ledge, reaching down. See if you can grab my hand. I'll keep talking till you get it. C'mon."

"I think I'm theya," said Balder, at length, below the voice still speaking. "Take the cup'n I'll swim on back." With his free hand he felt the slimy wall of the mountain, hard as granite but slick as an ocean ledge lined with algae or plankton. He held up the stemmed goblet and felt the big hand of Lt. Noruas touch his own as it groped with great care for the cup. That touch filled one of the strangest moments of his life with a surprising goodness and warmth. He had a great sense of relief and several images passed through his mind from memory's vaults: deep and forgetful moments of rest, laughter, and fellowship in 'Nam. Such times were richer than any he had known elsewhere. They had made him loose and happy, moments on end. Usually right before or after combat. He had been more alive then than in Gottheim since.

Have a nice day, he felt like saying to his old C.O. in parting, something like the ferryman had wished the consumers with on their way: Not with sarcasm but maybe with a wish for it to be so. He said into the thick fog, "Did you get it?" He heard the distant crying of the gulls and other birds flying above the remote green mount.

Did you enjoy the wonderful water from the Count of Time?

"Was the wahda still in theya fah you?" Treading the mist, Balder kept touching the slime-wall in the dark. Blinking, he peered up through dark vapor and saw nothing. He turned back to the island and saw the shade of Abner Bartlett standing small on the verge, an unmistakable silhouette with the Springfield musket, his legs spread some, but at ease.

"All but the last swallow..." said the Lieutenant. "...I want to savor it... —But yes, it was all there. There is no water like this water... and yet I can't say it's not unlike the mist, either. But you can't get enough of the mist to do much good. It's almost on your tongue — but isn't — or at least not enough to swallow and relieve your thirst.... Thank you, Simon.... I... appreciate your exertions... and this great gift."

"I'm about out of exertion, heah," returned the other. He was beginning to wonder how much he had left in him, and looked with longing toward the other place shining with glory in the midst of darkness, small and tender, like a rose made of sugar on a golden-green cake. He should take back the beautiful cup. But he said, "If it's still theya, you might pour out that last swaller.... Kinda thank you to God, hm? Used to do that in Nam... if no one was theya needed it."

Silence.

Balder tried to rest, treading the mist-dark but he wondered. What kind of rest is this? Nothing to cling to but slime. "Well guess..." he pushed off with his feet and began swimming toward the distant vision.

"Simon!"

He turned back.

"Take the last swallow. You'll need it.... I see that now. You need this to get back on. C'mon. I wasn't the best C.O., hell, y'fragged me! — Well *they* did. Blew me to bits and pieces in my tent. Please take the last swallow."

Sgt. Balder Simon swam back and, guided by the C.O.'s voice, found the stem of the cup and grasped it. He swallowed the live water and felt instant renewal. He thought briefly about the up-and-down, the back and forth, the cycle of opposites that showed the recession and renewal of life. Is good and evil like that? He could not tell. Maybe at home, in bed at *Simons Ledge*, he might think of it. Bed. He wondered how long it had

been since he'd fallen asleep, and awakened, upon the Count of Time....
How long??

Suddenly he heard the dribble of grit, and felt something coming down the ledge beside him. Here is Noruas's combat boots! Brushing his head coming down. The mechanic ducked. The man's legs were just coming alongside him. "Whad'y doing!" Balder yelped in surprise. He moved off.

"Don't worry. I'm not going to try hitching a ride back there with you," said the commanding officer's voice. "I'm well aware that my selfishness would get you killed. Take you down with me, that is. I'm not sure you *can* be killed.... Not like back in Nam."

The man was evidently hanging off the ledge full-length, now. His voice sounded flatly against the rock. "I'm holding here by my hands trying to get the courage to drop. I can feel just how heavy I am here …but even with the slime I might, just might, boost myself back up if I change my mind… but I doubt it. It's better hanging here, at least, till my strength gives out and I fall."

"But. You mean go to hell? Hell's down theya?!"

"It somewhere, that's sure." He sounded as though turning his head from side to side where he clung against the slime. "The ledge is too slippery. I don't think I can hold on."

Balder sighed within. He longed to swim back to the mount but he felt... compunction.

He resigned himself. "Well we got try'n get you ovah theya."

But he heard the man slip and cry, and knew he was gone.

Still clutching the cup, Balder clawed his way back through the mist, legs thrusting like a frog's. Wild-eyed, he came at last into the mist-light of the heavenly *Count of Time*. Abner reached down and pulled him upslope onto the green verge, where he lay gasping. He gasped with physical relief, emotional release, and with horror. It had just not seemed real when he and his guide were but talking of it before.

Abner had the ewer waiting for him. One exhausted corner of his mind thought, *That pitcher never seems empty.*

I wouldn't worry about him. He fell, that right?

But he did on purpose.

But that's good, Balder.

It is?

It was hopeful. On <u>his</u> part. Think of it: he volunteered for hell. He was always volunteering you guys for hell, in part because he himself was fearless and strong.

But he was also insane, merciless. And a glory-man. Covered himself— and us— in his own patriotic glory. The men didn't take kindly to it... as you learned.

He wanted to kill the enemy. Think—this was his last enemy. Lieutenant Noruas was his own last enemy.

But he went to... to hell!

What is hell?

"Whad mean, *What is hell*? Hell is — evah lasting fire!"

What is everlasting? <u>Who</u> is everlasting fire?

Balder closed his crying eyes. He thought, I don't get it.

Above him, Abner smiled. In the shade of his hatbrim the light of his eyes was gentle and pure.

'Board— the Inferno!

Abner Bartlett, the woodsman, scholar, and War of 1812 veteran sat on the grassy slope of the mist-lit knoll with Balder Simon, woodsman, mechanic, and Vietnam War veteran; having a conversation about nothing.

"*Is* there such a thing as nothing, s'pose?" Balder asked this of his guide.

"I think you just answered yaw own question, din't choo?"

Balder thought a moment, and grinned. "If it's a thing, how can it be nothing, y'mean."

Their backs were toward the white stone mansion with its Ionic columns. Above in the mist-light the white birds soared and hovered, wings spread and clinging to…. *What are their wings lifted by?* wondered the mechanic.

"Do the birds evah light? D'they eat grubs fom the grass? What do they live by?"

"Their Maker in heaven."

"Must be angels or sump'n, then." Balder grinned. He went back to thinking about nothing.

"Yes," said Abner. The heavy old Springfield musket lay long in the grass behind him. It was the first time Balder had seen it off his person.

"I give up," said Balder. "I can't think of nothing. They's no way to think of it without thinking o'sumpthin." He gazed into the mist darkness without seeing it. Every once in awhile the fire-seams in the distance shone out redly or faded and disappeared. And sometimes he thought he heard something, way down the gulf. But he forgot about it:

"Wait! —did you say *yes*? Yes, they ah angels?" He looked back at Abner.

"They are."

Balder lay back and faced upward, the gun barrel cool under his neck. "They look like birds. Shorebuds, seabids. Some kind of white eagles, sump'n."

Suddenly, as though at his summons, one dropped down toward him, enlarging, and he saw its face above his own, something like a man's, something not like; fierce, grave and at gaze as though seeing not the outer form of Balder, but his inner man. And the living gold-headed white-eyed creature was of a size with Balder's own. Then, at once it was gone. He looked. It was as a bird again—he thought above him, and Balder could not say which bird.

"It's gone," said Abner.

"Waya'd it go?"

"Down through the mist."

"The darkness? Down theya?" Still somewhat supine, he turned onto an elbow and pointed in the direction Lt. Noruas had fallen.

"They don't stay 'round long."

"These in't the same we saw comin' heeya?"

"Not one."

"What ah they doing? Why come'n'go? Wait —theya messengers. —What theya name means, angel."

Abner nodded, eyes faintly a'gleam beneath his hat brim.

"What is this, some kind o'way station?" He threw open an arm that included the grounds and great house with its portico and columns.

"Something like that."

Balder sat up. "I'm on my way to see Daniel," he said. "A long time has passed."

"Maybe not," said Abner.

"Where is the heavenly city he's in?" Balder stood, brushing at the minute mist droplets covering his mackinaw. He shook himself and jumped up and down. "Abner?"

"Let's talk about that."

Balder looked at him. "That doesn't sound good. Why'my heah? I thought I was gont see Daniel. Please." He said the last humbly and tried to quiet all impatience. He meant to speak his faith instead.

A light in the darkness, coming off his left shoulder, stirred the corner of his eye and he turned to see something moving through the dark, an orange gleam hardly piercing through the gloom. It increased and he heard the rapid chugging of diesel cylinders. The ferry hove into view. It went by and stood idling, and Balder saw the ferryman's strange dark head, with his old-time engineer's cap, craning out the cab. His eyes were lit with fire not unlike the mountainous seams across the gulf, but the look on his face was that of a wild uncomprehending innocence. There was nothing personal in the look but a fanatical unswerving endurance in the pursuit of duty.

Balder stared at him. The ferry operator's burning gaze was on the moorings below, near the verge. Balder had not noticed the moorings before. The human-inhuman operator cast the hawser over one mooring and called out in his highly stressed way.

" 'Board— the Inferno!! 'Board for the Inferno!!"

He shot out of the cab and ran aft like a maniac, flinging out a second hawser. He was actuated like a mechanism, his joints and limbs somewhat flailing but with an odd precision. The deep burbling of cylinders did not cease for a moment, idling. " 'Board for the Inferno!!" He called coming portside and peering at them from below with his red-burning wild and unsettling gaze. There seemed a quality of the highly devoted imbecile about him. To Balder he seemed a bit …developmentally disabled.

"In a moment!" called Abner.

" 'Board— the Inferno!!"

The ferry man's voice was carried in a shrieking incessant timbre that did not bode a pleasant ride for any passengers happening along. Balder barely recalled that he could indeed be silent in the performance of his calling, and recollected Abner calming him at the pulp mill where consumers and manufacturing chemicals were ferried across the dark river for production.

Balder said, "What's it doing heah? Get the day off? A busman's holiday, that it? The union don't like swapping jobs, but what do I care?"

"This's a barge reg'lar as clockwork in its schedule. Second shift: He follows his assignment without regard to the union. The union is quite limited outside of time, you'll find. Where Justice is folks don't care for such things."

"It's empty," noted Balder.

Abner smiled. "That can be a good thing."

"'Board for the Inferno!"

"Don't tell me," said Balder turning his face upward into the mist-light. He watched the messengers coming and going, crossing above the mansion roof, ascending and descending out of the light. "You waunt we should go with him. We ah going to hell?" He sat up.

"Not exactly."

"I get to stay here?"

The light limning Abner's eyes glimmered.

"But. Daniel." Balder frowns. He looked down at his boots in the grass. The grass made him think of that story, the one where the narrator goes to heaven, from hell, on a bus... and when he's about to go back, he learns that hell is down among the grasses or roots somewhere, so small that nothing of heaven can fit into it. One of heaven's crisp apples was too big and dense to go back to hell with them.

"Do you think they's enough room fah me down theya? What was that the C.O. said about being compressed— that how he put it? What's it mean?"

"I've never been too sure about the mechanics of these things. What if another dimension was found in a freckle between the hairs on your arm? Would you even know about it?"

"They showed things in Life Magazine recently, was it — no, on TV. The electron microscope showed vast intricate hallways in a molecule, I think it was. Think whad it be like to shrink down inside a protein molecule and try being recognized by the immune system. Makes my hair stand on end thinking of it, that molecule, felt all ovah to determine if it's okay to pass.... But, Daniel.... I hate to keep bah-thin you bout that but it's why I come, n' I got no interest in hell tell the truth. I been theya before, 'think. Why I waunt, voluntarily, see folks suffering so? Is that why God made in His image? So's he could just sit around up theya in heaven," he glanced up into the light, "watch'em twist 'n turn, getting crisp fah eternity? F'I'd got caught in Nam they'd put me in a cage not big'nuff to stretch 'n poke me with hot things evah once in awhile. But at least if they killed me they could do no moah. Think about it?—I have."

"'Board for the Inferno!"

"I think he's got get going, Abner. The clockwork schedule 'n all."

Abner had picked up his musket and was holding the barrel, fingering the cold steel, its brown smooth hickory butt in the grass. "Balder, I'm not forcing you onto the barge. I'm not talking you into it. Don't know f'I care if you get on or not.... Well... maybe some.... Fact is, what can you do? Here you ah on the Count O'Time...."

"'Board—the Inferno!"

"Yaw already 'tween two worlds. Now what? You caunt stay heah. You got go someplace."

Balder did feel the check on him here. The sense that he was excluded from whatever festival or worship went on inside the mansion.

"But what about Daniel? You ain't told the truth. I get to see him."

"I told you this was the way to see Daniel when we stotted."

"This?" Balder pointed down into the murk of the surrounding Gulf.

"I told choo you might see him...."

Balder sighed. "You didn't say by what route."

"'Zactly."

"But you *knew* I thought 'twas climbing, going *up*."

"'*Board— the Inferno!*"

"He's got go, hn?" said Balder. "I'll catch the next bodge when it gets heah afta we had this out."

Abner looked amused. The light round their rims disappeared then flashed out from the slits of his amused eyes. "Don't fret the clock," he said. "He's just doing his job the best way he knows.

"You allowed me to lead you downward into the earth, at the word of my promise.... You trusted me, might say."

Balder thought about this. He looked steadily at Abner's peaceable expression. "You was with me." He tried one last plea. "I in't certain...." He looked with apprehension toward the darkness and back at his guide again. "Guess I in't brave like Lt. Noruas.... Guess I knew that."

"Don't be sure on that ground. He had to get himself into an impossible situation before he could let go and trust. Or let say before he *had* to trust. On the whole you've done well since leaving Gott'im looking for Daniel.... Since... well, since being born in Gott'im, dying you might say in Vietnam, being reborn in Gott'im again. Not too bad."

Balder felt the tender relief, having it put so. We have to see corruption, he thought. *We have to suffer.*

"Balda, what does it mean to be made in God's image?"

"I thought of that off'n'on, time-to-time."

" 'Board for the Inferno!" The timbre of the ferryman's voice had not changed. It sounded apiece with an idiotic machinery that knew its own regularity. But Balder thought the operator was no machine.... Maybe a very earnest child.

He said, "If I'm the image of anything... what evah It is, It's fucked up. But I'm not too mad at It. I just don't understand. Does that mean I'm the image of what has no understanding? The image of what suffers and goes on, circles back to suffer some moah? The image of ignorance and want? Does It fight to be good, feel that It's not?... Feel hopeful again that It loves?"

Abner seemed more apiece of the light and mist than formerly. He was like a mist-light in human form.

"Don't dissolve on me, Abner. Don't go away in that light."

"I'm not, Balda. I'm happy. You've made me happy, s'all. I'll give a promise... since you have trusted me. I'll give you another t'keep fah me." He shifted the barrel to lean over, holding out his hand. "I will wait heah fah you.... Or some waya along. We will meet up again.... That do?"

Balder clasped his arm and shook, thumb on top of his wrist.

Surprised, Abner smiled. "The hippie shake," he said. "It came and it went, but it's good in the memory."

Balder stood on the barge slowly watching Abner, legs at ease and the musket upright between them; Abner disappearing as murk gathered round the barge. Balder felt no sensation at first but knew they were sinking because Abner dissolved above him, tiny, and the mist-light grew more indistinct.

He killed the monster, Balder said to himself. *He really did. Asa was telling the truth. There really was a monster to kill.* Balder began to pray.

Yet, though I walk through the valley of the shadow of death, I will fear no evil for thou art with me.

The mist-light dissipated to a point, as a star submerged in the cloud-murk, and was gone. Imagining the walls of the mountains ever higher above, Balder was left in shadow with only that sound of the diesel now enveloping him. He felt the greasy mist building and clinging to him. He could see and feel nothing else and wondered if, with sense curtailed, vertigo too would be his portion. He stamped the deck of the barge, even as he clung to the words in his mind: *Though I walk through the valley of the shadow of death I will fear no evil, for thou art with me.*

Then, strangely, he heard an owl hooting. *Ooo-ooo-oo-oooo. Who-cooks-for-you?* He heard the onomatopoeic, also, going through his mind with it.

The stench of the pulp-and-paper mill, something like chemically vulcanized vegetables, pervaded everything, striking him with unease as it had when he first went into the mill to work. Then he became aware of faint light from somewhere, and he turned to see two eyes of fire, red flame, looking at him through the greasy dark.

Yea, though I walk through the valley of the shadow of death, I will fear no evil for thou art with me.

He did not turn away from the eyes but held his gaze steady, even as the words went comforting through his mind. He found the eyes begin to shed light elsewhere and perceived new sights, things coming into view nearby; as though his own eyes were adjusting to the murk and dark, aided by those flame-eyes. He saw the outline of the cab behind the eyes-in-the-dark and wondered how that could be. He caught a glimpse of the wheel inside but was quickly riveted by the sudden appearance of a large platterful held before him in the long dark hands of the ferryman, whose gaze, while continuing on him, shone its reddish or infrared light down onto the plate and its contents. "Have some?" The voice said this over the burbling of the engine, its quality mechanical or automatic, as Balder remembered it from the salutation to commuters who were to be converted into paper.

Balder, as he gazed upon the ferryman and his offering, was some moments in understanding that food was proffered. He looked at the spread pale pile on the plate. It was something like Uncle Ben's rice in consistency, smaller grained, and thinly spread in a somewhat mealy-looking swirl. It seemed fairly obvious that the long charcoal-colored fingers holding the platter had scraped and spread the contents into it; and maybe added the spiraling decorative touch in an offhand but oddly whimsical way. An offering, he thought, looking up into the weird dark expressionless features with its two small red flames—something like a mentally disabled man's gift that may or may not be appreciated. Balder thought he had better have some of it, for reasons not the least of which was hunger. He found he was very hungry, famished.

Balder gazed on the pale stuff.

The operator seemed to respond to his unspoken question by scooping some into his own mouth with one of those long not exactly clean-looking spidery hands. Balder followed suit, steadying the platter as he did so. The meal was to his tongue as imagined Ambrosia; and was, at first taste, faintly sweet with a quality unmatched in his existence on earth. Then it became rich and dense and his mouth, like a bread that could stand on its own for an entire meal. He smiled with complete pleasure. "What is it?" His murky surroundings suddenly did not seem quite so bad.

"What is it?" said the ferryman.

Balder wondered. "You don't know either?"

"That's its name."

"What's its name?"

"What-is-it-?"

"That's what I want to know." Balder was a bit disturbed.

"Yes-I-see. You want to know what's the name of what-is-it-?"

"Ah you gont tell me, or not?" said Balder, ready to give up. He took one more helping, though really he did not need it. His first taste and subsequent feeling of heavenly nourishment had filled him pleasantly. The second handful was a shade less delightful. It was then he decided to stop— on principle.

"What-is-it-?"

Balder looked at him. The flame eyes, as well as glowing, were also flame shaped. The darkish face was narrow, the head capped in gray like an old-style engineer's, and there was an appearance of usefulness and innocence, the last again remarked by the mechanic. The operator was a bit taller than Balder.

"Oh," he said, unconvinced. "Well... —thank you. Tasted a bit like bread or cake baked in a light oil."

"It tastes like honey!!" said a small merry voice. Balder looked down. So did the ferryman, and in the light of his eyes Balder saw a little girl just behind the operator, half-peeking from out of the cab. She was dark of complexion with brown eyes and thick brown sausage curls banded with a blue ribbon. She wore blue print pajamas.

Balder said, "You had honey?" He was so surprised to see her there that he almost floated right off the barge, and the words came out solely in reaction.

"Everyone's had honey," she said matter-of-factly. She turned back into the cab. Balder craned round the operator and saw her standing on his pedestal seat at the wheel, her dark little hands holding it, for all the world, as though steering.

Does he know this? "She steering the bahdge?" asked Balder matter-of-factly, trying, and succeeding as any Gott'imite would, not to sound an alarm.

"That's-my-little-girl."

Management, the union know bout that? Though Balder said nothing, only looked at him. *They's a devil's union?*

The operator withdrew into the cab with his platter.

Balder, being uninvited, stepped close to the hatch and stood peering in. He would not, of course, go within without that invitation, as some in the mill might. He saw the pair at the wheel, the imbecile operator and his little girl, who looks and acts, again for all the world, like a normal little child. (Balder also then noticed a very small lit display screen above her.) She turned to smile at him over her shoulder with pearly teeth and big black pupils, set in starlight. Yes, he thought, those little teeth ah pearly. Like a new necklace, double rows of pearls.

"'Scuse me," he said. "That What is it?— waya'd it come fom?"

"The roof," she said, pointing upward. "Poppa says the waters put it there."

"The waters?"

"This!" Perched at the wheel, the child waved her arm about, perfect small dark fingers spread; stirring the gloom in the dim reddish light of her father's eyes. The murk swirled a bit.

Balder could not think how— ...Unless it was something like what happens at the narrows in the pond under certain atmospheric conditions. Every so often in winter he saw the rime, invisibly building with visible result, on the saplings and leafless brush. It, too, was fragile, delicate and sweet-seeming —like cake frosting. And when the sun shone, melting, it dazzled. This sight appeared in his mind with exquisite wholeness. Then he wondered how it could — simultaneous with this other: the glooming sight of his eyes. Each vision so real and true.

Just then he heard the owl again, distantly. …As he had heard it many many times off in the dark of the woods, beneath Simon's Ledge in the night. He could not imagine why a barred owl should be flying here in the fathomless murk of this great Gulf.... Such sound should come to them from a distance into this intimate space. The wheelhouse, and a bit of the barge, the engine next them under its housing: it was the *all*. But themselves, so isolated they seemed in the greasy gloaming here. Was it one of the messenger angels?

He wanted to ask her about the owl. Asking the operator was not Balder's impulse, so human/inhuman he seemed. While *she* seemed an every-child, the cleaving of nature in the ferryman made him all but unknowable to Balder. At moments his ego played with him, making the bargeman an object of dismissal or, conversely, a quotient unknown and therefore to be respected. Balder, on recognizing this, said to himself, *It's me that's strange. I'm the one I can't fathom. How can I be so awfully made?*

Then he thought about the word *awful*.

The child and her father had turned back to face out the windows, through which he himself could see nothing but their strange reflections with his own dim image behind. Were they looking at him in the light reflecting off the murky plateglass from those twin eye-socket flames of the operator?

"What's yaw name?" He asked it abruptly, in some desperation. For something to say, some kind-contact. His eyes were on her reflected murk-gazing expression. Again, he had no thought of addressing the ferryman. She was the sole comfort here.

She looked at the ferryman, wonderingly. He looked down on her, infrared lighting her face from above. He said nothing. She smiled at Balder over her shoulder and said, "I'm his little girl."

"Oh." Balder smiled in return, reassured. Must be like What-is-this-? Only without the question to it.

What he could see of the cockpit and barge in the ghastly reflected light— it was all he had to keep out of touch with vertigo, so it was hard to say: The barge *seemed* in general descent, without increase of power as against gravity. Now the operator reached his dark hand to the panel, cutting the engine off, much to Balder's surprise. The barge seemed to stop, rocking a bit, hovering in limbo. He waited, dealing with dismay:

discounting it, crediting it; waiting. His fingers gripped the grimy hatch-opening but not solely for the sake of footing. The barge had stopped. Where was the inferno?

Then Balder heard it. Birdsong. He recognized it immediately, the thin airy downward spiraling song. The veery!? A small speckled thrush. He heard another added to it, and another. Now there flowed such songs innumerable, some distantly, some close at hand: so much so that he worried over collision with them. "Wonder they don't hit us," he said. *Mother*.

That would be a reference to Elda Simon, Balder's mother, the animal rehabilitator. If you are a reader of *The God's Cycle*, you may recall from Israel Kimball's book, or from Jasper Mary's stories, or from me, Abner Bartlett, that she goes about with a pack, and sometimes a net with small weights, looking for animals in distress, you might say. Illness, injury, distress. Brings them back to the tree-mantled decaying old barn at *Simon's Ledge* for doctoring. You can't tell a story of Gott'im without animals. The beasts of the woodland, birds of the air, that sort of thing. I suspect she would extend her concern to the insects... if she knew how.

Veeries were passing very high. He listened to them far far above. And they passed low, too, under the barge. He felt wings graze his hair and eyes, heard the swift delicate song in passing. "Mind if I step in?" He asked, doing so without permission. "Please, what ah they doin'heah?"

"Those are the baby monitors. They fly with new souls in the breath. Did you feel the breath?"

"The *breeze*? —Just a bit. Thought it was their wings making it."

"They keep singing as they sail. So pretty that song." Her high voice itself was not unlike such a sweet song.

"You mean they ah goin'to mothers' wombs?" He was bemused. "In't this the wrong place fah them t'be though? Don't seem right. 'Board fah the Inferno'n all."

He wondered if any were headed with the birds toward Gottheim. But in fact one of these veeries was with the undeveloped soul of his own child sailing toward Gloria's fertilized ovum on the far side of the *Count of Time*, trilling its ethereal song; the song itself as a sweet slender breath on the breeze. This song brushed past him evoking for him, on this dark dirty barge, the sight of green flickering lights through leaves around *Simons Ledge*.

To me it seems a fairly infinite complexly interdependent process: Were I to tell you of the process previous to that of fertilization, called meiosis, I might also tell you of the process previous to that, and so on *ad infinitum*. So I won't trouble looking into that now. It is sufficient to say that meiosis cuts the chromosome load in half before fertilization, keeping the burden of genetic information from doubling with every human coupling. Without that would there be monsters among us? 'Twould seem so: every one of us a monster. The gametes had, as their name from the Greek implies, married one another to form the *zygote*: which would divide, and thus begin multiplying cells toward becoming the great round thumb-sucking form of the Balder-Gloria child. This, with proper care and nourishment, is how the elements of earth are reintegrated in human form.

But just now Balder knows nothing of this cellular marriage taking place in his girlfriend's body. For the long moments of his journey to Daniel and back again, he has forgotten the short ecstatic moments of life in the cab of his pickup after the netting of mate-seeking smelts at Indian Pond. To know of the cellular marriage now would only distract him from his quest. He has enough distraction, disturbance, and involvement on his way to the deeps he must descend... in order that he might rise again on the great mist/water cycle of creation/recreation.

How do I know? Because I too am in the cyclic journey, unbeknownst to him. I am Abner Bartlett, the monster killer, though I blush at the title. I only aided the mountain in killing the monster; and then I was also able to write about it. And I am telling you Balder's story now. The only part that concerns me, that is: No one human could tell the entire story of anyone. That is why we are born, each, into the world: in order that the GREAT LORD GOD might have but one tiny particle of humanity for the story He wishes to tell Himself. Our experience of that story is its telling. It may be given to Balder to see a metaphor for marriage itself in the meiosis fertilization cycle. It may be that Gloria will have no concept of this, as seems likely to me, what little I know of her.... But that is for another story, not this one.

"In't this the wrong place fah them t'be though? 'Board fah the Inferno'n all," he was saying.

The little girl made him no answer. And he saw then that her bright gaze had indeed shifted to regard him in plateglass reflection. She said simply, "I don't know everything."

In fact, this phase of the journey, too, was limbo. The Gulph. Limbo in another of its aspects which popular pagan and religious culture may fail to delineate. Let me call it a reversal of limbo, limbo inside out, limbo inverted, what have you. Here the invisible constituents of things may come together to form other things... for everything is made out of other things; things not always so readily apparent. I could give you an example of that out of your own body, call it the Earthen-Cycle-that-Thinks or some such thing: take your body apart piece by piece; cells, molecules, proteins, elements, atoms, subatomic particles, the whole breathing pile of you.

But, on second thought, why don't I just let the aging, dying, decaying forces do that for you as you experience it? We don't have much time for that here. We've got to keep up with this poor distressed man on his way to hell and back. So I won't trouble you with that now.

"Oh," said Balder grinning desperately. "I was just testin' the limits of yaw knowledge, see f'you knew or not."

She giggled, voice piping. "My Poppa does that all the time."

The thronging whiffling song passed away in the vast Gulph and the bargeman fired the engine. The burbling barge began with a gentle sinking feeling as in some elevator in Portland. Balder was not relieved and wished to call back the mystery and linger under it. The descent continued and he sought comfort or occupation for his mind. Not wishing to intrude on the family scene with his questions, he tried thinking what Limbo was. It seemed a sort of material oblivion; a place, if he understood the term, of obscurity, of beings forgotten and left alone or untended. He thought a moment if the babies fit that picture and decided that historically they did not but perhaps increasingly, yes. Take Gloria. *She does not want children because she does not think she can think of them as much as need be.... which is kinda wise. She told me they's too many in the world 'n I said that was God's business. She told me bout Malthus dismal theorem'n I said it's a dismal theorem all right so why not fahget it?*

He could not get used to this suspension of the laws of physics.... Was this what is meant by laws of an alternate universe? Some sort of language or semantic to cover the Monstrous Unknowable Unthinkable? He could not say the unbelievable: What did his belief or unbelief have to do with such physical laws? These thoughts were good for a moment or two but then Balder began to wish for another man to talk with. Someone to discuss things men talk of: hunting, fishing, the Sox, snowmobiling, engine repair, getting the wood in, stuff like that. You could share knowledge, learn a lot from other people this way. The conversation of other men, on such earthy subjects, was comforting to him. He might have spent several moments with Ansell over the skidder engine when they met up in the woods, especially if neither one of them had been grieving.... Long ago, oh so long ago. He liked to talk about things with people. Balder didn't like to get them talking so much about themselves but about what they knew, what they were doing in God's wide world. What if they had a problem or were in some kind of trouble or didn't feel well? It's not that he didn't like helping people but it was the uncertainty. What kind of help, how did you give it without messing things up? You give some help, you want it to be effective. If only there were instructions that came with it, like do *a. b.* and *c.* to fix it.

Now Balder was wishing that Abner had come with him solely for the talk. *That Springfield was a beautiful piece of art*, he thought. Its components practical and elegantly combined.

The little girl and her strange father looked peaceful and happy there in reflection on all three sides of the cab, the ferryman's dark hand on her blue-print pajama back where she stood close to him on the elevated seat at the controls. Balder thought of Daniel, and his inner man dropped low. He felt himself sinking deeper into the morass of sorrow. They had not known one another a year... and now he was gone. Will it be like he never was? Will he be like a phantom, a darkness over his heart each time his mind sought Daniel's memory?

The bright image of Dana came into his mind, Dana sitting, writing, on the green *Count of Time*. Balder felt a bit better.

The engine began slowing, then reversing itself just a bit. Now it came to a stop.

" 'Board for the Inferno!" The bargemen brushed by him onto the deck, calling his tenor singsong insistence that all were to board for the Inferno.

Why would anyone want to do that? Balder looked through the gloom and saw the dull purplish shadowy shapes of dockside commuters. He could see nothing else but this purple-dark murk. The operator was casting the hawser up front, then rushing to secure the stern.

"You want to get out here, don't choo?" said the bargeman coming past. "You want to get out here, don't choo?" said the bargeman. "They's someone wants to talk to you, in't so?" He was holding back the dark crowd with big hands waving, looking over his shoulder at Balder, the engineer's cap on the back of his head. He kept the chain across the open deck to prevent them entering. He continued staring over his shoulder, the two red flames of his eyes fixed, with what seemed unwavering dementia, on Balder.

Balder had stepped out of the cab and now he glanced back into it but the little girl was not to be seen. He would not get to say goodbye, or even see her happy contented being again. He sauntered over to the insistent authority, the halfwit bargeman, and with a quiet, but inwardly reluctant, bravado stepped over the chain. The shapes remained indistinct, mere dark ghosts, seeming part of the mist, murmuring a unified disturbance at being held up. As he entered with a shiver into their dim misty midst they parted. They seemed almost indistinguishable from the darkness. Why they evinced this shrinking at his coming was a mystery to him. Then they passed like a gust of darkness on either side of him onto the waiting deck. As the apparitions passed he thought he heard more than one whispering,

"Thank God."

Who were these forgotten beings? He wondered. *Were* they forgotten? Have they been remembered again?

Suddenly he smiled: Was anyone of them wearing his watchcap? He had forgotten, until now, about that lost thing, that watchcap gone in the dark scuzzy river in realms high above. Didn't it go over the falls, turn particles, rise, then flow downward on the mist?

He watched the shrinking ferry, a dark indistinct shape, its eerie light in the wraparound windows of the cab soon sinking out of sight. He was alone in the shadowy gloom. He could have expected a foghorn sounding, the sweep of a dingy beam from a lighthouse somewhere. But there was nothing.... Nothing save the slippery feel of the dock beneath his workboots. Then the faint whiff of sulfur and of sulfuric acid, as from the mill, drifted into his nostrils.

He was feeling Mother Nature's call. Somehow it did not seem right to answer it into the mist of the Gulf. Cautiously he made his way to the rocks and leafless scrub beside the dock, unzipped, and there let loose his stream. Then he moved back, again cautiously, again straining sight, trying to penetrate the mist and dark of the Gulf.

Why wasn't he going to the Inferno? Would he have to yet? Who wanted to see him? Was there someone here, truly? Or would he have to stand here in darkness, forgotten forever. As it now seemed.

His Brother Hoder

"Ic eom eower blind broðor, demende bedecian eower forgiefnes on þone ofer."

Balder turned at the sound of the strange soft voice. One, it seemed to him in passing, practiced in the art of chanting. He did not understand its speech. He saw nothing but shadow-murk, felt nothing but mist chilling him every part. He looked up as a flash of firelight split the dark and lingered far above him. Now he smelled hot caustic smoke, burning pyroclast. Then the fire widened. Above shone out like one of the roughly horizontal fire seams he'd seen on this same dark mountain where he met his C.O... across the Gulf from the green mount... now so high above and far away. This burning was also high above, giving him an impression or sense of the chasm in which he stood... between the mountain of Time were Gott'im lived and this mountain—was it Time's mountain too?

Are these mountains in the Land of Time? —Or is it Eternity'sback space two? But he scarcely thought of it, so riveted was his attention on the seam that kept pouring forth red brilliance. The mist high and low now shone with it. Mist mingled smoke and vapor, beginning to warm him. He was now very uneasy in the rapidly changing atmosphere. The seam dripped molten fire, great drops of it, in places thickening to rivulets running downward, cooling in color-tone as they fell. He heard faintly the tumult, the burning crackling popping of mineral constituents, but he was most taken by the silence of fire falling, oozing downward, along the reflecting flank of the splitting rock face. How long he watched he'd no idea. These were long long moments of mingled awe and dread followed by silent welling terror.

"Did you say sump'in?!" He hollered it several times—to anyone, in hope of human contact.

A great red pyroclastic blob, falling down, soon crusting in black, landed upon the rock away from the dock, catching his gaze, fixing it in fascination. He flashed back on Marine Pfc. Socotomah's burning flesh and hair, the friendly fire solely Balder's error, he felt sure —sometimes— though findings found him only in part responsible. The glob lay burning, encrusted; not far from the tiny river of molten stuffs thickening, and reforming the rocks about it, slowly flowing off down between small reflecting clefts. Closer to Balder the glob spread upon the softening rock like a crab or dark star, sprawling arms and legs. Then, to his terror, it stood and came toward him, unsteadily, as though a toddler unused to walking.

When it reached the wayside near the steaming dock, Balder standing fearful, hackles raised, saw it man-shaped like himself, but encrusted unevenly with fissures and breaks. It was dark and fiery at once. Its craggy face was practically no face; but having mouth and nose through which seethed breath, uncomfortably, as with torment. How great was the being's suffering!

Balder was harrowed by memory, fear and compassion; all. He could think of no way to relieve the being's pain but oh how he longed to do so. He felt he would not have another easy day so long as this being suffered. All the heroic deeds of the heroes in his company: They weren't the scenes that kept returning.

"*I am your blind brother Hoder come to beg pardon. Will you pardon me?*" Again, it was an oddly singsong hissing, as though with enchantment.

"'Cuss! 'Cuss, I forgive you! Whad you do? My brother? I got none. Oh please, please, for the Love of God be forgiven. God loves you! He sent Jesus dint He? In't he Jesus died fah our sins?"

"I slew you and now he's angry: The great god Odin my father is angry with me."

"You didn't. Look! I'm alive. Here feel my arm. See, touch it! I'm alive."

"You would let me touch you after what I did, slaying you? You would let me hurt you with these burning fingers?"

"Yes! Yes! C'mon!" Slipping over the slimy boards, Balder ran toward him where he stood burning on the rock of the quayside next the steaming dock. A small almost leafless bush stood near and caught fire by Hoder's burning feet.

Now it must be said here that Balder's consternation and terror were so strong he could hardly force himself forward. Here is Balder's thought, if that jumble of firing neurons can be called thinking: How in the world? — what in the world— how in the world do I help this soul? He had no clue.

A set of arms to burn? How is that going to help someone in this condition?

This is how it went with him. But to us sitting here reading, to Abner standing (so to speak) nearby, to Hoder tottering there burning, it seemed the mechanic ran straight to him with outstretched arms. "My brother, if-it's-you-say! Heah!" He thrust forth his arms.

It may be imagined that most of us would have run the other way. It may be imagined most of us would have jumped off the slimy steaming wharf into the murky sound and taken our chances with what we could not see. In doing so, would we have sunk beneath God's wisdom like stone, or drifted, treading, clamorous, slowly down through the murk? But Balder was of a different order. Or, if you don't think in these terms (orders of beings) then Balder was of a different *type*. Think about his type. Start with his name and looks, think of the story of his namesake, Baldr of the *Elder Edda*.

Balder will have much to think about when he gets back to *Simon's Ledge*. He will go into the Gottheim library to look up a few things or order some books on the interlibrary loan. Then he will read among the myths of the European North that his namesake had a blind half-brother named Hödr. Baldr was the fairest god, son of great Odin and Frigga, whom every god and order of being loved. (Except perhaps for the Giants.) It was impossible not to love the brightest fairest genial god who lived in a golden castle. The Norse were notoriously undemonstrative, therefore they all loved the warmest prince among them. But to her great terror and consternation, his mother Frigga had a dream in which he was taken from them. So she set herself to the arduous task of exacting from every living thing a promise to do no harm to Baldr. In this way, Frigga thought, lay his safety, for collision with things is what harms us. Even disease in its microbial or viral form is a collision of sorts. This is especially so for the immortals not subject to a mere deterioration of parts. All things love Baldr and were pleased to take part in the vow to do him no harm. She sought high and low and none escaped her attention accept the most harmless of things, namely the mistletoe. So insignificant a living thing need not be bothered with. Now began more fun in Valhalla because everyone wanted to fling things at Baldr, knowing that no harm could come to him. At feasts he was so full of charm and good humor that he doffed his mail and allowed every hit known to warrior and god: the iron mace, the broad sword, battering ram, shot put: All were flung with impunity. Even Thor's hammer could not crush him: Nothing could fall glad and mighty Baldr.

Naturally his half-bother Hödr, blind from birth, also wanted in on the fun, and the gods were willing that he should try; for thereby would their amusement be increased. Thus the whole hall full of gods and goddesses might throw themselves under the board or to the rush-strewn flags trying to dodge Hödr's wild thrusts and throws while Balder stood quietly grinning and smiling, giving no sounding of his position.

Finally, however, and much to the grief of everyone, the wily Loki slipped invisibly into the great banquet hall. Pitched beneath mortared stone with timbers and firelight, the rushlight glowing from great sconces, the great hall revealed not Loki's presence. He came up behind Hödr, who was just nocking an arrow to the string, hooked on a bit of mistletoe (innocuous parasite of the birch or great oak), and, as Hödr drew back the bowstring, the envious trickster placed hands on his blind arms, aiming the mistletoe. Hödr let loose and it flew straight into Baldr slaying him. He fell to the flags of the hall.

Hödr did not know whose hands had guided his, supposing it to be someone in fun. Later, when all was told, it became a parable that only (mysterious) love in the hands of Loki could kill Baldr. And now the mistletoe, drinker of mist, is used in token of this at the birth-of-Christ celebration when all are in the toils of Christmas feasting. But the blind Hödr is forever remorseful. He is doomed to meet the boat of every scheduled landing if anyone named Balder is aboard. This, however, is the first time a *living* Balder ever showed up, and Hoder is as surprised as our hero.

In the myth, Hel cannot give up Baldr from the dead until all, everything living and dead, weep for him.... But the Giants refuse to weep for Baldr. Not until Ragnarök, the last battle, will Hel give up her dead. Even the gods will fight and die in that battle, and all be destroyed and remade.

Who knows if this is a true story? It is a myth. According to the elemental nature of story—or even of cyclical nature herself— true it is. But for the doubters it will be as with those who ask if a prophecy is real or will come to fruition. Only if and when it does will they be able to say.

Hoder's arms took our Balder's in a burning embrace. For Balder mentally it was like hugging the formative molten earth itself: for his imagining flesh-and-blood—boiling, melting, calamitous. Balder cried out and the blind god released him. Both orders fell down on the rock, rolling and thrashing in agony, but when their movements ceased came a calm and cessation of burning. When he woke he found himself scorched, but his wool mackinaw had protected him. For all his agony passed—it and his beard were only singed and stank of burning hair.

He lay, brushing hastily at his beard and wool jacket. The heat of the embrace lingered, but slowly Balder turned on his elbow, slowly stood, looking upward to see the fiery seam cooling and darkening; the mist before it going dim. The leaking firefall had ceased and the smell of the mist, still somewhat caustic, renewed in his nostrils. He looked around for Hoder, still brushing at his arms.

What happened? How'my living?

"Hodah?" He said this low, truly querying if it had happened at all, though the heat of it poured off him in sweat. Above, the seam was yet more faintly to be seen, the mists wreathing and thickening; drifting, disclosing, then obscuring once more.

"Hodah?" Slowly darkness saturated everything, the fire streams of molten rock crusting over darkly and virtually ceasing to flow. The lurid glow dimmed and the darkness increased. The lip of rock where he stood was no longer warm with the presence of the blind god. The chill was descending again, but not as chilling as it had been far higher in his journey to the deeps of... of creation?— He wondered briefly.

"*...Here am I....*"

Balder thought he heard something.

"*...Here am I....*"

It seemed but a faint susurration, perhaps a sounding of the drifting dark mist. He looked around through shadows. He felt with his feet for the quay in the slippery mist and found it, stepped down off the rock with care.

"Hodah?"

Again it whispered, "*... Here am I....*"

Balder came closer, slid a bit, crossed yet more of the slimy planking toward the edge of the Gulf. "You heah?"

"*... Yes, here....*"

Only a whisper. Spooky and drifting so that Balder could scarcely tell if it came from the mist, the drift, the night; or his own ears, his own person, or thought.

"Waya?"

"*... On the edge of the dark. We are here....*"

Balder followed and, in what remained of the dim sulfurous gloom-glow, began to discern shapes, something humanlike, crowd-like, an insubstantial mass among the faintly dimly weaving mists.

These parted for the living being; but one stood unmoving. "I am Hoder," it whispered, and now there was no mistaking that one of the mist figures spoke to him.

"Ah you okay?"

There came a sense of drifting. "*... I am well, now.... Your forgiveness has remade me.... I give you many thanks....*"

Balder stood silent, peering through gloom at gloom, oppressed. He could sense nothing here but gloom... and... maybe a few faint particles of hope floating about... among the quiet ghosts surrounding him.

"What ah— how —?"

"I am a phantom...." He began in quiet musing. "Mist among the mists.... We are grateful... to be again in the cycle of droplets... waters that move and flow with more ease among the small things of creation.... As this we have hope to move more among the hopeful, released from the cycle of heavier elements, molten and fire-born, in making."

"You mean—rocks?"

"Yea.... many go down into molten heaviness, who wish to return to the sunlighted vapors and airs."

"But how—?" Balder found himself unable to verbalize his questions but the ghost before him understood.

"The rocks you saw making... of which I was one. The mountain is made of us... and remade of us.... We are part of the elemental cycle of making.... Your forgiveness frees us to move easier among the elements and... to escape into greater freedom from tormenting passions...."

Balder, the mechanic, thought a moment. "Like mist... only not so— misty?" He tried comprehending the difference between the phantoms and the murk (plied by the ferry), or the mist-light surrounding the *count of time*. Are these beings separate from the mist?

"What exactly happened to yaw body?"

"On our embrace I became cold and fell apart."

"You mean ...turned to particles?

"Motes. Specks."

"Let me get this straight: You become bits of dust around which water droplets form? Smoking particles of rock sediment adrift in the air?"

Balder was not far wrong in this surmise. These phantoms are like dust motes of their former selves, their regrets gathering the water in condensate, fuming upward into these shadowy forms of regret. In this way the two cycles, water and rock, coordinate. In concert: the elements of earth- air water and-fire at work sheathing and intertwining the human soul. For we, as earth, are breathed into to make of us a human soul.

This soul is the body's reason for being, the sum of creation. For God has made everything material (galaxies, stars, moons, minerals, earths, even dark matter and the energy of material processes and systems, and of biological life), in order to home the human soul: Being to commune with God in suffering, toil, and joy. The great wheeling of the universe, its spiraling galaxies and cycling suns fusing; the rapt monstrous abandon of making and remaking; this ecstatic, holy life- death and-resurrection—it is for nought without the human soul. Was it made to experience remorse? Maybe. Was it made to *contain* remorse. For a little while. But it was not made to *be* remorse. Regret is not meant as the human being entire, anymore, than, say, jealousy. It is but one feature of the psyche, expressed and forgiven, then gone. That is regret's proper sphere, its cycle. Being has a multitude of aspects to experience. Do not choose to stop, as Hoder did, on one ill-starred event. Move on, friend Balder, and having forgiven and been forgiven journey on. God grant we would not give up our being to remorse.

The Dream in the Book

He rode the barge down with the living shadows through deep black mist, full of greasy filth; he guessed from the industrialized elements of souls put to improper use. Billions of souls, he supposed, just might account for all this, but then he laughed at his imagining: *Whad I know?*

The operator was different, the barge different, if more dirty, from the last. Everyone ate the *what-is-it-?* passed around on plates, evidently scraped off the cab as before. Even ghosts can eat the *what-is-it-?* and, he saw, be satisfied. They did not overeat, either. He thought they must somehow be related to the strange delicious deposit or condensate: Weren't both in and of the mist? At first he wondered about this.

Balder leaned against the filthy humming cab and dozed. In his sleep he saw again every experience of this strange night begun in Gott'im and now continuing below Gott'im: experiencing, perhaps, even time and eternity. But he did not relive it.

Instead it was as though he were some other man, sitting reading about it, by his window at *Simons Ledge* where the tree limbs outside shone or dripped, and framed the sky as the seasons passed. He was, instead, some other reading about the man Balder who had lost his son and went to find him and bring him home safe again. He had sat in that room at times all his life, once for three years rarely leaving it, trying to process without much success everything that had ever happened to him, especially in Vietnam.

But now he sat peaceably drinking a cup of coffee and reading in the green light from the oaks and maples of summer, grownup outside the window since father quit farming and died. The book was spread open before him, and he was interested in everything this other Balder was going through and found himself hoping for the best outcome for that poor guy and his story, and that somehow that Balder would find and reunite in harmony with his son Daniel again. I have a son Daniel too, he thought. I know just how he feels, wandering around looking all over the side of Blackwell Mountain, asking his friends where Daniel could be.

I too would want someone smart as Abner to help me see him again if he had to die. I'd go down that rabbit hole. I hated *Alice's Adventures in Wonderland* but I'd do it for my son, if I had to.

I'd like to be able to encourage Alvin to try for God's attention. I always liked Alvin, who couldn't, I'd like to know? I went to work in the mill myself—and pretty much hate it—but I guess I could go by there again on my day off if it was hopelessly necessary. I always wondered about the founding of our country and what trouble that was and did we fulfill the promise they struggled, suffered, died to give us. I do wonder about that though. Seems we started not too bad but I doubt we are all we should be now. Maybe. Maybe not.

I guess the part I like best is this scene on the White House lawn. Wait, no, this is not the White House. It is the mansion at the *Count of Time*. I see what Abner is getting at with that. Or maybe not? He's made the mist-light like the *Two Trees*. How'd he know about that? It would've been so good to see Dana there like this with the other Poetry of God. I feel better just reading about it.

That poor Balder. Had to see his C.O. again. Hoo, I would not like that. Abner is helpful and kind but I'm beginning to wonder about him, letting Balder do that cup-of-water-trip and feel Noruas's fall. Then making him get on that barge for the inferno. It's almost like he tricked him. I wonder about Abner. Is he going to make the story, right? How *can* it be, really? Hell and all, I mean. The fire, of sorrow and regretting, hugging and taking hold of Balder like that. Who makes their friends suffer that way?

What's it all for and what will happen next?

Oh yeah. He wants to see Daniel. It has to work out right. It has to.

And then, sadly, Balder woke up from the dream of the book, the dream of green light and swaying branches and found himself again in bleakness on his way down to the inferno.

He had been leaning against the cab and woke standing there. The ghost of Hoder was beside him bleak and dim, and the silent shapes of other ghosts were there on the barge with them. Balder was so sad. He could not remember ever being so sad. His initial descent under the mighty fall of water, where the filth of the river water droplets were being cleansed, where the river was turned to mist—there had been sorrow of awful density and emotional dimension but its power encompassed the purging faculty wholly absent here.

"Why does my Father hate me?" asked Hoder so sadly. As before, he said this in the Anglo-Saxon yet Balder understood it even so. "I see now you are not my brother but you must look like him with his glad brow and bright hair. He was a glorious man who made me happy."

"But you couldn't see him? In't you blind? Can you see me?"

"Nay, I see you not. Nay, I did not see Baldr. All told me of his visage and I felt his glad countenance when he was near. I wanted always to be by him. That must be why my Father hates me. He must greatly have missed Baldr too."

"How'd it happen. How can a blind man do that?"

"Loki held my hands and aimed, he hung it with mistletoe. I thought it was right to let the arrow fly, but now my Father hates me. With a giantess he conceived and birthed, in one day, a monster to kill me. So that I died and came here and lived among the fire and became the fiery rock of my unending regret. But you released me and now there is this." The ghost beside him felt to Balder a fullness of rainfall, dreary and drenching. A complete atmosphere of murk and bewilderment of spirit. "My Father's hatred pursues me."

"What kind of Father can he be though? Fatha's ah'posed to forgive. Also, it don't seem quite right—maybe he'd be mad a little time, but it waunt done on purpose. Not like you knew what you was doing."

"Will you speak with him for me? Tell him these things?" Hoder said this with some hope and Balder felt the new, if slight, spirit immediately. He did not want to disappoint or perhaps send hope away with bungling, but he was worried: "He seems kinda unreasonable. Think he'd listen t'me?"

"If you are as beautiful as Baldr you he may not refuse. You have good fellow-feeling and those whom you know are the most fortunate of men."

Balder was silent, thinking. I'm on my way to see Daniel and Abner makes me come this way—well not makes—but what choice d'I have?... Now Hoder thinks he's my brother and wants me to go someplace. On the other hand the ferryman said I was expected, so maybe Hoder is part of it. Am I ever going to see Daniel? Got to believe the promise. Abner wouldn't lie. Balder said, "Is he at the Inferno? I'm kinda on a mission."

"He lives and does practice war in Asgard in readiness for the last great battle, Ragnarök. In *Gladsheim* within Asgard is Valhalla, not in the earth made of the giant Ymir in which you are a living man."

"—Wait. Ah you saying that earth is made out o'someone's body?"

"The uncreated one made the first ghost folk, the frost giants formed of the rime of the mist. This we ate from the scrapings of the wheelhouse, you wist. Like the what-is-it-?, he was begun out of the chaos of the *Ginnunga-gap*, where the cold mist moved and rose from the heat-sparks dropped of the flaming one's sword. The rime formed in layers to make him."

"Like the glaciers?"

"As you say. My father and his brothers overcame him and broke him apart and used him to make all the earth and mist-sky."

"I always thought 'twas the other way round, the body made out of the earth. Oh wait. I get it: the cycle. Evathin's made out of something else. But how do I get to Valhalla fom heah? Don't think I could even get back into *Time* without good directions. Uh, n'something, some sort of conveyance."

"People don't realize how worth it it is." Daniel said this to him. He was sitting in Decatur's Diner with Daniel. Melvinia had just set their Friday fish specials on the linoleum-covered tabletop in front of them. They sat across from one another. Daniel looked a little different. Balder could not put his finger on it. If he thought about it long enough maybe he'd think of it, but right now he had to listen to all his son was saying. Melvinia stood listening too, her earrings dangling and her head poised to shake. She was good at shaking her head. The fluorescent light overhead, and reflecting off the dark window, glared off her glasses. They were used to her and didn't remark. Daniel paused. He blew on a bit of fish and forked it steaming into his mouth. Some people were leaving, some were just coming in.

"Think I know what you mean," said Balder. "Afta I come back fom Nam I hed t'go through New York 'n saw thousands of people moving through the great terminal and that's what I saw... or maybe felt... or something. Love. Caunt explain it. Evahbuddy walkin' hurryin' dressed in black: Love. They's walkin' hurryin' looking, not-looking: whole place'n all, staff'n stuff. Trains coming, going, loudspeakers, hawkers, toll-takers, floor sweepers. Evahbuddy walkin' in this great Love. Thought maybe I's lifted't heaven, o' maybe heaven dropped down a second. Was I losing my mind? I thought, no, I'm getting it. This is my real mind. The one I keep missing. It's theya all the time but I don't know it."

Melvinia, standing there, listening, was thinking, *Shouldn't you be having this conversation in private?*

"Did you know Time is a Person?" Daniel had listened with great attention to all this about Pennsylvania Station. He did two things at once. He kept eating the fish and Balder could see he relished every bite, giving it his whole enjoyment. Something different about him, though.

Melvinia stood beside them next the table, her thin arms akimbo, order pad in her hand resting on her sharp hip; poised to shake her head. She shook it.

"Y'know I *did* think it once or twice," said Balder.

Melvinia shook her head. She said, "How can that be?" The earrings jiggled. "That's crazy." She looked over at the neon 1950s clock hanging above the elbow in the counter where Asa and Olive were sitting with their backs to the booths. "That's time: 6:45. Friday. 1980s. November."

Balder looked back at Daniel. "Is it God?"

"I'm not sure. I think so."

"Such a great thing—who can think of it—*must* be somebody that big, trustworthy. But—it says 'Time shall be no more.' How can God be no mo-ah?"

"Maybe God puts it on'n takes it off."

Melvinia was poised. "You mean it's one o'his outfits?" She shook her head.

From the elbow Asa Bartlett had turned in order to listen openly. His wife Olive still had her back to them, eating, but absolutely listening *no doubt*. Asa, of course, is the local historian and Congo churchtower clock-winder, twice a week without fail. Naturally he's interested. From up there at the top of the street, he surveys the length of Front Street down to the Minuteman statue tiny (as seen from the tower) in its small triangle of green lawn. Once in a while someone notices his bespeckled head popped out up there beside the Roman numeral XI. There is always some remark to be made. Once Lyman Bearce saw it and said to himself, *The old spook.*

"Maybe," said Daniel. He gave her his entire attention, same as with the fish, the clock, his father. He was alive, Balder thought, to everything. His eyes still had that solemn cast but they were lit with something... inner. Something... light. His skin was a more glowing brown, not so much sallow as before. It was more like Chrischana's, and Native American, now. She'll be grieving. Balder thought, *Chrischana should see him like this.*

"Mother will see me like this," said Daniel. "I'm glad you can talk about Vietnam now." He smiled his great smile. It was the sole time he had said anything that personal to his father. It may have been the only time he had seen his son's smile. Balder tried to think.

Invitation to Ragnarök

He woke up gradually, feeling the undulating movement of horse bones, muscle, flesh beneath him. He woke!

Balder sat the horse's rump behind the warrior maiden, gripping her. He leaned into her and clasped his strong arms around her massive form. He gasped. The movement of flight disturbed all the clouds and air about him with the rushing of many waters in tumult of storm. He turned his face aside against her great back. He saw another great maiden on a mighty steed, her charge lying dead in leathern armor before her over the pommel. All his darks were heightened to purple, umber, blue-blacks, and charcoal: it was the most color he had seen since the *Count of Time*. The coppery mist surrounding obscured still his watch. He thought he heard the horses neighing with wild abandon. Or was it the screaming storm?

Far below him Hoder looked up from the deck of the ferry. His eyes were opened and from the greasy barge on its way to Hel he saw, in silent shining variegation, the flight of the Valkyrs from beneath: It was the first thing vision had ever shown him. From there the storm of riders looked not unlike Aurora Borealis, its storm of dancing particles *clicking, snapping,* and *popping*. So it looked, but without sounding, to those in the north; in Norway where Balder's ancestors came from. And in the northeastern USA where Gott'im sits and looks up in wonder. But only when conditions are right; the magnetosphere grabbing and taking hold of particles in a grand way; grand like the smoke and flame of Ceylon Segar's tire fire burning and consuming the very ground. Some there think this flight the outflowing of plasmic particles from the sun, trapped in the ionosphere. Some, as did Daniel and Chrischana's native antecedents, think it ceremonial dancing of their ancestors around the celestial fire.

Balder had no idea how long they rode upon the streaming storm but to him it seemed long. He had no idea of lines of direction, but to him they seemed upward. As they descended higher the tumult of storm rose and he felt the tremor of song deep in the warrior before him, recognizing for the first time that she was singing a song of enchantment; a blending of song and chant; and that the others, surrounding them as though in stampede, and each laden with a dead warrior, were also joining the mighty tumultuous cadenced song. It rose shrieking and howling, whistling and swelling so that he became convinced he had been taken in a hurricane of lightning and cloud and would somehow be carried far and wide and dashed to pieces everywhere. Maybe, he thought fleetingly, dashed to the ice-bones, the stone bones of the giant Earth created in defiance and out of the constituents of Ymir, as Hoder had said. And, as they rose on the power of the storm, it grew brighter. Not an entire transmutation of light, but a gradual lessening of darkness so that the cloud-lights seemed now truly lights indeed; somehow not unlike the mist-light surrounding the *count of time*, but in other richer hues. Perhaps more of color, less of light.

At last, as breaking forth out of the somber-colored clouds, as upon a castle or keep of large stone and maybe apiece with the mountain, the storm-cloud and riders broke upon the lees of the castle-mountain, standing pale- and golden-gleaming: mighty waves surging, and with lightning, with thunder crackling, snapping, roaring and popping. Swift coppery light in shards lit everywhere: upon the battlements, upon the ramparts, upon towers too numerous to count. The Valkyrs' song reached a crescendo and they, as clouds and horses and riders of colored sound and light, heaved up around the walls, the great curtain wall of stones, and hurtled over in foaming light, suddenly too full for sound. Surging and falling with the mighty maiden, up and down, upon the great steed's rump, Balder felt the silence, abrupt, complete.

This sea of somber light subsided upon the vast stone floor of the bailey spread far and wide on either side so that Balder wondered. And he looked around him in this silence for the fortress towers. But they were gone. Receded into clefts and precipices distant and vast.

The steeds stood stamping and sweating in the expanse, and he looked and saw the maiden warriors all around him, solemn smiling and with no gestures, speaking their silent content in duty executed with the utmost of purpose, drama, and precision.

Oh Lordy Lordy.

He loosed the great Lady before him noting for the first time that her back was clad in gilded leather, not exactly gold, not silver gilded, but with a sort of combination of the two, and very dull.

Now, from every corner, and seeming at great distance, came streaming well-endowed and mighty serving people, as he surmised: They carried great trays and tankards wafting scents and deep rich fruity odors, and the sweetness of these swelling odors filled him full of sudden unexpected intoxication. As though he had drunk already, or eaten the contents of trays and tankards.

The maiden swallowed hugely from the great tankard up-handed her. He saw her massive white throat go up and down, as, beneath them, the leather-armored steed sidestepped upon the stone, its iron-shod hooves ringing with great clarity. The warrior half-turned and touched Balder with her white great finger, gloved to the knuckle, and he fell from her mount, great warhorse of awful height. He lay as though broken in every part upon the massive stones.... But he did not care. He was drunken with splendor, with drama, with sound. He had drunken with the Martial Muse and was overcome by her, filled with a great purpose that had nowhere to go.

He turned himself, dazed and blinking. He sat up, and looked upon the mighty cannons and fetlocks of the horses in the vast Bailey. He said, *"Lordy Lordy."* He said, *"Lordy Lordy."* He said *"Jeezus!"*

The warrior maidens looked down upon him with their great winged helms faintly gleaming. They laughed at him, their teeth shining; their great blue eyes as flames edged with yellow-orange. They spoke hilarity to one another in that tongue. The tongue that Hoder had spoken. Their warrior-burdens, heroes died in battle, slid to the flags and drank from great cups.

Balder thought, *Might be betta off don't drink the beer.* Mead. That mead in those mugs?

Two of the large and hefty serving folk lifted him swiftly. He stood uncertainly between a male and female, belted, wearing skin leggings and tunics, but he saw each had a short sword to their belts. He was still full of a mighty glad feeling and could not keep the grin off his face.

"To the judgment hall with him!!" cried the warrior maiden who had carried him. He found, as with Hoder's speaking, he could understand her command.

Judgment?

They picked him up by the arms and half-carried him, his feet working haplessly up the great stone stairs that widened suddenly out of a low wall nearby: he had not noticed before. Suddenly there was an antechamber opening before him, even as they entered and crossed it, and next he was lifted with great and easy strength into the golden great chamber before he could well grasp his position. He had stopped bothering about his feet and let them carry him. Before him now in the great hall ranged twelve thrones blazing with reflected light from torches in brackets ringing the gold and silver shield-work of the halls. The thrones were big as 18-wheeler chip trucks when their trailers were upended to puke out loads of chipped woodlands into the pulpyard at the mill. This comparison flashed into his mind and out again with no time to consider: He was overtaken by these mighty proportions, these dark and gleaming materials, the forged and hammered elements overlaying with glimmerness the monumental hewn stone. They stood him there between them on the cold stone floor flecked with darkly shining mica, and Balder's gaze filled with the hardness, dark burnishment of Gladsheim. The sight of the cold great empty thrones astonished him and he thought, *They need all this just fah me*? The intoxication had fled on their entrance, replaced by astonishment, awe, and dread in succession.

He felt their great hands tighten over his small biceps still covered in singed mackinaw; and, standing encircled by the thrones between two guards, thought of Hoder's story about the hatred pursuing him.

He tried to think how he'd gotten here.

I was talking to Hoder... then I was talking to Daniel.... No, that was a dream, another barge dream. Then I was with her, leaning into her... hours and hours....

Suddenly a golden-haired child ran into the chamber and stood before the gods' two servants, breathless. The lad had taken his red long-tailed cap into his hands.

"They call for him in Valhalla where the dead warriors are!"

Instantly they turned and lifted him out of the chamber, then out the massive stone building, and carried him forth into the city now built and furnished with every kind of human-seeming movement beneath the midnight of stars: so crisp and bright: They and this frosty mountain air stole breath from his nostrils and bosom. The Valkyrs and horses were gone from the Bailey. The great stone palaces surrounding the massive bailey-yard now appeared near and hewn from the mountains, and as though the mountains themselves had moved closer; the palaces' multitudes of leaded windows a'gleam with interior flame-golden lights.

Oh how, he thought. This heah Asgard is...! He did not finish his thought, but it had started into the territory of what Gloria may or may not be able to believe or imagine. The reader may remember that Balder's upper-middle-class glitzy girlfriend from away had been dabbling for sometime in her mishmash of neopaganism... perhaps in an effort to cleanse herself of her Baptist evangelical upbringing, perhaps to escape the routine of life... or, to be fair as Balder is, because she enjoyed it. Whatever the impetus he would only say to himself when he got back, *huh*. Guess I betta not say anathin. Don't guess I could get it ovah t'hah anaway.

On the slopes (where ringed the city), as they were ascending the hewn steps to the greatest of these monumental palaces, came another child running. She snatched her blue long-tailed cap from her head and bowed to one knee before them, saying, "He is to go to the bough *Lerad* outside the Hall of the Air, where decisions for the peace of the world are made!"

Again and immediately they lifted and turned him and carried him out of the city toward the blushing horizon where, in the distance, he saw another palace but overshadowed and shaded by the mightiest branch and tree the son of Elda Simon had ever seen. The moment he saw it he was beneath it, and so queasy he fell swooning between the guards. The blush of the horizon shot into his half-closed eyes reviving him. He looked up into the vast limb with its multitudinous tributary branches and saw the light of the sun, as he supposed, shining green and gold among the pattern of shadows; but the sun itself, he could not see. It was hidden below the horizon, and only its light in the leafy and limby pattern told of its existence in Asgard. They unhanded him. He stood in his red-and-black mackinaw, blue jeans and work boots, beneath the great hoary trunk so broad it was like a wall to him. And he perceived a vast expanse beyond its shelter, wide with this blush of the dawn. —Was it dawn or sunset? He had no idea of cardinal directions. Slowly, as his eyes adjusted to the deep contrasts of light and dark, he perceived a grouping beneath the great tree, picked out here and there with glimmerings as though gold and silver trimmed the garments of the assembled. Then, in a moment, he could scarcely take his eyes from them, so awful and burnished they shone.

And one, bearded and helmed, sat in their midst, the greatest. But next moment it seemed that One was not seated at all but had, in an instant, fumed upward, as if burning vapor full of breath and light, high into the tributary branches. 'Twas a great unfolding spirit among these branches. Balder saw in passing that the dark and bright leaves among this breath-burning of the god were compound leaves, yet so far away were they he thought he could but distinguish that they might be leaves of the ash, divided.

He went to his knees.

"All father," he murmured, and cast down his gaze in devastation. But where had they come from, these words? For Balder had never heard the chants of his ancestors round the fire, nor the epic poetry of the brutal and brave. And yet —he was the more afraid remembering how Abner had thrashed him for wrong worship.

Yet only, "Nay," said the voice full of power and warmth. "But that is unfounded, though thought of by many of your race. I am but Odin, or Woden, or Wuotan, some say."

Balder lifted his eyes and saw the great god of the Northmen seated beneath the massive rugged bole of the Mightiest Tree. He had taken off his helm. Balder had a complete sense, simultaneous with attention to the god, that there was more, far more to this tree than what he could see of it now. That, like all else in this world or realm he had come to, it defied both his comprehension and also his apprehension, so earthbound, small and human was he. He might not begin to understand, nor would his thought ever encompass, as his years passed, what the fragments of his experience here signified *of this Realm.*

"You think of the Tree, *Yggdrasil,* and you think of me."

Balder heard and understood the words, yet he was overcome: He could only raise his eyes and search the face of the great one who had spoken. His eyes were as the blue of Balder's eyes, were they lit with an inner fire of divine measure. The god's hair was tied back in a thong, curling and dark as was his beard, but the whole of hair and beard were mixed with threads of red; and he was handsome beyond description; and might, he saw, transfigure at will into live metaphor: so Balder had seen and heard in his burnished breath-voice-vapor. Tunic and cloak of blue and gray covered his form, yet his thews bulged with might. Balder before him could not help but feel for this Power an attraction coupled with a deep reverence or awe. His own small being was virtually forgotten and he wanted to worship, feeling his own inclination, yet recollected still Abner's injunction. If he could see *this one* there was One mightier still: One unseen who had fashioned and engendered *all might.* Both cloak and the garments were like the sky, blue adrift with clouds of gray; and dim with light, every thread. Upright in his hand was the infallible spear (as yet unknown to Balder). Behind him stood one, with the great helm in his hands: that helm fierce-faced with wings astride it like those of an eagle about to unfold. The blade of the spear shone and the helm with eagle eyes shone: But the shining was not as with the light of the sun. Nothing here shone with that light accept the leaves exceeding high above: He would recollect and meditate upon this fact again in his room at *Simons Ledge.* All lights in this place were almost as those at night: burnished as flames, burnished as metallic blues and grays and pewter. Upon his bed he would consciously breathe, and think of spirit-breath-wind. And he would think of great Odin.

"Allfather I am to the gods," said he, rich and deep of voice. "But to the races of men and women not so much. And this," he spread his powerful arms suddenly wide, "is Yggdrasil the world tree: holder together of worlds: of heaven-earth-hel. All its roots meet in the depths. The tree's boles and limbs lay claim to worlds-time-life. It is pasture for goatherds and deer, and stags without number whose horns drop dew and honey, feeding the rivers of earth.

"You have come to me here from the place of its unwithering roots where the rocks burn and flow and fashion forth the earth with turmoil and warping, and with heat unbearable for such as you are.

"You are called Balder, namesake of my son, Baldr, who was slain by the lowly mistletoe: proving that the gods themselves are not invincible and their lives any day may be forfeit by small things, by goodly and worthless humble things, by chance. —But. When I say worthless, have a care: I do not mean worth nothing. What is nothing?" He laughed and this sounding ruffled the leaves high above, and the cloaks and garments of the assembled whom Balder had yet to take in. The laughter was as the monstrous delight of water falling in Zambia, at Niagara, in Utigordsfoss. All about and beneath them roared and rumbled the laughter; and Balder could not tell if both the assembled and himself were laughter made flesh, or if the god laughed for and in all. But it amounted to much the same thing.

Odin.

"Speak, Balder. Stand."

Gott'im's Balder did not climb to his feet, shaky, with trembling, uncertain: He leapt. And stood before the Norse and Anglo-Saxon god.

Yet, as is the way with Balder, he felt his swift foolishness in the action while at once understanding its cause: simply, great Odin had pulled him up with his command! and there was such power in it: so!

"Uh. Dint choo say you called me?"

The god laughed—*Ah-ha-ha-ha!!* Then Balder was laughing, tumbling in the overcoming outpouring of the element.

At last he said, again with his foolishness: "Guess theya's no othah way to get heeya, sir!"

Have you ever heard a Mainer say, "sir?" You've probably heard one say *dear*, meaning perhaps nothing, meaning perhaps the opposite. But I doubt you have heard one say *sir*. Unless he or she were in the military… where a Mainer might deem saying it reasonable and right.

"Please, sir, I don't know how this happened. I guess I fell asleep on the barge with —." He stopped, suddenly remembering the commission assumed on Hoder's behalf. "—With Hoder. And he said he's your son?" He could not help the interrogative... nor the faint trembling he now felt in face of this terrible self-imposed commission. "I guess you know then I said you's unreasonable?"

Then Balder saw the assembled brighten forth around the great god, and he saw they also, in their terrible laughter, were gods. The ground shook with torrents, *of laughter*, as though in Iceland shaking, rolling, seaming and splitting, as though to vomit forth fire and earth. And they laughed at him as though he had told or *was* the best joke in creation. The strength of their mirth was so great that the palace in the near distance fell to the earth in ruin and the roots of the tree, as he watched, thrust up out of the rubble to wrap round and through it: first in brown hairy thongs but rapidly sending out shoots and those growing into trees: trees as great as any in Gottheim—and now more crowned and flourishing with limbs and leaves.

Gorry and *Jeezus*, he thought and fell to the ground covering his head with his arms, pulling up the mackinaw. Oh Daniel!

Oh, Gott'im! You must be in ruins by now. For it pressed into his mind that Time was cattawumpas and that centuries either dissolved in Asgard alone, or on earth in Gottheim as well. And that these were real gods, more real than his small self—whose look and whose laughter or anger could go on and on with exceeding power and devastation. *No wonder Hoder is so sad and troubled.*

Then, through the gaps in his mackinaw, he saw flashing like that of lightning. It hissed; it snapped and popped, lifting him with electrifying force from the ground. He stood on his feet, his eyes wide with astonishment, for there stood before him another, and the mightiest most frightful being he could never have imagined had it not been for Vietnam. The odd thought occurred to him unexpectedly as though he were sitting in Decatur's diner eating grilled cheese: He was not dreaming, he might never dream again. This was real life and life the way it *must* be.

The new god's face was cut fierce like an eagle's, his red beard blending as in feathers with his white wingéd helm. His beard was red as checkerberry, his eyes white and wild as lightning edged with blue, almost the opposite to the Valkyr warriors. And in his terrible expression—was it charged with wildness, with mirth: was it anger, was it holiness?—he shot sparks over the ground, among the assembled; and lighting on Balder's mackinaw, Balder's white sugarbowl hair and black beard. His gaze was bedizened. Hastily Balder brushed and shook his hair. The scents of ozone and burning hair, burning grass, filled his nostrils as incense and no longer alarmed him. He began to laugh with them, for how long he did not know.

They stopped their laughter and stood solemnly gazing at him until he could take thought to calm down.

Thor turned his back and spoke. Lightning flashed out again, lighting the face of Allfather. His voice was like power running through lines of force and spoke as had all here in the old language, the Anglo-Saxon. A moment he grappled with its vast atmospheric movement and sound, then Balder understood. It said,

"This peasant, this laborer, this warrior, this descendent of Norway is one of mine."

Balder looked from one Power to the Other, riven in spirit by the magnificent pair. The Powers with them seemed to go into a cloud, but not before he perceived, for the first time, the feminine among them.

"That is so, Eldest," said the greatest, "but you are even less sound and reasonable than am I." The laughter was submerged in the ensuing conversation: Solely through his spirit Balder perceived both it and their harmony. It was too irrational for his mechanic's mind. Odin continued, saying, "But one reason *will* I give. This is in the family, for here he is on blind Hödr's account. While seated and searching on *Hlidskialf*, I saw and took him; brought him hither from the midst of a dream. He rightly perceives this as true life and no wish of the fevered mind. I fear not to be thought unsound by him. But you, with those powerful hammer throws, and that white light, will not brook it: You will destroy him with your looks alone, it may be. Nevertheless, there is truth to your claim (that we might contend, for he has both Anglo-Saxon and Norwegian forebears). Let me, I pray thee Eldest, order the destiny of Hödr with him."

The other's nod was almost dauntingly imperceptible to Balder, so immediately used as he was to Thor's violent expression. But he did recognize it... so often was such a nod used in Gott'im.

Great Odin spoke again, his voice rich and deep as one of Gottheim's gem-filled caverns before they were played out: "Then we will set terms for the battle."

The battle?

"Balder, son of Everett, you a mortal man charge the god Odin— from whom even Christian kings and saints descend—of being unsound and lacking the love of a true father."

The god stopped speaking, his look on him. In Odin's look were many things Balder had not expected to see. Wildness, ferocity, love of battle for its righteous fervor and mayhem: Perhaps he expected these. But aided by his spirit, what he sensed also was a calm pure look exceeding comfort in its wisdom: complete in its utter lack of hurry and full of patience: as though Odin's was spirit unifying other things.

Balder took courage from him. "F'I 'memba right I said twas reasonable to be mad at fust, but then get ovah it: not like he did it on purpose. I mean, yes 'tother son's dead but what about this'n? —Caunt choo just bring 'tother Baldr back to life?"

There was silence. Great Odin looked on him with eyes blue as the skies over earth. He said, "This is well-spoken, you would say, Frigga?"

"Yes," came a deep but feminine voice from the cloud of Power surrounding the Allfather. Even Thor had disappeared into it, but Balder perceived him in its brighter and flickering parts. "But," the contralto feminine voice continued, "the first is not my son. I care but for the destiny of Baldr, from whom was taken his chance for heroic death."

The rose-gold light of the dawning persisted beyond the edges surrounding great Yggdrasil's trunk. It lit the leaves golden-green far above, but the light of the Powers seemed to take nothing from it. It seemed part of another world; or perhaps another age remote from his own. Balder noticed also the fragrance of every elemental thing, things elementary also with regard to type and word, but he heard the speaking deep feminine voice as one of these; and thought perhaps she was some portion of creation he knew but could not immediately place. Yet, he also vaguely sensed something of Chrischana in her voice and spirit, but had no time to much consider it.

Odin said, "Balder, son of Everett, has spoken true: I was wroth and conceived in my anger a monster with which to destroy my blind son."

"'N how'd Hoder get blind in the fust place?" Said Balder... and was instantly amazed at his bold speaking. "Uh, sir," he said. "Great uh sir."

Great Odin's blue gaze faltered not for a moment. After silence, as though answering Balder's question, he said, "Hödr was born blind. You say this is to be considered against the workings of my anger, as taking away from its justice. That also is well-spoken. Both Baldr, son of Frigga, and Hödr have suffered in the workings of these things. And Frigga has suffered and I Odin have suffered. I suffered both what flowed from it and, too, the overmastering feelings of my own anger. Then *Yggdrasil* put forth new roots boring places inside me for what did not before exist: what in your world you call love: I got over my storm of wrath but the outcome of it has not yet been fully assuaged. We will have to do with it. Hödr has felt my anger pursuing him, but this he cannot help, and this I do not long intend. His suffering in the making place of the deep is the work he does upon himself, but unknowingly, and that for the preparation of the battle. For such suffering he will, it may be, receive weregild in the day of restitution and vengeance. The enemy is not Hödr but my kinsman, Loki. Called also by some Loke, lie-smith, shape-shifter and others. Loki used my blind son to destroy my bright son Baldr and for this I am angry with anger that has not yet departed."

He stopped speaking. Balder looked into the sky of his gaze and saw shapes of blue flame edged with yellow and white: He saw shapes of dark vapor and smoke enmeshed in the shifting light of that sky. He saw the green of Yggdrasil pushing up among rice paddies and high among tangles of jungle, grenades exploding, B-52's dropping their fierce loads of fire: Thor bolting thither and yon between camps of opposing enemies: lightning strokes of great power and unintelligible speakings. The thought crossed into his mind that these powers were all antecedents of his family and faith; and he marveled that folks of the western world of his age, who were descending into the cycle of consumerism, triviality, futility and wimpiness were children of those who once were enamored of and worshiped these gods.

In the scenes blazing forward and back, and in this great gaze and laughter of earth in the making and remaking, he sensed then the riotous swirling of the galaxies and twining of stars entangled in the bright dust of the cosmos. Again he was tempted to worship, but the darkening look of the god himself forbade it and Balder fell quaking and shivering to the roots beneath the massive trunk and boughs of Yggdrasil. He cried tears for mercy. He cried for the shifting and roaring of contending Powers to cease.

"You are right," said the voice out of the making, "to wonder over those so used in your place and time: We are they who came before you—the eldest—for whom it is shame for man to die of old age or disease. Better even the last, for by suffering can be opened the thing in you that before did not exist."

Having assumed again in Balder's eyes the form of one he could talk to, great Odin said, "We ask of ourselves no less than of our descent: and why we are treating and inviting you—who gave of your own suffering the release of Hödr from molten making and remaking of his being."

Great Odin paused after making these speeches. Then he said, "Many of us here beneath Yggdrasil will die, not of neglect or old age but in honor upon the field of battle; and the great battle, our last battle with Giants of whom we descend."

"You waunt to kill y'grammy and grampie?"

Great Odin laughed and Balder hunched his shoulders and hid his head from the disastrous laughter. "Is it unreasonable, unsound in your world to want to die with your ancestors? *It is to be Ragnarök!* The last battle, the destiny and overshadowing of the gods. Let it be well-fought! And we invite you, Balder, son of Everett, to take part in it with us.... We have no right to command you, but the battle must come even so. Therefore, join with us, and not with Loki, for he will defraud you and seek to dishonor you for his own malice and pleasure."

Balder looked amazement at him, dismay. "You seem to know a lot'bout me. Then you know I hed m'war, and maybe still hev it. Dint do too good with that. Don't waunt n'other."

"Son of Everett gave his sound life for his country. You joined valiantly, fought— as well as you could, led them into battle, tried to restrain the berserkers: whom we sometimes disdain for their lack of wisdom. But they may give all to our service, forging panic in warfare. 'Tis useful. I can well use berserkers when they but follow my lead."

"But that war, turns out, was mistaken."

"May be. That may be. But your willing part in it was not

mistaken. Loki, the lie-smith, offered that war to those with the power, those given the authority, and they used it as he played. It will happen again."

Some reading this may wonder if Balder is about to be *bamboozled* again, this time not by a misguided government drunk on military hardware and power but by Loki in person. Some reading this will have grasped the wisdom and spirit of Balder and find it proof against this happening again.

He stuffed his hands in the scorched pockets of his jacket, jigged up and down slightly on the toes of his workboots and said, "You must know, you must o'seen me on the barge to the Inferno. There I got no interest in going, I got no interest in last battles. I want to see, as promised, or half-promised, or whatsoever, *Daniel*. My son. The one I care'bout. Outside the heavenly city, the light Abner showed me in the sky."

He stuck his head into the cloud, and found he had been granted the power to do so. He said, "...Ms. Goddess, in theya."

The creation about him shook with illogical laughter, but Balder saw her face looking down on him, unnerving, riven in great beauty and sorrow, wet with the mist of the Clouds—spinning out from her wet eyes, breath and hands, this cloud/vapor, enclosing the gods. He stood, his head only in the cloud, and let her suffering open up again the already existing places in his own heart.

Slowly, bringing his head out again, he stepped back. His face and beard were covered with tears. *Oh, Daniel!* He looked into the massive great bearded face of great Odin above him. Who said, "Thor's man. There will be battles and wars. You are invited to the Last Battle. Yet we do not know when Ragnarök will be. Now you have seen us, you will go back on your epic journey. But you will know when the time comes, and find your side then."

To the assembled gods great Odin spoke. "Balder will hear the horn blast of Heimdallr rousing all in heaven, earth, and *Nifl-heim* to the Battle." To Balder he said, "See him on the bridge yonder!" The god's bright blue glance showed the direction, and Balder looked away to see what before went unnoticed —if it had been there for him to see: a shining rainbow, whose limb struck through the earth but rose high beyond him. There in the sky-dark distance he saw a bright figure bestride *Bifröst*, the rainbow bridge made of colors of fire, air, sea. In his hand was a horn set almost to his lips, as Balder looked on and wondered. The Gott'im man saw but the bright contour, and the figure did not sound, but stood ready, poised as though listening for something and waiting. The contrast between the god Heimdallr standing on the shimmering elemental bridge and the deep dark of the sky moved him with a passion he felt in his inner man.

He thought, *Lord don't let me fall for these Nazis!* But great Odin laughed. He said, "Loki is the Nazi. Watch out for Loki! Know him. But, better, know your own God! The other's patriotism is false. Watch out for Loki!" Then he said, "Here comes *Gylfaginning* to guide you back to *Nifl-heim*! —To the mist!" He said the last words in answer to Balder's unspoken question.

Bounding toward them, out of the distant dark clefts beneath where the rainbow bridge soared, came a massive elkhound. He stopped before them, thickly furred, silver-blue and black, his sides heaving, his tongue hanging out his open gleaming jaws. He had a look of great intelligence in his eye, but his gaze was aloof. "Ride him! he deigns," cried great Odin. And Balder, hesitating but an instant, straddled the big powerful sides of the hound who took off with him as though after a deer. Balder clung to him, low, hugging the hound's neck in the wind, astonishing himself with his own glad, fierce, rejoicing.

I am alive, he then thought, *but going back to the dead.* They hardly have hope there, I remember. He buried his face in Gylfaginning's ruff. He saw the great dim-gleaming land of the Æsir no more but felt his own heart misgive him the more they moved. He felt the sinking and cooling and knew the hound brought him where willingly he would not go: no not with his feeling and longing to choose for him. But, yes, with his woeful and bedraggled assent, he sank beneath worlds— we know not for how long — and felt the dog land, heavily and scrabbling, its nails clicking and scraping the greasy iron decking. The animal wriggled away from him and was gone into the filthy murk before he could see. And Balder was left alone, blinking and inwardly whimpering on the deck of the barge. *Why'd I have t'live?* He wondered, *Why'd I have t'live?* Then he heard great Odin's laughter and began laughing himself. Balder laughed, and he cried, and he laughed some again.

What will Glory think if I tell her?

He lay on his back, knees bent, lounging, and propping himself on his forearms; fingers feeling the greasy pocks and nubbles of the decking. Already his hair was matted, his beard misted. The humming and vibration of the engine almost lulled him.

"That I'm crazy," he said aloud. "Not neopagan, just crazy. And I'd nevah get hah t'marry me."

Not that Balder would ever try to take her... or have her under false pretenses. That would be — would that be Loki? He wondered, and decided, *Yuht, that would be Loki.* I must be gettin' smotta by the minute.

Abna, f'I evah get my hands on you.... Wait. Yaw a ghost. No, I'm the ghost. No.... Now you got me confused.... This is bad. I almost fahget the gods and the warriors, and the Tree n'evathin, in this damned mist.

He did not know, of course, but I was right there all the time. Right above him, watching the whole thing. Who else was there to witness so as to tell his story? It is certain that Balder Simon could or would not tell his own story. He needed someone like me to do it for him. Some would-be poet who had— not exactly the same experiences, but not too dissimilar either. And... it should be someone, as well, who knows Gott'im. So I guess that about leaves me. I am Abner Bartlett. Some say I killed Gott'im's monster in 1808. I had help though. Believe I had plenty of help: help from suffering, help from the village, help from the monster's maker; from disease, from some very important sacrifices, and from Jasper Mountain. Don't forget Jasper Mountain. The monster could not have been slain without old Jasper Mountain.

Balder stopped thinking about Abner. Sitting there in the moving misty filth he thought about great Odin. *Odin or Woden or Woutan, did he say?* — Doesn't seem very Norwegian to me. He seemed more like some kind of potentate, a Sultan with about a hundred wives. Thor— he seemed Norwegian. They don't say much, those Scandinavians. I memba my grandmother Embla, the one named me. Don't recollect her saying one word though. Not one single word, evah.

Balder lay back, melancholy but resting, trying to detect movement of the craft, if any. It rumbled beneath him but as though idling or possibly checking a too rapid descent. If it were ever to come back up it would need that engine. Eyes closed, the cold nubbled decking beneath his head, he did not care to see who might be aboard with him. He doubted this barge was one he'd been on before but right now he did not care. Maybe a little. He put an arm under his head. From beneath his eyelids he saw the lurid light of the cab at the far end. The mist, if anything, seemed thicker than before. He lay, drifting with the barge.

He needed something to think about besides the way he felt, the hopeless pursuit of nothing, with the inferno at the end of it. He thought of great Odin, who talked as if being in the making himself, what with suffering opening up new places and all. He thought of great Odin being able to see him from — whatever he called that: a mountain, a tower, something. He had known Balder's thought. For some reason this got him thinking of Heisenberg's uncertainty principle, and the observer effect.

Balder is a smart man, wicked smart some would say, if they knew it. It was not too smart in the 1960s to think of college... unless you were also thinking of leaving Gottheim. What was there to do in Gott'im with concentrated formal learning and a degree? Nevertheless he had thought of it. Then Chrischana left, taking the incipient and unknown Daniel with her, and he, like most young in Gott'im before the war, joined up — but the war was on. The draft was, too. Some observers thought he should wait for that: the war then did not seem a good bet. Some observers thought Balder was none to smart for joining *in order* to go fight in Vietnam.

Balder has always been curious, has always read widely, and knew how to think about something; especially mechanical, applied; but also, if often unrequitedly, speculative. He didn't say much. He could make fun of himself — you might not notice this about him, but it was so.

You will have heard of the uncertainty principle. And of the related observer effect. Simply, if a subatomic particle can be pinpointed, the rate at which it's moving cannot be known; and vice versa. If one were able to observe these particles or their movements, the observing would itself change them or their movements. The instruments of measurement and observation would themselves work the change, making the data inaccurate to the reality of the observed/unobserved particle. Your findings would then be artificial. Or so says the observer effect.

Does that mean no one knows if these particles are of space-time at all? He wondered. And where would this barge, and the journey fit into it?

And, *Will I do or be different now I know great Odin is watching me?* Or — maybe he was just watching then because Hoder was there. Balder thought about his belief that God was watching him, watching every soul of man simultaneously. He believed God had made every subparticle and was ever principle, and so Balder had no trouble believing this. However he did not "know" or experience this in the way he had with great Odin. Face to face. He was drawn to the metaphorical conclusion that God was wise in keeping the knowledge of God's watching a secret from the creatures being observed. That experience with Odin had upset the whole works. Would Balder now be too concerned with great Odin and his presumed watching? How could he now live with this experience/knowledge?

From the slits of his eyes he lay observing the slight dark movements in the artificially lit cab.

If I think about this too much it will turn me into Theodora.

Maybe you don't remember Theodora. Balder too was trying to remember her. Except in his dreams, he could not recall much now about those left above. Theodora Prescott—Balder's old boss, the former mill owner and soon to be sister-in-law of Gloria; as Balder supposes. Maybe this is your first encounter with Gott'im's folk. Theodora is the townswoman so self-conscious that every personal encounter changes her surface. One never knows in reality who or what she is. However, like most observers, they remain unaware of this crucial fact. When she does something big they may say, "I never knew she had it in her." Or, "See that?—I knew all along she was quee-ah." Even Theodora does not know what she is. Often she thinks she's the observer-changing surface. Continually rearranging her fig leaves for social encounters, she nonetheless feels these movements are known, along with the pure nakedness underneath. Afterward she'll try to shrug and say oh well it's all me, fig leaves and nakedness, but then she breaks down and bawls. She's full of a lot of harebrained schemes and is happy in planning them, but often they result in dashed hopes and a lot of turmoil. To look at her from above, as I can do, is to see a work in progress that will all be scrapped in favor of something completely new and unheard-of. But Balder doesn't think of this. He just looks on her pityingly. If he did think it he'd say, Why all the trouble to her then? Why not just get her right the first time if you care so much about that? Which is a pretty good paraphrase of what he really wanted to say to great Odin about suffering Hoder, the whole god-thing, and the last battle.

Shucky

After a while, through the murkiness, Balder began to attend to the dark intermittently glowing movements in the cab at the far end of the barge. He also became aware that the murk around him was full of the dark mist-shapes he had seen on the barge carrying Hoder before he was taken to Asgard in the midst of a standing dream. Hoder was not here, but Balder was not alone after all. Then he wondered if perhaps he had not been acclimated enough, when he took the first ferry, to the presence of these ghosts. Maybe they had been there all along, right from the beginning, and he had just not been aware. He began to feel a bit lonesome in their midst and wanted to call out.

Why? He was unsure. Did he want attention? Simple notice? Did he want company? A touch of life? Friendliness? A party may be?

He laughed out loud at the thought. Some of the murk clouds turned toward him and he discerned faces, long faces full of melancholy and hopelessness. He began to feel so depressed that he wished for anything, even angst. If only he might see someone with enough spirit to show impassioned distress.

He looked on them all. "How long till we get theya?!" It was a declamation. Very loud.

"Three minutes, three hours, three days, what evah y'like!" This was said by a very gruff, almost growling, voice.

Balder had been lying back on his elbows, looking around on the sad shadow-clouds, but now he whipped his head back toward the cab and saw three large flaming eyes, like points of a triangle, staring at him in the dark. Though they were three, he knew them for eyes because they communicated intelligence. He sat up, instantly uneasy. He tried laughing at himself: He murmured. "I wanted angst, dint I?" The eyes did not seem set right to him. One was a bit higher and further apart than the others. He kept staring at them. His hackles rose till they could reach no higher. Then the eyes seemed to turn away, and redly light the cab again. He saw shadows there, swishing shadows, thick but contiguous and long, as though belonging to a single animal body. The movement reminded him of something. He watched. Then he knew:

Demon. Ferddy Sessions' hybrid wolf dog.

The movement in the cab was like Demon pacing on his chain in Sessions' dooryard. But bigger. Much bigger.

If you have read Israel Kimball's book, *Mystery Gottheim*, you already know the story of Demon and Dog-man. Dog-man, like his name implies, has the head of a man on a dog's body. 'Twas on this very night just past, in Gottheim, that Dog-man haunted the environs of the Town, *and* sundry of the townsfolk there—Lyman Bearce, the lumber baron, being one; and Demon, wolf-hybrid, being another. There were more but we won't go into that now—except to say that Elda Simon, Balder's mother, also saw the Dog-man and, being the local animal rehabilitator, was perplexed what to do about him, half man, half dog. They had gone a bit eyeball to eyeball and the Dog-man wasn't much interested. In truth he ignored her as beneath his notice, I guess. In her turn, she had to give him up as being beyond her powers.

Dog-man had got the wolf-hybrid to chase with him after the white deer named Sugarloaf—gont kill it—but he failed to lead Demon after Sugarloaf into the tire fire. So escaping Demon ran off. Dog-man, however, did go into the fire after Sugarloaf and its form along with thousands inside it was then burned up.... But I think I will tell you that that was not the end of it or them. I wish I didn't have to. However, the body of the pure white deer was *not* destroyed—so take heart.

In the schoolhouse of my childhood in Gott'im we were given a classical education without the classical languages, but if we went on with our schooling we learned the Latin and Greek and of their influence on the English as developed out of the Anglo-Saxon (or Old English).

We children found we had much of the lore of these great civilizations already embedded in our superstitions and stories supped round the hearth, the campfire, and the schoolyard. The devil hound was a favorite. You can find him just about everywhere story erupts, and he is very ancient and important. The Vikings told of Garm, whose breast was bloody, inhabiting the mists of *Nifl-heim* —when not at home seated before Hel, goddess of the unheroic dead. Howling, he signals the loosing of wolves upon the earthen realm, or Midgard. His fullsome howls are said to signal the onset of the Giant invasion of Asgard, which invasion, and subsequent war, is called *Ragnarök*—the gods twilight, worldwide destruction, and the remaking of all things. You might dispute his signaling the remaking... since that seems out his ken.

Then there are Cerberus and Black Shucky, the former being of course the Greek mythological hell-hound with the three heads and covered with snakes, guarding Hades' Gates. The latter, Black Shucky, whose name perhaps derives from Cerberus, succubus, *succa,* is shaggy, so maybe *that's* where the name comes from. Who knows? Shucky came to us Yankees a long time ago with our East Anglian Puritan ancestors' story-food. He haunted the East Anglian imagination with sightings that left his horrified victims alive to continue their apparently normal walks, but changed in some profound way. You never knew when or where he might appear. It is my opinion that this was he who showed himself to a few Gott'imites last night, the night Daniel died on the wooded mountainside. Those two incidents, the boy's death and the sighting, were unrelated.

On seeing Shucky Balder, I think, can use some help.

"Balda, I am heah. Don't be afraid."

"Huh?! That you Abna?!"

"Yuh*t*. I am heah."

"Waya?"

He looks all round trying to penetrate the mists and mist faces.

"I'm in the mist. Look fah my eyes. Maybe you can see them. But if not, fear not."

He looks around.

"Caunt. What is that thing? Horse? Giant dog? S'gut three eyes— like yaws but not like'em any."

I knew what he meant: the light of hell is not the same as that of heaven. But you knew that.

"That is Black Shuck. He was in Gott'im last night."

"He was?" Balder's gaze went back to the cockpit.

I conjured—or rather *gave*—him a few glimpses of Shucky, as Dog-man, appearing to Lyman Bearce and James Fay (the developer from away—Gloria's brother and supposed fiancé of Theodora). Also Cindabilla, who had Daniel's jacket, and Peter Prince, Daniel's currently lapsing common-law stepfather. Or, rather, he was beginning to lapse back into alcoholism until he saw the Dog-man.

"Gorry," said Balder. "A man's head!"

"Yuh*t*."

"What's he waunt with'em?"

"To tempt them."

"Huh? I'd think he don't look s'tempting. Fact, f'I could get away now, I would."

"Good. By some grace, maybe, they could see him and it scared each one. It's when he caunt be seen while present that he's most to be feared."

"Uh, —huh?"

"Nevah mind. His spirit is ravenous, gluttonous, greedy, that kind o'thing."

"Oh."

"Watch out. He wants you. Waunts match wits with you. Don't be afraid."

"Easy fah you."

"Go ovah'n talk t'him."

"... Abnah...."

"Go on. Memba yo-ah training in the Marine Corps. Game face, they call it?"

"Y'mean what I been using since I de-listed?" He grinned by way of example. "The one says I dare you to smack me?"

"That."

He sat there, gazing at the shadows pacing within the cab and its shifting lurid light. Slowly he stood and walked over the greasy pocked humming decking through the faintly parting murk-faces. He stood gazing into the wheelhouse. Light reflected from the wraparound windows as Shucky paced back and forth. The great dog stopped sometimes to look at him. Unnerving, disquieting. Balder gave no sign.

"You's in Gott'im last night?"

The three-eyed dog said nothing. Balder stood, his hand on the filthy steel doorframe, watching him. "Did you say sumpthin bit ago?—How long we'd be to the inferno? What's that s'posed t'mean? It don't make sense—three hours, three days."

Pacing there, turning his great narrow head this way and that, like a black afghan, Black Shucky did not look as he did in the glimpse I'd given Balder. Here he was all dog, about the size of Gylfaginning, huge as a pony, and otherwise dog except for the three flaming eyes. One of these eyes seemed more —infernal— than the other two. Balder did not like its fierce grinning light. He tried to concentrate on the lower two eyes, tried to think of them as being not too unlike my faintly light-limned eyes, but without much success. He kept trying. Pretending to be normal, not unnerved.

The dog stopped. "*Sense?*" Turning to the man, he said this in the gruff voice Balder had heard before, but lower. After all, the man was right there about four-five feet away. "*What's sense?*" He seemed to grin, his long pale tongue hanging out beneath his snout.

Balder was silent. Then he said, "Guess we caunt have a conversation then? They in't no real talking without it."

He had tempted Balder with this many times before. The great dark dog grinned. His eyes of flame, staring with stupendous arrogance at our hero. "That sounds like fun. For you I will pretend sense. I'll make as much sense as you please.... But, let me play the proper host: have some of the _whats-it_." The giant dog brushed past Balder, knocking him with great, but casual, careless force against the wheelhouse window facing the barge. Balder saw him rise on his hind legs and stand licking the honey-tasting rime off the roof, at first somewhat delicately but then with increasing vigor. He scrambled up and began rolling around the roof of the cab, twisting and turning as you have maybe seen your own dog do when it finds something dead to roll around in.

"If he doesn't stop that he'll fall asleep, wake up too soon, and then, it being his job to keep you out, you may not get into Hel. He wants you to stay on the bahdge and go back." Balder heard me say this as in his thought. He understood that it was my guidance and without sound or verbal construction. But he did not want to get into Hel so he stood there watching the great dog make a greedy ass of himself. I had to correct him. "Training, Balder. Unless you refuse out right, you _ah_ going."

"Better stop that," said Balder. "You could get sick."

The dog scrambled to his paws, great nails clicking, and jumped down; smelling stinky and wet. He ducked and went back into the cab. He stood front-facing, staring at Balder in the dark window reflection.

"Now you can use that greed when it's time. Save it till you get near Hel, see it glowing, then get him to gorge. But watch him: He won't be all lies, he won't be all truth: He's got plans for you."

Abner was silent and spoke to Balder no more.

"Have some?" said the dog.

Some no doubt will wonder why I encouraged Balder three or four times not to be afraid and then turned around and told him it was to fear. Let me make plain that, in its invisibility, the temptations of this creature do not inspire the proper fear. But when that cloak is removed and they see _this, then_ they may be too frightened to do the sinning. Fear of what the sin really looks like checks them and perhaps sends some away from it. But it had been better that I said with the Psalm, "Thou shall not be afraid for the terror by night."

Shuck sneered, part growl. "Don't you like the _whats-it_?"

"I do," said Balder. He reached to the top of the wheelhouse and coated his hand. He licked the _what-is-it-?_ off his long fingers with famishment, then slowly with delight. "S'good."

"Have moah. Have as much as you waunt. Theya's no end of it. Go on." The dog appeared to have little trouble getting his growly voice around his vowels, Gott'im-sounding words. He seemed, at the moment at least, to favor the softer yankee way of speaking.

Balder was casual, his neutral game face on. "Why'd you act like'd make you sick? You stopped when I said so. Should I get sick? That what you waunt?"

The dog grinned, tongue lolling.

"Just put you to sleep s'all. Like a nice rest?"

"I'd like to get into— waya evah it is yaw going."

The grin deepened. He stared at Balder. "Notice anathin?" it said.

Balder looked through the cab and saw the murk beyond glowing of its own accord. He looked around and overhead and saw the mist everywhere glowing, not harshly or brightly but faintly. A dull if coppery glowing murk. Again he felt his hackles rise.

"Theya's still plenty of time to fill up'n rest," said the dog. "We won't be theya yet fah nother hour. Don't worry..." The eyes in his long face grew brighter, particularly the top eye — so much more filled with intelligence. The other eyes were easier to bear: They but showed an unthinking animal fury: rapacity: something Balder could fight. "... I'll be sure to wake you. My charge is to bring souls to Hel... waya the lot belongs. You'll get into Hel—don't worry." The fire in his cunning eye brightened.

Right about then Balder desperately wanted a conference with Abner. He looked around. No Abner. The infrared mist showed with infrared faces now. The commuters on their way from limbo to hell. No Abner to help him sort it out. Could *anything* this dog said be believed? He tried to keep his orders clear: *Dog wants me out, I got to get in.*

Grinning himself, he kept licking his fingers though they were now clean of the mist-food. "What's in this hell, anaway? It the same as the Bible hell— like all the stories? Devils'n all, pitchforks?"

"Oh it's pleasant. Betta'n sunlit-lands, betta'n mist-land. Rather warm. You'll see. Have some?"

"No," said Balder frowning. "I've hed 'nough."

The eyes of Shuck flamed out. It growled. The lips of its muzzle, rising, exposed fangs.

A low compressed growl like the roaring of the tire fire from a distance, or the quaking massive pulp-digester with its load heating, as the blow valve begins releasing its pressure.... Or the first time —approaching the fields of fire in Nam. Balder began to sweat —something separate from the mist.

It said, "*I'm not taking you in theya less you gorge on it.*"

Balder stared at him, refusing intimidation. The dog bristled. Fangs bared, it seemed to think of physical attack, the third eye was thinking, governing the two eyes below. It stared at Balder, lightly growling, thinking. The glow through the windows and all about them grew. The roaring of the inferno was heard, blending with the growling of the Shuck.

"*This is for the unheroic dead. You want in there you gorge and die.*"

The man said, "Balder in theya yet? The real one, mythic, killed by Hodah? Was he unheroic?"

The great animal began pacing again, a great dark shadow against increasing light of the inferno. He stopped and looked at Balder. "His death was. Loki's triumph. Odin's Balder would have been a great hero if not for the theft of his death without the battle." It was said as though by rote, dispensed with. "Hel won't have you less you come likewise. A wise mistress—Hel." His top eye was quick with cunning.

"Tell you what," said Balder. "You hev some. I'll watch. *Then* I'll hev some. Kinda hard to resist it. But it's like when drinking sombreros— you waunt a buddy to drink with, huh."

The great dog hesitated. He looked at the mist-food above from the corner of his left eye. He fixed his smart eye on Balder. "What you want in there? Why do you *care*?" it said. Balder noticed that its voice was more angular now, more canine. He had dropped his us-folks manner.

"Have some?" Balder reached up and swiped the mist food off. He shoved it under Shucky's snout. Swiftly the dog licked it clean.

It said, "Why care, why care?"

Balder reached up. "Have moah n' I'll tell you all'bout it, buddy." He gave the dog to lick again but it scrambled up and began gorging itself, then rolling in it as before. Balder watched it, growing more and more amazed. The dog was feasting through its pores, licking the cab roof, licking his fur like a cat. Trying to eat every bit of mist food before it hardly had time to form. Before the supply had disappeared, however, the great dog rolled supine on the edge of the roof. Its great paws ceased waving. It crashed to the iron floor. Shuck lay in a stupor, grinning. He fell promptly to sleep.

Or maybe he had passed out. Balder, having leapt out of the way, now stepped back to check, but could not tell. It had that look of stone a sleeper did not have. As though if shaken it would not stir.

"Huh," said Balder, marveling. Probably like Ferddy Sessions unconscious on Sessions' kitchen floor.

He stepped back and turned to look at the mist-faces. They seemed as long and bleak as ever, staring at the comatose Shucky, or at nothing in particular. Balder glanced into the cab wondering what would become of them: Did this thing need its operator? Was Shucky it? But he did a double take on seeing the little girl at the wheel: the same little girl he'd seen before, wearing the same blue-flowered pajamas! How could that be? With her thick brown curls, fast she was becoming a shadow against the light of Hel. He stared at her small back, the glowing light of the approaching inferno gaining strength and color, a deep bright red. The strength of its roaring increased; the craft's engine now hardly heard.

He leaned in, saying loudly, "Is that you?"

She turned from the wheel, at which she stood upon the operator's stool. He could see the lights of her eyes. She was smiling. "It's me," she piped.

He said, "Waya'd you come fom? Is this the same ferry?"

She nodded and turned back, her small dark hands on the wheel. She was so friendly he did not hesitate to step in. He came to the control panel and stood looking out at the slowly increasing glow. Then he looked around the cab for her father but saw no one. In a corner, close by the door, was a narrow hatchway open with what looked like miscellaneous custodial equipment inside.

He said, "I'm confused. This the boat I's on then?"

Again she smiled at him, nodding. He thought, *Then Hoder's on the next one, behind this.*

"But waya's Fatha? Poppa, you said."

Her glimmer-eyes were so calm, contrasting against her dark skin. Happy undisturbed child's eyes. She seemed very glad to see him.

"He got off to go to the bathroom. But Shucky got on so I hid in the broom closet. It started us going. Pop said if it ever comes, go in there. It's not smart enough to look there, he says."

She faced forward out the window again. Her small contours, framed with sausage curls, were glowing.

Balder stood stroking his beard, mistrusting his senses. *Went to the bathroom?*

"Shucky's usually at the gate, but sometimes he prowls."

"I heard," said Balder. "What gate?"

"Hel's gateway. He guards it."

Like this girl, I will fear no evil. But he was afraid: "The mist don't— look s'dirty now."

"It's not dirty. Mist cleans the air and feeds things, Pop says. It's the barge that's dirty. The mist feels not too clean sometimes, but it is. The things that are dirty feel dirtier when their in it—"

"—Pop says." Balder grinned and she grinned back. "That explains why you nevah look dirty, only dewy." He thought: And why it feels filthy to me.

"Poppa says sometimes I glisten.... He's shy, did you know?"

"Yuh*t*." He had that thought about the ferryman: At first (on account of what Abner said about trickiness), he'd mistrusted if the big dark dog and the ferryman were the same, but then dismissed it. The spirit of each was too far removed from the other. "What happens when that happens?—Fatha gets off, Shucky gets on. This boatload, I mean? Will the dog stay like that long?"

"I don't know what that means exactly. Sometimes it eats too much and can't be at the gate. I can't move it off the barge, it's too big and heavy. Poppa says Hel gets mad but what can she do? He says it's part of being unhero... unhero-ic, and we can't do anything. I'd have to go back in the closet if he doesn't come."

"He'll be on the next barge, though," said Balder, glad to reassure her about her father. "I'll get the dog off fah you."

"Thank you!!" She smiled and now he saw her relief, though she had not betrayed any particular worry before.

Balder studied the control panel, trying to understand how the child navigated. "How'd you know how to get theya?"

She pointed to a small display, a screen no bigger than 12 x 12 centimeters, lit green and showing but two blue dots. "Poppa says we only need these two dots each time for the next station, and not to show any more. You see how this little one here, that's us, moves toward the bigger one? I do that with this wheel." She looked at him to see, not so much if he understood, but if she had explained well.

He nodded happily. "Got it!"

She smiled.

Now the mist was very bright and very orange-red. The roaring and screeching and clanking—industrial cacophony—almost drowned her out. "We're here," she shouted. She touched back on the throttle and he felt the crunch and heft of the craft against the dock. He had seen nothing but the reddish mist till now but things formed quickly out of the lurid mist-light. "I don't think I can get the hawsers," she said.

"I'll do it," said Balder over his shoulder, exiting the cab. He almost stumbled onto Black Shuck but stepped aside in time. Looking up he got a swift impression of redly gleaming lithic flanks, of mountains-sides or rock fortresses rising in monumental tiers. The rumbling, screeching of its engines. The sharp caustic smell of burning and sulfurous seethings stinging his nostrils and eyes. He squatted to work, putting forth his strength to shove the filthy creature through the luridly glowing mist-folk and off the greasy surface onto the dock. He spoke to the folk to keep them back but it was unnecessary. They seemed in no hurry to debark. Balder jumped back aboard and went forward, threw the thick filthy line over, and went aft to do likewise. He skipped off again to secure the barge then went to the dog and stooped over it. It stank like the mutilated corpse of an enemy on the battlefield.

Like a body left of its spirit. He pushed it to one side on the dock and motioned the folk off. They moved like the mist they'd become: bright red, or variations of same and particalized; a collection, each, of particles, it seemed to him. Then he looked after them. Maybe he shouldn't have ushered them.

They were now no more than up-drifting mist-glowing wavers of heat, rising toward a massive fortress wall in which gaped a rich red darkness, this great dark maw itself wavering in the rising fumes. The whole arduous face of the firelit mountain, in tiers rising and red-gleaming, was wavery and wandering in his gaze. It seemed at once ethereal and monumental, the foundations of a great dark world—the world above. Not so much crystalline but heavy and mafic; as though of monstrous solidity veiled with the contorted impressions of a dreamer. He looked down to grab hold his arm and squeeze but saw himself drenched in the wet of the mist that rose without surcease in the fuming heat. Where had all this water come from? Was it water of himself outpouring, transpiration of his fears? He wondered; before being carried away to other thoughts by his smoke-smitten gaze. He blinked rapidly and brushed at his eyes with his woolen-clad arm. He heard a crunching and grinding sound nearby, separate from the more distant pandemonium of hell.

Balder turned to look and saw the bow of another barge butting up to the first. The manic-seeming ferryman had jumped out and was hastily securing its bow. Balder saw another bargeman securing the stern, and the first now hurried, arms flailing, toward the gateway of his little girl's barge. He had to leap the dark carcass of Shucky, Poppa's long dark legs like pistons pushing. He ran to the cab and grabbed his little girl who, after a firm embrace, began giggling and squirming. She seemed to play over his form like a happy squirrel running up and down a tree trunk, as he stood tall and still, his eyes flaming, eyes moving as with her glee.

In his wake trailed a mist of glowing particles. It stopped and regrouped itself as a living form before Balder, saying, "I saw the Valkyr take you from me, brother. Blind I am no more thanks to your forgiveness. I thank you for speaking for Hodr to Great Odin."

As before, Balder heard his speech in the old tongue and understood it. He then perceived the ghost looking down on Shuck and was glad it could see. "That's okay," he said. "You know this dog?"

"Tis Garm, the Hel-hound, Hela's dog. He kept us in *Hel-heim*. But I was forced to go betimes to beg pardon, up through the molten Mountain as burning rock."

But Balder did not want to hear of it. His eyes grew misty and he bowed his head. Tears fell from under his lashes and he wiped them on the woolen inside of his arm.

"You won't hev t'go back now?"

"He is asleep. I will go down, it may be, on this ferry to the roots of the mountain and around up the other side. I would like to cross over at the Count of Time, and ship to the topside, where your monster killer has said is your son and descendant. But I do not think that will happen. I cannot tell what will become of me. Yet I must get away before Garm wakes. He has done this before," indicating his sleep, "and others get out by it. But I am unsure of my fate."

He drifted past Balder as the ferryman mechanically moved to loosen the hawser. Balder stared after him, amazed by his mention of Abner and Daniel's position. The engine began and some of the spirits just escaped from Hel came onboard. Balder wondered why there weren't more than but three or four to his seeming. He would have raised a crowd himself and gone out had he been kept in and saw a chance of escape. He waved to the little girl in the blue-print pajamas, where she stood at the wheelhouse hatchway waving back. He watched as the ferry drifted off and grew faint in a moiling of glowing mist and smoke.

Then he remembered he wasn't one of those escaping, raising the crowd to go with him. He was just a confused old Balder-boy supposed to go to hell for no reason. And Daniel was in a star on top of the Mountain of Time.

Balder Meets Hela

He closed his eyes standing there, wishing to see Daniel, trying to remember that Daniel had died and gone to heaven; wishing even to *recollect his face*, think how all this came about. Trying for all of this: and to think that he was, by some miracle he did not understand, supposed to see his son again.

And then, his eyes closed, Daniel's face was before him again: his brown solemn eyes lit, his mouth unsmiling. But Balder, eyes closed, saw in his son's face and lighted eyes the emanating spirit of love. Balder, standing below the ramparts of hell, felt himself melting: not from the heat of the inferno-fed mountain, not from the fumes of unconsumed hatred firing into the mist of the dark night far above. He was dissolving in the love of his own kinship with Daniel, feeling the great all-observing influence of the miraculous Spirit of Love. *Daniel.*

You can do it, fatha.

"Okay," said he aloud.

The face of Daniel faded. Balder opened his eyes. The great iron studded gate of hell ahead, straight up the causeway, was open. He left the ferry behind, with its mist-passengers he was himself now moving (but he in the flesh). He did not look back to watch the boat pass away, but went straight ahead, thinking of Daniel. Thinking of Daniel. Of Daniel.

The image of Daniel had vanished. He felt still the residue of the Love and took courage. *Maybe it won't be so bad.*

Then, as he walked:

It felt like the first time. And he was *back there* again…while walking up the stone and iron causeway into hell. His left hand had begun to throb and burn. He did not look at it. He was back there again and had made this mistake the first time he saw combat. When the ground shook and he was part of *it* he had the confidence in his training: He was *all there* in the combat, it was all working together, teamwork and training: But his training had failed in just one detail: firing: holding the barrel of his M-16 instead of its grip. Swelling, throbbing, burning. He looked down at it to make sure, and caught sight of the molten river, below, through the stone-held iron grating of the bridge. He thought, 'Without my rifle I am useless.'

The bright umbrage of the molten lake of fire beneath him, slowly moving, darkly crusted here and there—his throbbing hand was forgotten. He looked up, at the sweating glistening walls, then down again, his gaze and person drifting through the specters to the edge of the causeway. He looked over the parapet, saw that the vast fortress walls appeared lapped and plastic; lapped upon by living fire, plastic; melting but mysteriously still standing strong against the crusting molten lava.

Was the thing alive? This vast fortress: Was it floating? How can all these heavy elements, this dense elemental liquid, and heat of fuming particulate, seem so... so unlawful to their counterparts on earth? Maybe time was slower here, like it could be faster in Asgard with the Tree's awful growing? Again he realized he had no understanding of *time* on this journey. Maybe they were just taking longer to—. On earth, he felt sure, those walls would bleed and collapse into the molten mass so thick and viscous about their feet.

Or— is this lithic golden-red gleaming monstrous wall already in to its knees? How far below was the mantle of rock sinking into the burning pyroclastic flow of in these molten elements? Then he realized: This was the stuff of which Hoder had been made. Down there all the Hoders were mixed together, flowing.

He looked up again, his eyes blinking, nostrils burning, and saw the walls looming up, up out of his sight into ever deepening red-glowing darkness: the walls shaded with monochromatic dimness, keeping still their faintly glimmering sheen as they passed high above into fuming wavering darkness.... Up there somewhere opposite was the *Count of Time*.

The Gateway, through which he passed, was arched fire-sweating mafic materials, the iron spikes of its portcullis withdrawn but pointing downward. Within were seeming-guards, dark spirits of filth and fire, a bit larger than himself. They smiled on him with glee. He felt his naked fear without moving his features, his game face firmly in place. He would not acknowledge to their fire-faces what was inside him. He felt himself swell, rise to the occasion: It was none of their God-damned business, anyway.

Balder wondered that they did not try to stop him, as he had supposed they would. As Shuck might have. But as he passed, and heard their filthy jeering, he felt such hunger take hold of his entrails, stomach and gullet, that all questions vanished: He *had to eat!* Suddenly, his knees weak, legs like rubber bands, Balder looked desperately around for the mist-food.

There was none.

Only the great high walls above, shimmering and sweating.

He looked back at the fiery guards and saw them first abusing and then inhaling the fresh spirits who had come down from limbo and sunlit-lands on both barges. He saw a co-mingling of the true demons, as he thought them, with the spirits of humankind. The hunger he experienced in passing so near them was infection, influence, that passed off, eased just a bit, after he walked by. They did not try to molest him in any other way but he sensed that somehow they had done what they could with him: These were great phantoms of *need* and *want*. He remembered the consumers far above. He thought of the *What-is-it-?* As though it were even then on his tongue, but his belly felt wretched and sucked dry. He moved his tongue around, biting the insides of his mouth, sucking his lips and taking comfort from the memory of his last meal.

The great bailey before him diverged in three ways but he kept walking straight ahead where the middle way climbed through the rampart toward a great stair between intermittently gleaming rock walls. Passing toward it, on either hand he saw the ramps descending, and perceived that from therebelow issued the cacophony of the great engines of hell. *That's waya they do all the wuk*, he thought. *That's waya the orders fom the halls above go. The offices is upstayas, just like at the mill.*

He kept on toward the stairs, still in the midst of spirits, some darker, some bright, who followed lower on either side, or continued above with him, by some existential command he could not discern. He was so hot in their midst that, as he climbed the stairway, he thought to remove his mackinaw as fast as his fingers could fumble it off. But he heard, or had some sure impression, that Abner was somewhere saying, *Leave on the jacket. Don't remove the wool no matter what.* He was grateful to have the impression or thought. So sure and real in his being, it was like treasure: He felt instantly stronger and even a slight bit cooler and less hungry than he had been but a moment ago.

"Thank you," he whispered. *Thank you thank you.* He held the words of gratitude in his now less troubled mind, and they were, somehow as well, in his mouth. Nourishing.

It almost seemed he was falling asleep again as he climbed. He became less aware in some ways, the ways relating to thought, but more aware of things usually perceived as peripheral, such as uncoupled sensations and patterns, patterns surrounding him. He felt more than noticed the rise and fall of his feet, the turning of the stairway, its narrowing and widening, its conjunction with hallways and levels; heating and cooling, crowding of specters and thinning of crowds, the unending interconnectedness of rooms, chambers, passages and doorways. He could not seem to rouse himself, he did not think to know if he should. The odd disconnection of his thoughts began to perturb him, as though they were part of the pattern but should not be. He felt vaguely that perhaps they should connect up, connect with one another as the layout or pattern of hell seemed interminably to do. One thought seemed recurring, coinciding to the environment of this place, apiece with the pattern or structure or texture through which he moved like an automaton or disconnected particle that had not quite been pinned down or scoped out —maybe by theoretical science but not by the science of experimentation. The labyrinth. The labyrinth. …What was that Abner had said to Hoder?... Something —topside?

    …The labyrinth, the labyrinthine stair. Yes, that sounded familiar, the Labyrinthine Stair. Tolkien thought of it... and others, too. The "till we have faces" lady... and the plasma bolting hither and yon throughout the sun. *But*, he thought as he climbed ever upward (feeling the pattern of graviton-drag on his body and being), *the Labyrinthine Stair wound downward, down, not up*. Only the plasma went up... eventually... after about 20,000 years or so of the labyrinth.... And the great heroes Lúthien and Beren went down it to fetch back the Silmaril somebody lost... somebody or other... somebody or other.... And when they got down there they saw it in Morgoth's crown.... *Bloody awful* as the English would say. *Bloody awful's* what the Simon descendents'd say if they had stayed in East Anglia.... What's it doing in Morgoth's crown?

    He stopped. Sweating, Balder Simon looked around.

    He saw the great dark tail-end of what he took to be Black Shucky disappearing round the corner. Its stench, like that of rotting carcass, lingered. Balder took off after it, groups of spirits bright or drear parting or not for him as he ran. The dog was going through the doorway at the end of a torch-lit granite stone hallway, flecks of mica glinting, its hardwood floors dully gleaming as though recently waxed. Heedless, the mechanic followed. The thought flashed on him that Shuck had actually knocked him loose from his somnambulant and maze-patterned reverie. He remembered the great dog in Tolkien who, waiting outside the gates not far from the Thangorodrim, had taken off Beren's hand. Bit it clean, wrist, fingers, hand and all, where it held the divine light imprisoned in the fabulous jewel. Maybe he shouldn't have threatened the great dog with it, thought Balder: What would have happened if he offered to share?

    The thought, vagrant or not, made him laugh out loud, a happy chortling. With that every last spirit in the hall disappeared and Balder, the Gott'imite, millwright, Vietnam veteran, fishing fool, stopped short outside the door of the menace dog's escape. Maybe the dog wasn't escaping....

Why was I chasing it, anaway?

He looked inside. There was the three-eyed hell hound, half-sprawled, prone and panting—under a huge scrollworked desk. A great older lady calmly sitting there, eyed Balder in vast and earthy surprise. She was great, he felt at that moment, because her size was great. Great as great Odin's it seemed. She sat on a massive wooden— *throne* was the sole word he could find for it: It was a bit like the Morris chair in the front room but carven, and massive as herself, with posts to either side of her great mature yet smooth face. It curved high behind her back, a back that was regal, unstooping. Her great hands rested, belying the surprise in her eyes, on either massive wooden armrest. She spoke to the three-eyed creature in the ancient tongue and the man told by her cold tone, if not the words or expression, that she was not pleased. To Balder she said,

"Garmr left his post, you got in. He heaped worse on me in leading you, an outlander, right into my office."

There was, of course, no word for office in that tongue, but his head seemed to manage bureau or office and let it go with that.

He said, surprising himself as well, "In't he always up theya tempting people to hahm n'evil?"

"He is two places," she said shortly. "I am two places. You are two places."

"...I don't like the sound of it. That could make me beside myself."

There was silence but for the panting of Shucky. Slowly, very slowly, Hel smiled. Her gaze led him to step over the threshold. The great personification of Hel slightly smiled with genuine humor, no sarcasm, nor with malice, contempt, or even patronage: a real if brief smile. There was something familiar in it, in its matter-of-factness. A quality of naturalness that, along with its brevity and lapsing to silent neutrality, suggested to him the Scandinavian temperament familiar in his grandparents or in Olive Bartlett, Asa's wife. He thought, *Gorry. Am I dreaming?*

How can— Why would she run Hell?

But Hel was large, hefty, strong. Hel was bulk like a mountain of flesh. She was something like the Valkyries but not beautiful, muscular or, seemingly, active. She might bestride a Clydesdale with fitting proportion, but she would not ride one with every part of her being as did the women warriors. Her eyes were lit not with fire but ice, a gaze clear as shining blue ice he might say. Eyes that were not so much lit as perfectly clear and clean. He had to give her this: She had authority.

Shuck stared at him with those three flaming eyes, the brighter for being in shadow beneath her desk. The desk was as shapely as the desk chair, or throne—was it?—on which she sat: a large wooden table, of the antique type, with thick carved legs and carven struts shaped like upside down angel wings. They gleamed dully in fire-lights from sconces on the granite stone and oak paneled walls. On flanking walls flamed great hearths, their lintels overlaid with carved oak mantles, complementing other furnishings in the chamber. He glimpsed all and caught the flash of Shucky's yellow teeth, pulled back in a grin. He glanced around.

There were great others, also human-shaped as he, in this hall; but supine. He thought that odd but gave Hela his attention: It was the right thing to do.

She said, "He is out there, or up there as you call it, in spirit. He does not need to go there in the body. I need him here: He has duties in the body, same as you or I. He roams in spirit, even" — she paused a moment as if considering— "now." He saw her pondering the word. "...Searching out other bodies, other beings, to inhabit and school."

Habit, thought Balder.

She spoke slowly, calmly, but with consideration. In her ice-clear gaze he thought he saw her entirely present to him and yet... present somewhere other, too—was how it struck him.

She was a model of grave decorum, her grey-white hair swept up not tautly but neatly in a bun. Upon her desk stood a winged helm, but small, not ostentatious. She said, "He has other duties as well, but to leave his post, going off so, is sport to him." Balder felt the word was "fun," but sport was good, too. *Sport* he settled on.

He said, "We got sports passing through Gott'im all the time. They go in the deep woods fah game n'fishing. Brook trout I like the best.... But I see what y'mean. They's always someplace else as well. Maybe in the Hancock Building down theya in Mass. Maybe the World Trade Center—who's to say waya they work."

Again she slowly smiled. She said, "Not quite that... but something like to it."

"So...." he said and looked around. *Yaw the boss, that it?*

There upon a couch, nigh one hearth—part in shadow, part in light—reclined perhaps the most beautiful man, or large man-like being, that Balder had ever seen. He thought, *That's one they gods.*

The scent of burning wood smelled like incense to him. Balder felt a soothing silence in the room, accentuated by the fall of ash, a crumbling bit of ember, gentle crackle of a flame. He was surprised or thoughtful about many things here; as he stood nearer, both respectful and shifting slightly from one foot to the other, lightly restive yet done in; his right hand clasping his left arm in its wool mackinaw. (Balder had not been offered a chair.) Shuck was silent under the desk, its snout on crossed paws. It seemed asleep, but maybe not.

Balder did not notice the engines of hell far below unless he leaned an ear for the sound and listened. He could forget it in the other things of this experience: great figures sitting silently or lounging here and there about the chamber. There were many ladies, nobles, lordly even kingly, and he thought of various cultures, times. Some of them reminded him of artifacts Egyptian, Grecian, or portraits painted long ago of heroic men and women. Some wore suits and ties. She had papers on her great desk, and... *scrolls*,... one rolled open spread before her. Faintly shining candelabrum. Inkpots, were they? A steel nibbed pen? Not a quill, he noted. She had also large goblets, a great flagon. He thought not to think about the wine. He looked at Baldr. *Odd*, he thought. They need fire to be comfortable in hell?

"It's Odin's Baldr? Frigga's? Who's that with him?"

"That is Nanna, Baldr's bride." She also was beautiful and half golden, half in shadow, leaning toward her lover as in some gilt tableau.

He lowered his voice. "Looks like he's wounded."

"Yes. His blind brother slew him with the mistletoe."

"But waunt it really Loki done it?"

He saw something, a look elsewhere, passing through her gaze, through her straight clear eyes.

"Yes," she said. "Loki uses them like tokens."

"Even gods?"

"...If he can."

Balder glanced again at Baldr. He looked at him, wondering if it were okay. Was it maybe impolite to stare so; but he didn't mean to stare. He only wanted to look at Baldr.

As who would not, had they once seen Baldr? With a spirit of dejection, the god gazed at the polished floor agleam with reflected sconce and firelight. He was dressed in gilt and leathern armor through a chink of which was seen the wound, both scarred and partly weeping, maybe pus and blood, but dark: Balder could not tell. His hair flowed a golden mantle round his leathern armored shoulders. He wore still his winged helm; it also was more modest than those of the Valkyries and the assembled gods he'd seen in Asgard. His great gleaming sword, with straight blood-gutter lay near to his lax hand.

Balder wondered at the pair so beautiful. He expected, as it would on earth, that the scene would lose its initial power over his admiration each time he looked from Hel to Baldr and his wife, but no. Each time he saw them he was struck anew by their beauty and the pathos of their plight. There beside them on low tables were untouched cups of mead, wine goblets, fruits of every kind on platters, bread and hard cheese. The flickering lights picked out the gilt and bits of silver in their garments. He looked back at Hel, reluctantly.

"But Odin? Odin doesn't?"

"No. Not as a rule. Odin desires freedom, free service to his allegiance."

"But what about —..."

"His passion sometimes gets the better of him. But that is not the same. Loki loves to trick, beguile, seduce. It gives him the illusion of gaining what he does not, cannot, possess."

Balder considered this. He knew he would think about it again later, and again. He thought perhaps he understood it in its spiritual aspect. He had questions about many aspects of this experience, one of which was why he was here, why she didn't seem to want him here. There was lots about this conversation he would not understand... like many of the conversations he'd had in Gott'im. Maybe he would never understand. He wasn't sure he had a right to understand everything that happened... even to himself.... Let alone what happened to that Baldr there, the beautiful Baldr.

Balder lowered his voice again, looking away from the sad god toward her. He said, "He seems... not too happy. Odin says he can't be in the last battle...." This was, of course, by way of asking.

The goddess seemed almost without his notice to change a bit her look, her tone or manner. Perhaps her mood. He could not tell, and in truth did not really take much note of any change until the mood or whatever it was gained some.

At first she said nothing to this, but then, "Hermod came, the messenger seeking leave for Baldr, but my terms, though generous, could not be met."

Balder had been standing there before her at some little distance. His eyes sometimes turned to great now grinning Shucky; clasping his arm, the one above the hand he burned on the barrel of his rifle that first battle. Now he felt a bit of draft, from where he knew not. It may have been, like so much here (as he thought), from the goddess herself. Her gaze was very clear and so neutral it seemed cold. He could not say the gaze was cold the way a cold look went in Gott'im. It was somehow different: not a *show* of not caring... somehow it was other. He crossed and clasped his arms in either hand, shifted his stance.

He said, "The Last Battle." It was said with some heat. It came to him sometimes. Not often. There could be fire there... sometimes. He *held and used* it often in the war. "At least it's to be THE LAST." His gaze on her he knew was warm. He could not help it. "And what will you people do who revel in war, you gods? That all you know to do—fight wars?"

She looked at him.

"I can show you Loki…if you want to see him."

Huh?

"Yes, if you want."

He stared at her, then away. He felt the heat abate. After all, why is he here?

"Oh. Okay, sure. So he can trick me, too? Seduce me? I'm no smotta'n Hodah, you know."

"He will not be able to do that... as and where he is. But he is here. What you might call a … prisoner. Down below. We had to take certain measures."

Balder got the sense she meant the word certain at its true verbal meaning, though she did not emphasize the word. She seemed not to want to convince him, of anything. She had authority. She was immortal. He exercised no skepticism or doubt, but a kind of game bravado. He would be flip and curious to see the Nazi in his imprisonment... and if he were stupid, tricked, and trapped... well... he has been to hell and back before. He grinned. Much as he had grinned at Shucky before tricking him into a stupor.

"Cuss, I'll see that bastid! Lead me to'em! Looks like Hitler, I s'pose? Teeny mustache? He's two places, too, s'pose?"

"You'll need some of this, I think."

She poured out of the gleaming flagon into a great cup the size of those the warriors drank of. She moved it toward him, just a bit. Her voice was matter-of-fact, not inviting, commanding, or beguiling. "Rest first. Take off your tunic. Nourish yourself on this." There was a couch nearby she glanced at.

He caught its giant scent in her movement of the great cup. The scent alone did not intoxicate, as had the warrior maiden's brew, but smelled of power, of violence nonetheless. This scent was bigger, harsher. But— you recollect his famishment— he reached for it. *Just a swallow, just one.*

She moved it back slightly, it not yet having left her great white hand. "The tunic first. Your rest."

"This?" He touched the mackinaw. He stepped back.

"As you will," she said, removing the cup. "My dog, faithless cur, will show you where to find him." She leaned back a bit, but still trued in her great chair.

Shucky, with his fire-eyes and grinning muzzle, scrambled up and, paws clicking on the polished flags, led the way toward the door.

Balder, crossing its threshold stood and looked back at the beautiful god who had not moved, had not taken solace from either cup or wife. The Gott'imite looked at great Hela, and felt of her cold. The bitter cold of the northern ice and sun. He turned.

Her voice, neutral and like slate, followed him now, saying: "We will farm... afterward. After the battle."

He followed the dog, her words like wine, intoxicating. *Farm*. I always wanted to do that again.... Well not always. Just lately, though. *Simons Ledge*— my farmstead. That's what fatha did. He said it would be more fun if he could make the crops, not just grow them.

How does God make everything out of what does not appear? You may think that primitive humankind had been too busy to think about this: busy trying to get and keep a roof over its head, hunt and gather food, busy trying to take away the roofs of others, busy trying to stop the others taking away its roof. Perhaps the last two considerations are contained in the first but, by way of keeping your attention upon our predilection for war, I leave these in. It was Democritus who is recorded as the first to consider the halving of things. If you can cut a thing in half, you can cut its two halves in half and those halves also can be halved, *ad infinitum*. Where does it end, the Greeks wondered. They conceived of what we call the atom and said it was the last thing, indivisible: simply unable to be broken, and all were made of it. And thus you have the apostle declaring that God made all things out of things that do not in fact appear. This is one of the things the great Native American storyteller, Jasper Mary, saw Balder considering while he was holed up in his room after his honorable discharge from the United States Marine Corps. But the state of the atom was not strictly indivisible, and men set about to take it apart. Balder did not know much more about particle physics, subatomic particles, than your average layman: enough to be both charmed and scared.

Balder understood that when he had in his nostrils the musky scent of Elda's chipmunks—which freely she allowed to scamper through the house—that it was really bits of chipmunks lodged in his nose and signaling his brain. Not that chipmunk molecules, being several steps up the building-of-things, are as subatomic particles, which he surmised cannot be smelled. But something in them signaled anyhow.... At least he did not think it likely that electrons, positrons, gravitons and quarks have scents... or maybe there are no likely receptors for them on subatomic noses somewhere. He thought the photons, as particles of light, triggered signals via pigment molecules in his retinas to stimulate a picture in the visual cortex and enable him to see the enemy... or a friend... or Elda's chipmunks munching peanuts or dried mushrooms. He had seen the parts of which some of his buddies (and some of the Viet Cong) were made scattered through the fields of fire, and understood better than those folks comfortable at home in Gott'im how fearfully and wonderfully we are made. But the thought of these subatomic particles provoked no such visceral and agonizing upthrust in his psyche. Rather they spooked his imagination and troubled him with either an acknowledgment or a refusal of the void. How he went back and forth about this, how it gripped his mind. The argument clutched at him and squeezed, making his psyche a pit of dread. How can a particle, proportionally the size of a salt grain in some amphitheater of its surrounding atomic shell— what is all that space left over?! How can he or anyone be comprised of so much empty space?

Remember, this Balder exists in the 1980s: you, and I, the soul of Abner Bartlett, exist in the now. We maybe know a little more, in our popular imagination, but not that much more.

Most of the time Balder had no problem at all with subatomic particles. *I can take'em or leave'em* he thought. So what if my atoms, molecules, nucleic acids, cells are made of them. So what if my muscles and olfactories and such are made of these interactions? So what? What can I do about it? It's embarrassing but I'll just have to live it down.

Now, following Shucky on his way to see Loki, he watched along through the mizzling particles of murk and glow as the hell hound led him on. Eyes, ears, nose, tactile sensation, intuition and all were coordinated and tuned as though creeping, rifle at the ready, watching his way through the jungle; and yet his mind worked to defeat the devil.

Loki is probably just some weightless or massless theorized particle nobody's discovered yet. Think of the uncertainty principle. The observer effect. Maybe he is the mask of broken symmetry among quarks. Maybe he's a bunion on God's foot. That'd make anabody mad, even God.

The dog had been leading him back, it seemed, along the same dark mafic corridor lit by torches, and polished-floor reflection of torches— which he had taken in following it to Hela's office.

The giant dog's black rump moved, sleek and sedate, its long dark ragged tail moving faintly like it had no care; its head with that strange triangular set of eyes, turning every so often on him that look of cunning, the top eye checking the other two filled with mindless burning. Briefly Balder wondered how that worked: Did it yield some sort of triangulating vision? Did he Balder look 3-D?—or four dimensional, like some sort of swath out of time, five dimensional, or what? Am I six dimensional? He decided not to ask. He had nothing with which to understand an answer anyway. Instead he said, "So why'd she want you to keep me out? My particles hang too close together, I got cooties— what?"

Shucky grinned, the fire in his eyes grew fiercer.

He wasn't talking, but I will tell you: Simply, it's an irritating nuisance to know ahead of time that your temptation cuts no ice. And any time a live one comes, it means they will resist, are given strength enough to resist Hela's temptation.

They turned the corner and proceeded down the hallway several stories beneath where he first got bumped by Shucky passing to his mistress. Balder went back to thinking about the Loki particle. *Probably his name's spelled different when it's a particle. Its properties are more influential maybe and so they call it, spell it, Lokey or Lok-ee or something. Maybe it's a sub particle of the yet to be identified graviton. Gravitons are those subparticles, I think, that cause gravity. They have no mass which is odd because they seem to make weight, attract and shape things that have mass. Also, how can they be particles—if they got no mass? But forget that. Lokey, like the graviton, is in everything, only maybe he'd do something besides keep my feet in contact with the floor. One property of this Lokey sub particle is self, selfishness; another is repulsion. Lokey wishes to suck up and simultaneously repulse everything. But also another, stranger, property; a mimicking quality, influencing attraction. This particle Lokey is in everything, but his quantity or agency is somehow heightened in the proteins, molecules, cells, etc... to make the most of <u>sentient</u> beings — us. When everything and all energy is consumed and recycled this particle will not be... either in us, or as it was.*

When we get to where Loki is I will find he is maybe smashing into another particle in an accelerator...maybe a sucking black hole... or someone who looks like Odin or Hela.... If this mutt actually obeys its mistress.

So Balder mulled it over in his limited way, all the while his apprehension building, his senses tuned and restive, the strength, density and maze of Hel's architecture impressing him profoundly. They were descending back through the labyrinth; after what seemed hours or days, passing down to the main corridors which he conceived of as the main lobby of the skyscraping office towers where Hela was CEO. It was mortal hot and smazy. He expected the dog to turn left or right on the ramparts, perhaps leading him further down into the bowels of mechanized hellishness where maybe Loki was whipping the pulp makers or coal loaders into a frenzy; while, at the same time, off worshiping himself in some ghastly mirror universe, some other dimension, out of which extrapolated our own cosmos in spontaneous combustion.

But the dog led him past the insatiable demons sent to welcome the new arrivals with their hideous hungry torments: out the great gateway and onto the fuming causeway where: paws upon the wall and pausing briefly to look back in fury at the Gott'im mechanic, he leapt up and over into the molten sea below.

Balder, a few paces behind, could scarcely believe his eyes. Water gushing from his pores and dimming his eyes, slowly he moved forward putting his calloused hands upon the hot massive stone wall and craning forward. He gazed downward, eyes blinking and burning, but could not discern the dark dog in that turgid mixture of dark and light. The heavy viscous molten mass moved slowly but with great power, as though by convection currents, unseen and little understood, churning from depths and directions, sources, unknowable: This was the real hell, the inferno figured out of the powerful imaginations of our primitive ancestors: this great material fountain, crust of elemental making and remaking, out of which the purposes and plans for the plural universe were fashioned forth from the abyss. Shucky was gone.

Balder thought, *That settles'im. I'm not seeing Loki.*

He looked out past the ramparts toward the dock, expectant of a ferry waiting for his return. But it was not there. Suggested by Hoder's hope and worked out almost unconsciously while going up in the labyrinth, Balder's thought was that he would take the ferry down and around the mountain and back up again over the *Count of Time*, traverse the Gulf, and ship up toward heaven: his sole hope of seeing Daniel. A sort of three-dimensional or vertical journey in the shape of an elongated numerical 8, the *Count of Time* at its crux. *I'll go down and wait for the barge.*

Balder.

After a sort, I had to get his attention. He did not hear me with ears. He did not feel a tapping on the shoulder. In fact I was physically nowhere near him. But I was present all the same. He sensed, in his spirit, the impress of my call and knew I wanted him to jump in after Garm.

This was his most difficult moment.

…But Balder did not pull out the despairing arguments of intellectual resistance. He called out to Father God to help him. Balder climbed up on the wall, its various constituents pulsing with unbearable heat, and hurtled himself over — through the wavery distorting fumes into the living fire.

He was cooked before contact with the burning surface. It took and pulled him down consuming his Balder form but, borne away past the crux and onto the far side of *Time*, he himself was snatched up through cool pale-green brilliance to the shining gates of the Heavenly City: which gates are made out of light and crystalline elements bright with the glory of God.

Fatha, said Daniel, looking at him out of eyes full of hope and love.

They were close to one another, dissolving each into the other, becoming one spirit in blended sympathy and understanding; *and are.*

Where are we? asked Balder out of his wondering silence.

Said Daniel out of his silence, *This is almost, but not quite, where everything comes from.*

Balder looked at him, Daniel shining and happy as the child who had piloted the ferry to the gates of the Inferno. Father and son were one spirit. You could not tell them apart unless you knew both Balder and Daniel.

But where is Loki?

Abner the Monster-killer says his piece is about extinguished, exhausted. Subsumed into the burning fire of love that makes and remakes anew all its own desire. Love is not a thing but God, pronoun of existence, Who is wounded, Who wounds and reshapes all things.

Balder looked away, but a moment, from his son: up at the prismatic color-shining great walls of the City: up up soaring far from him and glistering, massive in varicolored splendor. Multitudes, beings of light, were scattering, coming and going through its great gates.

Will I go in there? he answered.

Even I will go in there, Fatha.

They took and held one another and were become one with the other in love.

I will never forget this, said Balder (without speaking—all had been said without speaking).

You will never forget, said Daniel.

And Balder was gone from there. And the Heavenly City was gone. And Balder was lying in the sodden leaves fallen with the year before: gazing up at the strange star as it faded and vanished off the side of Blackwell Mountain in the sun.

It alone, of all the other stars, had remained till now. Out the broken side of that other dimension, some call the void, the abyss, or wormhole: All those great stars and galaxies, full of gift and law; rotating, repelling and attracting; wheeling outward through space, that unknowably vast amphitheater of God; strewn with broken bits and pieces of God's body: *Take, eat, this is My Body broken for you.*

Balder looked up at the sky through woven branches. The sun had broken the night and bathed away myriad bits of starlight in morning brightness. His soul, and our soul, had been saved from the wrath of hell: which is the wrath of God. Love overcoming God's wrath: With hell he will punish, Himself and ourselves, no more.

He set up, looked around for me but I was not there. A bit above he saw the smoky reflected gleaming of his little fire-embers beneath the overhanging rock. Balder thought, Have to go home to *Simons Ledge* and prepare the garden. It had most grown to trees since he got back from his tour in Vietnam. *Think I'll plant that garden and call it Daniel's garden. I can make a li'l farmstead.*

The Mountainside in Gott'im

After meeting up and stopping to talk with Robbie the logging contractor, the two cousins' paths through the forest had diverged again. Now they were coming together once more in the continuing search for Balder's son. "I see'im!" Remotely, Hiram Robichaud's voice drifted down to Ansell standing poised and listening. Unlike Balder, they had not been out all night in the tire fire weather but had joined the search for Daniel in the a.m. while at work in the new day.

"Ovah heeya!"

The sun was up. Now they had sandwiches and coffee with them. The voice of his young cousin sounded far off his shoulder, and Ansell strode upward toward it. He climbed over a tumbledown rock wall blue-gray with lichen and picked his way toward the call.

"It's Balda!" He heard the other's voice drift to him as he went down into a dip, a small ravine. He saw the trembling figure against the tree when he reached the top.

"Give him this," said Ansell, starting to dig out the baloney sandwich. He saw the bruised cheek, the black-bearded blond man shivering. Ansell took off his jacket. He pressed it over Balder and knelt beside him to pour out coffee into the thermos cap. "Drink it, Balda." He opened up the wrapper and held out the sandwich while Balder drank down the coffee.

Balder roused. *God! That tasted good!* He looked up at Ansell, shivering, remembering his twin brother slipping off the barge into the greasy water separating the living from limbo. He looked just like him! How much alike! That dimple! He took the sandwich and began eating it. *Baloney. Baloney like... well that must be what prime rib tastes like.* He tried to grin. He couldn't.

"Goddamit, Balda!" Ansell twisted the cap back onto the thermos. "I think I love ya, man! Why'd choo wanna go lyin'heah gettin' killed in these woods. You nuts, man!?" He said it again: "I think I love ya!"

Balder now smiled. He said, "Yaw wawship is received, Ansell, but not b'me."

Hiram watched them with fear and astonishment. It had been a long strange dawning for him in the misty Dark forest by himself, once or twice getting turned around as one will in the woods. He started back, and fell thudding painfully against some rocks. There was something awful wrong here. Gott'imites don't talk like this! *Evah!* He scrambled to his feet and ran tripping through bits of blowdown and sliding down rocks, slipping on wet leaves all the way downhill beneath the tall oaks.

"We in't found'im I know of," said Ansell turning back from this spectacle to Balder. "Betta get up'n go home. He might be theya now."

Came a scrabbling through the woods toward them.

Ansell exclaimed, "It's one of the dogs from the hunt fah Daniel!" Robbie had heard about that over the radio. "Nevah seen one looked like that before, that breed." A Norwegian elkhound, silver and black, came bounding toward them. "Looks like he's got a mind of his own."

Stroking the dog's thick ruff, Balder remembered *Gylfaginning.* …And he remembered —he might yet go to the Last Battle?... It did not now seem too real, though. The one in the past, in Southeast Asia— that seemed real; and not really past. The black-and-silver dog sniffed the two men and ran off.

Ansell gave him a hand. Balder Simon stood uncertainly. His almost white hair was plastered to his head with bits of stuff in it. His watchcap was still balled up in his hand. He said, "Mind f'I keep this a bit?" He clutched the extra jacket around him. His mackinaw was filthy, he knew. "Don't worry I'll clean it b'fo-ah I give it back."

"I don't care f'you chew it d'bits'n spit it out again!"

"The sam'itch'll do me, I guess," said the other. He did manage that grin.

They started down the way Hi had gone. Balder wasn't shivering quite so bad. His legs felt like dead cedars that would pull out the ground if tugged just a bit. He was still chewing the last of the sandwich. "Got any mo-ah that coffee?"

They stopped, and he watched Ansell pour him another cup. "Bet it don't taste s'good's that first cup," he said.

The sound of baying dogs drifted east toward them, over the vast top of the mountain from the west.

Uh-oh, thought Ansell. He said, "Pro'lly not. But betta drink it." Balder was already looking at him over the upended last of it.

"Daniel died, Ansell," he said. He handed him the empty cup. "Show-ah?"

"You won't believe me but I saw' im—living, talked with'im....

Alvin, too." He watched his friend. He looked back down at the woolen watchcap –still in his hand. He held out his arms from under Ansell's jacket. The checked wool pattern was not singed. He thought, I'm two places. Before the throne of God, worshiping. And I have been all this time in Gott'im among the living and the dead.

The sun gleamed off Balder's head. So bright, that cap of Scandinavian-blond hair. Ansell looked at him. He said, "I believe you."

They looked at one another.

"I think I died a minute... maybe more."

Ansell looked away. He said to the distant tree trunks, straight and tall, "Yuh*t*."

They started back down, each deep in his own thoughts.

Just as they were finding the trail, Ansell found his voice again. He said, "Maybe y'betta not say so — about Daniel and Alvin."

Balder nodded. He said, "I'm okay— you knowing."

"Good," said the logger to the mechanic. "*I know*. N'that's okay."

The God's Cycle is set in the early mid-1980s

Guide to Characters

Asa Bartlett. Amateur historian, Congo Church clock-winder, millworker, married to Olive Lovejoy Bartlett.
Olive Lovejoy Bartlett. Caregiver, family woman, dowser, operates bed-and-breakfast, married to Asa Bartlett.
Lyman Bearce. Lumber baron, selectman, married to Rhetta Bearce.
Rhetta Bearce. Committee woman, married to Lyman Bearce.
Babette Buck. Dowel millworker, Ferddy Sessions' girlfriend.

Jeffy Decatur. Diner business owner-cook, bird hunter.

Gloria Fay. Graduate student, IICE facilitator, sister to James Fay, Balder Simon's love.
James Fay. Ski resort real estate salesman, brother of Gloria Fay, engaged to Theodora Prescott.

Harry Golding. Ski resort owner, maternal uncle of Amanda.
Julius Golding. Ski resort owner, maternal uncle of Amanda.
Amanda. Niece to the Goldings.

Jasper Mary. Historical and legendary healer, storyteller.

Israel Kimball. Town recluse, former academy headmaster, scholar.

Jim Nutting. The weekly *Village Voter* editor.

Eloise Potadoe. Artist, goatherd, homesteader.
Theodora Prescott. Mill owner, IICE participant, engaged to James Fay.
Peter Prince. Mechanic, common-law spouse of Chrischana Twitchell, father of Nathan, Benaiah, Daniel.

Robbie Robichaud. Logging contractor, father to Alvin and Ansell.
Alvin and Ansell Robichaud. Loggers, twins.

Celon Segar (pronounced Cigar by the locals). Tire dump owner.
Cindabilla Sessions. Niece to Ferddy Sessions, girlfriend of Daniel

Twitchell.

Ferddy (Ferdinand) Sessions. Town worker, Cindabilla's maternal uncle, boyfriend of Babette Buck.

Hannah Sessions. Farmer, domestic worker, mother of Ferdinand Sessions, grandmother of Cindabilla, sister-in-law of Nellie Sessions.

Melvinia Sessions. Diner server, domestic worker, distantly related to other Sessions.

Nellie Sessions. Dowelmill-worker, artifact collector, aunt to Cindabilla.

Balder Simon. Vietnam veteran, millwright, son of Elda, father of Daniel Twitchell, lover of Gloria Fay and Chrischana Twitchell.

Elda Simon. Animal rehabilitator, mother of Balder Simon.

Benaiah Twitchell. Adolescent son of Chrischana Twitchell and Peter Prince.

Chrischana Twitchell. Dishwasher, homesteader, common-law spouse of Peter Prince, mother of Daniel, Benaiah, Nathan.

Daniel Twitchell. Teenage son of Chrischana Twitchell and Balder Simon, friend of Cindabilla Sessions.

Nathan Twitchell. Youngest son of Chrischana Twitchell and Peter Prince.

Like this? Read also

Gott'im's Monster